THE
BRANCH
AND THE
SCAFFOLD

≈ AND ≈

BILLY
GASHADE

LOREN D. ESTLEMAN

FORGE®

A TOM DOHERTY ASSOCIATES BOOK · NEW YORK

THE BRANCH AND THE SCAFFOLD AND BILLY GASHADE

The Branch and the Scaffold copyright © 2009 by Loren D. Estleman

Billy Gashade copyright © 1997 by Loren D. Estleman

All rights reserved.

A Forge Book
Published by Tom Doherty Associates
175 Fifth Avenue
New York, NY 10010

www.tor-forge.com

Forge® is a registered trademark of Macmillan Publishing Group, LLC.

ISBN 978-0-7653-9355-5

Our books may be purchased in bulk for promotional, educational, or business use. Please contact your local bookseller or the Macmillan Corporate and Premium Sales Department at 1-800-221-7945, extension 5442, or by email at MacmillanSpecialMarkets@macmillan.com.

First Edition: March 2018

Printed in the United States of America

0 9 8 7 6 5 4 3 2 1

CONTENTS

THE
BRANCH
AND THE
SCAFFOLD

A Novel of
Judge Parker

This book is dedicated to the men who rode for Parker;
and to the memory of Douglas C. Jones,
who wrote about him.

I

A Dream of Justice

This reasonable moderator, and equal piece of justice,
Death.

—SIR THOMAS BROWNE
(1605–1682)

ONE

Two long blasts on the whistle, each bent in the middle by the wind on the river. It seemed to be shrieking his name.

"Well, they'll know we're coming." Mary Parker took her fingers from her ears.

"I think they know already."

Spotting the crowd on the dock, she drew in little Charlie and huddled closer to her husband. "Have they come with baskets of flowers or buckets of tar?"

"They're empty-handed. Come to see the carpetbagger."

"How soon can you prove them wrong?"

"Soon. I have my predecessor to thank for heightening the contrast."

"They cried for his impeachment."

"I studied his record. He's fortunate they didn't dangle him from his own scaffold."

"I should think a town with a fort would be an orderly place."

"The fort is closed. The town has thirty saloons and one bank. I am the order."

When the steamboat bumped against the hempbound pilings, the crowd eased back to allow the hands to erect the gangplank and bear trunks and portmanteaux to the dock for passengers to claim. Some newcomers were greeted and borne away amidst jabber, others escaped interest, looking for porters and transportation. Most of those gathered watched as Isaac and Mary Parker and their small son alighted. They saw a man in excess of six feet tall and two hundred pounds, wearing a sandy Vandyke beard, a soft hat, and a duster to protect his gray suit from cinders, accompanied by a large woman near his age in gloves, a cape, and a hat secured with a scarf under her chin. Patent-leather shoes showed beneath the hem of her skirt. The boy, in necktie, cap, and knicker-bockers, had a high complexion and kept close to his parents, although not from fear; he intercepted the curious glances of strangers with his father's level blue gaze.

"Your honor?"

Parker lifted his chin to confront the stranger. He was a man close to his own thirty-seven years, pale-eyed and neatly barbered, in a frock coat too heavy for the season, but he gripped Parker's hand with a dry palm.

"You're the first to address me so."

"William Clayton, chief prosecutor." He bowed to Mary and acknowledged the child with a nod but no interest. "Wel-come to Fort Smith."

It was a hot Sunday in early May. The family and Clayton boarded a waiting phaeton, sat with hands folded while the Negro driver and a porter secured their luggage, and rode down a broad street harrowed by hooves and carriage wheels to a fine dust that rose in clouds like flour and cast a scrim over a town built largely of unpainted wood, with neither sidewalks nor lamps to illuminate the streets at night. The saloons were shuttered for the sabbath, but wagons and horses lined the hitching rails, and stragglers from the dock dodged heavy oncoming traffic to run alongside the phaeton, staring at the occupants. Clayton tapped the driver's shoulder with his stick and he picked up the pace, leaving the rubbernecks behind but raising still more dust. Mary drew a handkerchief from her sleeve and held it to her nose and mouth.

"Isaac"—her voice was muffled, but still she lowered it a notch—"we've made a great mistake."

He patted her other hand. "No, Mary. We are faced with a great task. These people need us. We must not fail them."

Clayton spoke, distracting Mary's attention from a row of bright petticoats fluttering from a second-floor balcony like the flags of many nations. "No school yet, Mrs. Parker, but we hope to remedy that by the time the lad's old enough."

"He's seen our nation's capital and much of the continent in between," she said. "His education began early."

"How soon may I inspect the garrison?" asked Parker.

"Directly you're settled in. You'll welcome the early start. Many of the prisoners have waited months for their cases to come to trial, and eighteen are charged with capital offenses. If you can convene by the end of this month at the earliest, you just may clear the docket in time for Independence Day."

"As late as that?"

"Judge Story kept an untidy desk."

"I've heard it was worse than that."

"That's the popular view, but I wouldn't cast it about up at the courthouse. It's a Democratic stronghold and, begging your honor's pardon, you're an appointee of President Grant. Moreover—" He faltered, cleared his throat.

"I'm a turncoat. Everyone's aware of my original party affiliation, Mr. Clayton. The decision to switch has given me unique insight. I intend to keep politics out of my courtroom. I'd as soon hang a Republican as a Democrat."

"Isaac!"

He glanced at his son. "I'm sorry, my dear."

"People hereabouts would pay to see a thing like that," Clayton said.

"I understand they did."

"Judge Story suffered from sloth more than greed, although he had a chronic case of that as well. In fourteen months he managed to run up an expense bill of four hundred thousand."

"The taxpayers should be grateful he didn't show more initiative."

"At this point it's impossible to distinguish between simple attrition due to gross negligence and bald-faced theft. The Eighth is a big jurisdiction: all of the Western District of Arkansas and the Indian Nations, including places few white men have ever set foot on, and them that have you wouldn't want to meet out in the open. Prussia's smaller. A great deal can pass unnoticed in a responsibility that size. If Story was half as corrupt as he was incompetent, he could have made the Tweed Ring look like a First Street pickpocket. It will take most of the month for an honest man to begin to make sense of it all."

"Please be prepared to plead your most pressing cases a week from tomorrow."

The prosecutor's eyes flickered, the irises scarcely darker than the whites. "I don't see how you can do it, and neither will you once you've had a look about."

Three-year-old Charles Parker tugged at his father's sleeve. "Papa, when may we see the gallows?"

"It's the damnedest assignment any man ever undertook, or ever will," Clayton said. "All your judgments are final, hanging and all, with no appeal between you and Almighty God—not counting the president, who considering the human offal you'll be passing sentence on wouldn't touch it with a poker. It's instant history; and if you do it the way it needs to be done, it'll be the death of you."

"Are you attempting to frighten me off?"

"No, sir. A man ought to know what he's harnessing himself up to. My motives are less than Christian. We're to be partners, and a thing done no more than halfway by the one must be done one hundred and fifty percent by the other. I'm ambitious, but I ain't suicidal."

Parker's face registered disapproval of the deliberate lapse in grammar. His wife and son were unpacking in the Hotel Le Flore. Judge and prosecutor were seated in what was to be his chambers, a small square room barely large enough to contain a black walnut desk the size of a dining table, three tufted-leather chairs, shelves, and a credenza, with nary a horizontal surface not piled high with papers and bursting portfolios bearing witness to the disorganization of the previous administration. The curling leaves seemed to defy gravity, scaling the walls from floor to ceiling, their yellowed corners stirring in the breeze through the open window. Notwithstanding that, the air was stagnant, redolent of tobacco long since chewed and expectorated, and murky with the exhaust of the cigars the pair was smoking. A revolving bookcase leaned drunkenly to one side, stuffed with mustard-colored bound case histories with the hangdog look of children neglected and forgotten. A mausoleum of justice overlooked; a dead plant in a dry pot.

"Equal and exact justice," Parker said, when that image came to him. "Jefferson's words. If we can keep them in mind, we can dispense with everything else."

"Jefferson was a Democrat."

"What of it? Lincoln was a Republican. Together they freed millions. In any event, this is an oasis in the political desert. I explained that once." The judge broke two inches of ash into a heavy brass tray that performed double duty as a paperweight. "Thank you for the tour. My family and I will establish quarters in the commissary. Will you have someone see it's made ready as soon as possible? I don't wish to burden the electorate with a hotel bill any larger than is necessary."

"I'll attend to it. What did you think of the jail?"

Parker repressed a shudder. He'd served in Congress and fought with the Home Guard under Rosecrans, but the atrocities he'd witnessed were little more than an anteroom to the dungeon beneath his feet, separated into two sections by a stone wall that extended up through the ground floor, with prisoners sprawled on rough concrete, some in shackles, buckets for sanitary use. The stench was a permanent fixture. The rest of the building, two brick stories that had sheltered officers during garrison days, devoted half the surface level to court proceedings, the rest to the handmaidens of justice.

The judge addressed a different subject, somewhat to

Clayton's surprise; the attorney had placed him as a human-itarian, who would at least inquire about the possibillity of constructing a proper jail. "The scaffold," he said. "Is it as sound as it appears?"

"It would take a charge of powder to dismantle it. It's been struck once by lightning and survived."

This arrangement was visible through the window at a dis-tance of three hundred yards. It stood fourteen feet high on the site of the old powder magazine, extended for twenty feet, and supported a twelve- by twelve-inch beam suitable for hang-ing a dozen condemned men simultaneously.

"So far it's served only one," Clayton went on; "a half-breed named Childers, who slit an old man's throat for his horse. Old Judge Caldwell commissioned a substantial exam-ple of architecture to inspire fear in the territory. He under-estimated the highwaymen's resolve. Here in town they call it Sam Grant's wash line."

"Who is responsible for it?"

"Jim Fagan, whom you'll meet presently. He's U.S. mar-shal, and your chief law enforcement officer. I believe he assigns a man from time to time to apply whitewash and in-spect it for termites."

"The executioner should see to that."

"At present we've no one in that particular post."

"We should. I want to see personnel records on everyone who serves this court."

"I recommend you requisition a shovel." Clayton swept an arm along the mountain range of paper that surrounded them.

Someone knocked. Parker raised his voice, inviting the visitor inside. The door opened, admitting a small, narrow-gauged man in a blue uniform with a Sam Browne belt. He looked at the judge briefly, then at Clayton, and removed his forage cap. Strands of silver glittered in his broom-shaped whiskers and a shelf of brow left his eyes in deep shadow.

"Sir, we had a disturbance. I feared you may have heard it."

"What sort of disturbance?" asked Parker, before the prosecutor could respond.

When the man hesitated, Clayton said, "George Maledon, meet Judge Isaac Parker. Maledon's a deputy sheriff, helps out downstairs."

Maledon faced Parker. "Man threw his slops at a turnkey. I had to bust him." He patted the pistol on his hip.

"You shot him?" asked Clayton.

"No, sir, I used the other end. Doc Du Val says he'll live."

"Very well. We don't want another incident so soon after the last." To Parker: "Maledon shot an escaping prisoner last month. A single ball through the heart from a rifle."

"What is your experience?" Parker asked.

"Before this billet I was a policeman in Fort Smith five years."

"Would you consider resigning from the county and accepting a position in charge of executions in this district?"

Two tiny points of light guttered deep in the other's skull. "I would for a fact," he said. "Your honor."

TWO

"**O**yez! Oyez! The Honorable District Court of the United States for the Western District of Arkansas, having criminal jurisdiction of the Indian Territory, is now in session."

The tenor voice of Court Crier J. G. Hammersly, a short-legged man with a rooster chest, rang like a temple bell in the eternal twilight of the courtroom.

Parker, looking no more and certainly no less in authority seated behind a brawny cherry-paneled desk in his black robes, snapped his gavel. "The court is ready for the first case."

And, by God, thought William H. H. Clayton, *it is.* The

big regulator clock on the wall above the heads of the jurors twitched one second past eight A.M., Monday, May 10, 1875; eight days after Grant's new appointee set foot on dry land from the narrow Arkansas, like Moses from the mountain. At the time, his chief prosecutor had not thought the thing possible; but he'd learned a parcel about the man's character during the past week and would not repeat the mistake.

The clerk, Stephen Wheeler, baby-faced and without vocal inflection, rose and glanced down at the docket on his writing table. "The United States *versus* Daniel H. Evans. Charge, murder."

Evans, young and clean-shaven, was careful in his appearance. The suit and shirt his attorney had provided for him had evidently been selected by the client, for the collar and cuffs fitted him as if they'd been made to his measure and the coat lay smooth across his shoulders. He stood accused of having murdered a nineteen-year-old boy in the Creek Nation for his boots. When apprehended, the defendant had been wearing an uncommonly fine pair with hand-tooled tops and high, sloping heels, nearly new. He'd been tried before the previous judge, but the jury had disagreed on a verdict, and he'd been returned to jail. In the meantime the father of the slain youth had come forward, and in the presence of the jury he now identified his son's boots by some horseshoe nails the boy had driven to secure a faulty heel. Evans, who'd been jubilant and answered Parker's occasional remarks to him with polite banter, remained silent and pale throughout the man's testimony.

"The United States *versus* James Moore. Charge, murder."

Moore, whose deep sunburn had had little time to fade since his capture, plucked at his moustaches and glared at the witnesses against him, who identified him as one of the territory's leading horse thieves. While fleeing a citizens' posse led by two of James Fagan's deputies, the desperado had shot and killed William Spivey, the first federal officer to give his life in the service of the Eighth District court. On that occasion Moore escaped, only to be arrested by two more deputy marshals when he abandoned horse stealing for cattle rustling. A partner testifying against him gave evidence that Moore had been traveling with the owner of a herd, intending to murder him to gain possession, when he wandered into the deputies' hands. Shackled during the journey to Fort Smith, the defendant had boasted of having killed eight men.

"The United States *versus* Edmund Campbell. Charge, murder."

A Negro native of the Choctaw Nation, the heavy-shouldered Campbell had drunk himself into a fury over a hasty remark made by a neighbor, Lawson Ross, gone to Ross's house, and butchered the man and his common-law wife. He stared at the floor throughout the trial with angry eyes in a sullen face.

"The United States *versus* Smoker Mankiller. Charge, murder."

Unfortunately named for his present circumstances, the Choctaw sat broad and motionless at the defense table, not understanding a word of the evidence against him in English. For no reason ever given he'd borrowed a gun from an acquaintance named William Short and shot him to death with it. He'd been overheard proudly acknowledging the act, but since his arrest had changed his story, blaming it on two brothers named Welch.

"The United States *versus* John Whittington. Charge, murder."

The defendant was visibly ill, sallow-featured and shining with perspiration. The eighteen-year-old son of the victim in the case, John J. Turner, confirmed that he'd seen Whittington stab Turner's father along the Red River in the Chickasaw Nation, and had subdued and held him until help came to bring him to justice. Whittington and the elder Turner had been seen drinking in a low saloon on the Texas side of the river, where Turner had paid the bartender from a swollen leather poke. It was determined that on the way back home, the man under examination had bludgeoned his companion with a makeshift club, then brought his knife into play when the other had refused to stay down. When arrested, Whittington had had a large sum of money in his pocket.

"The United States *versus* Samuel Fooy. Charge, murder."

Fooy, Cherokee on his mother's side, had confessed to the slaying of John Emmett Neff, a schoolteacher in the Cherokee Nation whose skeleton had been found a year later with a bullet hole in the skull. Returning from the tribal capital of Tahlequah with three hundred dollars in back salary, Neff had offered the farm wife who had put him up for the night a five-dollar bill to settle the fifty-cent fee. Told she could not change it, the schoolteacher had struck out on foot for a nearby store to procure the silver. Fooy, a neighbor visiting the house, had gone out after him. When the victim was identified based on his name in a book found near the remains, the rest was legwork.

The six men were tried and convicted in a little more than a month. Judge Parker's charges to the juries left small doubt as to his sympathies, and Chief Prosecutor Clayton listened in wonder as the man behind the desk instructed them which way to vote. When the foreman in the Evans case informed him of the panel's decision, Parker thanked him in a tone of satisfaction Clayton hadn't heard from him previously. At his sentencing, the young man who had coveted a pair of fine boots even unto death stood tight-faced before the cruel voice from the bench. Execution was scheduled for September 3, 1875.

"I sentence you to hang by the neck until you are dead, dead, dead!" Parker banged his gavel.

And then he wept.

Clayton stood throughout each sentencing, accompanied by his assistant, a young, ham-faced man named James Brizzolara, who at the age of fourteen had risen to the rank of colonel in the insurgent army of Giuseppe Garibaldi in Italy. The judge's tone on these occasions remained level.

"There, on the morning of September third, eighteen seventy-five, you will be conducted . . ."

". . . on the morning of September third, eighteen seventy-five . . ."

". . . September third, eighteen seventy-five . . ."

". . . September third . . ."

"By God," Clayton was heard to mutter, when the date was repeated a fourth time. "By God."

On the sixth and last, young Colonel Brizzolara whispered to his superior, "They'll not make mention of Sam Grant's wash line after this. What do you think they'll call the infernal machine now?"

" 'Parker's tears.' " Clayton smoothed a cigar between his fingers.

Ropes were not difficult to obtain in Fort Smith, where cattle outfits from Texas stopped to lubricate their throats and replenish their equipment before swimming the herds across the Arkansas to the railroad depot. George Maledon, however, was particular, and incurred the impatience of clerks in half a dozen saddleries before settling on two hundred feet of the best and thickest hemp to be found east of El Paso. He procured linseed oil as well and spent hours working it by hand into the fibers until they were as pliant as a gentlewoman's hair and would glide around the coarsest neck until the gargantuan knot fixed itself beneath the mastoid bone behind the left ear and snapped the cervical vertebra like a stalk of celery; to the knot itself he applied pitch to prevent slipping. He'd paid close attention to the process when John Childers was hanged for killing a peddler, and obtained the technical information from Dr. Ben T. Du Val, who stitched up the prisoners when they got into fights and had timed Childers' moment of death against his heavy pocket watch for the official record. Forty-five, Bavarian-born, Maledon had been raised in Detroit, served with the First Arkansas Federal Battery during the rebellion, and been a city policeman before accepting a position as deputy sheriff of Sebastian County and a part-time appointment as deputy U.S. marshal to legitimize his service in the Fort Smith jail. He'd slain a man during an escape attempt and thought no more of it than he had of shooting Confederate rebels.

Two-hundred-pound sandbags manufactured for the purpose of damming the banks when the Arkansas River swelled in the spring were tied to ropes, and Maledon spent the weeks leading to the executions industriously, testing the single twenty-foot trap and the ropes' tensile strength several times daily. Soon, the *squee-thump* of the apparatus became as much a part of the sounds of Fort Smith as the creak and rattle of wagons and the tintack pianos in the Silver Dollar, the House of Lords, the Last Chance, and the whorehouses in the Row.

From time to time, as the settlement on the river entered the smothering heat of late summer, the little man paused to mop his brow and watch the steady stream of traffic turn up the dust on Garrison Avenue. Dust and traffic both grew heavier by the day.

A former military man who had taught tactics and strategy at a seminary in Pennsylvania, William H. H. Clayton stood absolutely erect at the window in Parker's chambers. From one angle showed Maledon's mighty engine of human destruction, from another the incoming tide of carriages, buckboards, and riders on horseback. Wheels locked hubs, mules balked, curses flowed.

"They've been coming in all week," the prosecutor said. "The hotels and boardinghouses are filled. The price of tent canvas has gone up three times in three days. I don't know how many more our little hamlet will hold."

"It's good for trade. Why should the saloons be the only

ones to profit?" The judge, in shirtsleeves and the black waist-coat he wore to church, sat behind the desk reading sworn affidavits. On Sundays it was his habit in this his first season on the bench to accompany his wife and son to Methodist services, dine with them at noon in the stone commissary where they had taken up residence, then report to the courthouse to bring himself up to date on the docket.

"There isn't a farmer in the state who's stayed home to bring in the harvest," said Clayton, "nor a civilized Indian in the territory who hasn't pawned his watch to make the trip. They've all read about the grand exhibition, or had an account read to them if they don't know their letters. Something about it appeared in the *New York Herald* last week."

"Splendid. A public judgment followed by public punishment is the swiftest way to clear the foul air left by Story and his cronies."

"The Eastern press seems to hold that the fate of these men should be private."

"An execution carried out in secrecy is no better than lynching from a dry branch."

"You ought to write that, and set the record straight. The journalists have all convinced themselves we're savages out here."

"They'll write what they please regardless. I used to see them on Capitol Hill, scribbling in their grubby little blocks before they'd been in to meet with their subjects. They have their forum and I have mine."

Clayton observed Maledon at work. The scaffold was visible from every building in the garrison. "How much more must he test? The man is a fanatic."

"Fanatics have their uses. I'm confident he'll serve this court well."

"No doubt. He's committed. I confess I preferred having him in the basement. The faces in the jail are milder."

"I didn't reassign him for his looks."

* * *

Spectators began entering the garrison at dawn. By ten o'clock, the hour scheduled for the execution, the grounds of the old powder magazine were no longer visible for the bodies that had pressed themselves in around the scaffold. Others perched like pigeons on porch roofs and hung like fruit from trees. Deputy marshals and guards from the jail, armed with revolvers and carbines, kept the central structure clear. The songbird colors worn by the women from the Row showed brightly among dark suits, overalls, and gingham dresses, and the stooped shoulders of the Reverend H. M. Granade drew a question mark at the top of the gallows stairs beside the brief apostrophe of George Maledon, turned out in a new suit and a gray slouch hat. His hands hung at his sides, within reach of the lever that opened the long trap by means of a simple gear. It was difficult to tell where his tangled beard ended and black broadcloth began. His eyes hid beneath a mantel of bone as substantial as the scaffold itself.

Parker's stolid figure stood framed in a ground-floor window of the courthouse. It was not seen to move.

On the stroke of the hour the condemned, escorted by deputies led by Marshal Fagan, shuttle-stopped their way from the jail, wrists shackled and irons on their ankles. They climbed the stairs and assumed their places on the paired planks of the trap, nooses stirring before them in the breeze from the river. Granade read aloud a pious statement dictated by John Whittington, the knife-murderer, then led the crowd in a hymn. Asked by Fagan if they had anything to say, only two of the men in shackles spoke: Boot-fancier Daniel Evans looked out over the crowd and said, "There are worse men here than me." James Moore, the horse thief, said good-bye to an acquaintance in the audience. Maledon left his post to adjust the black caps and fuss with the nooses. When at length he was satisfied with their placement, he returned to the lever and pulled.

Dr. Du Val, standing beneath the platform, inspected the six men for pulses, waiting two minutes for each with watch in hand. At the end of the month he would collect two dollars per man for this service.

He nodded. The man in the window turned away.

THREE

The day of a hanging was not a holiday at the courthouse. Sessions took place daily except Sundays and Christmas and were not suspended even on Independence Day, when Parker directed the windows be shut to reduce distraction from early fireworks explosions. On September 3, while the bodies unclaimed by relatives were being laid to rest in a plot behind the building, the judge signed witness- and juror-fee vouchers in his slashing hand, instructed clerk Wheeler to handle them with dispatch, and summoned James F. Fagan into his chambers.

The U.S. marshal's round Irish face retained its high color as Parker spoke. His hands hung at his sides. He considered crossing one's arms an indicator of weakness and standing with one's hands in one's pockets a breach of etiquette.

He listened with increasing wonder and no expression on his features. The judge was a man of clarity, who employed none of the ambiguous turns of phrase that Fagan had expected from a former member of Congress. When Parker stopped, he said, "Bringing the deputy census up to two hundred's a tall order. Washington pays two dollars per prisoner and six cents a mile one way. The nigger that cleans the spitoons in the Hole-in-the-Wall clears more than that Saturday night when the herd's in. Then there's the privilege of getting killed, like poor Bill Spivey."

"They're entitled to collect rewards offered for fugitives not wanted for federal crimes, so long as those activities don't interfere with their responsibility to this court. An enterprising man can shelter and clothe a family on much less. And this court isn't interested in what becomes of the chattel of the criminals they're forced to kill in the course of duty."

"They're fortunate if whatever it brings pays for the burial. Up to now they've been responsible for that if there's none else to stand the cost."

"So they'll remain. I don't intend to encourage the vigilante compulsion."

Fagan scanned the large-scale territorial map pinned to the wall behind the desk, divided into the five nations. "Two hundred deputies to cover seventy-four thousand square miles of raw country. It might be worth twenty dollars to the undertaker just to avoid the hazard of dragging some murthering scum all the way back along the Canadian without a citizens' posse for support."

"I can't challenge their discretion without witnesses to the contrary."

"You're safe enough there. If they won't peach on the killers, they sure won't come forward against them what killed them."

Parker thunked a dilapidated leather portfolio onto the marshal's side of the desk. "I've reopened the files on unsolved murders and other felonies extending back five years. Here are warrants for the arrests of the better known transgressors. Tell your deputies to bring them back alive or dead."

"Won't that encourage the vigilante compulsion?"

"You said yourself we won't be inundated with applicants. If we can't attract them with gold, we'll offer them a feudal system of independent action. That should appeal to the sort we require."

"Men like that are sure to have paper out on them somewhere."

"I don't insist upon appointing men of character, although if there's graft in the business it had better be small enough not to reach my ears. I detest men of violence, but that's what's needed to keep the peace in a place outside the jurisdiction of every local court. It's been let fester too long while men have sat here who by all that's decent should have been in shackles downstairs."

"If it's killers you're after hiring, you might consider going down there for your recruitment."

Parker gestured with folded spectacles. "Cowards and backshooters. Child molesters. Wife beaters and whiskey smugglers and howling lunatics. Animals who slew whole families of samaritans under their own roofs. I want the jail population to increase, and Maledon not kept idle. That means saturating the territory, and I can't do that with sixty men. Begin with the rangers in Texas. Find out who's restless and like to resign. Make contact with county sheriffs and city marshals who have worked with your office and whose performances meet your standards. Review every county election and city appointment over the past year, discover who lost by a hair or because he was unpopular for any reason other than corruption or incompetence. There's a limit to the first and I won't tolerate the second. Send the wires and this court will assume the expense."

"Is it your intention to strip every Western community of its protection?"

"That is not my intention, although it will likely be the result. My needs are more pressing. I don't want drunks and gamblers like that preening man Hickok, or bushwhackers like the gang in Dodge City. Such men are timid when they become separated from the pack. Pin that star on men of swift judgment and good instincts."

"It'll be the roughest bunch of hooligans this side of County Limerick," Fagan said.

Early on, as news of the sextuple execution in Fort Smith spread, rooted itself in the umber soil of the western Indian Nations, and grew into the solid stalk of legend, the men whom

Marshal Fagan appointed to swell the judge's standing army abandoned the practice of introducing themselves as deputy U.S. marshals. Instead, when they entered the quarters of local law enforcement officers and tribal policemen to show their warrants, they said: "We ride for Parker."

Sometimes, in deference to rugged country or to cover ground, they broke up and rode in pairs or singles, but as the majority of the casualties they would suffer occurred on these occasions, they formed ragged escorts around stout little wagons built of elm, with canvas sheets to protect the passengers from rain and sun for trial and execution. With these they entered the settlements well behind their reputation. The deputies used Winchesters to pry a path between rubbernecks pressing in to see what new animals the circus had brought. Inside, accused felons, rounded up like stray dogs, rode in manacles on the sideboards and decks. At any given time—so went the rumor—one fourth of the worst element in the Nations was at large, one fourth was in the Fort Smith jail, and one fourth was on its way there in the "tumbleweed wagons."

"That's three-fourths," said tenderheels. "What about the rest?"

"That fourth rides for Parker."

Charlie Burns had served as jailer under judges Caldwell— a good fellow, cheerful and kind to subordinates—Story—a distracted man with eyes too mobile in his head for trust— and now Parker, whose jury, to his mind, was still deliberating— and seen a number of things that few would accept as truth if they weren't part of the record that continued to grow on shelves and in pigeonholes upstairs, like mushrooms in the damp.

Burns had shot and crippled the horse thief Orpheus McGee during an attempt at freedom, but that was all in his capacity and was scarcely worth remarking upon. Smoking his pipe near the door to the outside, he'd been surprised to see John Childers, the murderer, approach the barred window dripping wet from the river, which he'd swum across to meet the terms of his bond, and had had to argue with him to get him to report to Story's clerk instead of just bunking inside; what'd he think Burns was running, a shelter for tramps? Childers had complied and commenced his incarceration with all the paperwork completed.

And the jailer had been present that legendary day when lightning struck the great scaffold at the instant Childers shot through the trap. A Negro woman in the crowd had fallen to her knees, crying: "John Childers' soul has gone to hell; I done heerd de chains clankin'." Well, he'd worn them on his ankles and wrists, so there was nothing to that, but a man of no more than normal superstition could not help but mark that it was the gallows' first attempt at its purpose, and that a bolt singling it out at that moment was no ordinary stray. It was a moment Burns returned to often, never without a shudder and a glance skyward at the source of the shaft and another at his feet to make sure the earth hadn't opened up to offer him a glimpse of the damned man's charred shade.

He'd seen his due share of the elephant, right enough, but nothing to give him a worse turn than the sudden appearance at his post of a lady of fine breeding, done up in the height of Fort Smith fashion, with one arm through the bail of a covered basket and a bunch of cut flowers cradled in the other.

"Mr. Burns, I think? Mrs. Isaac Parker. I'm here to see William Leach."

Leach was devilish bad on a scale that ran considerably higher than the eight-foot ceiling of the jail. He'd backshot a neighbor who had just left the hospitality of the prisoner's house in the Cherokee, attempted to burn the remains, and been apprehended while trying to sell a pair of boots that had belonged to his victim, well-cobbled boots being a popular article of commerce throughout the discalced Nations (Burns himself never ventured into the territory with anything on his feet but a pair of down-at-heels brogans, coveted by none). Leach was one of six scheduled for hanging the following April; the Eastern press had begun to circle.

Mrs. Parker was a large woman of the Irish type, pale-skinned, auburn hair pinned up beneath her hat, with eyes of the judge's same frank blue. She was not a pretty woman but a handsome one, and if the rank smell that permeated the granite foundation of the courthouse and hung like a miasma to a distance of ten feet around the perimeter caused her distress, she didn't show it. It was particularly ripe, too, with the stinkpot stove in each of the two long sections burning against the February damp, drawing the stench steaming from the prisoners' rags and the piss and shit that embedded the stones. Burns had known male lawyers accustomed to every description of prison, once they stepped across that invisible line, to bury their noses in handkerchiefs soaked in Bay Rum. The jailer himself, on days like this and in summer when the air squatted on its haunches like a Kansas City mule, jacketed himself against the olfactory assault with apple-scented smoke from his pipe.

"No visitors without a pass signed by the judge, ma'am." He gripped the cherrywood bowl between thumb and fore-finger and puffed the exhaust out the corner of his mouth.

Shifting the flowers from one arm to the other, she untied a reticule from her wrist, opened it, and withdrew a sheet of foolscap with a slender hand in an oyster-colored leather glove. Burns accepted the sheet through the bars and un-folded it. He recognized the judge's hand, as jagged as his lectures to the condemned. He grunted and turned a heavy key in the lock. When she placed a foot on the threshold, he blocked the entrance with his body.

"You read the letter," she said.

"Ma'am, I did. It don't say you can see Leach. This is no place for a gentlewoman. Not all the prisoners wear irons, and they won't run rusty to use you for their freedom. It places the guards in hazard too."

Fine Irish color climbed her cheeks; but she did not press the matter. She drew the checked cloth from the basket. The warm sweet odor of the fresh-baked cake inside found his nostrils through the jail's eternal fug. "Please take this and the flowers to Mr. Leach. I'll be back with more for the men who were sentenced with him."

"It ain't my place to say, ma'am, but it's too good for his like."

"That's my husband's view, but as you can see from the pass I'm a lawyer's wife. The wretch is forced to sit and listen to the fall of the trap every day. No Christian would deny him one moment of repose."

"Yes, ma'am." He took the basket and flowers.

"Don't take a crumb for yourself. The jailers' rations are more than sufficient."

"No, ma'am."

Outside, Maledon's apparatus squealed and thumped.

"That man is fond of his work," she said.

"Yes, ma'am. He took to it right off."

She turned up the collar of her cape and withdrew.

He shut the door, drew a finger through the frosting, and tasted. Leach was unworthy, but Burns's rebellion stopped there. The forces in opposition were too great.

FOUR

"Judge; a word with you after the services?"

Parker, seated next to Mary and little Charlie in their pew in the First Methodist Church, looked up at the man standing over him in the aisle. He was young, fair, and abundantly freckled, but he wore heavy handlebars and with his hat in his hands the bones of his skull showed through a haircut as severe as any in the military. The six-pointed nickel-plate star of a deputy U.S. marshal rode high on his waistcoat.

"Wilkinson, isn't it?" Parker asked.

"Yes, sir. I took the oath last month."

"You can have five minutes. My family and I are attending Catholic services later."

Wilkinson registered no reaction to this evidence of marital diplomacy. Following the sermon, collection, and announcements of community activities, they reconvened on the steps of the church while Mrs. Parker, Charlie's shoulders in her iron grip, engaged the minister's wife in conversation. The judge looked tired; older than his thirty-eight years, with silver streaks in his beard and dark thumbprints under his eyes. He'd recently presided at his second multiple hanging—only five this time, after President Grant had without explanation commuted the sentence of a savage killer named Osee Sanders—and the press from the States had professed shock and disapproval as always, while sending correspondents in number to record every grisly detail.

"It's this man Diggs, who split a drover's head with an axe in the Cherokee three years ago," Wilkinson said, without preamble. "I've been reviewing his case. He was held in jail for a spell, and when no witnesses came forward they sprung him. Story was in charge. I'd like a crack at him."

The corners of Parker's mouth twitched. "If it's idleness you despise, I've a drawer full of warrants for murders more recent."

"I've a line on where he is, and the names of some witnesses. If you'll renew his warrant and draw up summonses, I'd bet my badge the outcome this time will be different."

"Don't bet what you've yet to earn."

"Earning it is just what I'm fixing to do."

Parker concentrated on getting his cigar lit evenly, then blew smoke at the steeple. "I'll review the case tonight. Come to my chambers tomorrow morning before the session and if everything is as you say I'll have Wheeler give you what you need."

"Thanks, Judge."

"Thank me after you've come back with your man, and without a load of buckshot in your kidneys."

"Isaac!" Mary Parker clamped her hands over Charlie's ears.

"I'm sorry, my dear. I didn't realize my voice carried."

"You should. You've been preaching to the back of the gallery for more than a year."

The next morning, Wilkinson closeted himself with Parker for fifteen minutes, waited in the hallway outside for another hour while Stephen Wheeler prepared the necessary documents and the judge signed them, and with the papers in his wallet went out to assemble provisions and supplies and redeem his horse from the livery. He made his last stop at the post office, where he dispatched telegrams to peace officers in Kansas, Missouri, and various parts of the Nations, and as far away as Ohio and Michigan. In the three years since the murder, many of those who could offer evidence against Diggs had scattered, including Hiram Mann, who had been struck with the same axe as had J. C. Gould, a companion on the cattle drive, and spent months in recovery before decamping to Detroit. Wilkinson instructed his informants to address their replies to Marshal Fagan.

He swam his horse across the Arkansas to the train station, where he loaded the animal aboard a stock car and boarded a sweatbox day coach for the three-hour run up the Santa Fe line to Springdale. Soaked and enervated, he considered a bath house, a saloon, and a room for the night, but the experience he'd brought to his new job warned him that when the hunt was on the hunted grew wary, and that there was no time to lose. Diggs had left two fellow cattle drovers lying in a pool of blood over a matter of twenty-seven dollars in cash belonging to the man who had died. He had friends in the Nations who considered it a reasonable transaction, and neighbors who had little cause to place more trust in Fort Smith than in men whose faces were familiar; once in flight, the desperate man had a broad choice of barns, corn ricks, root cellars, and empty cisterns to fort up in, living on provisions smuggled in to him while armies of federal men combed the hills and haystacks and thousands of square miles of tangled wilderness. Surprise was more than half the fight, and Wilkinson pocketed his star and wore the kit of a cowhand looking for cattle to start his own outfit.

The deputy had been less than straight when he'd pled his case with Parker. He'd bet his badge of office with confidence as to finding the witnesses to the atrocity, but the rumor that its perpetrator was still in the Nations was smoky at best. It didn't bear following into that alien country, where every man's hand seemed to be raised against him. Better to confirm it by way of the invisible telegraph line that ran through the nomadic bands of cowboys who rode the trails from Texas to Kansas.

In Baxter Springs, across the Kansas line, he wet his whistle at last in a bar long enough to hang a month's wash and struck up friendly conversations with others dressed as he, hands just in from the first spring drives. He asked each if he knew J. C. Gould, an old pard of his who might be persuaded to go in with him on his enterprise.

The pickings were slim. A lot of heads shook, and he wasted time and expense money buying whiskey for a jabbery waddy who turned out to know the wrong Gould. That first session wore him out worse than the train and the horseback ride combined. He camped out north of town to relieve stress on the U.S. Treasury and took up his post the next day in a different saloon, with antlers on the walls. He didn't want to raise the suspicions of a bartender about a saddle tramp with too much time on his hands and too much silver to spread around. Barmen soaked up gossip like slops and wrung it out with both hands.

There he dipped his bucket into the same dry well for hours. Gould seemed to have been one of those faceless men who drifted from camp to camp making no friends and no impression. Wilkinson began to wonder if he'd exhaust every watering hole in town, and what the clerk back in Fort Smith would tell the judge when he saw all those drinks in the column. But along toward evening, when the place began to fill up with unwashed bodies and coal-oil smoke, Wilkinson found a man who informed him of his friend's sad fate at the hands of a companion.

"They hang the son of a bitch?" the deputy asked.

The man, a Texas drover with handlebars more swooping than his own and a little paintbrush of a beard, splattered a brown ribbon into a cuspidor and drew a sleeve across his lips. "No, he got carpetbagger justice. They rubbed his kinky head for luck and set him loose."

"This Diggs is a nigger?"

"Hell yes. I rode with damn fine folk blacker'n him on the outside, but his goes clean through. It's a piece of good fortune they didn't elect him governor."

"How long ago was this?" He always sprinkled his interviews with queries he knew the answers to. It kept him from appearing eager.

"Three years, maybe more. I ride drag when I pass through the Nations and thank Christ for every mouthful of dust I swallow, on account of I know no bastard's lurking behind to crack my skull for what's in my poke."

"I hear things are different in Fort Smith now."

"Not so's you'd notice. They're hanging Christian white men while that murdering trash is drinking corn liquor on Spring Crick in front of God, the devil, and U. S. goddamn Grant."

This was new information, and Wilkinson looked down quickly at the glass he'd nursed down to plain water to dissemble his excitement. The suggestion that Diggs was living almost on top of the scene of his crime was bold even for a man who thought he'd beaten the scaffold. "What's on Spring Creek?"

"A Cherokee squaw and forty acres her pa left her. They say the son of a bitch watches her plow all day and brags all night on killing a white man and making away with it. John Wilkes Booth should of busted a cap on that carpetbagging Lincoln before he freed his first nigger."

"Who says this?"

The drover's brows shot up. "Well, everybody in Texas."

"Not about Lincoln. About Diggs farming on Spring Creek."

"Who the hell knows? You hear talk." He leaned over the cuspidor and pursed his lips, but this time he didn't spit. He swallowed and fixed Wilkinson with mud-colored eyes swimming in blood. "Why do you want to know? What outfit did you say you was with before you went maverick?"

"The Double D."

"I know that spread. You know George Slaughter?"

Sensing a trap, Wilkinson ordered another round apiece and turned the conversation toward the drover's opinion of the quality of beef to be found in the Nations. Half an hour later, when the other left the bar to weave his way toward the outhouse, the deputy left. He was pretty sure he wouldn't be missed in the rapidly increasing population of the saloon, but on his way to camp stopped his horse often to listen for pursuers. A man who got to thinking he'd said too much to the wrong man was a contrary creature.

The next day, Wilkinson wired the headquarters of the Cherokee police in Tahlequah to confirm the presence of James Diggs, Negro, on or near Spring Creek. The tribal elders had no love for outside killers, and by that afternoon he had his reply. He took on fresh grain for his horse and crossed into the Nations at Quapaw. He wore matched Colt Peacemakers in suspender holsters crossed at his back and carried a brass-receiver Winchester that fired the same caliber and a Stevens ten-gauge shotgun with both barrels cut back to street-sweeper length in scabbards slung from his saddle, with a stubby British Bulldog in a pocket for a hole card. He shipped his ammunition in gunnysacks, rifle and revolver cartridges in one, shotgun shells in the other, and all five Bull-dog rounds in the cylinder of the pocket gun. Two canteens, jerked venison, and pemmican cakes answered for his provisions; he intended to keep a cold camp, with no smoke or smell of boiling coffee to draw attention to where he stopped. Tobacco for chewing only, to dampen his craving for cigarettes and his pipe. He was new to the marshal's service, but not to the business of tracking men. In the wild they acquired animal instincts on top of their natural human shrewdness and were more to be feared than grizzlies. Poor Bill Spivey's picture hung prominently in Fagan's office for a reason.

A spring drizzle stood sentry square at the border and stayed with him all the way along the Neosho River and after it bent west and away, water pouring from the curl of his hat brim as from a gutter and sliding in sheets off his oilcloth slicker. Both items of gear failed to keep him from being soaked through; no matter how reliable a man's umbrella, when it rained he got wet. At times he seemed to be hauling the downpour with him, as if it came from a nozzle that followed his progress, a moving spout surrounded by dry. When he camped he made a shelter of the slicker with cottonwood branches, wrung out his socks, and slept until he was awakened by his own misery. It was Ozark country, carved by glaciers and sandblasted from solid rock by a billion years of dust and wind and hollowed out by the relentless rain. He picked his way down draws, leaning back on the reins, and when the path became nearly perpendicular he dismounted and led his horse, his feet squishing in his boots.

His sore luck held when the sun mocked him by breaking out bright as fool's gold just as he entered Tahlequah and the promise of a sound roof and a change of clothes. He seemed to have spent all his good fortune in the saloon in Baxter Springs. In front of Cherokee police headquarters he left his horse standing in mud fetlock deep, went inside to show his star and his warrant, and got an updated description of Diggs printed neatly by a big Remington type-writing machine, the polished pride of the office. His man had picked up a scar on his neck since his first visit to Fort Smith; Wilkinson wondered if there was another dead man in that. He shook hands with the officer, a broad-faced full-blood with short hair and his badge, a star in a circle, pinned to blue flannel, and went out to serve his warrant, wet clothes and all. One man knowing he was in town was one too many; you never knew where personal loyalties lay.

He reached Spring Creek by nightfall and crossed at a shallow spot onto Diggs's farm, which consisted of a slant-roofed barn and house, both unpainted, some chickens, a milch-cow lowing in its stall, and rows of planted vegetables with wooden stakes at the ends. A subsistence place, supporting itself and barely; God help the odd transient with evidence of prosperity. The deputy tethered his horse to a cedarbrake and sat down with his back against one of the scrubby trees in the line to wait for full dark. He watched the dying of the light and then the orange glow of a lamp drawing on in a window. The last bird sang its sweet challenge to bash in the heads of interlopers and the first cricket struck up the band. An owl fluted. Wilkinson sniffed and wiped his nose and chewed tobacco and shifted his weight from time to time to pluck his damp trousers away from a fine case of red-ass.

When he could no longer see the toe of his boot he got up, stroked his horse's muzzle, slid the Winchester from its scabbard, and started toward the house, leaning forward on the balls of his feet and groping with one hand for unseen twigs and branches. Just inside carbine range a dog started barking, one of the yappy kind with a hysterical nature.

The lamp went out. He stopped. He'd been towing a path of silence through the crickets; they started in again, filling the night with their stitching.

He'd taken care to direct his gaze away from the light, to preserve his night vision. Now the shape of the house with its canted roof showed blacker than the sky behind it, an inverted check mark with dark clumps of trees standing well away from the perimeter. Diggs, or more likely his hardworking Cherokee wife, had made sure to clear the area of cover, forcing invaders into the open. He hoped his own silhouette wasn't as exposed as he felt.

Something moved against the foundation; his hands jerked involuntarily at the carbine. A chain jingled. It was the dog, stabbing its muzzle this way and that for a stray scent. A growling *woof* escaped its throat.

In a little while—it seemed longer—a hinge squeaked. The dog fell to barking frantically. There was a blow, a yelp, a whimper. Wilkinson saw this movement. Then something moved against the scarcely lighter oblong of the window and he made out a man's head and shoulders and something hovering above the hump of the one on the right: an axe.

Wilkinson raised the Winchester to his shoulder. A trickle of sweat sprouted between his shoulder blades and wandered down toward his belt, prickling like ants' legs. So far there had been no sign of the woman. He had little practical experience with Indians, had listened in fascination when men from the northern plains had told of the stalking properties of the breed. If she were behind him with some kind of weapon . . .

He fired. The silhouette jerked away from the window. He didn't know if he'd hit anything.

Light bloomed in the window.

"Goddamnit, douse that!"

The lamp went out, but not before he spotted the man who had shouted, crouched on his haunches in front of the far corner of the house right of the window with the axe leveled across his abdomen. Wilkinson charged him, sprinting, gaze fixed to the spot. He was within pistol range when a shape grew up out of the ground and ran straight at him, swinging up the thing in his hands. The deputy closed the distance in six strides and swung the Winchester. The barrel connected with a thump and James Diggs fell at his feet.

* * *

Parker listened, eyes half-shuttered behind their heavy lids, while the witnesses who had drifted in from East and West gave evidence against the slayer of J. C. Gould. They spoke for three days, at the end of which the jury retired briefly and then the foreman rose.

Diggs died on the scaffold December 20, 1878, beside John Postoak, a Creek who had killed a married couple named Ingley in the Creek Nation. Diggs's widow claimed her husband's body for burial on the farm that had belonged to her father.

II

A Prayer
for Ned Christie

What though the field be lost?
All is not lost; th' unconquerable will,
And study of revenge, immortal hate,
And courage never to submit or yield.

—**JOHN MILTON,**
Paradise Lost

FIVE

"That man is fond of his work."

When Mary Parker's remark to jailer Burns reached the ears of its subject—as such things will—George Maledon accepted it as a compliment, not being given to analysis of those factors that may lead to a conclusion; but had he known the particulars, he would have forgiven them in the spirit of good Christian forebearance. Abstract concepts such as honor and the rule of law were alien to her gender.

He did not experience satisfaction in being the instrument of a man's early end, or in the suffering that might attend it, whatever the fellow's transgressions. He believed, along with the judge, that it was the law that executed a man, and that their partnership in the act itself was nothing more than the practical application of a decision foreordained by an efficient system of justice. Maledon aspired to apply that same efficiency toward the swift and antiseptic extinction of the life force, with minimum pain and maximum effect. It was true that a man strung from a cottonwood branch with dirty twine and left to strangle wound up no more dead than one escorted to a straight drop and a broken neck from good rope on a proper scaffold; the great difference lay in the time involved, and the shame of a constricted windpipe and twelve minutes of convulsions. He had heard horror stories of botched lynchings that had made him weep for the reputation of his life's work.

In pursuit of proof for his theory, the little man with the grizzled beard and sunken eyes had burned many bowls of black shag in his long German pipe, poring over medical texts borrowed from Dr. Du Val, with their diagrams and colored transparencies of the human spinal canal, and worn his thumbs through those pages of farm and cattlemen's catalogues devoted to the quality of obtainable hemp. The sections set aside by Sears, Roebuck and Montgomery Ward for shed and barn maintenance—specifically pine pitch and the various grades of linseed oil—he had smudged with brown iron-gall ink his own annotations in the margins. These sheets he had torn out and anchored in a stack beneath the rough clay pot into which he knocked his dottles; it was his ambition, after he retired, at some long date, to publish a working manual on his craft, with chapters covering extensively these mundane details.

Yucatan sisal was stiff and stubborn and unresponsive to treatment, and so he ordered good Kentucky hemp from St. Louis, an inch and an eighth thick, compressed to an inch after the necessary stretching with sandbags. Sears and Roebuck offered lubricants of the finest grade, which when kneaded into the coarse cord provided the acceleration required, when the trap opened and gravity took its part, to slam the great knot into the sweet hollow below and behind the left ear. (Maledon, himself left-handed, set the standard for this prejudice.) There followed that crisp report that announced the preferred vertebra well and truly split, and the nerves that carried sensation to the brain severed clean. In short, Maledon's science bore the sureness and finality of a bullet through the eye. (The heart, he'd learned through bitter experience, was a slow messenger.)

On the day of execution, Fort Smith residents observed him striding up Garrison Avenue, trailing smoke from the pipe his father had purchased in Bavaria and carrying a market basket on one arm. He was somewhat more fastidious about his dress than he was about his burden; his black suit was carefully brushed by his wife and his boots glistened with blacking, but the basket was the least bit small for its contents, and on those occasions when several customers awaited him, nooses hung out from under the hinged lids on both sides. They dangled yet again when he returned home; good rope could be used many times, reducing stress upon the court's parsimonious budget, and when it came time to remove one from the rotation, he displayed it on the wall in his private study as a memento. The papered walls of the little room were covered with nooses, each accompanied by tintypes of the men who had worn them, when the likenesses were available. His penchant for retaining souvenirs, it was rumored, had led to high words and chilly relations between the Maledons, and on one volatile afternoon a number of tintypes snatched off their hooks and cast down a well. Days of silence in the domestic arrangement had followed.

His wife disapproved of his work, changed subjects whenever it arose in conversation, and hectored him frequently about applying for another position with Parker's court. What she failed to grasp, and what he lacked the vocabulary to convey, was that she was married to an accomplished slayer of men. He'd killed for the Union, shot men as a police officer under three chiefs, and would put down permanently a total of five prisoners attempting to escape the federal jail during his residency. The fate of the first, slain shortly before his promotion from turnkey to chief executioner, had filled him with remorse; not for the life wasted, but because it had cheated the scaffold, and by reflection the engine of justice he'd sworn to maintain. It had been a factor in his immediate decision to accept the judge's offer that first day in chambers. On the four succeeding occasions, he would not hesitate to draw and fire one of the paired Smith & Wessons he wore butts-forward on the belt he strapped around his waist (he remained a deputy U.S. marshal withal, which carried the responsibility of arming himself on duty and off), aiming from instinct for the vitals, the way he'd been taught, but he considered each instance a failure. Close observers would note that just before the hangings that directly succeeded those episodes, Maledon took extra time and care adjusting the nooses, as if to atone for whatever incaution had led to the prisoners' fancy that there was a way around Parker's pronouncements other than the vertical. He was a man of principle.

Beyond question, Maledon's wife disapproved of his work; but she inspected him for lint and loose buttons whenever he ventured out to perform it, like any good helpmeet, and corrected what needed correction on the spot, disregarding his protestations that it would make him tardy at his post. She would not be seen as a neglectful wife. These attentions bound her spiritually to Mary Parker, who baked cakes and cut flowers from her own garden to brighten the last days of the men her husband sent to perdition. They took tea together often, secure in their sisterhood.

Maledon had not that respite to vary his days. He worshipped Isaac Parker but respected his office—held it in awe, bestowed as it was by hand by the man in the White House; Ulysses S. Grant, the hero of Appomattox—and did not presume to overstep the invisible barrier that separated them. Deep within him he sensed a revulsion on Parker's part for his lieutenant's physical connection with the act of killing those who'd killed. He resented this in his turn, but chose to cloak the distance thus created in a pious German conviction in the difference between the classes. Women were a race unto themselves, unified by a common uterus, while men were divided like milch cows and beef on the hoof, geldings and studs. And so, once justice had carried, these partners in its carriage retired separately to their solitary reflections, the jurist to his case histories, the hangman to his ropes and tintypes. Unlike the military, the American judicial system there on the fringe of the frontier provided no club for officers of the court to socialize, commiserate, and find common ground. Maledon had not even the experience of a democratic upbringing to express his opinions on the situation even to himself.

Both men, however, shared the same low opinion by their wives regarding certain aspects of their calling.

In truth, apart from Maledon's profession and the eagerness he brought to it, his mate had little to complain about. Tobacco was his only vice, and he confined his consumption to his study and the outdoors to preserve her linens. He attended church every Sunday, a few rows behind the Parkers, ignored other women apart from raising his hat when he passed them on the street, and did not take strong drink, nodding in approval whenever a condemned man used his circumstances to deliver a lecture on the evils of alcohol to the restless audience gathered to see him in his throes. In public, Mr. and Mrs. Maledon behaved as if they were equal to Judge and Mrs. Parker, who had the good grace not to betray the presumption. Their daughter, Annie, played with young Charlie, sometimes tormenting him according to the laws of her sex; when the new school had opened, they were among the first in attendance. Younger siblings, when they came along, would spend much time in one another's company. The children were popular with their peers. Local opinion, led by the editors of the *Fort Worth Elevator,* did not hold with the clucking attitude of the Eastern press; those institutions represented civilized America, with a uniformed officer on every corner and space on the docket to parse out punishment one man at a time. Thanks to the judge and his most loyal servant, life was orderly there on the border, so long as one avoided the saloons and brothels, and the families of the men who stood for justice commanded respect.

George Maledon *was* fond of his work. He took pleasure in it for itself alone, with no more malice toward those most directly involved than a wood-carver felt toward an unfinished piece of pine, or a painter a blank sheet of canvas. During his long, long career in the faithful service of the Eighth District Court, he would know only two exceptions, when he thoroughly savored the anticipation of bringing extinction to a fellow traveler.

Both times he would be denied his subject.

Ned Chistie was the first.

SIX

The most widely circulated photograph of Ned Christie, taken in Fort Smith in 1892, does not do him justice.

He was born September 14, 1852, in Rabbit Trap Canyon in the Going Snake District of the Cherokee Nation, and was in his thirty-third year when his life turned full round on a pivot. Indians and whites acknowledged him an uncommonly fine-looking man, six-foot-four with black hair that reached nearly to his waist and Mandarin whiskers, well filled out for one who claimed Cherokee ancestry on both sides. He belonged to the tribal legislature—the Kee-too-wah—and with his frank eyes and easy smile had established a reputation for charming sworn enemies over to his side when it came to a vote. Women admired him, but he was devoted to his wife and children and kept close counsel with his father, a man widely revered in the nation as Uncle Watt, who knew little English but had seen that Ned became fluent. The son was indiscriminate in drink, but that was a general failing in a territory where alcohol was prohibited and as easy to obtain as a tick bite. Whether boring out a barrel in his gunsmith's shop or walking along a street in Tahlequah deep in conversation with a fellow lawmaker, Ned Christie turned heads, male and female.

Without question, his picture did not do him justice; but then, he was dead when it was taken.

Christie's cabin, in a clearing just inside Rabbit Trap with miles of dense black undergrowth at its back, was a regular stop on the local whiskey peddler's route. This entrepreneur, who had served ninety days in the Fort Smith jail for mistaking a deputy U.S. marshal for a customer, carried a rawhide-bound notebook scribbled in cipher that told him when Christie was paid for his service to the electorate, and on that day turned his wagon toward Going Snake. On the afternoon whose events would bring Christie to Judge Parker's attention it was payday, and he had purchased two squat earthen jugs of skullbender, distilled from water retrieved from the Salt Fork of the Arkansas, fermented potatoes, chewing tobacco, red pepper, and turpentine, with a pinch of gunpowder to taste. Christie carried the jugs as far as his front porch, where he and John Parris, Cherokee also, sat on split-bottom chairs passing the first jug back and forth, swigging, and taking target practice on trees and small animals with a pair of revolvers the gunsmith had brought home from his shop to test their sights. Christie's wife came out to call him in for noon dinner but he sent her back inside.

"Leetle off," he said, when he'd missed the pine knot he'd aimed at and gonged the bucket hanging on his well.

"Couldn't be that snake piss we're drinking," Parris said.

"Nope. I shoot better when I see double."

"How is that?"

"I sight in betwixt the two."

They laughed loudly. Christie's wife shut the window.

Something moved in the brush. Parris closed one eye and fired. A yelp went up. A moment later a scruffy white dog slunk out into the open on three legs. The left rear was shattered and bleeding.

"Shit. That's my neighbor's dog."

"He favor it?"

"It'll follow a coon right up a tree. Did anyway."

"He don't have to know a coyote didn't get it." Parris leveled the revolver again.

Christie backhanded the barrel. The bullet went skyward. The dog picked up its pace, panting and whimpering.

"Headed home." Christie pulled at the jug.

"You're too soft on critters. We better reload before your neighbor gets here."

"I won't shoot a man over a dog. I wouldn't shoot a dog over a man, come to that."

When in due course the neighbor appeared, the two were nearing the bottom of the first jug and weren't inclined toward patient conversation. Words were said, in English and Cherokee, and when the man turned around saying he'd see about that, Parris threw the jug at his head. Fortunately it missed; when it struck the ground, it was the ground that gave.

"See if there's any left," Christie told Parris.

Deputy United States Marshal Dan Maples rode out from Tahlequah in answer to the neighbor's complaint. The pair was still on the porch drinking. The sun was setting, the cabin's front and rear windows were in line, and the red orb seemed to be glaring from inside the walls. Maples had heard gunfire, but he knew Christie and stepped down with his Colt still in its hip scabbard. He was a smallish man but built like a prizefighter. He had a reputation back in Bentonville, Arkansas, of never having picked a quarrel, while putting an end to more than a few picked by others. People of the Nations considered him one of Parker's good ones.

"Ned, that dog had to be shot again and put down. A good coon dog's worth two dollars. You ought to square it with your neighbor. We'll just forget you tried to brain him."

"That was John, both times."

Maples heard Parris suck air in through his nose. The two didn't seem to like each other that much. Liquor was the common bond.

"I'll take your word on that, Ned," said the deputy. "It don't matter who pays, just so's it's paid."

"In that case, you pay him."

"It don't work that way. It happened on your property. That makes you responsible. Is this how you handle things in the Kee-too-wah?"

"Talk American. A white man talking Cherokee makes me puke."

"Cherokee's American, Ned. It don't get more American than that."

Liquid gurgled. Maples shifted his position to put the sun out of his eyes. Black and purple floaters obscured the outlines of the men seated on the porch.

"It's two dollars, Ned. You want to make a federal case?"

Christie barked. It was a close approximation of a dog. Out hunting, he could swindle a turkey with his gobble and an elk when he snorted. "That's right, Dan. I want to make a federal case. Why don't you step up here and take me back to Fort Smith and dandle me from Parker's tears because my neighbor's got to shinny up trees by himself from here on?"

Parris laughed, a high-pitched alcoholic giggle that sent snakes up the deputy's back. He thought if he could get Christie away from his companion he could make him see reason. A man wanted to appear tall to his friends.

Maples wound the reins he was holding around his wrist. "Let's go to your neighbor's place, just you and me. We'll all sit down and come to an understanding."

Flame spurted from the porch. Maples' horse swung its head, dragging him off balance. He heard the shot and right behind it a branch cracking not far from him. He raked out his big Colt from instinct. He saw flame again, but didn't hear the shot or anything else until his horse stopped dragging him and he lay on his back in the dirt and heard the noise the crickets made as dusk settled, fading.

Thomas Boles was the United States marshal in Fort Smith in 1885. Balding, with a graying beard that rivaled George Maledon's for length if not for bristle, he'd served as a judge in Arkansas, been elected twice to Congress, run the land office in Dardanelle for President Hayes, and been appointed to his current position by President Arthur. Those who knew him for his many kindnesses called him Uncle Tom. Others, impressed by his bearing, referred to him—always among themselves, never to his face—as the Old Roman. He was forty-eight and inclined to be sanguine, but when he read the

telegram from the Cherokee police in Tahlequah, he shouted
for his secretary, and when the young man presented himself handed him the wire and told him to get it to Judge Parker
right away.

"Sir, court's in session."

"I know that. Did you think I thought it was Sunday?"

"The judge—"

"He won't thank you for waiting until he adjourns. Give it
to the bailiff and tell him to deliver it to the bench at once.
Then come back here with the deputy roster. I want the name
of every man on duty in the Cherokee Nation."

The secretary left, shaken by the emotion in the marshal's
voice.

Parker was trying a case of rape. He scowled when the bailiff hurried up the aisle and stuck the yellow flimsy under
his nose. The victim, testifying in a voice barely audible, faltered and fell silent. The reporter covering the trial for the
Elevator noted that the man seated behind the big cherry
desk, gray now of hair and beard, drew his face taut as he read.
His hand found his gavel. He declared a recess of fifteen
minutes and was on his way to the door when the other men
and women in the room were still rising at Crier Hammersly's
command.

The judge entered Boles's office in his robes and found the
marshal studying a closely type-written list of names with his
secretary standing over him.

"Is it true?" Parker asked. "Is it confirmed?"

Boles nodded his great round head. "I know the man who
sent the wire. I thought I knew Christie, too, at least by reputation. He's been a credit to his tribe his whole life."

"His whole life is behind him. What about this man
Parris?"

"I don't know him." Boles handed the sheet to his secretary. "Wire Tahlequah. Tell them to locate the men whose
names I've checked and send them out to Going Snake. Start
there and turn over every rock west of Fort Smith. If they

don't know Parris, they're to be accompanied by someone who can identify him."

"What about Christie?" the young man asked.

"Everyone in the Cherokee knows Christie by sight. Go."

The secretary left. Parker asked the marshal the names of the deputies he'd selected.

"John Curtis, Joe Bowers, and John Fields. All good men, and they speak the lingo."

"Maples should have arrested both of them when he caught them drinking whiskey."

"If my deputies did that every time they saw it, there wouldn't be any room in the jail for murderers and rapists. The charge is a bargaining chip, to get information. Beyond that I won't comment. These men have to deal directly with the natives every day."

"Keep me informed. I don't care if I'm in the middle of pronouncing sentence."

Boles agreed. There were tears in Parker's eyes.

"I know Nancy Shell," Deputy Fields said. "I've bought a bottle or two from her myself, purely in the interest of criminal investigation."

Deputy Curtis didn't laugh. He'd been first on the scene after the killing and had pressed his ear against Dan Maples' cold breast. Inside the cabin he'd found Christie's wife with her children gathered around her like pickets, and had known before he asked his question what the answer would be. It was a waste of time trying to batter down that Indian barrier once it was in place.

He said, "Parris buys his whiskey there, when he's got the price. If I was him I'd run there if I couldn't run home."

"I'd feel better Bowers was along."

"He's with Chief Bushyhead, in case Christie takes it in his head to go back and get the Kee-too-wah on his side."

They crossed Spring Creek. Fields said, "Right around

here's where Jim Wilkinson put the irons on that nigger Diggs. Parker's friends are few here."

"Well, let's see if we can cut down on the enemies."

Nancy Shell received them in her parlor. She was some part Cherokee and several parts other things, with blue eyes in a round flat face, and her house was the same. Indian rugs and pots shared space with porcelain lamps, pictures in oval frames, and what had to be the only daisy-horn phonograph between Fort Smith and Texas. She got up from her rocking chair from time to time to change the cylinder, but it always seemed to be the same tin tenor singing the same song in Italian. The presence of two tall marshals in striped suits and weaponry made no impression on her features. She'd offered them whiskey, but they'd declined. She rolled a cigarette as they spoke, concentrating on getting the flakes of tobacco arranged evenly and sliding a sharp tongue tip along the edge of the paper. She lit it, blew smoke out her nostrils, and said, "John."

She hadn't raised her voice, but the curtains stirred in a doorway and a man ducked his head to clear the frame. He wasn't as tall as Christie, but he was on a level with the lawmen, and he appeared to be unarmed.

"Good morning, John," Fields said.

"I don't know you."

"Sure you do. Last time I seen you here I said I'd arrest you next time."

"I ain't had a drop. Ain't got the price."

"Well, things have changed. We're arresting you for the murder of Dan Maples. You're to answer for him in Fort Smith, or here if that's your choice." Fields drew his Colt.

Parris turned to run. Curtis, quicker to act than his partner, scooped out his Colt and slammed the barrel across the back of Parris' head. When he hit the floor, the phonograph needle scratched the cylinder.

"You boys want to wrassle, do it outside," Nancy Shell said. "I keep an orderly house."

Curtis got a grip on the unconscious man's collar, dragged him across the floor and down the steps of the porch, and dumped him into the burned-out yard, where he kicked him in the ribs until he came to and tried to roll himself up into a ball. Curtis caught him on the forehead with a heel and he jerked out straight on his back. Fields stood on the porch and lit a cigar.

"Easy on his head," he said, tossing away the match. "Maledon needs it to keep the rope from slipping off."

Curtis went around behind the cabin and came back hauling a bucket slopping water over the top. He slung its contents over the man on the ground. Parris spluttered, cursed in English and Cherokee, and sat up, his hair plastered over his eyes. Fields left the porch, slid his Whitney shotgun from its scabbard on his saddle, and threw it to Curtis. When Parris parted his hair like a curtain, both muzzles hovered six inches away. Curtis palmed back the hammers with a crunch.

"I didn't shoot him!" Parris shrieked. "It was Ned."

SEVEN

Ned Christie couldn't believe his luck; so he waited.

He'd beaten his way through heavy underbrush, crossed a field, and torn a hole in the knee of his trousers climbing over a fence in the dark to approach his gunsmith's shop from behind, to find no light in the windows and no signs of occupancy inside. The marshals were too smart— many of them, anyway—to give away their presence by striking a match, but he had a hunter's sense about such things and felt strongly in his heart that no trap awaited him. But he'd learned about the world outside the tribe in the mission school and placed his faith in things other than his instincts. Civilized man was a trickster and could not be trusted to behave according to the laws of the spirit. He had no soul, and therefore no scent. A place that contained him was as one empty.

And so he waited, on his belly like the spreading adder, sent to kill Sister Sun before she could annihilate the People for grimacing when they looked at her. This was a story his father knew and believed, and although Ned had been spoiled against it and all the others, he thought often in their terms. Watt Christie's simple faith and the travesty in Tahlequah, where the Cherokee raised points of order and recognized speakers from the floor and comported themselves like little white men, had made of his son a mixed thing, part Indian, part snake.

After some little time, measured in shades of darkness, Ned Christie rose and crept forward, drawing his only weapon, one of the revolvers he'd taken home to test in his other life, with two cartridges unfired. That was good if there were no more than two marshals, better if there was but one. He did not want to kill marshals. The second bullet would free him from his anguish.

The shop was deserted, he found when he broke the lock on the back door and no fire came from the darkness. Sheathing the revolver under his waistband, he moved surely in the gloom, feeling for the long guns in their rack, the assorted pistols and revolvers in their drawers, and the boxes of ammunition on the shelves, which he placed on the woven rug on the floor and tied into a bundle with his belt. He moved swiftly and noiselessly. With the bundle cradled in one arm he turned to leave, then remembered the bottle of Old Pepper he kept under the counter for days when business was slow. He was sober. His head timpanned from the late effects of trade whiskey consumed hours before. He moved aside the blanket that covered the door to the front of the shop—and snatched the revolver from his trousers. He smelled a man.

"Do not shoot."

The words were Cherokee.

* * *

Watt Christie watched his son tip up the bottle with the strange characters printed on the label. He himself had no taste for liquor and resented the universal notion that all Indians were born drunks, with a raging thirst for whiskey and no tolerance for its effects. It hurt him to see Ned undermining his argument. He was proud of his son's accomplishments, but he prayed each night to the old gods to free him from his persistent devil.

They sat in chairs near the cold stove in the front of the shop with the shades drawn and a coal-oil lantern turned very low on the floor at their feet. The orange glimmer left their upper halves in shadow, but kept Watt's despair from worming into his vitals. Ned made no protest. For him the whiskey seemed to produce the same result.

"I knew I would find you here." Watt spoke in Cherokee; English was one puzzle that eluded his wisdom. "I taught you never to go into the brush without a rifle. You never know when supper might present itself."

Ned said nothing. Clothing rustled. Whiskey gurgled.

"It is all over the Nation. Parris told the marshals you shot Dan Maples."

"I did not." Ned answered him in the same tongue. "John shot the dog and Maples, and he would have shot my neighbor too if the jug was not more handy."

"You must go to the Kee-too-wah and tell them this. They will see you to Fort Smith, where your version may be told. They say Parker is a fair man, sympathetic to the People."

"So much so that he has hanged thirteen of us in ten years."

"He has hanged more of Them than he has of us. It was not always so. You are too young to remember."

"I remember when you could buy your own warrant from a marshal for twenty dollars American. There is much to be said for the way it was."

"This is not my son I hear."

"You are deceived. We only have friends in Fort Smith until one of them is killed by one of us. They do not ask who. Any Cherokee will answer. I will not spend months in that shithole prison only to have my neck wrung like a turkey. If they take me I will not have even that choice. They beat John half to death to get that lie out of him, and they will beat me the other half. It is a hundred miles to Fort Smith and hell. I will not give *them* that choice. I will die here where I was born, with a rifle in my hand."

"Who will look after your wife and children?"

"The tribe will take care of them. Remember, I helped write that law."

"It is a good law. The white man has none like it." Watt took in air to the base of his lungs, then expelled it. "It seems years since you sat in town and made law."

"The white man's law ends where death begins. He believes in nothing thereafter, not even his angels and jabbery. He poisons everything he touches and calls it bread."

"You forget that it is a Cherokee who brought you to this pass."

"John Parris never liked me. He set himself out to make me as bad as him, and I fell in like the fool I am. Parker's marshals are not fools, but they chose him over me. There is no justice there. Even their tongue is twisted. From this day forth I will speak it no more."

"That is an unwise choice. The tongue of our ancestors is written on water. It will be forgotten in your lifetime."

"You overestimate my span. I will be dead before you sprout your next white whisker. But before then, they will know I lived."

"What can one man do against so many?"

"Others feel as I do. We will strike in number and then trickle away through the woods as water."

Watt wiped his eyes. "You say you are not a killer and yet you speak as one."

"I intend to break each of the laws I helped write. But upon your head I promise I will take no life unless mine is threatened. I will not shoot to kill, even if the man in my sights is a marshal."

"Where will you go?"

Ned drank. "Why? So you can tell your friends in Fort Smith?"

"That is unkind."

Here the translation falls far short of the original. The Cherokee language has relatively few syllables, but the arrangement is everything.

"I spoke rashly," Ned said then. "I am angry at myself. I became bewitched by the sweet scent of my own armpits and presumed to walk with my betters. I scaled a ladder like a squirrel thinking himself a man. The squirrel does not own the ladder. The man snatched it away. The squirrel fell to earth."

"My counsel now is worthless." Watt Christie unbuttoned his shirt, exposing a canvas money belt cinched around his middle. He unbuckled it and leaned forward to lay it in his son's lap. "That is every cent I have. Spend it on food, not whiskey. A man who has declared war upon the United States must keep his wits about him."

"I will steal what I need and slay what I eat." Ned lifted the belt and held it out.

Watt shook his head. "You are not as good a hunter as you think."

Which statement gave his son his first chuckle in many hours.

Deputy Joe Bowers, having satisfied himself that Chief Dennis Bushyhead and the Cherokee national council would not assist one of their own to evade the law, rode out to Ned Christie's cabin to serve the murder warrant. He did not expect to find him at home, but knew he would be lurking some-where inside Rabbit Trap, which was a good name for a can-yon that the closer a man rode to its tangled wilderness the more it looked like a place the smallest rodent could not penetrate. Yet the Cherokee had hunted it for generations, and those who had gone into private illegal enterprise had car-ried in their equipment piece by piece and assembled whis-key stills in clearings in the brush that had to be beaten back every few weeks to keep the forest from reclaiming lost ground. It was no place for a white man to go after dark, par-ticularly on Parker's business, and so he'd spent the night in Tahlequah while Fields and Curtis interviewed John Parris at Nancy Shell's. In the morning, after two cups of coffee and a plate of biscuits larded with gravy—a delicacy he found best to his liking in the Nations and nowhere else—he crossed into Going Snake.

The other two deputies had advised him to wait for them, but Bowers knew Christie for a reasonable man who would go quietly to Fort Smith to clear up what he himself was con-vinced was a misunderstanding. Even Christie's political opponents attested to his loyalty to the rule of law. Bowers blamed drink—the universal plague in that territory—and some kind of mix-up that Parker would set right.

He found Christie's wife, fine-featured for a full-blood with enormous mahogany-colored eyes, sewing a patch onto a pair of her husband's canvas trousers in their parlor, with a bone needle and a sailor's palm on her hand; the honey locust thorns and shagbark hickory played hell with the toughest and coarsest-woven fabric—and forgetting her English when he asked where Ned was and when she expected him back. He knew a smattering of Cherokee, enough anyway to ask the same questions, but not enough to sort anything out of the rapid-fire responses she knew damn well were too much for him. Leave it to a woman to find a way to cooperate with an officer of the court and flummox him at one and the same time. He admired her, and by extension Christie; he'd never known a woman who'd pay him half the respect she paid her man. It said a great deal about the man. Very soon he'd regret such carelessness, and continue to do so every time it rained or snowed for the rest of his life.

The children were at school, but he didn't consider waiting for them an economical use of his time. Cherokee youth obeyed its parents like three-day-old whelps, at least until it reached that damnable age when it knew all that transpired in the world and at the bottom of the wine-dark sea (Bowers read Homer the way Parker read the Old Testament, frequently and with pauses to commit long passages to memory), and held all who came before it as benighted and pathetic. The deputy thanked Mrs. Christie, put on his hat, and went out to beat the brush. Christie was two dollars on the hoof and a man had to pay for his biscuits and gravy.

He'd trafficked with Indians sufficient to know why they were the best hunters of game who ever lived: a white man, armed to the teeth and away from paying work, fretted about the time and expense and the humiliation that awaited him at the hands of his peers if he returned to civilization emptyhanded, while an Indian, nearly naked and carrying a bow, thought of nothing but his quarry. The difference separated the two by the span of three seconds, during which a turkey flushed suddenly and without warning fluttered either to safe harbor behind a tardy shot or crashed to the ground before its wings had chance to spread wide. Bowers was cogitating along these very lines when a high-pitched gobble sounded from a thicket to his left. *Supper,* he thought, and was in the act of unscabbarding his Winchester when a bullet struck him square on the knob of bone that stuck out the side of his left knee. Splinters of white-orange pain took away his breath, and he had to grab the horn of his saddle to keep from tumbling off his horse. The carbine fell—and added to Ned Christie's growing arsenal as the deputy raked at the flanks of his mount and galloped to safety like a wounded turkey.

That afternoon a Cherokee surgeon in Tahlequah spent an agonizing hour separating fragments of lead from shards of bone, wound gauze around the leg, and pronounced Joe Bowers a lucky man.

"Lucky enough to walk with a limp until God calls me home." The patient anesthetized himself from a flask of Old Gideon.

"Lucky enough to walk at all," said the surgeon. "Ned hits where he aims."

Deputy Fields told Joe Bowers he had balls bigger than his brains, and cursed him for a pettifogging fool all the way to Christie's cabin.

"Don't go out there in hot blood, John," Curtis had said. "Wait till we get what more we can out of Parris and we'll both go. You don't want to repeat Joe's mistake."

"Joe went out there to talk. That was the mistake."

He told Curtis to stay with Parris. The surgeon was wrapping their prisoner's broken ribs, and Fields didn't trust the man enough to leave them alone; Christie had friends all over and there were poisons on the shelf sufficient to wipe out an army of witnesses who could give evidence against him. He checked the loads in all his firearms and drew a fresh horse from the livery.

That idiot cripple Bowers had learned a bit of the lingo, passed a pleasant how-de-do with Christie when Christie was sober and disposed to behave like a senator from Michigan, and thought he knew the red man. No one knew a red man but another red man, and sometimes not even him. But Fields knew the depth of the chasm between civilized man's concept of justice and order and the savage's notion of right and wrong. He determined to camp out at Christie's cabin for however long it took him to return to the bosom of his family and to tell him, over the barrel of a carbine, how the cow ate the cabbage and that there was no help for it but to plead his case in Fort Smith, wearing irons all the way. One dead deputy was one too many when manpower was short and miles were long, and now another was on crutches.

He caught both kinds of luck. It was first light when he got to Rabbit Trap, and Christie was at home, asleep next to his wife, whose instincts were even keener than his. At the first clink of a bit-chain outside the cabin she nudged him. He leapt from bed, scooped up his Winchester in the same movement, kicked wide the door to the outside, and pared a rasher of bacon off the side of Fields's weathered neck as the deputy wheeled his horse to narrow the target. Fields, caught by surprise both by the man's presence and by his sudden appearance, rode hell for leather in the opposite direction, blood flying in a rooster tail from a flesh wound that would vex him for weeks, scabbing over and breaking open fresh every time he forgot and turned his head too fast; expecting any time during the ride the sudden slam of a bullet in his back. Christie held his fire, but the memory of that nightmare flight would haunt the deputy forever, ruining him for the life of an active peace officer.

Days later, a message from Rabbit Trap reached Tahlequah by Cherokee telegraph: "Tell the marshals to stop sneaking around and I'll stop shooting them."

When word got to Fort Smith, Parker didn't weep. The deputies were still alive, through no virtue of their own, and in any case after ten years on the bench he'd heard so much harrowing testimony and dropped the gavel on men of such abiding wickedness, rapists and debauchers, horse cripplers, slaughterers of families, that nothing short of the serious illness of his wife or sons—two, now, following the birth of Jimmie—could squeeze a tear from those weary ducts. His sentences now fell with the crack of a lash, and Mary's cakes for the condemned erected a barrier that separated man and wife along the very foundation of those things each held dear. Rumors persisted of days of silence in the Parker household after a hanging.

He did not weep, but interrupted court for only the second time on news from the territory to summon Marshal Boles to his chambers.

Boles regarded him across the walnut desk the size of a dinner table, scaped with writing paraphernalia, burst leather portfolios in heaps, and cigars standing to attention in a glass jar. "Christie's no ordinary outlaw."

"They're all ordinary," Parker snapped. "Possums are less common. Our purpose is to make them extraordinary, and as rare as dodoes."

"They say he's sworn never to kill an officer of the court."

"*They* say reams of nonsense about Jesse James and his kindness to widows. If Christie took such an oath, he should have done so before he killed Dan Maples."

"I wouldn't place a great deal of faith in the word of that man Parris. His reputation gives a bad name to Indians everywhere."

"An innocent man places his faith in a public trial. Some of the worst men who have trod the scaffold put up less protest than Christie."

"One deputy is dead and two wounded. I fear we'll lose more before he's run to ground, and that when he is he will never stand on the scaffold."

"If that's his choice we'll honor it."

Boles fingered his beard. "Is that a judicial order?"

"Don't flower it up with legal rhetoric. These are simple men, recruited by Fagan and you and your other predecessors from rough fields. Tell them to abandon the quaint conceit of taking Ned Christie alive."

EIGHT

In 1889, Judge Isaac C. Parker had commanded the Eighth District Court fourteen years, six days per week, with sessions often extending into the small hours of the morning, to be reconvened at 8:00 A.M. In that time, his dark hair and beard had turned silver, although he was not yet fifty, and close study of case histories by lamplight had left deep dents in the bridge of his nose from gold-rimmed reading spectacles. In that time also, five United States marshals had been appointed to direct the activities of deputies who patroled the Nations. It was a pork-barrel post, assigned by various presidents in reward for services rendered in electing them to office, with spoils attendant and no specific requirement beyond a talent for administration, and some were better at that than others, who left the details to a succession of anonymous secretaries and clerks. Terms in Congress, judgeships, and high rank in the military crowded these men's past professional experience, with little or no connection to fieldwork in law enforcement; the legend of the hard-riding, straight-shooting U.S. marshal was an invention of hack writers, who would also create the myth of the town sheriff. By and large these officials spent their days behind desks and their whiskers resembled those of elder buffalo, which grew them to the ground. Five marshals, with three to go before Parker's robes went up on the hook for good.

Gone was the courthouse in the barracks with its hellish basement jail. The building had been given over to jailers' quarters, and the former courtroom to the detention of female prisoners. Now Parker adjudicated from behind a high oak bench of the Eastern type in a stately three-story structure of red brick, with attic storage for physical evidence exhibited in criminal trials: stained axes, broken bottles, pistols, knives; common junk out of context, but each someone's tragedy.

Pair upon pair of shoes and boots for whose possession men had been slain; a museum of lore as sordid as a reliquary from the Spanish Inquisition. The building dominated South Sixth Street near the center of town, a block from Garrison Avenue and culturally miles from the old fort where Parker had condemned forty-three men; a little less than half the number he would eventually send to the most notorious apparatus of execution after the guillotine of Paris. This structure stood where it always had, on the grounds of the old powder magazine, but with a sloping roof now to protect Maledon and his subjects from the elements and a high board fence to keep out the uninvited. No longer would crowds stream in from remote places to buy chicken legs and bottles of beer from vendors and watch men die in ones, twos, and sixes. Parker disapproved, but had been trumped by Congress in deference to public opinion in the States; he believed now as he had from the start that capital punishment was a public affair, carried out honestly and in the open, and not behind cover, like a lynching in a barn. But men more persuasive than he had been chipping away at his authority for years. His decisions now were vulnerable to appeal to higher courts, although no attorney had as yet mustered the sand to seek another opinion on his client's behalf.

Even the redoubtable William H. H. Clayton, who had welcomed the Parkers to Fort Smith and introduced himself as the judge's partner in the prosecution of criminals from the Western District of Arkansas and the great Nations, had been forced to sit out the current Cleveland administration, pursuing private practice, while another pled cases for the U.S. in his place. Disregarding loyal local functionaries who had continued to serve him since his earliest days, Parker remained the single consistent and unifying feature of the federal court on the border, with one exception; George Maledon, more grizzled and bristly than ever, still climbed the whitewashed steps of the scaffold, bearing his basket of ropes and dropping two-hundred-pound sandbags from them through the trap.

As for those who had best cause to hate and dread judge and executioner, they awaited trial and sentence in a well-ventilated jailhouse that from a distance resembled a military barracks, with full hospital facilities staffed by a doctor and male nurses. Situated between Second and Third streets, it offered food and sanitary provisions far superior to the vermin-infested meat and foul buckets that once stood in the chimney wells of the old basement. Here, shackles were rarely used, a last resort for the violent, the escape-obsessed, and the suicidally inclined. Showers had replaced the bathtubs made from half-barrels, and ablutions were encouraged, rather than offered as a reward for good behavior. However, the *squee-thump* of Maledon's responsibility penetrated to its depths as it had those of the first jail.

Fort Smith had grown, away from its reputation as a Gomorrah for cowboys from Texas to drink whiskey to the point of insensibility and sample women of a particular type, toward a place where families settled in proper frame houses, attended the churches of their choice, and sent their children to school. There was talk of spreading macadam on the streets of mud and dust, of adding a second streetcar to the line. The discharge of a firearm in the Silver Dollar or the House of Lords or any of their twenty-odd competitors brought swift investigation, jail, and a fine. Row girls were prohibited from soliciting business in the saloons—indeed, even from entering—and a 9:00 P.M. curfew was strictly enforced upon them.

Fines levied for infractions swelled the treasury and helped finance the civic improvements. What passed without comment—for it was scarcely necessary—was that Fort Smith was growing on the broad shoulders of Judge Parker. With justice come to the frontier, settlers and the merchants who lived off their trade bought lots, broke ground, and built without fear for the safety of themselves and their children. When the Parkers rode to church in their fine carriage-and-pair, women on the street nodded and men removed their hats. For visitors stopping over on their way West, the spectacle was like getting a glimpse of the royal family in London.

Throughout all of these recent developments, these sweeping advances and reforms, Ned Christie remained at large.

Four years had passed since his declaration of war, and he had not been heard to utter a word of English in all that time. Around him he had gathered a small army of men who felt as he. Youths mostly, they were in open rebellion against their stoic parents, for whom the shameful story of the Five Tribes' eviction from the Eastern states at the stroke of a presidential pen, and the corpse-strewn Trail of Tears that had led them at bayonet point to this desolate place, were tests of the People by the Ancient. For their children it was an atrocity, and Ned Christie was their avenger. They abandoned their schoolbooks and the tools of civilized trades and joined him to raid corrals of horses, shops of supplies and provisions, and wanderers of cash. The only token required for induction into this society was a working rifle and extra ammunition. "With this," Christie said, hoisting a new Ballard above his head, "I live longer."

His cabin was stacked with weapons: Winchester carbines and Henry rifles, Stevens shotguns, revolvers from the factories of Colt and Remington in America and of Deane-Adams in England, belly guns, horse pistols, hideouts, guns that loaded through the breech and through the muzzle, guns that took cartridges and ball-and-percussion guns that required powder and bullet molds and yards of wadding, palm shooters shaped like mollusks and big-bore buffalo guns lethal at both ends; knives, daggers, bayonets, cavalry swords, and hatchets for close work. Christie's wife had to clear the table of cleaning rods, parts of weapons, and cartridge-loading paraphernalia to set out breakfast. Washing day produced a bounty of live rounds, empty brass casings, and copper firing caps from her husband's pockets. The house took on the aspect of the armory of the old garrison in Fort Smith.

Officers of the court who had visited the cabin and seen the kegs of powder and boxes and wooden crates of ammunition lying about suggested wistfully that a bit of flaming pitch hurled through a window would effectively disarm the West's most wanted fugitive; but the memory of January 1875, when a pot of Greek fire supplied by the Pinkertons blew up the Missouri home of Jesse James's mother, tearing off her arm and killing the outlaw's nine-year-old half brother, stayed the hands of the law in this regard. That incident had turned the countryside in James's favor and extended his career another seven years.

But it was agreed as far away as Fort Smith that Christie's longevity depended less upon warriors and weaponry than upon the network of generally law-abiding neighbors who kept him informed of preparations to invade his territory. Their sympathy for his situation, while not inviting cooperation in his vendetta, spoke of their faith in his innocence in the death of Deputy Maples. When deputies asked them if they'd seen Christie, they were polite, they offered them cups of steaming coffee in winter and dippers of ice-cold well water in summer (jars of moonshine if they knew them well enough), and shrugged their shoulders; then when the visitors left they sent their children running to Rabbit Trap. The deputies, slowed down by the tumbleweed wagon and disinclined anyway to fire up the locals by chasing down and boxing the ears of their offspring, chewed tobacco, watched them hurdling fences and splashing through streams, and soldiered on, rifles across the throats of their saddles in case of ambush. Most often the worst they found was Christie not at home, and that was the end of the matter until next time. He slept in his cabin most nights and took to the brush when the alarum was raised.

A photograph of Christie taken about this time, in a studio in Tahlequah, shows off his lean, rangy figure to best

advantage, with hair tumbling black and glossy well below
his shoulders, Mandarin whiskers trailing from his chin, a
clear challenge in his gaze, and about his person two Colt
revolvers and a Model 1866 Winchester. Unlike the case with
many a staged pose, weapons and the man appear familiar
with one another. The circumstances of its creation, in the
busy capital of the progressive Cherokee Nation, with deputies searching every Native face for his features and a price
of a thousand dollars on his head offered by U.S. Marshal
John Carroll, spoke volumes about the nature of the man and
the reasons for his legend.

Four years of assaults and escapes—hornet-stings about
Parker's furious head—lulls in the fighting, brief violent
brushes with the "marshals," and cold camps kept while men
searched the hills, caves, and thickets for some sign of his
passage, and Ned Christie's war was only a little more than
halfway to the finish. But his candle was burning low.

There came to Fort Smith a tall man, by appearances born
to the saddle, whose long hair, handlebars, and neat imperial
moved the more literary of his biographers to compare him
to D'Artagnan. At the time of his encounter with Ned Christie he was nearing forty and had settled into a practical and
comfortable working uniform of corduroy trousers, flannel
shirt, high-topped boots made to his measure, and a white
hat with a swooping brim, a fashion just then finding its vogue
after the example of Buffalo Bill Cody, inventor of the Wild
West. He spoke with a gentle drawl—foreshortened when he
barked instructions to his companions and commanded fugitives to come out from behind their barricades—and had
three children with his wife, who had packed them up and
returned to Georgia, where people placed family before duty.
He'd argued against the move, but had failed to prevent it, or
to persuade her to return. "You can't expect a woman to
understand or respect it when manhunting has got into your

blood," he told his few intimates. "I can't find fault with one who doesn't."

His name appeared in none of the rip-roaring dime novels of the age, and when pictures learned to move, with jerks and false starts like a child's, he would not be among the first ten chosen for dramatization, nor as the medium strode, ran, and found the power of speech, the first fifty, nor yet the first five hundred. Yet in his time everyone who read newspapers and many who could not knew his reputation. He was among the best and bravest ever to grapple with the challenges of the late frontier, and in a hundred years no star has replaced his in the firmament.

He was born January 6, 1850, in Oxford, near Atlanta, the youngest of twelve children, and roughhouse was his birthright. At age twelve he'd ridden dispatch for the Army of the Confederacy, and in his twenties he'd been shot in the face by a member of the Sam Bass gang during a train robbery in Hutchins, Texas; the scar was still visible after more than ten years. This incident had decided him to bring the fight to the enemy, and he'd joined the Texas Rangers and then the Fort Worth Stock Association as a detective, slaying two fugitives before throwing in with the marshal's office in Arkansas.

His name was Henry Andrew Thomas, but he seldom answered to it. His friends and even Judge Parker called him Heck.

NINE

Heck Thomas accepted bonuses and rewards. He had a wife and children to support, even if he never saw them, and for all its hard work and risk, hunting men paid poorer than clerking. After the doctor in Hutchings dug the bullet out of his face, making more of a mess than it had going in, the superintendent of the railroad line had paid him two hundred dollars; which decision Heck laid more to the twenty thousand dollars he'd managed to hide from the bandits than for the sacrifice of his youthful good looks.

He cashed the bank draught and went looking for employment that didn't involve swaying soporific over the rails in a windowless express car, half hoping for an attempt at robbery just for the variety, then getting his wish and a pistol round in the face and a recovery fee of one percent, which was what the banks were paying for the privilege of investing what a man earned by the sweat of his brow. Mostly it was the close spaces he objected to; he'd had his fill of that sleeping three to a bed at home and sharing a one-holer outhouse with his parents and eleven older siblings.

He found such a posting, all open air and a fighting chance, with the Texas Rangers. He answered to Captain Lee Hall, a man of few words and most of them profane, whose actions against the vigilantes in Goliad and against the bushwhackers who had fled Missouri to continue their war against the Union by way of banks and trains spoke louder than words. Many were in shackles and shallow holes, and the doors of Huntsville had clanged shut on John Wesley Hardin, whose career as a marauder had been largely responsible for reforming the Rangers, who had disbanded after the Comanches surrendered at Adobe Walls. Heck had learned most of what he knew about tracking desperate men from Hall, and all of what he knew about the finer details of detective work; the captain had been one of the first peace officers to compile and consult a criminal book, with likenesses, descriptions, and personal histories of fugitives in hiding, and his lessons had taught Heck to pay attention to such things as tracks left by horseshoes recently repaired, a man's preference for ready-made cigarettes over those rolled by hand, and the difficulty of disguising the shape of one's ears or the distance between one's eyes when whiskers and windowpane spectacles altered everything else.

Of chief importance, Heck had acquired the wisdom of

shooting first and shooting to kill. Most of the things that stopped a man when he was stopped were placed conveniently in the middle. It was an easy mark to hit, and the shooter's best insurance against getting shot himself.

He'd never warmed to taking orders, however, not even as a yonker riding for the CSA, and in time Hall's general lack of diplomacy in his dealings with subordinates wore thin. Heck took a handsome offer to work as a detective for the Fort Worth Stock Association, with steady pay, a free hand, and liberty to collect rewards. It came with an office, which appealed to Isabelle, his wife; she'd been riding him for a long time about his absences from home, and thought a fixed place of business meant a family reunited around the supper table every night.

It was that way for a time. In his sun-hammered room overlooking the cattle pens he kept track of known rustlers with pieces of colored ribbon pinned to a large-scale map of four counties tacked to the wall behind his desk, smoking the pipe of a settled man and moving the pins according to the latest communications made by wire and by drifters he struck up conversations with in the Alamo Sample Room; but when the pins drew near Fort Smith, he saddled up and rode out, often leaving word only with an acquaintance to tell Isabelle he'd be late for supper for a week or two.

He'd been gone longer than that, and closer to a month, when the episode took place that would bring him to the attention of Judge Parker's court. He'd picked up Jim Taylor, a friend from his express-messenger days who now rode for Parker in the Chickasaw Nation, and together they tracked Jim and Pink Lee, the notorious rustlers and road agents, to a house near Gainesveille, where Heck applied what he'd learned during his apprenticeship with the Rangers. When he and Taylor finished shooting, Jim and Pink Lee were dead. The sheriff in Gainesville saw the corpses laid neatly side by side on his porch, wrote out a receipt for the thousand-dollar reward, and handed it to Heck.

The Lees were killers, feared throughout central Texas and as far as the Nations. Heck was asked to run for sheriff of Tarrant County and offered a lieutenancy in the Rangers by Governor John Ireland, but he turned down both opportunities and asked Jim Taylor to put in a good word for him with the U.S. marshal in Fort Smith; Isabelle, left alone with the children for weeks at a time with no close neighbors, had wearied of Texas, and expressed the first of many veiled threats to find a better place, even if it meant excluding their father. (In time the veil would be lifted, replaced by an ultimatum.) Taylor said, "Christ, Heck, you don't need an introduction from me. Jim and Pink already took care of that."

Taylor was not a man to exaggerate. Heck submitted his application to the United States marshal's office in Arkansas, where such requests poured over the transom, scribbled by the sort of man who read pulp novels until his lips wore out, looking for the adventurous life of the Western lawman, and received a positive reply within a week. He and Isabelle made arrangements to send the bulk of their belongings to the Hotel Le Flore, packed bags and children aboard the Katy Flyer, and rented a house in Fort Smith, where Heck took the oath of office and received his first assignment, to accompany the tumbleweed wagon through the Nations, serving whiskey warrants and collecting army deserters and suspicious persons officially christened John Doe until they could be processed at the jail. He broke a chilly silent fast with his wife the following morning and followed the Arkansas into the Cherokee Nation.

His restless nature nettled him. In time, he grew weary of escorting the slow-moving prison van, palavering with storekeeps and paid informers, and rousting jail fodder out of low brothels, dugout saloons, and opium dens, and ferrying them back to civilization; his postman period, soul-destroying and Sisyphean in its monotony. Stagnating in Fort Smith following his testimony against a defendant in Parker's court, he presented himself to the marshal and asked for a crack at Ned Christie.

John Carroll, Thomas Boles's successor, was another gray-head who could tuck his beard into his belt, but he was of a more suspicious mien. Ambition put him on his guard; he owed his appointment to patience and loyalty to the Republican platform and equated impatience with arrogance. He interrupted Heck's carefully rehearsed request with a palm.

"Men more tested than you have taken a licking from Christie and his gang," he said. "What can you bring to the case that they have not?"

"I don't know Christie."

"You plead ignorance as a virtue?"

Heck said, "I've studied the record, and it seems to me they've all gone in with some notion that Christie's a civilized Indian, who if he won't listen to reason will at least defer to greater numbers and surrender. They don't take into account the fact that he's been on the scout for years, and thinks more like a cornered grizzly than a man of learning. I intend to do all my palavering with three good men and a wagonload of ammunition."

"Is it your aim to murder him as you did Jim and Pink Lee?"

"It will be no more murder than to hang him from Parker's tears."

"Judge Parker will debate you on that, and at length."

"I'd as lief rather debate it with Christie, after I've put a bullet in him."

Carroll had a leather portfolio flayed open on his desk. In it, Heck noted, as the marshal leafed through the contents, was a carte-de-visite of Christie, armed to the hair and daring anyone who regarded the image to try its subject. At length the marshal excavated a sheet of onionskin paper, upon which Heck could have read the iron-gall notation in hand backwards if he thought the effort worth it. In places the writer had torn the paper, so hard had he borne down upon the nib.

"That's Boles's recommendation, subtracting the legal fustian," Carroll said. "It's the official policy, though you wouldn't know it by the pattern of the investigations each time Christie's struck."

"They're all good men. It's hard to make the best choice when you've broken bread with the man you're sent to kill."

The marshal slapped shut the portfolio; Christie's picture escaped on a volume of air and drifted to the floor, from which he stared up mockingly. Heck—who was not a fanciful man—took it as a personal challenge.

Carroll sat back and laced his fingers across the base of his whiskers. "The farther east you go, the nobler Christie gets. I advise you not to read a word in any of the muckraking journals before you head out to Rabbit Trap. You can amuse yourself with them once he's dead or in custody."

Thomas nodded. He had not failed to note the order of his choices.

Heck hunted Christie off and on for three months. It seemed the outlaw had trained the owls and crickets to report on the deputy's progress in bucket-brigade fashion, for he was never at home, despite the evidence of recent repairs about the place that suggested a man in residence. Finally Heck let his beard grow out, trimmed it into a fussy Vandyke, put on his Sunday suit, and entered Tahlequah under cover of darkness. There he sought out a boardinghouse where he was unknown and introduced himself to the matron as a surveyor for the Missouri, Kansas, and Texas Railroad. He'd taken the trouble to secure a legitimate business card, but that effort was wasted because the woman was illiterate. He selected a room on the second floor back, as far away from her bedroom and parlor as the house permitted, paid cash, and met there after midnight with deputies Rusk, Salmon, and

Isbell, who rode in from Vinita, tied their horses out back, and crept up the back stairs with their boots in their hands. Although none of them could know it, the scene was eerily reminiscent of Christie's meeting with his father four years earlier, with a lamp burning low on the floor to keep from throwing their shadows onto the window shade. The war had turned on its head, with the fugitive roaming free and in the open and the manhunters forted up indoors.

"I feel like we're plotting to raid a bank." Isbell, a fellow veteran of the tumbleweed wagon patrol, popped a plug into his mouth and used his foot to drag over a white enamel chamber pot for a spitoon.

"It'll get more skulksome yet," Heck said. "This time we're going in afoot."

Rusk, a former working cowhand, registered his disapproval. "I didn't put in for this job to be no dadburn farmer."

"How are you at crawling on your belly?"

"I'm a fair hand. I'm married."

Isbell and Salmon responded, but were cut off in midcackle by Heck's hiss. "This whole nation is Christie's ear trumpet. We're wasting our time if we don't catch him with his pants down."

Salmon said, "I was wondering about them banker's whiskers. I thought maybe this was a retirement party."

He stroked them. "I figure this is my last shot at that renegade. I been back here so many times my face is getting to be better known than Lydia Pinkham's. One more trip and he'll be in Texas while my feet are still wet from the Arkansas."

"Well, we can't have that," Rusk said. "Texas has got bad men enough without importing more. Give me a cut off that plug, Izz. If I'm going to crawl on my belly, I need something to spit in a copperhead's eye."

Isbell cut three pieces and handed them all around. "Let's concentrate on spitting in Ned's."

Which turned out to be a prophetic thing to say.

* * *

They tethered their horses to scrub in the hills with plenty of forage in reach, walked into Rabbit Trap on the far blind side of Christie's cabin, and camped cold in the brush for three days, drinking from canteens and tearing off jerked beef and venison with their teeth. By daylight, when the frogs and crickets were silent and sound didn't carry, they moved toward the cabin, crawling sometimes, scrambling hunchback like crabs other times with carbines portaged on their shoulders. When mourning doves hooted and songbirds trilled, they listened for a human echo and decided the calls were not manmade. An hour before the sun came up on the fourth day, they closed in.

Christie had assembled nearly as many dogs as weapons. They all caught the scent at the same time and exploded into barking.

Heck raised his voice above the yammer. "Make a rush for it!"

Each took a side of the cabin and drew down on a window. Heck raised his voice again. "Christie, we're U.S. marshals, and there are too many of us to fight! Surrender!"

A plank flew out of a gable in the loft. A barrel poked out and sent a hunk of lead chugging into the earth at Heck's feet. Christie levered in a fresh round and fired right behind it even as every carbine on the ground slanted upward. The deputies' guns went off almost simultaneously, a prolonged roar like a freight train hurtling through a tunnel. Glass panes shattered, pieces of bark flew off logs, bullets gonged against pots and skillets and the iron stove inside. Heck cried for them to hold their fire.

"If you intend to fight, send out your woman!"

Six shots flew in rapid succession from the gable. Heck dove for cover. As the deputies returned fire, he scuttled behind a lean-to attached to the cabin, open to the rear with cords of firewood stacked inside. Heck erected a pile of kindling using sheets of loose bark, crumpled some John Doe warrants he carried from habit, and burned through three matches before getting it all to catch. When he had a strong flame, he fanned it with his hat until it spread to the wall of the structure and fled behind a hickory tree, bullets from the gable chewing up ground at his heels.

Fire from the ground trickled to silence as the deputies waited and watched the flames. The wind caught smoke as thick as cotton batting and slung it against the gable.

Christie had a coughing fit. Isbell, backing away from the cabin's deep shade to draw a bead on the gap where Christie had knocked out the plank, spun on one ankle and fell, a slug in his shoulder.

The cabin was burning merrily now. A figure leaped out the shot-away door. Rusk and Salmon opened up on it as it zigzagged into the tangled brush that encircled the clearing.

"Not Christie!" Heck bellowed. He'd recognized Ned's son, Arch. The youth was nearly grown and resembled his father, but was several inches shorter. Heck's cry went unheeded at first, and bullets tore at leaves and branches in Arch's wake.

In the loft, Christie rubbed the sting from his eyes, but the bandanna he'd soaked from a canteen and tied around his nose and mouth kept most of the smoke from his lungs; he'd coughed merely to draw a marshal from cover, and when Isbell stepped into the early light to see if Christie would poke his head out to breathe, Christie had taken swift aim, felt the Winchester push against his shoulder, and knew before the ball found its mark that it would shatter bone and reduce the odds against him by one. But as he fired, Heck Thomas glimpsed his profile against the lightening sky and squeezed off a shot that smashed the bridge of Christie's nose and tore out his right eye.

He lay for a long time in a swoon, with smoke filling the loft and flames snapping at the underside of the floor, which seemed to be sweating beneath him as the pitch boiled to the surface. He felt hands pulling at him and grasped for his weapon, but they were friendly hands, taking advantage of the smoke and Arch's diversion to rescue him. He was borne down the ladder, blind in both eyes from the blood leaking out the empty socket, carried on the run by his legs and shoulders, and dumped without gentleness into the bed of a wagon. Someone climbed in with him, embracing him; he smelled his wife. He held tight to her with one arm and with his other hand clutched at a sideboard to keep from bouncing out when the horses were whipped into a gallop. His pain was white and red and green. Belated reports crackled, a slug struck an iron staple on the side of the wagon and sang away. Whoever was on the spring seat knew the narrow passages through the thorns and brambles like a river pilot who had memorized all the snags in the current. His passenger felt as if he were being borne to safety in the talons of an eagle.

When an account of the fight reached Parker's desk, he put his head in his hands and asked Marshal Carroll if they were to settle for taking Ned Christie a piece at a time.

TEN

Three years of skirmishes followed, but Heck Thomas, either in punishment for his failure to kill or capture Christie or because he was too well known in Going Snake to breach the outlaw's early-warning system, was assigned to other duties. Another Heck, surnamed Bruner, assumed command of the investigation, and with deputies Rusk and others fought running battles with Christie's men in and near Rabbit Trap Canyon; three more deputies and several Indians friendly to Parker's court were wounded.

Whether Christie himself took part in these fights was a subject of heated argument in the saloons of Fort Smith, where veterans of the seven-year conflict gathered to show off their scars and swap war stories. Some said Heck Thomas had broken his spirit when he took away his eye and his good looks, others that he was still recuperating. Still others insisted he'd died of his injury and that his friends had entered into a conspiracy to keep his legend alive by carrying out raids and defensive operations in his name. L. P. Isbell, retired from service with a paralyzed shoulder courtesy of Christie, said the biggest mistake the deputies ever made was to destroy the cabin, and with it the one place the outlaw was sure to return to from time to time; now he could be anywhere in the miles of alien country, crouched in ambush behind the next fallen log or perched overhead in a tree.

"Time was you could rout him out with a rifle and a plan," he said. "Now you'd be lucky to take him with the Seventh Cavalry."

Which words would be remembered in the marshal's office later.

Christie had, in fact, recovered, with the treatment of the same Cherokee surgeon who had dug Christie's bullet out of Deputy Joe Bowers' knee in 1885; and if anything his spirit was more determined than ever. He, his family, and those who remained loyal to his rebellion had withdrawn to the far end of the canyon, chosen a site high in the Cookson Hills against a wall of striated rock with a view of every approach, and hacked a path between it and a steam-driven sawmill operated by an acquaintance, who provided wagonloads of hickory logs, enough to build a small settlement. Working from sunup to sundown, and drinking himself nights into stupefaction—the only rest he knew—Christie, with a bandanna knotted diagonally around his head to keep the sweat from burning his vacant socket, dug stones from the earth with his companions to erect a foundation and notched and stacked the logs four deep. When the walls were complete and a roof added (and rethatched with damp sod on a regular basis to resist catching fire from hurled torches), the low, dark building, with narrow ports in place of windows, was aesthetically inferior to the comfortable cabin the Christies had lost, but as a fortress its fame spread swiftly. By the time the legend crossed into Arkansas, it included a moat stocked with water moccasins and a standing army of fifteen of Christie's closest supporters. In reality, time, attrition, and Native impatience to waiting had shrunken his resources to his wife and family, lieutenanted by son Arch and a whiskey peddler and petty thief who called himself Soldier Hair; and Christie was afraid of snakes.

By October 1892, President Harrison had installed Jacob Yoes as U.S. marshal for the Eighth District. Yoes, a choleric Teuton several years younger than any of his predecessors and several times more ambitious than John Carroll, assigned seventeen deputy marshals to lay siege to Ned Christie's stronghold. It was the largest federal force ever assembled against one man, and Yoes took personal command of the expedition, the only marshal in Parker's long tenure ever to take saddle in the field.

"At least if we shit the bed this time we won't be alone," remarked one Christie veteran.

As the summons to report to duty shot out over the wires, deputies Bruner and Paden Tolbert traveled to Coffeyville, Kansas, borrowed a military cannon and personnel to help them load it aboard a flatcar, and escorted the gun by rail to Tahlequah. Army engineers in Fort Gibson transferred several cases of dynamite from the powder magazine to Yoes and took his receipt.

There was no longer need for secrecy. Christie was said to feel secure in his citadel, and in any case had broadcast his vow—translated from the Cherokee—to retreat no farther: "Like the bear, I will die where I was born." Indians in all five nations, and non-Indians who lived there by their leave, observed for days as men straddling glossy, well-fed mounts passed through their settlements, weighted down with pistols and big-bore rifles and belts of ammunition, stars flashing on their breasts. These witnesses laughed as Tolbert and Bruner cursed and whipped mules struggling to pull their artillery piece out of the mud. Then it hove to, gleaming in its ugly potential, and they fell silent.

An army was on the march. Some swore they heard the roll of drums calling men to muster.

Judge Parker, more aware than ever that the eyes of the East were upon him, broke precedent and assigned a press agent to the campaign. The bespectacled little German set up his tripod in a private coach and in the same sawmill where Christie had acquired his building material and committed the solemn, droopily moustached, self-important faces of the heavily armed men to glass plates. When the magnesium glare faded and sight returned, they rocked over the rails and took to their saddles, each to his own thoughts, and all of them trained on the days ahead.

"Fat men on fat horses loaded down with iron," said Soldier Hair, conversing with Christie in their native tongue. "I bet a case of whiskey they don't make it halfway through the canyon."

Christie swigged from a bottle of Nancy Shell's stock and passed it over. "Why not make it two? That's the last of it."

His wife came to stand over them. They were sitting on the hard clay floor of the fortress with their backs against the logs, which was how they spent most of their days, with their Winchesters across their laps. Christie had lost his taste for the card games the white man played, and both had forgotten the games enjoyed by their ancestors. *Part Indian, part snake . . .*

"Supper is on the table," she said.

"Eat it and tell us how good it was." Soldier Hair giggled and drank.

She raised her skirts and kicked the bottle from his hand, cutting his lip. He cursed and grabbed for his carbine, but was impeded by Christie, who lunged across him to rescue the bottle before it emptied. By then the long Cherokee tradition of female dominance had kicked in, and Soldier Hair sat back and smeared away the blood with the back of a hand.

"You are no better than that pig John Parris." She spun on her heel.

"Who is John Parris?" asked Soldier Hair.

A few days later, Christie helped his wife onto the seat of the wagon that had swept him away from his burning cabin, handed up the smallest of his children, and sent them off to her sister's house in Tahlequah. She fixed him at length with her mahogany-colored eyes, then gave the lines a flip.

Dawn came the color of metal on November 2, with the raw-iron smell of early snow. The dogs outside were barking and had been since an hour before daylight. By then the men on the grounds had all found their positions behind trees and in the brush. Christie had given up trying to keep overgrowth clear of the fort as a waste of time and energy; it marched relentlessly, more stubborn even than Parker's marshals, and at forty, after seven years spent on high alert and with the effort of keeping his balance with only one eye, he lacked the endurance, and Soldier Hair the ambition. Arch had grown into an arrogant young rebel who considered yard work beneath him. They were a fine gang of desperadoes.

The men in the fort had traded positions at the gun ports throughout the last dark hour, but had failed to find a mark to shoot at, and Christie was unwilling to snap off at mere rustles in the brush; his neighbors sometimes took it upon themselves to stand sentry uninvited, and in any case he was reluctant to shoot one of his dogs by accident. It was his soft spot for dogs that had gotten him into this pickle, but there it was: You could change a man's station over a trifle such as a misunderstanding, but his basic nature was bred in the bone. He contented himself with waiting for a proper target, and admonished Arch and Soldier Hair to do the same.

Ironically, when the challenge came, he'd dozed off; and when Yoes introduced himself, in a bawling voice best suited to a platform bunted for Independence Day, and told him there was nothing for it but surrender, it startled him into firing a shot through his own roof. He'd fallen asleep in a crouch against the wall with his finger on the trigger.

A quarter-hour's worth of racket ensued, with repeaters and buffalo guns and the deep bellowing roar of Stevens streetsweepers clearing the woods of birds, varmints, and deer for a mile about and tearing great yellow gashes in the logs, but otherwise doing no damage to his redoubt; there was nothing stouter on the Holy Spirit's green earth than native hickory, and no better workmanship than the Cherokee. A stray pellet of buckshot found its way through a port and broke in half a washbasin in its stand, but Christie had ceased to fret about his wife's nice things. That was a bit of freedom he hadn't counted on when he'd decided to abandon the life of the little white man and ride the high country. He loved the old girl, but there were times when the dungeon in Fort Smith seemed preferable.

Arch found the first target, but as far as his father could tell by the way the man in his sights retreated into the brush without staggering, the only pain would be felt by his tailor. Christie regretted never having had the chance to tutor his son in the manly art of marksmanship; an unforgivable failing in a skilled gunsmith. To plug the gap, he sent a round after the boy's, knowing the marshal had better sense than to withdraw in a straight line. It would be an insult to himself to assume otherwise. A man rated his standing by the quality of his foes.

"Fire!"

When the cannon opened up, from a cover built of cut branches on the edge of the woods like a deer blind, Christie grinned, like a child at a medicine show, at the gout of smoke and fire erupting from a sylvan patch—and laughed loud enough to be heard by his attackers when the three-pound ball struck a log with a thud he felt in his testicles and bounded away in a reverse trajectory nearly identical to the first, striking the ground just short of the woods and bouncing into them like a sphere of rubber cast by a titan playing jacks.

"Duck!"

That set the pattern for the next several rounds:

"Fire!"

"Duck!"

"Fire!"

"Duck!"

Each time, the ball struck the logs hard enough to rattle his teeth, only to plummet back toward its source. Christie took snap shots at exposed limbs as the marshals in charge of the cannon scrambled out of harm's way. While they were re-loading, he joined Arch and Soldier Hair in pestering the other marshals, using the smoke that blossomed from behind trees for a mark. Clouds of spent powder stung their eyes and a fog lay over the yard as in lithographs Christie had seen of Gettysburg.

Again the brush stirred in which the cannon was hidden; he braced himself for another blast. Then the brush parted and he saw the great blue-black muzzle for the first time, approaching the fort as if under its own power. It stuck out over the top of iron rails stacked in a square inside the wagon it sat upon, the rails shielding the men who were pushing it. As Christie drew a bead, hoping to dislodge the stack, bullets rataplaned off the logs near his gun port. He threw himself away from it. For the better part of a minute, all three defenders crouched in cover while the marshals laid down heavy fire at all the openings. Then thunder shook the earth as another three-pounder struck, harder than the others. Still the fort held.

Thirty times the logs were struck. That was more balls than had been brought, but some were used more than once because they had an accommodating habit of returning home after they had failed to stave in their target. Down on the ground, Marshal Yoes got the gunners' attention and slashed a hand across his throat. Bruner and Tolbert jumped out of the wagon and ran for the woods, unshipping carbines from their shoulders as they abandoned the artillery for the infantry. Yoes called for more fire and sent deputies Bill Smith and Charlie Copeland running to the wagon, carrying a crate of dynamite between them by the rope handles. The wagon containing the silenced cannon stood twenty yards from the fort, a miniature redoubt in its own right and the first armored vehicle in combat history.

With Tolbert and Smith hammering at the fort on one side and deputies Ellis and White doing the same on the other, Copeland dashed the sixty feet, trailing smoke from a burning fuse, and jammed a bundle of six sticks of dynamite into the space where two logs crossed at the corner, then ran a serpentine course back with bullets stitching the sod around him.

The roar of the explosion boxed the ears of marshal and deputies, pounding the ground and throwing eight-foot sections of log thirty feet in the air. Ellis, White, Copeland, Tolbert, and Smith charged the fort under cover of the smoke and dust, levering and firing as they ran.

A gap had been blown in the wall large enough to admit a wagon. The deputies vaulted over the debris and wheeled right and left, throwing down on shadows in the haze.

A volley of shots sent them to the walls. In the lull that followed, they searched for targets, but as the fog settled, they saw they were alone. Tolbert opened his mouth to shout this information to Yoes—then flattened against the wall as more reports crackled from nowhere.

"They're under the floor!" White pointed his Winchester down and slammed a succession of bullets through the planks, new and yellow and recently erected on a framework built on the clay beneath. The other deputies joined him, riddling the boards.

Outside the fort, Deputy Marshal E. B. Ratteree saw a man crawl out through a space beneath the floor, but held his fire in the murk of smoke for fear of hitting a fellow deputy. The man saw him and shouldered his own rifle. Before Ratteree could react, his face caught fire. Momentarily blinded by a powder flare whose mark he would carry for the rest of his life, he fired back.

Ned Christie bounded to his feet, whooping and gobbling. A space of silence, and then a dozen carbines rolled thunder. He pirouetted and fell, as loose-limbed as a scarecrow.

Arch Christie escaped once again, as he had from his father's burning cabin three years before. The deputies found Soldier Hair crawling on hands and knees under the floor and had to turn him over with a foot and shove their muzzles into his face to obtain his surrender; he was badly burned and both eardrums were punctured.

Jacob Yoes's deputies slung Christie's corpse into the wagon containing the cannon and carried it a hundred miles to Fort Smith like a trophy bear. They took a door off its hinges, leaned the stiff body against it, propped Christie's Winchester in his arms, and posed with him for the little German photographer; it was the closest any of them had gotten to him in seven years. After citizens filed past to look at the man who had declared war upon the United States, Watt Christie arrived to claim the remains and took them back to Rabbit Trap for burial and the traditional Cherokee plea for the disposition of his spirit.

III

A Woman in Her Time

These impossible women! How they do get around us!

—ARISTOPHANES

ELEVEN

J udge Parker congratulated Marshal Yoes, but had not the leisure to draw a breath of relief at the close of the longest hunt for a lone fugitive in American history. Privately he considered the expenditure of seventeen men, an artillery piece, and dynamite to exterminate one bandit an admission of desperation, and a failure of sorts. In any case, the docket left no space for reflection, and his enemies in Congress were threatening once again to slice up his jurisdiction like one of Mary's cakes for the condemned. Many of these meddlers had still been at school when he first took the bench; it was the privilege of youth to regard so venerable a fixture as an impediment to civilization instead of its instrument. The hanging of six more men in company on January 16, 1890, had revived all the old arguments, even though the private nature of the execution—attended by invitation only, with passes signed by the marshal—had drawn little fire from his old nemesis, the Eastern press. The eyes of the Union were drifting eastward, toward the robber barons of New York, and southward, toward the Spanish situation in Cuba, and no less an authority than Frederick Jackson Turner was about to declare the frontier closed. It was at such times that a man felt the world turning beneath his feet.

The strain of defending his territory, and of his punishing schedule, had whitened his hair and beard. From a distance he appeared to be wearing a polished porcelain bowl on his head, and when he bent over his papers in court he looked like an old woman in his robes. That impression evaporated when he lifted his chin and fixed the prisoner in the dock with the cold blue stare of an experienced killer of men. Seventy-one had died by his judgment.

The number should have been higher. Presidents would interfere from time to time, to placate certain wrongheaded contributors, and his opponents on Capitol Hill, carpetbaggers to the last, had granted convicted prisoners the right to appeal his decisions to the Supreme Court, after fourteen years of allowing him a free hand. For a time, no attorney exercised this right, knowing Parker for a fair man and not wishing to incur his displeasure by questioning his wisdom. Then J. Warren Reed, a prancing peacock of a man, Parker's opposite in everything but gender (and his silk shirts and wasp-waisted clawhammer coats obscured even that distinction; also, he was his wife's intellectual inferior), took the case of his client, a thief and murderer named William Alexander, to Washington. The Supreme Court had reviewed the evidence, ruled incompetent the testimony of a key prosecution witness, and ordered a new trial. This time, Reed went on the attack, splitting the jury five to seven; and William H. H. Clayton, Parker's friend and partner in justice from the early days, rusty and out of practice from his hiatus under Cleveland, had told the judge in confidence that he was pessimistic about the outcome of the third trial. (Next month, he would drop all charges.)

When Parker himself was still awaiting word of the decision in Washington, a groundswell of cheering penetrated the window of his chambers in the new courthouse, originating in the fresh construction of the jail, and he knew he'd been defeated. Minutes later his clerk, Stephen Wheeler—brigadier general, retired, in the Arkansas State Militia, still baby-faced behind his imperial whiskers—appeared holding a telegraph flimsy. Parker merely nodded. Somehow, the news had reached the men most directly affected by the appeals process before it entered the halls of justice. Predators were the first to sense weakness in the enemy.

But Fort Smith still loved its judge. The slapdash, temporary cowtown of '75 had gentrified with brick and mortar and
side entrances to the saloons for the ladies; electric lights
blazed in the federal courtroom, and although Parker thought
the wire the traction company men were stringing between
poles to electrify the streetcar line unsightly, it was one more
sign of progress, erected on the solid foundation of the rule
of law. Feared and despised in the jail, hated in the low dens
of the Nations, he walked the city streets unconcerned for his
safety, always allowing time to stop and converse with shop-
keepers and fellow members of the Methodist and Catholic
congregations and to pat the heads of their children and remark upon their growth. He was elected president annually
of the Sebastian County Fair Association, an office looked
upon with more reverence than mayor. Representatives of the
Eastern journals expecting to find an uncouth mountebank,
tobacco stains in his beard and a pistol in his belt, discovered instead a dignified and benevolent old uncle with the
head of a Roman senator. In interviews he was amiable and
watched with sly pleasure as they hastened to record his
learned theories in their grubby little blocks, knowing their
editors would butcher or bury them among advertisements for
cream separators and whisker balm.

At home, Parker dwelt upon his personal failures.

These came to him when his wife had retired. He'd finished annotating in his jagged hand the case histories he'd
brought home and sat in the horsehair chair in his study with
the lamp glowing on the Bible in his lap. Charles, his firstborn, had developed a wild streak, which he'd managed to
conceal on Sundays and holy days when Parker was home,
and which his mother was too gentle to remark upon even to
his father. By the time Parker learned of it, it had progressed
too far to reverse; but judging was his profession, he blamed
himself for overlooking the evidence when it was right under his nose. Charlie had spent time with Annie Maledon,

George's daughter. That had ended badly, and Parker had been too relieved to hear it was over to inquire into the details. He'd had too much respect for his chief of executions to express his disapproval, but he'd hoped Maledon would be aware of the class differences and put an end to the affair on his own. In this he'd disappointed his employer. But Fort Smith was a small town still, for all its advances, and Parker could not help overhearing rumors of other liaisons and caddish behavior, which if he had a daughter he would be sure to bring to the attention of the boy's father; but perhaps not, if the father were Judge Parker and he someone else. He hoped the boy had the character to come to a realization about himself and make the necessary adjustments. The iron was in the blood, after all; he was the son of a jurist and the great-great-grandnephew of a governor.

Young James was timid and lazy. His sensitivity came from his mother, who continued to deliver flowers and cakes to the men awaiting execution. Such a nature, determined to see decency where it did not exist, was less than equal to the challenge of disciplining a youth with no initiative or ambition. Parker himself could not remember when he'd last tasted one of Mary's cakes. The turnkeys, who could not resist sneaking samples, avowed that she had become an uncommonly fine baker through practice.

One man could bring order to a wilderness, provided he had vision and the sense of purpose the job required. One man could raise his sons to observe probity and devotion to duty and society, assuming he possessed those qualities himself and applied himself to the task. No man could do both. No man should be expected to try. Yet he had tried.

He removed his spectacles and rubbed his eyes, as if the weariness rested in them alone. The house was quiet but for the gasps of the fire dying in the stone hearth, the chimney cracking as it cooled. Mary, who had taken to drinking a glass of brandy each night to conquer insomnia, would be unconscious from the spirit's effects, and Jimmie would sleep around the clock if he didn't have to eat or get up to use the chamber pot. Parker didn't know if Charlie was even home. It was at times like this, here in the one place where a man should have the authority he reserved for the three hundred thousand people in his charge, that he gave himself permission to ruminate upon the past and find sympathy for that impossible woman Belle Starr.

Most of what was written about the West was rubbish, and more rubbish was written about Myra Belle Shirley from Arkansas than about Jesse James, Billy the Kid, and Buffalo Bill Cody combined.

The process by which a lank-limbed, crab-ridden consort of bushwhackers with a face like a log butt made the long climb from the brothels of Carthage, Missouri, to be coronated the Bandit Queen of the Border said more about the hacks who performed the ceremony than it did about their subject. To them, shut up in their whiskey-soaked furnished rooms in New York and scrawling in chair cars hurtling at forty miles per hour through the country they wrote about and never looked at, every desperado had a soft spot for orphans and kittens and every woman who strayed off the path of domesticity to follow the outlaw trail looked like the girls who modeled corsets in catalogues. The scribblers in soiled collars and beetle hats knew nothing of the conditions on the scout, and the unavailability of such refinements as face powder, dental hygiene, and soap.

Belle, at least, was real; which may have been the reason why her saga endured while the debutantes' parade of Indian princesses, Miners' Madonnas, Sirens of the Cimarron, and Buckskin Betsies, Bonnies, and Belindas had finished up back at the pulp mill. They'd sprung full-grown from the semen of their creators' pens and hadn't the blood in their veins to survive. There was no reason to believe either that at one time—say, twenty years before she made Judge Parker's acquaintance—she had not been comely. For certain her manners were those of a woman of breeding. But the nickel novelists would not have been interested in her in those days, because her story up to then wouldn't have sprung the collar of a pastor.

Well, there was the romance with Cole Younger; but a past without a spot of scarlet is a dismal thing.

She was the daughter of well-to-do Virginians in the Arkansas Ozarks, that feral land of green mounded hills and deep cuts exposing strata of granite and limestone, natural skyscrapers dizzying to behold from top or bottom, which stretching into the Nations would form the rear elevation of Ned Christie's fort. The family moved soon after, and by age eight Myra Belle was heiress to a mercantile empire in Jasper County, Missouri: hotel, livery, and blacksmith shop, maintained by John Shirley and his sons, Bud and Preston, the girl's brothers. In that year she enrolled in the Carthage Academy for Young Ladies, where she learned to pour tea, play piano, and read and write in Latin, Greek, and Hebrew. She took to horseback lessons with decorous skill; lithographs that appeared in *Frank Leslie's Illustrated Newspaper* many years later blundered in showing a flaxen-haired hellion galloping through treacherous mountain passes astraddle. The one equestrian photograph she posed for shows a middle-aged woman wound in yards of velvet, with a plume on her hat, a pistol on her hip, and both lower limbs arranged demurely on one side. Boasted she: "I did everything Cole and Jesse and Frank did, sidesaddle and wearing a bustle."

Federal troops taught her to hate. They burned Shirley's empire to the ground in 1863, charging that the hotel had been used to harbor rebels, and shot young Bud to death for protesting. In that year, most of Missouri decamped to Texas, and Shirley, an entrepreneur despite his grief, packed up the remains of his family and possessions and followed it to Scyene, where he and Preston bred horses for sale to cattle outfits intending to drive their beeves to the hungry postwar Eastern markets. This was when Myra Belle would learn the details of reproduction among mammals, and also the various techniques employed by start-up cattlemen to swell their herds. Hair branding, the running iron, and other methods and tools of the rustling trade became as familiar to her as the embroidery hoop.

It's unclear whether she met Cole Younger at this time, or if they'd known each other in Missouri, where he'd ridden with Bloody Bill Anderson's bushwhackers and acquired the skills necessary to rob banks and trains. As the brains of the James Gang, he was too sanguine to have trotted after Myra Belle to Texas, whatever her charms at the time, and so it's likely their relationship heated up there, as did most things. Both had lost beloved family members to the Union; great romances have been constructed on common ground less firm. It's a matter of record that she became pregnant, and whether the father was Younger or Frank Reed, whom she married, is open to speculation. Reed was a former guerrilla who had plundered Kansas and Missouri with the infamous Tom Starr. Myra Belle's preferences had become predictable.

Pearl was born in Bates County, Missouri, where Reed had rejoined Starr. The murder of a man named Shannon forced a temporary move to California. There a boy was born and scarcely christened before a mishandled stage robbery sent them back to Texas at speed. John Shirley lent them money to open a livery stable, but Myra Belle ran the business while Reed worked in the field to stock the stalls with stolen horses.

This was an unwise undertaking in a state where horse thieves were regarded with less favor than common murderers. On August 6, 1874, Lamar County Deputy Sheriff J. T. Morris shot and killed Reed. His widow placed the children with her parents and took up dealing faro in Dallas, on occasion crooking the game in favor of Jesse James, who had fled the posses in Missouri to spend some Yankee gold while on holiday. The arrangement was strictly for old times' sake; Jesse had nettled at Cole Younger's equal share of notoriety for the raids they'd pulled off together, and Myra Belle remained loyal to her first love. She considered Jesse a straitlaced hypocrite who preached the Ten Commandments and kept only the ones that didn't count, and Jesse thought her a harlot and a card cheat into the bargain.

Followed a stint in Galena, Kansas, playing house with Cole's cousin Bruce Younger, a gambler in the saloons of that cow capital. (Cole was at this time beginning a life sentence in the Minnesota State Penitentiary at Stillwater for the misguided robbery of the bank in Northfield.) When Bruce's luck ran cold, she decamped to a sixty-acre farm on the Canadian River in the Nations, assuming housekeeping duties as the wife of Tom Starr's son, a man nearly ten years her junior. It was at this point that she dropped the name Myra and became Belle Starr, on the advice of a Eufala numerologist; all her life the Bandit Queen considered herself a student of the modern sciences, refusing to travel without her astrology charts and a carved wooden head partitioned off like a butcher's guide with phrenological labels identifying the seats of humor, passion, culture, perversity, and patience. (She claimed for her own part a prodigious bump of loyalty.)

It was 1880, and the last golden decade of the authentic Wild West had begun. Within two years, Jesse James would be dead, shot in the back by a Judas; Pat Garrett would bust a cap on Billy the Kid, his confederate in the Lincoln County War; and Bob, Grat, and Emmett Dalton would learn the rudiments of keeping the peace for Judge Parker before deciding to try their hands at breaking it. Buffalo Bill would soon pimp the frontier for the entertainment of paying spectators in New York, Chicago, and Europe, Jesse's brother Frank James would beat numberless charges of robbery and murder and conduct ticketed tours of the James ranch, and Sitting Bull and Geronimo would surrender to the U.S. Cavalry. A nation of dime-novel readers, their thirst unslaked, would turn their attention to Belle Starr, whose likeness in *Harper's* and *Ned Buntline's Own* bore a closer resemblance to Jenny Lind than the horse-faced matron who rose in kid gloves, a hat with a veil, and floor-length skirts when Judge Parker entered the Fort Smith courtroom. Beside her was Sam Starr, looking decidedly less comfortable in a stiff town suit purchased by their attorney for the occasion, his dark Cherokee neck cruelly bisected by a starched white collar. His black eyes sought constantly for egress, only to come to a full stop at the calm, muttonchopped countenance of George S. Winston, Parker's private bailiff, and the butt of the Army Colt revolver rising ostentatiously above a cavalry scabbard strapped to his hip. He was a Negro, and Starr subscribed to his father's fear and hatred of the fighting freedman. He was precocious in his precaution; Winston's service to the court predated Parker's, and in several attempts at escape from that room, none had succeeded.

Belle was less impressed. When the principals and spectators were seating themselves, and before Parker could snap his gavel, she spotted an old enemy, and before Winston could react, she made a beeline for the penned-off section reserved for officers and the press, seized a little man seated there by his lapels, dragged him over the oaken railing, and slashed a red welt across his face with a riding whip Winston had not thought to confiscate from her. By the time the bailiff reached the scene, the man had slumped back into his seat, a hand to his cheek, and Belle surrendered her weapon without resistance. She left Winston holding it and returned to her spot beside Sam.

It developed that the little man—Albert A. Powe, editor of the *Fort Smith Evening Call*—had written some fanciful prose upon the $10,000 reward offered for the arrest and conviction of Sam and Belle Starr, with emphasis upon Belle's amorous adventures with the outlaw aristocracy, and she'd taken it upon herself to defend her honor without awaiting her husband's intervention. Parker, a man of surpassing humor and irony despite his reputation in the Puritan East, banged for silence, waggled a finger at the codefendant, and warned her, with subterranean forces twitching at the corners of his mouth, that another such digression from the dignity of the courtroom would bring a charge of contempt, and time spent in the women's detention in the old barracks. (Observers could not help but note, as she sank into a curtsey worthy of the Court of St. James's, that Parker cupped a hand over the unseemly reaction in the lower half of his face.)

Photographs had managed to capture the ravages of time upon the protean feminine face, but such reminiscences bear witness to the powers of seduction of those who have known beauty, and the wisdom that although it will not last, the memory that it once existed will continue to reap reward in the future. On this evidence alone, her loveliness stands beside Helen's of Troy.

The month was October 1883. Parker's power was at its height. Barring presidential intervention—and Chester Alan Arthur, whose likeness belongs in *Webster's International Dictionary of the English Language* beside the phrase "political hack," offered no such illusion—his pronouncements carried all the weight of the stone tablets from Mt. Sinai. But Belle was unimpressed. Parker was a man, by all accounts a gentleman, and once a woman has taken the measure of the brutes, the higher species are tame birds for the slaughter. The charge was horse stealing, a capital offense in that place, where to leave a man dismounted was to condemn him to death. But Parker had never marked a woman for hanging, and this prejudice encouraged her to believe that her danger was not mortal. The difference was the same that favored the gambler who could afford to lose. She bet everything on the hand that God had dealt her, and counted upon the odds to rescue Sam as well.

Thank God they had not been brought up on a lesser charge.

She had known many men, in and out of the Biblical sense,

and to each she had been faithful, until such time as fate and the astrological forces instructed her to shift her allegiance. For the time being, they directed her to stand by Sam. When prosecutor Clayton, a mattress-faced carpetbagger straight out of a political cartoon in the *Charleston Mercury*, berated Sam on the stand for his deficiency in letters, she sent lethal glances from the attorney to Parker, who—it seemed to her—flinched, and directed Clayton to restrict himself to the evidence. This was an epiphany. It was as if she herself were directing the trial.

Four days of this, the pendulum swinging between conviction and acquittal as the pettifogging lawyers parsed out the facts, evicted the jury while the finer points were dissected, squabbled over, and both counsels silenced like unruly children by the waggling finger behind the bench, and then Parker lectured to the panel at stultifying length and bade it retire to consider its verdict. No suspense there; had Parker simply said, "Guilty," and thanked the jurors for the waste of their lives, the result would not have been different. After a brief recess—briefer, perhaps, if the clock were not so near noon, and luncheon not promised for the deliberators—the farmer in the foreman's seat, solemn and monkey-faced in his clean overalls, stood and let fall the stones of doom.

"You will listen to the sentence of the law," Parker told the couple, "which is that you, Sam and Belle Starr, will spend not less, nor more than one year in the Detroit House of Corrections, in penal servitude for your crimes against the citizenry of the United States." Or some such babble; Belle paid little attention beyond the price.

She caned chairs for nine months, in the stone building on the Detroit River (in the language of the pavement, *up the river* would survive its source by many years). None of the matrons complained about her behavior, and Sam was as docile on the men's side. They were released on the same day, whereupon they left the Siberian Michigan wilderness for the opportunities still to be found in the Nations.

TWELVE

She saved Blue Duck's life, after Isaac Parker, Jesus Christ, and Blue Duck himself had laid it to rest. It was a thing to take pride in, even if the life itself wasn't worth a broken stay, and would likely play itself out behind walls of stone doing God-knows-what with his fellow prisoners.

Belle liked his looks and grooming. He was a white man despite the name, spent fifteen minutes each morning trimming his pencil moustache with a pair of nail scissors, used pine needles to clean his teeth, and changed his shirt twice a week. He never raised a hand to her, even when she striped his face with her riding whip for laughing when she used a mounting block to board her favorite mare.

She was still married to Sam Starr and would remain so for the rest of her brief life, but by 1884 that relationship had cooled, and she'd moved in with Blue Duck in a house in the Cherokee Nation, where they lived without an Indian residency permit, a misdemeanor in Parker's court. Deputies escorting the tumbleweed wagon carried warrants to arrest them next time their route passed near enough to take the trouble to bring them in. But before that, Belle's companion moved himself to the top of the priorities list when he got drunk on trade whiskey in the Flint District of the Cherokee, remembered an old insult, and emptied his revolver into a farmer named Wyrick. Whooping and whirling his horse, Blue Duck reloaded and snapped off a wild shot at an Indian boy working Wyrick's field, missing as the boy ran for cover. He was equally off the mark minutes later when he fired three times at a neighbor named Hawkey Wolf, frightening him seriously but causing no physical injury. None who heard of this incident could come up with a reason for the visit, so it was decided the shooter was only amusing himself on this occasion.

Blue Duck committed the additional indiscretion of boasting of the Wyrick affair over a jug of busthead in a store near Vinita. One of his listeners sent for Deputy Marshal Frank Cochran, who arrested Blue Duck and a friend said to have accompanied him on his raid. The friend was acquitted, but the jury found against Blue Duck. He was sentenced to mount the Fort Smith scaffold on July 23, 1886.

Belle Starr was in the gallery when the sentence was pronounced. Some who knew her and were not influenced by her purple press said she had dead eyes, cold as wax, but there was plenty of fire in them that day, all of it directed at Prosecutor Clayton, who had humiliated Sam on the witness stand when the Starrs were tried for horse stealing three years before, and his remarks upon Blue Duck's character during his turn in the dock had to her mind gone beyond the purpose of merely convicting him. Had Bailiff Winston not taken care this time to disarm her of the riding whip she carried everywhere as a sort of trademark, she'd have given the man a good lashing and she didn't care how many chairs she had to cane in Detroit to square things with Parker. She considered Clayton a coward who used the safe cover of the courtroom to assault men who if he crossed their path in the Nations would make him wet his drawers with a hard look.

It was a quirk of Belle's nature that she carried no such passion against the judge for condemning her man, or for any of the five times she herself stood accused before him. She thought him a man who did his job, no more and no less than that, and he seemed as quick to lecture Clayton as his opponent at the defense table whenever he strayed over some line. For his part, Parker seemed more bemused than angered by Belle's offenses against justice, and was possibly a bit starstruck by her reputation in the yellow journals. Certainly the sentences he passed upon her were milder than those he'd brought against men who had committed similar crimes. Belle considered him a gentleman, with all the contempt a woman of her background felt for that breed; she had, after all, acquired some of her most effective weapons at the Carthage Academy for Young Ladies. She took particular care selecting a dress and some delicate scent for her appearances in court.

The gavel came down on Blue Duck's case at the end of January. While he was in the old jail, listening to George Maledon testing the trap and his ropes, Belle returned to the Nations and Sam Starr.

Sam had never lost his interest in her, and had demonstrated the point by trailing a man she'd dallied with shortly after their return from Michigan and removing his face with a charge of buckshot. The outlaw wasn't as shrewd as his infamous father, welcoming her back without question. Blue Duck's blunder and conviction seemed to him sufficient cause for her affections to fade. Sam was still in this frame of mind some weeks later, when he fled a posse of Cherokee Lighthorse over some old difference of opinion and jumped his horse off a twenty-foot cliff into the Canadian River. The dive was reckoned the longest in equestrian history, and the fact that horse and rider survived and swam to freedom gave him the edge for a while over old Tom Starr.

This episode, and Starr's enforced absence thereafter, threw Belle's plans seriously out of gear. Her real motive in coming back to him was to assemble a new criminal enterprise and raise money for a brilliant lawyer to appeal to President Cleveland for Blue Duck's pardon.

Despite the stories told about her, Belle was strictly an adjunct, and no leader. She was arrested in short order after she and three men of Sam's acquaintance were accused of robbing an elderly man named Farrell and his three grown sons in the Choctaw Nation. She was said to have been dressed in male gear at the time—a man's wide-brimmed hat, high-heeled boots, and duck canvas shirt and trousers, as endemic in that country as lederhosen in the Swiss Alps—but still riding in ladies' fashion, with one knee hooked over the pommel. However, at a preliminary hearing in Fort Smith, none of the four victims could identify the woman attired in the height of that season's style as their bandit, and she was released, only to be brought in again a few weeks later for stealing horses from a ranch belonging to a man named Mc-Carty. In restraints on the way back to Arkansas, she wept bitterly; but since that was inconsistent with the legend they'd created for her, the hack writers ignored the report. She failed Blue Duck and was certain he'd hang while she was still fighting this new charge.

But there was no sign of tears on her face when, free on bail, she entered the office of J. Warren Reed and sat in the embossed leather chair in front of his desk, resting a large carpetbag on her lap.

Reed was a vain man who wore corsets to accommodate his snug coats and pointed his handlebars with Pearson's Wax. In the woman's blue velvet dress and Sherwood Forest hat trimmed with ribbons—itself a fat two-dollar item in the proliferating millineries in Fort Smith—he saw the possibility of a substantial fee, and something to his account at the tailor's to keep himself out of small claims court. Her frank flat stare, and her notoriety, gave him no qualms. He was the kind of man who cut across cemeteries after midnight and feared nothing worse than a bruised shin on an inconveniently placed headstone. He'd determined to beard Old Parker in his den at his first opportunity, but had no intimation that the opportunity was so close at hand.

"I'm familiar with your case, Mrs. Starr," he said. "I read all the city and territorial newspapers. This rancher McCarty has a reputation for casting a wide loop when it comes to foals belonging to his neighbors. With his testimony in tatters I feel I can win you an acquittal, if not indeed a directed verdict in your favor."

The corners of her lips twitched upward in a parched, thin-lipped smile that reminded him of some portraits of Elizabeth the Great, another mannish woman who just might possibly have lived up to her reputation. "Anytime I can't twist my way around Judge Parker is time I took up lacework in St. Louis," she said. "I'm here about Blue Duck."

"Blue Duck? I'm afraid I'm not—" It wasn't often he was dismasted in his own office.

She filled him in on the particulars, with scarcely a word wasted. It occurred to Reed that she would have made a fine legal secretary. And as the details seeped into the honeycomb material of his singular brain, J. Warren Reed caught the bittersweet scent of challenge. He could not wait to tell his wife of this day. She was the only woman in the world who was more ambitious than he, and damn few men could match him for his faith in himself and his future.

"I can't promise anything," he said, once Belle had finished speaking and the regulator clock on the wall opposite his desk, a twin of the one in Parker's courtroom, had clonked twice in the vacuum. "I'll need to study the transcripts. Offhand, the fault most consistent in the judge's method lies in his summations to the jury, and the language he chooses when he pronounces a sentence of death. The first is often prejudicial—shockingly so—and there is an element of sadism in the second. I truly believe the old hypocrite enjoys the role of Jack Ketch."

"I don't know who that is, but if you can get Blue Duck clear of the scaffold, I'll pay the freight." She stood up, inverted the carpetbag above the desk, freed the catch, and dumped stacks of banknotes bound with India rubber bands onto the leather top.

Reed, managing to dissemble the pounding in his chest, didn't trouble to count the notes in her presence. He slid them together into a block, dipped a horsehair pen into a squat bottle of iron-gall ink, and wrote her out a simple receipt stating that her account was paid in full. She surprised him then by offering him a limpid hand in a kid glove—the reward tendered a gentleman by a lady of fine breeding, and not at all the hearty grasp of a woman who rode, cursed, took the

Lord's name in vain, and generally trafficked in the same vices as men.

"I'm stopping at the Hotel Le Flore," she said. "You can report to me there, if I'm not tied up in court or in Parker's Dungeon of the Damned."

She demolished the government's case, as she had predicted; although she knew little of the labyrinthine passages through the American legal system circa 1886, she had the measure of Judge Parker and the drab, simple men who sat on the panel—farmers, mostly, with dirt under their nails and no conception of a lady lathed in the mills of society beyond a furtive glance at forbidden sections of the Montgomery Ward catalogue—and felt confident in the revolutionary allure of her saga reprinted endlessly on brown sawtooth paper bound between crimson-and-yellow covers; the callow public defender she'd drawn in the lottery had little to do but allow the jurors to compare his client's refined posture in the dock to rancher McCarty's slumped figure and yellow-stained beard in the witness box to secure the exchange Belle had foreseen:

"Gentlemen of the jury, have you reached a verdict?"

"Sure thing, Your Honor. We—"

"Wait until I ask, sir. How do you find?"

"We find"—the man in overalls and a rusty funeral coat consulted a scrap of paper in his horned palm—"we find the defendant not guilty as charged in the within indictment."

Parker slapped his gavel, dismissed the jury with thanks, and shooed Belle Starr from his courtroom. His calendar was filled with cases to try.

J. Warren Reed drafted and redrafted his letter to the White House, gave it to his wife to transcribe in her refined hand on good rag paper—she made improvements and corrections from her own extensive knowledge of the law—and posted it by special delivery. He sent word and a copy of the letter to his client at the Hotel Le Flore and waited. He had not met

with Blue Duck and had no intention to seek a personal con-
ference. The man had nothing to offer that would help obtain clemency, and much that could prevent it. Anytime an
attorney for the defense could work the system without
soiling his cuffs on an actual defendant was cause for self-
congratulation.

Grover Cleveland's situation was complicated. His Republican rivals, who had been slow-roasting him for two years
over his personal morals, were sharpening their blades for the
congressional elections in November, the railroads were pres-
suring him to pressure Congress to assign them rights-of-
way to build more spurs in the Indian Nations, and his support
among his fellow Democrats was eroding. Many of them
were sworn enemies of Isaac Parker, who had deserted the
party a dozen years ago, and their diatribes on the grisly
situation in the Eighth District had been reported at gassy
length in the columns of the *Congressional Record*.

Reed had known all this when he'd composed his plea, and
also that Cleveland had robbed Parker of a record-setting,
scaffold-testing eight-man hanging on April 23 of that year
by commuting the sentences of six of them to life imprisonment in Detroit. Once the presidential pen had been whittled
to so fine a point, an experienced petitioner had but to strike
before the momentum slowed. Within two weeks of its posting, his letter brought Cleveland's reply, signed in his heavy
hand. Blue Duck was ordered to be transferred from the jail
in Fort Smith to Menard, Illinois, there to begin a life sentence in the federal penitentiary.

If Reed expected one of Belle's rare George Washington
smiles when she returned to his office in response to his note,
he was disappointed. Her skirts rustled across the floor in a
straight line and she leaned forward to rest both hands atop
his desk, the famous riding crop in one.

"Blue Duck is no good to me behind bars," she said. "I
need him pardoned."

The lawyer was amused. "My dear madam, what you're

asking has happened only once, and the man was convicted of rape, not murder. Chester Arthur had already been defeated for the Republican nomination, so he had nothing to lose. This president's friends and enemies take a dim view of killing farmers. They need their votes."

"I don't follow politics. It isn't a ladies' game. How much have you got left from what I gave you last month?"

"It isn't a matter of what's left. I'm paid for my time, and the amount of that I'll need to reopen the case, interview witnesses, and establish grounds for a presidential—"

"Draw what you need from what's left. I'll be back with more." She walked out, the crop under one arm like a folded parasol.

THIRTEEN

S am Starr, fresh from the legend of his twenty-foot plunge into the Canadian River on horseback, rode the same splendid animal between tall stacks of September corn smack dab into the same Cherokee Lighthorse officers whose pursuit had led to that stunt. This time, Starr charged straight into them Missouri guerrilla fashion, his reins in his teeth and Colts barking in both hands. They parted, giving him the right of way, then wheeled their horses and took out after him. A slug killed the most celebrated horse since Comanche of the Seventh and Starr was captured, only to be rescued by confederates from the farmhouse where he was being held for the tribal council.

Informants told Belle that the Lighthorse and marshals both had had their fill of Sam Starr and his like and were recruiting a small army to kill or recapture him and burn down the homestead on the Canadian that Belle had named Younger's Bend, where criminal gangs were known to congregate. Without a base of operations, her plans to raise funds

to pay Lawyer Reed were worthless. She advised Sam to surrender to the marshals, who would give him a fairer hearing
through Parker's court than he'd find before the Cherokee
council. Sam was disinclined to reverse the policy of a lifetime, and their debate on the matter was overheard, some
said, as far as Going Snake; which was scarcely possible, but
then business in the Nations showed small regard for the laws
of man and God. In any case, Ned Christie had begun his
campaign against the United States, and if the row reached
his ears in Rabbit Trap Canyon he ignored it, because he had
more personal concerns to occupy him. But Belle's temper
was waspish, she had a mule's own disposition, and Sam's
people-handling skills were restricted to others of his gender. On October 11, Deputy Marshal Tyner Hughes watched
in wonder, drawing his pistol and working his jaws on a plug
in his cheek, as the most wanted man in the Nations rode
up to him in front of the jail, stepped down, and spread his
coat to show he carried no weapons.

Many years later, when Parker was dead and buried and
oil had been discovered in the State of Oklahoma, men who
as children were present on that occasion, and some who
weren't but claimed the distinction anyway, told of the day
the great Sam Starr, wearing the butternut coat and sweat-
stained campaign hat in which his father had ridden with
Captain Quantrill and Bloody Bill Anderson, trotted a fine
sleek racing stallion straight up Garrison Avenue while every marshal and Indian policeman was scouring the Cherokee for him and calmly handed himself over to the mercy of
Parker's court. The members of the Eastern press who had
come to interview them in their newfound wealth waved aside
such ancient history; they were more interested in why an old
red man in a motheaten blanket had decided to buy himself
a private railroad coach with no tracks to run it on.

The coda to the affair was anticlimactic. Starr was ar-
raigned, posted bond out of Belle's tight budget, and rode
back to Younger's Bend, scratching his head, to await trial.

He considered the law a contrary critter and harder to predict than a badger.

Belle remained behind in Fort Smith, where Parker one day beckoned her to join him in his chambers. She hesitated, but the absence of an armed escort assured her she was in no trouble, and the tea service on his desk bespoke hospitality rather than incarceration. She watched him fill the delicate cups with his fine pink hands, as hairless as an old woman's and calloused only where the fingers gripped his pen, and wondered if he had brewed the tea himself; there was something spinsterish in the judge's manner that escaped his demonizers back East.

They sipped. Belle noticed that the judge preferred his justice strong and his tea weak. He cleared his throat, cleared it again; his Adam's apple dented the careful crease in his cravat. He appeared ill at ease in a social situation; one, at least, in which his gavel served no purpose. "You know, perhaps, that I am president of the Sebastian County Fair Association." His manner begged an affirmative reply.

"I don't come to Fort Smith often, and not usually by my choice," she said. "You could claim you ran the fire brigade and I couldn't contradict you." She was enjoying his discomfort.

"I can't claim that distinction. As one who has the honor to attest to the former, I hope to persuade you to play a part in the festivities."

"I've never been good at raising hogs. When one gets big enough to consider showing, I slaughter it. Sam is partial to ham steak."

"I don't judge livestock. I haven't the credentials." He betrayed something of the impatience he reserved for audacious attorneys. "Would you consider leading a mock raid on a stagecoach, purely for the entertainment of spectators during the event?"

She rotated her cup in its saucer. Had she been drinking, she felt she would have choked.

"It's a grotesque spectacle," he hastened on, oblivious to

her reaction, "one I should not have given my assent to five years ago, when such atrocities were far more common and carried out in deadly earnest. However, I suppose it's a signal of progress that we should put forth the thing as an attraction instead of something to be eradicated."

"I've never robbed a stagecoach. I wouldn't know how to go about it."

He smiled in his beard. The man had a sense of humor, rare enough in his position and remarkable in his circumstances, which she knew to be unique in its challenges from high and low. "It needn't succeed. The object is to provide noise and color, with blank cartridges and the usual theatrical claptrap on the order of Buffalo Bill's extravaganza. Your"—he tasted the word—"notoriety will draw customers. If you're concerned that I'm asking you to play the clown, I must tell you I'm placing my own dignity on the line as well. I've agreed to be a passenger, and Mr. Clayton has consented to accompany me, along with one or two other officers of the court."

Belle reflected later that she must have been singularly in possession of her poker face. Any light that appeared in those lifeless eyes at that news would surely have caused Parker to reconsider the invitation.

She set her cup and saucer down on the desk with a thump. "I'll do it. I never could resist a fair."

The exhibition was gay even by the standards of that jaded city, where until recently inebriated cowhands had ridden their string ponies up the steps of the Two Brothers Saloon and recalcitrant Comanches had terrorized visiting tenderheels with their scalping knives and a snootful of Old Pepper. Covered wagons clogged the streets, bearing all the comforts of home for those who had arrived too late to book rooms in the hotels, the girls in the Row worked double shifts, and vendors prowled the boardwalks, selling ice cream and cotton candy for prices that would have made the dollar-an-egg merchants of Creede and old San Francisco curse the lost opportunity. Patent-medicine showmen burst the hinges on their strongboxes with banknotes before they were sent on their way by city policemen, a Frenchman spent a night in jail for sorcery on the evidence of a demonstration of pictures that moved. A bicycle salesman from St. Louis made his case for the obsolecensce of the horse. Opium dens on First Street exhausted their inventory and substituted pipes filled with loco weed scraped from the soles of boots fresh from Texas. From his window on the ground floor of the old courthouse, Judge Parker looked out upon the barbarism of his age and recalled his wife's early judgment: "Isaac, we've made a great mistake." Then a string of firecrackers went off with a volley that reminded him of the tense days with the Union Home Guard, spooking a horse into spilling a cartful of some vendor's baked potatoes, and he returned to his desk to review a case of rape, robbery, and murder on the Osage reservation. He burned a cigar over the explicit details. It was a wicked world.

Belle had not lied about her inexperience; holding up stagecoaches was a distinct gap in her resumé. She researched the method with all the solemnity that poor Cole, rotting away cording jute in Minnesota, would have brought to the enterprise. Quietly and without ostentation, she polished a live cartridge on the velvet of her skirts and inserted it into a chamber of her borrowed Colt among the blank rounds charged with powder and harmless wadding, singing to herself softly: "Old Bill Clayton lies a-mould'ring in his grave . . ."

On the day of the event, Belle, got up in a pulp-writer's idea of female-bandit regalia—flowing skirts, frilly lace bodice, and a cocked hat with an imitation ostrich plume of dyed turkey tail feather—trotted up Garrison Avenue sidesaddle aboard a fine sorrel stallion, and reined in beside the requisite politicians' platform draped in red-white-and-blue bunting with town dignitaries pressed against the railing in silk ties and sashes of office. She posed obligingly for a little German photographer, soon to be anointed with the responsibility of committing Ned Christie's conquerors to the graphic record, then spotted a fresh opportunity for legend. Albert A. Powe, he of the *Fort Smith Evening Call,* an unpopular local reputation, and a celebrated whipping at the end of Belle's riding whip, made the mistake of showing up, and was seized by citizens and borne, short chubby legs kicking, to within Belle's reach. She uncorked her rare, compressed smile and lent an arm to help haul him up onto the cantle. She quirted the reins across the horse's withers, and as it pounced forward, the little man threw his arms around her waist, gasping asthmatically as she galloped around the fairgrounds at a Sam Starr pace, depositing him at last in a whimpering heap in full sight of the spectators around the arena. "The pen," wrote one journalistic rival, "may indeed be mightier than the sword; but it is no match for the Bandit Queen of the Indian Territory aboard a prime example of Arkansas horseflesh." She did not fail to note that the jackals of the press tore into their own with the same relish they reserved for everyone who fell into their den.

Her scholarly studies had informed her that few successful stagecoach robberies had taken place entirely from horseback; when the crisis came, the true highwayman relied far more strongly upon his own resources than those of an animal with a brain the size of a turnip and all the courage of a journalist. As the lacquered red Concord trundled out onto the grounds, she gave the crowd its money's worth, whooping and hollering with the tame Indians from the Nations in their beads and feathers, then leaned back on the reins, leapt from the saddle with the force of the horse's momentum, and bore down on the coach, snapping the hammer on the punk cartridges and keeping count before she came to the live round with Clayton's name on it.

Live cartridges had a will of their own, and found their way despite the best intentions. But she never had a chance to put that explanation to the test of an inquest. Clayton's arrogant bewhiskered face failed to appear among the three passengers sharing the facing seats with Judge Parker. She held her fire one short of the fatal round.

Clayton had bowed out at the last minute, claiming the burden of his caseload. She didn't accept it. Parker's was heavier, yet he had found time for digression in the interest of his community. There in the clamor of cheering and dust and the driver's gees and haws, her gaze locked with Parker's, as cold and blue as drift ice in the Arkansas in January; and she knew that she had underestimated the old buzzard. It was a defeat for him as well as for her, for she would not repeat the mistake.

The Hotel Le Flore, relentlessly Parisian, cloaked its dining room in tatted curtains, framed rotogravures of the French capital, the *Mona Lisa,* and the gardens at Versailles, and featured thick slices of veal swimming in champagne sauce with hearts of artichoke looking like little vaginas floating in pools of red wine. The menu was engraved in French on paper as thick as a Creek blanket, with the prix fixe appearing only on the copy handed to the gentleman. Reed's eyes went directly to the bottom, recorded the information with the crunch of an adding-machine lever inside his skull, and lifted his gaze without reaction to his client's. "How do you prefer your oysters?"

"With Blue Duck on the side." Her eyes were like open graves. She wore widow's weeds, black as fresh tar, with a veil pinned to her hat with bow-tie flourishes that looked like tiny suspended bats. He could not know that she was in mourning for her lost opportunity with Prosecutor Clayton. "What's the news? I reckon it's good, or we'd be eating greasy fish on paper down by the Arkansas."

"It's good. Escargot good, with a burgundy chablis, if they have it and you don't mind eating snails."

"I've eaten wolf's liver, still warm with the wolf studying

my throat. They're a long time giving up the fight. Me, too. When do I get to take Blue Duck home?"

"Let's not get premature. There's a deal of paperwork to make out, and two or three bureaus to put their stamp on it. Let's just say for now you'll be celebrating the anniversary of the birth of our Lord with your friend, in the place of your choice, with none looking on. I don't expect Judge Parker to pray for my immortal soul come Christmas morning, but I gave up on his friendship when I came to Fort Smith."

"Does that mean you've got the pardon?"

"It does, barring unforeseen delays. Um—"

"Um," she said. "I've picked up half a dozen tongues in the Nations, but I wouldn't know how to translate 'um' for a one." She made room for her carpetbag on the linen-draped tabletop, hauled out bricks of currency, and arranged them in neat avenues between the candle and his bread plate. "Are we square?"

He looked around quickly, meeting the gazes of neighboring diners, and scooped the banknotes into his leather briefcase. "I am always at your service," he said. "You're the only client with whom I've never had to bring up the delicate subject of compensation."

"Take care I don't steal it back," said Belle.

FOURTEEN

Mrs. Lucy Surratt ignored her neighbors every day of the year but one, when the bleak winter on the Canadian River got to her and she invited them into her husband's home to commemorate the anniversary of the birth of Christ. On the Friday before the holiday, 1886, Belle Starr got tired of watching Sam drink and fret about his upcoming trial, threw him a clean shirt, and announced that they were going to the party.

She needed the change. J. Warren Reed had underestimated the stalls in Blue Duck's case, her daughter Pearl had told her she was about to become a grandmother out of wedlock, and son Ed was in jail in Fort Smith for peddling whiskey in the Nations. Belle blamed her absences from her children's side for the way they'd turned out, despite whipping them with extra enthusiasm during visits to make up for the neglect. As a result, Pearl was terrified of her mother and Ed hated her.

Sam Starr was a hostile drunk whose every brush with the law had followed a session with busthead. He was snarling when he and Belle drew rein before the Surratts' past sundown, and once inside proceeded to find fault with the punch, the close climate on the dance floor, and the way the fiddler played. When a bottle made the rounds he emptied it and hurled it at the poor musician, striking him on the neck and ruining "Jack o' Diamonds."

"Simmer down, Sam," Belle said. "We need the music."

Sam responded by wheeling their hostess out on the floor and jostling the other dancers. One lunged toward him, but was restrained by a companion. Everyone knew Sam bit when he foamed.

It was Frank West's poor timing to come in from a smoke out back just about this time. The Cherokee Lighthorse policeman wasn't wearing his uniform, but Sam recognized him from a previous encounter.

"You're the son of a bitch shot me and killed my horse that day in the cornfield."

West regarded him with oak-colored eyes. "That wasn't me, Sam. It was Chief Vann and Marshal Robberson done that."

"You're a liar." Sam drew his Colt and shot West in the neck. It was Sam's night for necks.

Blood spouting from his jugular, the policeman pulled a short-barreled revolver from the pocket of his overcoat as he fell. The powder flare caught Sam's shirt afire. The bullet shattered his heart. Male guests helped Belle load him into her carriage. The next day, a hired hand moved a cord of wood to dig a hole in the only unfrozen patch of earth at Younger's Bend. Belle laid a bouquet of dried lady's slippers on the mound.

When the report of Sam Starr's death reached Judge Parker, he told Stephen Wheeler to strike his name from the docket. The clerk noted the relief in his superior's tone. He had seen often the traces of dust on the judge's knees after he had prayed for the souls of the men he had sent to the scaffold.

The cabin at Younger's Bend yawned large and empty without Sam's larger-than-life presence. Belle missed Blue Duck more than ever, but his case was still crawling through the logjam in Washington; Grover Cleveland had troubles of his own that season, with a hostile Congress and the worst winter on the plains in a hundred years driving the price of beef through the roof and threatening another panic. On an impulse, Belle wired her children to join her, the telegram to Ed reaching him in his cell where he was finishing out his sentence. She warned Pearl not to bring her bastard with her when she came. The lessons of the Carthage Academy for Young Ladies died hard. She could abide any sins except those against social decency.

For a time after the passing of Sam Starr, a pall of peace settled upon the Indian Nations. Of all the chronic felons wanted perpetually in Fort Smith, Ned Christie now stood alone. Five years, and the health of several deputy U.S. marshals, would pass before he made his final stand. The wild West lurched a step closer to tame.

Belle meanwhile settled into the quiet life of widow and mother. Those who knew her by sight paused as her apparently dutiful son helped her down from her carriage when she went to McAlester's store for provisions and supplies; those who knew her by reputation only professed disbelief that this plain woman decked out in the pinnacle of Eastern fashion was America's own Bandit Queen. They turned again to the

Valkyries borne of the fistulous imaginations of self-styled journalists, who never disappointed.

Blizzards laid claim to the prairie. Thousands of cattle froze in huddles, children lost their way, crouched, and turned crystalline scant yards from shelter. Meteorolists—a new term for readers of the Eastern sheets to wrap their lips around—cleared their throats at podiums and predicted a new Ice Age. Evangelists dusted off Revelations. Chicagoans brawled over tins of corn and peaches in markets, convinced that a cellarful of foodstuffs was all that stood between them and starvation when the snow drifted to the roof of the Mercantile Exchange. But on the Canadian, Belle Starr rocked on her front porch, drew her shawl about her shoulders, and warmed her vitals with coffee laced with brandy, obtained through the ladies' entrance to the House of Lords in Fort Smith (the skullbender they sold in the Nations tore her up inside). At forty-one she considered herself retired from the adventurous life. It was a good bargain, given her history and the lies everyone told about her; Wild Bill had made only thirty-nine, Jesse thirty-five, and poor Cole had been buried alive since age thirty-two up in squarehead country. That little fat nance Albert A. Powe had let his mercenary instincts get the better of his fear long enough to approach her with a proposition to help her write her memoirs.

She rocked and thought about that. It was a story worth telling, better than anything she'd heard about the pack of howlers that Judas Pat Garrett had published about Billy Bonney, who it seemed to her she could have set on the right path with a sound whipping the first time he'd strayed. There was war in the thing and betrayal, and Sam's twenty-foot plunge horseback into the river; she hadn't been with him on that occasion, never went out on raids except when he was unavailable to lead them, but Powe didn't know that and neither would the readers until she told them, and she wasn't about to let truth get in the way of the record. Those Missouri wildwood boys had taught her a thing or two about stretching yarn. She wondered if publishing paid better than highway work.

Seasons changed while she was contemplating the literary life. The snows out west receded, leaving behind carcasses in heaps and scattered corpses, the spring rained hard and the summer ran hot and dry. Lawyer Reed wrote her a litany of Grover Cleveland's travails that made her wonder if he wanted her to transfer her concerns from Blue Duck to the president. Another harsh winter hammered the continent all the way to New York City. Entrepreneurs in that wicked town charged elevated train passengers two dollars a head to conduct them down ladders from their stalled positions to the street. Belle shot a deer and had to quarter it to get it up the drifted hill from the river.

Spring again, and she put in corn and potatoes and fattened a hog, whether to feed her grown children or to enter in Parker's fair she wasn't certain. She wondered if she'd have been free to slop and till if Clayton had been aboard that stagecoach. It would have made a dandy chapter, and an object lesson to cowardly counselors. She might write it regardless. Clayton had sure showed the white feather there.

Her children made her feel old. She took up with Jim July, a nephew of Sam's, and gave him harbor when the marshals and Cherokee Lighthorse sought him for horse rustling. He wasn't as loyal as Sam, disappeared for days at a time while she suspected he was seeing other women, but she was realistic about her prospects and made no scene when he returned. When during one reunion she learned he'd fled a tumbleweed wagon and hid out overnight in a ditch, she told him he ought to follow his uncle's example and turn himself in; the jail in Fort Smith was no less comfortable than a ditch, and the meals were regular. "And Sam never spent a day," she added.

"That's because he got shot."

"That didn't have anything to do with the business."

"It just seems to me a powerful lot of men wind up shot around you."

"Well, I didn't shoot them."

"Not seeing nobody else did comes to the same thing."

Belle had no answer for that that wouldn't have started the row all over. It was her first indication that Jim resented her as much as her son Ed. Of all the people under her roof Pearl was the most trustworthy, and she'd betrayed her by running off and getting with child. Belle still caught her from time to time, staring out the window and mooning over the bastard girl she'd left with friends. This domestic existence had nearly as many snares as the bandit life. Such was the course of her thoughts as she curried her mare, Venus, clawing away fistfuls of dead hair and wishing all the dying things in the world were disposed of as easily, exposing the glossy fresh growth beneath.

She heard skulking outside the barn and challenged the intruder to show himself, curling her fingers around the handle of a pitchfork leaning in a corner of the stall. When the man entered the doorframe she recognized Edgar Watson, a neighbor. He was good-looking, in a dissipated way, broad-shouldered and straight in the legs, but he had a wet mouth and bitter little eyes like buckshot, and was one of those men who trailed their pasts behind them like snails. She'd ridden with his kind, dishonest men twice over who broke common bonds with no more thought than they showed when they broke the law. It didn't do to show them one's back.

"I been wondering if you changed your mind about leasing them twenty acres," he said.

"You wasted a trip. I'd as soon let them lie fallow as let you take a plow to them."

A whining note entered his tone. "What the hell did I ever do to you?"

"Not a thing, Watson, and you won't as long as I refuse you the opportunity."

She'd had too much experience with his breed to give him specifics. Wives kept a loose hitch on secrets when there was another woman around to confide in, and Mrs. Watson was a refined Easterner who knew good breeding and trusted in it, although too late for her relationship with Edgar. Belle had learned from her that her husband had fled a murder charge in the Florida wilderness. It wasn't the killing that bothered Belle so much as the length of his flight to avoid prosecution. Where she came from, a road agent placed his faith in his neighbors and in his knowledge of familiar terrain to confuse posses and make them lose heart and turn home. A man who abandoned his neighborhood to the enemy never stopped running. She saw a field half-tended when trouble came and no money to collect from a man on the scout.

"You're lying about letting that land lay fallow," he said. "I heard you got a tenant."

"You heard right. We've entered into a contract, so go skulk about someone else's barn."

Watson produced makings from his overall bib and built a cigarette. He made as shoddy a job of it as he had his life. "He was to bust that contract, you'd have a summer's worth of brush to clear away next growing season."

"He'll keep to it. Not every man is as slippery as you."

"Trouble dogs you like a whipped hound. If Parker's men take you down for this or that, the territory will claim your spread, and there's a parcel of seed gone to crows and such and nothing to show for a broken back. Might could be he'd see reason when it's put to him and cut his losses."

"We'll see what they have to say about that in Tahlequah, and Fort Smith if it comes to that. Conspiracy to violate a signed covenant is a matter for the courts."

"I reckon the Nation and Parker's court have enough on their hands with Ned Christie and the like not to trouble me over it."

Belle lost her temper. That wet mouth and what it was doing to that sorry cigarette infuriated her sense of the social graces. "I don't suppose the United States officers would trouble you, but the authorities in Florida might."

Watson, it seemed to her, turned green. With shaking fingers he took one last slobbery drag on his smoke and dropped it onto the trodden hay at his feet, where it might have caught the barn on fire if she hadn't mashed it out as soon as he left. "The sun don't shine on the same dog's ass all day long," was all he had to say in parting.

Months passed. Her unplanted twenty grew over in weeds and juniper and she made plans to sell it in the spring. Younger's Bend was poor enough ground for crops, and with Sam's old gang scattered to the winds it was a useless space of God's forsaken earth.

Reed sent her a copy of Blue Duck's pardon, signed by Cleveland. It was months old, and she had yet to hear from the man she'd worked so hard to set free.

On February 2, 1889, she was one day short of her forty-third birthday. Her gift was Jim July's sullen acquiescence to her prodding; men were weak creatures, after all, boys at heart, and the legend of Sam Starr's bold surrender sent him over at the last. She watched him assemble the rags of his best finery, an old guerrilla shirt whose linen ruffles she'd put to the iron with care, a slouch hat without too many stains and a snakeskin band, and a fine pair of stovepipe boots, and agreed to ride with him as far as San Bois in the Choctaw Nation, thirty miles from the Canadian. They stopped for the night at the home of friends, dined on biscuits and gravy, boiled radishes, and Arbuckle's coffee strong enough to raise a blister on a bullhide, slept fitfully on a featherbed, and parted at sunup on Belle's birthday, Jim to Fort Smith and Belle back to Younger's Bend. At 3:00 P.M., saddleworn and hungry, she put in at the house of Jack Rose, a neighbor, and partook of fare similar to the previous evening's. She could not help but remember Reed's promise that she would celebrate Blue Duck's freedom over French snails and red wine.

In her physical and emotional exhaustion, her loneliness,

Belle was only partly aware of Edgar Watson's presence in the yard. Everyone knew everyone else in the eastern Nations; friends were friendly with enemies, and enemies observed truces in the name of Christian forebearance. She recalled, as she saddled up for the ride home, that the men who had met to slay one another in Tombstone, Arizona, in 1881, had played a convivial game of poker the night before. This was too much complication for the dullards who wrote cheap novels, but was entirely in keeping with standards in the territories. In any case she considered Watson beneath contempt and outside serious consideration; the mere mention of Florida had been sufficient to bring him to heel. She jerked tight the cinch, mounted modestly to the side, and quirted her trusty whip across Venus' withers.

Her way led around Watson's poor farm, where a fence required her to detour through low scrub to pick up the road that led to Younger's Bend and her cabin, which stood one hundred fifty yards from Watson's house. A figure stood behind that fence as she passed. She gave it no heed other than to spur Venus into a lively trot.

The first charge struck her full in the back, tipping her from the saddle as the second raked her neck. She knew it for turkey shot, not nearly as heavy as the pellets meant for buck deer, but the force of it stunned her as she struggled to roll onto her back in the road. She knew from observation that people who fell on their faces invariably died in that position, like limp rags with one arm crumpled beneath them. The fire to survive burned fiercely within her.

Thus she had a full view of the killer who leapt the fence and poured a freshly reloaded barrel into her face and throat.

But the fire still burned. She was conscious when a neighbor brought Pearl to her mother's side many minutes after the shooter left her in a wallow of bloody mud. Belle managed to string syllables into one or two words that meant nothing to her listeners—*Open your ears!* she screamed in her skull;

Understand me!—then coughed up a jiggerful of blood and sank into darkness.

Marshal John Carroll noted that Judge Parker moaned and closed his eyes when the word came in of Belle Starr's death. After deputies reported the details, he called for the detention of Edgar A. Watson, Belle's son Ed, and Jim July.

"Your Honor, July was on his way to Fort Smith when it happened."

"You of all people should know better than to underestimate these border raiders when it comes to hard riding. He could have doubled back, then dug in his spurs for town after the murder was done. Some men get to brooding over good advice from a woman when they're let alone."

For July's part, when the news arrived he procured a fresh mount, lathered it up clear back to the Canadian, threw down on Watson, and brought him in to jail himself. But the man never faced trial. Neighbors declined to testify against him at his hearing, and communications with Florida failed to produce a warrant for murder or any other felony. The charge was dropped, and July's action removed him from suspicion. No one was ever indicted in the death of Belle Starr.

Parker permitted himself a moment to remember a woman he would miss in his courtroom. Belle Starr had won the granite heart of Cole Younger, called Jesse James a hypocrite to his face, beaten justice in Fort Smith, yet withal maintained the outward appearance of a woman of culture; she'd read *The Iliad* in the earliest Latin translation, while Parker himself had struggled with Pope's popular version in English, ridden the High Country in the pirate tradition of Mary Read and Jeanne de Belville, and very nearly had shot the best prosecutor in the United States out from under his hat in full view of the citizens of Sebastian County; she had romanced a Texas banker, it was said, and left him with a thirty-thousand-dollar shortage in his books; a male citizen of the Cherokee Nation had been forced at the point of her gun to retrieve her hat when it blew off her head, which action she explained was a lesson in good manners. Belle had had her troubles with her grown children, as who had not, and brought two of the Eighth District's most infamous bandits to the hobble in Fort Smith. She had known how to reload at full gallop and which spoon to use when she stirred her tea. Parker's world was a more orderly place without her, and so much more drab. He wept.

IV

A Flaw in the System

Revenge is a kind of wild justice, which the more man's nature runs to, the more ought law to weed it out.

—FRANCIS BACON

FIFTEEN

A hangman had feelings.

He was a man for all that, and fretted about bills and cracks in the cistern and whether he was a good husband and father. The pests who swarmed in to plumb his depths and make them public had paid entirely too much attention to the "hang" and none at all to the "man." But they were less than human themselves, and so when they came to call he filled his pipe and let them fondle his rope collection and dropped before them his pearls of wisdom burnished with Bavarian graveyard humor. "Haunted? No. I have never hanged a man who came back to have the job done over."

They took it all down like monkeys pretending to be stenographers and still managed to get it wrong. He read that he'd smiled grimly (a difficult expression to carry off; he'd tried before and his son had laughed at him) and said, "No, and if one ever came back to haunt me I'd hang 'em again." They compared his deep-set eyes to sockets in a bare skull; his beard was "noose-shaped," his build cadaverous. To a man they plundered the mortuary advertisements in their own newspapers for terms to characterize him. An editorial cartoonist in Baltimore had rendered a vile likeness in pen-and-ink, a humpbacked Reaper grinning in his hood with a pile of human bones at his feet; he'd thrown it in the fireplace before Annie could see it.

She'd been little then, and by God if he could turn back the clock he wouldn't hesitate.

It grieved George Maledon that his daughter had in all probability lost her innocence to the one young man in Fort Smith who did not fear him. Charles Parker was a self-loving dandy, and enjoyed an easy popularity among fellows of his own age that went no deeper than the white enamel on a wash basin, beneath which was brackish zinc. Under it they liked him no better than anyone else and professed friendship merely to declare independence of their disapproving parents. Their gibes, good-natured on the surface, bore an adumbration of contempt for themselves as well as for him. In that society, Charles alone was immune to self-loathing.

Fort Smith had grown beyond all prediction since Maledon had first set foot on the scaffold, but it was like an onion that had grown too swiftly by way of heavy unseasonal rains, with the outer layers wrapped loosely around the solid inner bulb, wherein resided the small rough town of 1875, where every citizen knew all the others and news of their least consequential actions was more current and reliable in the barbershop and around the barrel stove in the Mercantile than in the *Elevator* and the *Evening Call* combined; there, he had learned of his daughter's unchaste reputation. Young Charlie had claimed her virtue, then turned from her to fresh challenges, and rather than picking herself up from the dust and shaking it from her skirts she had continued to drag herself through it with whoever's son was willing, and with one or two who were no longer anyone's son, with wives and children Annie's own age at home. Saddle tramps she had had, half-caste Indians from the Nations, and men who had come to town to face Parker's justice for misdemeanors in the territories. She had wasted little time after her humiliation, with the result that when her father learned of her infamy, it was far too late to take a razor strop to her with any promise that it would raise any more than welts on her legs and sweat on his brow. He took it down from its hook above the basin, held it for a time, and returned it to its place, years older than when he had unhooked it.

"What did you expect?" asked his wife, when he confronted her. "Did you think she would come to you with her pain, you in your study with those nooses all around and pictures of the dead men whose necks you put them on?"

"It was the law did that. I only took out the suffering."

"Did you think the suffering began when you sent them through the trap?"

"Where is Annie?"

"I haven't seen her in days. How many days before that did you see her?"

He said no more. Since the day his wife had chucked his first tintypes and ropes down the well, he'd known it was impossible to argue with a woman on the basis of logic. You asked them a question and they responded by asking another that had no answer.

Disloyally—so he admitted to himself—he blamed his late wife for his daughter's beauty. Plain women had little to fear from predatory males, and had Annie inherited her father's bony brow or her stepmother's unornamental features instead of the wealth of black hair that glistened unfettered to her waist, the striking eyes and Cupid's-bow lips, the figure that needed no corset to lift the breasts and narrow the waist, she would have remained at home. She was also too intelligent for her gender, becoming aware at an early age that the woman whose responsibility it became to rear her from childhood cared more for their son, James; and that, together with her father's dread reputation that kept respectable suitors from their door, had forced her into the gravitational pull of young men whose histories demonstrated their lack of fear of the engine of justice he helped to maintain. Children brought up in divided households were rebellious by nature. What better way to declare one's independence than to take up with the enemies of domestic tranquility?

Of all his acquaintances, restricted as they were by circumstances to the officers of the Eighth District Court, there was one alone who might be expected to understand his plight and offer counsel. He put his forage cap in hand and called upon Judge Parker in his chambers.

Parker sat him down with the reserved cordiality he'd shown Maledon from their first meeting, in that same room so redolent with the memory of good cigars, disintegrating leather bindings, and the fading phantoms of sour mash and expectorated tobacco left by the conflicted men who had sat before him behind that great walnut desk. Reading his guest's expression with those eyes that had recorded the characters of a hundred or more defendants and hundreds more who had given evidence for and against them, the judge excused himself, and returned moments later with a stout bottle of brandy and two crystal glasses clutched in his hairless pink hand and poured them each two fingers of honey-colored liquid. Maledon, who read men as easily, and who as Parker's closest ally in the hundred years' war against chaos knew his host better even than William H. H. Clayton and the army of men who had ridden for him in the Nations, recognized this as an act without precedence. The brandy, of course, came from Mary Parker's own store, procured through the ladies' entrance to the House of Lords to bring on the sleep that would not come to her otherwise. The woman kept impossible standards, and would have been far more content wedded to a store clerk or a postal carrier, whose most important decisions did not involve the lives of men. The same was true of Maledon's own wife. He and Parker were twins from the same exacting mother, however much the judge feared and detested his chief executioner's proximity to the consequences of his pronouncements of sentence. Parker's fingers never touched their necks.

For all that, Maledon had spent less time in that room than anyone else in the district's service. There was the brief interview that had led to his promotion from turnkey to hangman, and two other confrontations, when he'd asked to be excused the abhorrent duty of hanging a fellow veteran of the Union Army, and when he'd rebelled against sacrificing his time with family to operate the gallows at night. (Much good that had done him.) Parker had agreed both times, handing the first assignment to a guard from the jail and postponing the second to a daylight hour. Parker was reason personified, distilled as purely as the spirits they shared upon this occasion. Parker for his part took a healthy sip in commemoration of the singular nature of the event; Maledon, whose lips had not brushed liquor since the early days of his service to the Army of the Potomac, dampened his moustache merely and left the remainder of the contents of his glass untasted.

"Annie—" He cleared his throat.

"Yes."

Parker, he now saw, with the rush of disillusion that comes to a disciple when the fog lifts and he sees his idol for a creature of clay, had invested all the penitence of a degraded sinner into that single syllable. In it his listener heard a paragraph of apology and confession. Charles Parker was a cross to be borne only by the lowest of God's creatures.

The silence that followed fell with the thud of a charge from a Confederate mortar. It was not to be borne, and so Parker filled it with a slap of his palm upon the stack of leather portfolios that made an impenetrable forest between him and the desk's inlaid top. Maledon did not deceive himself that the records there contained had direct application to the business at hand; it was symbolic of the towering evil that faced Fort Smith.

"Marshal Yoes's men keep a vigilant eye upon the recidivists who pass through this jurisdiction," Parker said. "I won't blaspheme so far as to say that I mark the sparrow's fall, but through them I flatter myself to say that I know rather more about what goes on in the district than the gentlemen of the press."

Maledon made no expression, his head tilted forward and his beard on his chest, as he learned that his daughter had been seen in company of late with a man named Frank Carver, at twenty-four her senior by six years. Parker's description, detailed and factual, painted a picture of the sort of young man who attracted the attention of impressionable girls: tall and slender, with barbered imperials and a taste for fine clothes, including the splendid boots that had led so often to covetousness and tragedy in the Nations, which was where he made his home. He spent money far too ostentatiously to have come by it through honest labor.

"What does he do?"

"He's pleased to call himself a gambler, but that isn't his only source of income." Parker turned his glass in its wet circle on the desk. His eyes remained on his guest. "He receives an annual allotment of eight hundred dollars from the Indian Bureau as a husband of a Cherokee with two children of Cherokee blood."

The hangman lowered his head another inch.

"His family's in Muskogee, where he's been arrested twice for possession of alcohol. His drink of choice is Jamaica ginger. You may have heard it called Ginger Jake. It's a scourge in the territory."

Maledon nodded. This was a flavoring extract obtained from ginger, intoxicating in the extreme and lethal if ingested in large quantities without diluting it with water. Banned in the territory, it was readily available across the Texas state line, where retailers and wholesalers proliferated, well aware that most of their customers transported their purchases back to the Nations for sale or personal consumption. Carver had been acquitted both times he'd been tried in Fort Smith; it was difficult to convince a jury, to whom the offense itself was a trifle, that a young man who presented so fine an appearance in court had anything in common with the sots who came through on that charge.

"Where are they now?"

"Charlie Burns, who checked Carver into the jail twice, saw them at the slip last week, waiting for the ferry. They could be anywhere in the eastern Nations by now, although I suspect not too close to where his wife and children are struggling to survive without their allotment."

"Can you send someone after them?"

Parker looked more uncomfortable yet. "At present, I've no sufficient cause to issue a warrant for Carver. Annie is past the age of consent in the State of Arkansas, so the white slavery laws don't apply. I've no doubt he's guilty of defrauding the United States by appropriating funds intended for wards of the government, but without evidence I can't authorize his arrest. Old friends in Congress are just waiting for me to make that kind of mistake. I am sorry, Mr. Maledon, truly I am."

Maledon combed his fingers through his whiskers, over and over. "I must go after them myself. If I talk to her I can make her see reason."

"You're sixty, and in no condition for such a journey. Where would you search? If you were fortunate enough to stumble upon them, Carver would be within his rights to send you away."

"You've forgotten I'm not exactly helpless without my ropes."

"Shooting down an escaping prisoner and shooting down a man in his own neighborhood are not the same thing. I should not want to sentence you to die on your own scaffold, but I will if you do murder, and there will be no phrases of comfort when I make the pronouncement. You are not a cold-blooded killer; you must disabuse yourself of that notion." The judge's expression had softened. Then it went flat. "In any case, your presence is needed in Fort Smith. There are four capital cases awaiting your attention." Parker hooked on his spectacles and opened one of the portfolios on the desk. They were acts of dismissal.

Maledon rose and went to the door.

"George."

In seventeen years, neither judge nor executioner had addressed the other by his Christian name. Maledon gripped the knob and waited.

"I'll direct Yoes to have his men maintain a weather eye for Carver and Annie. Some of them know the girl by sight, and his face is familiar in the Cherokee, but I'll see descriptions are provided. They can report how she is faring. She may get homesick in the meantime. Most runaways come back under their own volition."

Maledon left without responding. He spent the rest of the day on the scaffold, oiling the gears that operated the trap and inspecting the mortises and tenons for cracks and dry rot. He did not return home until after dark, and then he locked himself in his study without speaking to his wife. There in the company of his ropes and the faces of old customers he smoked pipe after pipe, filling the room with noxious vapors.

In March, John Thornton mounted the steps to the scaffold for the murder of his daughter in the Choctaw Nation, whom he had shot through the head, presumably in a fit of rage after she'd deserted him for a husband. The condemned man offered no words of explanation or farewell. When he dropped, the rope whizzed around his neck, the knot caught in the hollow behind and below the left mastoid, and blood geysered like water from a hydrant as the vertebra snapped clean through and the muscles of his neck, too weak to support his superincumbent weight, tore apart. Jerking, his body remained connected to his head by the tendons alone. Several officers of the court, who had reported to that enclosure many times to witness the fulfillment of sentence, never returned to see another. A few resigned. Thornton's coffin dripped blood from its seams as it was lowered into the Catholic cemetery.

George Maledon had not been present. Some said he'd refused to participate because Thornton had fought in the uniform of the Union, others that Parker's partner in punishment had lost his taste for the business. Said one, "That's like Old Scratch losing interest in snaring souls." Wagers were proposed, but no one offered to approach him for the truth, and nothing was to be gained by asking the judge to betray what went on in chambers. Deputy Marshal George S. White,

whose inexperience while filling in for Maledon had produced the gory spectacle, pledged to adhere to his other duties henceforth.

Soon afterward, Fort Smith society learned that Annie
Maledon and Frank Carver had left the Nations for far Colorado. No one knew just when the news had reached her father.

SIXTEEN

Eighteen ninety-two was a big year in the Nations. Apart
from the scandalous flight of the Prince of Hangmen's
only daughter, that twelvemonth witnessed the explosive end
of the low comedy of Ned Christie's war, and in Coffeyville,
across the Kansas state line, the annihilation of the Dalton
Gang after three years of train robbery, some sixty thousand
dollars spirited away from righteous hands, and the lowest
casualty count of any of the desperate associations of the era.

The brothers—Bob, Grat, and Emmett—had first taken to
the adventurous life in the service of Parker, riding with their
eldest brother, Frank; then leapt the fence after whiskey
smugglers slaughtered him from ambush in 1887. For a time,
they had partnered with smugglers and rustlers while still
wearing badges, but when warrants were issued in Fort Smith
for their arrest, they fled to California, where they struck the
Southern Pacific Railroad but failed to break open the safe
in the depot. Back in the Nations—Oklahoma Territory, now,
with Sooners busting clods on homesteads once divided
among the Five Civilized Tribes—they took on four new
members, including Bill Doolin, and carried away fourteen
thousand dollars from the Santa Fe Limited at Wharton in
the Cherokee Strip. Other raids took place in Lelietta, Red
Rock, and Adair; their take now rivaled that of their distant
cousins, Frank and Jesse James, who had been seventeen

years at the enterprise, but that wasn't enough for leader Bob, a bucktoothed, jug-eared criminal mastermind shot through with the sin of vanity.

Under the influence of busthead whiskey, Bob proposed a shift from trains to banks, which he reasoned had the advantage of standing still, and added that an experienced band like theirs could split up and assault two such institutions at the same time, doubling the plunder and eclipsing the infamy of the James Gang forever. Moreover, he suggested Coffeyville, a town known to the brothers since infancy, as the place to benefit from their plunge into legend. He sobered up later, but having parried aside the others' arguments was reluctant to withdraw his scheme in the cold light of wisdom. His solution to the intelligent point that the residents of Coffeyville knew them as well as they knew Coffeyville involved false beards and farmers' overalls. The town met them in force with scatterguns and squirrel rifles and laid them out on a boardwalk to have their pictures taken. Emmett alone survived to begin a period of lengthy imprisonment in the Kansas State Penitentiary at Lansing. In Fort Smith, Judge Parker read the details in the telegraph column of the *Elevator* and put away early plans to hang three brothers at once.

His jurisdiction was shrinking. The new homesteads were part of the United States, with local magistrates put in place to adjudicate disputes and violations of the criminal code. Congress and the Supreme Court had assigned crimes among Indians to the tribal courts, which forced Parker's deputies to parse out complaints according to what constituted an Indian: full-blood, half, eighth, sixteenth? Mistakes were made, carrion-eaters of the J. Warren Reed stamp swooped, and the judge was brought to task in Washington. He accused the justices of splitting hairs, was quoted, and bitter invective circled about him under the Capitol dome. Open letters signed by Parker and officials in the U.S. Department of Justice appeared in the press. Reporters described the contretemps, borrowing colorful verbs and adjectives from the boxing columns. Washington whittled away at his fiefdom. Circuit courts were allowed to review all capital cases tried in the Eighth District, inserting yet another wedge between Isaac Parker and God Almighty. Colleagues helped themselves to cases that for years had gone directly to his desk, yet his docket grew no lighter: He mounted the bench every morning at eight, Monday through Saturday, and often did not descend from it until past midnight. The dark smudges beneath his eyes looked like bruises, the last brown hair on his head turned white as filament. He was fifty-three years old.

At home alone, her sons pursuing activities outside her ken, Mary Parker drank brandy to lay her cares to rest and bring on sleep. One bottle no longer lasted her a week.

Parker's men, led now by the legendary Three Guardsmen: Heck Thomas, Chris Madsen, and Bill Tilghman, rode through the Nations alongside the tumbleweed wagons and left them behind to scale the Winding Stair Mountains and the walls of Rabbit Trap Canyon, rooting out rapists and murderers and whiskey distillers, swapping lead with them, and occasionally stopping slugs. Those who failed to rise decorated the walls of Marshal Jacob Yoes's office with their likenesses.

And George Maledon worked oil into good Kentucky hemp with his strong hands and waited for news of Annie and Frank Carver.

In Colorado, Carver found work on a cattle ranch. The wages were minimal, but he supplemented them by gambling, at which he was sufficiently adroit to show a profit without arousing the suspicions of his opponents, who tended to try suspected sharps on the evidence of circumstances alone and punish them, according to their humor or the charms of the defendant, on a scale with stripping and flogging at one end and lynching at the other. Aware of the delicacy of his situation, Carver drank in moderation and held Annie's interest with gifts and loyal attention. When after two years the ranch foreman was forced to cut personnel and Carver's luck at the tables turned bitter, the pair returned to the Cherokee Nation, where Frank boarded Annie with a colored woman eight short blocks of the house where his wife had taken in washing and sewing to support herself and their children; he did not return to his wife, however, hoping to persuade her to grant him a divorce on the grounds of desertion. This she refused to do, and since there was little honest work to be found in that vicinity and money that might otherwise have been spent at cards and dice went toward foodstuffs and house repairs, the pressure to provide income compelled Carver to ride the rails to Texas, preying upon passengers with friendly games of chance and spending most of what he won on Jamaica ginger in Texas.

Annie was not the sort of mistress who embroidered pillowcases in her man's absence and sold fresh-laid eggs to earn her board. She transferred bags and baggage to the home of another Frank, surnamed Walker, and there made sport with the Maledon name and the manly reputation of him who had forsaken respectable domesticity for her sake; so Carver regarded the situation, as Annie and Walker learned weeks later, when word reached them that Carver had returned.

In Fort Smith that season, the interruption in the Maledon family unit faded into the background as Parker considered that the Dalton episode had not so much come to an end as begun a new phase under the command of Bill Doolin, who had joined the gang in 1891 but had not been present in Coffeyville when it was torn apart a year later. While the bodies were still on display, and a surgeon was still plucking lead from Emmett Dalton, Doolin assembled a rich association of colorful nicknames in the persons of George "Bitter Creek" Newcomb, "Tulsa Jack" Blake, Oliver "Crescent Sam" Yountis, Richard "Little Dick" West, Roy "Arkansas Tom" Daughtery, George "Red Buck" Waightman, and two others, including Bill Dalton, eldest brother of the demolished family, who had forsaken the California legislature for the lure of his blood after Coffeyville had destroyed his hopes for high office. These lurid appelations crimsoned many a gray column and Western Union bulletin board as banks and trains fell to assaults throughout Kansas and the newly minted Oklahoma Territory.

But these were not the Nations of memory, where a desperado might reasonably expect to retard the consequences of his calling in the wild scrub of the Cookson Hills and the root cellars of neighbors who still held the United States to account for the Trail of Tears. The great Land Rush of 1889 had introduced thousands of white settlers into the extremities of the Eighth District, who tore up the scrub for potatoes and built ricks to store corn, not fugitives. Among them was a thirty-eight-year-old former Iowan named William Matthew Tilghman.

Tall and rangy, with swooping moustaches and eyes that went from kind to vengeful as quickly as clouds slid away from the sun, Tilghman had shot buffalo at eighteen, served as a deputy sheriff under the legendary Charlie Bassett in Dodge City at twenty-three, and divided the next ten years between his ranch near Fort Dodge and a succession of positions keeping the peace in the roughest cowtown in Kansas. When Oklahoma opened to homestead, he'd quit his job of city marshal and staked out several lots in Guthrie, whose quickly expanding population elected him marshal. Two years later he laid aside that badge and took up the simple six-sided star of deputy U.S. marshal under Jacob Yoes and Judge Isaac C. Parker.

Tilghman's experience needed tempering yet, for the territory retained a vivid sense-memory of untamed wilderness; Ned Christie was not long in his grave, and in many districts the quality of a man's boots was worth more than his life. Heck Thomas, who had failed to apprehend Christie but

had since sacrificed marriage and family to the service of
Parker, taught the new man the basics of manhunting in hostile country. An ordered, military approach to what amounted
to enemy lines came courtesy of forty-one-year-old Chris
Madsen, who had served in the Danish Army, the French
Foreign Legion, and the United States Fifth Cavalry, with
which he had ridden into the Battle of Warbonnet Creek and
covered Buffalo Bill Cody while he slew Chief Yellow
Hand and tore from his head the first scalp for Custer in
1876. A hard man with flint in his beard, a plug in his cheek,
two grown children, and already a string of dead fugitives
in his portfolio in Fort Smith, Madsen bridled only when
younger deputies addressed him as "Pops," cuffing their ears
hard enough to make them ring and unleashing a string of
Scandinavian curses. His Danish accent became pronounced
when he was excited, which he almost never was; a quickening of his jaws as he chewed was for those who knew him a
clear indication that the moment was tense. He was a chief
deputy, and even Thomas called him "Mr. Madsen." (Parker,
practically a contemporary, hailed him by his Christian
name.)

The people of the Nations would come to know them
as the Three Guardsmen: Madsen, hard and silent on the
trail; Thomas, eyes bright when he caught the scent of human prey; Tilghman, easy in his manner but cat-swift in his
reflexes. A trio of killers.

In the spring of 1893, the Doolin Gang raided a bank at
Spearville, Kansas, divided the plunder, and split up to hide
out until posse fever passed. Entering the Cherokee Strip,
Crescent Sam Yountis lost the use of his exhausted mount,
challenged a farmer riding a fresh bay to surrender his animal, and blasted him off its back when he demurred. The
bandit caught the reins before the horse could bolt, vaulted
into the saddle, and galloped on to his sister's farm.

The killing took place near Guthrie, where Heck Thomas

and Chris Madsen rode circuit for the federal court. Madsen knew all the farms in the vicinity. He collected Thomas, laid siege to the farmhouse, and shot Yountis with a Winchester when he emerged from the house and fired at Thomas, who kicked the revolver from the dying man's hand as he struggled to rise.

"Too damn bad I didn't get you," Yountis said.

"You came close enough, by golly." Madsen put his boot heel on Yountis' throat and held it there until he finished struggling.

The gang struck a Santa Fe express in Cimarron soon after, and bettered the Daltons' final adventure by dividing its ranks and holding up two trains simultaneously at Wharton. This, Parker reflected, represented a new phase in frontier outlawry: the drive, beyond mundane material gain, to make one's own mark on the historical record and imitate in life the swashbucklery that incarnadined the popular press. Frequently, tardy raids upon hideouts abandoned by wanted men, and saddle pouches confiscated from captured bandits, yielded small libraries of tattered paperbound novels with whole sensational passages underscored heavily in pencil; blueprints for adventures yet to be undertaken, and the bar raised to first-column level. When Charley Pierce, a charter member of the Doolins, was recognized and shot to death by fellow hands on the ranch where he was hiding out, his pockets were found to be stuffed with yellowed cuttings from Texas and Arkansas newspapers chronicling the gang's depredations. Over a cup of tea while addressing one of his wife's social clubs in Fort Smith, Parker remarked drolly that it was just a matter of time before some progressive band of border ruffians applied to St. Louis for a press agent. Only Mary Parker, who maintained a barometer of her husband's passions, detected the depth of his despair over the public lionization of the element he had sworn to banish from his jurisdiction.

In September 1893, the Doolins cut loose at thirteen deputy U.S. marshals surrounding a house where they'd holed
up near Ingalls. The return fire shattered windows, knocked
shingles off their hinges, killed a goat, and shot away the
front door, but three deputies were killed and all but two of the
gang got away: Arkansas Tom, who surrendered, and a teen-
age prostitute named Jennie Stevens, whose horse Bill Tilghman shot out from under her as she leapt a fence toward
freedom. The tiny Stevens and a friend, Annie McDougal,
had been selling their favors to the Doolins for months, don-
ning male dress to act as lookout during some robberies and
stealing eggs and chickens to feed them when they were in
hiding. Tilghman, exasperated at the size of his catch, spanked
Stevens over his knee before placing her in custody. After a
bank in Pawnee gave up ten thousand dollars to her friends,
he and Steve Burke, another Parker deputy, captured McDougal, but not before she'd shredded Burke's face with her nails,
knocked off his hat, and torn tufts of hair from his scalp.

"Little bitches," said Burke, upon depositing her in the
women's quarters of the Fort Smith jail beside Jennie Stevens.
A reporter overheard and, either misunderstanding him or in
deference to decorous editorial policy, dubbed the dwarfish
Stevens "Little Britches." Not to be outdone, his colleagues
anointed McDougal "Cattle Annie," and the pair enjoyed a
brief scarlet vogue in half-dime novels before history lost interest. Parker damned the Fourth Estate for making romantic figures out of petty thieves and cheap harlots.

The comedy was light enough, and too much so for the
grim record. In one afternoon in Ingalls, the Doolin Gang had
slain more men than the Daltons had managed to do in three
years, and in the same gesture slaughtered more peace officers than the Jameses and Youngers combined. Parker raged
at his new marshal, George J. Crump. The rewards mounted.

The gang spread out. It slew a sheriff during a robbery in
Canadian, Texas; an auditor in a bank in Southwest City, Mis-

THE BRANCH AND THE SCAFFOLD

souri (witnesses identified Bill Dalton, reformed politician, as his murderer); and returned to Dover, Oklahoma Territory, robbing the Rock Island line and shooting to pieces several innocent bystanders during the getaway. Rumor held that Red Buck was mustered out of the association for this atrocity; casualties among noncombatants played hell with romantic legend. (In Thieves' Valhalla, Jesse James played faro with Belle Starr and chuckled, stopping the hole in his head with a palm to preserve the resonance.) After Tulsa Jack was stricken dead on that ride, and Bitter Creek Newcomb and Charley Pierce fell victim to reward-conscious ranch hands, the gang was decimated. Raids spread as far as California and Iowa would be laid at its door in reporters' desperate attempts to stretch the gravy, but their editors grew restless; it was true that they wrote for morons, but morons had been known to rebel, as witness the election of Benjamin Harris to the office of president, which error had been rectified by the return of Grover Cleveland. With more pressing news streaming in from economic panic in the East and the Spanish situation in the Caribbean, and nothing fresh from the vanishing Nations, the name Doolin slipped to the inside pages, then away.

But Bill Doolin was still at large, and his final chapter would be the strangest of all, although none would know its truth for many years.

George Maledon followed the saga listlessly in the company of the dead men who shared his tiny study. His interest in criminal activity in the Nations, which he had once kept track of as avidly as a farmer tracing the path of a blight that would one day be his personal concern, had evaporated, and with it his zeal for his profession. He began to consider retirement. Then in the spring of 1895, three years since Annie had left the shelter of his roof, his wife came to him in his study to say that his daughter had been brought to St. James Hospital in Fort Smith with a bullet in her spine.

SEVENTEEN

In the Nations, Ginger Jake was known as the Great Divider: You never knew how it would affect a man under its influence, or indeed if it would affect the same man twice the same way.

Sometimes, the distillate made the drinker more the way he was when sober, creating a kind of caricature. If he was angry and given to violent outbursts, it might make him react to the smallest slight with savage blows or a weapon; if he was gentle and good-humored, he might meet the vilest insult with a jest or an offer to buy a drink for his calumniator.

At other times, a complete reversal of personality was the result. Many of the men who employed the opportunity of George Maledon's scaffold to deliver oratories on the pernicious poison of strong drink and women of ill fame before they swung were by reputation God-fearing men of good conduct who had turned bestial on the authority of Jamaica ginger. A number of their fellows had lost their lives refusing to defend themselves against assailants, imagining themselves to be more peaceful men than they were when sober, and trusting in all mankind.

Frank Carver, soft-spoken and clean in his habits, liked by men and admired by women, belonged to the most dangerous category, a changeling who depending upon the amount drunk, the strength of the mix, and the phase of the moon, might laugh off an injurious remark or horsewhip a stranger he suspected was talking about him behind his back on no evidence at all. Those who had seen him on benders had learned to give him distance or flutter on his perimeter, waiting to see which way the frog jumped before pressing their acquaintance. However, this last course was perilous, because his mood was likely to shift with the speed of a striking snake, but with less warning. There were men in Texas who could confirm that, if their shattered jaws didn't get in the way of their speech, and a divorced woman in Okmulgee with a scar that pulled her face out of line when she tried to smile.

Most of what went into the record about Carver's last meeting with Annie Maledon came directly from the written statement she had dictated before she died, eleven weeks after a round from his revolver lodged in the soft tissue of her spine, where no surgeon could get to it without causing more damage. Her last days had been spent in a state of semiconsciousness, with morphine in her veins to ease her passing over.

Carver, she said, returned from Texas while she was in residence with Frank Walker, a man known to them both, and called upon her there several times when Walker was out. Harsh words were spoken, resulting twice in threats against her life if she did not come away with him. Annie explained that by this time her former lover was in a state of constant inebriation, and that she feared to be with him, as she had seen how quickly his humor could change from affable to morose. The most frightening thing about him in this condition, she said, was that he managed to walk straight and speak without slurring under circumstances that would have reduced a man of much greater height and bulk to a gibbering idiot without a rudder; one had to know him as intimately as she to recognize the hazard.

On the night of March 25, 1895, Carver sent word to meet him on the east side of the tracks belonging to the Missouri, Kansas, and Texas Railroad in Muskogee; the note informed her that he was leaving for Texas forever and that it was the last time she would see him. She suspected his motives, but was reluctant to ignore the invitation and give him cause to change his mind. However far she had drifted from the lessons of home and family, she still prayed every night, beginning with the prayer that Carver would go away and never return. She persuaded Frank Walker to accompany her to the assignation.

Carver's appearance under the light of a tallow streetlamp

reassured them both. He never failed to put on a fresh collar, drunk or sober, but his boots shone, his coat was brushed and pressed, his whiskers trimmed, and for the first time in weeks the whites of his eyes were clear. Annie leaned forward from the waist just far enough to smell the sweet scent of the pine needles Carver used to pick his teeth, and determine that there was no liquor on his breath. She satisfied herself that he had broken the shackles once again and nudged Walker, who stepped forward and shook Carver's hand.

The three agreed to bless Carver's departure with a last night on the town. In the first place they stopped, Carver immediately began drinking, and as they moved on to the next, Annie clung closer to Walker, who curled his arm around her waist comfortingly; he did not know the man well enough to recognize the signs of moral disintegration hidden beneath his clear speech and steady step. While leaving the third house of notorious reputation, Carver leaned close to Annie and whispered in her ear: "Honey, you're done for tonight. I'm going to kill you before morning."

"What did he say?" asked Walker, when she clutched his arm.

Carver produced a heavy-barreled revolver from beneath his waistcoat and fired it into the air.

"None of that, Frank," Walker said. "You'll have the Cherokee Lighthorse on us all."

Carver grinned and returned the revolver to his belt. They walked another square. Then he jerked out the weapon and fired twice at a streetlamp. The second bullet came closest, brushing the flame. When Walker opened his mouth to protest, Carver leveled the revolver at Annie, who whimpered and turned into the other man's arms. There was another report and she shuddered and sagged in Walker's embrace.

Carver fled, but returned moments later as a crowd gathered around the young woman lying in the street with Walker supporting her head with a hand. "Oh, Annie, are you dead?"

cried Carver. "Who has done this?" Then he ran away again.

Annie Maledon's former lover was arrested that night in the home he was once again sharing with his wife and children and removed in shackles to Fort Smith, with the deputies in escort speculating aloud as to whether George Maledon would attend to his humanitarian duty or let Carver strangle; George White, whose blunder while serving in Maledon's capacity had led to the beheading of John Thornton, described that affair and said he wondered which was more distressing for the man in the noose. Carver arrived in Fort Smith pale and shrunken in his restraints.

Frank Walker had not been seen since the night of the slaying; rumors insisted he had a wife in Texas and had likely returned to her, but no one knew the address or if he lived there under the same name. While the prosecution was preparing its case, Carver's brother and other relatives pooled their resources and retained J. Warren Reed to plead for the defense.

In the years since his successful fight on behalf of Belle Starr's lover, Blue Duck, Reed had if anything adopted more resplendence in his dress, with velvet facings on his lapels and ornaments of fraternal affiliations dangling like tiny scalps from his watch chain; his girth had increased as well, and he had foresworn at last the discomfort of a corset. His persistent preference for clawhammer coats caused the citizens who saw him strutting the boardwalks brandishing his gold-headed stick to remark upon the way his backside thrust out his tails like a rooster's. These same observers gossiped that his remarkable wife, Viola, who had studied for the bar in West Virginia but had been balked by the barricade of her gender, was the more accomplished lawyer of the pair, and that without her application and counsel, the popinjay whose very name turned Judge Parker's gaze glacial would still be defending chicken thieves in the Appalachians. But Parker himself, while enjoying this assessment, knew it to be unfair; Reed was an aggressive debater, predatory in the extreme, and a polished thespian whose stage was the courtroom. He could charm and repel by turns, and in so doing deflect attention from the evidence most damaging to his client.

Before 1889, the Reeds of the world had been helpless against Parker's suzerainty. With no fixed system of appeal in place, the judge could turn the stampede over the facts with a snap of his gavel, a threat to consign the transgressor to the basement dungeon for contempt, and what amounted to a directed conviction during his instructions to the jury. But Washington had cut the ballocks off the old bull; such tactics were grounds for reversal, and Reed, who knew he stood no chance in Parker's court the first time around, had but to goad the old man into committing a judicial indiscretion that would earn a second trial. A baseball enthusiast, the attorney was determined to keep fouling off pitches until he wore down the fellow on the mound and belted one deep into fair territory. That had been his strategy throughout his first seven years in practice in Fort Smith, and of the 134 men he had represented in capital cases, only two had hanged. The rest had been discharged during preliminary examination, acquitted by juries, or had their sentences reduced or commuted by order of authorities higher than Parker. The letter signed by President Cleveland ordering Blue Duck's pardon hung in a frame in Reed's office opposite a steel lithograph of the martyred Abraham Lincoln.

In Walker's absence, conviction depended heavily upon the deathbed statement of the victim. Reed here was in his element: As handy as Blue Duck's isolation had proven in structuring his pardon, he valued even more the testimony of an eyewitness who could be cross-examined without its author offering a word in rebuttal. He went to work on the several inconsistencies in the rambling, agonized text, drew numerous objections from the prosecution, sustainments and warnings from the bench, and made copious notes for his request for appeal of the verdict and sentence he fully anticipated. The prosecution, less savage following the retirement of William H. H. Clayton in favor of a judgeship in the new central district in McAlester, was vigorous nonetheless, and the jury voted to convict. On July 9, Parker sentenced Carver to hang on the first day of October.

Throughout the proceedings, George Maledon, who seldom attended court, sat in the gallery, keeping his own counsel and directing his sunken gaze toward the back of the head of the man who sat at the defense table beside Reed. He was among the first to leave when the verdict was announced.

Fort Smith society, which convened without exception to retry all of Parker's cases in the Silver Dollar, the brothels on First Street, and the sewing circles on Garrison, pondered over whether Maledon would set aside his professional considerations and select common balers' twine and a shoddy choke-knot for the man who had stolen his daughter's innocence (this against anecdotal evidence to the contrary) and her life, so excruciating in its prolonged withdrawal, with spinal fluid staining the winding-sheets; but it had underestimated the depth of his dedication to the machinery of justice. He determined on using virgin rope, and rejected two shipments of Kentucky hemp that he pronounced substandard because of heavy rains during the growing season before deciding upon the third. His discrimination in this detail rivaled those of connoisseurs of French wine, who knew vineyards and their climate with biblical scholarship. The fibers that would separate Frank Carver from this pale would be the finest in Western agriculture, and the measure of pitch and linseed as precise as a chemist's when preparing a purgative for a close family member. Like Parker, whose reversals and disappointments had honed his judicial decisions to a razor's edge, America's Executioner was devoted to the highest principles in this personal affair. He applied these same attentions to the scaffold, ordering the replacement of certain joints that appeared quite servicable on the surface and supervising the sanding down of the finish by convict labor and the application of a fresh coat of whitewash.

The infamous scaffold had by this time acquired a slant roof to protect it from rain. When viewed from behind in its high enclosure, it resembled nothing more sinister than a storage building for harnesses or grain. The black scars of that vengeful bolt of lightning at its inauguration had long since been concealed by cosmetic attention. Parker's Tears had never looked more decorous.

These attentions were lost on the Supreme Court, whose members had not forgotten the injuries inflicted upon it in public by the pen of the man in charge of the Eighth District Court. They reviewed Reed's writ of error, pared to the basics by the coolheaded Viola, considered the implications of a sentence of death carried out by the father of the victim in the case, reversed Parker, and granted the defendant a new trial. Smelling blood, Reed launched a fresh attack on four points of conflict in Annie's statement, and this time secured a victory more apparent to him than to most of those who followed the trial: While the first jury had voted in favor of Carver's execution after four short hours, the second required two full days of deliberation before agreeing upon a verdict of murder in the first degree.

Maledon, frustrated only by the protraction of justice, restretched his rope, dismantled, cleaned, and reassembled the gears that operated the trap, and made the mistake of confiding to an acquaintance that he was looking forward to this execution. The remark reached Reed, who conveyed it to certain supernumeraries with the ear of higher powers in the system. Meanwhile he filed a second writ of error. A third trial was granted. The additional time enabled the attorney for the defense to assemble a set of witnesses who offered testimony confirming Annie Maledon's faithlessness to most of the virtues. This jury ruled in favor of murder in the second degree and recommended life imprisonment.

At the sentencing, Parker hesitated, fingering his gavel, and was seen to review his prepared remarks, sliding his spectacles up and down his nose as if the words he himself had written were foreign to him; which in fact they were. He was weary, visibly so, he had a pain in his belly and a heart that beat all out of cadence with the consistency of his moral principles. Each new reversal of his decisions had plagued him with the unfamiliar malady of second thoughts and self-doubt. At length he tightened his grip on the handle his palm had polished to a high gloss, ruled in favor of the advice of the jurors, and commended Frank Carver to the custody of the penitentiary in Columbus, Ohio, for the rest of his natural life. The gavel cracked.

George Maledon that day petitioned Judge Parker for his retirement. The request was granted. After a brief attempt at the grocery business in Fort Smith, where his wife kept the books and wrapped the customers' purchases with care, he bought an eighty-acre farm in Fayetteville, Arkansas; but Mother Nature proved as harsh a partner as the justice system, and he gave his acreage to the weeds and joined a carnival tour. There in a tent not much larger than his study, he exhibited his collection of ropes and tintypes and made his case for the certainty of punishment in a scripted speech cribbed largely from Parker's comments to the press and accepted questions from his audience. Spiritualism was in the ascendant; most of his interviewers were curious about the shades of the men he had slain. He combed his fingers through his beard and said that if any of them were disposed to return, he would simply hang them again.

Back home, his wife and son turned away reporters asking for details of human interest about the domestic life of a celebrated hangman. They said there was nothing of interest, and pressed shut their door.

V

A Promise to Punish

That virtue is her own reward, is but a cold principle.

—SIR THOMAS BROWNE

EIGHTEEN

"**W**hich Cherokee Bill is this? It seems to me this court encounters one every couple of months." Judge Parker trayed his cigar to review the request for a warrant.

"The worst of the lot so far," said Colonel Crump. "His right name's Crawford Goldsby. It stands to reason 'Cherokee Crawford' didn't answer, though he could claim 'Greaser Bill' and be closer to the mark. There's Mexican and Sioux in his blood, and I'm told his mother was black as Jed's boot. There's Cherokee on her side, too, but it'd bleed out if he were to nick his little toe. He looks like he ought to be butchering chickens in Nogales."

"I didn't inquire into his ancestry. He rides with the Cook brothers. I was under the impression we had them on the run." Parker paged back and forth through the record. Crump's reports were closely written and maddeningly chronological, a product of his army training.

The marshal, a second-term Cleveland appointee who had succeeded Jacob Yoes, adjusted his beard the way another man might straighten his necktie. He put more pride in his military background than in his present spoils position, and Parker considered him competent, although he had a prejudice against him for replacing George Winston, who had served the court as bailiff since before Parker's own appointment, with a Democrat. He suspected Crump distrusted Negroes, and therefore that he harbored disloyal opinions of the judge as a carpetbagger.

"Jim's in custody in Tahlequah," Crump said, "or was. The word is he escaped, but God help the white man who tries for a straight answer from the Cherokee courts when they soil their britches. Brother Bill's still at large. The posse that took Jim lost a man; Goldsby's tagged with that killing. That's neither here nor there, since he was Lighthorse and it's Indian jurisdiction, but Goldsby's a rotten little egg of eighteen. They say he shot his first man over a woman at a dance."

"In Fort Gibson, I see. The man recovered." Now came details of Goldsby's adventures with the Cooks and their band. "Chicken. Dynamite Dick. The Verdigris Kid. I wish these fellows read something other than *Ned Buntline's Own*. Why haven't I heard of Goldsby before this?"

"Up to now it's been by guess and by God. There was the man at the dance, who pulled through, and any of a half dozen Cherokee Bills might have been responsible for that Lighthorse affair. A conductor named Collins on the Katy Flyer took one through the heart because Goldsby forgot to buy a ticket, but go find a coach passenger who'll admit he saw anything if it means coming to Fort Smith. This time, though, we've got Cherokee Bill's own word for what happened in Lenapah."

Bill Cook kept a loose hitch on his brother Jim's gang. Two members, thought to be Cherokee Bill and the Verdigris Kid, cut out to rob Schufeldt & Son, a store and post office in that busy town in the Cherokee. The Kid laid down fire outside to discourage interference while Cherokee Bill ordered John Schufeldt to open the safe. When the man in the street called for shells, his partner searched the store, spotted a curious housepainter named Ernest Melton peering through a window on the alley, and shot him in the face. The bandit then filled his pockets with money from the safe and fled on horseback with the Kid.

Crump thudded a finger on a passage in his report, attributed to deputies W. C. Smith and George Lawson: *An informant in our employ, acting upon instructions, sought out "Cherokee Bill," who said, "I had to kill a man at Lenapah."*

Parker signed the warrant, and a petition calling for a reward of $1,300 from the Justice Department for the capture or death of Crawford Goldsby, *alias* Cherokee Bill. The request was granted, as he knew it would be; Crump had recently traveled to Washington to plead his case with Attorney General Richard Olney to encourage public cooperation in bringing an end to such as the Cooks, and the Department of the Interior had become involved in the interest of establishing a territorial government. A pen-and-ink likeness of the bandit drawn from witness descriptions appeared in train stations and telegraph offices throughout Arkansas, Texas, and the Nations: Cherokee Bill's broad Hispanic face and flat negroid features peered out from beneath the broad flat brim of a pinch hat.

"If these efforts fail," Olney had announced, "it is assumed that the military will be called into requisition."

Parker glowered at the suggestion. To Crump he said, "These United States have entered a new chapter: We no longer declare war on countries, only men."

"Whatever help we get is all to the good."

"The difficulty is in persuading it to leave once it's served its purpose."

The judge authorized wires enlisting the aid of the Cherokee Lighthorse and the Indian police in the Choctaw, Creek, Seminole, and Chickasaw nations and on the Osage reservation, and drafted a personal invitation to the directors of the Rock Island, Santa Fe, and Missouri, Kansas, and Texas railroads to lend their detectives to the cause. These men responded swiftly and in the affirmative. With Crump's deputies placed on alert, some five hundred men had joined the hunt. It had taken only seventeen to run Ned Christie to ground. This time, at least, there would be no cannons.

The killing in Lenapah had shifted Cherokee Bill's accomplices to the background, with $250 offered for each, dead or alive. Deputy W. C. Smith, who had helped connect the bandit to the murder through his own words, remarked to his partner, George Lawson, that the price of shooting housepainters had risen steeply since he'd come to the territory.

When a small party of manhunters crossed Bill's path and shot his horse out from under him, Bill took to the scrub on foot—and vanished. They tracked him until his trail doubled back on itself, then gave up the chase. Stories of his Sioux blood got into the newspapers, a biography ran many columns, attributing more killings to its subject than to the Doolins and Daltons combined. Writers in the East borrowed from it heavily to fill out space between garish paper covers. With all the hostile tribes subjugated, popular fiction in the 1890s turned toward road agents and guerrillas. By Christmas 1894, Cherokee Bill was nearly as well known as Kris Kringle.

A trio of Cook associates was surrounded by deputies and Indian police outside Sapulpa. Two were killed and a third was taken to Fort Smith and tried with another man captured during the robbery of a bank in Chandler. Parker sentenced them to ten to fifteen years in the Detroit House of Corrections.

The rest of the gang migrated west, away from their pursuers, but not in such haste they failed to attend to business. In the Seminole Nation, they waylaid a family of German settlers on their way to Tecumseh, robbed the father of his money and a gold watch, stole the horse from the wagon, and raped the man's daughter. The hunt for Cherokee Bill had improved communications; deputies trailing the gang from the scene of the atrocity wired the Texas Rangers, who captured three members near Wichita Falls without firing a shot and held them until the deputies arrived to remove them to Fort Smith. Parker sent one man to Detroit for thirty years and the others for twenty years apiece. Some who witnessed the proceedings muttered that the judge was mellowing.

"He's saving his teeth for Cherokee Bill," said one.

The rumor furnace was stoked and putting out heat. Cherokee Bill had raped the girl; Cherokee Bill was nowhere near the Seminole at the time of the assault, but was robbing a train at Red Ford; Cherokee Bill was taking a holiday in Nowata, openly courting a girl named Maggie Glass. It was a signal of a desperado's rise to stature that the laws of space and time presented him with no greater challenge than those of man. Few who followed his adventures could encompass the fact that neither his name nor his alias had yet appeared in print scant months earlier. The stuff of legend now traveled at the speed of Morse code.

He was, in fact, in none of the places attributed to him at the time of the Seminole incident, but sleeping long hours under the attic roof of a farmhouse near Talala. Neighbors who remembered the farm's first ownership referred to it as the Frank Daniels place. There, Bill found cartridge-loading equipment and sent his sister, Maude, who worked the farm with her husband, George Brown, into town to secure powder. Brown, a wolf-lean man several inches taller than his guest, had during their tenancy established the house as a regular stop on the local whiskey peddler's route. When Brown's store ran out before the peddler's return, he saw giant rabbits for a time, then after the shakes passed grew quiet and relatively amiable; Bill during these periods considered him better company than he'd been running with, and the pair smoked and swapped stories on the front porch evenings when the wind didn't blow from the north while Maude washed the supper things inside. It was only when the peddler had come and gone and Brown made up for lost time that the farmer lost his affability and made cutting remarks, usually at his wife's expense but sometimes at Bill's; the recurring complaint was that his brother-in-law considered him a hotelier, and slept all day "like a hog" and kept Brown up all night with his bullet-rammer chunking directly above the bedroom where the Browns rested. "How many shells does a man need to defend an attic?"

Cherokee Bill's host was not the only one to take note of his nocturnal activities. In Talala, Deputy Lawson, who knew

Bill's sister lived nearby, had spread money around town against information on any change in the Browns' routine; he had aspirations regarding collateral rewards offered for the fugitive dead or alive, but found business too confining to stake out the farm. Informed of Maude's recent black-powder purchases, he wired Tahlequah for reinforcements from the Cherokee Lighthorse for a raid on the homestead.

Brown's sneering remarks seemed to have no effect on his houseguest. In the days before his infamy, Crawford Goldsby had been thought by some a typical dumb greaser, and probably a coward. The vilest insult to his face made no change in his expression and brought no retribution. These witnesses had not been present when Bill was with his sister, his confidante in the early years when his father took out his mixed-blood miseries on the only other masculine member of the household, first with his belt, then when Crawford grew too large to present his backside without protest, his fists. When Brown grew weary of trying to get a rise out of Cherokee Bill and took a horsewhip to Maude over the matter of an overcooked ham, Bill dusted the black powder from his palms, loaded his revolver with six newly minted rounds, stuck it under his belt in back, and went downstairs.

He found his sister curled into a fetal position in the corner next to the stove and Brown standing over her, panting like a hound, the whip dangling from his hand, exhausted from his exertions and sweating pure skullbender from every pore; he smelled like a still in ninety-degree heat. Streaks of blood stained Maude's dress where the lash had shredded the material.

"George, let's go out for a smoke."

Brown looked at him, his features stupid. He appeared to take a moment to recognize Bill. "I'm fresh out. You smoked everything in the house but the rat shit in the potato bin."

"I've got cigars." Bill patted his shirt pocket.

"What'd you do, steal 'em? You spent every penny you stole on whores. I ought to've put Maudie out on the line herself for all the use she is around here." But he dropped the whip and started toward the door. He had one foot on the porch when Bill drew the revolver and shot him in the back of the head.

Maude screamed and began blubbering widow's incoherencies. Bill went to a cupboard, emptied a coffee jar of household cash, reached down to pat her shoulder, saddled up his horse in the barn, and rode hard for the Cimarron with his saddle pouches full of fresh cartridges. It really was a shame what she'd done to a fine Arkansas ham.

The new year of 1895 was barely a month old when the story, reported widely in newspapers as far east as Chicago, was retold in *Cherokee Bill's Gamble,* in which the Bandit Prince shot a stranger's cruel husband in a fair fight and upended a bank bag filled with greenbacks onto the woman's kitchen table before taking his leave.

Deputy Lawson, in the company of the Cherokee Lighthorse, had found Maude Goldsby Brown seated hollow-eyed at that same table, bare but for a worn oilcloth cover, with a dead man on the porch under a rug to discourage flies. He borrowed a shovel to bury George Brown while the Indian policemen watched, smoking and retelling old jokes in Cherokee.

Cherokee Bill's story so overshadowed that of the Cooks', the worst gang ever to plague the Nations until the coming of Rufus Buck, that when Jim Cook resurfaced, years after the capture and imprisonment of his brother Bill, journalists suffered his company only to ply him with questions about Cherokee Bill, who had joined the band too late for Jim Cook to offer any recollection of him. In the early years of the twentieth century, Jim formed an alliance with Al Jennings, an Oklahoma train robber recently released from custody, to film a series of fanciful photoplays about the wild days on the border, only to be cast out of the company for his inability to embroider upon historical fact. He passed from the record, penniless and forgotten.

Cherokee Bill, it was said, traveled with a small library of his exploits, seasoned like a cookbook with exclamation points and purple adjectives; he'd grown up reading similarly embellished accounts of Ned Christie's vendetta and took almost carnal pleasure in his own ascension into that company. In the meantime he'd taken his amusement at the expense of banks, stores, a train or two, and the odd complacent traveler, and made sport of the humorless men who gathered, heavily armed, to write his final chapter.

Judge Parker, who maintained a close watch on everything that appeared about events that took place in the Nations, expressed little outrage over the distortions in *Cherokee Bill's Gamble.* By the time he learned of them, Cherokee Bill was in the Fort Smith jail awaiting justice.

NINETEEN

The new courtroom reminded some visitors of a giant humidor, wainscoted four feet high all around, with stout rails separating the gallery from the proceedings, straightback chairs for the jury, a paneled box for witnesses beside the judge's high bench, and pews polished by the shoulder blades and backsides of those who sat to spectate, bored and mesmerized by turns by the inexorably turning gears of justice. The furlongs of polished oak smelled strongly of furniture oil, which on hot days when the slow swoop of the electric ceiling fan failed to stir the heavy air blended with sweat and the stench of mothballs from woolen suits just out of storage.

Others compared the place to a church, and the analogy was not inept. For all the men who had been removed from that insular chamber to the new federal jail, there to await their appointments with George Maledon on the old scaffold, and the men and women who had been escorted from there in manacles to trains bound for penetentiaries in Michigan, Ohio, Illinois, and Little Rock, there were nearly as many stories of innocence established, wrongs reversed, families reunited, and unions sanctified: Parker had performed weddings there and at his home. Accounts of these happy occasions found their way into the social columns of the *Elevator* and the *Evening Call,* but died on the telegraph wires between Fort Smith and the newspapers in the East, where multiple executions boosted readership far more dependably, although not so much as in the days when the engine of the law had chugged away in the old military barracks; with the escalating situation with wicked Spain in Cuba and the Philippines, America had begun to fancy itself a world power, and business was more pressing from the eastern half of the globe. The Shah of Persia was dead by an assassin's hand, the British were mired in the Sudan, the Turks were slaughtering Armenians in gross lots in Constantinople. The Hanging Judge seemed as quaint as knee breeches.

Nevertheless the scaffold was maintained in working condition. Mollie King, who with two of her lovers had murdered and buried her husband, Ed, in the Cherokee Nation, had been found guilty and scheduled to hang, but as her four female predecessors had had their sentences commuted or their cases pardoned, and J. Warren Reed had taken up her standard, Parker doubted he'd be executing a woman that season. Still other cases considered settled in Fort Smith hung like overripe fruit on the tangled branches in Washington while the dates set for final disposition came and went. His enemies in Congress and on the Supreme Court had engaged him in a war of nerves, a staring contest in which he was determined not to flinch. The gray nonentity from the staff of deputy marshals who had assumed Maledon's responsibilities upon his retirement oiled the trap, treated the ropes as prescribed by the man he'd succeeded, and dropped sandbags to stretch the hemp and test its strength, the *squee-thump!* blending as always with the other routine sounds of Fort

Smith. One never knew when the men in the capital might decide the old gargoyle on the bench was right for once, and the equipment must be equal to expectations.

Parker meanwhile attended church each Sunday—sometimes twice, in deference to Mary's Catholicism, although not as frequently as when her brandy bill was not so high and her tread more steady. There were weeks when she didn't imbibe, and accompanied her husband to meetings of the Social Reading Club, of which he was president, and which met in the homes of members. They read and discussed *Uncle Tom's Cabin,* General Wallace's *Ben-Hur,* the poems of Rudyard Kipling, and *The Prisoner of Zenda,* which Mary defended with passion, but which the judge considered a cheap imitation of better works by Dumas the elder. She recited poetry—*Wet the Clay* was the favorite—and Parker, buoyed by an unexpectedly favorable finding in Washington and a saturation of Sunday bonhomie, sang "She'll be Comin' 'Round the Mountain" in a rich baritone while the organist from the Methodist church played piano. The husbands shook his hand with enthusiasm and their wives expressed surprise at the strength of his voice. They avoided the indiscreet depositions in court and had never heard him condemn a prisoner to his face with all the thunder of a damnation in the Book of Exodus. ("Old Thunder" had become a term of endearment applied to him by deputies who had been present during sentencings.)

Charlie and Jimmie Parker still attended church with their parents, but did not ride with them in their carriage on the way home or to noon dinner with friends, finding their own amusements in town; it was painfully evident that timid, pliable Jimmie had fallen victim to his older brother's sinister influence. Father and firstborn rarely spoke. Having spent his wrath in court, the judge hadn't the energy to pursue it at home, even were it still possible to change the course of events. Isaac and Mary drove in silence and separated inside the door, the judge to his study and his pile of portfolios, the wife to her sewing room and the squat bottle she kept on the shelf behind the wicker basket containing needles and spools of thread. She was as likely to take to it in the morning as in the evening, when sleep eluded her, with predictable results; she had given up baking cakes for the condemned after disastrously substituting salt for sugar on one occasion, and arranging and delivering bouquets of flowers to the new cells aboveground presented the obstacle of climbing stairs to one who could no longer trust where she put her feet. Her husband had questioned her drinking early in its course, but she had made no response other than to return the bottle to its place with the cork secure. Later from the dining room he'd heard the tiny clink of the neck touching the edge of a glass. She was the partner of his youth, the strength in his early struggles; he could not lecture her as he did the principals in the trials over which he presided. When along in the evening the light went out beneath her door and she passed to bed, Parker continued to read and smoke until the hall clock told him he had just eight hours to rest before morning session.

With little opportunity for casual discourse at home, he found congenial company in his officers, particularly deputies like Madsen, Thomas, and Tilghman, whose tirelessness and insistence upon obtaining proper warrants best exemplified his dream of justice in the Eighth District. When he encountered them in hallways, in chambers, and in the marvelous hydraulic perpendicular railway that conveyed passengers between floors in the brick courthouse, he addressed them by their Christian names, while maintaining the customary formality behind the bench. (These officers in their turn called him "Your Honor" always.) In private they discussed baseball and the county fair, and in the lift one day Parker related the amusing anecdote of the time Belle Starr treated unsuspecting deputies to a meal of fried rattlesnake. More and more he discovered that exasperating woman's record a source of pleasurable exchange, and it occurred to him that something of the heart had gone out of outlawry when she'd been blasted into legend. At such times his pallor and snowy whiskers took on the mien of an indulgent grandfather.

His listeners this time were Chris Madsen and Bill Tilghman, who chuckled good-naturedly at a story they'd heard several times before in differing versions, from a half dozen deputies who swore they were present at Belle's memorable dinner. It happened that the pair were on their way to the attic to review some items of physical evidence before testifying in the trial to which they'd been summoned, and they stayed aboard the car after the judge stepped out. The doors were not soundproof, and as the contraption continued its ascent, Parker overheard the following:

Tilghman: "How old you figure the old man is?"

Madsen: "Not sixty yet."

Tilghman: "He's started in repeating himself."

Parker grunted. Perhaps he had. That was what came of having to defend one's every decision time and again.

The room where he spent most of his life was seldom less than two-thirds filled, even during such routine events as public drunkenness and a final divorce decree, for the theater of the courthouse was the town's biggest attraction, and one never knew when a bit of drama might break out, such as the details during testimony of a romantic indiscretion or an attempt at escape; Maledon himself had ended five of those with his pistols, with which he was ambidextrous, although left-handed at table and on the scaffold. Then, too, there were the judge's impassioned soliloquies when it came time to hand down his final judgments. Before his arrival, the men and women assembled chattered happily, offering one another apples and other cold victuals from sacks in hot weather and passing around vacuum bottles filled with soup or coffee when frost nibbled at the windows, but fell silent and rose at Crier Hammersly's command when the white-haired man in black robes strode in and took his place in the leather-embossed chair. The smack of his gavel was superfluous as

to establishing order and served no purpose other than overture.

Once he claimed that familiar position, Parker's humor
changed, for as many cases claimed his attention as had from
the start. His sphere shrank by the day, it seemed, with such
business as Mollie King's held up in debate over whether it
belonged to the authority of the Cherokee court and not Fort
Smith, but his docket remained elephantine, the largest in the
United States and its territories, and larger than the famous
Assizes of Great Britain. If anything it was increasing. It was
as if the jackals who had preyed upon the people of the Nations had sensed the end of days, and become ferocious in
their determination to squeeze the region of its last drop of
innocent blood before the curtain fell. When the unassigned
lands of the Cherokee Strip opened to homestead, some fifty
thousand pilgrims had swarmed in to break ground, and in so
doing offered the ruthless element that many more potential
victims. Robbery remained steady, a staple of the venue,
while rape and murder rose in direct proportion to immigra-
tion, the details becoming more grisly; clearing the room of
women was not an option, and it distressed him to observe
how many genteely dressed matrons and their daughters did
not abandon their seats when such things unfolded—leaning
forward, in fact, lest something be missed. He thought of his
loyal executioner, retired now to shopkeeping, and was grateful that he himself had sired no daughters.

It didn't help trim the schedule when sensational novels
trumpeted the heroic exploits of murderers like the Daltons,
Bill Doolin, and Cherokee Bill, while readers who might
have benefited by Parker's efforts to protect the people he regarded as his flock had to make do with indignant editorials
and the *Congressional Record*. Contributors to that journal,
fusty in its appearance yet as purple in its prose as *Buffalo
Bill's Leap for Life* and *Deadwood Dick, Prince of the Road,*
included as many enemies as ever, as new antagonists rose

in place of old ones who had retired or died. The opposition now was bipartisan: Whereas the aging Old Guard of Democratic imperialism had never forgiven him for switching sides, his tormentors now were as likely to come from his own side of the aisle. They saw in him a disgraceful relic of buccaneering days, to be flung overboard to improve the party's chances in November, and this November in particular. Cleveland's second term had been plagued by economic panic; the Republicans smelled blood.

The world, it seemed, shared those pews with the curious loiterers, waiting for something to happen, for the Old Man of Fort Smith to stumble. It made a man slow and deliberate in his movements, forced him to retard the workings of his mind, like a phonograph winding down to a guttural growl. It was no good for the cylinder, and no good for the heart. His was winding down. He knew it, and all the strength he retained would be required to keep the predators from knowing it as well.

The clock struck. He folded his spectacles, put aside his reading, and retired to prepare for fresh battle in the morning. So had it been for going on twenty-one years; but never before had he found it so difficult to rise from his bed when six o'clock came around.

He had, however, one victory left in him, won on enemy ground, and one flight of judicial oratory that would stand up to examination for a century and beyond. The old man still had all his teeth.

TWENTY

Funeral bells were breaking up that old gang of Bill Doolin's.

Early in 1894, with the Nations alive with deputies, Indian policemen, and bounty killers hoping to retire on the rewards offered for the death or apprehension of him and his companions, Doolin married Edith, a minister's daughter, and settled down to the life of a gentleman farmer in the Comanche and Kiowa Nation. There he read in the papers of the slaughter and arrest of close friends, raised horses for racing purposes, and hired hands to plant crops and string fence. His split of the plunder would not hold out long in this fashion, but with five thousand dollars on his head, Doolin thought clodbusting beneath him.

In his semiretirement he learned of the passing of old associates: of Charley Pierce and Bitter Creek Newcomb, spotted by nobodies, tracked down by wire, and slaughtered by federal men in a farmhouse. That was bad enough, but the wind from the twentieth century had brought a new indignity to death, the postmortem photograph. Doolin heard an undertaker in Guthrie had peeled down the sheets that covered their corpses for a man with a camera to record them in their nudity, hair slicked back with water and their livid multiple wounds obvious to see. Charlie had had bullets in the soles of his feet, for Christ's sake. Was ammunition as cheap as that, that the blood-crazy marshals would go on pumping lead into a man as he lay on the ground already shot to pieces? In Vinita he'd seen a cabinet photograph of Bob and Grat Dalton and Tim Evans and Dick Broadwell, propped up on a barn door with a Winchester across Bob's and Grat's laps and all their boots off. Bob's big toe stuck out of a hole in his sock. Doolin turned his head and spat when he thought how close he'd come to going along on that foolish Coffeyville job. But what of it, if any ignorant saloon swamp or nigger that swept up horse apples in the street could tag him for the reward and later spend a penny of it on a picture of him with a hole in his sock and slugs in his belly?

It was dangerous to train a contrary creature like a horse with such thoughts distracting him. He took a holiday from work and wife in Eureka Springs, Arkansas, whose Victorian gimcrackery and steaming mineral waters soothed his raveled

nerves and improved his breathing; he had contracted consumption somewhere in his breakneck travels through icy
downpour, sodden heat, dusty wasteland, and pox-ridden settlements where a man who rode the owl-hoot trail might find
peace at the high price of his harbor. It was the coughing
and the retching and the general feeling of weakness that had
turned him off that trail more than fear of the law; a fit of
hacking in the middle of a holdup was just what some nance
of a clerk needed to give him the Dutch courage to clobber
Doolin with a spitoon and hold him for the authorities.

That trail had taken him as far West as New Mexico Territory. One of his hosts there was Eugene Manlove Rhodes,
a young adventurer with literary aspirations whose celebrity
would come a generation later with publication of *Paso por
Aqui*, the tale of a fugitive's flight to avoid arrest; Rhodes thus
became the first in a long line of writers who championed
desperate men in quest of personal publicity and raw material. For his part, Doolin found him unnerving company,
always staring at him when he thought Doolin wasn't looking.

Only in Eureka Springs could a man be truly alone with
his thoughts. Subsiding into the smoky waters that brought
out prickles of sweat like fire ants on his forehead, he swigged
from a bottle of Old Pepper and considered himself on the
road to health. Naked, he lay out of reach of the .38 Colt in
its scabbard hanging on the back of a wooden chair when
Deputy U.S. Marshal Bill Tilghman kicked open the bath-
house door and threw down on him with a .44. He was out-
dressed and outgunned and surrendered himself without a
fight.

"Where's the rest?" he asked, dressed and in shackles,
when they were outside.

"I'm the shebang," Tilghman said.

"Well, hell. If I knew that I'd of put up some kind of argument."

"I wish you had."

"Where we headed, Fort Smith?"

"Guthrie. You must answer for Ingalls."

"I wasn't in on that."

"Your horse was. Lafe Shadley shot it out from under you and you gunned him down for it."

"He was a good horse, but I wasn't riding him that day. I loaned it to Little Dick West for a fresh mount and rode into Guthrie to see the elephant. I wasn't at Ingalls."

"You can tell that to the judge in Guthrie, and thank your lucky stars it ain't Parker."

"I'd as lief it was. Guthrie's a far piece to ride. I'm a sick man." He coughed for emphasis; which was a mistake. It led to a fit. The waters had not had their chance to finish the cure.

Tilghman untied Doolin's horse from the hitching rail. Everyone knew his saddle rig on sight. "You can ride sitting up or hog-tied on your belly. It don't make no difference to me either way, but one's more pleasant for you."

"What'd I ever do to you to get your back up against me? I wish it was Heck took me instead of you."

"You'd get the same from him or worse. Now step into leather."

With Parker's court in division, Guthrie held jurisdiction over Ingalls, where the Doolin Gang had slain three deputies during the siege on their hideout. Doolin was housed in the federal jail there, charged with the murder of Lafe Shadley, a deputy. He thought Tilghman unreasonable on that point. Heck Thomas had plenty of bark on him as well, but was less inclined to take such a thing as a necessary casualty personally. Doolin and Heck had always liked each other, apart from their professional differences.

That ride—long and hot, with infrequent stops to rest and frequent prodding at the point of Winchesters belonging to the officers Tilghman had recruited to help with the escort, men who shared his unreasonable attitude toward decisions made in the heat of battle—erased the progress Doolin had made in the springs. Slick with sweat and pale, wheezing and spraying pink drops on his shirt, he fell into hallucinating in the wagon they'd dumped him into to discourage any hot ideas about breaking for freedom, and struck up a conversation with Grat Dalton, dead these three years. At the jail, Dr. Smith, the resident physician, fed him spoonfuls of a black gluteant made from tamarack bark, spikenard and dandelion root, hops, and honey, with a drop of coal oil substituted for brandy, which was banned from the institution. It was a tribute to the prisoner's strength of will that he recovered from both his relapse and this treatment; but since the evidence rested upon a mass jailbreak led by his patient, Dr. Smith was not disposed to congratulate himself within anyone's hearing.

On July 5, 1896, several prisoners overpowered and disarmed a guard, opened cells, and spilled out, fourteen strong, into the countryside. The news reached the private telegraph station in the room in St. Louis of a successful contributor to the popular press; he paused while composing *Bill Doolin Pays His Debt* to decode the message that came tapping out, crumpled and threw away his pages, and began writing *Bill Doolin's Flight to Freedom*. Heck Thomas, apprised at home in the house he shared with his second wife, Matie, hitched his suspenders up over his shoulders, loaded his Winchester, and went out. His grown son, Albert, already an experienced apprentice manhunter, rode beside him. Back home in Atlanta, Albert's mother fretted. Heck had told her posse work was in the blood.

Rufe Cannon, a deputy marshal who had taken part in the Ingalls raid, joined the Thomases in their camp below the Cimarron, not far from where that bloodbath had taken place; Doolin, who ranged wide but always returned to old haunts, had set up his horse ranch in that vicinity. In the Nations, men of low character were like stubborn mule deer, seldom grazing more than a few miles from where they were born, and dying there more often than not; it was the terrain and the cooperation of their neighbors, not distance, that kept them out of custody for such long stretches. Edith Doolin was still in residence, cooking for the hands and promising to pay them when Bill came back and found a customer for his horses. Heck took advantage of his own friends in the community and greased the palms of promising strangers to keep a posting on what took place there. Slowly as erosion, personal profit and the changing population had worn away at loyalty in the face of a common enemy. Heck thought it sad to see, as he respected a hardworking criminal ahead of an opportunist, but you couldn't stop the world from turning.

After dark on August 23, a rider entered the deputies' camp to report that Doolin's wife had brought a team to the Noble brothers' blacksmith shop in Lawton to have them reshod. It was a rush order; the horses were needed by morning. Cannon and the Thomases mounted up at dawn.

Passing the Doolin spread, they spotted fresh wheel ruts turning into the road. That meant a household packed into a slow-moving wagon. They eased their pace to conserve horseflesh. Sometime past two P.M., they were met by the Noble brothers, who had sent the message. They had passed Edith Doolin's covered wagon, heaped to the sheet with furniture, a cultivator, a plow, and a wooden coop filled with squawking chickens, headed toward Old Man Ellsworth's store.

"How do you know that's where she's headed?" Heck asked.

Charlie Noble answered. "Brother Bob spotted Bill Doolin's saddle rig on a horse in the shed behind the store."

His brother, a hulking youth with a wispy fair beard like spun sugar, confirmed this.

The posse took the long way around to avoid meeting Edith Doolin on the road. Below a hill overlooking Ellsworth's store, with living quarters in back and the shed behind the building, they tethered their mounts and crawled through the grass on their bellies, then took turns peering through a pair of field glasses Heck had confiscated from Bill Cook at the time of his arrest. There was a deal of activity going on about the store, but none of the men milling around came close to Doolin's spindly build and stooped shoulders. The possemen shared plugs of tobacco and twists of jerked beef and waited for dark.

Nearing sundown, a wagon with a canvas cover hobbled in, creaking and clucking, and a woman in a bonnet and long dress stepped down from the driver's seat and stretched her back. Heck knew Edith Doolin by sight. She went into the store, leaving the horse in the care of a man who came out carrying a feed bag. He stroked the animal's neck and strapped on the bag, making no move to release the animal from its traces.

"They ain't stopping here." Rufe Cannon turned his head and spat a brown stream onto the ground.

Heck took back the glasses, looked, then gave them to Albert. He traded his Winchester for Cannon's eight-gauge shotgun and told him to work his way down behind the house. "Shout out after me," he said. "Don't make a sound till then."

Heck Thomas' report of what followed read like a story a man told the first time he told it, without colorful detail or interesting asides, and never took on any of those things all the times he told it afterward. With the moon shining bright and just off the full, Bill Doolin emerged from the shed, leading his horse with the reins wrapped loosely around his wrist and his Winchester held in front of him in both hands, ready for use. Later the manhunters learned that the people who'd been spying on Mrs. Doolin had been unsubtle and he was prepared for ambush. It was Bill for sure, skinny as a withered rail and favoring his left leg, which poor Lafe Shadley had broken when he'd shot Doolin's horse out from under him in Ingalls, and for which he'd given his own life in return.

Heck waited until Doolin was halfway between the shed and the road, then rose with the moon in front of him and behind the bandit. Albert rose with him. Heck shouted for Doolin to surrender. Rufe Cannon echoed the words from behind Doolin.

The man with the horse fired from reflex. Heck heard the

bullet chug into the ground in front of him. He swung the heavy shotgun to his shoulder, but he was unfamiliar with the weapon and fumbled at the hammers. Doolin fired again. By then Cannon and Albert had him in their crossfire and his second shot went wide. Heck's palm found the hammers and raked them back. Doolin's carbine sprang from his hands as if yanked by a wire; one of Cannon's slugs had struck it. The bandit scooped a pistol from his belt. The others claimed later he squeezed the trigger, but Heck had no recollection of hearing the report or seeing the flash. The shotgun bellowed, punishing his shoulder.

". . . the fight was over," Heck concluded.

That was his account, the one that was accepted in Guthrie and by Judge Parker in Fort Smith, and he never wandered from it, not even when he was an old man and reporters and historians pressed him for a version with more color and closer risk. Another version, suggested first in Lawton near the scene of the shooting, spread rapidly through the Nations, carried in gusty whispers like an off-color joke, but found no life beyond the borders of Oklahoma until it stumbled into print in 1920, thirteen years after statehood and eight years after Heck's death at age sixty-six. It went like this:

When Heck got tired of waiting for Doolin to show himself, he posted his companions on lookout and went down to knock on Ellsworth's front door. At length it opened; he pushed his way through the store to the living quarters in back, swept past Edith Doolin when she tried to block his path, and found Bill lying stripped to the waist on a mattress stained black with sweat and hemorrhage. The desperado's arms were spread, his head was tipped back with the mouth open in mid-gasp and the eyes fixed on the ceiling. Heck felt for a pulse in his throat, which was still warm and moist to the touch. He took his hand away after a minute. Doolin's consumption had stalked him to his end.

Moments later, a shotgun blast rocked the house.

When the body reached the undertaker's parlor in Guthrie (the same one where Charley Pierce and Bitter Creek Newcomb had lain), Dr. Smith, summoned from the jail to conduct the postmortem examination for the record, counted twenty-one shotgun slugs in the chest and abdomen.

"Not much blood," he said.

"A scattergun don't give you much time to bleed," said Heck.

"Still." But Smith signed the death certificate.

The same photographer who had made immortal the remains of Pierce and Newcomb arrived with his box and tripod and case of glass plates. He had Doolin tilted forward on the wicker preparation table and struck his likeness, turkey-necked with his beard black as soot, with the round punctures vivid on his naked torso. At Edith's request he took another in a display coffin with the corpse fully dressed in his Sunday suit of clothes. She had no other photos of him for the family album. Bill had avoided flash pans throughout his career.

People streamed in from Kansas and east Texas and from as far away as Doolin's birthplace in Johnson County, Arkansas, to file past the bier where the King of the Oklahoma Outlaws lay in state. His hair was combed, his beard trimmed, and a small piece of gutta-percha had been inserted beneath his upper lip to give him a hint of a smile, as if he were dreaming of easy banks and slow-moving trains. A bouquet of blue lupine, handpicked by Edith, stood in a pot on a metal stand. Beside the registration book lay a wooden strongbox with a slot cut in the top for coins and banknotes to be deposited for the widow and Doolin's small son; it was said Mrs. Doolin had spent her last penny on the funeral arrangements. Heck Thomas, who had shared with his posse a reward in the amount of $1,435 offered by Wells, Fargo, the Missouri State Legislature, and various citizens' groups for Bill Doolin's death, never responded to the rumor that half his cut wound up in the box at Doolin's services.

TWENTY-ONE

"Where's papers?" Cherokee Bill asked.

Ike Rogers, turning from the door to follow Bill's swinging stride through his front parlor, hesitated; as always, his visitor bore with him a brimstone stench of burnt wood, leather, horse, and spent powder. He carried his Winchester in one hand and slung his bedroll into an upholstered chair with the other. Snow slid from it, thawing on contact with the red velvet seat and staining it as dark as ink. "What papers are those?" Rogers said.

"*News*papers, what you think? I ain't seen one in a month."

"I used them to start a fire."

Bill bit back a curse. Rogers had family in the house and he considered himself a gentleman bandit. "The marshals got the telegraph to tell them what I'm about. What've I got to tell me what they're about, except the papers? You knew I was coming. You sent word."

"I guess there's some in the outhouse."

Bill went out through the back. When he didn't return in two minutes, Rogers figured he'd stopped to take a shit. He wasn't fooled by any excuse Cherokee Bill might offer about his interest in the press; he just wanted to see if he was mentioned. Right now there would be three or four cheap novels with his name on the covers rolled up in his blanket and slicker.

Sitting on the icy seat with his trousers down and his flap unbuttoned, his breath curling, Bill slid his finger down the smudged columns smelling of mildew. There was a stack of them on the floor for a man to wipe his ass with when the corncobs in the bushel basket ran out. The basket was empty, and Rogers seemed to be partial to front pages. He looked in vain for his name. He read that Bill Doolin was in custody in Guthrie. With Jim Cook on the run and Bill Cook on his way from New Mexico to Fort Smith in shackles, he'd hoped to join up with that bunch, but not if Doolin was absent. The great Ned Christie was dead; Henry Starr, the latest road agent to bear that celebrated surname, had been taken in Colorado. It was up to Cherokee Bill to keep the war going against order in the Indian Nations.

It was the central tragedy of Crawford Goldsby's life that he'd been born too late to "ride the high country" during the Golden Age of frontier banditry. He'd been just seven months old when the Jameses and Youngers were shot to pieces by squareheads in Minnesota, by which time old Wild Bill, who for all his service to the law and the Yankee army had tinkered his share with the life of the road agent, had been dead barely a month, slain in cowardly fashion from behind. Give him just ten years and Crawford would have prevented Bob Ford from killing Jesse in that same yellow mode, or at least avenged him face up, with both of them armed and a bullet in Ford's black heart when he wavered, as cowards did without fail, and another in his white liver to show the world his intention.

Concealing himself from his father's wrath, behind the barn with wick turned low and his face two inches from the rough sawtooth page, young Crawford had read of these atrocities in *Beadle's Dime Library* and fantasized about "calling out" the brutal old man who had sired him, "throwing down" on him with the "hogleg" he wore high on his hip, and blasting him into hell; after which he would go "on the scout," separating high-interest banks and arrogant railroad barons from their soiled coin and distributing it among their victims, or failing that into his own pockets and saddle pouches and living the "high life" in saloons and "dance-halls," where beautiful women in brief costumes admired his straight legs and square jaw and told him of the men who had "ruined" them (he knew not just how, only that the act was disgraceful and its effects permanent), whereupon he sought the blackguards out and deprived them of their lives. There was usually profit involved; invariably the men were thieves who lived in close proximity to their "ill-gotten booty," and didn't it say somewhere in Scripture that robbing a thief was no sin? If it didn't, it should have.

The early move from Texas to Fort Gibson, on the western boundary of the Cherokee Nation, had made a showdown with his father unnecessary; but it had exposed him to the truth of his Native blood and opened his ears, at the impressionable age of ten, to whispers of Ned Christie's war against the United States. When the marshals set fire to his cabin in Rabbit Trap Canyon and shot out Ned's eye, the boy had transferred his hatred to Fort Smith, and longed to join Christie in his new fortress, defying the government in Washington with his private army and vast arsenal; when after seven triumphant years Christie fell and his body was dragged to the federal courthouse for exhibit, Crawford asked his acquaintances to address him as Cherokee Bill and laid an elaborate plan to assassinate Judge Isaac Charles Parker. The thing seemed easy enough; it was said that in his arrogance the old murderer paraded up and down Garrison Avenue with neither weapons nor bodyguard, in full view of God and the Devil, openly inviting disaster. The bullet that sent him to hell would assure immortality to the man who fired it. Why no one else had thought of it was one of those mysteries that alienated generations.

He came across a social piece about Parker uniting a young couple in "wedded bliss," and considered the ease in which a personable young man dressed for the occasion might produce a short-barreled Colt from a shoulder rig beneath his swallowtail coat and unite the man holding the Bible with the men he had sent to the scaffold. What a reunion that would make in the pits of Hades.

But business had become too confining for all that. (He had read *The Authentic Life of Billy, the Kid,* attributed to Bonney's slayer, Sheriff Pat F. Garrett, and consigned to memory the Kid's response to Garrett's call for surrender: "Can't do it, Pat. Business is too confining," and yearned for the day when he could make it his own.) Bill had slain a man at a dance over some little thing, and "lit a shuck" toward the outlaw life with the Cooks, as stupid a pair of brothers as had ever taken to the outlaw trail, although he'd admired the viciousness of their dedication. Notoriety had followed hard, depriving him of the anonymity necessary to stalk the streets of Fort Smith unnoticed. And so he'd taken his vengeance by proxy, preying upon the institutions the carpetbagger in the courthouse held dear. The situation carried its compensations, right enough; every ounce of gold diverted from Parker's salary spent sweetly in the brothels of the city that had sprung up around McAlester's store, where Bill experienced at firsthand the results of the "ruination" he'd read about, to his immediate satisfaction, and with each double eagle he spent toward his education scored deeper his contempt for organized society. Compromise signaled manhood as much as pubic hair and the muscles that spread a man's shoulders and strengthened his resolve. Let Parker hand down his decisions and wait timidly for confirmation on high. In the Nations the name Cherokee Bill, with weapon in hand, carried certain death, with no appeal between it and the Prince of Darkness. He saw himself the judge's dark twin.

"I thought you fell in," said Ike Rogers, when Bill reappeared in the parlor.

"Where's Maggie?"

"She'll be here directly. Her people have her on a close halter."

Maggie Glass had aroused the bandit's interest. A handsome combination of Negro and Cherokee, she was the sixteen-year-old daughter of Christian folk who placed little faith in the men who came to their door requesting her company. Ike, who was a quarter white, was a cousin who enjoyed their trust, and therefore the opportunity to open his home to *rendezvous* between her and Cherokee Bill. (Bill had first heard the term from Maggie, who read novels dolloped heavily with passages in French; he liked the sound, which if you broke it into thirds came out like Cherokee.) The bandit supposed he'd ruined the girl, although she didn't seem to hold the fact against him.

Bill appeared to consider what Rogers had said. He still had on his deerskin coat and flat-brimmed hat and was holding his Winchester. At that moment Rogers' wife, a full-blood Cherokee, came to the door that led into the kitchen and announced that supper was on the table.

"Put down your rifle, Bill," said Rogers, "and let's eat."

"That's something I never do."

Rogers wanted to say, *What, eat?*, but didn't. In their acquaintance he'd never known the highwayman to smile at a joke or tell one of his own. He wondered if he saved his humor for those he trusted. It was a source of doubtful conjecture that Bill remained unaware of Rogers' official connection with Fort Smith. He'd been commissioned a deputy marshal by Colonel Crump, with rewards attendant upon the capture or death of Judge Parker's chief object of interest that season. A peaceable man by nature, Rogers had of late taken to carrying an antique ball-and-percussion revolver beneath his clothes wherever he went, and kept loaded the Stevens ten-gauge shotgun mounted above the stone fireplace in his parlor. Reluctantly he left that dependable piece where it was and preceded his guest into the kitchen. Bill was good with that Winchester indoors and out, handled it with the ease of a pistol; Rogers couldn't hit a gallon jug at close range with anything but a scattergun.

Maggie came in while they were seated around the oilcloth-covered table. January was in full charge, rattling the frosted panes with gusts loaded with needles, and her color was high beneath the brown pigment as she untied her bonnet and removed her cape. Bill stood up quickly, nearly tipping over his chair, grasped her by the wrist, and hauled her toward the bedroom, carrying his rifle in his other hand. She made some pretty noise of outrage but offered no resistance.

Rogers accepted a bowl of potatoes from his wife and lowered his voice to a murmur. "He knows."

"If he don't, Maggie's telling him. I saw the second she came in she suspects."

Bill returned, too quickly even for a man who'd gone months without feminine companionship, and sat down in his chair. He'd removed his hat and coat, but he still had the rifle. He leaned it against the table. Rogers saw all over again how big a man he was. People who didn't know him took him for a Mexican through and through, but his size was against it. He was strong, too; Rogers had seen him hoist the carcass of a two-hundred-pound elk and hold it while Rogers finished tying it up to a limb to gut and drain. That was before the commission, before he'd gone and had that rifle grafted to the end of his arm. Rogers watched him tear a piece off a loaf of bread with his big, heavy-veined hands.

"Where's the kids?"

"In bed. It's late, Bill."

"I thought maybe you'd sent them away."

The Rogerses exchanged a look. "No, they're in bed."

Bill got up and carried the Winchester out of the room. The door to the children's bedroom squeaked. Rogers started to rise, but then Bill returned and took his place with the rifle close to hand.

Maggie came in, smoothing her skirt. When she sat down, Mrs. Rogers placed a plate of fried chicken in front of her, took a pitcher of milk from a windowsill where it kept cold, and poured her a glass. For a time the only sound was the click and scrape of flatware on crockery. Rogers pushed the food around on his plate, then shoved himself back from the table.

"Not hungry, I guess," said Bill.

"I don't eat as much as I used to."

"Stay put a bit."

Rogers rested his hands in his lap. The butt of the big pistol was gouging a hole in his back. Maggie nibbled at a chicken leg and drank some milk. Bill sopped the grease from his plate with a piece of bread and ate in silence. Outside, the wind hummed around a corner of the house.

The host leaned down from his chair. Bill stopped chewing and watched him lift a jug from the floor.

"You know I don't drink, Ike."

"I thought I'd have one myself, but I changed my mind." He returned the jug to its place. "How about a hand of cards?"

Maggie helped Mrs. Rogers clear the table while Rogers dealt from a dog-eared pack. They played several hands without any conversation unrelated to the game. Afterward they adjourned to the parlor, where Bill's bedroll had been removed from the chair and placed in a corner. Rogers sat in the chair and his wife knitted in the rocker while Bill and Maggie sat together on the settee, talking in low voices with her head on his shoulder and his arm around both of hers. His other hand rested on the Winchester leaning against his knee.

"It's a rotten night, Bill. Why don't you stay over?"

When Bill smiled, nothing moved but his lips. He had fine teeth. "Why, I believe I will, Ike. I'm obliged you asked."

Mrs. Rogers returned to the kitchen to wash the pots and pans she'd left soaking. She dropped one, making a racket. Rogers chuckled. "All thumbs, I guess."

The clock ticked on the mantel below the big ten-gauge. Outside, the wind rose and fell. Rogers patted back a yawn. "I think I'll go on to bed and leave you two to catch up."

"I'll go with you."

"To *bed*? I don't like you that way, Bill." He tried to grin. He was aware that his wife had come to the door and stood there wiping her hands with her apron.

"You only got two beds," Bill said. "Mrs. Rogers can bunk with the kids and I guess Maggie can make herself comfortable in here. This bench is too short for me."

Ike Rogers figured he would remember that night as long as he lived. He and Bill stretched out fully clothed on the mattress, the Winchester next to Bill on the other side. Rogers lay in the dark with his eyes open, listening. When Bill's breathing became even, he slid toward the edge.

Bill sat up, his hand on his rifle. "What's the matter, Ike?"

"Just restless." He sank back.

Twice more during the night he tried again. Either Cherokee Bill was the lightest sleeper in the Nations or he'd learned to do without sleep entirely. It was no wonder he'd remained at large when so many of his fellow travelers were in jail or dead. Rogers began to ask himself what had made him think he could succeed where so many others had failed, often at the cost of their lives. He thought about his wife and children.

In the morning—the slowest in coming Rogers had ever known—Clint Scales, a big Negro who helped out around the place, joined them at breakfast. Clint, who knew the situation, took one look at his employer's exhausted face and nodded his head a quarter of an inch. Bill was filling his cup from the big two-gallon pot that stood on an iron trivet.

Rogers' boy and girl ate crisp bacon with their fingers, asking Bill questions about his life on the scout. The guest, who had had no childhood of his own, liked children. He told stories that opened their eyes wide. Any one of them was enough to hang him. He kept his gaze on Rogers as he spoke. His host began to realize the stories were meant more for him than for the little ones. Most of them seemed to have to do with the price of betrayal. When he paused between anecdotes, Rogers turned to his children and asked them if they'd like to go next door and play.

"We want to stay and talk with Uncle Bill," said the boy.

"Bill can't hang around anyplace for long." He got up, Bill's gaze following him, and took a cartwheel dollar out of the jar of household accounts. He held it out to Maggie, who had barely touched her plate; her appetite didn't seem to be any better than Rogers'. "Why don't you take the kids next door and leave them and buy two chickens? We'll have them for noon dinner."

"We had chicken last night."

"I'll stew them," Mrs. Rogers said. "We've plenty of milk for gravy."

Maggie and the children bundled up and left. Rogers saw her glance at Bill from the door. Bill made a sandwich of bacon and a biscuit and appeared not to notice.

When he finished eating, Bill stood and picked up his rifle. "I best get going. Tell Maggie I'll see her in a few days."

Rogers said, "Sit a spell. She'll be back in a minute."

"Why'd you send for me, Ike?"

Mrs. Rogers paused in the midst of scrubbing dishes.

"Why, to see Maggie," said Rogers. "Her folks are in Nowata. I knew they wouldn't miss her if she stayed the night."

Bill seemed to turn that over, standing big as a cast iron boiler in the low-ceilinged room holding the Winchester. Then he leaned it against the wall, took makings from a shirt pocket, and rolled a cigarette, twisting the ends. When he lifted a lid from the stove and set fire to a piece of kindling for a light, Clint Scales turned over his chair, scooped a chunk of hickory out of the woodbox, and swung it with both hands. It made a nasty thump when it struck Bill's temple and he fell to the floor with a crash.

TWENTY-TWO

In August 1895, an event of monolithic proportions occurred in the Eighth District. Judge Isaac Charles Parker took his first holiday in twenty years.

This decision shook the court to its soul. It was as if the stately brick building on Sixth Street had lifted its stone skirts and waded across the Arkansas to visit with the train station.

Parker's doctor, who had diagnosed him with a weakened

heart as a result of a dropsical condition, had ordered the change of scenery and routine on pain of death ("You will listen to the sentence . . ."). The couple decided to visit Charlie, who had begun the practice of law in St. Louis, and left young Jimmie in charge of the brick house on Thirteenth Street, to which they'd moved from the old commissary. The younger son was studying for the bar in the State of Arkansas, and expressed eagerness to be alone with the choice legal library on the shelves in his father's study; the proprietor of the House of Lords prepared for his nightly commerce on the judge's credit. Unlike his brother, Jimmie was a morose drinker who kept to himself at the end of the bar and frequently had to be slapped awake at closing and pointed toward the exit. The bartenders who filled Mary Parker's brandy order through the ladies' entrance said he came by his habits honestly.

Citizens gathered on the platform to watch as His Honor, wearing a cinderproof cape and carrying a stick, his white leonine head covered by a soft felt hat, saw his wife aboard a Pullman car and submitted his elbow to the support of a porter to join her. They noted that his face was gray with fatigue and that he made more use of the stick than just for fashion.

They stopped to rest in Little Rock, then pressed on. Parker sat in on a case Charlie was defending in the St. Louis courthouse, where he disapproved of his son's arrogance, which brought objections from the prosecution and several admonitions from the bench, but after the habit of years chose not to criticize him personally. He remembered his own early mistakes and counted upon the legal system to shape his son. He and Mary enjoyed the comforts of the Planter's House, whose gilded dining room displayed prominently a large portrait of Charles Dickens, an early visitor, and when the judge felt energetic enough to venture out in the evening they attended a performance of *The Pirates of Penzance* at the opulent Olympic Theater. As the days passed the lines smoothed out in his features and they resumed the marblelike quality that had inspired some observers to compare them to a profile on a Roman coin. He had by this time taken to brushing his snowy hair in a dove's-wing swoop over the right side of his forehead and combed out his beard so that it was broader at the base than at the top, and others thought he resembled a minor poet. He and Mary strolled the levee; passersby, alerted by the city's social columns that the famous Hanging Judge of the Border was visiting, made note that his linen was acceptable and he did not strike matches on the seat of his trousers. They found his wife "blowsy," wearing last season's dress, but her expression was pleasant and she was kind to street vendors no matter how aggressive. When she opened her reticule and gave a coin to a one-legged veteran, her escort frowned. He and St. Louis appeared to share the same opinion about encouraging vagabonds.

At length Parker felt rejuvenated enough to grant an interview to a local reporter, who soon learned that one did not so much ask questions of the judge as sit and record his instructions to the jury; in this case, readers of the *St. Louis Globe Democrat*. The subject was Cherokee Bill, who after two years of committing depredations against the residents of the Indian Nations was now in federal custody waiting out his appointment with the noose.

"What is the cause of such deeds, do you ask?" said Parker; although in truth the young man had not. "There are now fifty or sixty murderers in the Fort Smith jail. They have been tried by an impartial jury; they have been convicted and have been sentenced to death. But they are resting in the jail, awaiting a hearing before the Supreme Court of the United States. While crime, in a general way, has decreased very much in the last twenty years, I have no hesitation in saying that murders are largely on the increase. I attribute the increase to the reversals of the Supreme Court."

Here the reporter made so bold as to ask if His Honor did not believe in the appeals process.

Parker drew on his cigar and broke an inch of ash into the crystal tray in his suite. "I have no objection to appeal. I even favor abolition of the death penalty"—the young man's ink-pencil scratched furiously, as his subject leaned forward in his armchair—"*provided* there is a certainty of punishment, whatever the punishment may be, for in the uncertainty of punishment following crime lies the weakness of our halting justice.

"This court is but the humble instrument to aid in the execution of that divine justice which has ever decided that he who takes what he cannot return—the life of another human being—shall lose his own."

The reporter made private note of the fact that Parker seemed to carry his court with him everywhere, like a pocket flask, and uncorked it any place he found suitable; but filed the story as written, or rather as it had been dictated to him.

It ran in long paragraphs of uninterrupted monologue, with Parker's tacit endorsement of an end to capital punishment—outlawed in far-off Michigan alone in all the world—buried in its text. St. Louis society deliberated but failed to agree upon a verdict for or against the man in the *Globe Democrat*'s dock. Generations had passed since the city's unruly adolescence, and tales of lynchings and river pirates were repeated in the arch melodramatic tone usually reserved for parables from the Brothers Grimm. Its citizens were loath to surrender their perception of the ogre perched on its mountain of skulls.

Parker read the article, sensed the interpretation, and sloughed it off with a roll of his shoulders, turning to the telegraph columns for news from Washington. Mary, sipping a cordial, saw this reaction and rejoiced. She wished, without disloyalty, that Isaac's dropsy had presented itself years earlier, as nothing but the threat of death and permanent abandonment of his responsibilities would have forced him from the bench for more than a day, that day being Sunday or Christmas. They took long carriage rides, dined at the

homes of local dignitaries, and watched Fort Smith fade like
the details of a troubling dream, the jail and scaffold last in
line. Mary Parker began to entertain the timid hope that her
husband might retire. They would live in St. Louis, and
Jimmie would join Charlie in his practice.

Modern communications were against her. The news that
came by wire to the local papers contained new encroach-
ments by Congress ("haggling at my jurisdiction," was Isaac's
phrase) and atrocities in the Oklahoma Territory. Isaac grew
restive, unresponsive to the sights and sounds that surrounded
them; his temper became short, his fingers drummed. Came
the morning she drew on her robe and left the bedroom to
find him standing fully clothed in their sitting room with a
message from Western Union spread out on the writing table, and she knew their idyll was at an end.

Back in January, Ike Rogers had found himself having the
Devil's own time collecting the reward on Cherokee Bill.

Clint Scales, his hired man, had taken a mighty swing at
Bill's big head; the chunk of hickory had made a thump when
it connected that Rogers himself had felt in his testicles, and
Bill had dropped like a turd, shaking the house and shower-
ing plaster from the kitchen ceiling. Rogers reached to catch
Bill's Winchester, but missed, and before it struck the floor,
Bill was up in an animal crouch, his hat gone, his hair in his
eyes, and blood trickling down the side of his face. He lunged
for the rifle. Rogers flung both arms around Bill's waist
and Scales, who had dropped the piece of firewood, caught
Bill's throat in the crook of his elbow while Mrs. Rogers,
who had been watching from the sink, bent, scooped up the
Winchester, and ran into the parlor.

Bill writhed and bit and straightened his legs with a
snap, carrying all three men across the room and into a wall,
knocking a skillet off its nail, pinning Scales backward,
and emptying his lungs with a woof. Dazed, the hired man

relaxed his grip. Bill raised both hands above his head, closing them into a ten-fingered fist, and brought it down onto the back of Rogers' neck with the force of a club. Rogers' knees went weak, but he held on to the bear hug despite two more blows to his head and shoulder, the second of which numbed him all down one side. He felt his hands slipping, and Bill twisted free. In so doing, he raised one foot from the floor and Scales, recovering himself, hooked Bill's other ankle with one of his own and snatched it out from under him. The three fell into a heap with the bandit on the bottom. Scales and Rogers beat at him with their fists. Bill turned over to shield his face and got both hands beneath him to shove upward and dislodge them, but Scales screwed a knee into the small of his back and forced him flat. Mrs. Rogers came running back in with a pair of manacles. The men jerked Bill's hands behind him and Rogers hooked the cuffs around his wrists, ratcheting them tight. At length the man on the bottom stopped struggling, his breath whistling in and out.

"Got him a head like a pine knot." Scales, panting also, rolled over and sat on the base of Bill's spine.

Rogers rose, wobbling. His wife asked him if he was all right. He sent her for the Winchester and told Scales to hitch up the team.

"Where we taking him?"

"Nowata. Marshal Smith and Marshal Lawson's been waiting on delivery since sunup."

Bill caught his breath, gulped, and spat. "They'll wait till hell if they're waiting for me."

Scales went out, passing Mrs. Rogers coming in with the rifle.

When the wagon was ready, Rogers prodded Cherokee Bill outside and told him to sit in the bed. Rogers then swung up and latched the tailgate and mounted his horse. He rode behind with the Winchester across the throat of his saddle and Scales driving the wagon. He slid the clumsy useless burden of the big ball-and-percussion pistol out from under his belt and stuck it in a saddle pouch.

Turning into the road—his wife, that good woman, watching from the porch—Ike Rogers felt easier than he had in days, when he'd first decided to set his snare. That night in bed with the worst killer in the Nations had nearly unmanned him, and in the kitchen he'd fought with the blind savage terror of a kit caught in the jaws of a wild boar, but in the end it was Bill's time that had run out, and Bill knew it, too; he'd gentled right down once the cuffs were on. Rogers thought if he could remember what he'd done with that badge they'd given him he'd pin it on.

The sun was out, headache bright on the snow. They crossed the Verdigris River basin, the horses stepping high to clout a path through the drifts, and climbed out of it onto the plain leading flat as a poker table to Nowata. Rogers saw Bill struggling with his shackles now, the big muscles across his shoulders bulging like pumpkins. The boar still had some piss in him after all.

"Lay off that, Bill. You'll rub yourself to the bone."

"They're too tight, Ike. You want me to get the gangrene?"

"The reward notices don't say nothing against it."

"You're a Judas son of a bitch."

"Times are hard, Bill."

The prisoner relaxed. Moments later, he started in again. His temple resumed bleeding as he strained against the short length of chain.

"Bill, you're stubborn as—"

Bill braced his feet against the tailgate, his back against the headboard, and heaved. Something snapped. Rogers thought it was the tailgate latch, but then Bill got both hands on the sideboard and threw himself over. *Jesus, he's strong.* He landed on his feet, but his momentum combined with the wagon's almost pitched him forward onto his face. He stumbled, found his footing, and broke into a sprint, the sun glinting off the broken links dangling from his manacles.

Scales hauled back hard on the lines; the team tried to rear. Rogers drew rein gently, taking his time. Three hundred yards of open plain separated the running man from the cover of the nearest cedarbrake. Rogers levered a shell into the chamber and raised the Winchester to his shoulder. The sound crackled loudly in the sharp air. The fugitive ran another couple of yards, then slowed to a stop.

"What's the matter, Bill, restless?" Rogers called out.

Cherokee Bill turned around and walked back toward the wagon. Taking his time.

Deputies Smith and Lawson listened to Ike Rogers' account, grinning all through the details of the previous night, and fitted the prisoner with irons for his legs, which were heavy enough to hobble a buffalo. After holding him for a while in the back room of a store, they took him, shuffling in his chains, to the Arkansas Valley Railroad yard and locked him in a cattle car. The train was a while leaving; people gathered around to peer through the slats at the man seated on a pile of straw. He leaned forward and cut loose with one of Ned Christie's trademark high-pitched turkey gobbles. That sent them scrambling. He sat back and closed his eyes, sore in every muscle with his head pounding and fatigue settled deep in his joints. If he'd shot Ike Rogers last night when he'd been in the mood, he could have taken his rest then and been in Rabbit Trap Canyon by now, defying the Lighthorse and marshals from the ruins of Christie's fort, where at fourteen he'd crawled over the charred logs, making popping noises with his mouth and tumbling enemies left and right.

He awoke with the train moving. He had no idea how long he'd slept or how far he'd traveled. The scenery sliding along the openings between the slats was unfamiliar. He'd never been so far east. He was freezing. He wiggled his toes to draw feeling back into them and huddled deeper into his coat, moving awkwardly in his shackles. His belly gnawed. He'd eaten breakfast at Ike's, so a fair number of hours had passed, but without knowing just when the train had begun rolling he remained disoriented as to space and time. He'd always preferred traveling by horse, which put a man closer to the earth and more in harmony with it. He wondered if someone would come to feed him and whether he'd be armed and what measures might be required to separate the man from his weapon, but the train kept going at a steady clip and no one came. It passed through low scrub and gullies spanned by shallow trestles and might have been crossing the face of the moon for all any of it signified.

Finally the wheels slowed, trash and hovels accumulated alongside the tracks, and the train belched and farted to a halt beside a low frame building with a plank sign swinging from chains stapled to the roof: CLAREMORE. The platform was jammed with people. As the steam settled they moved in and pressed their faces to the gaps between the slats. Eyes swiveled his way, jaws hung slack. For a time he enjoyed the attention, feeling like Sam Starr and Bill Doolin and the Daltons rolled into one. Then the novelty wore off and he lowered his chin to his chest, placing the brim of his hat between himself and the gawkers. He was glad when a couple of railroad men banged at the side of the car with coupling pins to back them away and the train lurched into motion.

Monotony set in. His car passed through a string of small settlements without stopping. He learned to anticipate civilization whenever rusty buckets, empty beer bottles, piles of sodden newspapers, and shacks built of mud and lath began to congregate.

At Wagoner, the train stopped again and four men gathered on the cinderbed to cover him with Winchesters while a fifth unlocked the car; this was Clint Scales, Ike Rogers' hired man, who'd brained Bill with a chunk of forewood and sat on him. One of the others ordered him to step down and change trains. He recognized Marshal Bill Smith and behind him, back a pace and to the side to shield himself behind the marshal, Rogers in the flesh, looking more weaselly than usual with his moustaches standing out in stiff bristles. Bill didn't know the other two, but their coats hung open showing stars on their waistcoats. One wore a Colt in a suspender rig under his arm.

Hobbling along with the rifles at his back, circulation needling back into his legs in their irons, he was ordered to stop when a little man came puffing across the platform hauling a camera on a tripod and a black leatherette case. As he set up his equipment, the marshals and Scales lined up on either side of Bill.

"Not by Rogers," Bill said. "I won't be photographed standing next to snake shit."

The marshals were accommodating. Bill maneuvered himself next to the man with the underarm pistol; he found out later it was Dick Crittenden, who had joined the party at Claremore with his brother Zeke. The little photographer gestured to them to press closer together. Bill threw a friendly arm across Crittenden's shoulders. Just as his fingers touched the Colt's grip, the marshal shoved him away.

Cherokee Bill shrugged and posed with his hands in his pockets. The sun was too bright for the photographer's inexperience; the picture was overexposed, and badly retouched later to bring out the men's features, but Bill never got to see it. He was in jail in Fort Smith by sundown.

August hung heavy as stink in Fort Smith. When an officer of the court met the Parkers at the station, he found little sign of recovery in the judge's face, which appeared as pouched and gray as when he'd left for St. Louis. Cherokee Bill, whom he'd sentenced to hang for the murder of Ernest Melton, the housepainter, had made a break for freedom, and slain a man in the attempt.

TWENTY-THREE

Crawford Goldsby, as he was named in his indictment, retained an attorney whose name was known across the Nations nearly as well as his own. "Cherokee Bill and J. Warren Reed," a source close to Colonel Crump was overheard to say. "No one's seen a combination like that since Frank buried Jesse."

Counsel for the defense arrived just after Bill, in leg irons but wearing the too-tight suit and cutthroat collar Reed had procured for him, was seated behind the oaken table facing the bench. The lawyer surrendered his silver-headed stick at the door but retained his shimmering silk hat, which he removed with a Vaudeville twirl and set bottomside-up on the table. He tossed his gray kid gloves inside the crown, touched his cravat, flipped up his tails like a concert pianist, and sat down beside his client. Only then did he look at Bill, turning his head just far enough to wink at him.

Parker came in, and Cherokee Bill laid eyes for the first time upon the man he'd once sworn to kill. He looked like an old lady in a black dress; Bill had known one or two in Fort Gibson who could have grown a set of whiskers just like his if they let them go long enough. He was fussy, too, just like a hag, opening his leather folder and arranging the sheets just so, wiping his pen with a little piece of stiff cloth and nodding as his clerk whispered in his ear. Then he smacked his gavel and looked at Bill while the charge was read. He hadn't appeared to take any notice of the defendant before that, and there was nothing in his expression to indicate he thought any more of him than of anyone who had wandered into the gallery to take in the show.

The pews were packed. People who'd come in less than half an hour before the proceedings stood at the back. Some of them wore stars, but mostly they looked like store clerks and day laborers, ordinary folk there for the entertainment. More than a few of the spectators were women, all dressed up in gloves and hats and little fur-trimmed jackets; they sat in a special section thought to be out of earshot of the more explicit testimony, but this segregation only called more attention to their distracting presence. The newspapers called it "Beauties' Row," and Parker was said to disapprove of it, chiefly because of the almost tangible wave of sympathy that washed the jurors' way from that direction when the defense was pleading the prisoner's case. But no loophole existed in the phrase "speedy and public trial" for the exclusion of women.

Cherokee Bill was the draw. He'd heard some of the early birds had made a day's wage in an hour by selling their seats, and someone had tried to bribe the bailiff to hold a place for him near the front. In the press section, reporters from as far away as St. Louis and Denver crowded in beside the gentlemen from the *Elevator* and the *Evening Call*. Attempts had been made by some of them to barter their way into the jail for an exclusive interview with the desperado, and when those had failed they'd filled their columns with all manner of nonsense about him to keep the story alive. Bill didn't know it, but he and Parker shared contempt for the breed, although Bill enjoyed seeing his name in print when someone from outside gave a turnkey tobacco to get a paper into the jail; it seemed half of Fort Smith's transient population was made up of friends in federal custody. Bill traded rations for a peek now and then, but the fun was going out of it. If this kept up, no one was going to give credence to the things he *had* done.

And would do yet.

Trial began at noon. A parade of witnesses appeared and identified him as the man who had robbed Schufeldt's store and shot the housepainter point blank when he'd showed his face at a window. Everyone in Lenapah, it occurred to Bill, had picked that hour to do his shopping, and a good deal more than had been present, or he'd not have had room to raise his rifle. He muttered as much to Reed, who waved off the intelligence as a thing of no consequence. Bill began to have doubts about the man he'd heard so many favorable things about from acquaintances on the scout: The road agent's friend, they'd called him. Gin blossoms on the attorney's cheeks had raised his suspicions already. Cherokee Bill had never found a taste for the stuff, and considered the "blue ruin" the flaw that had led to the demise of such as Ned Christie. When it came down to brass tacks, the fellow who chose to ride the high country had only himself to rely on.

His opinion altered not at all when the prosecution rested and Burns called the first witness for the defense: Bill's own little brother, Clarence Goldsby, whom he hadn't seen since Hector was a pup, and whom he knew rather less than the men he'd ridden with. He remembered a scrawny lad who'd wet his pants whenever their father lurched into the room, stoked high on Ginger Jake and resident evil. The slight young man who took the stand and stammered with his hand on the Bible lent no confidence to the case.

Reed rose, but made no move to stray from behind the defense table, standing with his hands in his pockets jingling his loose change. A man who had to reassure himself he had the price of a drink was no good in a crisis.

"You are the brother of the defendant," Reed said. "Where does he live?"

Clarence mumbled a response. Parker asked him to speak up. He cleared his throat, leaned forward, and said, "Fort Gibson."

"How long have you lived there?"

"About seventeen years."

"How old are you?"

"About seventeen years."

Bill's contempt calcified. He saw the gray-whiskered jasper at the prosecution table scribble a note. A man who wasn't certain about his own age could not be expected to give certain evidence of anything.

"Do you know where your brother was on the last day of November eighteen ninety-four?"

"That morning, before daylight, he was at home, as near as I can remember."

Bill started to count on his fingers the months that had passed since he'd seen Clarence last. A sharp clank of the coins in Reed's pocket made him leave off.

"How long had he been there? How many nights?"

"Two."

"Where did he stay in the daytime?"

"Somewhere up in the hills."

"When you talk about the hills, that would be the Grand River Hills where he was?"

There was some business during which the prosecution objected about leading the witness. Parker said, "Sustained," and directed Reed to rephrase the question. Reed nodded, and established through Clarence that the Grand River Hills were indeed where brother Crawford had been at the time of the robbery in Lenapah. Bill saw his course then; he couldn't believe the thing was so simple, and a glance at the men in the jurors' seats, ox-faced and likely counting their fees, told him nothing.

Bill's mother and sister were in the gallery, seated close to the rail that separated America from Judge Parker. Bill turned to look at them from time to time, putting his hand on the back of his neck as if it were stiff. They looked as if they were attending a tent service. He couldn't bring to mind just when he'd seen them last. There had been roast turkey and some stewed greens. Studying Parker he was unable to tell if he was even aware of their presence. It all seemed a waste of time and train fare. Bill would have to kick in a fat bank just to get them back home.

The prosecutor thought so little of Clarence's testimony he didn't ask him any questions of his own. Reed rested; Bill knew he'd been betrayed as surely as if he'd retained that yellow snake Ike Rogers to represent him. He'd bored holes in

Ike's face all the time Ike was testifying, and taken grim satisfaction when the court laughed at his account of his night in
bed with the man on trial; he'd as good as admitted he'd shit
the bed. Even the old lady behind the bench had smiled. But
now here Bill had gone again and built his trust on loose
gravel.

The opposition's summation to the jury painted a picture
of the defendant as scarlet as any cheap novel's: He was a
plague, a blight, and probably a cornholer, conceived in Texas
and puked out onto the unsuspecting people of the territory,
and Ernest Melton a hardworking family man who farted
roses and left a widow and two half orphans to fend for themselves. (Bill was prepared to concede all of that, even the
roses, but a fellow with a wife and kids ought to have sense
enough to keep his head down when caps are being busted
and not go peeking through strange windows.) When the
graybeard prosecutor finished and sat down, twelve faces cut
square out of bedrock turned Bill's way.

Then Reed rose, hooking his thumbs inside the armholes
of his silk waistcoat and poking out his belly, and Bill found
out what he was paying him for.

Seldom raising his voice above conversation level, and
balancing its timbre against the counterweight of his heavy
handlebars, the gentleman from West Virginia poured honey
onto his accent and proceeded to dismantle every one of the
statements the United States had made against the poor Indian boy in the dock. He was a victim, not a disease, the son
of a brutal father who'd deserted his family, and a sickly
mother unequal to the challenge of rearing three children
properly in the wicked Nations. (Mother and daughter, in
bonnets, lowered their gazes to their folded hands; Clarence
lifted his brave chin.) Nevertheless, Reed said, the boy was
the sole support of them all. Where was counsel for the
prosecution when in his desperation the lad fell in with low
company? (Bill thought Reed was trying to cut the pie both
ways: He wasn't there when the housepainter got it, but if

he was, it wasn't his fault.) He spat words like *calumny* and *canard* at his esteemed colleague on the other side of the aisle and was generally as entertaining as any of the spellbinders with the Chautauqua; Bill hadn't always understood what they were saying either, but it was thrilling to let himself be swept along by the torrent of syllables. Finally, harboring no illusions about his chances against the combined might of the U.S. marshals and the court in Fort Smith, young Crawford had appealed to a friend for shelter, only to be betrayed, beaten with a club, and thrown into a cattle car, where he was exhibited like a beast for the thirty pieces of silver on his head.

Bill thought it a whizbang show, especially when Reed punctuated *betrayed* by jabbing an accusing finger at Ike Rogers in the gallery, reddening his face and making his whiskers twitch like a water rat's. The Beauties were moved, too; some of them sobbed aloud. But when the attorney took his seat the jurors regarded the defendant with pitiless eyes. White men in suits, the bunch, not an honest pair of overalls among them.

Parker told them how the law worked. He sounded tired, as if it were him who'd been measuring the floor of a cell for a month, and Bill, who'd heard stories of his sermonizing, was disappointed after the performance he'd just witnessed. Choking off a man's life in his prime had become a daily thing and meant no more to him than moving his bowels.

The jury left, to return twenty minutes later, hardly long enough for a hand of pinochle. Bill stood to hear the guilty verdict, and damn if the man standing next to him didn't tip him another wink.

There were cards in jail, and time enough for Bill to learn every new game. He was one of fifty-nine men waiting to hang. Sometimes he was taken from Murderers' Row, where the condemned were segregated from the general population,

to sit down with Reed. The attorney had applied to the president for clemency, but Cleveland hadn't any on hand, so Reed
had put in an application to the court in Washington with the
claim that seven witnesses had come forward to swear that
Cherokee Bill wasn't in Lenapah at the time of the Melton
killing.

"Where was they when I was on trial?"

"The same place." Reed touched his temple.

"What the hell use is that?"

"Patience, boy. I save my best business for the curtain call."

His mother visited. Bill made arrangements with her to finance Reed's inquiries and some other things and took a few
dollars for the comforts. He'd been too busy stealing money
to spend it, and she was his bank.

Parker had set his execution for June 25. The date came
and went by his order while the high court was reviewing the
letter that Reed's eloquent wife had composed for him. Bill
had his picture taken with Deputy Lawson, who lent him an
unloaded Winchester to pose with, like a dead grizzly stuffed
and set upright with its claws raised. It was a fine weapon
with an action as smooth as a sewing machine's; he worked
the lever rapidly several times and asked who owned it.

"Houk, the postal inspector."

"That is a waste." Bill returned it to Lawson with a sad
smile and something growing inside him.

In July, a former Doolin hanger-on named Ben Howell
escaped from the Fort Smith jail. He'd begun a ninety-day
sentence for stealing groceries in Ingalls, and as a short-timer
had been allowed to wander the yard outside the building.

In his cell, Cherokee Bill heard the row. Within minutes
he had the details. He crawled under his cot, slid a broken
brick from its place in the wall, removed a loaded Colt revolver from the recess, and replaced the brick, using his hands
to spread out the loose mortar dust. Then he crawled back
out and put the weapon in his slop bucket where the turnkey
would be sure to find it.

TWENTY-FOUR

The dismal dungeon—the fetid, dripping purgatory of old Fort Smith, malarial and in a state of perpetual eclipse—still existed as a jail only in the East, where *progressive* was never a term applied to anything connected with Isaac C. Parker. Its successor was a marvel of government architecture and late nineteenth-century technology, all sandblasted brick and polished steel, with the cells stacked in tiers—a cage inside a box—and a gear-driven mechanism that secured them doubly once their doors were locked with a conventional key. A bar ran the length of each row of cells, and when a lever was thrown, the "brake" slammed into place with a reverberating bang. Officials from throughout the federal penitentiary system traveled many miles to tour the facility, and of course to see the sinister scaffold; the splendid waterworks that hydrated the city rated a poor third. They had their pictures taken with the first two, like the deputy marshals with their quarries alive and dead, shining in their reflected glow.

Veteran residents of both the old and new institutions agreed that the sanitary arrangements and ventilation were vastly improved, but there were some who said that the chuckle and squeak of the old gridiron gates did not sicken the heart nearly as much as when that pitiless shaft slammed shut like a mighty breech. It was as if the entire weight of the massive engine of U.S. justice had fallen on them from above, burying them alive. They preferred the rats and stink to the impersonal working of the machine, the measured exchange of fresh air for old breathing through the ductwork day and night as in a steam-powered lung. The coming century gleamed bright as cold steel, and thank God for Parker's Tears that they wouldn't live to see it.

Lawrence Keating had been a night guard at the jail for

six years, and for three years before that in the old basement keep; the newer men lingered in the guards' quarters past their shifts to hear stories of the convicts old George Maledon had gunned down trying to escape. He liked the late hours, "when the boys are all asleep and look just like angels." One of the oldest officers in the system, he was as white-haired as Judge Parker, with a magnificent set of moustaches and four children at home he let pull on them. Charles Burns, who had presided at Fort Smith's very first hanging, had liked him, and "Uncle Dick" Berry, who had assumed Burns's duties as head jailer upon his retirement, regarded Keating as his most dependable man. The prisoners considered him a mellow old gentleman who used no weapon when he struck them for calling him "Pops." Fort Smith approved of him warmly; it was still a small town for all its modern conveniences and growing population, and a man who helped out on the pump wagon when fire broke out and tended bar in the beer tent on Independence Day was known to all.

Campbell Eoff—"Oaf" to his intimates, a garrulous Scot with a heavy burr, altogether too foreign for popularity—worked the day side in Murderers' Row, a lower tier that discouraged suicidal leaps. He presided over the evening lockdown, securing the cell doors with a set of keys on a ring the size of a croquet ball preparatory to throwing the brake. In deference to the Caribbean heat of Arkansas in July, the hour had been pushed back from 6:00 to 7:00 P.M., and with old Larry Keating keeping pace outside the bars that lined the corridor, Eoff unbuckled and hung up his gun belt and let himself inside with his ring of keys. Keating's shift would begin when this ritual was completed.

Cherokee Bill occupied Cell No. 20, third from the far end of the corridor. Bill rested against the door with his hands through the bars and smoke scrawling from the end of a hand-rolled cigarette between his fingers. Next to him in 19, Dennis Davis, a Negro sharecropper who had shot a neighbor to death in the Creek Nation in a dispute over shares, lay on his cot singing a tune with neither lyrics nor melody. Four court-appointed attorneys had sought to have him declared not guilty on the grounds of insanity, but he'd been convicted and consigned to the scaffold.

Eoff stood before the door to Davis' cell. He turned his head to call over his shoulder to Keating. "There's something wrong here."

Keating stepped up to the bars that separated him from the corridor. Eoff was struggling with the key to No. 19, which was stuck fast in the lock.

The door to No. 20 swung around on its pivot and crashed against the bars of Davis' cell. Bill stepped into the corridor, leveled a revolver at Keating's face, and rolled back the hammer. "Throw up and give me that pistol!"

Keating jerked his sidearm from its scabbard. Bill fired twice. The guard staggered back.

The unarmed Eoff swung about and ran toward the opposite end of the row of cells, leaving his keys dangling from the lock, which had been stuffed with a wad of paper. A bullet struck sparks off a bar to his right; another went between the bars at the end of the corridor and spanked the brick wall beyond.

Eoff reached the end, grasped the bars in both hands, and rattled them. "Jesus, let me out!"

Cherokee Bill's cigarette smoldered in the corner of his mouth, stinging his eyes. He spat it out and drew careful aim between the guard's shoulder blades.

Someone jostled him hard from behind; he almost fired wide. George Pearce, a murderer awaiting execution and Bill's nearest neighbor to the gate on that end, charged out carrying a bludgeon fashioned from a table leg in his cell and advanced upon Eoff, blocking Bill's line of fire.

"Step aside, George!" Bill called out.

"Keys!"

"They're stuck in the goddamn door!"

The door in the wall beyond Eoff's end burst open and four

officers came through with pistols. One was Deputy Marshal Lawson, who had taken Bill off Ike Rogers' hands and lent the prisoner a Winchester in order to have his picture taken with Cherokee Bill. The first thing he saw was Larry Keating, swinging around the corner of the cage with one hand supporting himself on a bar and the other holding his revolver. The front of his uniform was soaked and slick. Eoff was spread-eagled on the end gate, banging it in its hinges and shrieking to Jesus. Ignoring the new arrivals, Keating raised his weapon to aim between the bars at the man standing with gun leveled at the far end of the inside corridor. He hesitated; Pearce had stopped halfway down holding his useless club, blocking the guard's target. The revolver was slippery in his hand; he had no strength to grip it. It fell. He felt himself sinking. His knees were bending on their own. "I'm killed," he said.

Lawson aimed between the bars and fired at Pearce. The bullet rang off steel and Pearce flattened himself against the line of cells on the left side. Billy McConnell, one of the guards who'd entered with Lawson, shot at Cherokee Bill, who returned fire twice, snapped the hammer on an empty shell, gobbled like a turkey, and scrambled back inside his cell as the officers assembled opened a fusillade. Bullets twanged off brick and steel, spent themselves, and rattled on the floor like shelled corn. A cell door halfway down the row swung open, drawing a volley of lead and spitting sparks where it hit; the prisoner inside stayed put. Bill had thrown the lever on his end, hoping for cover when the men poured out. But they appeared contented to wait instead for the rope.

There was a lull while McConnell tried to revive Keating. Bill had shot his wad, and the officers spread out to cover his cell from all sides. Then three rapid shots fanned out from inside and they ducked for cover; he had reloads.

Now the area outside the cage filled with armed men summoned by the sound of gunfire. Deputy Marshal Heck Bruner emptied the barrel of a shotgun, the characteristic boom followed by the skittering sound of falling buckshot. The air was a blue haze.

An unspoken truce was declared while the smoke cleared.

"Hey! Hey, goddamnit!"

This was a new voice, coming from a cell near the far end from Bill's.

Bruner poked a new shell into his empty barrel and slammed shut the breech. "That you, Henry Starr?"

"Who in hell else would it be, Heck? You're the son of a bitch dropped the lid on me."

"I just thought you was a gallows grape by now."

"I'm waiting on my appeal."

"Well, good luck with that."

"What if I brung you Bill's pistol?"

Bruner remembered he had a cud in his cheek. He shifted it to the other side. "I don't draw no water in Washington, Henry. I couldn't promise a thing."

"All I ask's a word on my part."

The deputy raised his voice. "How's that set with you, Bill?"

Cell No. 20 was silent while chambers were reloaded all around. Then: "How many's out there?"

"Right around twenty."

"Start Henry, then."

"It's your funeral, Henry," Bruner said. "I'll say a kind word to the judge or at your graveside, one or the other."

Bruner's ears rang. He strained for the reply.

"Is it true Maledon's quit?" Starr asked then.

"Hanging *and* storekeeping. I hear he's put his hand to busting sod. The new man's okay, but he's been known to strangle one from time to time."

"All right, then. Bill, you go to shoot me, you make it clean, you hear?"

"Sure thing, Henry," Cherokee Bill said. "That damn wash line's took too many good men."

"Don't shoot," Starr said, and crept out into the corridor, hands above his head.

Bruner told the officers to hold their fire.

Starr walked slowly. When he passed George Pearce half-way down, words were spoken, too low for anyone to over-hear. Starr walked on without pausing.

He stopped in front of Cell 20 and lowered his hands. The men watching strained to listen, but only a stray word or two of Cherokee reached them. Starr stepped inside; they braced themselves to fire. When he turned back toward the corridor, his hands were raised again, and a heavy Colt dangled by its trigger guard from his left index finger. He went across and eased it between the bars into the hand of an officer.

Keating was dead. His body was carried out gently, and no more words were spoken until after the cage was opened by a spare set of keys, letting out a lank and spent Camp-bell Eoff. Cherokee Bill was in manacles, and his cell was searched for contraband beyond the handful of loose car-tridges they found on the cot. They discovered the broken brick, and space behind it for two pistols, including the one Bill had put in the bucket for the guards to find when they went through the prison after Ben Howell's escape. Bruner split Bill's cheek with the butt of his shotgun, and still noth-ing was said. The officers were saving their words for when their kids asked the old man about the time the great Henry Starr set out to disarm Cherokee Bill.

A hundred shots had been fired, one man slain, and none wounded, which was considered some kind of record. The noise had emptied the shops, homes, and streets of Fort Smith. By the time Bill's irons were in place, the crowd outside the prison was larger than any that had gathered there since the order had come down to restrict the audience for hangings. Larry Keating's fate was common knowledge before it went out over the wires to Judge Parker in St. Louis; within thirty minutes of the shooting, all the old man's faults had been eradicated from memory and he was reckoned to have been the best Christian the community had ever known outside of the judge himself. His best friends would fill the county fair. It was hot as hell and lynch fever spread like diphtheria.

Parker was livid. He went straight to the courthouse from the train station, leaving Mary in the carriage to go home and unpack.

He found Colonel Crump in the same humor. The mob had been broken up, and at his request the city police were enforcing the curfew an hour early to prevent unhealthy gatherings. Crawford Goldsby was confined to his cell, shackled hand and foot, with turnkeys keeping watch on him in round-the-clock shifts.

"Those last three measures should have been taken when the gun was found in his cell," Parker said. He sat facing the marshal's desk, still in his traveling cape and hat.

"I asked Jailer Berry why they weren't. He said it made the prisoners unruly in the heat. The truth is he assumed the crisis was passed when the gun was found."

"That's just what Goldsby counted on. Who smuggled it in to him?"

"Berry questioned all the trustees at the time and took away their privileges. Much good that did him."

"Lynch talk, and in Fort Smith! This is what comes of meddling in Washington. The citizens have a keen sense of justice, if they know nothing of statutes and precedents. When I came here I promised it to them, and I kept my word, in the face of a firestorm from Washington and brickbats from the press. This fellow Reed and his tribe have managed to tear down in less than seven years what it took me fourteen to build. And now here's a good man slaughtered and a peaceful population determined to string his slayer to the nearest branch while a proper scaffold gathers dust."

Crump smoothed his beard and weighed suggesting another of Parker's popular open letters when his secretary knocked, entered, and told him his presence was requested at the jail.

"Berry?" barked the judge.

The secretary hesitated. "Yes, sir. Your Honor."

Parker waggled a finger at the marshal. "Either he's gotten to the bottom of the business or he's written a letter of resignation. Accept nothing in between." He left while Crump was lifting his hat off the peg.

They reconvened in chambers. Parker had removed his hat and cloak and looked up over the tops of his spectacles from the portfolio he had flayed open on his desk.

"He didn't resign." Crump's face was flushed, either from the heat or from some other stimulant.

"Indeed."

"Goldsby's a coward once his fangs are drawn. He knows now there's nothing between him and a steep drop but that letter to the Supreme Court."

"As of Friday night it's a penny wasted."

"Even so he's a penitent. He's prepared to swear out an affidavit identifying Ben Howell as the man who smuggled in both weapons, the decoy included. Goldsby claims that idea as his own. It was pretty smart at that."

"Refresh my memory."

"There's no reason you'd place Howell. You gave him three months for pilfering tins and such from a store in the Cherokee. He walked away from a work detail two weeks ago; there's a warrant out on him next time someone spots him from a prison wagon. We'll raise the ante on that. As I see it, he let himself get caught just to ferry those guns in to Goldsby. Berry fired the turnkey who was supposed to search him directly he found out."

"The man should be up on charges."

"Berry thinks he was careless and that's all there was to it. It was a ninety-day bit."

"Still too long for Howell; but I imagine he had money waiting for him. Who made the arrangements?"

"Goldsby isn't saying."

"Give me the benefit of your professional experience."

Crump brushed again at his beard; heat and moisture were making it curl. "Who else? His sweet, sickly mother."

J udge Parker spread out his sheets of foolscap and smoothed them in that pernickety way that had caused Cherokee Bill to mistake him for something less than Lucifer. He was a full minute at it, and Bill suspected he'd read his thoughts on the matter and was bound to twist the knife once or twice more before shoving it home. At last he rested his pink, naked hands on the bench and looked at the man who stood before him, with irons on his wrists and ankles and two feet of chain linking both sets. Then he folded his spectacles and recited the long text from memory. His blue eyes were glacial and no mercy lived in them.

"You have taken the life of a good man," he said, "who never harmed you; of a faithful citizen, a kind father, and a true husband. Your wicked act has taken from a home its head, from a family its support. You have made a weeping widow; your murderous bullet has made four little sorrowing and helpless orphans. But you are the man of crime, and you heed not the wails and shrieks of a sorrowing and mourning wife no more than you do the cries for a dead father of the poor orphans. Surely this is a case where all who are not criminals or sympathizers with crime should approve the swift and certain justice that has overtaken you.

"All that you have done has been done by you in the interest of crime, in furtherance of a wicked criminal purpose. The jury in your case has properly convicted you; they are to be commended for it, and for the promptness with which they did it. You have had a fair trial, notwithstanding the howls and shrieks to the contrary. Your case is one where justice should not walk with leaden feet. It should be swift. It should be certain. As far as this court is concerned it shall be."

The harsh voice stopped. A throat caught in Beauties' Row with a faint mew. Parker made no sign he heard it. Now he shuffled his pages, bringing one to the top, and placed the steel-rimmed spectacles astride his nose.

"You will listen to the sentence of the law, which is that you, Crawford Goldsby, *alias* Cherokee Bill, for the crime of murder committed by you, by your willfully and with malice aforethought taking the life of Lawrence Keating in the United States jail in Fort Smith, be hanged by the neck until you are dead; and that the marshal of the Western District of Arkansas, by himself or deputy or deputies, cause execution to be done in the premises upon you on Tuesday, September tenth, eighteen ninety-five, between the hours of nine o'clock in the forenoon and five o'clock in the afternoon of the same day.

"May God whose laws you have broken and before whose tribunal you must then appear, have mercy on your soul." Parker flicked his gavel and turned away.

The sharp crack broke the string that had bound the assembly into a taut bale. A woman sobbed openly, and a capacity crowd exhaled as one. Pencils scratched paper in the press section. Even the big electric fan overhead seemed to resume its slow swoop after a breathless pause. Colonel Crump stood two rows behind the defense table, near enough to hear the wet trickle when Cherokee Bill opened his throat to swallow saliva. Apart from that he showed no reaction to the damnedest example of oratory the marshal had ever witnessed, in and out of war and politics.

He watched two of his deputies conduct the man in chains out of the courtroom and opened his watch, marking the time without quite believing it. The judge had spoken exactly twice as long as J. Warren Reed had taken in summing up the case for the defense, yet that earlier address had seemed fusty and long-winded by comparison; the peacock had commenced to molt. Trust Old Thunder to use the machinery of judgment to dispatch another of his infernal open letters and save himself a penny.

TWENTY-FIVE

In 1896, following the snail's progress of appeal, and after standing idle for more than a year, the great scaffold in Fort Smith claimed the lives of nine men between the middle of March and the end of July. Not since 1876, when only God and the president had the power to challenge Parker's will, had so many capital sentences been carried out in that jurisdiction, and no other year came close. A black cloud of despair descended over Murderers' Row; it seemed to the condemned, and indeed to the nearly half million people in the Eighth District, that Washington had broken itself at last on Parker's granite shore.

The high board fence that had been erected around the place of execution strained against the turnout for each event. Colonel Crump, anticipating an escalated demand among federal employees, local luminaries, the press, and ordinary citizens for the final disposition of a case involving the murder of an officer of the court and a popular neighbor, had tripled his standard print order for passes to the hanging of Cherokee Bill; these were exhausted quickly, and he handwrote more on government stationery for late applicants who could not be turned away. Come the day, people began streaming into the compound two hours before the time appointed. By the time Deputy Lawson and Campbell Eoff, whom Goldsby had tried to kill, escorted the prisoner up the steps, the sea of hats, caps, and bonnets awakened memories of the public executions of the early years when anarchy ruled in the Nations.

Cameras were banned. However, the march of invention had replaced the cumbersome equipment employed by professional photographers with handheld Kodaks available to all, and one such item, smuggled in under a coat, captured the image of the young desperado whose two years on the scout had mobilized more officers than had skirmished with Ned Christie for seven, hatless, with arms and legs in restraints and one cheek still healing from its encounter with the butt of Heck Bruner's shotgun, the noose snug around his neck. The plate was lost, but not before an artist named Gannaway copied it in charcoal. Lithographic prints sold briskly in Fort Smith for weeks following the event.

At Cherokee Bill's request, the Reverend Father Pius of the Catholic church prayed for the soul of Crawford Goldsby. The marshal then asked if Bill had anything to say.

"I came here to die, not make a speech."

He said good-bye to an acquaintance in the crowd. Then he turned to Lawson. "The quicker it is over the better."

Lawson fitted a black hood over the prisoner's head. Eoff, who had not hesitated to volunteer for the duty, grasped the lever worn smooth as polished ivory by the hand of George Maledon and dropped Cherokee Bill into history.

Four months later, on the same day in July, the five members of the Rufus Buck Gang followed him. Small-time offenders who had all spent time in the jail, Buck, a Ute Indian, Creeks Sam Sampson, Lewis Davis, and Maomi July, and Lucky Davis, a Creek Negro, had scourged through the Cherokee Nation on a gin-driven frenzy of rape, robbery, and murder, and been brought to ground in a gun battle with one hundred deputies, Lighthorse policemen, and outraged citizens in the summer of the previous year. The Supreme Court had rejected their petition for appeal with a shudder, and with one jerk of the lever, one of the more depraved bands in the bloody chronicle of the Oklahoma Territory went to oblivion. Buck and Lucky Davis outlasted the others by several minutes, convulsing in the throes of slow strangulation. Parker turned from his window and missed Maledon.

The attendance on that occasion equaled Cherokee Bill's. By spectral telegraph, it was understood that this would be the last mass execution by the judge's order, and likely the last in the long tradition that had begun when Peter the Great took up the axe to aid in the extermination of the Streltsys; for the troubled century was drawing to a close, and Parker's ailments could no longer be concealed. His absence was noted at the Methodist service on Sundays; he was said to lie abed, conserving his energy for the Monday session. He had been seen frequently to close his eyes during testimony against the Bucks, and the language of sentencing, as wrathful as when he had consigned John Childers to his death three times over in 1875, had been read in a dreary monotone from his notes without his once looking at the wretches who stood before him. The engine of justice in Fort Smith was winding down. Old Thunder's lightning had lost its blinding white flash. Those doddering citizens who in their cynical youth had pressed in around the phaeton carrying the callow jurist whom Washington had sent to deliver them from ineptitude and corruption wandered the streets wearing figurative bands of mourning on their sleeves. The coming century promised nothing but an empty hole cut out in the shape of Judge Parker.

George Pearce, who with his brother, John, had killed a man in the Cherokee to gain possession of a mare and a colt, and who had unwittingly spoiled Cherokee Bill's shot at Campbell Eoff in the federal cage, stretched the hemp beside his brother on the last day in April, and this, too, drew a mass audience, due in part to George Pearce's connection with Cherokee Bill's desperate gamble.

James Casharago was born on a farm in Arkansas of an American mother and an Italian father, who died from a fall when Casharago was a boy; his stepfather despaired of teaching him discipline, declaring that the love of hard work that existed in the Mediterranean races had in Jimmy's case been extinguished by the American side. The boy was a petty thief who grew up to become an experienced forger of documents turned easily into cash. Unmasked and driven to flight, he was captured and jailed in Faulkner County, but escaped and went to high ground in the northern part of the state. As George Wilson, he worked as a stock clerk in a country store, where he robbed his employer of a pistol and cash. In his twentieth year, sheriff's deputies arrested him for breaking into a store in Obion County, Tennessee, for which he served three years in the state penitentiary at Nashville.

Upon his release he returned home, borrowed a mule from his stepsister, and sold it to buy a wagon, which he mortgaged to obtain a team and merchandise and turned peddler; it was remarked upon later that had he set his sights higher, his talent for swindling might have earned him the acclaim of a Vanderbilt or a Morgan and a brownstone mansion on Fifth Avenue in New York City instead of a cell in Fort Smith. He was arrested again, but broke out of jail and fled to the shelter of an uncle, in tears and declaring his intention to lead an honest life thenceforth. The uncle provided him with a letter to Zachariah Thatch, a friend in Washington County, introducing his nephew and asking Thatch to give him work on the farm.

Casharago was twenty-five, a personable young man in full possession of his health. Thatch, aged and infirm, enjoyed his company, and in April 1895 asked him to travel with him on a horse-trading expedition into the Creek Nation. Casharago loaded a wagon with camping gear, hitched up a team, and tethered the trade horses, including a splendid stallion, to the tailgate. They started out, and on May 13 reached Buck Creek near Keokuk Falls. There Casharago split open Thatch's head with an axe, weighted down the body with rocks, and threw it in the creek.

Nearly two weeks passed before the bloated corpse broke loose and floated downstream toward discovery. A search on foot ended at an old campsite where a fire had been built atop a bloodstained patch of clay. Thatch and Casharago had been seen together, and deputies matched the description to a man found driving a wagon in Sapulpa, who gave his name as

Wilson and who when taken to see the body said he'd never known the man. Asked about bloodstains in the bed of his wagon, he said he'd killed a prairie chicken for supper some days before. He was taken to Fort Smith regardless, and there his story disintegrated when acquaintances identified him as James Casharago, the murdered man's hired hand. Simultaneously a neighbor of Thatch's examined a fine stallion that Wilson had sold to a breeder of racing horses in Sapulpa and declared it the property of Zachariah Thatch.

"James Casharago," Parker said, "even nature revolted against your crime. The ground cracked open and, drinking up the blood, held it in a fast embrace until the time that it should appear against you. The water, too, threw up its dead and bore upon its once chaste bosom the foul evidence of your crime."

The apparatus of justice in Fort Smith was now firmly connected to the sprawl of gears, pulleys, and plunging piston rods that stretched across civilization and ended in Washington. Automatically the Casharago case entered it, and in course of time the justices of the U.S. Supreme Court passed around the particulars, forcing Parker to order a stay of execution pending a ruling. It was at this time that he began to stay home from church, and as the days of the week lost their light to recess cases that traditionally he had tried late into the night. His face was pallid almost to the point of transparency; he appeared to be fading away like an old photograph.

The justices upheld his decision unanimously. The Fort Smith papers crowed that the gray lion had shown his teeth and the nine old men had recoiled. Parker was at home and could not be reached for comment.

On July 30, 1896, an officer of the Fort Smith jail tugged a black hood over James Casharago's head and stepped away from the trap. For twenty-one years, Judge Parker had stood at the window in his chambers to witness the execution of sentence; he was as much a fixture on the appointed day as the dread solid scaffold. When a second officer pulled the lever, many in the packed crowd turned their heads to look at the window on the third floor of the courthouse. It was empty.

Isaac Charles Parker had hanged his last man.

"Oyez! Oyez! The Honorable District and Circuit Courts of the United States for the Western District of Arkansas, having criminal jurisdiction of the Indian Territory, are now adjourned, forever. God bless the United States and the honorable courts."

J. G. Hammersly stood now with the support of a wooden cane, and the golden bell of his tenor had long since turned brazen and harsh, but it didn't crack even on this occasion. He glanced from habit toward the man behind the bench, but it was not Parker who slapped the gavel; a nobody from South Dakota had been appointed to sit in his place. Parker lay on his deathbed.

Parker lay on his deathbed, propped up with pillows, and responded animatedly to questions put to him by Ada Patterson of the *St. Louis Republic*. It was warm for September, and Mary stood beside the bed fanning him slowly with a palm leaf; Miss Patterson reflected, not for publication, that he looked like an aging sultan in his figured dressing gown. The cap of chalk-white hair—luxuriantly abundant despite his travails, as if it fed directly upon that immense legal brain, irrigated by the waters of Jordan—fit him as closely as a turban. These fanciful thoughts she kept from the record, which was demonstrably the final testament of a great man, greatly flawed. She leaned over in her chair to make shorthand notes in the light of an electric lamp on the nightstand; the curtains were drawn, creating a twilight condition at odds with the squeak and jabber of busy Fort Smith outside the window, a Fort Smith he had done more than anyone to create in his own image.

"When President Grant appointed me, I didn't expect to stay but a year or two," Parker said.

"You said that, Isaac."

"It bears repetition."

"It was the greatest mistake of your life. It has broken your heart and your health." Mrs. Parker turned to the journalist. "He's only fifty-eight."

Miss Patterson made note of the figure, ignoring the faint scent of strong spirits that drifted from the judge's wife.

"It wasn't a mistake."

"My readers want to know how it feels to have hanged so many men."

"I've never hanged a man. It is the law that has done it."

Followed one of those monologues Miss Patterson had been warned about, as Parker summed up his case before the jury of public opinion. "Do equal and exact justice," he finished. "Permit no innocent man to be punished; let no guilty man escape. No politics shall enter here. I have this motto in my court."

"But you have no court."

"No." His head leaned back, his eyes closed. Blue veins showed in the paper-thin lids. "But the court has had me."

"Please don't print that last part," said Mary as she saw the woman out through the parlor. "It will start the whole thing all over again."

"What do *you* think of capital punishment, Mrs. Parker?"

"I've never believed in it since I read *Eugene Aram*. It was the first novel I ever read."

The journalist looked for the book to read on the train, but there was not a copy to be had in town. In St. Louis she checked it out of the library, read the first chapter, and skimmed the rest, stopping here and there to read a passage. She tossed the book aside. It was a silly romance about a man on trial for his life and presented only the case for the defense.

* * *

Parker lay on his deathbed, marking time by the gong of the hall clock and the ebb and flow of traffic in the street and the passage of the filtered sunlight as it crossed the papered ceiling. The counterpane felt heavy, making breathing difficult, but he hadn't the strength to adjust it. It was hard to concentrate on anything for more than a few seconds; for him, who had listened to testimony for hours on end and noted when a small detail had changed before an attorney did and raised an objection. Charlie visited, in the middle of a busy legal season in St. Louis, and that was a certain sign. The Reverend Father Smyth, pastor of Mary's church, came; at Parker's request he kissed and put on his vestments, baptized Parker into the Catholic faith, and performed the last rites. His convert thanked him and closed his eyes. The sheet covering his chest rose and fell shallowly.

In the Fort Smith jail, the men on Murderers' Row smoked and waited. They had only the sounds of the building for distraction; the echo of a turnkey's footsteps on the iron-oak floor, the sigh of the foundation settling, the current of air passing in and out through the ventilation ducts like the tenuous breathing of a dying man. The scaffold stood idle once again; no *squee-thump!* to stand one's skin on end and make him drop ash.

Parker lay on his deathbed. He found he could center his thoughts on numbers, cold and intractible in the face of relentless arguing on the part of opposing counsels: 13,490 cases tried, not counting 4,000 petty offenses settled in preliminary. Of 9,454 convicted and pled guilty, 344 were capital in nature. One hundred sixty-five of these had ended in conviction, with 160 sentenced to hang. Upon the dissolution of the court—Parker's court, as securely his own as the British Empire belonged to Queen Victoria—seventy-eight jurisdictions had sprung up to hear complaints civil and criminal; one fewer than the number of men he had caused to suspend from the scaffold. Two others had swindled the system through natural death behind bars, five had died in escape attempts, dispatched by George Maledon's brace of pistols. The rest had been spirited away through appeal, commutation, and presidential pardon. He did not count those prisoners who had managed to escape or forfeited bond; one must make allowances for the natural will to survive. The respect and love of those wards of the United States government he had pledged himself to protect from marauders from inside and outside the Nations lay without the realm of cold mathematics, and so exceeded the grasp of the remarkable brain whose whorls had worn smooth, like the grooves on the tips of the fingers of a postal clerk through whose hands had passed many thousands of letters and circulars and memoranda from the postmasters general in Washington.

The progress of his crusade was measurable in terms of time. The James Gang had confounded the Pinkerton National Detective Agency and peace officers in five states for nearly twenty years. Ned Christie had hung on for seven, the Daltons for four. Cherokee Bill had managed two, and through the railroads and the telegraph and the iron determination of the pioneers, Rufus Buck and his assembly of perverts had faced justice after just two weeks. Decades had been distilled to days. The wheels now ground as small as at the beginning, but swiftly rather than slow. The time was near when mere hours separated the miscreant from the inevitable. He had done his part, minuscule as it was. A footnote was preferable to blank space.

Was it?

Of course it was. A man who failed to inspire love and hate in equal measure might as well have run for public office, or taken up arms against order and the rule of law.

Isaac, we've made a terrible mistake.

No, Mary. We are faced with a great task.

You will listen to the sentence of the law . . .

* * *

George J. Crump, colonel of the Army, retired, United States marshal for the Eighth District Court, which no longer existed, sat smoking a cigar in his office in the Fort Smith courthouse and considered the task of assembling boxes in which to place his personal effects, that the man who succeeded him would not have them removed to the attic, there to gather dust among the bloodied axes, arsenal of firearms, and pair upon pair of handsome boots, each of which represented a man struck down before his time and family and friends in mourning, that a killer would not go unshod. He thought also of that jackanapes J. Warren Reed, doomed to dull his blade with no Parker to grind it against, and the junior senators in Congress deprived of their devil; for surely there was nothing so ludicrous as St. George without his dragon. Crump had disliked the old bastard, but he hadn't a friend as constant.

He thought of calling his secretary to crank up the disturbing new telephone instrument and inquire after the health of Judge Parker. Then he became aware of an unearthly groundswell of noise from the direction of the jail.

He rose, threw up the window sash, and felt the whooping from Murderers' Row like a hot wind upon his face. He'd been told the same thing had happened the first time the Supreme Court reversed Parker. If he lived to be a hundred in the service of the United States Department of Justice, he would never learn how the lowliest convict in the system became aware of momentous events ahead of the official channels.

A SUMMATION FOR THE DEFENSE

In writing *The Branch and the Scaffold,* I've departed from the example set by Sir Walter Scott and told a historical tale without any fictional characters. Coupling invented people with real events serves to heighten drama, which is unnecessary in the case of Judge Parker and his remarkable court. Every figure in this book is real.

It's the privilege of the historical novelist to make certain adjustments in the interests of animation and clarity: I've introduced manufactured dialogue into episodes the record reports only in narrative, altered the order of some events, installed bits of business where details are spotty, and in the case of Deputy U.S. Marshal George Lawson and Will Lawson, a guard in the Fort Smith jail, consolidated two minor players into one. Such measures were seldom called for; the story provides so much that's required to entertain and instruct that it's a mystery so few writers have undertaken to retell it.

Beginning in 1875 and until his death in 1896, Isaac Charles Parker tried civil and criminal cases in the Western District of Arkansas and the Indian Nations—an area larger than today's United Kingdom—every day except Sunday, Christmas Day, and one brief period of rest ordered by his physician, made even shorter by Cherokee Bill's attempt to escape from the federal jail. During his first fourteen years on the bench, Parker's sentences were not subject to appeal except directly to the president of the United States. He hanged seventy-nine men, and an examination of the record suggests far beyond a reasonable doubt that all were guilty of murder or rape or both. Sixty-five deputy U.S. marshals were slain in the line of duty during his tenure. His charge to the jury at the end of Cherokee Bill's trial for the murder of Lawrence Keating (too long and specific to include in this book) is still cited in legal references as a model of understanding and explanation of the law as it applies to murder in the first degree.

But Parker's story is more than just a legal thriller. Any drama that employes Belle Starr, Heck Thomas, the Dalton brothers, Bill Tilghman, Ned Christie, Bill Doolin, Cherokee Bill, Chris Madsen, "Cattle Annie" McDougal, Jennie "Little Britches" Stevens, and the fascinating and sinister George Maledon—the Dr. Kevorkian of his day—ought to run on Broadway for at least as long as Parker sat in judgment. All are legends, and the real wonder of the thing is they all played out in the same geographic locale within a span of two decades.

Unlike most of the tales associated with the American West, these are closely documented, in thousands of pages of trial transcript, period newspapers, many of whose editors prided themselves on accuracy, and three volumes that are absolutely essential to the solution of the enigma that was Isaac Charles Parker:

Hell on the Border, **by S. W. Harman.** Three years after Parker's death, Harman, a defense counsel in his court, published this massive chronicle, with names, dates, and all the pertinent details attending the most notorious cases that came across the Fort Smith bench between 1856 and 1896, with photographs and tables listing defendants, charges, victims, and dates of trials and sentencings, noting commutations, pardons, retrials, and their results. The book is indispensable, and is the major source of most that has been written about Judge Parker.

He Hanged Them High, **by Homer Croy.** An anecdotal and highly entertaining account of Parker's life and work (even the index is amusing), Croy's book draws its material from Harman, long-buried transcripts, and contemporary newspaper accounts, with valuable new information gathered from interviews with surviving personnel and direct descendants of the principals, many of whom were still alive when the book appeared in 1952.

Law West of Fort Smith, **by Glenn Shirley.** A prolific and popular Old West historian, Shirley distilled information from the Harman and Croy sources with research of his own among newspapers, court records, and biographies of figures peripheral to his subject to create a chronological and highly readable history. He is, however, casual about some facts (asserting that both of the Parkers' sons were present when they first came to Fort Smith, when James had not been born yet), and the lack of an index among more than one hundred pages of appendices, notes, and bibliography is irksome to researchers.

Although to my knowledge *The Branch and the Scaffold* is the first novel to present Judge Parker as its central subject, he has played an important supporting role in a number of works of historical fiction. These are among the best:

Cherokee Bill, **by Jon and Tad Richards.** This comes closest to being a novel about Parker. The judge shares nearly equal space with Clarence Goldsby, with the rest of the volume divided more or less evenly among J. Warren Reed; his wife, Viola; and, of course, George Maledon. It's a rip-roaring read, authentic in detail, with much navel-gazing on the part of its eponymous protagonist.

Hanging Judge, **by Elmer Kelton.** Despite its title, it's mostly about Justin Moffitt, a newly sworn deputy U.S. marshal assigned to Parker's court, and his relationship with another fictional character, Marshal Sam Dark. Kelton, heir to the

"King of the West" mantle that once belonged to Louis L'Amour (and a better writer than L'Amour by far), is known for his intimacy with historical detail, fully drawn characters, and compelling plots, and his subject matter here delivers in all three departments.

True Grit, **by Charles Portis.** The book is best known as the inspiration for the movie that won John Wayne his only Oscar; but the role would not have been so meaty had it come from the brain of a Hollywood screenwriter. An Ozarkian, Portis draws from primary sources and his own relationship with the locale to create a seminal work in the literature of the frontier. The early scenes in Fort Smith are worth the price of the book, but what follows is pure entertainment, and "true grit."

Winding Stair, **by Douglas C. Jones.** Jones, an Arkansawyer, hit the national bestseller list with *The Court-Martial of George Armstrong Custer,* postulating what might have happened had Custer survived the Battle of the Little Bighorn, but here he plays it straight, with a lengthy cameo by Parker and a brief but unforgettable glimpse of Maledon in a plot based loosely on the manhunt and final disposition of the Rufus Buck Gang. Eben Pay, the fictional lawyer hero, is naive and a bit prissy, but Jones' creation of Deputy U.S. Marshal Oscar Schiller is his best contribution to the pantheon of Great Western Characters Who Never Existed.

Parker has been represented in the cinema with spotty success. James Westerfield was too old and bald in the movie *True Grit,* but played the role with an admirable balance of authority and irritability; John McIntyre, another fine character actor who donned the robes in the dismal sequel, *Rooster Cogburn,* was also much older than Parker lived to be, but was closer physically; at least he had hair. The best Parker in Hollywood was Pat Hingle, who in *Hang 'Em High* bore a close resemblance to the judge during his early years on the bench, and characterized him with an Old Testament clarity of purpose tempered with conscience—rendering inexplicable the decision to change his name and even the name of Fort Smith. (Fun fact: One of the men Hingle sends to the scaffold is James Westerfield, *True Grit*'s Parker!) The film and *True Grit,* book *and* movie, borrowed heavily from *He Hanged Them High.* Dale Robertson's gunslinging Judge Parker in a TV movie, *The Dalton Gang's Last Ride,* was claptrap, although it's entertaining to see Parker shoot down bounty hunter Jack Palance in a quick-draw contest at the finish.

Bloody business connected with the Indian Nations did not end with the breakup of the Eighth District Court, and a number of mysteries that took place in its jurisdiction are still unsolved.

No one ever stood trial for the murder of Myra Belle Shirley, better known as Belle Starr. The likeliest candidate, neighbor Edgar Watson, was arrested, but released for lack of evidence, only to be shot down by a citizens' posse in his home state of Florida in 1910. Ed Reed, Starr's shiftless son, remains a strong suspect. In 1971, a man named Robinson reported that his grandmother, Nana Devena, had confessed on her deathbed to slaying Starr in a case of mistaken identity involving a feud with another neighbor.

No hard evidence supports the controversial theory that Heck Thomas did not kill Bill Doolin but peppered his tubercular corpse with buckshot in order to claim the reward and split it with Doolin's wife. Glenn Shirley, in *Heck Thomas, Frontier Marshal,* called the story "scurrilous," and in *Bill Doolin, Outlaw O.T.,* Colonel Bailey C. Hanes suggested it was fabricated by an enemy of Thomas' to discredit him, but Dennis McLoughlin, in his entry on Doolin in *Wild and Woolly: An Encyclopedia of the Old West,* asserts on the authority of his research that Thomas acted from altruistic reasons and talked Doolin's penniless widow into accepting part of the reward after the fact. Whichever account is true, in a chronicle jam-packed with stalkings and gunfights, the postmortem-shootout theory is the more intriguing, and deserves further investigation.

Emmett Dalton, youngest of the bandit brothers, recovered from severe wounds suffered during the addle-pated attempt to rob their first two banks simultaneously in their hometown of Coffeyville, and was paroled from the Kansas State Penitentiary in 1907. He became a building contractor in Hollywood, moonlighting as a writer for the silent screen. His memoirs, *When the Daltons Rode,* were filmed in 1940, three years after his death from old age, but censorship required that the man upon whose autobiography the script was based die in the robbery along with the others.

George Maledon retired after the appeals process cheated him of the satisfaction of stretching the neck of the man who'd murdered his daughter. After failing at farming and shop-keeping, he toured the country with his ropes and tintypes and a piece of the original mainbeam of the Fort Smith scaffold, lecturing on the theme that crime does not pay. He died in Johnson City, Tennessee, on May 6, 1911, a few weeks short of his eighty-first birthday.

Ike Rogers did not long outlive Cherokee Bill, with whom he'd shared a bizarre night in bed and the next day turned over to Parker's deputies for the reward. In August 1897—by chance, some said—he stepped out of a railroad coach onto the platform in Fort Gibson and was shot fatally through the neck by a revolver in the hand of Clarence Goldsby, younger brother to Cherokee Bill. Goldsby, who, incredibly, was employed as a payroll guard at the time, dove under the stopped train, sprang up on the other side, and ran away from his pursuers, who were probably not that keen to begin with; Rogers had been overheard boasting that he would kill Cherokee Bill's brother.

James Parker, the judge's second son, committed suicide in 1918. It was said he never got over the loss of his father.

Charles Parker, his firstborn, married a daughter of Prosecutor William H. H. Clayton. She left him. He hadn't many friends beyond those of the drinking variety and few turned out for his funeral when he died of cirrhosis of the liver in Durant, Oklahoma, in 1925.

Mary Parker buried her sons and returned to Fort Smith, but the generation that had grown up since her husband's death did not remember the town's former first lady. She went back to Durant, where she had lived with Charlie, and died a year later. She was interred beside her husband in the National Cemetery in Fort Smith.

J. Warren Reed lost his enthusiasm for the practice of law after the passing of his nemesis. ("Our beloved judge has fallen asleep," he told a reporter for the *Fort Smith News-Record*.) He began a book about the court, then lost interest in that too and turned his notes over to S. W. Harman, who used them for *Hell on the Border*. Then Reed lost his wife. He retired to a life of senile dementia in Muskogee. In 1912 he joined Viola in Fort Smith's Oak Cemetery.

Ned Christie presents as great a challenge to history as he did to the Eighth District Court. Depending upon the source, he was either an innocent or a fiend or remarkably stupid; and the last two are insupportable by the evidence. Slipshod sensationalists have charged him with multiple robberies and as many as eleven murders, but when pressed for details fall silent. That he was cunning is inarguable. Accused of murdering a federal officer, a crime which then as now invited swift and savage retribution, he managed to remain at large for seven years, with every deputy marshal and Indian policeman in the territory knowing where he was, and when they finally converged upon him in his self-built fortress, a cannon failed to dislodge him and his ingenuity trumped even dynamite. Did he kill Deputy Daniel Maples? The picture is murky; I introduced a canine atrocity in lieu of specifics about the "disturbance" that led to harsh words between them. The long record of skirmishes with Parker's men, several of whom Christie shot but none fatally despite ample opportunity, casts doubt on his guilt in the Maples killing. I'm inclined to believe that had Christie gone to Fort Smith to tell his side of the story, he might have been released. Popular history, of course, would have suffered.

Henry Starr, no doubt in part for volunteering to disarm Cherokee Bill in the federal jail, was allowed to plead his murder case down to manslaughter and served five years at hard labor. Paroled again in 1913 after robbing a bank in Colorado, he caught Dalton fever two years later and took a bullet through a leg while trying to rob two banks in Chandler, Oklahoma. He was sentenced to serve twenty-five years in the state penitentiary, but was granted a pardon in 1919. (By now his adventures had begun to appear in serial form in Sunday newspaper supplements, where they were devoured by little Charles Arthur Floyd, who was not yet known as "Pretty Boy.") In February 1921, Starr left his automobile running in front of the People's Bank of Harrison, Arkansas, adjusted his snap-brim hat, and with pistol in hand swaggered into a shotgun blast courtesy of the manager. He died the next day, the last of the old-time Oklahoma badmen.

Defending Isaac Charles Parker from detractors is a staple of books about him. However, modern opinion of his record is more moderate than it was in his own time, particularly in the East. The fact that as many men (counting local peace officers and Indian police) died in the court's service as were condemned by it suggests that circumstances were far from overbalanced in the court's favor, and judiciary reviews have for the most part supported Parker's rulings. Certainly the men and women he felt duty bound to protect experienced no ambiguity in the matter; they showed up in the hundreds to pay their respects at his graveside service. Wherever one stands on the thorny subject of capital punishment, it is tempting to hope that such as he will sit in judgment in a case of personal interest.

As for the Fort Smith scaffold, silent since the dissolution of the court, the suggestion that it be sent on tour with Maledon horrified the citizens, who were eager to forget it ever existed. The city council had it burned and the ashes buried. Two generations passed in near ignorance of the court and its great engine of death; then, with mock gunfights being staged in Tombstone, Arizona, and pilgrimages being made to the scene of Wild Bill Hickok's murder in Deadwood, South Dakota, the city had a change of heart and reconstructed the scaffold on its original site to draw visitors. It stands in the shadow of the courthouse, directly under Judge Parker's window.

BILLY
GASHADE

For KEVIN AND KIMBERLY,
my children, delivered to me full-grown;
and for DEBI,
their mother, my world

Full lasting is the song, though he,
The singer, passes.

—GEORGE MEREDITH

AUTHOR'S NOTE

This song was made by Billy Gashade
Just as soon as the news did arrive.

It is possible that the above lyrics have never been sung by anyone but their composer. Yet in the saloons and parlors of the trans-Mississippi West between 1882 and the turn of the twentieth century, the song in which they appear, "Jesse James," was requested as often as any of today's million-selling hits, and is still a folk staple. Ironically, almost nothing is known of the man who wrote it.

The following is a work of imagination.

I

A Selection of Hells

ONE

My birth name doesn't matter, although that wasn't always the case. If you've patience enough to page through the New York Social Register—and in my time there were many who built entire careers on doing no more than that—you're sure to come across someone or other who bore it clear back to Peter Minuet.

No, my birth name doesn't matter, and I won't tell it now, even though all my enemies are dead. The truth is I've gone by Billy Gashade for so many years—full four times as many as I answered to the other—that if someone were to address me by the name under which I was baptized I'd keep on walking as like as not.

In any case, neither name displaces much cargo now. If you're the kind of moviegoer who sits through the opening credits instead of going out for Cracker Jacks, you won't find me listed there, despite the fact that I wrote three songs for Gene Autry to sing in *Phantom Empire* and two in *Tumbling Tumbleweeds*, and composed the entire score for a Porky Pig cartoon. Not bad in a Depression year for a man of eight-and-eighty.

I pocketed the cash for this work and let others slap their brands on it, not because I'm modest, but because any kind of attention sooner or later gets back to New York and I didn't want to take the chance of one of my old blueblood acquaintances recognizing my features in a wire photograph after all these years and spreading the news through the season boxes at the Met that the judge's son is making his living as some kind of Tin Pan Alley songster in Hollywood, California. I don't care a damn what they say, but my father always did, and I respect that dead gent too much to let those hypocrites have the satisfaction of dragging his name through horseshit.

It isn't a bad living at that. There are no summers in Newport or autumns in Europe, but I've a small apartment I find comfortable at Pacific Palisades with a dandy view of the ocean when I stand in the northwest corner of the living room and crank my head, a two-block walk to the bus stop, and at an age when most men require strained turnips and a bedpan I have my health. Not to mention a pretty young blonde named Myra to bring me my meals on those occasional days when I'm too stove up to go out. Her mother, my landlady, carries my rent when the studios aren't calling and floats loans to her oldest tenant when his less understanding creditors come around. But then I've always had the good fortune to make the acquaintance of generous ladies.

You'd know this one. Not so long ago, when pictures didn't talk, she did her communicating with Rod la Rocque, Valentino, and a score of other pop-eyed foreign male leads by means of a black lace fan, usually to their ruin in the last reel. She was billed as Annique Deriger, which if my drawing-room French isn't too rusty translates as Annie of the Erection; and she had her day right up until she tested for her first role in a talkie and her Flatbush accent landed her on her girdle square in the middle of Hollywood Boulevard. Since then, along with a dead husband and property, she's acquired a fair approximation of a Parisian way of speech, which only deserts her when one of her succession of bad housekeepers neglects to clean an apartment she wants to show a prospective tenant, or she encounters a word ending in *r*. Underneath that voluminous gypsy scarf and pound and a half of makeup she's a good old gal with a heart as big as a Tennessee Walker. Daughter Myra's more steely-eyed, with a clearer view of what she wants out of the film trade and how to get it than her mother ever had, but she's sweet-tempered and more patient with an old man's guerrilla ways than most people her age. I think she's been an extra in a couple of programmers over at

Fox. I know she sleeps with an assistant director there, and that's more than her mother knows. Women confide in me. Always have.

A deal more than three thousand miles and seventy-two years separates my palm-lined neighborhood from the Fifth Avenue of my youth, where I recall strolling home one day, a boy of sixteen, with my father from his club, and stopping to converse with one George Frederic Jones, a courtroom acquaintance of Father's, and his wife Lucretia. Jones was six feet and bore himself erect beside his birdlike and exquisitely seamstressed wife, who was pushing a perambulator. Its occupant, a grave little girl about a year old in a sparkling white linen dress and a starched bonnet trimmed with pink lace, took no notice of the conversation, appearing to be preoccupied with the gold elk's tooth depending from my father's watch chain, which dangled tantalizingly at her eye level when he stooped gallantly to retrieve the wood rattle that had dropped from her hand to the sidewalk. Ten or twelve years ago I was amused upon reading *The Age of Innocence*, by Mrs. Edith Jones Wharton, to learn that the Pulitzer prizewinning novelist had retained her fascination with such details more than half a century after saying farewell to perambulators and rattles. How different our lives have been. I've known associations whose gold teeth were extracted with a blacksmith's tongs from the jaws of their previous owners; but I am getting my verses mixed up. I'll sing them in their time.

My father was an expert jurist in a court system that routinely awarded the black robes to men who had simply managed to avoid personal scandal. Before that he was a brilliant and dedicated attorney with a firm whose partners had ascended to their positions by arranging not to be stillborn. So much genius and industry might have been regarded as unseemly in the New York society of the middle of the last century but for his celebrated family. That, together with my mother's line, less illustrious but nearly as old, guaranteed him membership in all the best clubs, and by projection the finest of musical educations for his only son.

I don't know how old I was when I first clambered aboard the stool of the Steinway grand in the conservatory of our Fifth Avenue town house, but I am told that at age three I was pecking out the opening chords to "Will You Come to the Bower?" without benefit of sheet music. My parents lost no time in engaging a tutor. One of my earliest memories is fearsome: A child with legs too short to reach the pedals attempts the bridge to the "Moonlight Sonata" over and over while an ancient dragon of a Viennese piano master with a Louis Napoleon goatee hovers nearby, keeping time with malacca stick raised as if to strike at the first false note. It never fell that I recall, but the implied threat remained, and to this day I am unnerved by men with thick European accents and chin-whiskers.

By the time I turned sixteen—at which point my song begins in earnest—I had performed in a number of successful recitals, and it had long been assumed that my future lay not with the law but with music. Although this was a subject of some ungallant gossip in a class that looked upon any sort of public exhibition as vulgar—this despite the fact that the beginning of the social season coincided with the Academy of Music's first opera production of the year—my parents were undisturbed: "Follow your strength" was a favorite axiom of Father's, and he would no more presume to turn me from the path that was obvious to me than he would have allowed my grandfather, a former head of surgery at New York Hospital, to suggest to him a course in medicine. The complacent belief was that in time I would take my place as a soloist with the great Philharmonic Orchestra.

Fate, however, is seldom complacent.

In May 1863, with the Civil War in full savage swing, President Lincoln proclaimed the military draft to be in effect. The selection process, based upon a list of men of eligible age compiled from the tax rolls and voting registers, began in

New England several days before the lottery wheel spun in New York for the first time. The declaration that the draft was unconstitutional, made by a number of politicians and several esteemed judges—with whom Father chose not to include himself, believing the war a necessary horror in which each must take his part—had led to a number of demonstrations and minor civil disturbances in Boston, Massachusetts, and Troy upstate. Therefore the police were out in force when a crowd gathered before the Enrollment Office on the corner of Forty-sixth Street and Third Avenue on the morning of Saturday, July 11.

The event was anticlimactic. Neither the city patrolmen nor a squad of wounded soldiers assigned to assist them in maintaining the peace were so called upon. Spectators remained peaceful, although there was a murmur of surprise when the names of several firemen from the local Black Joke Engine Company No. 33 were drawn. Since firefighters were exempt from service in the state militia, it was assumed they would be spared placement with the Union. Nevertheless the crowd dispersed quietly when the doors closed at six o'clock.

Monday, July 13, dawned placidly enough for me, if unpleasantly warm. In other years the family would some time since have repaired to Rhode Island and the cooling sea breezes of Newport, but this year my mother, never a sturdy woman, was confined to her bed with strict physician's orders to avoid travel of any sort, and Father had chosen to employ the enforced stay in the completion of one of those legal tracts that were always so well received from one of his stature in the profession. This time he had honored me by requesting my assistance, and so I made no complaint about the heat and grime of the city in summer as I struck off on a research errand to the library.

I have ever been curious, an incurable affliction and nearly always personally disastrous. When I was five I climbed by means of a construction of ottomans, pillows, and the works of Sir Walter Scott to the top of an eighteenth-century chifforobe in my parents' bedroom, only to burn my hand badly in the pretty blue flame of the gas jet that had inspired the ascent. Alas, it was not a learning experience. As many times since then as my Need to Know a Thing has landed me in foul soup, I would in my present extremity sooner chase a siren than dine on pheasant. In 1863 I nearly died of this condition.

Brief though the walk was to the library, I boarded a horse-car to avoid exerting myself in the punishing heat. It seemed to me as I paid my fare that the driver, an old campaigner in a battered shako with an inch of cigar screwed into the corner of his mouth, looked me over with more than the customary suspicion of the confirmed urbanite; but then I had been brought up to regard these denizens of the world outside the rails that connected our parlor, the opera house, our friends' dining rooms, and Father's clubs as nothing more than fixtures in the scenery, and so gave his behavior no great thought. However, as I found my way swayingly to a seat I overheard gossip among some of my fellow passengers that set my pulse throbbing.

Reports had spread that members of the city's Irish element, sworn enemies of the Republican administration that had created the draft, had been gathering in saloons and public halls since Saturday to grumble about the situation. Bad tempers and cheap alcohol was not a mix to be considered lightly, particularly when there was usually a derby-sporting agitator from rival Tammany Hall on hand to buy the drinks and keep the conversation from drifting in less volatile directions. Several horsecars on Second and Third avenues had been stopped that morning by rough-dressed men armed with cudgels and iron bars, forced to unload their passengers, and turned back to their barns with instructions to the drivers to go home from there. Other men had been seen with axes, chopping down telegraph poles in the same vicinity and along Forty-sixth Street. Plainly the objective of these activities was to seal off the Enrollment Office. Trouble was in the air as thick as cinders.

It was a spectacle I was determined not to miss. I got off at the next stop and headed east on foot. As I did so I had no way of knowing that twenty years would pass before I returned home.

TWO

The rumors I had heard proved true the moment I rounded the corner onto Third Avenue.

There the carriage traffic, normally brisk at this business hour, was halted. A city policeman stood in the middle of the street holding things in check with an upraised hand while a party of laborers in overalls and flannel shirts black with sweat strained to lift a fallen telegraph pole from the macadam to the sidewalk. Impatient oaths arose from the stranded travelers, as might be expected, but it seemed to me that there was an added edge to the cries this day. The work progressed under the supervision of a second policeman, glum and moustachioed, who stood slapping the business end of his billy stick into the palm of his free hand while rotating his helmeted head constantly in search of interlopers who would hinder the operation for reasons of their own. That he was an Irishman was stamped plainly across his features; that his native sympathies and his professional sense of duty were in conflict appeared equally plain to my (admittedly prejudiced) eye. How divided we were then, and it was nothing so simple as abolition *versus* slavery, or an arbitrary line drawn in cold black ink across a paper map. Republicans and Tammany, Irish and Negro, rich and poor, assemblymen and suffragettes, the socially acceptable and the morally unredeemable; had a political cartographer set his pen to a chart of our tiny island of Manhattan it would have resembled a butcher's diagram, with all the sections outlined in angry red.

All this is clear enough to an old man who has seen the best

and worst of his species at their most typical, but to a boy of
ten-and-six whose most daring recent act was to take the
March air in the back of an open phaeton without bringing
along a lap robe, an unplanned excursion into the belly of the
beast was jolly good sport, a prime anecdote to drop casually
into the conversation next time the Reverend Eustace Aberna-
thy's son Reginald brought up the weary subject of his sailing
holiday in Puget Sound. Even Thurlow Rainsford, whose
treasures included a brown withered scalp said to have been
taken by his grandfather from a Huguenot captive during the
French and Indian wars, would have to take second chair to
the boy who brought a bloody riot still dripping to the circle.

The building, an unprepossessing two-story brick structure
officially known as the Ninth District Provost Marshal's
Office, was not the scene of pandemonium I had anticipated,
although a sizable crowd had converged in front of its doors,
blocking the street with their numbers and obliterating the
sidewalk. Elsewhere, I learned later, hardware stores were being broken into to procure broadaxes for the continuing destruction of the local telegraph system, the tracks of the
Fourth Avenue railway had been torn up with crowbars by
the wives of prospective Irish draftees, and Superintendent
of Police John A. Kennedy had been identified and bludgeoned within inches of his life by a gang of protesters; but
for the moment, thanks in part to a show of force by some
sixty police officers cordoned around the building, order
reigned at the center of the tempest. As I stood straining to
see over the heads of the crowd, the lottery wheel began turning inside, and each name as it was drawn was announced in
a clear ringing baritone by a draft official standing atop the
front stoop in gartered shirtsleeves and a straw boater.

I was not surprised that I failed to recognize most of the
names. Percy Vandergriff's was called, but as he had just
returned from Princeton to accept a position as junior vice
president in his father's bank, I had no doubt but that he would
report promptly with the three hundred dollars required to

remove his name from the rolls. This provision, a bone tossed by President Lincoln to the Congress to secure passage of the Conscription Act, was the point of sharpest contention between the measure's supporters and detractors. It was said that it singled out the poor for military service while excluding the wealthy.

Chaos, when it came, arrived all of a piece. After about fifty names had been called, a horse-drawn hose cart with the legend ENGINE CO. NO. 33 splashed in elaborately serifed gilt letters upon its side panels swung around the corner, scattering pedestrians as the wheels ground to a halt in front of the office. This was the company from whose ranks several members had been selected on Saturday to serve the Union. On board were a score or more of firefighters in leather helmets and slickers and boots laced to their knees, carrying hooked axes. At sight of them a police whistle blasted and the uniformed patrolmen closed ranks, joining hands to seal off the entrance to the building.

There was a pause, and then a shot rang out.

At the time I thought someone had been shot *at*, and like many of my fellow seekers after diversion I scrambled away from this latest amusement for my own safety; but I have since concluded that the report was merely a signal for action. Instantly the firemen spilled from the wagon, exposing a bed mounded over with fist-size rocks, ideally suited for hurling. A window shattered. A second projectile knocked a policeman's helmet askew and he went down, either grazed or seeking cover. Emboldened, the crowd surged forward. I tried to hold my ground, but the pressure from behind was too great. With my feet scarcely touching the earth I was swept with the tide up the front steps. By now I heard wood splintering. The firemen were battering down the door with their axes, bound for the lottery wheel and any draft volunteers unfortunate enough to be standing in their path.

I saw a despicable thing.

A city policeman, sent to his knees by a thrown rock or a

blow from an axe handle, his face scarlet from a gash in his brow, attempted to rise, only to be shoved sprawling by a booted foot planted against his chest. The firefighter behind the boot, an ogre with huge red muttonchop whiskers and a great blue-flanneled belly pushing out through the opening in his slicker, braced himself then and swung his axe. The fallen officer thrust up his billy club in time to deflect the blow. However, the axe cut cleanly through the stick and the flat of the blade struck the policeman over one eye, stunning him. I thought that was the end of it, but again the axe came up. The fireman spread his feet. It was clear that he was about to do murder.

I am not a large man, and in that summer of my sixteenth year I had not yet reached full growth. I was lithe, however, and hours of daily exercises at the keyboard had made my fingers abnormally strong. With no thought at all I threw myself into a gap between bodies and caught the axe handle in both hands just as the blade reached the top of its arc. Using the momentum of my spring, I wrenched it from the man's grip before he could react. He stumbled, caught his balance, and turned my way, his face black with rage. I raised the axe and he hesitated.

For an eternity we stood facing each other across a space of three feet while humanity boiled around us, shouting and shoving and tearing at the shutters and flower boxes with which some aesthete of a civil servant had decorated the windows. Then the firefighter's marble-blue gaze flicked beyond my shoulder, and light came into them.

"Shoot the fuzzy son of a bitch, Brennan," he said in a brogue thick with Old Sod. "He's got me chopper."

I thought it to be a trick to get me to turn away, and I was loath to fall for it. At the same time I was acutely aware of two things: That my back was without protection of any sort, among hundreds whose sympathies lay with the man whose murderous intent I had thwarted; and that through schoolboy caprice I had waded chin-deep into a business that had noth-

ing to do with me, in a place where none of the elaborate
mechanisms that had seen me safely to my present age were
likely to have any effect. I turned; and in that one movement
saved my life and changed its course.

I nearly missed seeing the new danger, at that. He was a
small, rat-faced fellow, not much over five feet and eighty
pounds in a tight-fitting striped suit and child's-size derby
cocked over one eye. He had one of those spade-shaped black
beards that I continued to associate with my tyrannical early
music tutor, who was by then either retired or dead everywhere but in my nightmares. This man posed a more real
threat. He was sprinting straight toward me up the front steps
from the sidewalk with a short-barreled black revolver gripped
in his left hand.

Pinned to his right lapel was a gold badge in the shape of
a shield, of that scroll-encrusted variety that is shriven out to
certain municipal employees by the handful. Since the man
I had disarmed was one of these, and since he had hailed the
newcomer in a tone of friendly familiarity, I took no heart
from this discovery, but stepped forward to defend myself.

The sequence of the next several events eludes me after all
these years, as indeed it did at the time.

Flame pounced from the revolver's barrel. I swung the axe
in a short unsatisfactory arc, not having had time to lift it
above my shoulder. I felt the jar when it connected. Fireworks
burst inside my head, red and yellow and then black, black.
My knees folded. My insignificant role in the New York City
Draft Riots was over.

"Michael *J.* Brennan?"

"Himself."

"*Jehosophat* Brennan?"

"The same."

"Well. When this young sprout comes around I'll be asking him what he's got against doing a thing by half."

"*If* he comes around. That potato-eater knotted him good."

"Tupper, if you weren't so good to the girls I'd have Zebulun throw you out back with the slops. You know bloody well I was born in Limerick and ate my fair share of potatoes on both sides of the water."

"Ah, but, Arleen, you're one of the good ones. You never pull a cork before ten and you got the vote out for Jimmy Lynch in the Fourth Ward."

"Not so loud, boyo. Tweed's got long ears."

That this conversation, overheard dimly as through cotton batting, made little sense to me came as no great surprise. I had for some time been passing in and out of a dream state peopled with angels and ogres from my early childhood to times much more recent, and as they kept changing faces, confusion had become my customary condition. I wondered if the echoes of crashing wood and exploding glass would always be with me. When I turned my head, broken pieces seemed to slosh around inside like shards of glass in an earthenware jug.

"You lose, Tupper. It's God's grace you ain't a betting man. It looks like our lad has a brainpan as thick as Bob's bunions. Slide that basin a little closer."

A scraping noise was followed by a wet smacking as of water lapping the sides of a vessel. Something soft and damp slithered across my forehead. A somewhat soiled blossom opened inside my skull, bearing with it a dull brown throbbing. I opened my eyes, squeezed them shut hurriedly against the light as the pain went from brown to bright red, opened them more slowly.

I was lying on a rough mattress in a room papered in yellow. There was a water spot on the ceiling, vaguely swan-shaped. Although the room was oppressively warm, the single narrow window was shut and shaded and a coarse brown blanket covered me to the chin. In the light of a tin lamp burning on the nightstand, a stoutish woman in a high-necked seersucker dress with sleeves puffed at the shoulders sat wringing a flannel face cloth over a basin on the stand. Her black hair was piled high with spun silver at the temples and her face was as pale as bone china under a modest application of rouge. Her eyes, when she turned them upon me, were of a deep shade of mahogany, almost black. She belonged, I was to learn, to that curious race known as the Black Irish, who, lacking the red hair and blue eyes commonly associated with their countrymen, betrayed their geographic origins only when they spoke.

"Welcome back, young sir," she said without smiling. She never did in the time I knew her, but her eyes had a way of puckering at the corners when she intended lightness that made up for the omission. "Are the devil's garters really red?"

I flinched a little at the emerald lilt in her speech; the association was not a happy one. I responded, alarmed at the hoarseness of my voice. How long had it gone unused? I couldn't tell if it was dark or light out. "Am I shot?"

She exhaled, a short blast—redolent with fermented sour mash—in a semblance of laughter. "The ball went wide, Tupper says. You got your headache from behind. Fist or forearm?" She glanced up.

"Fist, and a good thing it was. That big red-whiskered Mick had wrists as big around as beeves."

I had been aware of someone standing in the corner by the headboard, but I knew instinctively if I tried turning my head that far, the pain would make me swoon. The man had no accent that I could determine, which was something of a relief. I was not entirely in the hands of marauding Celts. "The fireman hit me?"

"Not soon enough, I'm sorry to say," said the woman. "It would've gone a good sight easier for you if he'd got you before you made kindling out of Jehosophat Brennan."

"If you mean the man with the badge, I was defending myself. He meant to shoot me."

"Probably he was just out to nick you." This from the man called Tupper. "Brennan hasn't the stomach for murder. It was the wheel he was after. You just happened to be standing in front of it."

A horrendous crash shook the building. The woman winced. "What's keeping them broken soldiers of yours, Tupper? In a little while there won't be anything left to save."

"On their way, old gal. Yours isn't the only disorderly house in the neighborhood."

"What place is this?" I asked.

Her eyes puckered. "That's Shakespeare." To Tupper: "See, I know a little more than what the pictures tell me in *Frank Leslie's Illustrated Newspaper.* Lad, you're a patient at the East River Society House at Twenty-third and First. The physician in residence is 'Doctor' Bridget Arleen McMurtaugh, but you're free to address her as Bridey. Everyone else does except the general here."

The other occupant of the room stepped forward. I jumped at the sight of him, shooting a white-hot bolt of pain to the top of my skull. His face was unlined, but his hair was pure white, long for the fashion of the day, and streaked with filth. His clothes were smudged as well, blue wool with brass buttons and a belt with a U.S.–engraved buckle cinching the tunic; the uniform of a Federal infantryman. Soiled bandages covered his right eye and ear and that entire half of his head from crown to jaw. My first thought was that it had been carried away by a cannon shot.

He bowed his head briskly, his single eye twinkling. "Corporal Templeton Deane," he said. "Late of the Eleventh New York Fire Zoaves, serving with the First Army Corps at Gettysburg. Assigned at present to the Invalid Corps of Volunteers."

"Tupper was a hook-and-ladder man," said Bridey. "It's why they sent him to the Enrollment Office yesterday, to deal with them Leatherheads, and a good thing for you. He skidded a ball past the ear of the man what brained you and ran him off."

"Yesterday!" I sat up—and fell back in agony. Father had expected me at his chambers by noon Monday at the latest.

Bridey bathed my face. "Smooth your feathers, boyo. You've had a fair knocking."

I was loath to ask the next question. "The man with the badge; is he—did I—?"

"Split his gun arm like rotten oak." Tupper's grin wrinkled the grotesque bandage. "He may pull through. We'll hope he does. Brennan's a fire inspector, and Boss Tweed's man. Tammany will hound you to your grave if Jehosophat dies. Maybe even if he doesn't. Once it starts you may damn me to the devil for interfering."

THREE

The thought that I had maimed a man, and possibly killed him, made me ill at my stomach and incapable of comprehending the rest of the information Tupper provided on that first meeting. Even when it was explained to me later I found it incredible. A native New Yorker, exposed by my parents from an early age to the tailcoat-wearing gears and diamond-bosomed cogs that ran the machinery that governed our lives, I was now made to realize that they were but parts of a clockwork toy compared to the dynamic forces into whose path I had stepped with a single impulsive act.

It's true that in that third year of the terrible War of Secession the name William Marcy Tweed was still unknown to most of my fellow citizens. Born on the Lower East Side of the city, the son of a Scots immigrant chair maker, he had served as an alderman, a member of the county board of supervisors, and chairman of the Tammany general committee, but except for a single term in Congress he had spent his entire public career in the obscurity of that bureaucratic maze

peculiar to our municipality, a conundrum fully as impenetrable to the political layman as a Chinese box. By the end
of the decade he would parlay the twin posts of street commissioner and state senator into a pattern of influence-peddling
on a grand scale, wresting control, with only an occasional
nod-and-wink to the democratic process, of the entire city,
and by reflection Greater New York State. At the time I first
learned of his existence, he was just beginning to be spoken
of as "Boss Tweed," and eager to repair the damage caused
by his loss in the last sheriff's election to James Lynch by
means of whatever opportunity came his way.

This proved to be the draft riots; and while no one ever suc-
cessfully tied Tweed to that week of horror, no one questioned the fact that when the smoke blew away and the dust
settled, he and that band of cronies who would shortly be
known throughout the Union as The Ring stood all alone atop
the rubble.

And I, a beardless society sprout with musical aspirations,
had injured a Tweed protégé.

On that first day, however, there were more immediate concerns. Hardest to ignore was the din of destruction that
continued to drift up from the floor below.

"That would be the breakfront," announced Bridey in response to a prodigiously drawn-out splintering of glass and
wrenching of wood directly beneath our feet; and reading the
question on my face, explained: "Looters. Jackals. In another
few minutes they'll be up here, looking for the millions we
hostesses are known to stuff into our mattresses. Damn your
eyes, Tupper! Your invalids never had trouble finding this address in the past. You must have told them I sent my ladies to
the Port Authority till things blew over."

"Shush, old gal. I think I hear them." The bandaged corporal limped to the window and drew aside the shade. Outside was darkness. I now realized I had spent most of Monday
and all of Tuesday in that room, insensible. The judge would
be tearing his hair. "You'll learn to trust me yet!" Tupper ex-

ulted. "That's the Zoave regimental they're whistling. I taught it to them the whole time I was laid up."

Bridey rose, all rustling seersucker, and joined him at the window. "I hope you taught them to throw away their torches before they come inside. I'd as soon the foxes burned the place down as the ferrets."

"I must get word to my family," I said. "If I could trouble you for a pen and paper."

"Tupper here'll do the writing when it's time," said the mistress of the house, turning. "You'll trouble me for oxtail soup and eight hours flat on your back."

I had begun to protest when my stomach rumbled audibly. The creases at the corners of Bridey's eyes settled the argument.

Two more days passed before I left the agreeable confines of the East River Society House, in the course of which my world had altered irretrievably. The reports that reached me from outside were monstrous, and would have been inconceivable had I intercepted them in the cosseting shelter of my parents' Fifth Avenue town house instead of there in the eye of the cyclone. By the end of its first day, the disturbance that had begun at the Enrollment Office had taken a far more ugly turn. Policemen were hunted down, stripped of their uniforms, and beaten faceless; the homes of private citizens not involved in the protest were plundered and set afire; defenseless Negroes, blamed for the war that had given birth to the draft, were hung by their necks from flagstaffs and streetlamps; and the Colored Orphan Asylum on Fifth Avenue between Forty-third and Forty-fourth streets was torched by a demented mob, its innocent occupants rescued from a hideous burning death at the last minute by volunteers who hustled them out a back door to the nearby sanctuary of the Twentieth Police Precinct. These vicious attacks upon the most vulnerable segment of the population were especially indefensible in view of the fact that black men were as accessible to conscription as anyone, and more than most, few possessing the wherewithal to buy their way out. The Age of Reason was extinct.

Noncombatants were victimized by both sides. On Tuesday, a female bystander and her child were slain by a howitzer blast directed at a throng of demonstrators on Second Avenue. In retaliation, rioters seized the man responsible for the order to fire and tore him to pieces. This was Tupper's own commander, Colonel Henry O'Brien of the Eleventh New York Volunteers. The whole bloody business built to a ghastly crescendo late Thursday afternoon when shots were fired into a company of volunteers on the Upper East Side. With rifles and bayonets the soldiers drove the crowds shrieking to the roofs of the surrounding tenement buildings and over the edge to their deaths.

Revolted as I was by these events, I was not a complete innocent. I readily guessed the nature of the transactions that were conducted under the roof I shared with Bridey McMurtaugh and Zebulun, her huge and laconic black manservant. Indeed, I had been aware for some time that such things went on in the city. I congratulated myself for concealing my pious sense of moral superiority from my hostess. I am embarrassed to relate, however, that at one point my damnable curiosity got the better of me and I inquired as to what arrangements were made for the care of the illegitimate children who were bound to result from so many sexual liaisons.

Bridey, who was spoon-feeding me oxtail soup at the time, paused to daub at my chin with a folded linen napkin. "For some, there's always room in the sweatshops. Why don't you ask your father's friends what becomes of the rest?"

She was by this time aware of who my father was, and was awaiting a reply to a telegram she had sent him informing him of my fate. Although I failed—or refused—to understand the full meaning of her words, I read in her mahogany-colored eyes a subtle condemnation of the values of my class. I was so far insulted as to refuse another spoonful of her rich and greasy brew.

She gathered her skirts and stood. "You're strong enough now to feed yourself, anyway. You'll find fresh clothes in that wardrobe. I had Zebulun air and brush them. The man who occupied this room before you was much your size. I'm sorry to say your own suit of clothes was ruined. Join us below and we'll put you to work. There's a deal of clearing and cleaning that needs doing." She took herself out.

I arose, troubled by her judgment of my people and somewhat ashamed of my anger. She had shown me great kindness, which I supposed entitled her to certain liberties, preposterous as was their foundation. I was clad in only a nightshirt—no doubt the former property of the room's late tenant, who I had been given to understand had succumbed to an apoplectic seizure shortly after paying his first month's rent. This was a sum calculated to overcome Bridey's prejudice against boarders and silence her questions about his motives for not paying a much lower rate at a hotel. The wardrobe, in addition to three shirts, two changes of socks and underwear, and a multiplicity of collars, contained two suits—one plain serge, one checked—high-topped shoes, and a derby hat with a red silk lining, wrapped in blue tissue. I chose the quieter of the suits, which although tight in the shoulders fit well as to sleeves and length of trousers, tried on the hat, and returned it to its shelf when it proved too small, setting my head to aching all over again when I pried it off.

The shoes were snug but serviceable. Just before going out, I put my hand in the right coat pocket and brought out a dozen small rectangular pasteboards pressed in a worn pigskin folder. This was a collection of gentleman's calling cards, all bearing the same name. I put them back in the pocket and left the room for the first time in three days.

Shambles greeted me downstairs. The front door hung on one hinge, its lock shattered and all but one of its panels battered in. Not a single windowpane had survived the attack. Shards of glass and crockery and pieces of plaster covered nearly every square inch of the broad oak planks of the floor.

Great ragged cavities yawned between the studs where some-one had kicked holes in the walls—whether searching for hidden treasure or for the pure deranged joy of destruction, there was no determining. A number of surprisingly tasteful oil portraits (I had been given to believe that such establish-ments were decorated solely with cheap reclining nudes and obese nymphs romping with satyrs) had been torn from their hooks and slashed with knives, their gilt frames smashed or stolen. It was a sight to sicken the soul.

From the foyer I passed into a parlor whose curtains had been ripped down, doused with coal oil—the stench was unmistakeable—and set afire. Someone, perhaps a member of Tupper's Invalid Corps, had put out the flames before they could spread to the rest of the room, but the fine Brussels car-pet was scorched beyond repair. Here I found Bridey, in a long white apron with her hair tied up in a kerchief, fretting over the ruins of an upright piano. The front panel had been demolished as by an axe and the ivory keys blackened, likely by the same pyromaniac who had set a torch to the curtains. Big quiet Zebulun, appearing embarrassed by the tears shin-ing on his employer's cheeks, shook his great head absently and went on sweeping up the debris.

"O, the bastards, the bloody misbegotten whelps of Jeze-bel's runt bitch," she was saying, in a chanting tone not un-like that of a heartfelt prayer. "Why didn't they tear me heart out instead? This piano was the only thing my father left me. It was the one thing he wouldn't sell, including his only daughter Bridget. He had it shipped over from Londonderry with the money he made laying brick. It took him five years to set enough aside. O, the purity-spouting, two-faced sons of Grendl out of banished Cain."

"Perhaps I can get it to play," said I.

She turned suddenly, and seeing me there made haste to swipe a forearm across her eyes. "You walk as quiet as a sav-age Apache. What's a judge's boy know about repairing pianos?"

"I play. And I've watched the tuner at work. There isn't much to it, actually. All you have to know is what to listen for." I approached the keyboard and rippled a forefinger down its length. It was abominably out of tune; several of the ivories gave up only a thud. "Have you a tuning hammer?"

"I've a hammer."

"Too hard. A cork will suffice, and a knitting needle."

"Will you knit me a new instrument?" Her eyes crinkled, but there was a line between them. "Do you really think you can fix it?"

"It depends on whether any strings are broken." I doffed my borrowed coat and turned back my dead man's cuffs.

"Zeb, go up to Charity's room and see if she left her sewing things. Bring them down."

Zebulun went out, returning moments later with a small wicker hamper. Bridey meanwhile had gone to the kitchen and brought back the stopper from a bottle. It smelled of brandy. I rummaged through the hamper, retrieved a needle about eight inches long, transfixed the cylinder of porous material with the point, and tested it by holding the needle as if it were a handle and thumping the cork against the heel of my hand. It was a crude substitute for the precision tool required, but I felt the need to return the kindness of my nurse and hostess in whatever way presented itself, no matter how small.

I removed the ruined panel and was pleased to observe that none of the strings had parted. Evidently the vandals had been interrupted, possibly by the arrival of Tupper's fellow invalids, before the destruction was complete. However, several of the stops were stuck fast, jammed as if someone had pounded with both fists on a number of keys at once. I set to work to free them with blows from my makeshift tuning hammer.

While I was thus engaged, Tupper entered the parlor. He was much changed. The disreputable-looking campaigner of Tuesday night had bathed, brushed his uniform, and changed his dressing. His collar-length hair gleamed white against his deep sunburn and the fresh antiseptic bandages lent him a rakish quality, as of the eye-patched pirates of old. His expression, however, was grim.

"I got this from a derelict on Twenty-second," he told Bridey without greeting. "He had a stack of them. He said a gent in a derby gave him half a buck to hand them out."

She took the stiff sheet of paper he held out and stared at it for a thoughtful moment. "It's a fair likeness. Who drew it?"

"Tammany has journalists on its payroll, why not artists? If Brennan was sound enough to provide a description, it could be a good sign; on the other hand, they might've gotten it from that redheaded fireman."

"What's it say?"

"Forgive me, Arleen, old girl; I forgot." He took the sheet from her and held it out to me. "Tell her, will you?"

The handout, printed on the thick white stock usually reserved for election bills, contained a reproduction from a woodcut made from a drawing that resembled my face not a little, along with a written description and a legend offering a hundred dollars in cash to the individual who reported my whereabouts to the proprietors of Delmonico's Restaurant. I was sought, it said, "for the unprovoked Battery upon the Person of Michael James Brennan, a Fire Inspector of this City, with intent to do Murder."

"Saints preserve us!" exclaimed Bridey after I had read this to her. "There are wharf rats in this neighborhood would slice up their mothers for less than a hundred."

"I don't understand the part about Delmonico's Restaurant," I said.

Tupper lifted his single exposed brow. "You *are* a show pup. Delmonico's is where Tweed hangs his hat. You'll find him there more often than you will at City Hall."

I returned the handbill to him and buttoned my cuffs. "I must turn myself in."

"The devil you will!" This from Bridey.

"My father will represent me. I have nothing to fear from a judge and jury."

"You'll never see either! Tupper?"

The soldier's domino face was expressionless. "You'll be locked up in a precinct house while they make ready to send you downtown to the Tombs. Long before the paddy wagon comes, a mob will storm the precinct house. You will be dragged from your cell and strung from a lamppost. Commissioner Acton will express his sincere regrets to your family. Mayor Opdyke will announce an investigation. Aside from that you'll be just another victim of the riots, and as dead as Tim Coogan's cat."

Had a man of Corporal Templeton Deane's appearance and demeanor told me of these things a few days previously, I would have known him for a mountebank and given him no more of my time. The events of the past seventy-two hours had unsettled all my preconceptions of the world as an orderly place. When a duly appointed military commander could be beaten to death in broad daylight by his own fellow citizens, no outrage was impossible.

"I wish Father would reply to that wire," I said. "He'd know what action to take."

"Damn! That Johnny Reb saber carried away more of my brains than I thought. I met the boy on the walk." From inside his tunic, Tupper drew a yellow telegraph flimsy and gave it to me.

MY BOY

YOU ARE IN GREATER DANGER THAN YOU KNOW STOP
ARRANGING PASSAGE FOR YOU FRANCE UNTIL SITUATION
CHANGES STOP I PERCEIVE YOU ARE IN CHRISTIAN HANDS
AT PRESENT

YOUR FATHER

"Christian hands, Tupper," preened Bridey after I had read the wire aloud. "Pipe that. And me father excommunicated."

Tupper was grave. "Don't change your money to francs just yet, young fellow."

I inquired what he meant.

"Tweed may know your name by now. If he doesn't I wouldn't bet a copper against a double eagle he won't by the time that tide goes out with you on it. Your throat will be cut before you're halfway up the gangplank."

"Still, the old boy's right about new scenery."

We both looked at Bridey. She laid a finger beside her nose.

FOUR

Casting back over the terrain of my life, its summits and valleys, I find it appropriate that my departure from New York and from the only life I had ever known should have been conducted under circumstances that would shame the producer of a tenth-rate melodrama.

Before providing details, I would tell of my parting gift to Bridget Arleen McMurtaugh, gracious proprietress of the East River Society House and the lady who found time amid a great turbulence to return an impudent boy to health and strength. Having managed to repair the piano while Bridey was upstairs preparing to implement the plan she had yet to share with either Tupper or myself, I wiped off the keys with a rag soaked in kerosene, drew up the stool, and, after loosening my fingers with a few simple exercises, launched into Chopin's Waltz #3 in A Minor. To be sure, it was an ambitious selection for an instrument that had been used so hard, and which likely had been long past due for tuning before that; but it was a favorite of mine, and after such an unaccustomed time away from my practices and so many mortal blows to my complacency I needed reassurance that my skills had not deserted me.

My fears were groundless. After an awkward beginning, my fingers found the proper chords from memory alone. Chopin will not be put off by inferior equipment. Very soon I was transported. Climbing, gliding away, then climbing again toward the crescendo, I was unaware that I had attracted an audience. Without pausing I slid into a tune from my childhood, one better calculated to please the heart of the mistress of the house. I had barely begun when a voice, pure but untrained, the clear and guileless falsetto of a young girl, picked up the verse behind me:

> *Through streets broad and narrow,*
> *she wheeled her wheelbarrow,*
> *crying, "Cockles and mussels, alive, alive, oh!"*

> *Alive, alive, oh!*
> *Alive, alive, oh!*
> *Crying, "Cockles and mussels, alive, alive, oh!"*

I continued through "Molly Malone" with Bridey keeping pace—she knew all the verses, even the most obscure—and finished to a double ovation. When I turned, she and Tupper were both in the room, the soldier leaning against the door frame. Bridey flicked at both her eyes.

"I've not heard that played in more years than you've been on this earth," she said. "Are you so sure you haven't a bit of the Old Sod in your family past? Perhaps a free fumble behind the stables with a groom named Murphy?"

I shook my head. I can truthfully say that at that moment I was ashamed of the fact for the first time. "I had a governess whom I liked very much. Enid was her name. She taught me the song. She said no child in Dublin learned his numbers until he could recite 'Molly Malone' from start to finish. Father fired her for filching drinks from the whiskey cabinet."

"A native failing. Even so it was a small enough price to pay for your first music lesson. How is your head? Will it travel?"

I replied that it would, although it remained sore.

She nodded curtly. "Drucilla Patakos is more sister to me

than friend; has been since we slept in doorways and nicked turnips off pushcarts to eat. She married well and took off for California, but the odds caught up with her in Kansas. Indians butchered her man and cut her up fair. She's running a house in Lawrence with a Creole who calls himself LaFitte or some such fancy frog name. She wrote me last year. Here's my answer." She removed a sealed envelope from the pocket of her dress and gave it to me. "Tupper helped me get the words down. It says you'll work hard in return for a roof and found. Don't make Bridey out a liar."

I looked at the envelope, which contained no address. "I'm going west?"

"There are worse places," Tupper said. "There must be. Just don't press me for names."

"How will I find her?"

Bridey exhaled. "Ask the nearest wharf rat, bullwhacker, or saloon swamp. Unless Dru's changed her method of doing business, any one of them will give you directions you could follow in the dark."

"When can I return home?"

"When Tweed dies, or his fortunes change. He's a Scotchman, remember, and a politician to the bone. He never forgets a favor or a wrong. He may seem to, but it's just the grudge going underground. Them that's thought otherwise ain't here to share their wisdom."

I felt bleak. Save for the annual trip to the Continent, I had never been so far from home, and then I had been accompanied by my parents and at least two family retainers to lessen the shock of new surroundings. This journey proposed to insert a thousand miles between me and familiar things, with no indication as to how much time must pass before we were reunited. "When do I leave?"

"Tonight."

"So soon?" It was evening. I had expected to spend the night and depart sometime the next day.

"It may already be too late," Tupper said. "Tammany has

more spies than the Confederacy has fleas. They'll be searching house to house before we know it."

Bridey said, "There's the eight-fifty to Chicago, and then
no more trains till morning. Just time to get ready if we don't
dawdle."

I stood. "Won't they be watching the stations?"

"Like sparrow hawks," she said. "But they're looking for
a young man."

Something about her words, and the puckering of the skin
around her eyes, put me on my guard; but I was too much in
her debt, and perhaps too wary of the answer, to question her
further.

What transpired during the hour that followed I still find
repugnant to relate, after a lapse of more than seven decades.
I am, however, far too close to the Great Truth to dissemble
at this juncture.

I was then beardless, and more delicate of feature than
time, exposure, and the circumstances of my life would
render me. With my short hair covered by a sturdy bonnet
of the type designed to protect against cinders, and a broadcloth cloak concealing my masculine attire, I'll warrant
I might have passed for a young woman in the shadows of
a railroad platform. The "improvement" was not accomplished without a great deal of resistance on my part. Bridey
threw up her hands at last and threatened to cast me out to
find my own way through the hazards awaiting me. It was
Tupper, the professional man of violence, who made me see
reason.

"You know Dumas?" he asked. *"The Count of Monte
Cristo?"*

I replied somewhat stuffily that I had read that great adventure in the original French, although the relevance of the
conversation escaped me.

"After all those years of imprisonment, do you seriously
believe that Edmund Dantes would have refused to trade
places with Faria's corpse had his friend been a woman?"

"I cannot help but think that I am hiding behind skirts," said I, after mulling this over.

"What do you think you've been doing since Tupper fetched you here, all filthy and trampled?" Bridey flared. "Jesus, Mary, and Joseph! Why you men set such store by your precious trousers is beyond my grasp. What you carry there leads you into every manner of a fix, and all for what's inside a woman's skirt! Yet you call us weak. It don't signify."

I had never been spoken to with so much earthiness. That the speaker should be a woman made my cheeks hot. I made no more protest, lacking the words.

"No rouge, Arleen," put in Tupper. "We want to deflect interest, not attract it. A trackside seduction might cause complications."

She shrugged and put away the pot while I sent a silent message of gratitude to the corporal. He winked his good eye.

We squeezed into an enclosed hansom for the ride to the Fourth Avenue station. The streets were quiet, eerily so for our metropolis of four hundred thousand souls at that hour on a fine summer evening. Here and there, peeping around the leather curtain, I spotted physical evidence of the revolt that was even then still winding down in various parts of the city: the boarded-over windows and charred front of an abolitionist newspaper office, a gaslit gleam off the polished barrel of a rifle in the shadows of a doorway where a homeowner stood guard against roving bands of looters. As we turned the corner onto Fourth Avenue, I saw a sight that haunts me still: the corpse of a black man in laborer's overalls, dangling from a rope made fast to an awning post in front of a darkened clothier's, the rounded shoulders, lowered head on the broken neck, and drawn-up legs describing a question mark three feet above the sidewalk; the terminus of a tragic query.

I changed then. Although I would see horrors as bad or worse in the weeks and years to come, none would have as profound an effect upon me as that lonely tableau, gone from my sight in a moment, but branded in my memory for all time. Often in recent years I have seen it afresh, particularly whenever a self-ennobled Northerner born since the war has held forth within my hearing on the depredations visited upon the black race by godless Dixie. I have met only contemptuous disregard when I explain that the first Negro I had ever seen lynched was in New York City.

Civilian pedestrians were few and moved furtively. Squads of soldiers in uniform, some with bandages and slings identifying them as members of the Invalid Corps, but most without such encumberances, patrolled the streets openly, rifles at the ready. Tupper, veteran that he was, pointed out the insignia of the Twenty-sixth Michigan Volunteers and the Seventh and Sixty-fifth regiments of the New York Militia. Rumor had it that with Robert E. Lee's army reported broken at Gettysburg, Secretary of War Stanton had ordered five more regiments of the Army of the Potomac to report to New York and put down the insurrection. When I asked if that meant the war was over, Tupper pulled aside the curtain on his side of the coach and spat out the window.

"I watched fifteen thousand of Lee's men hurl themselves against our artillery on Cemetery Ridge for an hour. No sooner had we mowed down one line than another sprang up, charging through the smoke with bayonets fixed, to be mowed down in turn, line upon line. Of that fifteen thousand, not a hundred made it to the top of the ridge, every man jack of them full of piss and fire and ready to fight hand-to-hand. Broken?" He spat again. "Not as long as there's a Virginian still standing with blood in his boots."

The station was more crowded than the streets, evidence that an exodus was in effect, at least among those with means to quit the troubled city. There were soldiers here as well, and policemen in numbers to prevent further uprooting of the rails by those bent on extending the pandemonium. Still other vigilants were present, these more sinister to my own predicament. In the arched entrance from the street, and at each end of the westbound platform, men in derbies and tight suits stood studying closely the faces of travelers and well-wishers through wreaths of blue cigar smoke. One or two held a square of stiff pasteboard and consulted it from time to time as the throngs passed.

"Chin high, my girl," whispered Bridey at my side, thrusting an elbow into my ribs as we approached the waiting cars. "Ladies of good family don't skulk about with their eyes on the ground like a common tart."

I obeyed, feeling the color rise in my unrouged cheeks—and locked gazes with a derby man standing by the caboose. My heart stood in place as hard interest came into his eyes— then resumed beating when his moustache came up on one side and his right eye closed in a lewd wink. I flushed deeper still and looked away quickly.

Bridey exhaled, the closest thing to a laugh she knew. "Don't take on airs. Them ballot-boxers ain't particular as to what they take between the sheets. Last year when half my ladies were down with the grippe I fobbed off a scrub-drudge with one good ear and two teeth in her head on an alderman. He came back."

Mortified, I said nothing. I truly hated her then, if only for an instant.

At the steps to the car I raised my foot, only to be boosted aboard by Tupper, who handed me the carpetbag Bridey had packed with a change of shirts and other necessaries, including a hundred dollars in cash, which I swore I would repay. Shielding the movement with his body, the wounded soldier pressed something cold and smooth and solid into my other hand. "Something to tide you over."

I swiftly secreted the object under my cloak.

"Good-bye, Maisie, dear, and remember me to Uncle Liam." Bridey raised her lips to kiss my cheek. When I bent forward she whispered, "Don't write, don't wire. If anything changes I'll let you know. And think of a name. You can't use the old one."

"I've thought of one." I handed her a card from the folder in my suit pocket.

She stared at it uncomprehending, then showed it to Tupper, who laughed shortly and told her what it said, standing close to make himself heard over the train's whistle. Listening, she scowled. Then, for the first time, something came to her lips that I can only call the phantom of a smile. It was my last image of her.

The card read:

Billy Gashade

Entertainments

FIVE

Every seat in the day coach was taken. The brass racks were stacked high with parcels and portmanteaux, and in the dreary orange glow of the lamps sixty passengers sat hunched beneath the burden of their own weariness. The air stank of perspiration and stale defeat. It was in every sense a refugee train, making ready to propel a shipment of frightened and disillusioned souls into an uncertain night. This intelligence, that I was not alone in my situation, should have given me solace. Instead it filled me with despair. What had I in common with these wretches? I was the scion of a distinguished family, and by all rights on this summer evening belonged home, reading my Browning or practicing an étude, perhaps looking forward to Sunday morning, when Cook would bring buttered scones and a pot of steaming coffee to my room. When would I know these things again? Nothing I had heard or read of the country where I was bound included any mention of such benchmarks of civilization.

At that juncture the thing from which I was fleeing seemed not so formidable after all. Really it was no more than a misunderstanding, one which a generous contribution to Tammany, and perhaps an endorsement from my father, must set right. Encouraged by these reflections, I think I would have turned around and gotten off the train but for what happened at that moment.

I was standing in the middle of the car and in an ideal position to scrutinize the two men who entered at the rear from the next car up the line. One, tall and beefy, his great belly prying a gap of striped shirt between vest and trousers, pawed at the backs of the seats on both sides as he lurched my way, swiveling his big derby-hatted head to peer into the faces of the seated passengers. Those who were alert enough to return the gaze quickly averted their eyes, so intense was his expression. Without warning, he stopped and snatched the hat from the head of a young man dozing not half a dozen seats from where I stood. When the young man blinked up at him, he muttered an oath and lumbered on, dropping the hat on the runner.

His companion, moving more slowly behind him, was identical in height and girth, but carried himself with so much more gravity, leaning heavily on a gold-headed stick, that he gave the impression of outweighing the other man by a hundred pounds. His paunch—solid, prodigious, counterbalanced by the backward tilt of his shoulders—was contained in the black wool of a superbly tailored suit far too heavy for the season, although he didn't appear in the least uncomfortable, perspiring not at all in a starched collar and soft hat with the brim turned down jauntily on one side. His face, above a fine auburn beard chased with silver, was pale and unremarkable but for the eyes. These were large, dark, and set deeper than any I had ever seen, and seemed to burn steadily like embers in the belly of a black iron furnace. They were predatory in the extreme.

I had no doubt that I was in the presence of Boss Tweed. I was as certain of it, in fact, as I was that the man walking in front of him bent on identifying every passenger in the coach was the same red-whiskered fireman whose axe I had confiscated before he could swing it upon a defenseless policeman, and which I had employed in my own protection against his superior, Fire Inspector Michael "Jehosophat" Brennan— Tweed's own man and the only plausible reason he was here in the company of a witness capable of pointing out Brennan's attacker.

The firefighter stopped directly in front of me. His breath was strong with whiskey and bad teeth. Beneath my woman's cloak I closed my fingers around the smooth polished handle of the pistol Tupper had pressed upon me. My pulse thudded between my temples.

Abruptly, with a gruff attempt at some lesson of manners half forgotten, he fisted the brim of his derby, raising it a fraction of an inch, and bustled past without once having looked me full in the face.

The disguise Bridey had engineered had held fast!

I was denied the luxury of immediate relief; for without the obstruction of the fireman's ungainly form, nothing remained to separate me from the source of all my troubles.

Time cannot measure how long Tweed and I stood there while he turned the searching, speculative heat of his gaze upon me. He seemed to see clear through to the roots of my hair. His expression, what there was of it, evolved from bland curiosity to keen suspicion to perplexity, and finally bemused resignation, as of the philosopher who has spent the better part of a potentially productive day contemplating the unknowable, consoling himself at last with the certainty that where he has failed to go, none may visit. At this point a set of admirably manicured fingers lifted his hat entirely from his head, which was bald to the crown.

"Your pardon, miss," he said, rolling his *r*s slightly in the Scots fashion. Inserting his expansive rear into the space between two seats, he made what room he could for me to pass.

Galvanized suddenly, I slid through, brushing the front of his person hard enough to jostle his heavy gold watch chain— terrified lest I disarrange my cloak and expose the man's suit I wore underneath.

I managed to avoid this disaster and hurried on to the end of the car, feeling those incendiary eyes upon my back until the whistle shrilled again, indicating that the train was preparing to leave the station, whereupon a shifting of the floor told me he had turned and moved on.

Witnessing my approach, an elderly man with white handlebars rose from the rear seat, tipped his hat, and graciously offered me the place he had vacated. I shook my head quickly and went through the door to the platform between the cars. Here, out of sight of my fellow travelers and shielded from the loiterers at track-side by shadows, I tore off the bonnet and cloak and stuffed them inside the carpetbag. I tugged the pistol from the waistband of my trousers, thinking to do the same with it, then thought better of that plan and shifted the weapon to a more comfortable position in front of my left hipbone. I was still in Tweed's New York, after all, and far from "out of the woods," as my late benefactors might put it.

The next coach was less crowded. I found a window seat near the front and space overhead for my bag and, bone-weary suddenly, collapsed in a heap into the horsehair upholstery. On the other side of the glass I spotted Bridey in her light wrap and broad-brimmed hat tied with a scarf under her chin and beside her Tupper in his infantry uniform with his kepi canted over to the side to make room for his head bandage. From this little distance I noticed for the first time how small Bridey was; the crown of her hat barely cleared her companion's shoulder. Strange to reflect that the most powerful personality I had known aside from my father should come in so tiny a parcel. Another sixteen years would pass before I saw the phenomenon repeated, in the person of young William Bonney.

The pair were searching the windows of the train, apparently hoping to catch sight of me. For the third time the whistle sounded and the train lurched into motion. Their eyes moved in my direction. I raised my hand to wave—and immediately withdrew it, slumping down in the seat, as Tweed and his flame-whiskered accomplice came into sight farther down the platform. They, too, were watching the windows, the fireman's face all grimace and darting glances, Tweed's composed and without expression, the embers of his eyes fixed steadily at window level, letting the train do the work. As I was carried into their field of vision, I distorted my features by yawning broadly and pretending to rub the sleep from both eyes with my fists. I could not be certain that the subterfuge worked, but as the train kept picking up speed I assumed that I had, for the time being at least, "dodged the bullet." I believed then, and I believe now, that the man responsible for tending the flow of money and services that kept the machinery of the city in motion was capable of having the train stopped and searched thoroughly, and to the devil with the schedule.

Many hundreds of miles would roll away beneath the wheels, however, before I ceased to expect that I would be removed at the next stop, and yet the next, to face Tweed's retribution. The memory of those days is still potent. Even today, whenever a streetcar slips its cable or congestion ahead forces the taxicab in which I am riding to slow down or brake, I become acutely agitated. Dead these fifty years and more, the Boss of Tammany haunts my dotage.

It would be false to claim that the experience was entirely negative. Despite my longing for the comfortable and predictable life I was forced to leave behind, and trepidation over my uncertain prospects in a place—a direction, actually—about which I knew nothing beyond hysterical tales of Indian atrocities and bandit outrages, I could scarcely contain my excitement. The adventurous yarns of Dumas and Victor Hugo (to say nothing of a number of cheaply printed pamphlets concealed in an unlocked pantry by an Australian majordomo named Halliard) had made me eager to experience at first-hand the great vulgar world without.

Like Melville's Ishmael, I was seized with wanderlust. I could not then know that I shared the condition with nearly a third of the nation.

The pull was strong indeed to survive the rigors of travel across country in 1863. After the war, Cornelius Vanderbilt, like Tweed the son of poor parents, would acquire the New York Central Railroad, employ his self-made fortune to annihilate most of his competitors and merge their operations with his, making it possible to ride the same car directly from Manhattan to Chicago; but in those final days before the rise of the great robber barons of the Industrial Age, the same process required changing trains no fewer than fifteen times, with interminable waits on hard depot benches in between, and worse to come west of the Windy City.

On one such bench, in the decidedly flat and singularly undiverting town of Indianapolis, Indiana, I was roused from a half doze late in the evening by a mountainously fat man in a gray striped suit smelling of mothballs, who deposited himself beside me amid an audible settling of chins and buttocks-flesh. After fixing me for some little time with a glare that had perhaps been described to him one too many times as hawklike, he cleared his throat and said:

"Where sits the knights' master? By what name is he called?"

"I beg your pardon?"

"Come, man! Who keeps the sword of the covenant?"

I sat up, clutching at the handle of the carpetbag in my lap and cursing myself for my lack of foresight. Finding the pistol uncomfortable and thinking it no longer necessary to keep close to hand, I had transferred it from my trousers to the bag. "I think you have me confused with another party," I said. "My name—"

"Not *your* name, confound it! Are you not of the Circle?"

"To what circle are you referring?"

For a moment he remained still, glaring in a way that I might have found disconcerting had I not but lately known a gaze far more impressive. Divining at length that he had failed in the effect he sought, he muttered something unintelligible, pushed himself with a grunt to his feet, and waddled off to give his attention to the chalkboard containing the day's schedule of trains. Five minutes of that, and then he consulted a turnip watch on the end of a chain clipped to his handkerchief pocket, swept a glance around the sparsely populated interior of the train station with the air of an obese bird of prey, and took himself out the door.

No sooner had he departed than a pair of men who had been smoking cigars in the corner by the ticket window came over to where I sat. Both had on slouch hats and ankle-length dusters—the attire of the seasoned traveler, easily maintained and useful in protecting faces and clothing from the ravages of dirt and blowing cinders—but aside from that they bore little resemblance to each other. One, whom I judged to be in his twenties, was moonfaced and clean-shaven, and affected a splendor of dress not often seen in railroad depots, including a beautifully embroidered vest and tooled boots with flaps on the toes to prevent scuffing. The other, twice his age and sallow, wore a rumpled suit with a soiled collar and chin-whiskers in need of trimming.

"Stand up, please," directed the younger man.

He spoke politely, but I was slow to comply, being weary. By the time I rose, his companion's face was white with anger. "Inspect him!" he barked.

With a swiftness that made resistance impossible, my arms were flung up by the elbows and a pair of practiced hands stroked and patted my clothing from armpits to ankles.

"Nothing, sir."

"Name," demanded the man with the whiskers.

Intimidated by the turn of events, I very nearly gave my true name. "Billy Gashade."

"Proof."

I produced the leather folder and held out a card. He made no move to accept it, drawing on his cigar and letting the smoke drift into my face. His eyes were small and hard. After a moment his companion took the card, read it, and showed it to his superior, who glanced at it, then removed the cigar and flicked ashes to the floor. "What kind of entertainments?"

"I am a musician." In truth I had pondered over that advertisement and drawn a sordid conclusion.

"What tunes do you know besides 'Dixie'?"

This bizarre query left me dumb for an answer. The burring *r*s of the older man's Scottish intonations, so reminiscent of Tweed's, had convinced me that Tammany's long arm had reached me at last, but I could find no place in the hypothesis for this reference to the anthem of the Confederacy.

Now he replaced the cigar and stepped close. He was slightly taller than I, and the hot tip burned within inches of my right eye. I cringed away. "These Copperheads are getting younger by the day," he said. "I expect they'll be changing diapers in Elmira before the fighting's over."

"What were you and Major Johnson discussing just now?" inquired the other, not unpleasantly.

"Major Johnson?"

"The fat man. The conversation looked intense."

"He mistook me for someone else. He asked questions I didn't understand." *Like you*, I added silently.

"What sort of questions?" rapped the older man.

"Questions that made no sense, about knights' masters and keepers of the sword."

The moonfaced man stroked his smooth chin. "The sword of the covenant?"

"Yes. He wanted to know if I was with the Circle. He left when I asked what he meant."

"Pah!" A ball of poisonous smoke stung my eyes. "No one's that ignorant. Search his bag."

The other man opened the carpetbag on the bench where

I had left it, rummaged through the contents, and removed the pistol. "Sir."

Triumphantly, his companion seized the weapon, a handsome nickel-plated European revolver of the five-shot variety with ivory grips, and examined it. A furrow appeared between his eyes when he noticed the engraving on the backstrap, which read: "To T.D., Jr., from T.D., Sr.; The Union Unsundered."

"Who did you take this from?" he asked.

"I did not take it. It was given to me by a friend. His name is Templeton Deane. He is a corporal with the Invalid Corps."

"Do you expect me to believe that?"

"Sir, the things Johnson asked him are part of the Circle's identification ceremony. If they'd never met before, it's possible he made a mistake."

"It is if we take this whelp's word that's what they talked about."

"It's a *secret* ceremony, sir; or they flatter themselves it is. If this young fellow were a member he wouldn't divulge any part of it to strangers."

The other fell into a silent contemplation of the revolver. The younger man regarded me with a mild expression, which I was only then beginning to consider more sinister than the other's scowl. He had pale eyes without discernible brows and his lips, full and curved gracefully, turned up at the corners like a cat's. "How old are you, Billy?"

"Eighteen," I lied, not wishing to be taken for a runaway.

"Indeed. I'd have guessed younger. Where are you from?"

"New York City."

"Bound where?"

"Kansas." Feeling a sudden need to dissemble, I added, "City."

"I'm from Chicago myself. I work there. Jack Fabian. I'm a captain with the Pinkerton National Detective Agency. This is my employer, Allan Pinkerton."

Incredible as it seems now, none of these names held any

significance for me at the time. No one could have convinced me of the importance they would assume.

I ventured a question of my own. "What is the Circle?"

He nodded. "You do come from far away. The Knights of the Golden Circle is a secret society of Confederate sympathizers. Their aim is to hinder the Union here in its own territory. Mostly it's an excuse for grown men to play at pirates. Now and then they leave off the secret handshakes and coded messages and take up arms. Something of the sort took place here a couple of months ago. That's when we came on the case. We answer only to Mr. Lincoln."

"What do you do?"

"Just now we're following Johnson. It's easy duty. He's hard to miss when he's on Circle business. The rest of the time he's a barber."

"I assure you, I have no Confederate sympathies."

"If you haven't and you're eighteen, why aren't you in Union blue?"

This harsh question, breaking Pinkerton's long silence, took me unawares. I stammered out that I was on my way to visit my aunt.

"That's no answer."

Fabian was soothing. "What's your aunt's name, son?"

"Drucilla Patakos." I had run out of fictions.

The sensuous lips turned up another notch. "I believe I know your aunt. I've visited her establishment a time or two on Pinkerton business. However, the last time I was there it was still in Lawrence, not Kansas City. Has she relocated?"

Thus caught in a falsehood, I said nothing. Pinkerton threw down his cigar and crushed it out with his toe. "We'll ask this whelp some of the same questions in Chicago. We tend to draw straighter answers there."

"I think it would be a waste of time, sir. Young Mr. Gashade knows nothing we can use."

"Then we'll take him there on principle."

"It would be just our luck to have Johnson make some sort of move while we're gone."

The older man's tongue bulged his cheeks in a scouring movement, as if the cigar had left a foul taste. "Perhaps you're right, Captain."

"Of course I'm right. The fellow's a musician, not a spy. What instrument do you play?"

"The piano."

Fabian asked his superior for the revolver. When Pinkerton hesitated: "He's headed for Jayhawker country, sir. It's no place to be without a smoke-wagon."

Pinkerton handed it to him. Fabian offered it to me, butt foremost. When I reached to grasp it, he spun it around, bringing the muzzle into play. I stopped, paralyzed. Again he rotated the weapon. This time he held it by the very end of the barrel.

"You've just had your first lesson on life on the border," he said. "When a man offers you a pistol, make sure his finger isn't inside the trigger guard. Go ahead, take it."

I did, and threaded the barrel down inside my belt. The Pinkerton man nodded approval. "I'm in Lawrence often on agency business. I look forward to dropping in at Drucilla's and hearing you play."

The pair left, presumably in pursuit of the fat barber.

SIX

New York, New York
23 July, 1863

Dear Son,
In the week that has passed since the tragic events of July 13–16, little appears to have been resolved. The Irish newspapers, in particular the *Tablet* and the *Metropolitan*

Record, continue to trade accusations as to who was responsible for the disturbance, the Republican government in Washington or certain unassimilated Irishmen loyal to Tammany Hall. Meanwhile many parts of the city remain in ruins, and pledges of funds totaling $12,000 from such as A. T. Stewart and Leonard Jerome (whom you will perhaps remember as the "Uncle Leonard" who presented you with the hobby horse carved in Austria on the occasion of your seventh birthday) promise to make little progress toward clearing away damages and claims now estimated to exceed 1.5 million; and in any case will probably find their way into various personal pockets long before they reach those most in need. A Committee of Merchants for the Relief of Colored People Suffering from the Late Riots, whose members include numerous Irish repelled by the behavior of some of their countrymen, has begun to collect donations, but many are agreed that they will have to work swiftly, as the period of shame and expiation among New Yorkers is notoriously brief.

Although some hysterical reports tally the deaths above a thousand, more reasonable assessments place the figure closer to five score. The feeling in the clubs is high that in spite of the several investigations that have been announced, few if any of the true criminals involved will actually be brought to justice. The district attorney, Oakey Hall—familiar in certain quarters as "Elegant Oakey"—is a Tammany man through and through, and an outspoken opponent of the draft.

Michael J. Brennan, the man with whom you fought before the Enrollment Office, is rumored to be in stable condition at St. Vincent's Hospital, but direct inquiries to that institution are turned away with the explanation that details concerning the patients' health are restricted to members of the immediate family. As this is not the policy of most hospitals, one can but assume that a conspiracy to obfuscate is in effect.

The man Tweed has been on view in Delmonico's Restaurant almost constantly since the riots, holding court at his customary table in back. Despite his association with those principles which sparked a now-unpopular revolt, his power increases daily. It has been bandied about that that great unlettered horde of immigrants whose ballots maintain the Tweed ring were sufficiently impressed by Tammany's challenge to the Lincoln administration to redouble their support, saturated as they are from birth with the mystery and ceremony of the Church of Rome. A more earthy interpretation counters that the wholesale plundering which went on in the city at the time of the troubles has enriched the graft. In either case the Scotsman's star is decidedly on the rise, and sources in the courthouse where I adjudicate inform me that if Tweed carries out his threat to prosecute "the person or persons responsible" for the attack upon his man Brennan—some sort of relative, I am told, by marriage— acquittal will be impossible.

And so, my dear son, I must counsel you as I have been counseled, to take no action at present. I am assured by one of my more reliable (if less clubbable) informants in the enemy camp that the sun is not privileged to shine upon the same dog's backside the entire day, by which I take him to mean that circumstances are bound to shift in our favor if we can but possess our souls in patience.

The McMurtaugh woman, who has agreed to forward this letter, refuses adamantly to divulge your whereabouts to me lest I attempt some rash act that will lead the wolves to your threshold. While I disapprove of both her assessment of my prudence and the immoral way she makes her living, I sense that she holds your best interest at heart. This one thing we share.

Your mother asks me to send you her love, and to remind you to stay clear of noxious weeds, which irritate

your sensitive skin. My sole request is that you conduct
yourself in a manner that will not shame you to relate to
me upon our reunion. Awaiting that event I remain

Your loving father

The letter, creased and scuffed all over from the many
hands through which it had passed and its shifting position
in one canvas mailbag after another, bore my father's familiar and precise calligraphy, yet it found me strangely detached, as if I were reading a missive addressed to someone
I knew but slightly. In truth, I was not the person for whom
it was intended. I had taken my first step away from that individual when I reached up to wrench the axe from the hands
of the murder-bound fireman, and each one since—my stay
at the East River Society House, my face-to-face encounter
with Boss Tweed aboard the train to Chicago, my conversation with Allan Pinkerton and Captain Jack Fabian in the depot at Indianapolis, and most especially my first two weeks
in Lawrence—had carried me that much farther. I missed my
strong and resolute father, my distracted and often ailing but
always affectionate mother, the hum and whirr of the City on
the Hudson, but these people and this place that had circum-
scribed my world for all but the last twenty-one days of my
life had already begun to soften at the edges, like a childhood
dream so vivid in the dreaming that I could no longer separate it from the memory of real experience. And the realization
that they were slipping away so swiftly made me bleak. To
this day a letter addressed to me in a familiar hand fills me
with the kind of dread that most people who are unaccustomed to receiving telegrams feel when a messenger from
Western Union rings their bell.

The party who had brought me the letter from the Lawrence landing, though I had known him scarcely two weeks,
was a good deal more real to me at that juncture than the man
who had sent it. A short man, thick in the torso, with the
bowed legs and rolling gait of the lifelong mariner, he wore a

visored cap of the fashion worn by Mississippi riverboat pilots and an absurd long military greatcoat over a red-and-black-striped shirt and duck canvas trousers, the last indescribably filthy and stuffed into the tops of stovepipe boots that gleamed with a blue-black vengeance. The boots were the only items of apparel he paid any attention to, and when he propped them on a table or porch rail while sitting, the soles and heels showed evidence of having been recovered many times by cobblers of widely varying degrees of skill.

His face was as dark as any Negro's, but the undersides of his wrists were fair, demonstrating that he had not been born to the pigment but had acquired it through years of exposure to the sun. When he grinned—which he did almost perpetually—his teeth stood out in his snarl of black beard like oyster shells in a bed of Spanish moss. His full name, as he confided to me over a cup of the vile rum, as thick and black as molasses, that he preferred above all other forms of libation, was Robert Leslie LeFleur. Everyone who knew him called him Panama Bob.

He was born thirty-six years previously on the French-held island of Martinique, had taken to the sea as a cabin boy at age ten, and captained his first craft at nineteen. For ten years he had smuggled slaves from the west coast of Africa to New Orleans, eluding ships of the British Navy whose masters were trained to identify and confiscate slave vessels and hang their crews from the yardarms for violating the international embargo, until an incident at sea "showed him the light," after which he became a dedicated abolitionist. As he explained it:

"Off the Canaries, it was. We caught the eye of a man-of-war a week past, and thought we shook it as many times as I have the fingers, but then a fog would lift or we'd crest a wave and there she'd be, all sprit and sheets to the wind, coming on like Jesus at the temple, and us with a hold full of niggers. It was our necks if they boarded.

"It wasn't my idea, nor anyone else's I could name. It just came up, and we took a vote. Over the side they went.

Sixty-three there was, men and women, and didn't they put up a squawk when they saw what we were about. Some of those bucks were strong as rhinos—we picked them for strength, you see, good field hands commanding the highest price—and it took three good men to put one over, chains and all. Sometimes when the wind blows right I still hear them wailing, I see those dark heads bobbing in the wake.

"I did terrible things, Billy"—to him I was always *Bee-lee*—"damnable things, things worse than that. But it all stopped that day. It wasn't the wailing and carrying on that did it, either, or even any of those we put over the side. It appeared one of the negresses we threw in belonged to this one buck, and before it came his turn he fought his way to the rail and threw himself in after her. Not to save her; he must have known if he even got her back on board we'd just turn around and pitch him back in. He wanted to be with her, that was all. He wanted it so bad he put himself over before his turn. She was away back by then. I greatly doubt he even got close before they both went under. Blacks don't float for *merde*, you know; not for shit or tin coins."

He paused to relight his pipe, a penny corncob with a mended stem. We were sitting on the front porch, and, soporific in the afternoon heat, I was mesmerized by the sight of an enormous horsefly perched upon his right cheek. No amount of movement of his head or facial muscles would shake it off, but then Bob appeared in no great haste to be rid of it. He was the laziest human being I have ever met, and one of the most evil.

"By the time the limeys pulled alongside," he went on, "there wasn't a thing on board to tie us to the slave trade. Or almost. They asked about the bedding straw in the hold and we told them we'd delivered a load of goats to the Canaries and were off to the Azores for lemons. Mind, they didn't believe a word of it, but they needed proof to hang us, and they weren't half going to haul us all the way back to the Canaries to look for goats. The Brits are hell for keeping the calendar.

"Right about then this runty second mate let out a whoop and fished a Bible out of the straw, one of that hidebound kind the missionaries gave out. I said it was mine. The captain, a skinny old crane with blue veins in his beak, thumbed through it and handed it to me and told me to read from it."

"Did you know how to read?" I asked.

"Oh, I had my letters and could chart a course through a cargo manifest. But only in French. It was an English Bible." He put his head back and blew a smoke ring, enjoying the moment. The blue oval hung on the sultry air for an improbable length of time, then drifted streetward. "The last ship I took before my captain's papers came through was a sealer out of Baltimore. The master was a Presbyterian, and a deacon in the church during the off season. Sundays he insisted every man aboard sit still for Scripture. Being a seafaring man he was more than passing fond of chapters seven and eight of Genesis. He read from them six Sundays out of ten for two years. I'll wager there wasn't one of us who sailed with him didn't know it forward and backward by the time we reached port. I opened the book and said:

" 'In the six hundredth year of Noah's life, in the second month, the seventeenth day of the month, the same day were all the fountains of the great deep broken up, and the windows of heaven were opened.

" 'And the rain was upon the earth forty days and forty nights.

" 'In the selfsame day entered Noah, and Shem, and Ham, and Japheth, the sons of Noah, and Noah's wife, and the three wives of his sons with them, into the ark;

" 'They, and every beast after his kind, and all the cattle after their kind, and every creeping thing that creepeth upon the earth after his kind, and every fowl after his kind, every bird of every sort.

" 'And they went in unto Noah into the ark, two and two of all flesh, wherein is the breath of life.' "

This passage he delivered without hesitation in the clear,

ringing chant of a veteran of the pulpit, drawing curious stares
from more than a few passersby on the sidewalk below the
porch. Listening, I felt a deep burning shame, as if by merely
providing him with an audience I had made myself an accomplice to a great blasphemy.

"The British captain said no more, but left after poking his
beak into my cabin aft and the forecastle and galley. For the
rest of the day the man-of-war trailed us, but it was gone
come dawn. I have carried that Bible ever since. It taught
me the rest of what English I now know, and a great deal
more." Again his voice rose to a chant. "'And when thou
sendest him out free from thee, thou shalt not let him go away
empty; Thou shalt furnish him liberally out of thy flock, and
out of thy floor, and out of thy winepress; of that wherewith
the Lord thy God hath blessed thee thou shalt give unto him.'

"That is how I came to be in this great free state of Kansas," he said, knocking out his pipe against the sole of a boot.
"Certainly I couldn't continue in my former profession, and
so I became a Jayhawker and an *entrepreneur*."

This term, which he pronounced in the French manner,
with obvious relish, was as close as he ever came to explaining his function; for I never saw him do anything around the
establishment operated by his partner, Drucilla Patakos, beyond take naps and diminish its stores of rum and tobacco in
wondrous volume. When he became restless he would black
his boots and walk down to the ferry landing to see who came
in and what they brought with them. (That was where we had
met, the day I alighted in Lawrence for the first time and accompanied him back to the house.) If he felt energetic he
might pick up the mail.

For cleaning and maintenance Drucilla employed a maid
named Isabel, who I suspected had performed other services
until she grew too old and stout to bring in sufficient capital
to justify her continued residence, and the odd handyman
around town, who more often than not took his pay in trade.
Drucilla herself kept the books, scratching the credits and

debits precisely in their columns in the light of the single lamp she kept burning in her room at the top of the house. She seldom left it, and the thick curtains that covered the windows were never opened. There were sound reasons for this eccentricity, as I shall presently explain.

Lawrence was just nine years old when I came to it, but in contrast to the monotonous succession of raw log and clapboard hamlets through which I had passed since leaving the Chicago sprawl, it had a look of permanence about it, from the brick and frame and stone buildings that lined its orderly streets to the earthworks that surrounded it, erected as high as seven feet in places as protection against border ruffians. Proud it was, declaring its abolitionist principles on signs advertising the Free State Hotel and the city's two newspapers, the *Herald of Freedom* and the *Kansas Free-State*. Meanwhile that state, like the nation itself, was more or less evenly divided upon that very point, with the predominantly pro-slave Missouri border only a day's ride to the east.

Such was my safe haven in August, 1863, the Year Kansas Bled.

SEVEN

I had been in residence—if keeping to the ground-floor parlor with my carpetbag close at hand can be spoken of as "in residence"—in the house at 98 Massachusetts Street for fully two hours on my first day in Lawrence before I was allowed to meet my hostess. It was a fine three-story brick colonial with a well-tended flower bed in front, an iron-railed balcony encircling the building on the second level, and heavy wooden shutters reinforced with iron on every window, which Panama Bob told me had been added after border vandals raided the town in 1856, hurling torches through the windows of homes belonging to prominent abolitionists.

A gently curving staircase with an Oriental runner and an elaborately carved newel post swept into a spacious foyer, with a curtained archway leading into the parlor to the left. This was a good-size room rendered small by a superabundance of furniture and decorations: upholstered rockers, straight-backed chairs, overstuffed settees, pedestal tables, music stands, ottomans, and cabinets of china commanding nearly every foot of floor space, with a handsome pump organ occupying the place of honor against a long wall hung with painted fans and square and oval portraits in gold-encrusted frames. Every flat surface was covered with a shawl, and upon every shawl stood a forest of vases, candles in holders, and pictures on stands. The atmosphere, in a country most often described by returning excursionists as wide and open and empty, was suffocating.

Instructed by the austere, bell-shaped Isabel to wait there while she carried the letter of introduction I had brought from Bridey McMurtaugh to her mistress, I entertained myself for a time with a number of books and periodicals, treated myself to a tour of the gardens of Versailles and the canals of Venice through the magic of the Stereoscope, dozed in a wing-back chair pinned all over with doilies and antimacassars, and to restore my circulation paced carefully among the bric-a-brac, studying the paintings of dogs and pilgrims and bewhiskered elder statesmen depending from the picture rail. At length, bored beyond measure, I took the stool before the pump organ, adjusted it for my comfort, and, after executing the scales a number of times until I became accustomed to the operation of the treadle, played from the sheet on the tilt-board in front of me. It bore no title or any other legend, just chords that seemed to make no sense when I read them, but which came alive in the playing; a strange, exciting composition I had neither played nor heard before I attempted it that day. It was novel and original—not quite brilliant, perhaps, but unforgettable once encountered. I played it all the way through with the intention of repeating it, only to be dissuaded before the final note ceased to resonate by the sudden appearance of Isabel at my elbow.

"Madame will see you now."

I followed her out of the parlor and up two flights to an unlit corridor whose features I could barely make out, the window at each end being cloaked in heavy velvet curtains of either deep red or black. There I nearly collided with the maid when she stopped abruptly before a door near the end of the hall and tapped softly on a panel. A voice on the other side bade her enter. She didn't, but merely opened the door and stood aside. I stepped into pitch-blackness.

The room was not as dark as that, as I saw when my eyes adjusted themselves to the change; but with the windows swathed and its only lamp turned down to an orange glow, its larger contents, including a four-poster bed and corner wardrobe, were but solid blocks of shadow and the walls were invisible. The effect was of a dying star in a limitless universe, or if not that a universe made up entirely of limits, created and defined by them, as is a coffin. Far from brightening the atmosphere, the low oil flame directed attention to its gloom.

"Close the door, please."

I obliged the unseen speaker, completing the sense of isolation. A minute dragged past, possibly less. Then the flame came up, illuminating first the glass chimney and then a globe-shaped area the size of a cantaloupe. Now I saw that the lamp stood upon a small writing desk equipped with a brass inkstand. A creased sheet of paper lay unfolded on its top, which I supposed was the letter I had brought. The hand resting upon it, small and dark—although not as dark as Panama Bob's—wore an enormous garnet ring on the index finger. Darkness above that, and then a smear of reflected light on the frontal bones of the face of the woman seated at the desk with her chair turned to face me. I saw the corner of a mouth, downturned and pulling a sharp crease from it to the base of a nose with a slight, strong curve, an eye with a heavy lid, an arch of brow, as thick and dark as a man's. All else, including the entire right side of her face, was obscured.

"Bridget. She is well?"

Her voice was deeper than that of some men I had known, and she had an accent that returned me instantly to the winter I had spent touring the Mediterranean with my parents, measuring equal value to vowels and consonants. I answered in the affirmative.

"I am glad. I have close relatives in Athens who mean less to me."

"I owe her my life."

"As do I. And she hers, to me. More times than either of us can count. Which I think cancels the debt."

This made me uneasy. Was she preparing to turn me away? I knew not a soul in the whole of Kansas. What remained of the money Bridey had given me, after meals and various bathhouses, would not pay my fare back to New York, even if it were safe for me to return.

"Was your journey unpleasant?"

"At times," I replied. "There were many delays. We were stopped twice by Union troops and once by Confederates, each looking for the other."

"Were you frightened?"

I hesitated, then nodded. "Often."

"Are you always this candid?"

"I was taught to regard honesty as the first of virtues."

"You will find the opposite to be true here on the border." She glanced down at the letter. "Bridget says you are gifted musically. I am inclined to agree. Do you know the name of the piece you played just now?"

"No."

"I was told it has none. Had you ever heard it before?"

I said I had not.

She seemed gratified by this response. She nodded very slightly, then drew a deep breath and released it. "The man to whom I was married claimed to have written it for me. He was a good violinist, but not always reliable in the things he said. You are the first person I have had the courage to ask if it was original."

"I have never come across it before today, and my training has been extensive."

To this she showed no reaction; suspecting, perhaps, my eagerness to say what pleased her. "I suppose Bridget told you he was killed?"

"She said you were set upon by savages."

"Savages, yes. Not Indians, although some of them were painted and wore feathers to leave that impression. They were Missouri trash, and whiter than I. Gareth had too much to drink in Kansas City and let slip how much cash we were bringing along to see us through to San Francisco. They followed us across the river and fell upon us as we made camp. Gareth's throat was cut before either of us knew we were not alone. I fought, but there are only so many times you can be slashed with the knife that took your husband's life before you will lie still and let them do to you what they like.

"They left me for dead. It was an easy mistake. Robert thought I was a corpse when he found me."

"You were rescued by Panama Bob?"

"The inspiration was not his. He bent over me, searching what clothing remained on me for valuables. I slid his belly gun from under his belt, placed it against his groin, and whispered that he had straddled his last woman if he did not agree to take me to a doctor. The nearest doctor happened to be in Lawrence."

Appalling as I found this narrative, I was yet the same curious youth who had interfered in an affair not his own in the city of his birth, and thus set in motion the circumstances which had brought him west. "If you came here with nothing—"

"Nothing except five hundred dollars in gold double eagles

in a sack hidden in a barrel of flour. The murderers threw off the barrel while they were ransacking our wagon, but did not think to sift through its contents. This was of some assistance in persuading Robert to comply with my request."

"Surely, in your condition, he could have overpowered you and taken the gold."

"You have taken him for a shorter-sighted scoundrel than he is. People often do. By this time I think he saw possibilities in our partnership if I survived. If I did not, the five hundred was his for the picking up. The gamble paid off for us both. He has made many times that amount in our years together."

"And you?" I was bold enough to ask.

She lowered her eyelid almost demurely. "Scoundrels are more useful than you know. In his time he has shown himself well worth every cent he has stolen from me." Stirring, she refolded the letter and returned it to its envelope. "I cannot afford to employ a man to do nothing all day so that he can play the organ at night. Isabel requires help with the heavy cleaning, and there are repairs to be made and errands to be run. The room next to the kitchen is vacant. You will have clean linen weekly and three meals by the day. We shall discuss salary once you've shown you are worth these things. Isabel will show you the room."

I turned to go. Remembering that I had not thanked her, I turned back just as she reached over to lower the lamp's wick, and saw the right side of her face for the first time. It was slashed cruelly from the ear to the mouth and from the hairline to the chin in a ragged, livid X, and amateurishly stitched. Healing, the skin had puckered at the edges, pulling her lip up into a grimace that exposed teeth and tugging down the lid of her right eye—bisected by the vertical gash—into a grotesque caricature of a wink. There were other scars, mercifully disappearing into her high black lace collar, and all were white against the natural olive hue of her skin, like maggots. The result was a torn and tragic mask, barely human.

Involuntarily, I gasped. Instantly her hand went to the damaged half of her face and she drew it back into darkness. I saw the pain in her good eye when it fell upon my revulsion, which I was unable to dissemble in time. The unimpaired side of her visage went rigid with controlled fury.

"Is there something else?" Her tone was as cold as metal.

I shook my head and let myself out quickly.

My room was tiny but clean, containing a narrow cot, a chest of drawers with a brick substituted for a shattered leg, and a wash-stand with a small mirror above it suspended from a nail. It had no window, and had probably served originally as the pantry. The nights were hot, almost unbearably so Mondays and Thursdays, when the cookstove was stoked and banked for the next morning's baking. My native modesty was an early casualty. That Monday night I slept without a nightshirt for the first time in my life, lying naked and awash in perspiration on top of the sheets.

I had little time for homesickness. Isabel—housekeeper, cook, and now head of the household staff—kept me busy chopping and splitting wood in the backyard, filling and carrying in buckets of water from the pump, scrubbing the windows inside and out (with the exception of those on the top floor), feeding the chickens that scratched inside the fenced-off area behind the house and raiding their nests for eggs, and buying supplies and provisions at the mercantile nearby, called simply the Country Store. In between these regular chores, I replaced the odd broken hinge, pounded home the occasional rebel nail, and cleaned and refilled the lamps. These operations were time-consuming, as I had scarcely held a hammer or a screwdriver in my life, and poor Isabel was forced to take on the added duties of nurse to my swollen thumbs and burst blisters.

The food was unadventurous but hearty: salted ham, boiled potatoes, steamed greens, and white biscuits that flaked apart at a touch, smothered with gravy and heaps of melting butter and washed down with pots of scalding coffee, followed by peach cobblers, mincemeat pies, and strawberry shortcake. My appetite, indifferent at best in New York, became robust due to increased exercise, and I gained weight rapidly, which is not to say that I grew fat; I was a reedy youth to begin with, and still growing. At night, exhausted, I became senseless the instant my body made contact with the mattress and slept without dreaming straight through to dawn, when my day would begin all over again with morning chores and a breakfast of eggs, sausages, corn bread, and pancakes with honey.

Manhood came to me during this period. Stimulated by the motion of the axe and the weight of the water buckets, the muscles in my back and shoulders took on definition and strained the shoulders of my blue serge when I donned it in the evenings to play the organ. And I felt a man's desires.

The four women who shared the house with Drucilla and the maid were bound by a city ordinance regulating the conduct of women of their calling never to appear below the second story less than fully clothed, with all buttons fastened and ankles and bosoms decently covered. My duties as handyman without portfolio took me to every floor, and it was my fate to stand for no small amount of feminine sport, which in the hands of women whom society has already declared outcast can devastate the sensibilities of a burgeoning male.

For helping me to resist bewitchment I was grateful to my father, a man of the world whose jurist's-eye view of human frailty had given birth to the frankest and sternest advice a man could provide for his son. At the time it seemed that he had foreseen everything, and even now I can detect only merit in his proposed mechanism for the prevention of surrender and disgrace.

However, not even Father could prepare me for what went on at 98 Massachusetts Street while western civilization crumbled around it like so much wormy bread.

EIGHT

The *inventory*—for such was the term Panama Bob employed in reference to the women who resided on the second floor at Drucilla's, enamored as he was with the *entrepreneurial* life—was at its low point when I discovered it. Serena, who held greatest seniority after Isabel and Drucilla herself, was away visiting her brother in a Baltimore hospital, where he was recovering from injuries received at Gettysburg. Another, Zoe, had deserted the profession for the Church, which Bob assured me was a common nuisance, "whores spending as much time as they do staring up." Two more had wed soldiers with the Tenth Missouri Volunteers and were following that body south behind General Sherman. The reformed slaverunner was confident, however, that Drucilla would soon find more applicants than she had rooms in which to put them up. "War widows," he confided, grinning despicably in his tarry beard.

Of the four women who remained, Ada, a fleshy, motherly sort with sunset-colored hair caught behind her head with combs, busied herself the day long darning the hose of her fellow residents and lecturing them good-naturedly upon such practical matters as the importance of not powdering one's neck too close to the collar of one's dress to avoid frequent laundering; Carmel, pale, black-haired, and slender—nearly translucent by lamplight—spoke with a soft and cultured Southern lilt that cracked upon occasion, when she would deliver an oath more suited to a Biloxi alley than a plantation ballroom; Rachel, a tall octoroon with haunted eyes and a pronounced addiction to snuff, held herself aloof from the others, a mode of behavior not calculated to win their admiration, particularly in view of the fact that she was known to receive black freedmen at the back door when she wasn't engaged with a white customer in the parlor; and

Veronica, the youngest and freshest, upon whom Isabel doted, contrary to her habitual attitude of reserved contempt for the world and its population, dressing the girl's strawberry-blond hair in the sausage curls then fashionable among young ladies of the local aristocracy and outfitting her in frothy dresses of pale blue and champagne pink trimmed with lace.

Veronica. Close to my age, bright, feral-eyed, and determined after the manner of the indisputably spoiled to satisfy her basest desires at the moment they occurred, this tiny creature caused me more vexation than the other three combined; but not, as it turned out, my undoing. That dubious prize went to another.

Saturday nights were busiest. Lawrence was a recruiting center for the Union Army, and when the guards deployed to protect the enrollment office fell out, with no place for them on the duty roster until the following Monday, the foyer and parlor became a sea of Federal blue. Isabel carried their names and calling cards upstairs to her mistress, who considered them and arranged assignations in order of rank. Those who were forced to wait were made as comfortable as possible in the seats available while the maid passed among them with glasses of brandy and trays of sandwiches. I performed requested tunes on the organ, and in so doing learned a great deal about the musical preferences of men stranded far from home and family.

I expected that their tastes would run toward the bawdy and boisterous, and indeed there were those who fulfilled that expectation; but their suggestions were shouted down almost invariably in favor of the sentimental and, as the evening wore on and the liquor had made the rounds several times, the mawkish and maudlin. Complying, I wondered idly what the gentlemen's bordellos back home would make of "Aura Lee," "The Riddle Song," and "The Gypsy Laddie." To be sure, when these homely ballads of love and faith and purity had reduced every man within earshot to helpless tears, someone would call for a "right rouser," and elicit no protest. In this category, "The Arkansas Traveler" was the clear favorite, followed closely by "Jeannie with the Light Brown Hair." On those occasions when the group's spirit became martial, the selection was less likely to be the belligerent "Rally 'Round the Flag" or the righteous "John Brown's Body" as the melancholy and pensive "Darling Nellie Gray," about a slave girl sold away from her lover's side. What they sang about in the barracks I cannot say, but I came to conclude that with physical fulfillment so near—literally, the distance of a single flight of stairs—these trained and experienced men-at-arms found the security to indulge themselves at long last in reflections on what they had left behind.

Carmel, she of the spectral complexion and Delta drawl, sang between her upstairs appointments, disclosing a choir-trained voice and what amounted to an inexhaustible memory for lyrics, no matter how obscure. She stood close to the organ without moving, hands clasped below her bosom, the scent of her personal blend of lilacs and jasmine (with the slightest hint of the camphor she and the others employed to prevent inconvenient pregnancies) drifting my way, and to this day I find that I cannot play "Wondrous Love" or "Lucy Locket" without detecting that delicate combination; or pass a scent shop that features it without hearing one of those tunes in my head. She had a lovely voice, which worked to rob her favorite gutter expressions of their intended effect. Raised in song, it never failed to subtract, for some little time, the bleakness of combat from the haggard faces of her listeners.

This was Saturday. Sundays we closed, and on weeknights business was sporadic, the clientele checkered. It was then, when the troops were confined to the post, that I learned how well known Drucilla's establishment was outside the city of Lawrence. Although hardly the only disorderly house in this community of twelve hundred, it was the one located closest to the eastern limits, and as the first encountered by visitors from across the border, the one most familiar to Missourians traveling west.

"Look livesome, Bee-lee," was Panama Bob's advice to me the first time one of these individuals was shown into the parlor with me at the keyboard; whereupon the former slaver left the room, to return a few minutes later carrying a single-barreled shotgun, which he leaned conspicuously in the corner near where he sat drinking from his ubiquitous cup with a bottle of black rum at his elbow.

This ostentation wasn't entirely superfluous. The stranger who had prompted it, a long, bony specimen of the great outdoors, with the raw neck and knoblike knuckles of the life-long farmer, wore a shining black slicker—for it was raining heavily—over a curious knit pullover buttoned to the neck, and although he surrendered his hat to Isabel, muttered that he would keep the coat. This was unconventional, as the atmosphere in the overfurnished parlor was close and the weight of the oilcloth on his shoulders must have been uncomfortable. I divined immediately that he was "packing iron," and unwilling to expose his weaponry to the strangers present. His untrimmed hair and day's growth of beard aged him, but I placed him in his early twenties. His eyes were older.

It appeared that he had stated his wishes to Isabel, for when that grave lady returned he rose from the edge of the hard seat where he had placed himself and accompanied her through the curtains. His spurs clanked when he walked. Leather creaked.

"Freebooter," spat Bob when he had gone. "Pro-slave Missouri murdering trash. I cannot think why she countenances it."

"Who, Drucilla?" I went on playing.

"Any of them. A whore who lies with a pig hasn't far to go to touch bottom."

"How are you certain he's from Missouri?"

"He has the guerrilla stink all over him. Did you mark that business with the slicker?"

"He is armed, of course."

"Show me a man who is not. This one didn't leave anything behind. I want his horse. Any animal that can haul that much iron across the river on a wet night like this could pull boxcars. What's that you are playing?"

"A fugue. Bach."

"Well, I don't know what language that is, but our cutthroat friend seemed to like it."

"I noticed he was watching my hands."

"He was watching everyone's hands. That's how you know a killer."

"I thought it was the eyes."

He showed his startling teeth. "You have read too many of the penny dreadfuls. Eyes do not kill."

"Perhaps he didn't care for the music after all."

"He cared. It would surprise you to know how simple a brute is, and what may tame him. I know of one, surrounded by enemies, who hesitated to whip his horse through a gap that might have saved him because he feared to trample a stray dog. His death was messy."

"A horse? I thought all your adventures took place at sea."

"It is a story I heard," he said.

I had no opportunity to pursue the point, for he left the parlor shortly thereafter, and when I asked about him the next morning I was informed by Isabel that he had saddled his horse and left during the night. When he returned some days later, exhausted and covered with mud and dust, he was uncommunicative, but after some sixteen hours' sleep and an enormous breakfast he was again his convivial, anecdotal self, although he made no reference to where he had been or what he had done, nor would he be drawn out on the subject. Ada, ever the fount of information on the doings of the household, told me over her darning egg and needle that Panama Bob's frequent unexplained absences were a point of much discussion among "the ladies," some of whom held the opinion that Drucilla had a rival on the Missouri side of the border.

"And what opinion does Ada hold?" I asked, mocking her habit of referring to herself in the third person.

"Ada's older and less romantic. For Drucilla to have a rival, she'd have to be interested in Bob to begin with, and you'd easier breed a Kansas mare with a barnacle than get them two together over anything more tender than a cash box."

"Then where does he go, and what does he do once he gets there?"

"I'd only be guessing. I've not seen Bob with his drawers down—he likes 'em young and skinny, thank the Lord—but I'm thinking if I did I'd not be shocked to see his limbs are bright scarlet."

This was not as enigmatic a remark as she may have intended, thinking me an ignorant Easterner. In fact I had overheard a great many conversations in the day coaches and depots on my way west, and had gleaned something of the long history of raids and counterraids into each other's territory launched by the pro-slave Missouri night riders and the abolitionist Kansas "Jayhawkers." There were men on both sides who took advantage of the breakdown in law and order to settle private scores and carry away plunder. These jackals were known universally by a colorful and sanguinary nickname.

"Bob's a Redleg?"

I could not see her expression, bent over her work as she was; but the hand holding the needle hesitated between stitches, then resumed moving with a fresh purpose. "I'll never get through my sewing for all this jabber. I thought you came for the bedding."

I gathered the soiled sheets and pillowcases from her iron-framed bed and carried them out back, where Isabel was scrubbing the laundry in a great cauldron designed for scalding hogs; the amount of washing to be done among even that reduced workforce having long since outgrown an ordinary wooden tub. I was filled with thought. My initial judgment of Panama Bob's character—that he was a blackguard masquerading as a soul reformed—was correct, and I should have felt some satisfaction. However, I had experienced at firsthand the special horrors of wickedness done in support of a creed, and found it more distasteful than blind, unthinking evil. LeFleur the unregenerate pirate and slaverunner would have been easier to accept than Bob the Bible-quoting night rider, espousing by day the virtues of freedom for all and looting the homes and businesses of known or suspected pro-slavers under cover of darkness for his own aggrandizement. Very possibly he had committed murder: The story of the man gone to a bloody death for love of a dog had sounded like an incident witnessed rather than a rumor heard. I thought it conceivable that Bob had been among his slayers.

There was no one in whom I could confide my feelings in this matter. The issue in this part of the world was heated, and I could not be sure of a sympathetic ear. Drucilla alone, on the evidence of our discussion on the day of my arrival, might have handled the situation with reason and logic, but I was quickly made to understand that our meeting in her quarters was unprecedented, and would not be repeated. Isabel, who brought her meals and carried out the chamber pot, was the sole resident allowed regular access to that darkened room. Even Panama Bob visited there by appointment only. Its occupant seldom ventured out during the day, and never appeared below the top floor before dark. On hot nights when sleep was slow in coming, I would hear the squeak of a floorboard outside my room or the scrape of a chair, and I would know that the mistress of 98 Massachusetts Street was abroad in the house, carrying a lamp from room to room, surveying her monarchy at the only hour during which she felt secure enough to expose her ruined face outside her self-enforced exile. After many years spent searching my soul I can say with confidence that it was not fear of her deformity that prevented me from getting up and opening my door when I sensed her presence just outside it, but respect for the privacy of the only person who had shown me charity west of Bridey McMurtaugh's East River Society House.

At other times I showed my gratitude in a way less passive.

Some nights, when the last customer had drifted out the door on a cloud of personal satisfaction and the "inventory" had retired, I would produce the stained and yellowed sheet of music that had greeted me the first time I sat at the organ and play, as softly as the instrument allowed, the composition left by Drucilla's slain husband. I was certain that its strains reached clearly to the top of the house, where its subject sat at her writing desk entering the evening's transactions in the ledger and waiting for the hours to grow small, and yet I received neither word nor signal that she had heard; which I took to mean that she did not disapprove. I never played the piece at any other time. Indeed, though I know it by heart, I haven't played it in twenty years, not since the news reached me that Drucilla was dead.

When I state that she was my only source of charity, I am not forgetting the contribution made by the women of the second floor, which carried a price. As the sole male on the premises apart from Bob, who had sampled the charms of all save the matronly Ada—with special attention to the octoroon Rachel, whom he seemed to have convinced himself he was freeing, if only a little bit at a time—I was their "meat," particularly desirable because of the shared view that I was a virgin, and the first such in the vicinity since Shiloh.

Subtlety was not a weapon in their armory. A visit to an upstairs room to deliver clean linens or to unstick a swollen window was invariably a fresh lesson in the mysteries of the female anatomy, as I was forever "surprising" the occupant in an advanced state of deshabille, despite conscientious knocking at the door. I learned, among other things, that Carmel had a small tattoo on her right hip that she thought was a pineapple, but which I, being familiar with that overemployed symbol of Victorian hospitality, should have thought more closely resembled a thistle; that Rachel—cool, distant Rachel—was the same even butterscotch color all over, with the exceptions of her palms and the soles of her feet, which were pink—and that Veronica spent most of the money she earned ordering lacy black undergarments from a company in New Orleans, whose catalogue Panama Bob had brought with him across the continent for the purpose of starting fires.

This youngest of Ada's "ladies" had been such a reliable customer that the firm had sent her, free of charge, a sampling of its most popular scents with its last shipment. These she insisted on daubing upon inaccessible parts of her person and asking my opinion of their value. This I declined to do, but it would be less than honest of me to assert that I was not tempted. She was an extremely pretty girl, well formed in the slightly overupholstered fashion that passed for feminine beauty in those innocent days, and framed to perfection in the best artifice of Beechlove's Parisian Stays & Garters, Ltd.

Honesty eludes me yet. I did not decline. I fled.

Out of her room and down the hall, still carrying bunched under one arm the blue-and-white counterpane I had brought, fresh from an outdoors airing, for Veronica's bed. Down the hall, and into a near collision with Ada, who curled her fleshy arms around me, cooing and whispering phrases of motherly comfort, and drew me into the sanctuary of her room.

NINE

This was Thursday, August 20, 1863; a date that many another who survived to tell of it would remember for reasons other than a boy's first experience with the physical act of love.

As I lay, thoroughly spent, in Ada's slumbering embrace in the old gold light of a late-summer Kansas afternoon, another young man, only ten years my senior, with Quaker-ish long hair and the sparse beginnings of a ginger-colored moustache, was preparing, at the head of a column of three hundred men, to cross the border from Missouri and de-stroy whatever illusions I retained that I lived in a Christian country. His name was William Clarke Quantrill.

I had heard the name exactly twice since coming to Law-rence, both times in the form of a jest. Once, awaiting my turn at the counter of the Country Store behind an enormous farmer in dirt-smeared overalls and thick-soled boots laced up to his knees, I overheard the farmer inquire of the clerk, Jim Perine, if he had seen anything yet of Captain Quantrill.

Perine, a long-faced, stoop-shouldered man who never smiled when I was present, lowered his left eyelid in a sol-emn wink and replied, "No, but yesterday's receipts came up three cents short, so I expect he's been in."

The farmer hoisted his sack of flour and went out past me, shoulders shaking.

On another occasion, as I was sweeping the steps in front of Drucilla's, a portly, white-maned gentleman in a frock coat, whom Panama Bob had pointed out to me as a Judge Carpenter, paused in mid-stroll at the end of the block to ob-serve a bearded fellow unloading a crate from the back of a buckboard in front of Palmer's gun repair shop. Cupping his hands around his mouth, the judge cried: "Watch your back, Ed! Quantrill's behind you!"

The man swiveled, face expressionless, with the crate bal-anced on his shoulder. He burst out laughing at the sight of a scruffy yellow dog raising its leg to urinate on the wagon's left rear wheel.

"Sorry, Ed!" called the judge. "Honest mistake."

Bob, who made it his business to know every affair not connected with the day-to-day drudgery of keeping Drucil-la's house prosperous, explained to me that the rumor had been abroad for months that the Missouri guerrilla chief was planning to attack Lawrence, slaughtering prominent

Jayhawkers and burning the city to the ground. For a time armed guards were stationed at all the roads leading into town, but when nothing happened after several weeks the panic subsided and people began to joke about the threat they believed had passed. The guards were withdrawn, and Lawrence resumed its routine as a backwater of the war.

Quantrill's hatred of Kansas was legend. At age twenty-six, having pursued the variant careers of Sunday school teacher, horse thief, and gambler, this Ohio native had nursed a grudge for the state since his expulsion in 1858 for stealing from his fellow Johnson County settlers. Another story, believed by many to have been invented by Quantrill himself, held that his older brother had been murdered in a raid led by Senator Jim Lane, the Jayhawker chief later responsible for the burning of Osceola, Missouri. Whatever the story's truth or lack of it, the sack of Osceola was reason enough for the embittered irregulars who rode with Quantrill to harbor a loathing for Lawrence—home to Senator Lane, whose raw-boned frame and head of flame-colored hair were celebrated locally with the fervor reserved for the native son who had distinguished himself in the world.

Commissioned a captain of partisan rangers by no less an authority than General Sterling Price of the Confederacy, Quantrill commanded a cavalry of 150, hardened campaigners all, their souls afire with the will for vengeance, plunder, and death to any abolitionist who crossed their path. An equal number of men led by Confederate Colonel Holt joined them at Lone Jack, and together the forces crossed the border south of Kansas City at five o'clock in the evening. Above their heads snapped the black flag of the damned.

I knew none of this at the time, of course; and if I gave any thought to the man Quantrill at all, I suppose I considered him a half reality at best, largely an ogre fabricated for the purpose of frightening children lest they stay up past their retirement hour or neglect the greens on their plate. No, as I lay partially dozing in the arms of Ada (who snored, I am unchivalrous enough to report, like a teamster), smelling of her not inconsiderable ardor, my reflections were those of discovery. So this, I thought, was what all the stir was about; the low whispers between husband and wife that ceased abruptly when a child entered the room, the sniggering speculation of filthy little boys on a street corner, the indecent jests and bellows of coarse laughter shared by grown men in rooms filled with smoke and ferment, out of ladies' earshot. After so much anticipation, I found it oddly unsatisfying, somewhat depressing, and, to one of my fastidious temperament, untidy in the extreme. And I felt that I could not wait to experience it again.

I was watching Ada's face when her eyes opened. She blinked away the blurriness, recognized me, frowned, and remembered. I smiled tentatively. She disengaged an arm, fumbled on the nightstand for the decorative watch she pinned to her dress when she went downstairs, held it close to her face, mewed, and threw aside the covers violently. I watched uncomprehending as she stooped and slid something out from under the bed. When she hiked up her nightdress and squatted on the chamber pot, I swung my feet to the floor and put on my clothes quickly. Not a word had passed between us from the moment she took me into her room until I let myself back out into the hall.

Thus was my initiation to the pleasures of the flesh. Women to whom I have related its details are usually unsympathetic. I am told that the aftermath is not often different when the man is the seducer. In any case, I have been with many women since, and knowing from experience the sting of being cast to one side immediately upon conquest, I have tried always to make the coda as tender as the overture. However successful the result, it is a scrap of wisdom I owe to Ada, who little realized what she had wrought in her fever to beat her younger, prettier rivals to the finish, and who I suspect would not have cared had she known.

Am I guilty of hindsight when I maintain that I felt an impending Something when I descended the stairs that evening to take my place at the organ? Very likely. An old man's recollections are not entirely to be trusted. Yet I distinctly remember noticing the way the hairs on the backs of my hands stood erect when I ran through the scales, and feeling acute discomfort for the first time at being forced to sit with my back to the parlor entrance. I found myself glancing back over my shoulder often. Hindsight perhaps. The fact remains that I was watching the curtains when the tall, bony young man came through whom I had last seen the night Panama Bob disappeared on his most recent mysterious excursion. Tonight he wore a duster in place of the oilcloth slicker, and this time he was not alone.

Fiends I have known in plenty, and yet I never met a man I feared at first sight as I feared this new stranger. In attire there was nothing to mark him from the usual customer who drifted in of a weeknight: slouch hat with a broken brim, canvas coat darned and patched all over and fraying at the cuffs, ticking trousers reinforced with leather along the inseam, dusty boots run-down at the heels and nearly worn through at the toes. His face was another matter. Fine-skinned if deeply burned, the features even and recently shaved, it belonged on the shoulders of a marble statue but for the eyes. These were pale, startlingly so in their dark setting, and stared straight ahead without blinking, seeming to see everything while making contact with nothing, and giving nothing back. The eyes of a corpse, and not one who had surrendered its shade peacefully. Behind them raged the fire that burned without consuming.

I was playing, I remember, "Sally in Our Alley," much to the delight of the local visitors, whose preferences varied in a backward direction from those of the soldiers. Colonial songs were greatly prized, possibly because they invoked thoughts of the gentler times of their grandfathers, or at least a time when the enemy was foreign—a Brit, nothing less, who wore a scarlet coat and honked through his nose like a gander when he spoke—and less likely to be a close relative from a slave state. Carmel being engaged upstairs, a number of the men had gathered around the organ and raised their not entirely incompatible voices in an approximation of Henry Carey's lyrics. Some of them tended to rush the melody, while others lagged behind, and as it required concentration not to fall into their bad habits I lost track of the two newcomers until I heard a voice close to my ear.

" 'Bonnie Blue Flag.' "

The request was a whispered sibilant, and affected me as would a venomous snake dropping from the ceiling to my shoulder. I missed a beat, let two more go by before I picked up the chord, and shook my head without taking my eyes off the music sheet. I knew without looking that the man who had placed the request was the man I have just described.

" 'Bonnie Blue Flag.' " This time the whisper was accompanied by a metallic click.

I smelled sharp oil and felt the cold of the steel behind my right ear. The stranger was standing behind me and to the right, with his body twisted to the left, shielding the pistol from the others, who were declaring that if it weren't for Sally they'd rather be slaves and row a galley.

I was in a quandary. I had no doubt, based on the stranger's frightening appearance, that he would not hesitate to squeeze the trigger if I ignored his demand to play the rebel march. At the same time I held no illusions that the boisterous good fellowship of these Kansans and Free-Staters would not turn to violence before the first verse was out. Their initial inclination would be to tear to pieces the same musician whose skills they were now celebrating so loudly.

"I don't know it," I said at last.

"You got thirty seconds to learn. After that you won't have brains enough to finish that piece you're playing."

I longed for Panama Bob and his shotgun; but I had not seen him since morning, at which time he had already made serious inroads in his day's allotment of rum. Ada had told me it was ever thus when he returned from a protracted absence: "Three days flat on his arse to each one in the saddle. That's the count, and there's no changing it."

"You are one stubborn bluebelly," said the man with the pistol.

I shrank from the blast I knew was coming. Then a new body blocked the light from the corner lamp. I thought at first it was Bob, and turned my head that way in relief. My heart went sour when I recognized the gaunt young man who had come in with my tormentor.

"It's no good, John." His voice was thin, with the clear high twang of the Missouri hill country. "There's four of them to a man."

"Brings the odds just about even," said the other, but after another moment the hammer snicked back into place and the muzzle was withdrawn. Deliverance flooded my veins.

The pair left, and the rest of the evening was uneventful. Exhausted by the day's momentous events, I retired as soon as the last customer was out the door, unaware that the next day would be the longest of my life.

I couldn't know at the time, but as I turned out the downstairs lamps the bloodshed was beginning. At around eleven P.M. the main body of guerrillas swept through the village of Gardner on the Santa Fe Trail, firing buildings and shooting down the half-dozen or so men who came running to put out the flames. Four hours later they kidnapped a boy in Hesper and forced him to agree to guide them through the well-bottom blackness of a moonless night to Lawrence. In the gray light of dawn, the column trotted bold as brass down the main street of Franklin, four miles to the east. There they were spotted by a handful of citizens who mistook them for Union cavalry, and thus failed to report their presence. When they were two miles from their destination the Missourians galloped into the barnyard of the Reverend Snyder, a Federal officer on leave who commanded a company of colored troops in the field. He stepped out, rifle in hand, into a wall of bullets. The band set fire to the house and barn and left him writhing in a muck of dirt and blood.

Stopping at the Lawrence city limits, they were intercepted by two scouts Quantrill had sent in the night before, who reported that all was quiet. These were the two men I had encountered in Drucilla's parlor.

Four hundred Union soldiers were camped north of the Kansas River outside town, separated by the ferry from a few dozen more on the Lawrence side. Quantrill dispatched a detail to take possession of the ferry and prevent the enemy's main body from crossing. The others were slaughtered in their tents.

I awoke to a rattle of gunfire, which I have since decided belonged to the action described above. I was groggily reaching for my trousers when my door burst open. Panama Bob, barefoot with his braces dangling and no shirt on over his stained and faded long underwear, rushed in gripping a long-barreled revolver with an enormous bore. Around his narrow waist he had buckled a belt with a scabbard containing a curved saber, its handle chased with gold.

"Your pistol, Billy! Where is it?"

"In my bag," I managed to stammer. His great Gallic eyes were wild, his black hair and beard more tangled than ever. I felt myself in the presence of an aroused and cornered beast.

"Put it in your hand and come with me! Hurry!"

"But who—?"

"The Philistines!" With that he was gone, crossing the kitchen with long loping strides.

I finished dressing quickly, inspected the charges in the cylinder of the five-shot, and went out behind him. Ada and

Rachel, in their dressing gowns, were huddled in the foyer by the open door, and I was aware of Carmel and Veronica standing on the stairs. From outside came a din of splintering glass and drumming hooves, punctuated by pistol reports and a hellish scale of unearthly, high-pitched shrieks: the rebel yell. I went outside.

Massachusetts Street was in uproar. A plunging, rearing stream of men on horseback filled it from end to end, whooping and quirting their reins across their mounts' withers, twisting this way and that in their saddles to shoot at men and windows. Some carried torches, some waved sabers. To a man they were dressed in the butternut gray of the Southern Confederacy. I saw campaign hats and kepis, ostrich plumes and gold braid and the black flag on a staff. They shattered panes, punched holes in watering troughs, riddled signs, and shot at everything that moved. No sooner had I appeared on the porch than the lantern hanging above the discreet sign that identified the house as Drucilla's exploded not a foot from my head. I ducked as a shower of glass pelted my shoulders and went down inside my collar.

"Over here, Billy!"

Bob was crouched in a corner behind the railing, using a small dogwood growing on the other side for cover. The barrel of his pistol rested atop the railing. I joined him, keeping low.

"Rebels?" I asked.

"Worse. Bushwhackers. Captain Q's black devils, or I am damned."

"How can you tell?"

"I get one and show you."

Before I could stop him, he rose, extended the arm holding the revolver, picked his target, led it, and fired. A horseman sweeping past the steps threw back his head and cartwheeled out of the saddle, landing in the strip of grass between the porch and the street. Bob made a triumphant noise in his throat—a growl, really—shouted, "Cover me!" and scampered down the steps. While the enemy thundered past an arm's length away, the reformed slaverunner made a brief examination of the fallen man, then belted his pistol and backed up the steps, dragging the man by his Sam Browne belt. A rider, spotting him, shouted a curse of indescribable filth and took aim at him with a bone-handled revolver. Before he could fire another horseman came between him and his target. In another moment he was swept out of effective range, and Bob was back behind the dogwood with his trophy.

The whites of Bob's eyes glittered in his dark face as he studied me. His chest heaved. "Is that what you call giving cover?"

"It was all too fast," I said.

"The next time a fellow shoots at me I will ask him to slow down." With a final exertion, he turned the dead man over on his back between us. I was astonished to see a beardless face, spotted with acne on the chin and forehead. He was not much older than I. His blue eyes were open, but they saw nothing and would never see anything again.

Bob wasted no time looking at the boy's face. He seized the front of the gray tunic in both hands and tore it open, exposing a mass of ruffled white linen peppered with blood.

"Guerrilla shirt." He sat back on his heels. "You'll not see a fancy rig like that on any honest man-at-arms. Most of them never wore anything but homespun before they joined up. It's the first thing they buy once they get their hands on plunder." He hawked noisily and spat into the ruffles. Then his head flew apart.

It was as sudden as that. One instant his face was before me, and the next it was a red smear. Something stung both my eyes; I tasted salt and iron on my lips and spat it out in an automatic reaction. Much time would pass, and with it many a bar of coarse brown soap and several layers of skin, before I felt that I had cleansed myself of the last of Panama Bob's brains. He slumped forward across the corpse of the boy he had killed, and I looked up, my face dripping, into a pair of eyes as dead as the boy's.

I knew the man at once, though he stood on the porch against the red glare of the morning sun and had exchanged his worn canvas and ticking of the night before for the belted gray coat and single-striped trousers of a Confederate officer. Under the broad brim of his hat, pinned up on one side and decorated with a plume, were the icily classic features of the man from the parlor. Smoke was still twisting out of the end of his revolver when he turned it upon me.

"I reckon you'll be playing 'Bonnie Blue Flag' next time on a harp," he said, drawing back the hammer.

"Step to the ground."

The low, Greek-inflected tones drew those empty eyes toward the open front door, and mine just behind. There, in the full light of day, stood Drucilla Patakos, in a handsome embroidered dressing gown with the stock of Panama Bob's shotgun pressed to her ruined right cheek. The sun's searching rays brought the scars into brutal relief.

The man assessed the situation at a glance. "There's right around three hundred of us," he said. "What you fixing to do once you empty that barrel?"

"It will not be any concern of yours, since I intend to empty it into you."

"Too thin, old lady. I'm calling your hand."

Hooves rataplaned up to the porch. The lanky young farmer I had seen on two previous occasions swung down from the back of a racing bay. He, too, had switched to rebel gray, but of a much simpler design, without insignia or frivolous ornament. He wore two pistols on his belt and a saber in a scabbard. Standing on the bottom step he glanced quickly from the woman with the shotgun to the guerrilla on the porch. "I wouldn't, John. She ain't bluffing."

"Balls, Frank. You couldn't take a pot with a hogleg."

A shot rang out very close. I'm ashamed to say I wet myself, for I thought the report belonged to the weapon pointed at me. In fact, both he and his friend were looking away from Drucilla and me, at a resplendent figure leaning down from the saddle of a tall blue roan to peer under the roof of the porch. Long-maned and heavily bearded, he wore his hat at a dandyish angle and a scarlet sash around the waist of a tunic with captain's bars on the shoulders. I counted three pistols on his person—two in the sash, a third gripped in his right fist pointed skyward and smoking—and had the impression there were others I didn't see. I assumed that so flamboyant and abundantly armed a figure must belong to Quantrill himself. I was wrong.

He spoke quietly, and I realized for the first time that the street was quiet. The slaughter had abated temporarily. There would be more, so much more; but even the devil must pause betimes for breath.

"No women killed or harmed, that was the order. Which part do you find unclear, Lieutenant Thrailkill?"

"It ain't the woman I want, Captain. It's this key-plunking son of a bitch."

The bearded man appraised me, not missing the pistol in my hand, which I myself had forgotten. It wasn't likely to assist me in any case. "Sergeant James?" He looked at the farmer.

"He's no threat, Captain. Plays the organ at Drucilla's."

Now he looked at Drucilla. "You prize him so, madam?"

She said nothing. The shotgun remained steady.

"Plays well, does he?" he asked Sergeant James then.

The farmer surprised me by grinning. Then he surprised me a great deal more. "Bach. Sir."

"Bach?"

"Yes, sir."

The captain appeared to consider. Then he thrust his weapon into the sash with the others. "Bring him."

II

Nocturne for Night Riders

TEN

As it was with the New York draft riots, casualty reports connected with the sack of Lawrence by Quantrill's raiders were exaggerated hysterically. The world may never know how many men died—all the victims were male, by decree of the commander, who thought himself chivalrous—in that community between the hours of five and nine A.M., when the last of the invaders departed. None of the accounts I've read make mention of the young guerrilla shot down by Panama Bob in front of Drucilla's, and since most of them point to a former preacher named Skaggs as the only Missourian slain, I have come to doubt all the statistics cited by "experts" who were not present that day. I do know that a mass funeral took place there on the day following the attack, and that throughout the rest of the war a double row of naked chimneys and broken sections of scorched brick wall were all that remained of the business district.

Gone were the Eldridge House and the Johnson House, hotels and popular meeting places for the Free-Staters; the Country Store was burned to the ground as well, also Palmer's Gun Shop, the latter with the occupants still inside. When the kegs of black powder stored in back went up, they took the roof with them, along with every window on the street not already broken by gunfire. Several stables and granaries went to the torch, for no apparent reason other than that they burned so easily. I am told that for days afterward a cloud of smoke hung above the settlement like the black pall of doom.

Mayor Collamore was dead. So too were State Senator Thorpe and editor Josiah Trask of the abolitionist *State Journal*, gunned down in front of their wives when they came out of their houses to surrender. Judge Louis Carpenter, who had jestingly pretended to mistake a stray cur for Quantrill, was shot down like a dog in his home. Dozens more, strangers to their assailants, died for the crime of being male and of age in the Jayhawker capital of Kansas.

Ironically, Senator James Lane, whose Redleg raid on Osceola, Missouri, had inspired the assault, escaped harm by concealing himself in a nearby cornfield until the danger had passed. Guerrillas searched his house, questioned his wife, and rode away after leaving their compliments. It was that kind of war.

All of my information regarding the aftermath of the grisly events of August 21 came to me secondhand, and long after the fact, for I was not there. This was not Drucilla's wish. She did not lower Panama Bob's shotgun when the showily dressed captain instructed Sergeant James and Lieutenant Thrailkill to bring me along; instead, she moved it slightly to bring the captain within range of its broad pattern. The hand that wore the garnet ring did not quaver.

"The young man will stay," she announced. "You will not carry him away so that you can murder him in private."

The man on horseback lifted his brows. Then he laughed—a genuine, deep, guttering sound that issued from the base of his chest and carried to the watching guerrillas, all of whom joined in, with the notable exceptions of Thrailkill and James. But for their silence it was as if someone had told a Homeric off-color joke at a gentlemen's smoker.

Suddenly the captain stopped laughing. Just as suddenly, before anyone could react, he drew the revolver he had recently shoved under the sash about his waist, cocking it in the same motion, and fired.

A townsman I knew by sight but not by name, middle-aging and running to fat in a dusty morning coat and wire spectacles, cried out, clutched his abdomen with both hands, and fell from the section of boardwalk between Drucilla's and the house next door. Evidently hoping to escape attention, he had emerged from the neighboring shallow doorway and begun inching toward the narrow passage that separated the two buildings. The man in the saddle had made no sign of noticing him until he put a bullet in the fellow's stomach. Lying in the street, the wounded man pitched and rolled, groaning and kicking with both feet.

"Maddox," said the captain.

A bearded guerrilla sitting his horse near the suffering man leaned down and shot him through the head. The wretch arched his back, then slowly subsided. He lay still.

One or two of the watching Missourians sniggered.

The captain levered the device attached to his revolver to extract the spent powder from the two chambers he had fired recently. "Captain Anderson, madam," he said, pausing to touch two fingers to the brim of his hat. "Some of the boys call me Bloody Bill, and I guess I've earned it even if I don't answer to it. I have never busted a cap on a man in private in my life. If I intended to kill this young man I would have shot you just now instead of that sneak, and finished the job at my leisure. You would have died with your finger on the trigger."

"What do you want with him?" Her voice was even. I could not tell if she were dissembling, or if her past experience with border killers had so hardened her to the sight of a man's death in cold blood that it left her unaffected. As for me, it seemed the more of it I saw, the less I was prepared for it. The fact that I had not had breakfast was the only thing that kept me from retching.

"An army, madam, requires three things to remain an army: God, music, and the will to fight. The damn Union has given us all of the last we need, and we have more preachers in our ranks than General Lee has whiskers. We are rotten short on music. Corporal Taylor's squeeze-box doesn't answer, and Lieutenant Yeager's mouth organ is an abomination before God. We have a piano at headquarters and a trunk full of good Southern music going to waste."

"What are you offering him in return for all this entertainment?"

"His life. It's poor enough coin in these times, but it's all we can spare. Everything else goes to Richmond."

"You lie as easily as you do murder, Bloody Bill."

The look in Anderson's eye told me that he had run out of words. I rose to my feet, Templeton Deane's pistol dangling from my hand. "I will go."

"Don't be foolish, Billy. It is a secessionist trick." The shotgun had begun to sway. Soon she would find it too heavy to hold.

"Thank you for the hospitality of your house, Mrs. Patakos. It's time for me to move on."

She was silent for another moment. Then, slowly, she lowered the shotgun.

Anderson began replacing his charges from a pair of leather pouches he drew from his tunic. "Thrailkill."

The guerrilla kept me covered. "He's still heeled."

I offered him the butt of the revolver. After a pause he holstered his weapon and reached out to take it. I rotated the pistol.

Now he was staring down the muzzle. He bent his elbow to redraw, stopped. It was his own uncertain swiftness against the velocity of powder and ball.

Fast as thought, Anderson spun his own cylinder buzzingly with the heel of his hand and "threw down" on me. On the street a dozen or more hammers crackled in reply.

Again I spun the five-shot, and this time I slid my hand down to the end of the barrel.

Thrailkill hesitated, then took hold of the grip. When his grasp was secure he tore it out of my hand viciously.

Someone whooped. Laughter Gatlinged through the mob of killers. Even Sergeant Frank James grinned. Looking quizzical, Bloody Bill Anderson took his pistol off cock and returned his attention to the fired chambers. "You're rusty, Lieutenant," was his only comment.

The humiliated guerrilla thrust my revolver into his belt, wheeled, and stamped down the front steps in search of his horse, shoving James out of the way.

Beyond doubt, executing the border spin against John Thrailkill was the most foolhardy thing I had done since leaving home. I had been practicing the maneuver in private ever since it was shown to me by Captain Jack Fabian of the Pinkerton National Detective Agency, and in the rush of the moment I had surrendered to the impulse to demonstrate how well I had learned it. In the course of things I had made an enemy for life.

I was allowed, under the close supervision of Sergeant Frank James, to roll my few possessions into a borrowed blanket—for the carpetbag was too bulky and awkward to carry on horseback—and say my farewells. My reception varied according to whom they were said.

Ada, distracted by the turmoil but still glowing over her conquest, smiled self-satisfaction at the flush that came to my face when I spoke to her, and pinched my freshly scrubbed cheek. "Sweet boy, listen to Ada's advice: Don't fire first unless you're in the field."

Veronica was openly hostile and left the parlor abruptly when I entered it. She had started the race as the favorite and was not of that breed that accepts defeat with grace.

Rachel was either haughty to the end or acutely conscious of her mixed blood in the presence of so many rampaging pro-slavers, for she did not come to her door when I knocked.

Of that crew, only the marble-skinned, raven-haired Carmel was cordial. The contest for my virtue had been a lark to her, nothing more, and we had shared too many a successful parlor concert for her to express anything but sweet sorrow at my leaving. She curtsied in the best Southern fashion and kissed me upon the cheek.

Isabel, stoic tyrant of the mop and dustpan, received my

words of parting with a granite face. She appeared unmoved by the events of the morning. Panama Bob's death seemed not to concern her except perhaps for the fact that now she would have to clean up the mess herself. In her way, she was as ruthless as Quantrill.

Drucilla had retreated to her third-floor sanctum. When a full minute went past without an answer to my knock, I turned to go. Just then the lock snapped and the door opened inward six inches. The left half of her face alone was visible. Her eye went from me to the guerrilla sergeant standing behind me and back to my face. "Yes?"

"I am going now," said I.

"Yes."

"I am sorry about Bob."

Nothing changed in her expression.

"I wanted to thank you again before I left. But for you—"

"Yes."

The door closed. The lock snapped to.

"Women." James hooked his thumbs inside his gun belt. "Once they get started you can't shut them up."

Massacres do not cease for the sake of a hostage. I was escorted from Drucilla's to a house around the corner and shut up in the potato bin in the cellar with a guard posted outside while the raid continued. There in the humid darkness, accompanied by the smell of earth and vegetable decay and the occasional inquisitive rummaging of a rat, I sat on the end of a barrel and listened to the shots and cries from outside. What became of the people who lived in the house I did not know, but I suspected the worst. Later I learned that, far from a random and unplanned act of vengeance, the attack on Lawrence had been organized to the last detail and carried out according to a strict time schedule, with squads of guerrillas assigned to particular sections of the city, equipped with maps upon which the homes and businesses of individuals singled out for special punishment had been clearly marked. Quantrill himself had led the group that searched Senator Lane's house, and his parting request to Mrs. Lane to give his regards to her husband reflected a kind of restraint for which he was not generally known.

I did not mourn the loss of Robert Leslie LeFleur, *alias* Panama Bob; although I did feel responsible for his death. He was a thoroughgoing scoundrel, and if he indeed felt remorse for the black slaves he had drowned to spare his neck, as he had claimed, that same conscience had not seemed to plague him for the wrongs committed by the Redlegs with whom he rode. Murder and pillage in the name of freedom from chains did not strike me as more noble than similar injustices performed for the sake of states' rights. However, to remain idle with a weapon in one's hand while a man with whom one has lived and broken bread is slain horribly is not an act to look back upon with pride. True, I was confused and upset, and my brain was still saturated with sleep. Was the situation so different from the one in front of the New York Enrollment Office, when I had stepped forward without thinking to save the life of an unknown policeman, and then struck without hesitation to save my own? Had the horrors to which I had been exposed since that day broken my courage, rendering me unable to take decisive action when the danger became personal? These were not thoughts designed to comfort a boy trapped in the vile dark with visions of Bob's exploded head for company. I could still taste his gray matter upon my tongue, musky and sharp, like iodine.

Sunk in these reflections, I knew not how much time passed, and failed to notice when the hellish noises from the street began to fade. I came out of myself only when the hatch above my head was flung open and daylight gushed in, dazzling me.

I was aware of a number of figures standing between me and the light, but I could not tell how many, nor make out details of their faces or costume. Then one of them trotted down the short flight of rotting steps, kicked the barrel out from under me, sending me over onto my back in a pile of black dirt and desiccated potatoes, and snarled in John Thrailkill's voice: "Stand for Captain Quantrill, you Jay-hawking son of a bitch!"

ELEVEN

In the matter of making the actual acquaintance of men and women whose reputations precede them—of being bitterly disappointed as opposed to finding all my expectations fulfilled—my score sheet is nearly even. Greta Garbo and Buffalo Bill Cody in person were even finer physical specimens than either their photographs or their legends suggested, while Sheriff Pat Garrett was a tall, stoop-shouldered gawk with a hook nose and an Adam's apple the size of a croquet ball, and none of the costly perfumes with which Lola Montez drenched herself, gifts of Austrian emperors and vice presidents of Mexico, could disguise the fact that she smelled like a coyote bitch in season.

William Clarke Quantrill—Antichrist, Death Angel, Avenger of Osceola, Slaughterer of the Innocents; call him what you will according to your sympathies—belonged to the category of disappointments.

When I first saw him he was a shadow against the sun, and even when I had ascended to ground level and stood before him he remained vague and largely without feature. He stood at average height, a slender figure in his tailored Confederate coat, belted at the waist and reaching to mid-thigh, with captain's bars on the high collar. He wore his reddish hair long and brushed back over the tops of his ears, and in the shadow of his tasseled campaign hat his complexion was fair beneath a smudge of dust and spent powder, his mustaches sparse and darkened with wax. His lids overhung his eyes, which were murky and indirect; dreamer's eyes, and not at all what one expected of a self-appointed seeker after retribution. The strongest impression I received was of a scent, faint but definite, underneath the mingled odors of horse and perspiration and sulfur, of violets.

I have looked in vain for a record of Quantrill's life that mentions the violets. I now believe I am the only man living who knows of them, and of the thin glass phials he carried inside his coat so that, riding at the head of his odoriferous column, he had only to reach inside and crush them to his chest to deliver himself from the stench of his own fellow guerrillas. These many years later, violets remain my least favorite fragrance, associated with sweet corruption.

"He's disarmed?" he asked, without looking away from me.

"Yes, sir. I took this off him." Thrailkill held out the ivory-handled revolver.

Someone snorted. I recognized Sergeant Frank James among the group. The lieutenant gave him a poisonous look.

Quantrill glanced at the weapon without taking it. He returned his attention to me. After an awkward moment Thrailkill put it back in his belt.

"Did Anderson happen to say why he wants this boy?" asked the guerrilla chief.

James spoke up. "Sir, he said we need somebody to play the piano back at headquarters."

A smoke-filled silence followed this information. My eyes began to sting.

Finally Quantrill stirred. He slid a pair of kid gauntlets from under his belt and pulled them on, taking care to press the material tight between the fingers. "Make sure he understands the prisoner is his responsibility."

"Yes, sir," James said.

"Personally I detest music."

"Yes, sir!" barked Thrailkill.

"What o'clock is it, Sergeant?"

James produced a watch from inside his tunic and popped open the face. "Quarter of nine, Captain." He snapped it shut and put it away.

"Tell the men to mount up. We're leaving." Quantrill turned and, surveying the smoldering ruins of the buildings across the street, astonished me by slipping into Latin:

> *"Impia tortorum longos hic turba furores*
> *Sanguinas innocu, non satiata, aluit.*
> *Sospite nunc patriâ, fracto nuncfuneris antro,*
> *Mors ubi dira fuit vita salusque patent."*

In that barbarie arena, surrounded by creatures whom Panama Bob had correctly identified as marauding pagans, I could not have been taken further aback had a hydrophobic dog raised its lathered and bloody chin and quoted Shakespeare. As if quizzed by a tutor, I voiced an automatic reply:

> *"Nil sapientiae odiosius acume nimio."*

Quantrill's head snapped around. Interest flared in his eyes for the first time; interest, and something else that until I knew him better I would hesitate to name, but which in another I should have called jealousy. He banked the fires quickly. "A scholar," said he.

"Merely a student," said I.

"Lieutenant, see that this man is treated with the courtesy reserved for a captured enemy officer."

"Hang him?" Thrailkill was eager.

"Not that kind of officer. I mean make him comfortable."

"Yes, sir."

When Quantrill left, the lieutenant snapped at James to carry on and stalked away. The sergeant took my arm and we started off down a street clogged with rubble and dead bodies in heaps. I spotted Jim Perine, the clerk from the Country Store, sprawled atop one of them, one eye clotted with blood and his toes poking through a hole in his left sock. Flies had begun to convene in great glittering clouds.

"That was Roman you two was talking," Frank James said proudly. "I know a line or two myself. My pa was a Baptist minister and a man of learning. That old man was hell for Bach. I didn't catch none of what you said, though."

I translated Quantrill:

"Here the wicked mob, unappeased,
long cherished a hatred of innocent blood.
Now that the fatherland has been saved,
and the cave of death demolished,
where grim death has been, life and health appear.

"It was a Royalist inscription, popular at the time of the Bourbon Restoration in France. It was a colorful choice." My voice sounded shallow in my ears. I was fighting to keep down my bile. Already the day was growing hot. Soon the corpses would begin to turn.

"What was that you said back?"

"It is from Seneca. 'Nothing is more disagreeable to wisdom than too much cunning.'"

He laughed, a short high bray. "That's the captain down to the ground. Always lets on to know more than he does. I'd bet a silver dollar to a horse turd he didn't feature a word."

"Why do you follow him if you do not respect him?"

"On account of he hates Yankees even more than I do."

We crossed Massachusetts Street in silence. The roof of the Eldridge House, a few doors down from Drucilla's, collapsed with a noise like a great tree falling, sending up a geyser of sparks and flaming debris. I was gratified to see that the house where I had spent the past three weeks was untouched. It appeared that unlike New York, where such establishments had been prime targets for vandalism and looting, on the border they were treated as neutral territory. In time I would come to regard those evenings of sentimental music in the parlor, and the pleasures upstairs, as a furlough for combatants weary of the killing fields.

"I daresay neither you nor your commander hates as deeply as Lieutenant Thrailkill," I said then. "He seems to abhor the universe."

"Well, he's got better reason than most. This here's your horse. Sorry I couldn't catch you a thoroughbred."

I recognized the sergeant's muscular bay hitched to the rail in front of the City House hotel, which remained intact, beside a swaybacked gelding with shaggy fetlocks and a milky eye. A worn blanket had been flung over its back, but nothing else.

"Where is the saddle?" I asked.

"Same place as the spring-wagon with the fancy red wheels. You're lucky you got a horse. It was Thrailkill running the show you'd be afoot, and barefoot besides."

"I haven't had much riding experience."

"Well, you come to the right place to get it."

Despite its truculent reputation, Quantrill's command was a miracle of military discipline. Every man was in his saddle with reins gathered by the time I finally got a leg up over the gelding. Bloody Bill Anderson, in charge of the division that included Thrailkill and James, trotted his roan to the end of the block and waited, pocket watch in hand, for the others to fall in, which they did with a minimum of confusion, considering that their saddle pouches and blanket rolls bulged with what was euphemistically referred to as the spoils of war. I saw silver candelabra, yards of gold chain coiled like lariats, and bolts of brightly printed fabric stashed behind candes and bundled and strung from pommels. One red-whiskered corporal had tied a dozen white geese together by their feet and slung them across the throat of his saddle, their heads dangling like pompons from their wrung necks. A bellow of command, picked up and carried by relays to the rest of the column, and we were in motion. I rode sandwiched between Frank James and the rest of the division, hanging on tight to the rope hackamore with all my worldly *accou-*

trement in a duvet tied at the ends with cord and balanced across my lap, a prisoner of a war for which I had no taste and in which I had no personal stake, and which a scant month earlier had seemed a thing as remote as an uprising in Russia. I had never felt farther from home, nor more abandoned by my God.

And then I felt ashamed; for as we moved down that street of glowing timbers, of bodies spread-eagled on the boardwalks and draped like quilts over the hitching rails, I saw the smudged, sweaty faces of widowed women and orphaned children staring out with vacant eyes at the moving column from alleys and through the windows of the buildings left standing, and knew myself fortunate to be alive. They were as dead as their husbands and fathers, many of them doomed to wander the place of their former happiness and security, gaunt shades of what once they were. And I knew then that any calculation of casualties, no matter how accurate, was only half the truth, that no battle ends with the last to die, and that no war takes place so far away from him who hears of it that he is unaffected by it. It scars us all as deeply and permanently as that part of Drucilla's face she turned from the light.

Lawrence was no longer the proud and orderly place I had come to at the end of July; nor would it be again, notwithstanding new construction and improved fortification. Its landmarks were in ruins, the surrounding corn and wheat fields intended to support it through the long winter set to the torch. In weeks its streets, once so well kept, would fill with beggars. All this was reversible and would be corrected in time. What could not be fixed was its stubborn Jayhawker heart. It had been torn out by the roots, spat upon, and trampled, and the watchworks that replaced it would not answer. This was Quantrill's legacy, and that of the war that spawned him: the murder not just of a city, but of the bumptious pioneer will upon which it was built.

Lawrence was dead. I was alive. I could not help but wonder which of us was the more fortunate.

TWELVE

A s fate would have it, I was not to see the guerrilla headquarters or its piano for some time.

We were less than a day's ride east of Lawrence, moving at an easy canter to spare the horses, when one of the men Quantrill had left behind to watch the back trail came galloping up on a lathered gray and reported breathlessly that Union troops were five miles to the rear. In less time than the most pessimistic predictions had allowed for, troops of the Eleventh Kansas Volunteer Cavalry out of Emporia had linked up with the Federals who were stranded when Quantrill took the ferry and were coming on hard under Colonel Preston B. Plumb. A number of stragglers at the rear of the guerrilla column were already in skirmish with the pursuers; the snap and pop of sporadic gunfire could be heard to the west. The commander's single-word order bounced back through the ranks like a ricocheting bullet: "Disband!"

Frank James quickly inspected the loads in each of the .36 Navy Colts he carried in a pair of scabbards attached to his saddle, then returned them to their sheaths. "It's every hog to its own tit, youngster," he said, gathering his reins. "Come or get lynched."

"But I am not a guerrilla!"

"That don't signify to the Eleventh Kansas. Them boys is mad as yellow jackets about now. If it's betwixt them and the border and it ain't wearing Lincoln's blue, they'll string it up or ride right on over it."

"Where are we going?"

"I'm going home. You don't have to come, though you'll be giving up the best corn bread in Missouri for a short trip from a high limb if you don't. Personally I don't give a possum's ass what you do, but as I got on Johnny Thrailkill's black side to save your scalp I figure I got to make the invitation. I damn sure ain't waiting for them Kansas boys to show up while you're deciding."

I was in turmoil. Sore from the ride and sickened by the events of that morning, but light-headed after nearly twenty-four hours without food, I was hardly in a state to make a lightning decision that was bound to affect my life. I don't know what I would have told him had not the clear ringing note of a bugle, warped by wind and distance, reached me at that instant from the direction of the sunset. I had a sudden, sharp vision of the Negro I had seen hanging from an awning post in New York, his head lolling from his broken neck.

"Which way?" I asked.

James grinned. "Where the Yankees ain't. Hang on!" Taking the ends of the hackamore from me, he tied them to his saddle ring and raked the bay's flanks with both spurs. It whinnied and bolted, and behind it the gelding, which would have pitched me off if I weren't hugging its neck with both arms. Around us the column had broken in three directions, some of the riders casting aside their heavier plunder in the interest of speed. For all that, it was an orderly rout. I remember thinking that if the enemy's *irregular* cavalry was this well organized, the Union would be a much longer time putting down the rebellion than was commonly believed back home. Then I noticed that we had turned, placing the sun directly to our left.

"Isn't this north?" I shouted.

He ducked to clear the low-slung limb of a sycamore. "Was last time I looked."

"That's Federal territory!"

"Where's the last place *you'd* hunt for Johnny Reb?"

At dusk we camped in a stand of trees at the top of a small hill. I was exhausted, for we had ridden hard for an hour and my tailbone was without feeling; but James handed me a canvas bucket and his canteen and told me to walk down to the narrow creek at the foot of the hill and bring back water. "Don't wander off, now," he said. "These woods is full of two-legged coyotes'd slice off your pecker for a pipe."

When I returned, panting from the exertion, he relieved me of the bucket and handed me a hard biscuit. The surface was as sandy as granite.

"Soak it from the canteen before you bite into it. That is, unless you like spitting teeth."

The water softened the biscuit to the consistency of harness leather. The hinges of my jaws ached from chewing, but I ate every last morsel, to ease the feral clawing in my stomach. I asked if there was more.

He finished watering the horses and produced another biscuit from inside his tunic. "Just this, and it's mine. I'd fry up some bacon, but I can't risk a fire. Here." Reaching into the tunic again, he took out a dark oblong the size of his thumb, sawed off a piece with the bone-handled knife he carried on his belt, and held out the piece.

I took it and examined it, then tried to return it. "I don't chew tobacco."

"Didn't ask if you did. Chaw on it anyway. It'll give your juices something to work on besides your own gut." He put away the knife and tobacco plug and sat down on a moss-covered rock to eat his biscuit. "I guess you'll live on less before this war's done. Folks in Jefferson City was down to eating wallpaper when that son of a bitch Fremont declared martial law."

The tobacco was vile, as I was certain it would be: brackish and bittersweet to such a point that my stomach tried to reject the biscuit I had eaten. The juices backed up and filled my nasal passages, making my eyes water. Inadvertently I swallowed some and got up, retching, to purge what remained of the plug. I leaned heavily against a tree, hacking and sputtering and wiping my mouth with the back of my hand.

Frank James chuckled. "You put me in mind of my little brother. He's about your age; couldn't stomach the stuff neither. Last time I was home he begged for me to put in a word for him with Captain Quantrill. I said, 'Now, what kind of a guerrilla would you make? You can't even stick a piece of chaw in your mouth without heaving up your guts.' Well, he's got our ma's stubborn blood. I expect he'll be chawing and spitting like a muleskinner when I get back."

"Is that where we're going?" I felt dizzy and pale. I was afraid to abandon the support of the tree.

"Clay County, Missouri." He licked the crumbs from his fingers and cut himself a plug. "Poorest farm country you ever did see. Our pa never could raise hell on that plot of land we got. I reckon that's why he went to California and got himself dead. It was just too slow the other way."

"I thought you said he was a minister."

"That's even slower than scratching in the dirt. Preachers' kin lives on what the flock gives them. A piece of pigshit don't go no farther in Clay County than anywheres else. He went to dig for gold and dug his own hole instead. Pneumony, they said."

"Your mother and your little brother work the farm alone?"

"We got us a stepfather. There was another one in between, but he hurt my brother's arm and I stuck him with a hay fork and he went away. Doctor Samuel, this one is. I never seen him do no doctoring, so I don't know if he's any good at it, but he's a fair enough farmer. Better anyhow than our pa ever was. This one grows things."

"What does he think about your riding with Captain Quantrill instead of staying home and working the farm?"

"Oh, he's for anything that's against the Yankees. So's everyone else in Clay County. It was a choice of go to the devil or turn Yankee, there ain't a man or a woman there wouldn't grow horns."

I pushed myself away from the tree at last and turned. "I'm a Yankee."

He spat a glittering stream and wiped his mouth. "That's because you don't know better. Where you from?"

"New York City."

"No shit. Where's that?"

"A long way from Clay County."

That was the end of the conversation. We spread our blankets on the ground and wrapped ourselves in them against the cold night air; for along with destruction and slaughter, Quantrill's horde had brought winter's first chill to the State of Kansas. Before drifting off, Frank James slid one of the Navy Colts from its scabbard on the saddle he was using for a pillow and laid it on his chest with his right hand closed around the butt.

I had thought that my first night ever on the stiff cold ground would be sleepless, but I was more tired than I was sore and hungry. I dreamed that I was back in my comfortable bed in my father's town house, awakening from a nightmare that I had been banished to a barbaric land. I waited for the soft knocking that told me Cook was outside my door with my breakfast on a tray. Instead a booted foot kicked my ankle and I opened my eyes to total darkness.

"On your feet, youngster," Frank James said. "It's coming on first light."

I rose staggering, stiff in the back and legs and shivering in the raw damp. My breakfast was not scones and coffee but a long icy draught from my keeper's canteen, intended to fool my gnawing stomach that it contained something more substantial. I watered the horses while James scuffed about, eradicating all signs of encampment, and then we were riding, guided by the first blade of metallic light in the east.

By dawn the pain in my insides had grown so sharp I feared my condition was serious. I had never before experienced true hunger of the life-threatening kind, had not imagined that it actually hurt so that one could think of nothing else; and I wondered what must it be like to go for days in such a state. Thirty-six hours only had passed since my last meal, I had had a biscuit in the interim, and I was in agony. I thought of the beggars I had passed so many times in the doorways and alleys of my home city, their heads wrapped in scarves and their grubby fingers protruding through holes in their gloves, and knew I had earned a week in Purgatory for each open palm I had passed without leaving a coin. Perhaps this was that penance.

The sun was above the trees when salvation arrived, though I failed to recognize it. We were riding down a shallow decline ending in a boggy marsh when James drew rein suddenly and leaned over to grip the gelding's makeshift bridle.

"Sing out if you lay eyes on anyone."

He took off at a canter before I could question him. Soon the marsh closed in behind man and horse, and for a quarter of an hour I was alone with the whistling birds and the occasional rustling from the direction of the bog. I nearly fell off my horse when a flock of grouse exploded from the tangle with a noise like a locomotive charging out of a tunnel. I remember wondering, when I recovered, if they tasted like partridge.

Presently my companion emerged from the underbrush, leading the bay and holding his campaign hat cradled in the crook of his free arm. As he drew near I saw that the hat's inverted crown was filled to the sweatband with blackberries.

"Bears live on this shit," he said as I dismounted and dug in with both hands. "You never hear of no bears starving to death. Slow down, now. You'll bloat up and bust like a horse. They don't know when to stop neither."

My fingers—and, I was sure, my face as well—were stained purple by the time I stopped eating long enough to speak. "I wondered why you didn't shoot those grouse."

"I didn't want to risk the shot. Anyway, we can't build a fire for the smoke. You can get mighty sick eating raw bird. They carry grubs and shit."

When we had both eaten our fill, he tied up the remaining berries in a bandanna and hung it from the horn of his saddle. "Ma might make a pie." He mounted. "We'll be eating grits and fatback by sundown."

We had swung east at morning, and crossed the Missouri border below Kansas City around noon. James said we'd go on to Independence, stake out a spot where we could see the ferry landing, and if no Union troops were in sight we'd cross the Missouri River and head straight north for Kearney and the Samuel farm nearby.

"Home," he said. "The air smells better already. In Kansas I hold my breath the whole time."

The road to Independence was hardpack, with dense forest on both sides. Our hoofbeats echoed off the wall of trees, the echoes feeding upon themselves and multiplying, as if we were a dozen instead of just two. The effect was mesmerizing; which may help to explain what happened next.

The road was too narrow for two horsemen to ride abreast comfortably, and so we had formed an Indian file with the guerrilla in front. Something pricked the back of my neck, I slapped at it automatically, and looked down at the smashed mosquito in my palm. When I flicked it away and looked ahead again, Frank James and his bay were gone.

I blinked like a child at a conjuring trick. That a horse and rider could just disappear without my seeing or hearing them was a phenomenon outside my experience and understanding. Yet the road in front was empty, and when I turned to see if they had somehow fallen behind I saw nothing but a ribbon of beaten clay with the branches of the trees latticed overhead, forming a natural tunnel. And the beat of my gelding's hooves came back and mocked me like malevolent spirits chuckling in the shadows.

And then I was not alone.

Thirty yards farther on, the road broadened where trees had been cleared for some civilizing project that had probably been cut short by the war. Just beyond where it began, moving like ghosts, noiselessly and with unearthly precision, two horsemen from one side and three from the other came out into the road from the thick cover and turned their animals to face me. They were dressed in blue, and each man held a side arm in his free hand.

"Well, I'm damned," said one as I drew rein before them. "Look what the wind blowed up from the south; and us with all these pretty trees to tie a rope to."

THIRTEEN

The speaker was a six-stripe sergeant with the largest pair of handlebars I had ever seen, swooping past his ears and up at the ends on a level with his kepi. All of his companions sported facial hair as well, though none so impressively, and this together with an unmistakable look upon their sun-stained features identified them as veteran campaigners. I had perceived the identical quality in the visages of the men who rode with Quantrill: of having passed through a fire that had left their bodies intact while burning away their humanity. I saw little difference between them and the dumb resigned war-bitten faces of the horses they straddled.

"You see, boys," resumed the sergeant, "that's what I dislike most about Missouri: You can't walk in any direction without stepping in a mess of muleshit, and you can't step in a mess of muleshit without kicking up a bushel of secesh maggots like what we got here."

"I am no secessionist," I said.

"Shut your cake-hole and get them hands in the air."

I complied, protesting that I was unarmed.

"Horseshit. There ain't a one of you guerrilla trash don't pack more iron than a sow's got tits. Pat him down, Syke. Day's half shot already and we got us a lot of necks to stretch before we lose the light."

"We ain't got time to stretch even one, Sarge." The man mounted at the sergeant's right had a lean, simian face half-shadowed with beard. "We got to be in Kansas City by dark."

The sergeant let out a lungful of air. "That's a disappointment. Things have sure gone to hell when you can't take a minute to strangle a grit-eating bushwhacker. Well, hell." He raised his pistol and sighted down his arm.

A high-pitched shriek tore through the alley between the trees. A cloud of startled birds took to the air with a panicky chatter and a whoosh of wings. The horses pitched and reared. The sergeant hauled back on his reins, almost losing his grip on his weapon.

A hundred feet beyond, Frank James sat aboard his racing bay in the center of the road. His reins were clamped between his teeth and he held a Navy Colt in each hand.

"Yellow rebel trick!" cried the sergeant, turning his horse to meet this new threat.

While the others followed suit, I leapt to the ground and led the gelding up the bank into the trees. From there I had a clear view of what I like to call the Battle for the Independence Road.

The five were still turning when James galloped straight at them, coattails flying, muzzles flashing, a grinning Angel of Death charging through the smoke of his own fire. The Union men returned fire, but as they were still in the midst of regrouping none of them had time to take aim. The man called Syke cursed shrilly and clawed at his shoulder. Another man fell out of his saddle, and still another lost his kepi, but I could not tell if he was hurt. The smoke was as thick as cotton by the time the opposing sides met. For an instant I could not see what was happening. Then the guerrilla came out the other side, leaning back on the reins and heeling over to turn the bay. While the Union riders were untangling themselves, he leaned forward, dug in his spurs, and vaulted the bank not ten feet from where I crouched holding on to the gelding's hackamore.

At the top he stopped long enough to leather his revolvers

and take the reins from his teeth. Then, with a significant look in my direction, he took off through the woods, keeping his head low to avoid the boughs.

I mounted and followed, kicking into a gallop when a rattle of belated reports sounded from the road. I could hear the pistol balls skipping through the branches overhead.

We rode hard for two miles. Then, in a broad clearing rutted with the overgrown furrows of an abandoned field, James stopped to let his horse blow. I stopped alongside.

"Won't they keep coming?" I was gasping for breath.

"No. They got wounded to see to, and Kansas City to make before sundown. That kind don't put theirselves out if they don't have to. It was just our sore luck to stumble right on top of them. My fault. I let down my gate when we left Kansas."

"But you knew they were waiting for us. That's why you left, to circle behind them."

"I guessed. It was a likely spot for what they had in mind. I should of seen it sooner."

"You used me as a decoy."

"Had to. They heard us coming, though they didn't know how many we was on account of the echoes. I needed something to keep them occupied. Lucky that sergeant's a talker."

"I don't mind telling you I was terrified."

"Don't never stand still for it, that's my advice. If you come on hard enough and fast enough, folks will generally clear you a path. Nobody wants to die when you come down to it."

"I'm not angry for what you did," I said. "You could have kept going after you left the road."

He cut himself a chew and offered me the plug, shrugging when I didn't take it. "Don't set yourself up too high, youngster. I didn't join up with the captain to turn tail and run when I see Yankees." He returned the tobacco to his tunic and took up his reins. "Also I aim to hear me some more of that Bach." He clucked the bay into a walk.

* * *

The sun was close to the horizon, spreading molten copper light over the swelling country below, when Frank James leaned down from the saddle and unlatched a whitewashed wooden gate bearing a sign whose hand-painted legend read:

SAMUEL FARM

NO TRESPASSING HUNTING PEDDLERS

"Are you expected?" I asked.

"Nobody's expected me anywhere since 1861."

As if in confirmation, drawing within sight of an L-shaped one-story frame house with a corral and barn standing nearby, we were greeted by a thick-waisted, brown-haired figure in a simple dress standing on the long front porch with a twin-barreled shotgun raised to her shoulder.

"Around here we pay attention to signs!" the woman called out in a voice surprisingly strong and full of timber.

James drew rein, signaling for me to do the same, and cupped a hand around his mouth. "You're getting old, Ma! I remember when you could pick a coyote out of a dog pack at a thousand yards."

"Alexander Franklin, is that you?"

"I asked you not to call me that in front of company, Ma."

"Who is that with you?"

"Well, promise me you won't blow him out from under his hat and I'll introduce you."

She lowered the shotgun. "Come ahead, then."

We approached at a walk. James swung down before the porch and mounted the steps to embrace his mother, who rested the shotgun's butt on the boards and patted his back with her free hand. When they parted, she studied him from head to foot. "You've been forgetting to eat. How do you expect to kill your share of Yankees if you will not keep up your strength?"

"Why don't you rustle up some of your fatback and corn bread and put me right? I been bragging on your cooking to Billy here for sixty mile."

Now she turned her attention to me. A large woman with a straight back, she gave the impression of having been weathered by care and hard work rather than age—for I placed her close to forty, although she could have passed for older—with graying hair and sharp lines in her broad forehead and at the corners of her eyes. I had the suspicion that if she untied the black ribbon that held her hair in place behind her head her face would collapse. As she turned, I realized with a start that she was in a family way; the swelling in her abdomen beneath the plain dress was slight but unmistakable. I averted my eyes. Pregnancy in those days was a thing to be endured behind closed doors.

Her gaze remained on me, bright and wary. "Who is Billy?"

I removed my hat, an old sweat-stained felt with a flop brim, borrowed from Drucilla Patakos' store of male garments left behind by their owners. "Billy Gashade, ma'am."

"Say something more."

I searched my brain. "You have a handsome farm."

"I don't like the way he talks."

"It ain't his fault, Ma. Billy's from New York City."

Her grip tightened on the barrels of the shotgun. "Yankee?"

"I brung him from Lawrence. He's a prisoner."

"You brought a Yankee to our home?"

"He plays piano, Ma. Wait'll you hear him."

She slapped his face. The noise was like a pistol shot.

"The Yankee militia was here in the spring," she said without emotion. "They claimed we were carrying information to the guerrillas. They tied a rope around your stepfather's neck and hauled him up in that tree four times to get him to talk." She pointed at a heavy-trunked pecan in the yard. "When he refused they kicked him on the ground and broke his ribs. They called me names I would not call a nigger, and me carrying your stepfather's child. Then they rode out to the field where your brother was plowing and slashed him with quirts. Last month, with Reuben still bedridden and your brother in Kearney buying flour, they came back and arrested me and put me in jail in St. Joseph."

"How'd you get out?" He stroked his cheek, which bore the red imprint of her hand.

"They let me out when they saw it wasn't going to do any good. They knew when they put me in I wouldn't say anything. They just wanted to bring me down. That's the Yankee way. They respect neither women nor honor. And now you've brought one to our house."

"Billy ain't one of them, Ma. Captain Anderson seen that himself or he'd of let Johnny Thrailkill blow his brains out when he was busting to."

"Bill Anderson stopped him? Bloody Bill?" She looked at me now with curious interest.

"'Bring him.' Those was his exact words."

"Were," she corrected. "I did not give up an hour after supper every night for eight years teaching you grammar to hear you speaking like Jayhawker trash."

"Yes, ma'am."

She was still studying me. "Well, he knows enough not to step down uninvited."

Frank James risked a grin. "I reckon even a Yankee respects a Southern woman with a scattergun."

"Tell him to step down. I cannot cook with a crick in my neck."

I alighted from the gelding, grateful to be on my feet once again. In addition to sores on my backside, I had developed an irritation inside my thighs from the rough material of the blanket and the salty lather shed by the horse.

"Your brother will be along directly," Mrs. Samuel said. "He and Leander are out with the team, pulling stumps."

"Ain't the doctor up to it yet?"

"Isn't. He is a slow healer. You will find the basin out back. Wipe your boots before you come through the kitchen. I will not have you tracking Kansas into my house." She looked at me. "I apologize for my inhospitality, Mr. Gashade. Prisoner or not, you are here at my son's invitation. You will be treated as a guest." Swinging the shotgun under her arm, she turned toward the door. "It's good you're home, son."

"You'll never know how good, Ma."

We led the horses to the barn and rubbed them down with burlap sacks hanging on the stalls. Frank pitched hay down from the loft with a three-tined fork that might have been the one he had used to drive his first stepfather from the farm, and we carried our belongings around to the back of the house. There we found a young black woman in a faded print dress with her hair tied up in a kerchief pouring water into a blue enamel basin on a plank laid across two sawhorses. When she finished she curtsied before each of us, then hung the bucket on the spout of the pump nearby and went inside through the back door.

Minutes later, scrubbed, buttoned, and our boots duly wiped on a straw mat outside the door, we followed her. We were in a spacious, immaculate kitchen, with broad pine floorboards scoured white, a black iron stove with a warming oven on top, and a square painted table with a red-and-white-checked oilcloth and ladder-back chairs all around. The young Negress was setting the table with blue china and Mrs. Samuel was at the stove, stirring a pot. The mingled smells of hot grease and warm bread reawakened the dormant gnawing in my stomach.

When we entered, a tall, spare, white-bearded man, many years Mrs. Samuel's senior, came forward from the opposite doorway and switched hands on his cane to shake Frank's hand. His gray homespun shirt was buttoned to the throat and he wore his woolen trousers supported not with braces in the manner of a farmer or a store clerk, but with a broad brown glossy leather belt.

"I hear you gave those Jayhawkers what-for," he said by way of greeting.

"I never will feature how news travels twice as fast as a good horse."

That ended the conversation between stepfather and stepson for a while. The two appeared ill at ease in each other's company, without being hostile. Frank introduced me briefly. Dr. Samuel nodded with what seemed genuine courtesy, but did not offer his hand. I saw that he had a house pallor, yet the leathery look of his face told me he was accustomed to being outdoors. I thought of his ordeal at the hands of the militia. Many a healthy Easterner would have died from a lesser shock.

We were just sitting down at the table when the back screen swung open and a youth about my age walked in from the yard. He wore dirty overalls over a stained shirt and his longish brown hair was slicked back with water from the basin. I recognized his mother's fineness of feature, but the disconcerting directness of his gaze—apparently a James family trait—was developed to an even greater degree than his mother's and his brother's. A handsome boy with a girlish complexion, a proud lift to his chin, and something of a whiff of brimstone about him which at the time I attributed to his daylong exposure to the sun while clearing his late father's land for crops. It was a scent that would never leave him until his last days, when its absence would prove fatal.

But his grin was as bright and guileless as any boy's when he laid eyes upon his brother. "Buck!"

Frank leapt to his feet with a rebel whoop and bounded around the table to seize the youth's hand. After a minute or so of horseplay, pummeling shoulders and attempting to lock their arms around each other's head—cut short by a sharp word from their mother—the brothers, farmer and guerrilla, stood side by side facing the table. Frank said, "I want you to meet the pet Yankee I brung you."

"Brought." Mrs. Samuel passed a bowl of steaming boiled potatoes to her husband.

Frank ignored the correction. "Jesse, this here's Billy Gashade, from New York City. Billy, this here's my baby brother, Jesse James."

FOURTEEN

Mrs. Samuel was as good a cook as advertised. Unaccustomed as I was to the rich, heavy food of that region—pork slices dripping with fat, biscuits swimming in gravy, and pies of every description—I filled my plate twice and mopped it clean both times with spongy corn bread. After supper Nettie, the Negro maid, washed the dishes while the rest of us retired to the well-appointed parlor. There, under clouds of smoke from Dr. Samuel's cigar, I sat at the piano, a fine old upright with inlaid ebony panels and polished brass pedals, and played a host of songs from a dog-eared stack of sheets tied together with ribbon, which Mrs. Samuel took from a cedar trunk. These included such standards as "Amazing Grace," "The Blue Tail Fly," and that exquisite medieval folk ballad "Barb'ra Allen," which had also been a favorite at Drucilla's among those whose parents had left ancestral homes in England and Ireland to settle the area. There were others with which I was not familiar, such as "The Gospel Train" and "The Hunters of Kentucky," a rousing celebration of the Battle of New Orleans that had accompanied Mrs. Samuel from her Kentucky birthplace after she wed the Reverend James.

And to show my gratitude to Frank for having saved my life on the Independence Road, I played "The Bonnie Blue Flag." I thought it significant that this was the only selection of the evening to which the assembly did not give voice, listening instead in the heavy silence of their own reflections. I was learning that the closer one moved to the actual fighting, the less likely he was to hear others sing of its glories.

Young Jesse had a particularly good voice, light but broad-ranged, and indescribably sweet during those passages where he overcame his natural self-awareness. His brother's was deeper but confined to a single half octave, and their mother, a contralto, dropped out on the high notes. Dr. Samuel had no ear at all and hummed when he didn't know the lyrics, which he frequently did not. Of that family, I felt its youngest member had the best chance at a career in music, provided he received the proper training. I have always believed that the world lost a good tenor when Jesse James took to robbing stages instead of appearing on them.

One song that was not to be found in the stack, and which I was never asked to play in all the time I spent with Confederate sympathizers, was "Dixie." I now attribute this to the song's Northern origins, to its composition by a Yankee named Daniel Decatur Emmett in New York, and, somewhat confusingly, to its popularity in Richmond. Along the border there existed a native distrust of the rebel capital and of all things Virginian; and if the anti-abolitionist element in Missouri chose to stand with the Old Dominion against a common foe, as had the Irish with England in the time of Napoleon, this did not erase the common feeling among these simple farmers, many of whom had never owned nor even seen a slave in the flesh, that Jefferson Davis and his West Point generals held themselves above the ordinary run of soldiers with dirty fingernails who fought and bled for the "land o' cotton."

Many years later this information enabled me to spot a fraud. In my early days in Hollywood, the bistros teemed with colorful old characters cadging drinks from gullible listeners with their blood-and-thunder "personal" accounts of life on the old frontier. One white-stubbled scarecrow, wearing a moth-eaten Confederate greatcoat and shouting "Dixie" at the top of his lungs, was rescued from a sordid walk-up speakeasy on Yucca Avenue by an executive producer at RKO, who hired him as technical advisor on a Civil War film on the strength of his boast that he was the last surviving member of Quantrill's Raiders. My attempts to discredit him based on his fondness for a tune despised by all true guerrillas were failures: Telephone calls to the executive producer went unanswered, an assistant director kept me waiting in his outer office for two hours, then listened to me for five minutes before glancing at his watch and announcing he was late for a luncheon appointment with John Gilbert. A letter to Will Hays, president of the Motion Picture Producers and Distributors Association of America, brought a polite reply that since the employment of a bogus night rider did not violate the Production Code he was not in a position to do anything about it, but asked me to keep an eye on the project and report "anything of an indecent nature." At this point I abandoned my crusade. Sometime later a writer with *Photoplay* unmasked the charlatan as a retired streetcar conductor from Ohio who before his sixty-fifth birthday had never ventured west of Cincinnati. The unpleasant publicity frightened off the bankers, the production was shelved, and the executive producer took a job in radio. All because the people in charge chose to ignore the wrong old man.

I should point out that this prejudice against Virginians did not extend to Robert E. Lee, whose framed lithograph occupied a place of pride in the James-Samuel household between an age-varnished miniature of one of Zerelda Samuel's Scottish ancestors ("Zerelda" being the mother's Christian name, and one of frequent recurrence in the family) and Dr. Samuel's diploma from the Kansas City School of Medicine. Like many of her neighbors, Mrs. Samuel, who boasted a great-grandfather from the pluckier Virginia of the American Revolution, considered General Lee a noble throwback to the spirited men and women who led the first fight for independence. I have seen two wars since those days of North versus South, and read of many more, and none has shown so many sides.

My first evening in Missouri was a success. Frank slapped me on the back, and this time the doctor shook my hand. Mrs. Samuel unbent so far as to apologize for having to put me up in the barn for lack of room in the house. "I will have Nettie bring you blankets. The nights here are capricious in late summer."

Jesse said nothing. His eyes spoke volumes. Plainly, it had been a long time since music had been heard in that house, and longer still since he had been able to behave as a boy of sixteen, as he had during the roughhouse with his brother Frank, whom I never heard him address by any name other than "Buck." My memory of Jesse at this time is of a shy youth, awkward and unsure of himself in the presence of strangers, yet one who seemed older than his years. As much as I had seen and been through since leaving behind my life in the East, I sensed that bleak scenes and personal hardship were to him a part of the natural order. His whipping in the field, the abuse of his mother, and his stepfather's torture were not unique in the county of Clay. He was and always would be just outside my ken. Friendly we would be, but we would never be friends. All this I suspected within minutes of our first acquaintance.

I slept well that night. The blankets brought to me by the black girl, together with the sweet-smelling hay in the vacant stall where I made my bed, insulated me against the dampness of the night and cushioned my sore muscles. With my belly full for the first time in days I drifted into a warm black void. Months would pass before I dreamed again of home, by which time its details had acquired the pastel, unreal quality of an illustrated *Alice*.

"We are a brand of brothers, and native to the soil;
fighting for the property we gained by honest toil.

And when our rights were threatened,
the cry rose near and far:
'Hurrah for the Bonnie Blue Flag that bears a single
star!
Hurrah! Hurrah! For Southern rights hurrah!
Hurrah for the Bonnie Blue Flag that bears a single
star!' "

In the bronze light of midday, with the gold and emerald belts of wheat and corn stretching to the hardwoods that crowned the hills to east and west, the evening's melancholy was forgotten, and stripped to the waist, the muscles in his lean back working, Frank James shoveled shit through the back door of the barn into a big pile outside and sang of war's glories. In the yard I sank the axe into the chopping block and bent to scoop up some pieces of split maple that had rolled off the heap and collected around my feet. I was becoming an adept at the chore of chopping wood.

"What do you do with the manure when the pile gets too big?" I asked.

"Well, the corn that made the meal that went into that bread you been eating didn't just grow from sun and rain and please-God."

"Oh."

"Everything a farm produces it uses." He fished a red bandanna from his hip pocket and mopped his face. "The shit goes into the corn, the corn goes into us, the shucks go into the horses and come out shit."

"What about the cobs?" I grinned.

He showed me his teeth back. "You been here three days. Don't tell me you ain't seen the inside of the outhouse by now."

Had anyone told me a week before that I would soon be living with one of Quantrill's bushwhackers, much less enjoying my stay, I would have assumed he'd been into Panama Bob's rum. My days were filled with hard work and substantial food prepared by a cook as good in her way as any chef in Manhattan; my evenings were spent at the piano, where at Frank's request I worked the fugues of Johann Sebastian Bach in among the sentimental compositions of Stephen Foster and rough-hewn Ozark ballads by anonymous but gifted illiterates dead since before Yorktown; my nights were pleasant oblivion, thoroughly earned for perhaps the first time in my life. I imagined myself to be growing lean and muscular, my voice deepening. It was a fact that when I scrubbed my face over the basin in the backyard I encountered cottony wisps on my cheeks and upper lip that told me I would be borrowing Frank's razor before long. In this I was more precocious than Jesse, who watched me stroking my face with envy in his whole carriage. Despite his twelve-hour days working in the sun with Leander, the Negro farmhand employed by the Samuels, his skin remained fair and fine on the underside of his jaw and across the top of his forehead where his hat rested, and he had yet to sprout his first whisker.

His jealousy was misplaced. When it came to life in that open country he excelled in areas where I could hope to be no more than adequate.

His horsemanship was one. Frank and I looked up from our toils to see Jesse racing in from the far field aboard one of the mules he and Leander had hitched to the wagon that morning: Head down, back hunched, his knees drawn up to his chest, he whipped the old gray jack up over the last hill and into the yard, where at the last second he leaned back on the reins and leapt off. He hit the ground running and stopped six feet short of the barn.

"What'd you think?" he asked his brother. He was out of breath, his face aglow.

"I think you better not let Ma catch you riding old Pete that way. They're eating mules younger'n him in Vicksburg."

"You know what I mean. I can ride as well as any guerrilla, and you know I can shoot."

"Can you chaw?"

"Cut me a plug and I'll show you."

Frank winked my way. "I ain't real sure there's going to be any more guerrillas, Jess. We done broke up after Lawrence. There's going to be hell to pay from the Yankees when we bunch up again."

"When you do I'm bunching right up with you. If you try to leave me behind I'll just follow you."

"If you try it you'll cross your own trail so many times you'll meet yourself both ways."

"Buck, there isn't a man alive who can throw me off his scent."

"You're a good tracker, for a fact."

"I'm the best you ever saw."

"It don't signify if you are. The Yankee army ain't hard to track." Frank tipped me a grin. "What you say, Billy? If I show up at headquarters with this sprout, is the captain going to strip me to my boots and run me over the border on a splintery old rail or what?"

"What are you asking him for? He's a Yankee, and greener'n gooseshit to boot."

That took the starch out of me, for I thought I'd done a fair job of assimilating in a short amount of time; but then there is no deceiving the child of pioneers. As rough as my outer skin became in later years, frontiersmen to the manner born frequently guessed my origins. In the places and situations God had in store for me, that intangible thing my father always spoke of as good breeding would often work to my detriment.

"He's green, all right, but he knows enough to keep his yap buttoned about things he don't know from a squirrel's ass, which is more'n I can say for a certain baby brother."

"Who you calling baby, you horsetail-faced monkey?" Jesse shot back; and in another moment the James boys were grappling in the dust and manure inside the barn.

"Stop that right now! I thought I raised two sons, not a pair of razorback hogs."

Fascinated by the spectacle of two healthy hillmen locked in combat who knew more than a thing or two about wrestling, I had taken no notice when Dr. and Mrs. Samuel rattled into the yard on the seat of the family buckboard and braked to a halt. Immediately the boys broke off and climbed to their feet, brushing the debris from their clothes.

"Ma, I didn't expect you back by daylight," Frank said, striding out to meet them. "Did you pick up some Levi Garretts?"

"Never mind your damn tobacco! What if we were the militia? You'd both be strung up like hams by now. I'm surprised you've lasted this long with no more sense than you've acquired serving with Captain Quantrill."

Zerelda Samuel continued in this vein for another minute, lifting the dark skirts she wore into Kearney to climb down from the buckboard. The cloak she had donned to disguise her pregnancy had collected dust in the folds, testifying to a hard ride from town. Dr. Samuel kept his seat—preferring to wait there, evidently, for his wife's decision to go inside the house rather than stand around supporting himself upon his cane. I listened in silence, struck dumb by the intensity of her diatribe. I had never heard her curse before that day. Her sons were equally cowed. I shall forever retain that picture of Bloody Bill Anderson's loyal sergeant, who scant days before had been up to his elbows in slaughter, and his brother, whose name would one day sear across the Western states like a flaming brand, standing with heads bowed while an irate woman enumerated their sins against intelligence. I fully believe I am the only man living who saw them so.

"What happened in Kearney?" Frank's question, dropped meekly into the ringing stillness that followed the censure, was as a pebble come to rest atop a rockslide. It had the curious effect of tranquilizing his mother, who replied in a tone of icy calm.

"They are posting these all over." She drew from beneath her cloak a cylinder of stiff paper, which Frank unrolled, then read aloud from the text printed upon it. The words were black and smudged, but they might have been written in letters of fire for the information they contained.

FIFTEEN

A mong my small collection of souvenirs from my early days on the frontier is a brown and flaking document, disintegrating along the folds, headed "General Order Number 11." I here record its main provisions, which had the devastating effect of an artillery barrage directed against the homes and businesses located in four Missouri counties in the summer of my sixteenth year—and, by projection, upon the history of the Western United States for the next two decades:

Headquarters District of the Border,
Kansas City, August 25, 1863.

1. All persons living in Jackson, Cass, and Bates Counties, and in that part of Vernon included in this district . . . are hereby ordered to remove from their present places of residence within fifteen days from the date hereof.

Those who within that time establish their loyalty to the satisfaction of the commanding officer of the military station near their present place of residence . . . will be permitted to remove to any military station in this district, or to any part of the State of Kansas, except the counties of the eastern border of the state. All others shall remove out of the district. Officers commanding companies and detachments serving in the counties named, will see that this paragraph is promptly obeyed.

2. All grain and hay in the field or under shelter, in the district from which inhabitants are required to move,

within reach of military stations after the 9th day of September next, will be taken to such stations and turned over to the proper officers there. . . . All grain and hay found in such district after the 9th day of September next, not convenient to such stations, will be destroyed. . . .

By Order of Brigadier General Ewing.
H. Hannahs, Adjutant General.

"What's it mean?" asked Jesse when his brother had finished reading.

"Confiscation."

Four pairs of eyes swung upon Dr. Samuel, who rarely spoke up on any subject of importance. The head of the household sat stiffly erect on the buckboard seat, face taut, his knuckles white on the crook of his cane.

"Confiscation is the legal term," he went on. "The military calls it requisitioning, or commandeerment. However you say it they mean to claim the western district from the citizens of Missouri. Some of the grain and hay will be used to feed Federal troops and their stock. The rest will be sold back to us at three times its value and the profit will go into the Red-legs' pockets. Some of the houses and barns will be used to quarter officers and horses and supplies. They will put the torch to the others. General Ewing means to eliminate those places where guerrillas may find concealment and rest, if it means starvation and exposure to hundreds who never raised a hand against the damned striped banner.

"That's the Yankee way," he finished, averting his eyes, as if embarrassed by the attention he had drawn.

"He is right," said Mrs. Samuel. "It is just an excuse for looting. Posting their intentions doesn't change anything."

Frank rerolled the document and bent it in the middle with his fists. "I reckon this is the payout for Lawrence."

"It doesn't mention Clay County," I said.

Now I became the attraction. My presence appeared to have been forgotten.

"That don't mean it don't touch us," Frank said.

I felt shamed and foreign. New York, with its self-contained town houses, neighborhoods, and immigrant communities—four hundred thousand individuals sequestered upon an island seven miles long and three miles wide, yet cordoned off into independent units as thoroughly as the hundred principalities of Europe—was a far cry from this country of cousins. Prick the skin of one, and hundreds bled.

Mrs. Samuel said, "The militia will be back here with blood in their eyes. They will take this to mean the Federals are behind them. This time they will not be content with abuse and torture. They will ransack the house and barn and ride down the rows with sabers."

"This time we'll be ready," Jesse put in. "I'll take off the head of the first Redleg that sets foot on our property with a double load of buckshot."

His mother shook her head. "You will not be here to do that."

"I'm sixteen, Ma. I'm not going to crawl down some hole and hide like a rabbit."

"Of course not. You have Cole blood in you, and no member of my family ever ran from a fight with right on his side. You are going with Frank."

Frank lifted his eyebrows. "Where am I going?"

"You are going back to Captain Quantrill. Do not pretend you don't know where he is. Guerrillas always have a plan."

"When was you ever a guerrilla?" Her older son was amused.

"Were. I was born a guerrilla, of guerrillas. My great-grandfather was one before there was a name for it. Your father taught you to turn the other cheek, like Jesus, but it was I who read you the story of Jesus at the temple. He was the first guerrilla."

Jesse said, "What will happen to you and the doctor here alone?"

"We will let them search the farm. The God-fearing have

nothing to hide. They know from the last time your step-father will tell them nothing even at the end of a rope, so they will not try that again."

"You can't be sure of that," Frank said. "A yellow dog will go after the same porcupine before his snout is through healing."

"Not if he is shot first." Zerelda Samuel raised the double-barreled shotgun from under her cloak.

"You took that to town?" Frank was grinning.

"She took it into the dress shop," said Dr. Samuel. "She had it with her in the changing room."

"Hell, Ma, why don't I leave Jesse here and take you with me? The captain can send half the boys home for Thanks-giving."

She shook her finger in his face. "Don't blaspheme."

Still grinning, he shook his head. "Sprout, I reckon you're in. I sure hope you can shoot Yankees the way you pick jars off a fence."

"The first fight we get into I'll shoot one for each of the welts on my back." Jesse's brow was dark.

"Shoot one for me while you're at it," said Dr. Samuel.

Now Jesse smiled, but there was still no mirth in him. "I'll shoot four for you. That's how many ribs they broke."

Frank said, "The first time you get inside gun range of a Yankee trooper, you'll be bare-ass lucky to come away with your hide. They don't just stand there like turkeys."

"Neither will I," his brother assured him.

Mrs. Samuel looked at me, and her eyes warmed. "Billy, you are free to leave anytime you choose. This is not your war."

"Ma, what am I going to say to Captain Anderson when he asks what become of the piano player? My mother let him go?"

"Tell him he broke away. God didn't give Billy music to see him slain on a battlefield for a cause that means nothing to him."

"He didn't give it to him to see him swinging from some old sycamore neither. He won't get two miles before some

abolitionist bastard hangs him for a secessionist or some ignorant bastard hangs him for a Jayhawker or some just plain
bastard hangs him for the shade. I seen a lot of necks but
I never seen one looks so easy to stretch as Billy's."

"If he stays here the militia will hang him," his mother
pointed out.

"I will go with Frank and Jesse."

Once again I became the center of the small gathering.
This embarrassed me. Then as now, the only time I felt
comfortable under public scrutiny was when I made music.
"Forgive me for speaking out of turn," I said. "I don't covet
being talked about as if I were not present."

Frank had cut himself a plug during the discussion. Now
he nearly choked on it laughing. "You're no guerrilla nor ever
will be," he said when he recovered. "Jesse ain't, but he's so
mule-headed he won't fall down the first ten times he gets
shot, and that's what makes a guerrilla. First time you get
shot, you won't be able to think of nothing to do but die."

"I don't plan to fight. As Mrs. Samuel said, this isn't my
war. My weapon is the piano. That's what Captain Anderson
wanted me for in the first place."

"I was just joshing when I said that. He won't remember
you. Anderson carries six pistols at a time. He don't check
the loads. When he wants to know is there a live round in a
chamber he points it at the nearest Yankee and jerks the trigger. See, he counts Yankees cheaper than the ball and patch
and powder and cap. He sees you, maybe he wants to hear
you play piano, maybe he wants to see if he remembered to
reload. That's why they call him Bloody Bill."

"Does Captain Quantrill encourage that?"

"Hell, for all I know he *taught* him that."

"Don't you want to go home, Billy? Your mother must be
sick with worry." Mrs. Samuel rearranged her cloak to cover
the shotgun.

"My mother has been sick for as long as I can remember.
My coming home won't make her well."

"That isn't what I asked."

"I want to go home," I said. "Trouble is waiting for me there, but that's not the reason I won't go back. If I do, I'll be living in my father's house, taking music lessons my father paid for. When I have learned enough to make my living as a musician, my first appearance will be arranged by a friend of my father's."

"Runs you from pistol to finish, does he?" Frank spat a stream of brown juice at the base of the woodpile.

"Only because I have never tried to run on my own. The trouble I got into was the first thing I have done in my life that was not his idea. Until recently I thought it was a mistake. If it weren't for that I wouldn't be doing what I'm doing now."

"It was a mistake all right. There's plenty worse jobs than chopping wood but if I had my choice I'd watch somebody else chop it for me."

"All my life someone has chopped wood for me, cooked for me, dressed me and washed my clothes. All the time my country was ripping apart at the seams I was complaining to my valet about the crease in my trousers. I didn't know the significance of being alive until I saw my first dead man hanging from an awning. Look." I showed him my palms.

Frank took one and rubbed his thumb over the fresh blisters. "Them ain't nothing. A little goose grease'll take the sting right out of them."

"I don't intend to do anything with them. I want to feel what it's like to have calluses." I took back the hand. "My father judges men for his living. I wonder how he would judge me if I were to go back now and take up my life exactly where I left off."

"You cannot live for your father," said Mrs. Samuel.

"I cannot live because of him, either. Or I shouldn't. I don't know how else to put it. I don't think I could stand to watch my hands grow soft and smooth as if I'd never swung an axe or hoisted a sack of grain to my shoulder or pointed a pistol at a man."

Frank looked down, then walked two yards to the corral and scraped manure off his boot heel onto the bottom log of the fence that enclosed it. "I reckon I just don't feature you, Billy. I seen more men hung than I got buttons on my underdrawers, and the onliest thing I ever got from it was a bucket of glad it wasn't me up there dancing on top of the weather."

Mrs. Samuel put a hand on my shoulder. "Frank and Jesse's father proposed to me in a convent. I never looked back."

"When do we leave?"

Jesse's impatience was obvious, as was his resentment that someone else had claimed center stage. I had already observed in him a strong need to be the object of everyone's consideration. It would be the pattern of his life until he was no longer in a position to change.

"Don't saddle up just yet, Jess. We still got wheat and corn to get in and a heap of wood to chop for winter."

Mrs. Samuel said, "Leander will see to that. If he requires help we will hire a temporary hand, perhaps a boy from one of the families that have been turned out. We shall have our pick of those soon."

"What's the matter, Ma, we getting on your nerves? We got two weeks."

"The Yankees have never been true to their word in the past, written or spoken. There will be troops crawling all over the county by the end of the week. If you leave within the hour you should be across the Middle Fork by nightfall. By Friday you will be in Arkansas."

"What makes you think we're headed that direction?" Frank asked.

The look Zerelda Samuel gave her son might have been one she had used when he was slow to grasp a lesson after supper. "Everyone in this part of Missouri knows Quantrill winters in Texas."

"Everyone except General Ewing," remarked Dr. Samuel; and for once he had the last word in a family discussion.

SIXTEEN

Texas!

The very name was exotic to a native New Yorker, as remote-sounding as Babylonia and Old Cathay, and filled my imagination with heroic figures and images: Davy Crockett, Jim Bowie, and Colonel Travis defending the ramparts of the Alamo; running battles between the Texas Rangers and Comanche Indians; Sam Houston and the victory of San Jacinto. Those two syllables were synonymous with the deeds of tall men with big guns and knives and eyes like shards of flint in faces burned brown by the sun. All through our preparations to leave and during the journey through the breathtaking steep green Ozark hills of southern Missouri and Arkansas and the plains and creeks of the Indian Nations, I had visions of vast deserts and brilliant sky, of ferocious sandstorms and acres of cactus and painted savages on horseback with scalps fluttering from their lances.

The reality was far different, although hardly less dramatic.

Our leave-taking was brisk and, considering that one of us was a boy going off to war for the first time, not overtly sentimental. Zerelda Samuel divided a salted ham three ways, baked biscuits, and wrapped them in greased paper and oilcloth, and these we stored in our blanket rolls. She embraced her sons affectionately but with no great display of emotion, and when she took my hand to wish me well I felt no diminution of the warmth she had shown Frank and Jesse. Dr. Samuel shook our hands, reminded Jesse of his promise to shoot a Yankee for each of his broken ribs, and told him he had to sit the dun mare high if he didn't want to be pitched off the first time the horse put its foot wrong. Jesse said he would, rolling his eyes to indicate that he had heard the same advice many times before. As we rode out of the yard the couple stood on the porch waving at us with their hands at shoulder height as if they expected us home the next morning. I gathered that partings were nothing new for them, and that the demands which recent events had made upon their human feelings had taught them the importance of conservation.

I never saw either of them again in the flesh, but I have only to close my eyes to summon Zerelda Cole James Simms Samuel sharp from behind the occlusion of decades: erect, intelligent-eyed, resolute. She was everything my mother was not, and possessed many of the qualities a son looks for in his father. The brothers James could have sprung from no other stock.

Three days out we crossed the Red River into Texas. The water was too deep for wading. I had never swum a horse before, and the gelding sensed my fear. Halfway across, the current struck us and tried to turn us around. The horse's head went under water. It came up screaming and spluttering and I lost my grip on the bridle Frank had donated from the tack at the Samuel farm to replace the hackamore. I slipped beneath the surface, but I was able to grab a fistful of mane and haul myself out of the depths. I had water in my eyes and could not tell which direction we were swimming. Then the water exploded close by, something reddish-brown struck the gelding on the opposite side, turning it crossways to the current, and an arm in a sleeve soaked black with water stretched out and grasped its bridle. I got my free hand up and under the harness on my side, and between the four of us—Frank James, his veteran bay, the gelding, and myself—we kicked and clawed our way to the point where the horses made contact with the gravelly bottom on the south bank. I hung on tight and allowed myself to be pulled up the incline and onto dry land, where I knelt gasping and vomiting water from my lungs.

"You are a bucketful of green," observed Frank when I flopped over onto my back and looked up at him standing tall and dripping against the Texas sky. "You're mighty lucksome the river's so low."

"That's low?" I hawked and spat. The water stung inside my nostrils.

"You ought to see it come spring." Shielding his eyes with a hand, he studied the sun's position. "This ain't camp. We got fifteen more miles to cover, and only four hours of daylight to do it in."

As I dragged myself back into my borrowed saddle, I glimpsed Jesse astride his stepfather's dun mare. He looked triumphant. I had begun to realize that competition was the only scale by which this child of three generations of pioneers measured his relationship with his fellow male creatures.

That part of the Lone Star State did not differ appreciably from much of the country we had been traveling through since leaving Clay County. Green, rolling, and heavily wooded with sassafras and spruce and black walnut and magnificent sequoias, the last towering as high as two hundred feet and as big around as houses at the base, it contrasted severely with all my expectations. I confess that I had little concept then of the state's great size, or of the fact that any territory as large as all of Western Europe must encompass as many different kinds of topography, vegetation, and climate. Thus the adjacent communities of Sherman and Mineral Springs, to which we were headed, bore no more resemblance to the storied settlements of San Antonio and Amarillo as London bore to Madrid, and Madrid to Berlin.

Mineral Springs was a place of uncommon beauty, compromised somewhat by the presence of tents, smoldering campfires, and the blight that accompanies large assemblies of men in a close setting: stiff "long-handled" underwear suits jittering on lengths of rope stretched between trees, heaps of rubbish, and a long slit trench at the far edge over which men squatted with their trousers down to their ankles to void themselves. Beyond all this climbed steep rocky slopes carpeted with hardwoods and evergreens, with the crystal waters of the springs glittering down cuts gouged in the limestone millions of years before the first Indians laid eyes upon them.

We had just moved within sight of the tents when a rifle cracked close by. Frank drew rein and signaled for Jesse and me to do the same.

"Get them hands in sight!"

The disembodied voice was nearly as sharp as the report. Jesse and I raised our hands.

Frank kept his where they were. "Jim Younger, that you?" he shouted.

There was a pause, then: "Frank?"

"Well, who else'd come riding smack-dab into your sights a mile after he seen the sun flashing off your rifle?"

"You never did! I got the sun behind me!"

"You don't know the sun from the moon, you cross-eyed son of a bitch."

A handful of pebbles skipped and skidded down a steep limestone slope twenty yards ahead and to the left, and a figure separated itself from the rock, a thick torso balanced on bowed legs in a Confederate uniform with a long-barreled rifle braced against one raised thigh. The face beneath the sail-brimmed hat was a dark oval against the sunset.

"I reckon I ain't so cross-eyed I don't know the moon's got no business being in the same sky with the sun," said the man. "Who's that with you?"

"My brother Jesse and Billy Gashade. He plays piano."

I began to think my tombstone would bear that inscription.

"Which one plays piano?"

Frank produced his plug and sawed at it with his knife. "Does it matter?"

"Not to me. I don't know piano music from a washtub falling downstairs. Throw me a chaw, will you? I'm out and the captain won't let us go to town."

"Where's that dollar you bet me I wouldn't get out of Lawrence alive?"

"Crawling under a boardwalk till the fighting's over don't count."

"Chew grass, you turd-kicking bastard." Frank put away

the plug and took up his reins. "You going to shoot us or let us pass?"

The man spat, then rubbed the spittle into the rock with the toe of one boot. "You scared a cross-eyed man shoots better than you think?"

"I'm scared you'll draw a bead on Jesse and blow my ass off. Where's your brother?"

"How the hell would I know? I stopped tagging after him when I got my first hard-on."

"We're coming ahead, Jim."

"Come if you're coming. It's staring into ugly faces like yours crossed my eyes in the first place."

We walked our horses past the rock. When I looked back, the sentry had blended into the hillside once again. "Aren't you afraid he'll shoot you in the back?" I asked Frank.

He leaned over and shot a stream of tobacco into the grass beside the trail. "Jim Younger's just about the best friend I got, next to his brother Cole. And the best rifle shot in Missouri."

We were passing the first tent when I had one of the surprises of my life. A woman stepped out through the flap carrying an enormous dead rat by the tail and threw it into the road. My gelding shied and I choked up on the reins to keep from falling off. The woman, a gourd-shaped Indian in a plain blouse and dark ground-length skirt with her hair in braids, stared at me with bottomless black eyes as I rode past.

Farther on we saw more women, scrubbing laundry in large wooden tubs, stirring kettles suspended from makeshift tripods over open fires, and sitting on canvas stools before their tents, smoking cigarettes and sewing buttons on shirts. Most were white, but several were Indian and a few were black. Many wore men's hats and coats. One or two had on muslin shifts only, with round-toed boots too big for their feet, and the sun behind them showed that they wore no underclothing. I felt my face growing hot and avoided their

knowing eyes when they looked up at the three newcomers
riding past. I guessed their function.

A cry, shrill enough to cause Frank to jerk one of the Navy
Colts partway from its saddle scabbard, turned all our heads
in the direction of a tent several yards ahead, where a young
woman stumbled out through the flap, barefoot and clutching the ruins of a garment to her chest. She wore nothing
above the waist. Running with her head turned to look back
over her bare shoulder, she would have collided with Frank's
horse had he not yanked back on the reins, emitting an ear-
splitting whistle through his teeth as he did so. Startled, the
woman looked in front of her, saw the hazard, and tried to
stop. She lost her footing and fell into an undignified sitting
position on the ground, losing the torn garment and exposing a pair of small breasts with large brown nipples. The sight
set my pulse hammering. Ada had lit a fire back at Drucilla's
that I knew would continue to smolder into old age.

When I looked back at Jesse, his face was averted and as
red as rouge. It gave me some small satisfaction to learn that
I had the advantage over him in this one area.

An instant later a familiar ogre emerged from the tent and
took two long strides toward the half-naked girl before he saw
us and stopped. Instinctively, Lieutenant John Thrailkill
reached for the big revolver in the holster on his hip, then
changed directions when he recognized Frank and hooked
his trailing braces over his shoulders. He wore no shirt over
his long underwear, which clung like a second skin to the lean
sinew of his arms and torso. His classic features were blurred
somewhat by his disheveled hair and a two-day growth of
beard, but his dead pale eyes were clear.

"Thought you'd deserted," he said.

Frank ignored the taunt. "I see you're still hell with the
ladies, Johnny."

"It ain't what you think. I wanted her to model, but she
thought I wanted something else."

The young woman got to her feet and stood with eyes downcast, clutching the tattered cloth to her chest. It had been a blouse, a becoming one printed with flowers. She had long straight black hair like an Indian's, but her features were fine and the skin of her breasts was blue-white.

"Women," Frank said appreciatively. "They're each one different, and all the same. I never seen one so eager for it she wouldn't stop to unbutton a pretty piece of cloth like that there. Especially not with a war on and goods so dear."

"They get queer notions. They think nothing of dancing bare-ass in front of the whole camp, but ask them to take their shirt off in a tent so you can paint them and they fight like a badger." Thrailkill put a hand to his face and took it away to look at it, and I saw a row of angry red scratches on his cheek for the first time. "I reckon I got impatient."

"Hell, Johnny, I don't care what you do with them in your tent. I just don't want you scaring my brother."

"I see you brought more than your brother." The empty eyes turned my way. "We ain't got no piano here."

"You got something else that belongs to Billy, though. That pretty pistol he loaned you."

"I ain't got nothing don't belong to me."

"Sure you do. You just forgot. As I recall it was his decision to let you have it for a while. He damn near gave you the business end of it, and you with your jaw hanging down past your balls."

One of the half-undressed women watching from the tents cut loose with a loud guffaw. Thrailkill threw her a look that choked it off.

"He wants it back he can come get it." He turned his eyes back upon me. It was like looking into a pair of open graves.

"You shouldn't be that way, Johnny. Captain Quantrill won't like it. Any more'n he won't like hearing how you treat your models. You know how soft he is on women."

"Maybe what Quantrill likes or don't like don't matter no more."

Frank straightened in his saddle. "That's foolish talk even for you."

Thrailkill turned his way, and it seemed to me he grew taller. "Things ain't what they were when you lit out. There's been a whole new shuffle since Lawrence. A fresh king's on top."

"And who might that be, you?"

"No. Not him."

This was a new voice; or perhaps, when we looked at the man standing in front of the tent across from Thrailkill's, not so new after all. Bloody Bill Anderson looked up at us from the revolver he was wiping with an oily rag. The other five he wore in various holsters and slings were clearly visible with his coat off.

SEVENTEEN

They said two women were the cause.

The situation was more complex than that, of course. Money, jealousy, and conscience were also involved.

Fletch Taylor, one of the fiercest of Quantrill's lieutenants, had defied the custom of dividing plunder equally among the men, claiming for himself six thousand dollars in United States currency taken from Lawrence. Appeals to Quantrill were useless; the guerrilla leader, who lived for revenge, was sated temporarily and not inclined to take interest in a squabble over finances. Captain Anderson, commanding as much loyalty as Quantrill, and whose blood lust was even more pronounced, stayed aloof from the dispute while news of the inequity spread through the ranks like a cancer.

Others, sickened and disillusioned by the bloodbath in Kansas, had deserted for their homes or places with the regular army. William H. Gregg had pulled out with a substantial number of followers to join General Jo Shelby's brigade in Louisiana, and it was rumored that Cole Younger, a Quantrill man almost from the beginning, was considering a Confederate post. Those who remained were undecided whether to stay with the status quo or throw in with Bloody Bill. All that was required was a shift to one side of the scale or the other.

After Lawrence, Quantrill had acquired a mistress, one Kate King, who in a kind of common-law ceremony of marriage took on his middle name of Clarke. The pair were often absent from the day-to-day military life at Mineral Springs, pursuing their dalliance. At about the same time, Anderson had reported his desire to marry in nearby Sherman at his earliest opportunity. Quantrill, who seemed to think himself the only guerrilla privileged to permanent female companionship, ordered him to put off his wedding until after the war, whereupon Bloody Bill declared his intentions to pull out for Sherman, and issued a blanket invitation to as many of the men who cared to accompany him to get their gear together.

This was the situation when Frank and Jesse James and I entered the guerrilla camp on the eve of September 1863, never realizing that we were scaling a powder keg until we were sitting on top of it.

Much of our information came courtesy of the brother of the fellow who had challenged us at the edge of camp. After taking our leave of Lieutenant Thrailkill and Captain Anderson, we spotted a man standing up to his knees in a pool of crystalline water down the hill from the first cluster of tents, twirling a length of stout cord with a bent pin attached. Frank watched in silence while the weighted end arced up and out and disappeared into the water with a gulp.

Then: "Them better be Yankee fish you're hooking, Cole Younger."

The man, whose back was turned toward us, didn't flinch, but reeled in the cord slowly with a practiced winding motion of both hands. "I'm safe, then. I ain't hooked a one since before noon."

"Maybe if you washed your feet before you waded in, they'd still have a appetite."

"Maybe if damn fools didn't keep yelling fit to scare a crazy wolf, we'd have catfish for supper instead of Texas rattlesnake. How the hell are you, Frank? I heard you deserted."

"I heard the same thing. Bet we both heard it from the same place. I thought Johnny might simmer down a little after Lawrence."

"He'll simmer down when they pat him in the face with a spade. Me, I had my fill and then some. I'm getting out."

"I heard that too. What you fixing to do with Shelby you can't do with this bunch?"

"Walk on my hind legs, for one. I'm sick of slanching around like a wormy dog." He coiled the cord neatly and resumed twirling, feeding out a little more with each pass until the makeshift hook whistled out in a flat circle eight feet from his head. Then he let fly. This time the end plunked beneath the surface three yards beyond where it had landed the time before. Again he commenced reeling it in. "I seen Thrailkill plug a man full of holes hiding in a cornfield on the edge of Lawrence with a baby in his arms. Left him dead with the baby still there squalling. I picked it up and took it into town and gave it to the first woman I come to. She spit on me. No woman ever spit on me before," he added.

"You shoot her?"

"Why? She didn't do nothing I didn't do to myself when I agreed to ride into that damn town."

"You felt that way, how come you didn't shoot Thrailkill?"

"I didn't get to him in time to save that poor bastard in the cornfield. Anyway you ain't done much when you've shot a man that's dead already."

He'd snagged something. He jerked the cord taut to set the hook and hauled it in hand over hand. In another moment he held up the ugliest fish I'd ever seen, twelve inches long and black, with tentacles sprouting like whiskers from each side of its working mouth. It flapped desperately, splashing him with water from its fins and tail.

Frank whistled. "That's an elephant. I wonder what's the record around here."

Holding the fish by the gills, the man in the water worked the hook out of its mouth. He stood studying it for a moment, then with an underhand flip threw it back into the water.

"Not hungry, I reckon," Frank said.

"I ain't et all day. I ain't so bad off I need to bash in some poor slippery cat's brains to make my dinner. Not tonight anyhow." He looked down at the coiled line. Without hesitation he threw it in after the fish, turned around, and waded toward dry land.

Sturdily built like his brother, but taller and more evenly proportioned, Cole Younger sported a handsome set of chestnut-colored chin-whiskers, perhaps in compensation for the thinning of his widow's peak, though I judged him to be no older than Frank James. (He was in fact several months younger.) He was in his shirtsleeves—plain homespun, no guerrilla ruffles—and shapeless tan trousers rolled up to his knees, and wore no hat. I never knew him to wear one afterward, no matter the weather; there was a belief at the time that covering one's head encouraged baldness, and as he had a keen interest in scientific theory I always suspected this had something to do with his decision. Once out of the water he stooped to pick up a worn pair of stovepipe boots and dingy gray stockings, but before he put them on he came the rest of the way up the bank and reached up to shake Frank's hand. Such scrupulous observation of the courtesies was so rare in my recent experience that I goggled. Here, I thought, was something new in night riders.

"Jesse. I heard a parcel about you from your brother," said he when the other James was introduced.

Jesse murmured a greeting of some kind. He seemed to be

in awe of the big man, and I assumed that Frank had told him at least as much about Younger as he had told Younger about his brother.

Jesse James and Cole Younger. I have pummeled my memory for something dramatic about that historic first meeting. All I saw was a boy and a man exchanging polite words.

Frank said, "This here's Billy Gashade. You two got a thing in common, Cole. Billy's old man is a judge."

He turned friendly eyes on me. "What jurisdiction?"

"The eighth District Court of Manhattan," I said.

"That's a long way to travel to fight for the South." He sounded mildly surprised.

"Oh, Billy don't fight. He's a musician."

His smile upon receiving this information was reserved but warm. He had a wide, thin-lipped mouth that seemed always ready to smile or frown; a blank canvas waiting for the first stroke of the brush. "The organist at Drucilla's. I heard. Do you play any other instruments?"

"The piano," I said.

"Sorry to hear it. I found a guitar in Lawrence and I been looking for somebody to play it ever since, to make me feel less the damn fool for carrying it all this way."

"Hell, learning the guitar's got to be easy after the piano," Frank said. "It's just five strings against eighty-eight keys."

"Where is your father's bench?" I asked Younger, changing the subject.

His smile faded. "Six feet under some of the best topsoil in Missouri. Federals killed him last year."

"I'm sorry."

"Not half as sorry as the Yankees," said Frank. "Judge Younger backed the North. They made one fine fair Johnny Reb out of Cole in one night."

Younger sat down on the ground and began pulling on his stockings and boots. "You're welcome to ride with me to see Shelby, Frank. The regulars need good cavalry."

"Your brother going?"

"Jim likes it here. Bloody Bill promised him a commission. Shelby's got more lieutenants than he needs."

"I reckon I'll stick for the same reason. I been in it too long to start taking orders from a shavetail with pimples on his dick." Frank leaned over and spat tobacco.

"Suit yourself. When the Yankees catch you and hang you I'll send flowers to your old ma."

"Well, don't pick 'em just yet. You get any of that Kentucky sippin' I heard Fletch Taylor found in the cellar of the Eldridge House?"

"I been saving a bottle for a special occasion."

"It's my first Texas sundown. If that ain't occasion enough, I don't know what is."

Cole Younger stood and stamped his heels into his boots. "I reckon it is, at that. My tent's this way." He started walking, and we coaxed our horses into his path.

Seated that night on the ground before Cole Younger's tent, eating salted ham and biscuits and passing around a plain unlabeled bottle of mellow rye whiskey—not my first taste of hard spirits, but certainly my most substantial to date, warming my insides and lifting my thoughts free of the gravity that chained my body to the earth—I learned most of what I still know about the men who rode with Quantrill and Anderson. It was a story as old as Homer yet as fresh as the Union and Confederate blood staining the ground at Chancellorsville and along the Shenandoah.

I know not to whom he told it, or whether he was telling it to anyone at all. At the time I assumed it was for the benefit of the newcomers, Jesse and myself, but upon reflection I wonder if he was attempting to fit together the pieces in his own mind, and if the rest of us were merely eavesdropping. He sat with his legs crossed Indian fashion, staring into the small fire he had built to ward off the evening chill and moving only when his long-stemmed clay pipe required recharging. His voice was low and pleasant, changing pitch as the narrative demanded, in the old storytelling tradition.

As he related, most of the men with whom he had spent the past twelvemonth held personal grudges against the North and those who had allied themselves with it. Cole and his brothers, James, Robert, and John, the latter pair still too young to take up arms, had been deprived of a father when Union militiamen robbed and murdered Judge Henry W. Younger in retaliation for his son's guerrilla involvement. Shortly after the murder, Cole's sister and a female cousin were incarcerated in Kansas City by order of James Walley, a militia captain. Walley accused them of espionage, but in fact he was angry over having been scorned by the sister at a dance. When the ramshackle jailhouse collapsed, crushing the cousin to death among others, rumors flew that the building had been undermined deliberately to prevent the Younger girls from testifying against Walley. Another of the women who died in the disaster happened to be a sister of William Anderson, thus setting that individual on the violent road that would lead him to the sobriquet of Bloody Bill. Accident or otherwise—and I heard too much testimony afterward to disregard entirely the accusation that the hand of man was involved—this tragedy had within the space of a few minutes created two enemies whose acts of vengeance would plague the Union for years.

John Thrailkill's reasons to hate the Yankees were as good as anyone's and better than most. I scarcely credited it at the time, but before the war he had been an artist, and a good one. Engaged to marry a beautiful girl whose family sided with the South, he was locked away in his rented studio laboring with his brushes and easel to make his paintings salable to support them both when militiamen paid a call upon her at her father's home. When they left, the invalid old gentleman was dead, the young woman violated and out of her head with grief and shame. When Thrailkill finally emerged from his artistic exile, he found his fiancée laid out in her prettiest dress on the sofa in her parlor, she having slit her wrists and bled to death in her bath. After kissing her cold lips, the young man swore to avenge her and her father. At the time I met him, he had slain eighteen of the twenty men who had been present at the time of the murder and her disgrace, and if the blood he had spilled had quenched his fires in any way, the flame at the start must have been prodigious indeed.

"It's difficult to believe that two more deaths will restore his humanity," said I at this point in the story.

Cole looked at me over the bowl of his pipe. "Seen any of his paintings?"

"Does he still paint?"

"Sometimes late at night I get up to use the latrine, I see a lantern on in his tent with his shadow jumping around. That's when he works, never outside during daylight like I hear he used to. I seen just one of them, when he went out and left his tent flap crooked. I don't know what his pictures looked like before the war. Maybe they was all like that, but I doubt it or he'd of gone up like a plugged barrel long before he did."

"What did it look like?" I asked.

He shook his head. "I can't tell it so you'd see it. I just hope I never dream nothing like what I seen on that canvas. I reckon he does, though, all the time."

Jesse's eyes were fixed upon him, pupils wide and shining, like a child's during a bogey tale. "What does he do with the paintings?"

"Burns 'em, I suppose. Or buries 'em. There sure ain't room for them in his traps when we move on."

"Why go to all the bother of painting them just to destroy them?" Jesse asked.

Frowning, Cole knocked out his pipe against a flat rock next to the fire. "I read this piece once in *Harper's*, about getting things out of your skull before they have the chance to fester. Maybe that's what he's doing. I know I sure wouldn't want to walk around with a thing like that stuck under my hat."

"Dogs!" Frank moved his shoulders up and down and reached for the bottle. "I wisht you had a piano in your tent. I'd like to go to sleep thinking about Billy's Bach instead of them paintings in Johnny Thrailkill's skull."

"Your mind made up against that guitar?" Cole was looking at me. "I'd as lief not pack it all the way back to Missouri. I'll bust it up before I let some Yankee find it and pluck out 'John Brown's Body' or worse."

Perhaps it was the whiskey. Perhaps, like Frank James, I preferred to insert something physical between my dreams and the dark visions that came out through the bristles of Lieutenant Thrailkill's brushes. In any case I told Cole I'd give the guitar a try. As he got up to look for it, I heard Jesse sigh. Plainly he resented the interruption. I wondered if the young would-be guerrilla dreamed, and if his dreams had the power to terrify him. Nothing else appeared to come close.

EIGHTEEN

Here my narrative accelerates. The primary responsibility of the storyteller is to hold the interest of his audience, and while lengthy periods of physical and intellectual stagnation are as much a part of war as destruction and death, it would serve no purpose to recount in extended and redundant detail the long flyblown days and stale sultry nights that stretched unbroken between the horrors that continue to season my dreams. Sufficient to say that there is little more diverting in a sticky summer night spent in the open, prey to mosquitoes and chiggers, than is to be found inside a moldy tent in winter, with rain leaking in and two healthy Missouri farmboys sleeping within arm's length, passing gas and snoring loud enough to wake Gettysburg's fifty thousand dead.

The days were hardly better. In effect, with Union troops turning over every rock and leaf in Missouri and Kansas for the men responsible for the Lawrence outrage, we were in hiding, counting upon the Texas alliance with the Confederacy to protect us from retribution. As a result, we were inactive, which was not a situation calculated to rest lightly upon the shoulders of men who had gathered around the standard of the black flag to ride, fight, plunder, and kill. With no enemy within reach, the guerrillas' natural disposition turned inward. Fights broke out daily, challenges were issued and accepted. The object of a squabble might be a missing poke full of coins, a razor borrowed and not returned, or the affections of one of the female camp followers. Broken jaws and gunshot wounds were treated with frequency at the "hospital tent"—two soiled cots overseen by a former St. Louis intern denied a license to practice medicine for reasons of drunkenness.

By and large, these sporadic eruptions were welcome distractions from unbroken days and nights of boredom. There were card games and horse races, shooting contests, and betting; but these things required energy, and each day spent apart from the war that raged in the East drained the stores like coal oil leaking from a neglected barrel. *Morale*, a term of French origin just then beginning to seep its way into the military lexicon, was low, and getting lower by the day. Desertions were reported on a regular basis.

Late in September, Bloody Bill Anderson left Mineral Springs for Sherman, completing the breach between him and Quantrill. Frank, Jesse, and I rode with the men who accompanied him, a number comprising nearly half the remaining command. The change of scenery was a relief. We left the tents behind and took up permanent quarters in the Christian Hotel, where the three of us shared a room.

By this time I had begun to conquer the guitar. The instrument, enameled red and bearing the initials W.G.B. burned into the wood on the back, had six strings rather than five, and I had spent the better part of the first week learning how to tune it properly; but by the end of the second I was plucking out "Amazing Grace," earning for the effort an angry bruise on my upper left arm one midnight when Frank James flung a boot at me in the darkness of the tent and requested I put the damned thing down and go to sleep. Although I still had much to learn, when I slipped the hand-tooled leather strap across my shoulder, my fingers flocked to the frets and strings like birds to a telegraph wire. After the first month I discarded the chip of firewood I had fashioned into a pick. The calluses on my fingertips had grown thick enough to take its place. I was fast forming a bond to rival my lifelong relationship with the keyboard.

Meanwhile, dissension and *ennui* among the men boiled over into the surrounding communities. Fletch Taylor— acting, it was charged, upon orders from Quantrill, who quarreled frequently with the authorities in Texas—led a band of guerrillas to a house north of Sherman and robbed and killed one Major Butts, a Confederate officer. Quantrill, reversing himself under pressure, suggested turning Taylor over to the regular army for court-martial, but Anderson, with whom Taylor had ridden from Mineral Springs, refused to betray the guerrillas' oath of self-government. He had the major's widow escorted into town for her own protection and put her up at the Christian Hotel.

The situation fermented and festered. On Christmas Day, guerrillas loyal to Quantrill charged into Sherman, firing their pistols at whatever targets tempted them, chasing pedestrians off the boardwalks, and riding into stores and public buildings, destroying merchandise and terrorizing employees and patrons. One group, acting with single-minded deliberation, galloped into the lobby of the Christian just as Mrs. Butts was coming downstairs to investigate the commotion and shot the ornament off her woolen cap. Laughing, they turned their horses and rode back out.

A citizens' committee appointed by the town complained to General Henry McCulloch, commander of Confederate troops in the area, asking him to capture and punish the men involved in the attack. With the pressure building, Captain Anderson rode into McCulloch's camp and officially accused Quantrill. In March 1864, William Clarke Quantrill was ordered to report to the general's office and placed under house arrest.

On the last day of March but one, I elected not to leave the hotel room when Frank and Jesse invited me to go walking with them. Things had quieted considerably since the incidents of Christmas—grown soporific, in fact—and with nothing but the guitar and Jesse's personal Bible for entertainment, I was feeling depressed and lethargic. Early spring was a time of awakening in New York, beginning with the raucous frivolity of the St. Patrick's Day parade and quickening with the first warm breezes from the harbor and the height of the theater season, when cabriolets and broughams filled the streets and Fifth Avenue became a sea of high silk hats and ladies' floriated chapeaux. By contrast, March in northeastern Texas was merely wet. Dirty gray skies rolled down almost to the ground, releasing sheets of gluey water like fly paste and churning the streets into troughs of yellow-brown mud knee-deep. Mildew formed on everything, and the quest for dry feet took on all the fanatic importance of the search for the grail. I had not received a letter from my father since Lawrence. I was certain he had written, but I was equally certain his letters had been returned in lieu of a forwarding address. General McCulloch had shut down the post office in Sherman, decreeing that henceforth only military communications would be allowed between the territory under his jurisdiction and the East. I was suffering from a severe head cold, and I was more homesick than ever.

Abetted partly by a medicinal draught from a bottle Frank had purchased in a local establishment of a whiskey he called "Texas tanglefoot"—not by any means to be confused with the smooth, aged spirits we had shared in front of Cole Younger's tent on our first night in Mineral Springs—I drifted from my funk into a deep sleep. When I awoke it was dark.

I coughed, stirred, and thought at first that the cold had settled in my chest, realizing but slowly that the weight I felt there was real.

I smelled fresh whiskey. Evidently one of my roommates, most likely Frank, as I had yet to see his brother drink anything stronger than the bottled water from the springs, had returned heavily under the influence, crawled into bed heedless that it was already occupied, and gone to sleep with an arm draped across my chest. I struggled into a sitting position, groped on the nightstand until I found the box of lucifers placed there for the purposes of lighting the lamp, and struck one on the bedrail. The white flare blinded me at first, then as the sulfur burned away and the flame turned yellow, I saw a slender naked arm stretched across the quilt, and beyond it, nestled into the hollow between my neck and shoulder, a head with an abundance of long black unfettered hair. Neither the arm nor the hair belonged to any guerrilla of my acquaintance. As I stared, waiting for the clouds to clear, the head lifted and a pair of dark pretty eyes regarded me in silence.

The flame stung my fingers. I gasped and dropped the match, then slapped desperately at the sheet lest it smolder. While I was thus engaged, another match flared. A hand lifted the glass chimney of the lamp on the nightstand. The hand holding the match started the wick glowing. Frank James's face, demonic in the light from below, floated in the darkness surrounding it. "Happy birthday, youngster. Sorry I didn't get time to wrap your present."

I looked from him to the grave young woman lying against me. She was the same one who had fled from John Thrailkill's tent the day of our arrival at the guerrilla camp. I knew without investigating that she was naked beneath the quilt we shared. Now I looked back at Frank. "How did you know?"

"You told me the date. You wouldn't remember doing it. You was drinking that good Kentucky rye of Cole's. Wonder how he's getting on with Shelby? From what I hear there ain't a dime's worth of difference betwixt him and Captain Quantrill." He shifted the plug in his mouth, found the cuspidor at the foot of the bed, and used it. "Don't get too attached to the filly. Johnny's bound to miss her come morning."

"What am I supposed to do with her?"

He grinned. "You're seventeen now, pard. I reckon you'll come up with something."

"Is Jesse in on this?"

"Jess has a stick up his ass over this kind of thing. He don't hold with it. There's a load of our pa in that boy."

"I can't," I said.

Just then the dark-haired girl slid her hand under the quilt and grazed her fingers down my bare torso. Our faces were inches apart. No smile came to her lips, but her eyes reflected the light from the lamp. Her hand stopped, fondled. I took in my breath.

Frank withdrew into the darkness. "Where are you going?" My voice was strained.

"Little brick house on the west end of town. I know somebody there." The door opened to the hall.

"What are you going to do?"

I heard the grin in his tone. "Celebrate your birthday, what else?"

Alone with the young woman, I fumbled at the nightstand, found the glass tumbler I had set there, and drank. I choked and coughed. Someone, probably Frank, had poured out the water and substituted Texas tanglefoot. As I recovered, gasping, the girl took her hand from under the covers and held it out.

"Can I have some?" Her voice was shallow and breathy, a little girl's snared in a woman's body.

I handed her the glass. She drank off half the contents in a long draught and gave it back. Her dark gaze met mine. She seemed to flush a little, but it may have been the effect of the spirits.

"What is your name?" I asked her.

"Nowata."

"Are you an Indian?"

"I'm half Cherokee."

I took a careful sip from the glass. The whiskey warmed me and calmed my nerves. "Which half?"

She smiled then for the first time.

The war came back with the fury of a mad beast suddenly set free.

On the night of my seventeenth birthday, March 30, 1864, as I lay with Nowata, William Clarke Quantrill overpowered the two Confederate soldiers assigned to guard him, locked them in the clothespress of the room where he had been held, and made his escape.

Alerted by General McCulloch, with whom he was cooperating at present, Bloody Bill Anderson ordered his men to mount up and pursue his former commander.

Quantrill, riding at the head of the small band that had remained loyal to him, fled into Missouri, where he eluded his persecutors and entered upon a series of minor but violent skirmishes that would continue to make his name synonymous with war at its worst.

Anderson, by contrast, aligned himself more closely with the regular Confederate Army, coordinating his command with that of General Sterling Price in a series of devastating raids against Union forces in Missouri.

Although I accompanied the guerrillas on these forays, I saw little of the actual fighting, riding at the rear of the column with the women and other noncombatants, including the young boys and stove-in soldiers who fetched water and performed other necessary chores: repairing boots and harnesses, carrying supplies, trapping and shooting game and preparing it for consumption, driving the ammunition wagons. When we camped, I produced my guitar, played requested tunes, and introduced a few that were unfamiliar to the company. The selections I chose from Vivaldi quickly became favorites, but Liszt left my listeners cold, and they were positively hostile to anything by Rameau, whose bold experiments in dissonance had found little more approval in the French salons of the eighteenth century. To be fair, I must point out that I was playing their compositions from memory, upon an instrument I had yet to master. However, the same was true of the Scottish mountain ballads I attempted to reproduce after hearing a few bars hummed by those members of my audience who asked me to play them, and these seldom failed to spark applause or an impromptu jig. Unsophisticated though these fierce fighters and their women were in the area of musical criticism, I found gratification in their acceptance even as their displeasure mortified me.

Billy Gashade, read the packet of calling cards I still carried in my pocket; *Entertainments*.

A number of the Missourians I had known since the beginning had passed almost beyond my ken.

Anderson, far up front directing murderous flank attacks at the Federals to divert attention from Price's frontal assault, was a source of rumors and legend as farfetched as if his exploits were taking place in another hemisphere and reported in relays, growing with each retelling. At Pilot Knob he was encircled by enemy forces ten times his strength, but slashed his way to freedom with bayonets and sabers; at the Missouri River he charged a Union encampment and forced the troops into the swift waters, where most of them drowned. Homer would have found few heroes in his repertoire to stand beside Bloody Bill as he was described to us at the rear.

Cole Younger, some said, was in California, utterly disillusioned with the war and with his failed efforts on behalf of General Jo Shelby to recruit mercenaries in Mexico for the rebel army. When next he loaded his pistols, it would be for no cause but his own.

John Thrailkill was particularly active, and the stories that drifted back from the fighting, of women and children cut down by his shot and steel, of villages razed and Negroes lynched, curdled the blood. I did not care to see what fearsome paintings sprang from his twisted soul during this period.

What little news I received that I regarded as truth came from Frank James. I had my own tent now, left by a deserter, and he visited often, to enjoy a chew without having to listen to one of his fellow night riders boasting of his prowess and to hear me play. Although I had heard wild tales of his feats fighting at Anderson's side, he seldom spoke of himself, preferring to pass on bits of gossip and share glowing reports of his brother Jesse's performance under the command of Lieutenant Fletch Taylor.

"He's a scrapper," Frank was fond of saying. "Even Bloody Bill says he's the keenest and cleanest fighter he's got. He don't swear nor drink nor pay attention to lewd women. I reckon that's where he finds the energy."

For two weeks in August, Frank did not come around. We were in Carroll County, a wild place of thistles and thorny locust trees forever scheming to reclaim the land from the farmers who did battle with them every day with scythes and axes; combat with militia and Union regulars had been heavy and hot along the Ray County line, and rumors of victory, defeat, and casualties had been contradicting one another furiously for days. I feared that my friend and sometime protector had fallen. Then, on the anniversary of the Lawrence raid, a gaunt, hollow-eyed specter of Zerelda Samuel's firstborn shambled into the light of my fire and stood swaying before the camp stool where I sat picking my way through "Tenting Tonight." His beard was untrimmed and the front of his faithful knitted pullover was caked with something that in another place and time I should have assumed was mud.

"Jess," he said; and without waiting for a response, turned and shuffled back into the shadows.

I followed, of course. He had tied his racing bay, panting and flecked with foam, to the picket line, and despite his clear exhaustion was in the saddle by the time I joined him in the torchlight. My gelding was already saddled—standing orders whenever the war was in full cry—and though I lost no time in mounting, I had to kick the horse into a brisk trot to catch up with him. I had brought my guitar without thinking. Not knowing what else to do with it, I slung the strap across my shoulder.

We covered perhaps two miles. The distance seemed greater in that wild country with no moon and only dusty starlight to guide us around chuckholes and low saplings. At long last we stopped within sight of a small log cabin with a smear of light in a greased-paper window. After a moment spent in silent scrutiny of the building and the clearing that surrounded it, Frank slid one of the Navies from its scabbard and fired it twice at the sky. Again we waited while the echo of the reports growled among the distant hills. Then a fresh crack of light appeared to the right of the window—a door opening—and a muzzle flashed vertically, followed an instant later by the crash of a rifle. Frank scabbarded his pistol and coaxed his tired mount forward. I fell into step behind.

"Who's that with you?"

Our challenger, dimly outlined on the cabin's tiny front porch, wore bib overalls with a piece of twine holding them up on one side where the strap had broken. The light from indoors made haloes in the dents on his bald scalp. An ancient flintlock musket rested on its buttstock with his hand holding the barrel.

"He's with me, ain't he? Any change?"

"Nope. That boy's a goner for certain."

"The hell with you, Rudd," Frank flared. "You're a good Christian and I thank you for all you done, but the hell with you."

Rudd said nothing. We dismounted, handing him the reins, and went inside. A rag rug lay on the dirt and there were a few sticks of furniture and a fireplace for cooking, but aside from that the lone room appeared empty and uninhabited.

Frank led the way around a worn quilt hung from a rope strung across the end.

Jesse James lay on an old feather mattress in a bed made from pine planks. Flies crawled on his face in the light of a lantern hung from a nail in the wall. Where the counterpane had slid down, a slash of white bandage slanted up over one shoulder, Roman toga fashion. His skin was pale and appeared clammy.

"Jess?" Frank's tone was a murmur.

Jesse didn't stir. His eyes remained closed.

"Minié ball ripped a hole in his chest big as a barn door on the twelfth," his brother said. "That cork-pulling sawbones didn't give him till the end of the first week. Takes an hour to get a bowl of broth into him. He'll swallow; he just won't wake up. I tried talking and singing and yelling. I don't want to shake him. Sawbones says it wouldn't do no good anyhow."

"I'm sorry."

He looked at me. In the illumination from below, his face was deeply etched, with shadows hammocked in the pockets. He looked three times his age. "Play for him, will you, Billy? Jesse likes your music."

"On the piano," I said. "I'm still learning the guitar."

"That don't matter. If fingers was all there was to it, any teamster ever handled a six-hitch rig could make music. It don't come from the fingers." When still I hesitated, his face grew hard. "I don't like to call in markers. I figure you owe it to me for the Independence Road."

I slid the guitar around. "I cannot promise anything."

He brought me a wobbly cane-bottom chair, and I played for Jesse: "Amazing Grace," "The Bonnie Blue Flag," "The Gospel Train"; as many of the tunes from Zerelda Samuel's cedar trunk as I could remember, along with those I had learned since and those I had brought with me from New York. I played deep into the night, started awake in the gray wash of dawn, and resumed playing. Jesse remained motionless.

The doctor, a young man in everything but outlook, with hands that shook slightly and broken blood vessels in his cheeks, came to examine the patient shortly after sunrise, shook his head, returned his instruments to his cylindrical bag, and spoke to Frank on the other side of the hanging quilt. Frank's voice rose harshly above the guitar music. To avoid listening, I concentrated upon my fingering. I was tired and hungry and sore from my night on a chair not designed for sleeping. I counted ten fingers on one hand. I closed my eyes and went on playing.

". . . the Hunters of Kentucky."

Jesse's singing voice was scarcely a whisper. I opened my eyes, half certain I had dreamt hearing it, and met his gray-blue gaze.

I cried Frank's name. He came running, followed closely by the doctor, who looked into Jesse's eyes and measured his pulse against a battered steel watch. Again he shook his head, this time in disbelief. For all that he seemed no less grave than before.

After the doctor left, Frank and I went outside while his brother rested. Rudd, who apparently had slept on the porch, was busy drawing water from the well in the yard.

"Jesse's strong," I said. "He'll recover."

"I know it." He cut himself a chew.

"I doubt it was anything I did. He'd have awakened sooner or later."

"Maybe not."

I slung the guitar behind my back. "I'm tired. I guess I'll go back to my tent."

"Leave it."

I waited. He was leaning on his forearms on the porch railing, shifting the plug back and forth in his mouth. "Go back to New York. Go to California, like Cole. This ain't your war. Never was."

"I want to stay." Even as I said it, I realized it was untrue.

"You ain't listening. You been sucking this tit too long. Hard enouch feeding them that pull their weight."

I watched Rudd carrying the wooden bucket toward the house, throwing out his free arm for balance. "It's going to get bad, isn't it?" I said. "Worse than it's been."

"Leave the gelding. You need a horse can outrun the militia when you stumble smack into them like you're bound to. I don't reckon Jesse will mind too much if you borrow the dun mare."

"What's going to happen?"

"What do you care? You'll be in New York. Or California." He spat a brown stream over the railing.

"I care."

"I know it."

"Thanks." I stuck out my hand.

He regarded it, then extended his across his body to take it. "One thing you need to remember about that mare."

"I remember. Sit her high."

He grinned.

III

Ballad of a Wanderer

NINETEEN

Frank James was prescient. It did get worse.

On September 27, 1864, Anderson and 225 guerrillas pulled Union troops off a passenger train in Centralia, Missouri, lined them up on the station platform, and forced them to strip to their underclothing to provide the night riders with disguises for future activities. Bloody Bill, it was reported, stalked up and down the line of captives like an officer reviewing his troops, then turned to John Thrailkill and said, "Muster 'em out." Thrailkill and Arch Clements, another Anderson lieutenant, shot down the first four prisoners without help. The rest of the guerrillas assembled then joined in. When the acrid smoke cleared, twenty-four soldiers of the Army of the Potomac lay dead.

It was not the most heinous act to take place in that darkest theater of the war, but it was among the most widely reported, and its grisly details unhinged the reason of some Northern campaigners who had hitherto displayed nought but cool logic under fire. Upon learning of the outrage, Union Major A. V. E. Johnson later that day made two costly mistakes. First, he divided his command, leaving part of his mounted infantry to secure the town of Centralia while he took off in pursuit of Anderson with a reduced force. Second, upon catching up with the guerrillas in open country, he ordered his men to dismount.

John Thrailkill was credited with leading Johnson into the ambush, allowing the company to pursue him, seemingly a lone fugitive, to a grassy hollow where a portion of Anderson's force stood around watching their horses graze. No sooner had the Yankees dismounted than the guerrillas leapt into the saddle with a rebel yell. Thereupon the rest of the command charged over a hill, shouting and shooting and outnumbering the enemy nearly three to one. Johnson's company was virtually annihilated. Only the men dispatched to the rear to hold the horses escaped.

Major Johnson was an early casualty. Reports identified his killer as a seventeen-year-old guerrilla recently returned to active duty after recovering from a war injury. Jesse James was his name.

News of the Centralia massacre and the battle that followed reached me in Abilene, Kansas, a greenwood settlement a hundred miles west of Lawrence consisting of a post office, a hotel, a blacksmith shop, and a mercantile store where the male residents gathered to drink whiskey and wonder aloud at the deranged fantasies that had brought them to this desolate place. I confess that I knew little more of my own reasons for coming, other than that the farther I traveled in the direction of the setting sun, the fainter grew the din of war. There in the flat, sparsely grown scape of the Great American Desert, the struggle to wrest a living from the granite soil was far more dramatic and personal than the clash of men and ideals taking place only a two-day ride to the east.

Back in Missouri I had traded the gelding to Rudd for a slab of bacon, a gunny sack full of dried beans that rattled like buckshot when I loaded them aboard the dun mare, cooking utensils, and a small sack of Arbuckle's coffee. The mare was strong, and war had trimmed it down and sharpened its instincts; we had attracted enemy attention just once, when a band of militia spotted us near the Kansas border, and we had eluded them easily, outrunning them on the flat and losing them in a stand of trees. I remember wondering, as pistol balls clattered among the branches behind me, what my old horror of a childhood music tutor would think if he saw me then. *"Pianissimo*, young master," he might say, gesturing downward with his stick; "we are running away from the Yankees, not charging up Cemetery Ridge."

I had stopped in Lawrence overnight, and almost immediately regretted coming there.

Although it was late morning when I arrived, the streets were empty. The mare's hoofbeats echoed off the fronts of the boarded-up buildings as off the walls of a canyon. Curtains moved in windows, but when I looked at them they were still. Furtive fluttering movements behind the crumbling walls of burned brick buildings left to fall on their own ceased when I turned my head their way. The busy, boastful farm capital I had first seen barely more than a year before was gone. This was a broken place haunted by frightened phantoms.

At first I failed to recognize Massachusetts Street. Thinking I had miscounted my blocks, I turned the mare and retraced my steps to the corner, where the sign assured me I had not. The absences of the Eldridge House, Palmer's Gun Shop, and a half-dozen other establishments whose names I had already forgotten left blanks in the skyline that altered the shape of the neighborhood nearly beyond recognition. Further, the street where I had lived for three important weeks had bespoken life in its every detail, from the flower boxes in the windows of the houses to the sparkling display windows and bright awnings of the storefronts, whereas these blank board faces and weedy overgrown foundations suggested nothing so much as a cemetery lot filled with the remains of people whose survivors had themselves passed on or moved far away, leaving none to care for the mausoleums and markers.

Stopping before Drucilla's, I sat still for a full minute, fighting the urge to sink my heels into the mare's sides and canter on. The house was untouched. The windows were intact and uncovered, the discreet sign still swung from its staples under the eave of the front porch; yet I knew without checking that I was viewing a corpse whose soul had fled. On a warm morning in the last week of August, the windows should have been open—all but those on the top floor, where

Drucilla kept her twilit exile—and Isabel, grim maidservant and *majordoma* of the establishment, should have been visible through them, charging from room to room straightening slipcovers, shaking out dust mops, and just generally storming through the daily exercise required to make the house glitter from attic to basement. The building was sealed tight, and if any activity took place there at all, it was far too subtle to have anything to do with that resolute old dragon.

I dismounted, tied the mare to the hitching rail in front, and climbed the steps to the door. As highly as I regarded the august disfigured lady whose personality still clung to the brick and gingerbread, I had other business that precluded my going off to preserve my memory of the house as it had been in happier times.

My first knock went unanswered. When after a minute the door remained closed to my second attempt, I tried the latch and found it open.

A trapezoidal patch of sunlight lay on the floor of the foyer. In the grayness to the right of the staircase leading to the second story stood a small boy holding a pitchfork with a shattered handle, the tines pointed at me. He was barefoot and his clothes hung in rags. His eyes were huge and hostile and terrified in a face smeared with dirt.

"I am looking for Drucilla," I said. "Does she still live here?"

For answer, the boy jabbed at me with the fork. As six feet separated us, I did not move. He was seeking only to keep me at bay.

"Are you alone here?"

He jabbed again. His breathing was loud and sibilant. I could not tell if he understood my words.

"He ain't alone."

I peered up at the staircase landing. The woman standing there was barefoot as well, in a faded housecoat that she held together at her throat. Her dark shoulder-length hair was streaked with gray and needed combing, had needed it for at least a month. She held a large-bore pistol braced against her right hip with the hammer cocked.

I raised both my hands. "I used to live here. My name is Gashade. I was asking your boy about Drucilla Patakos."

"He ain't my boy."

It occurred to me that she might have seen me through a window when I was hitching up. The mare looked too healthy for a war-ravaged city whose residents could barely take care of themselves.

"I am not a guerrilla. I am looking for an acquaintance, nothing more." For emphasis I spread my coat, revealing my lack of weapons.

"It don't matter. We got nothing to steal. We busted up all the furniture to burn last winter. I had a house," she added. "Bushwhackers put the torch to it and killed my man. This boy was just here when I come to get in out of the rain. I don't know his story. There wasn't nobody else around. You can't take nothing from me or him ain't already been took."

I believed her. Her tone was without life, producing words with the grim tired inevitability of factory machinery. She resembled the buildings of the town, boarded over and left to the weather.

"I wondered if any letters had come for me," I said.

She was silent. Then: "In there." She waggled the pistol barrel in the direction of the parlor.

I took a step over the threshold. The boy jabbed at me, then moved back the same distance I had advanced. I came in the rest of the way and turned toward the room where I had earned most of my keep.

For the second time that morning, I felt that I had turned the wrong way. The curtains had been pulled down, the organ and carpet and most of the furniture was missing, and the floor was caked with dried mud. I could not picture this barren room as the place to which so many men had gravitated, lonely and needful and far from home, in search of a respite from their wretched condition: That corner, where a rat or a squirrel had gnawed a hole in the wainscoting; was that indeed the spot where a grizzled sergeant with buckshot burrowed in the side of his face had wept aloud at the end of "Darling Nellie Gray"? More immediately, I saw nothing that resembled the bundle of correspondence I had come there hoping to find.

Or perhaps I did.

The fireplace, a narrow brick arch of the design then popular, was heaped with ashes spilling untidily onto the hearth, as if new fires had been kindled atop the remains of the old with no cleaning in between—an intolerable state of affairs were Isabel still in residence. I approached the heap with a sinking in my vitals, slid a poker from among the implements leaning against the chimney, and crouched to turn over the layers of calcined paper and unburned sections of molding that covered the grate. Some of the sheets retained their original shape, although the heat had turned the cursive white while blackening the surface upon which it was written. I recognized my father's hand, my old name; a phrase, "despondent by the day." Putting aside the poker, I reached out with both hands and attempted gently to lift the burned leaf. It crumbled into cinders.

"Find your letters, did you?"

When I came back through the foyer, the woman had descended the stairs partway. Now she leaned on the railing with both hands, one of which still held the revolver, although she was no longer pointing it. Her eyes were alight, triumphant.

I said nothing, but kept walking toward the door.

"Fires don't start by theirselves!" She laughed. "Paper's the thing!"

Something stabbed me in my lower back. I whirled. The boy was on the other side of the staircase now, the broken pitchfork in his hands. I saw in his face the same expression worn by the woman. I felt blood trickling into my trousers. In a rage, I seized the handle of the fork near the tines and twisted it, breaking his grip. He leapt back, hissing like a cat, and flattened himself against the curve of the staircase. His eyes were as wide as dollars.

I stared back for a long time, breathing hard. Then I threw the fork clattering into the opposite corner, turned, and went out. As I hastened down the steps of the porch, reaching back with one hand to grope at my injury, I heard the woman shouting.

"See what it's like to lose all you got! Just see!"

My wounds, as I discovered when I stopped to wash them at the Kansas River, were superficial. The boy had been too timid or in too much of a hurry to put his weight behind the weapon. The worst of the three punctures was less than a quarter of an inch deep. I flushed them out with water, rubbed them with a piece of the salty bacon to purify them, and applied a patch cut from the tail of my spare shirt with sticky tree sap, as I had seen Frank James do after a saber had slashed his thigh at Pilot Knob.

I felt no anger toward the woman or the boy, nor did I pity them. And I knew then that I had changed. Not grown; for one who has lost the ability to feel sorrow for those who are made to suffer through no fault of their own cannot be said to have advanced in his journey through life. Too many had died, too many had lost limbs and friends and family to the monstrous obscenity through which we were traveling for me to expend what remained of my humanity upon any one individual. In time, perhaps, I would begin again to share the pain of my brothers and sisters, and there commence the odyssey back to where I had started. Until then I could not return home, for fear that if I tried, I would find that place not to be my home at all. When that bundle of ashes had fallen apart in my hands, it had been a bridge collapsing. It would take much time to rebuild, and what I found at the end when I had rebuilt it would depend upon what sort of man I was when I started back.

On the riverbank I built a fire, cooked a piece of bacon and some beans in Rudd's rusty old skillet, then used the skillet to make coffee. When I finished cleaning up and packing, the mare's head was pointed west. I mounted and rode in that direction.

TWENTY

Abilene, when first I saw it, was not the place it would become in three short years. Then, the coming of the Union Pacific Railroad along the south bank of the Smoky Hill River, and the ballooning postwar cattle trade that would make a Mecca of every railhead between Chicago and El Paso, would render unrecognizable the little farming community where I stopped to rest and replenish my supplies on my way to the frontier. I found there a ragged cluster of a dozen or so log buildings on a prairie road, where the arrival of a stranger on horseback was entertainment sufficient to bring the residents to their doorways to study the phenomenon. I sensed, as I tied up before the mercantile and mounted the boardwalk, that the guitar slung behind my back might as well have been a live ostrich or a third arm for the interest it attracted. A number of the local men had followed me on foot along the walk and formed a knot in front of the door through which I was forced to make my way in order to gain access to the building.

The interior was dim, lit only by the sun coming through the small front window, with a floor made from half-sawn logs, merchandise stacked on shelves, a plank counter at the back, and a partition to the right with an opening cut through and a number of tables and chairs visible beyond. There, I assumed, drinks were served, discreetly separate from the mercantile side and the wives who browsed among the goods offered there. As I made this discovery, a plan began to form in my mind. I prayed I had the sand to pull it off.

The man behind the counter, lanky and sheathed in a white apron from neck to knees, lifted his thick brows as I approached. I suspected his curiosity was not directed so much at me as at the crowd I was towing behind me. Presently he smoothed back his black patent hair with the heels of both hands, swept a knuckle at each of his waxed moustaches, and asked what he could do for me. Plainly he had concluded he was in the presence of some great visiting personage— Secretary Seward, perhaps, or Charles Dickens at the least. As I drew near, however, and he became aware of both my youth and my somewhat travel-worn appearance, both his brows and his moustaches fell.

Quickly, before he could ask what was the meaning of this queer procession, I produced the scrap of soiled paper upon which I had scribbled my list of provisions. "A ham if you have it, sir, or two pounds of bacon if you do not. A sack of coffee, three pounds of flour, and a dozen fresh apples."

He hesitated, glowering, then slid a tablet in front of him, wet the tip of a stub of yellow pencil with his tongue, and totaled the purchases. "Buck twenty-three," he said. "I'm fresh out of ham."

I assumed a regretful expression that was not all the result of artifice. "I haven't even the twenty-three cents. However, I have a proposition to offer, if you can spare thirty seconds to hear it."

"Proposition." He tasted the word. "That better be some kind of U.S. currency."

"It can be."

He glanced sourly at the crowd that had gathered in his little store. I could read his thoughts. No man wants to take the chance of looking the fool before people he must face daily. "No."

"You have not heard the proposition," I said.

"All I want to hear is silver clinking on this here plank. If you can't do that, get going. I don't give credit to drifters."

"Aw, hear him out, Floyd," came a voice from the group behind me.

"What's thirty seconds?" came another.

Floyd's brow darkened. "Higher'n you can count, Gunderson." For a moment he was silent. Then his gaze lit upon a brown glass jug at the end of the counter. The label, printed black on manila, read:

DR. BEAN'S WORMER
For Permanent Relief from Ringworms,
Cutworms, Tapeworms, Roundworms, Pinworms,
Flatworms, Whipworms,
Hookworms, Seatworms,
and Filariasis

With one motion he hooked the jug up by its handle, upended it, and balanced it upon its cork on the counter. The contents, a glutinous mass, began to ooze down the side of the container toward the cork.

"You got till it settles." He folded his arms across the bib of his apron.

I slid the guitar around to the front, trying to keep my eyes off that migratory sludge as I explained to him, with carefully chosen hyperbole, the benefits of music to the alcohol trade: how a sentimental ballad (strumming a few bars of "Barb'ra Allen") can turn a man reflective, ordering drinks to sharpen a pleasant memory or deaden a painful one; how a sprightly quadrille ("Cindy") can erase his troubles, lifting his spirits and inspiring him to call for a round for the house to celebrate; how a patriotic march ("Hail, Columbia") can remind him of his proud national heritage and raise his freshly filled glass to the Founding Fathers; finally, how a song from one's own former homeland can return him to a place and time of innocence, thus mellowing the flavor of the rawest red whiskey.

For the last, presupposing an Irish origin for Floyd, I selected Bridey McMurtaugh's favorite, "Molly Malone," singing:

Alive, alive, oh!
Alive, alive, oh!
Crying, "Cockles, and mussels—"

"Time's up." The counterman snatched up the jug and set it back down on its base.

There were angry protests, which Floyd stilled by reaching beneath the counter and slamming a two-foot section of iron bar onto its top. Evidently this bit of persuasion had been used to settle arguments before, as with a chorus of muttered halfhearted obscenities the group broke up and began drifting toward the door. I followed, crestfallen. I think now that I was less disappointed by the prospect of being forced to leave without the provisions I so desperately needed as by the knowledge that my first serious attempt to become a professional musician had been soundly rejected.

In front of the building, I found my path blocked once again as the group of horn-handed men in threadbare overalls boiled past on both sides and turned to confront me. I could not tell one anxious bearded sunburned face from another; work and weather and hopes worn as thin as their clothing had sculpted them all as alike as rocks in a canyon.

While we had been walking, they had all been talking at once, each trying to attract my attention ahead of his fellows. Now, as I offered it to them, they fell silent, shifting their weight from one foot to the other and avoiding my gaze. At length one of them, a big fellow with the rounded shoulders of an ox and hands the size of gunny sacks, swept off his shapeless felt hat and stood kneading it as he spoke. His drawl was as slow and thick as sour mash.

"Mister, I ain't heard 'Lubly Fan' since I left Alabama. I sure would—"

" 'Froggie Went a-Courtin'!" piped up another, a long drink of water with an animated Adam's apple.

There followed a cacophony of song titles, and again I was assailed by a mix of Eastern and Southern dialects, flattened by their distance from home and roughened by cursing at horses and mules hitched to plows and harrows. To quiet them, I slid my guitar back around and began strumming "All Hail the Power of Jesus' Name," which I thought just the thing to placate these simple God-fearing tillers of the soil. Indeed, they stopped jabbering and backed away to give me room to play and air to breathe.

And as I played, a remarkable transformation occurred. That circle of worn and dirty faces, so similar when first I saw them, drew inward, subsiding into forgotten expressions, so that by the time I reached the final bars each countenance was separate and singular, and tied to its place of origin: Here was the great State of Alabama, honest and enduring; there was Maine, courageous, pragmatic, and Puritan; over there, Illinois, Ohio, and Michigan, and the oaken strength of the Northwest Territory; and all those other places left behind in the rush to conquer new worlds, and lost in the dust and desolation of the discovery that a plot of earth in Kansas is pretty much like all the rest, worse than some, and in any case no repository for dreams of grandeur. I had come upon a pack of dumb brutes and uncovered a group of men.

I did not stop there, but went directly into "Lubly Fan," then "Froggie Went a-Courtin'," and as many of the asked-for tunes as I could recall, adding a few from my expanding portfolio and occasionally helping out a supplicant who could remember neither the name nor the lyrics of the one he wanted, and so hummed a chorus until I found it on the strings. The light that dawned on his face upon hearing the first notes was precious to behold. I felt as a missionary must feel when he sees some benighted soul embrace the Word.

All this was too much for the counterman, who came out to find the entrance to his establishment obstructed by a musician and his enraptured listeners, the latter sprawled upon the bench outside the door and leaning against the posts that supported the porch and seated on the boardwalk with their legs dangling over the edge. He spun upon me, his moustaches bristling, and slapped the palm of his free hand with the iron bar gripped in the other.

"Just saying you ain't welcome ain't enough for some, looks like," he said. "Some folks need to have it spelt out." He drew the bar across his chest for a backhand swing. I shrank away, raising the guitar as a shield.

"Floyd, I see you ain't changed. You ought to take some of that wormer you buy by the barrel for a quarter and sell by the gallon for a dollar. Something's eating your guts for sartin."

Here was a voice to stop a riot or a stampede. I had never heard one to rival it and have not heard one since, though I have sat in the front row when Caruso sang in San Francisco and once pawned my guitar to hear Richard Mansfield deliver the soliloquy from *Richard III* at the Standard Theater in New York. Not quite a bellow, this; that implies exertion on the part of the speaker, and it came out too naturally for that. It was loud enough to drown out a herd of cattle, yet it sounded effortless, and left no room for doubt that it would be understood and heeded.

Certainly this was true in Floyd's case, for he froze on the spot, bludgeon cocked, eyes searching for the source of the interruption. Presently they settled upon the man standing in the middle of the street, one hand holding the reins of a buckskin horse some sixteen hands high, with shaggy fetlocks the size of melons and a mane that nearly swept the ground.

Man and horse were built to scale. Towering well over six feet in scuffed Wellingtons and a coat too heavy for the season that swung below his knees, he was a white-bearded length of gristle under a pearl-gray hat of the style referred to, for reasons that eluded me, as a "Wide-awake," with a brim almost as broad as his shoulders. It was plain to see from the dark, grainy texture of his skin that he was no stranger to the great outdoors. I placed his age around sixty.

One feature he possessed that I could not help staring at was an enormous goiter swelling above his collar. The inflated growth was nearly as large as his head and made him look for all the world like a two-hundred-pound bullfrog.

"Well, Bridger," Floyd said, much of the conviction gone from his tone, "I guess this ain't your affair."

"I know it. But I'm a meddlesome old coot. I come too late to hear this boy play, but he can't be so bad he needs his brainpan cracked open with a big old piece of metal."

"He's spoiling my business!"

"You run the only store in town. They'll be back. I'm asking you to put aside the bar."

When still Floyd hesitated, the man he called Bridger sighed heavily and unfastened with one hand the single button that closed his coat. The right side dropped away, exposing the leather-bound hilt of a knife at least fourteen inches long on his belt, its broad blade sheathed in a scabbard covered with Indian beadwork.

It seemed to me hardly the best weapon to select at a distance of not less than twenty feet, but it had its effect upon the counterman, who lowered his arm, muttering something I assumed was a curse in German. I closed my eyes at my own stupidity. Instead of "Molly Malone," I should have chosen *"Eine Kleine Nachtmusik."*

Bridger caught the eye of the man from Alabama. "What do you say, Yarbo? Should I of let Floyd put a window in the lad's skull, or can he get anything out of that box that don't scare half the game out of Dickinson County?"

A chorus of denials from the others overtook Yarbo's negative.

Bridger nodded. He seemed to take genuine satisfaction out

of having made a just decision. "I'm partial to 'Greensleeves' myself. My first wife liked it a heap."

Recognizing a request when I heard one, I turned my attention to that old troubadour's favorite. To my chagrin, my hands were shaking too badly to make anything but a mess of the melody. I looked at him with an expression I knew was tragic.

The anticipation in the weathered old face set like the sun. "Well, it's got a parcel of notes." To Floyd: "Last time I went to Saint Louie this direction, I didn't see three people in your place. Seems to me you'd be a sight better off paying this boy to gather crowds inside." He buttoned his coat, chuckling softly. "Just a dumb notion, mind. I notioned myself right out of my own trading post on the Black Fork of the Green River."

Floyd glowered down at the boardwalk, swinging the iron bar idly at his toe-tops. "Can't pay," he said without looking at me.

I said, "Two meals a day and a cot will suffice. I'll earn my travel expenses in tips."

"That'll come to twice nothing. Last time a nickel showed itself here, folks rode clear in from Uniontown to get a look." He went inside.

And so I joined the musical profession, with Jim Bridger, the greatest mountain man and Indian scout of them all, as my first booking agent.

TWENTY-ONE

In the fall of 1864 the war was still there, but it had not much longer to run. Events began moving rapidly the moment I was no longer intimately associated with them. As with anything that is flying apart, shreds of war information reached me in Abilene, carried by travelers on their way west.

One month to the day after the Centralia massacre, Bloody Bill Anderson fell. Reports said he was leading his column along a road half a mile north of Orrick, Missouri, in the southwest corner of Ray County, when he was ambushed by Union infantry, who riddled him in their crossfire. They then lopped off his handsome bearded head with a saber, dragged his body by its ankles through the streets, and impaled the head atop a telegraph pole to serve as a warning to his fellow guerrillas.

Soon afterward, General Sterling Price, deprived of his best flank commander, withdrew his troops from Missouri. Without the protection of the regular Confederate Army the raiders who had served with Quantrill and Anderson were forced to disband permanently. Six months later, inside a modest brick courthouse in a town named Appomattox in Virginia, General Robert E. Lee surrendered his saber to General Ulysses S. Grant, bringing the Civil War to its conclusion. After four years, the great silence that ensued was as a void in the air following the prolonged clangor of a thousand great bells.

It was shattered one week later when an assassin's bullet ended the life of President Lincoln at Ford's Theater in Washington City.

Despite that tragedy, there was celebration in the North that the long nightmare was over. Although I raised my glass along with the Union sympathizers gathered in Floyd's saloon annex when the surrender was announced, I had seen at close hand the hatred and bitterness attending the conflict, and knew that it would require more than a formal declaration to close the gaping wound that divided our republic. News of the president's murder confirmed my suspicions. A great deal more blood would stain the hands of North and South before they joined.

Meanwhile I was a success. Men did not come to a saloon to drink. If whiskey were all they wanted, they could purchase a bottle for far less than they paid for the same amount by the glass and consume it at their leisure in the comfort of home. When in Abilene they passed through that door from the mercantile side, they sought a neutral place where the hard work and heartbreak of grappling with the land for their existence could not follow. They came for the cool dimness, the company of other men who shared and understood their travails, the strong drink—and the music. Afternoons, evenings, and particularly Saturday night, when they left their fields early to come to town for supplies and to clear their souls for church the next morning, I took my place on a chair near the plank bar and played the guitar and sang. My voice, while not gifted, was pleasant, furnishing a welcome change from the braying of their mules and the disconcerting clang when a plow blade struck yet another rock to be prised up and carried to the edge of the field. When, courtesy of the odd transient who brought with him the lyrics of a new song from the metropolises in the East, I presented them with a melody and words they had not heard before, they pummeled my back and bought me drinks and behaved as if I had tapped into a secret underground spring that would irrigate all their properties and make them rich.

The late Stephen Foster's "Beautiful Dreamer" was just such a discovery. Released from among the composer's papers after his death the previous year, this bucolic selection set my listeners' faces aglow and quickly became the tune requested most frequently, as much as a dozen times in an evening. I still find myself humming it when my mind goes drifting, of all the thousands of refrains that are stored there.

In spite of the fact that I was responsible for the steady flow of business to the saloon side of his establishment, my relationship with Floyd remained cool, bordering upon hostility whenever I helped myself to a bowl of rabbit stew, chicken soup, or a slice of ham from the table he arranged daily for his customers. His senior partner, I learned, was Charles H. Thompson, the community's chief developer and tireless promoter, who was usually away in St. Louis or Kansas City, attempting to interest investors in his self-styled Eldorado. Thompson had introduced the free lunch to Kansas after the fashion of saloons in New York, Chicago, and San Francisco, about which he had read in *Harper's Weekly*, but his partner, whose duty it was to prepare the food and pay for it out of the meager monthly profits, disliked the idea intensely. That I, a non-paying customer, should benefit from it, irritated him further. I ignored his black looks and partook heartily.

On my first full day there, I inquired when Mr. Bridger might drop in. I was grateful to him for helping me land my position and looked forward to treating him to a better rendition of "Greensleeves" to make up for my erratic attempt of the day before.

The counterman, who was busy placing a number of rat traps behind the foodstuffs on the shelves behind the counter, grunted. "You got plenty of time to practice. He left for Saint Louis at first light."

I asked when he would be back.

"Who the hell knows that? *Bridger* don't know. Six months, a year. Never, maybe. When he heads back West it might not even be through this part of the country, and then as like as not he'll probably get his scalp lifted by some damn injun. The time to expect that rawboned old son of a bitch is when he's standing square in front of you." Just then the spring trap he was setting out snapped, catching his thumb and sparking a cry in German that was no doubt vile.

I withdrew, sharply disappointed. I felt that I owed the great frontiersman his one request, and it dissatisfied me to think that he might go on the rest of his life believing me unequal to it.

At that time, I took the fact that Jim Bridger was a great frontiersman on faith. Before I met him I had never heard his name, but he was old, he had the look of a man who knew his way around rough country, and the bloodcurdling tales I had heard about life in the Western territories assured me that

the very act of growing old there was in itself a great pane-
gyric. Later I would hear the whole story, and know that I
had been privileged to meet a man without peer, both in his
own lifetime and beyond it.

Until then I subsisted. Floyd's parable of the nickel that was
celebrated in the region for its rarity was not as much of
an exaggeration as I had hoped. Popular though my music-
making was, the gratuities that came my way were seldom
tangible. My hand was shaken, my back slapped. If I accepted
every third drink offered me, I would have been in worse
shape than the occasional tragic soul who camped upon the
porch since before dawn waiting for the establishment to
open, hugging his knees lest he shake himself to pieces for
want of liquid stimulation. Although I squirreled away what
coins I was able to lay hands upon, hoping to collect enough
to outfit myself for my intended journey west, the fraying of
my collar and cuffs and the holes in the soles of my boots
reminded me by the day that if I did not soon pay attention
to them I would finish up barefoot and indecent. I commenced
to wonder if I would ever get enough ahead to leave, or if this
drab community where so many dreams had languished
represented the end of the line. These were burdensome
thoughts for a boy of eighteen.

I'd passed that mark almost without noting. One year earlier, thanks to Frank James, I had laid to rest my seventeenth
in the sweet, fierce company of Nowata, the half-bred Cherokee romantic interest and sometime artist's model of Lieutenant John Thrailkill, and learned a number of things that
could not have been taught me by any of the debutantes to
whom my parents would have introduced me had I stayed in
the city of my birth. This day began before dawn, when my
slumber was interrupted by Floyd's rummaging among his
baking utensils, which he habitually threw into a pile behind
the stove in the cramped kitchen where I slept. (Very early
in our arrangement I came to miss the relative privacy of my
little pantry at Drucilla's.) I went outside, washed my face in

the Smoky Hill River, in which splinters of ice floated, took a brisk walk to restore circulation to those portions of my anatomy grown numb from their contact with the floor through the thin straw pallet that served as my bed, breakfasted upon ham, potatoes, and coffee in the saloon, and was halfway through my morning guitar practice before I remembered the date.

I fancied that I appeared older than my years. I had grown an inch in the past twelvemonth—assuming my sleeves and the legs of my trousers had not shrunk—I was leaner, and when I stood away from the razor two mornings in succession, the shadow upon my cheeks accentuated the bones in a way I flattered myself was handsome. Once again I pledged to grow a beard as soon as I could be certain it wouldn't be one of those spun-sugar absurdities that made a young man resemble a boy in costume for a church pageant. My voice had dropped a full octave. Two or three of my regular listeners had commented favorably upon the change, which had taken place over a period of a month, with none of the grotesque breaks and squawks that often accompany that passage, and one of the farm wives who patronized the mercantile made so bold one day as to compliment me upon my singing, which she had overheard one afternoon while trying on straw hats from a recent St. Louis shipment. She was half her husband's age, and I thought I detected a note of cautious flirtation in her tone. It has since been my observation that youth and a pleasant singing voice present powerful challenges to the sacred oaths.

In spite of such diversions, my outlook during the first spring and summer of peace was not cheerful, particularly as the heat grew oppressive, accentuating the conviction that I was shut up in a close room without air. On one such day toward the end of July, I was perched upon my chair in shirtsleeves, my collar limp with sweat, strumming some lifeless melody in competition with the buzzing of a soporific fly, when one of my listeners came forward and said, " 'Rally 'Round the Flag,' please."

"I don't play war songs." I continued playing without looking up. I noticed he wore ornate boots with tooled shanks and protective flaps over the toes. A vague memory stirred at the sight, but I hadn't the energy or the inclination to ponder it. Of course he was not a native; a pristine pair of boots in Abilene could only be on their way to some other destination. Likely he was one of those scavengers swarming southward with official documents in their carpetbags empowering them to seize property from former secessionists for their personal agrandizement. I had no sympathy for these carpetbaggers, and hoped this one would go away before I was forced to air my views upon the subject.

He dropped a coin into the cigar box I kept optimistically open on the end of the bar. "You choose, then. Anything but that dirge you are playing. Your talents are wasted upon it."

I glanced with annoyance toward the copper I expected to find in the box, only to see the gold glinting off a five-dollar piece. It was more than I had collected there in the past month. Startled, I looked up—and recognized instantly the moon face, pale, brow-less eyes, and gracefully curved lips of the young man who had taken me for a secessionist in the train station at Indianapolis on my way west from New York. Was it only two years ago?

"You remember me," he said. "I'm flattered."

"You were with that sour detective fellow. I've forgotten your name."

"Jack Fabian. Mr. Pinkerton is abrasive, I agree. Still, there are advantages to working for him. He's in Chicago while I am here. That's one."

"I thought you worked in Chicago."

"Not anymore. I've been operating out of the Kansas City office since April. At present I'm on my way to Texas."

"You are dressed for it," I said ironically. Under his linen duster, he wore a tan twill suit with a striped vest—ideal for a Sunday row, but less than suitable for a hard ride across the Texas plain.

He ignored my gaucherie in a way I found conspicuously well bred. I caught myself wondering about his origins. "I seem to remember your saying you played the piano," he said.

I rested my hands upon the guitar. "Where I have been, they burned all the pianos to keep from freezing to death. Your war has been ruinous to culture."

"*My* war. Does this mean you are a Copperhead after all?"

"Sides are not the issue. It doesn't matter to an orphaned child which flag flies above his father's grave."

The corners of his lips curled upward in their catlike way. "You've learned much since Indianapolis, Billy Gashade." Something about the manner in which he pronounced the name suggested that he knew I had not been born to it.

I made no response. Outside the sun was going down; more customers had begun to shuffle in from the mercantile. The Pinkerton man stepped closer and lowered his tone.

"Quantrill is dead."

"I hadn't heard." I felt nothing. The guerrilla chief and I had met but once, and he had not impressed me.

"It happened two months ago, in a place called Smiley in Kentucky. Union cavalry tracked Quantrill and his band to a barn and shot him off his horse when he tried to escape. The rest of his guerrillas surrendered, except for a few. One of those who did not was Frank James."

His pale eyes were fixed on me as he imparted this information. I met his gaze. "Who is he?" I asked.

After a pause he moved his shoulders. "The agency has a warrant for James's arrest for the murder of a Kentucky Militia commander named Barnette. The incident took place after Appomattox, and so is not sanctioned by the articles of war. Our information is he and the others fled to Texas after the death of their leader. I am tracking his brother Jesse as well, and a guerrilla lieutenant named John Thrailkill." He described the three, down to Frank's auburn beard, Jesse's blue eyes, and Thrailkill's classic jaw. "I was wondering if they passed through here."

"I saw nobody who looked like that."

"I thought not." He sighed. "They would be avoiding civilization. According to our informants they are on their way to meet up with Cole and Jim Younger in Mineral Springs, do some recruiting, and return to Missouri. Lee's surrender meant nothing to them. They intend to continue murdering and plundering until they are stopped."

"That will not be easy," I said. "According to what I have heard."

"It would be a good deal less difficult without the protection of their friends."

Under his deceptively mild scrutiny, I picked out the opening bars of "Kingdom Coming" on my guitar.

His lips curled farther. "Good choice." Reaching into a vest pocket, he produced a card and another gold coin and placed both in the cigar box. "You can wire me at this office if you should see any of the men I described. Someone will forward the communication. The agency is offering a reward of five hundred dollars for information leading to their capture."

"For one or all?"

"That point is negotiable," he said. "Short of extortion."

"What if they are not captured, but are killed instead?"

"The result is the same. All our client wants is to be rid of them."

"Your client?"

"The people of the United States of America."

"The Union I knew was not disposed to post human bounty," I said.

"The Union you knew was seriously injured at Fort Sumter. It took a mortal wound at Shiloh and died at Gettysburg. We buried it at Appomattox."

"Thank you, Captain Fabian. For your contribution." I reached over and flipped shut the lid of the box.

"We are old acquaintances, Billy. Call me Jack."

"I prefer not to."

He took off his slouch hat, creased the crown between two fingers, and replaced it. "Then I shall call you Mr. Gashade. What is a name, after all? One changes it as readily as his shirt."

He left, and I was told later that he mounted a blaze-face black tethered in front of the building and rode west leading a chestnut loaded down with packs. Alone that night, stretched out on my pallet, I examined his card in the light of the lantern I used for reading. It contained, in addition to the name "J. T. Fabian" and an address in Kansas City, a single, wide-open eye with an accusatory arched brow, and beneath it the legend:

"WE NEVER SLEEP."

TWENTY-TWO

Floyd clamped each of the gold coins in turn between his teeth and studied the results. His expression was as somber as if they had shown themselves to have been made of lead.

"Nobody's had any gold around here since Jed Oxley pried out his fillings to pay for a plow," he said.

"Will it cover my outfit?" I inventoried the items spread across his counter against the list I had made by the light of my lantern the night before: flour, coffee, apples, beans, bacon, a canteen, halter leather to secure packs and make repairs, two flannel shirts, two pairs of whipcord trousers, a blanket, a corduroy coat, and a good pair of riding boots. It had been my pleasure to watch the counterman's moustaches droop when I added the five-dollar pieces to the bent and tarnished coppers and nickels I had hoarded away over the course of a year.

"You got change coming." It was clear he was loath to surrender the point. I never met a man more disgusted by his own honesty than Floyd. I assume he died penniless, and I doubt he was very much surprised. "You headed for China, or just Africa?" he asked.

"Both, perhaps. After I have seen all of this country. I'm off for the frontier."

"What you want to go out there for? All that's there is injuns and rattlesnakes."

"Have you been there?"

"A man don't have to go to the North Pole to know it's cold." He balanced my change in the palm of his hand and squinted one eye. "I could let you have an old Colt for the difference. The action's so loose you got to hold the cylinder back against the frame or the firing pin won't engage, but it beats spitting in some red buck's eye when he's cutting your throat."

"I am done with pistols. I'll take the chance."

"You'll get scalped."

"I'll wear a hat."

"How you figure to get food when your cash runs out?"

I slapped the guitar. "I shall sing for my supper."

Snarling, he tipped the change into my hand. "I was starting to get used to you. I ain't heard a complaint about that noise you make in a week."

"Why, Floyd, are you saying you'll miss me?"

"Go to hell."

I left Abilene with no plan other than to follow the Smoky Hill River, putting in at Fort Harker by dark, and there find out about the situation to the west before venturing farther. I had no map and only a vague sense of the geography through which I would be traveling. Reckless though this may sound in our day of detailed highway routes and auto club directories, there was nothing else for it then. Maps in those days were difficult to obtain, and so unreliable (based as they were upon speculation and hearsay) that to have one proved more often a hindrance than a help. The entire central section of our continent from western Kansas to the border of California was usually drawn as an enormous blob labeled the Great American Desert, and was said by some to contain all manner of curiosities and hazards, from quicksand seas the size of New Jersey to two-headed cannibals and snakes that took their tails in their mouths and rolled downhill. The only way to cross it was to proceed to the next dim light of civilization and then the next, picking up information at each place about the next day's ride.

Fort Harker, when I came to it, was still in the early stages of construction. Muleskinners and bullwhackers hitched their teams to fresh-sawn logs and whipped and cursed them to the top of a hill overlooking the river, where army engineers sharpened the logs with adzes at both ends and sank them into the earth to form a stockade. Stripped to the waist, their backs brown and glistening, they put me in mind of Egyptian slaves raising the pyramids at Giza. The oaths with which they performed their labor, however, were decidedly Anglo-Saxon in origin.

An Irish sergeant who acted as foreman of the crew, prematurely white-haired, with muttonchop whiskers and a pattern of blue-black spots beneath the skin of his right cheek that I attributed to the shotgun barrel of a Confederate La-Matte pistol, directed me to a corner inside the stockade where I could spread my blanket. That night, as I sat cross-legged upon the blanket playing before a small fire I had built of twigs and bark that had fallen from the cut logs, the sergeant came over and asked if he could join me. I informed him that it was a free country and that since the heat coming from the other side of the fire was going to waste anyway, he was welcome to have a seat.

He lowered himself carefully, making the faces that went

with having a stiff back, and rolled a cigarette. "Nice," he said of the piece I had just finished. "It ain't English, I hope?"

"It's German, as a matter of fact. I got it from a farmer in Abilene, who learned it from his grandfather. It's about a man who takes his own life because he believes his wife to be untrue."

"Sad."

"The farmer had occasion to remember it. His wife hanged herself in their cabin while he was outside plowing his field."

"Was she untrue?"

"No. Merely tired."

"That can do it." He lit his cigarette with a stick from the fire. "Headed west?"

"Yes."

"Texas?"

"I don't know."

"Everyone's going to Texas, seems like. Some to Mexico. There's a revolution going on down there, as if four years of that up here wasn't enough. Lord, Lord." He shook his white head. "You want to watch your topknot. One of our patrols seen dog soldiers as close as Larned."

"Dog soldiers?"

"Renegade Cheyenne, answering to nobody or nothing. Ever since Chivington give Black Kettle what-for at Sand Creek they been hot as hornets. Savages."

I played through the silence that followed this pronouncement. Then: "I should think the troopers at Fort Larned would be able to contain these dog soldiers."

"You can't contain what you can't catch. Injuns is all yellow. They won't fight when they can run."

"If they're so cowardly, why does the army bother to build forts?"

"They ain't forts, they're fences. Being yellow, injuns take out their mad on women and children and pilgrims traveling alone, like you. We build these here fences to put the women and children and pilgrims inside so they can keep their scalps."

"The stage is coming," I said, "and after that the railroad. Your fences can't protect all the women and children and pilgrims they will bring."

The sergeant grinned around the cigarette clamped between his teeth. "The red bastards can't run forever. When we finish putting up fences they won't have no more *room* to run. That's when we start picking them off, like flies on horseshit."

I studied his face in the firelight, all pouched shadows and polished bone and buckshot beneath the skin like spots of mold. I said, "I'm turning in now, Sergeant. Thank you for warning me about the dog soldiers."

"It's early yet. I'd admire to hear that piece again about the farmer's wife that hung herself."

"No, in the song it was the man who took his life."

"I liked it better when it was the woman. A man that would pull his own cork on account of he found out his woman was peddling her ass ain't no kind of man in my book. He should of pulled *her cork*. There's something worth singing about." He got up with a grunt and flicked his cigarette into the darkness. "Sleep fast, young fellow. One night's all you get. This ain't the Palmer House."

Left alone, I considered Captain Jack Fabian's dry eulogy for the innocent nation slain in the war. Something had expired in me as well: the faith in the basic goodness of man that would have been troubled by the sergeant's philosophy of hate. I slept well in spite of him.

When the first steel rays lanced above the horizon, I fixed myself a breakfast of bacon and coffee and went to the picket line to untie the dun mare. I asked the man who was guarding the horses, a trooper with a face like a grave monkey, how far it was to Fort Larned. He told me if I headed south I would reach the Arkansas River by midmorning; following it west would bring me to the fort by nightfall. When noon came and went and I had not come within sight of the river, I decided either the distance had been greatly underestimated or I was lost. The heat was punishing. When I found the river at last I let the mare drink and got down on my stomach to fill my canteen. When the ripples on the surface of the water smoothed out, I saw three fearsome reflections staring back at me.

Startled, I looked up. In the river near the opposite bank, three horses stood up to their knees drinking. Their riders, nearly naked, had smooth, hairless torsos and were painted to the waist in broad swaths of black and vermilion. All three cradled long-barreled rifles across their laps.

Back in 1932, during dinner at William Randolph Hearst's preposterous castle at San Simeon, I chanced to hear the diamond-plated wife of a studio mogul seated near the end of the long table declare that she regretted the purchases she had *not* made more than the ones she had. I reflected that this was definitely true in the case of the old Colt I had elected not to buy in Abilene. However, if I had indeed bought the pistol, I most certainly would have grabbed for it at the moment I saw that trio of Indian warriors, and been shot down for my trouble. As it was I merely placed my palms against the ground and pushed myself to my feet without taking my eyes from the newcomers.

For a time after I rose, there was no movement save the rush of the water and the four animals drinking. Then one of the Indians turned his head slightly in the direction of the man mounted nearest him and spoke. The other laughed shortly, then raised his rifle to his shoulder and pointed it at me.

The crash of the report was like a physical blow. I staggered, certain I was hit. Then I saw the Indian who had aimed at me reel. He dropped his rifle into the river and would have fallen in after it had not the man next to him grasped his arm and pulled him upright. The stricken brave was wounded on the right side, the blood smearing his paint. Yipping like an angry terrier, the third Indian wheeled his horse, braced his rifle along his right forearm, and snapped a shot toward the opposite bank. The others turned as well, bounding their horses up and over the bank and galloping away toward the south. The wounded man had recovered himself enough to

ride, but from the angle he was leaning, it was clear he would
not have his seat long.

Dazed by the sequence of events, I turned—and ducked
immediately behind my mare for protection. A rider was bearing down hard upon me from the north aboard a tall buckskin whose long mane and tail fluttered behind it like black
fire. He did not slow down as he came near, but swept past me
at full gallop, shrieking at the top of his lungs and swinging
his long rifle in one hand above his head like a club. Man and
horse hit the water with an explosion. They were nearly across
the river when the man drew rein and stood in his stirrups,
waving the rifle and shouting what I assumed were imprecations at the departing Indians, for he spoke in gutturals
and consonants which for me held no meaning.

At length, apparently satisfied that they were not coming
back, the man lowered himself into the saddle, turned his
horse in the current, and started back in my direction. Now
I recognized his long coat, so incongruous in the heat, his
scarred, high-topped Wellington boots, and the great sweeping brim of his gray sombrero. More to the point, I recognized
his gristly, white-stubbled face and the goiter on his throat,
so like the sac of a harrumphing bullfrog. As he kicked the
buckskin up the bank on my side of the river, I saw by the
glint in his small steely eyes that he knew me as well.

"Mister *git*-ar man," greeted Jim Bridger, reining in to look
down at me. "I sure hope after going to all this trouble I can
count on you being all practiced up on 'Greensleeves.'"

TWENTY-THREE

Injuns ain't yellow." Bridger used his clasp knife to whit-
tle slices off a wild onion into the skillet where our bacon and beans were frying. "Some are, I reckon, just like
some whites. They ain't no better nor no worse'n the rest of

us, and they ain't all one way or all t'other. They don't like things starting out like this and winding up like that. That's the reason them three taken off when one got shot. That weren't cowardly. That was just plain good sense. Nobody but a fool fights when he don't know what he's fighting."

"A sergeant at Fort Harker told me they only attack those who can't defend themselves."

"White-headed jasper? Buckshot in his cheek?" I nodded. "That'd be Mulcahy. He's got balls as big as boulders and brains the size of these here beans. He wouldn't know a *Wōhksēh 'hētăniu* from a digger Pawnee."

"All the same, I am grateful to you for rescuing me from those dog soldiers."

"Who said they was dog soldiers?"

"The sergeant—"

"Them weren't renegades. The whole damn Cheyenne Nation's on the prod, and they're all of them as fired up as any of the dogs. That bloody mess at Sand Creek last fall killed any chance of peace with Black Kettle." As he spoke, he became agitated. The knife moved faster and faster. Some of the onion shavings fell outside the pan.

"Chivington," I said, echoing the name I had first heard upon the lips of Sergeant Mulcahy.

"*Colonel* Chivington, he calls himself. Bloody butcher is more like it. Some of them he kilt was sucking their mother's teats. There's yellow for you."

Profiled in the firelight, the cords in his neck stood out and the growth on his throat appeared more puffed-up than ever. I considered that so much tension was dangerous for a man in his sixties, even for one as hearty as he. Leaning back against my saddle—we were camped fifteen miles upriver from where we had encountered the Indians, in a stand of dogwoods whose branches shredded the smoke of our fire and whose trunks deadened its glow lest we attract the attention of more hostiles—I pulled over my guitar. I played "Greensleeves," of course, this time the way it should be played, or at least as well as it can be without a mandolin, as it was originally intended. A few bars into the sylvan melody, Bridger's entire body began to slacken. His shoulders relaxed, his tendons retreated, he settled back on his heels. The deep lines in the weathered old face smoothed out.

"My first wife was rotten partial to that song," he said, using the blade of his knife to turn over the thick bacon slices. "She was a Flathead, which is a civilized tribe. They make the best wives. I'm powerful sorry I doubted your ability to play it."

"How many wives have you had?"

"Three."

"All Flatheads?"

"No, the second was Snake. If you can't get a Flathead, you can do heaps worse than a Snake. They're gentle as a kit fox when they're gentle and full of piss and vinegar when you want them that way. Sometimes when you don't. One time she brained me with the blunt end of a splitting maul. I was out for six days."

"Did you divorce her?"

"No, she died. The Flathead died too. I sure hope the Arapaho I'm married to now keeps her health. I don't think I could go through another injun wedding ceremony. Grub's ready."

I put the guitar aside and held up my tin plate while he scraped food from the skillet. A slice of the bacon and some of the beans fell into the fire and he cursed. "Better hold it a mite closer. This child's eyes ain't what they used to be up close. Not for far neither. Time was when I could see signal smoke ten miles before them army shavetails could pick it up with their damn glasses. Don't never get old, son, that's Bridger's advice. Oncet you're there they ain't no place else to go but dead."

I could see he was brooding, so I tried to cheer him by complimenting him upon his cooking. I didn't need to exaggerate. I could not see how the mere addition of some wild onions he had picked along the trail could so transform the meals I'd been eating since leaving Abilene. Indeed, I've never sampled cooking to compare with the old mountain man's, and I've dined in the best restaurants our two coasts have to offer.

He shook his head. He ate directly from the skillet with his fingers, and a more fastidious eater you've never seen with a knife and fork. He made me ashamed of the utensils I was using. "You ain't et spaniel the way a Sioux woman can roast it in a clay pot buried in buffler shit. Melts in your mouth like sweet lard."

"Cocker spaniel?"

"Well, mostly. Them injun barkers ain't too particular what they mount."

The talk shifted to our immediate plans. I asked him about Wyoming, where he was employed as chief of Indian scouts at Fort Laramie with the rank of colonel.

"It's sweet country if you like wind that won't quit and rain coming down like iron stoves and heat so hot you can fry bacon on the back of your neck and cold so cold you piss icicles. But you can ride for a week without passing a thing on two legs and that suits this child."

"This one too. I've just been through a war, which is about too many people fighting for too small a plot of ground."

"Wyoming ain't for you." He took a gulp of scalding coffee from his battered cup.

"Why not?"

"That *git-*ar's your hunting rifle. The saloon's your range. With Red Cloud all painted up for war in the Big Horns and Black Kettle the same in Colorado, everybody that likes his scalp is doing his drinking at home. You'd best bide your time in Kansas till the army flushes them out. I'm on my way to meet this carpetbagger colonel named Carrington to do just that. It shouldn't take long, provided I can talk him out of this foolishness of dragging a wagon train with him everyplace he goes. You got to catch up with injuns if you want to force a fight. Otherwise they trickle away into cracks and holes like spring runoff." He chuckled then, a dry rustle in his swollen throat. "Just a dumb notion, mind. I notioned myself right into a Blackfoot arrow trapping the Missouri in thirty-two."

"One of your notions kept me from starving in Abilene," I said. "I have had my fill of Kansas for a while. What is the situation in Texas?"

"That's like asking what's the situation in South Americky. Which part?"

"The Southwest. I've been to the Northeast."

"Mexicans, Comanches, and Apaches. The first ain't got nothing to put in your *see*-gar box and the rest'll cut off your balls and wear 'em for earrings. Either way there ain't much future there for a man in your trade. You might try Fort Riley."

"Where's that?"

"You must of passed it on your way to Abilene. It weren't much to look at then, I expect. They beefed it up since for the same reason they're building these others, to guard the overland stage and then the railroad, if they ever get started on it. Talk is they're getting a new commander, one of them ninety-day generals from the late unpleasantness. He's a young fellow, I hear, and likes his fun. He's sure to put up an officer's bar where you can work for scrip. Some carpetbagger kind of name. I disremember it just now."

"If you think it's best." My disappointment showed in my tone. To reverse directions now symbolized for me a regression in time, when what I wanted most was to put the past behind me.

"Don't take it so bad. You're young, you got time to walk around the world twicet and stop for noon dinner besides. All I got to look forward to is another arrow in the right place this time, or a hunnert and sixty acres of dirt in Missouri if I ain't that lucky. The plow's all there is when you can't read sign no more. Care to trade?"

I said nothing, depressed not only by my own prospects,

but by the old mountaineer's self-pity as well. They were a dour lot, these veterans of the frontier.

Suddenly he smacked his knee, startling me with the noise. "Custer!"

"I beg your pardon?"

"George Custer. That's the name of the fellow that's set to take over Fort Riley. You ought to give the place a whirl. Talk is he's headed for tall things."

TWENTY-FOUR

At age nineteen, George Wymore, a student attending classes at William Jewell College in Liberty, Missouri, found a curious kind of immortality. On February 14, 1866— St. Valentine's Day—he walked around a corner into a fusillade of bullets and was dead when he hit the ground, the first fatality of the first daylight bank robbery in American history.

A few minutes previously, two men wearing slouch hats and dusters walked into the business office of the Clay County Savings Association, drew revolvers on Greenup and William Bird, father-and-son employees of the bank, and stuffed a grain sack with cash from the vault. After shutting up the two employees in the vault, the pair joined ten of their confederates guarding the street outside, mounted their horses, and rode out hard, firing their pistols at windows and the sky and yelping like wild dogs. It was at this point that the hapless Wymore stepped from the obscurity of undergraduate academia into history. When a young physician with ancient eyes examined the body later, he declared each of its four wounds fatal. This represented a quality of marksmanship unheard of before the war, and while the victim's friends and family mourned his loss, the newspaper-reading public swiftly concurred on the specific arena that had turned out sharp-shooters of such skill and daring.

The amount reported stolen was also unprecedented: sixty thousand dollars. Rumor held that the editors of the St. Louis *Missouri Republican*, while setting the story in type, argued over how many zeroes the figure entailed. Of course this tale was apocryphal. Four years of casualty counts had educated an entire nation upon the configuration of thousands.

A group of hastily deputized citizens mounted upon their own horses and armed with personal weapons, referred to as a "posse"—after the Latin term *posse comitatus*, meaning "force of the county"—tracked the bandits to a country church, paintless with paper tacked over the missing panes in its windows, where bill wrappers bearing the bank's name told them their quarry had stopped there to "split up the take." After that they lost the thieves' trail in a fierce blizzard.

That the men involved in the raid were former guerrillas was accepted without discussion. Much time would pass, and several more thousands would disappear into grain sacks, before names were publicly applied to the faces behind the bandanna masks they wore. For my part, I suspected who they were as soon as I heard of their noisy method of retreat. The remnants of the band that had followed the black flag of William Clarke Quantrill and Bloody Bill Anderson had not changed tactics since the sack of Lawrence.

I remembered Jack Fabian's report that Frank and Jesse James and John Thrailkill had been on their way to Texas to meet Cole and Jim Younger, planning to return to Missouri and their old habits.

News traveled slowly across the prairie. By the time I learned about Liberty, I had been at Fort Riley several months, wondering what had persuaded me to stop there for more than a day. It was November, not my favorite month by twelve; and November is a particularly miserable time on the Kansas plain, when the great sweep of emerald grass has gone the dead brown of beetles' wings on a dusty windowsill and the first raw winds of winter blow straight down from Canada, chilling equally the townsman in his woolen muffler and the trapper in his buffalo coat. Unlike the bitter, flinty cold of December and January, which numbs the skin upon contact and flees on pins and needles in the presence of a warm fire, November's cold is damp and cloying, and separates itself from one's spine reluctantly, like a leech being pulled away from its host. In the sutler's store where I spent all my time when I wasn't huddled in my unheated lean-to outside the stockade, many a liquid cough and snuffling intake of breath told me I was not alone in my wretchedness.

The knowledge was cold succor. The store, a poorly chinked log hovel, was overheated to compensate for the imperfection, giving the occupants the choice of loitering near the walls and shivering in the draughts that whistled through the holes between the logs or moving closer to the center and suffocating in the soporific glow of the pig-iron stove. The air was thick with the mingled stenches of unwashed wool, tobacco juice, raw whiskey, and urine, the last from the corners beyond the lamplight where drunken troopers relived themselves into the sawdust when they were too unsteady to walk outside. A clapboard partition separated this room from the officers' bar, a slightly less feral atmosphere from which the click of colliding billiard balls announced an additional diversion for the men who commanded other men. Admission to enlisted men and nonmilitary personnel was by invitation only. I had found the officers of Fort Riley a distinctly unmusical lot, and so I played for those troopers and noncommissioned officers who upon rare occasions were moved to contribute a creased and stained rectangle of the post currency known as army scrip to my cigar box. The scrip was redeemable for goods at the store, and so kept me from starving.

I had by this time acquired a second instrument, to whose recourse I turned when the guitar had ceased to draw a reaction from the stupefied relics of human refuse who had drifted into the service since the cream of the nation's youth was sacrificed to the soil from Richmond to Bull Run. The banjo had been among the personal possessions left behind in the barracks by a trooper who had deserted while out on patrol, whose sergeant had offered it to me rather than throw it out or lose it at poker. I had taken to it more quickly than I had to the guitar, and through its more impudent sound discovered life in a number of tunes I had hitherto employed only as a bridge between greater crowd pleasers. It was singularly suited to an Irish drinking song taught to me by a former Killarney resident who told me he had enlisted in the U.S. Army during a campaign to fill the Union register in Ireland, then learned while his ship was anchored in New York Harbor that the city Enrollment Office was paying a hundred dollars to each new recruit, whereupon he jumped overboard, swam to shore, and enlisted again. Shortly after teaching me the song, he deserted.

He had company. Post life for the most part was hardship and boredom, and with the fighting ended in the East and South the ranks filled with filth and degenerates, fortune hunters, adventurers, men sought for crimes committed under other names, and no small number of disillusioned rebels, who "lit a shuck" for home or the various frontier towers of Babel as soon as they were issued clothing, a weapon, and a mount. Those who remained included hard-drinking Irishmen, misfits from the East like myself, pederasts, cardsharps, and confidence men, many of whom hung around only to prey upon their inmates. Morale was low. Fistfights occurred daily; troopers were sent to the guardhouse on a regular basis for drunkenness while on parade; and there were dark rumors that the fort's new commander was a *dilettante* and a notorious "welsher" when it came to paying off his poker debts. Although the circle to whom these wagers were owed contained such forgiving types as his wife, his younger brother, and a number of friends of long-standing, the unpaid markers were a point of harsh conjecture among the perverts and putative murderers who discussed them in low tones with sidelong glances whenever the commander hove in sight.

His gaming practices aside, the C.O.'s credentials were sterling. A splendid figure in tailored uniforms who affected the sail-brimmed hats and fringed buckskin coats of the frontiersman, with coppery locks flowing to his shoulders in defiance of the hostile Indian's predilection for handsome scalps, he had, for courage and audacity in the fighting at Blue Ridge, been promoted from first lieutenant to major general, at age twenty-three the youngest man ever to attain that high rank. Although he had been forced to surrender that brevet position at the end of the war to assume the rank of lieutenant colonel, he continued to be addressed as "general" according to the military custom and held himself as if he had not stepped down at all. In residence at Fort Riley for just over a week, he had through strict adherence to the manuals of arms and swift punishment for offenses against the code of conduct—slovenly appearance at muster, for instance, meant lugging a heavy length of tree trunk upon one's shoulder around the parade ground for as long as twenty-four hours; two lengths for a second offense, and a saddle and full kit for a third—established himself as a man to obey before God and government. He was probably the most admired man I ever came to know—and the most poisonously hated.

Coincidentally, I was reflecting upon all this as I picked my way through the Irish air when an erect figure stepped in front of me, very nearly clicking his heels to get my attention, and I looked up into the callow, wispily moustachioed face of Lieutenant Myles Moylan, the commander's adjutant.

"Mr. Gashade, I am sent to ask if you are not too busy if you would care to join General Custer in the officers' bar."

George Armstrong Custer was seated in a chair near the parlor stove that warmed that scarcely more genteel side of the establishment, idly scratching one of his four great greyhounds behind the ears and balancing a glass of what appeared to be lemonade upon his right knee. I'd heard he was a teetotaler, though I had hardly credited the information based upon what I had observed of the army's bibulous ways, and wondered how much of this abstemious display was a pose for the ranks; later I learned that the leader of the newly formed Seventh Cavalry had no capacity for liquor whatsoever and, being Custer, had chosen sobriety over looking the fool. The other three dogs lay or sat about his feet, one of them industriously licking its genitals. They were gaunt, stupid creatures with narrow heads and long curved snouts like rats', and were forever getting lost on the prairie when their master took them out upon his beloved hunts for deer and buffalo, forcing him to dispatch a patrol to find them and lead them home. I detested them thoroughly, and as a rule I like dogs.

For a full minute after I presented myself before him, the general said nothing, watching me and scratching the dog at his side, which rolled its eyes and grinned dementedly, showing its eyeteeth. Custer was then about twenty-six, but his prominent bones, deeply sunken blue eyes, and the heavy, horseshoe-shaped moustaches whose weight drew his skin taut made him look older. His celebrated curly hair was receding, twin horns of pink scalp appearing alongside his widow's peak.

"Gashade," he said suddenly. His voice, a clipped, clear tenor, actually made the glasses ring behind the bar. "A name of French derivation, is it not?"

"I believe it is," I replied.

"Civilized people, the French. Terrible soldiers. Bonaparte used up the best of them. I expect the current Bonaparte will find that out soon enough. What was that tune you were playing just now?"

"A carousing song. The man who taught it to me said the Royal Irish Fusiliers played it to taunt the French troops storming the beach at Tarifa, Spain, in 1811. The Irish turned back the attack. Perhaps you were right about the French."

"Does it have words?"

"Yes."

Custer stretched out a leg, hooked a vacant chair with his ankle, and scraped it toward me. "Sing it."

I thought of refusing. The Boy General, as he was referred to by those who were unaffected by his not inconsiderable charm (when they weren't calling him names less printworthy), seemed not to have recovered from the meteor-swing that had carried him overnight from shavetail to the top of the ranks; plainly he expected everyone within his orbit, soldier and civilian, to snap to his command after the example of his dogs. However, the officers' bar was heated more evenly than the enlisted men's, and I was no longer diverted by the curious sensation of roasting upon one side whilst freezing upon the other. I took the seat, placed the banjo in my lap, strummed the melody, and raised my voice above the popping in the stove:

> *Let Bacchus's sons be not dismayed,*
> *But join with me each jovial blade;*
> *Come booze and sing, and lend your aid*
> *To help me with the chorus—*
> *Instead of Spa we'll drink brown ale,*
> *And pay the reckoning on the nail,*
> *No man for debt shall go to jail*
> *From GarryOwen in Glory!*
> *No man for debt shall go to jail*
> *From GarryOwen in Glory!*

I played and sang it through from start to finish, all seven verses, inserting the chorus after each. Doing so extended my time by the stove, as if by soaking in as much heat as possible I could store it through the night in my clammy quarters. The significance was not lost upon me that with each change of location since leaving New York I had descended a full stage in sleeping arrangements, going in three short years from coffee and scones in a four-poster to a discarded army blanket in an abandoned corn crib, with a pint of raw whiskey to prevent my blood from freezing in my veins. Perhaps that was why I feared to quit Fort Riley. My next berth might be a shallow doorway or the naked ground of the prairie, where I would be prey to coyotes and hostile tribes. For hostile they all were now, from Oregon to the Gulf of Mexico, the Sioux and Arapaho and Cheyenne and Comanche and Apache nations having declared war upon the railroads, the telegraph, pioneers, cattle companies, and the U.S. Army.

I must say in my defense that I tried no one's patience. In fact, by the third refrain, nearly everyone within earshot had joined in to sing "From GarryOwen in Glory"—the half-dozen officers present, the white-coated corporal serving drinks behind the bar, and a number of men on the other side whose bodies could not follow their voices through the door that separated them from officers' country without facing discipline. Custer alone held his silence. It was impossible to tell what was going on behind that monolithic countenance, all hollows and ridges with his eyes burning like blue-gas flames in the shadows.

"A carousers' song indeed," said he, when I had finished and the members of my impromptu choir were congratulating themselves upon their harmony. "What is Spa?"

"Mineral waters, General." I had nearly addressed him as *sir*. "I'm told the song originated in Limerick, which was famous for its springs."

"Do you agree that hard liquor is superior to the healing waters of Mother Earth?"

"Not having sampled such waters, I wouldn't know." I rose and shouldered my banjo and guitar. It was clear I'd overstayed my invitation.

"Where are you going?" he demanded.

"To bed. It's late, and I have been up since reveille."

"Why? You are not employed by the garrison."

"Your bugle doesn't know that, sir." There it was, curse him. "It's as loud for a civilian as it is for a soldier."

He stopped scratching the greyhound's ears. The dog looked at him, then lowered itself to the floor with a prolonged sigh. Custer applied the same slow, pensive stroking to his moustaches. "Would you consider teaching that song to the regimental band?"

I opened my mouth, then shut it. Then I had to open it again to speak. "I wasn't aware there was a regimental band."

"What is that? W-what is that?" Agitated, he began to stutter. "There is no glass in the west windows of the married officers' quarters, either; Libby and I have had to stuff them with rags to keep out the cold. But glass is coming, and so is a band. I shall start you on trooper's wages tomorrow. You will continue to draw pay while the band gets set up and until they have the tune down. Do not try to draw it out, mind. Out you go when the job is done."

"Does it include quarters?"

"You will bunk in the barracks. You are not Paganini. You will be issued a blanket and clothing, and you will dine with the men at mess."

"I accept."

"Of course you do. Perhaps a good drinking song is what's needed to make a regiment of this vermin. Lord knows the Temperance League would starve here. Lieutenant!"

"Yes, sir!" This time Moylan really did click his heels.

"See that Mr. Gashade gets what he needs."

"Yes, sir."

That night, stretched out upon my plank bunk in the cavalry barracks with a stove at either end, flanked by a trooper whose sinus condition rattled the windows and a corporal masturbating under his blanket, I crossed my arms behind my head and wriggled my toes, luxuriating in my good fortune. I only hoped that Frank and Jesse James and John Thrailkill never found out I was working for the Union.

TWENTY-FIVE

We are the boys that take delight in
Smashing the Limerick lamps when lighting,
Through the streets like sporters fighting,
And tearing all before us.

Instead of Spa we'll drink brown ale,
And pay the reckoning on the nail,
No man for debt shall go to jail
From GarryOwen in Glory!
No man for debt shall go to jail

From GarryOwen in Glory!
We'll break windows, break the doors
The watch knock down by threes and fours;
Then let the doctors work their cures,
And tinker up our bruises.

(Chorus)

We'll beat the bailiffs, out of fun,
We'll make the mayor and sheriffs run;
We are the boys no man dares dun,
If he regards a whole skin.

(Chorus)

Our hearts, so stout, have got us fame,
For soon 'tis known from whence we came;
Where'er we go they dread the name
Of GarryOwen in Glory.

(Chorus)

Johnny Connell's tall and straight,
And in his limbs he is complete;

He'll pitch a bar of any weight,
From GarryOwen to Thomond Gate.

(Chorus)

GarryOwen is gone to rack
Since Johnny Connell went to Cork,
Though Darby O'Brien leapt over the dock
In spite of judge and jury.

(Chorus)

An unregenerate crew, those fusiliers; but they and their Homeric Connell and O'Brien had nothing upon the men of the Seventh, as drunken and belligerent a gang as ever served a lemonade-sipping commander. Punishments for intoxication while on duty and brawling were meted out with all the predictability of the spoonfuls of castor oil the post surgeon issued to the long line of malingerers who appeared before him each morning, feigning every variety of illness from Blue Balls to smallpox, to avoid work assignments. At times the men "walking the Ring" with logs upon their shoulders outnumbered those on parade drill. Desertion continued to be a problem throughout the stiff winter of '66 and muddy spring of '67: Offenders, when captured, were stripped naked and paraded across the compound before their fellow soldiers, with their heads shaved and the livid letter *D* branded upon their left hips, to the jeering accompaniment of "The Rogues' March" provided by the regimental band. When their sentences in the stone guardhouse were finished, they were put outside the stockade with neither money nor horse nor provisions, no matter if the sun were shining or a great door-battering blizzard were pushing the drifts to eighteen feet and snapping off trees like birthday candles.

At that, I imagine they felt themselves well shut of Fort Riley. The work was hard, the commander a martinet, the boredom paralyzing, and the food—bitter saleratus flour, spoiled meat, concrete hardtack, and watery soup—was barely acceptable. Vegetables and sugar were impossible delicacies associated with Easter and Christmas, and scurvy was a common complaint. There wasn't a full set of teeth or an uninflamed case of hemorrhoids in the ranks. I was told the general himself stationed a sentry outside the outhouse to warn him when anyone approached, particularly an officer's wife, that he might refrain from groaning until she had passed; and now that I pause to read that, I realize it's the first I've seen on paper about Custer's piles. I should think it would go a long way toward explaining his behavior at the Washita and Little Big Horn. However, there I go again, placing the lyric ahead of the melody.

The monotony, at least, found respite late in March 1867, when Major General Winfield Scott Hancock—"Old Eagle Eye," "Hancock the Superb," "The Thunderbolt of the Grand Army of the Potomac," "Old Bull Nuts," call him what you will according to your experience of him—arrived at Fort Riley with twelve hundred men and a pontoon train, assembled four companies of the Seventh Cavalry and one company of the Thirty-seventh Infantry, and set out in April for Fort Harker at the head of a column of fourteen hundred, not counting a colorful band of Delaware Indians acting as scouts, guides, and interpreters, with their faces painted for war and bandoliers of ammunition strung across their naked chests. The expedition was bound eventually for Fort Larned, there to meet with a delegation from the Cheyenne, Arapaho, and Apache nations to request safe passage for the Overland stage and employees of the Kansas Pacific Railroad, who had by that time lain track to within a few days' ride of Fort Riley. In actuality (so went the talk in the barracks and at the sutler's), the excursion, complete with regimental band blaring martial airs and bicolored guidons snapping above the ranks of men in brass buttons and fringed white gauntlets, was intended to frighten the Indians into submission with the largest show of military force yet exhibited upon the plains. Farther north, where the real fighting was taking place, Colonel Carrington (abetted, one assumed, by the scouting *savvy* of Jim Bridger) was holding the Bozeman Road against Red Cloud's Sioux, flush with their victory over Captain William J. Fetterman, who had gone down with his entire command of seventy-nine men southwest of Fort Phil Kearny last December. In selecting Black Kettle's Cheyenne to look on his works, it was said, the Thunderbolt was in effect demonstrating solidarity with the demonic Chivington and the massacre at Sand Creek.

"The Sioux'll thank Old Bull Nuts, and that's for sartin," declared one old campaigner on the eve of the expedition, throwing in his cards and leaning back to strike a match on the sutler's stove. He was a side-whiskered trooper with a vivid inverted V on the sleeve of his tunic where a sergeant's chevron had been. He claimed to have fought the Comanche as a Texas Ranger before heading north to join the Union. The Seventh was full of liars, but none with a scar like the one that bisected his face from the right side of his forehead to the left corner of his jaw.

The man to whom he had surrendered his hand, a tall jasper hard on thirty with ringleted hair longer than Custer's and a set of silken moustaches that would have made a Chinese mandarin envious, raked in the chips on the table with his left forearm, retrieved the deck, and shuffled. A new arrival attached to Hancock's brigade of civilian scouts, he was a ripe dandy, fitted out with a big sombrero, buckskin trousers, knee-length boots with Mexican spurs, and a Zouave jacket of scarlet and black fastened with gold frogs. Cinched about his waist was a yellow sash with a pair of ivory-handled .36 Navy Colts thrust down inside.

"They're bound to fight sometime," said he, dealing. "We'd best do it now while we still remember how."

"Tell that to Fetterman's ghost. Three." The former ranger discarded three pasteboards.

The dandy dealt him replacements. "Fetterman was a horse's ass. Mr. Stanley?"

The third member of the party, a mild-looking fellow, tidy in his dress and habits, replied that he would stand pat. Henry Morton Stanley's soft Louisiana mode of speech belied his British birth. He had joined the campaign as special correspondent for James Gordon Bennett's New York *Herald*, and as an emissary from that city, brimming with news of its late fortunes, promised enlightening company if I could but separate him from his poker-playing companion. Two years had yet to pass before he would find his own place in the columns by approaching a British physician-explorer deep in blackest Africa with the absurd statement that he presumed he was making the acquaintance of Dr. Livingstone.

There were raises all around, and then it was Stanley's turn to fold. Called by the dandy to show his hand, the man from Texas grinned for the first time since he had sat down, displaying an Eldorado of golden incisors, and spread his cards face up on the table. "You're a right judge of horse's asses, Mr. Hitchcock, but you can't bluff for shit. Full house, jacks over deuces."

Before he could rake in the pot, however, his gaudily attired opponent showed four treys.

"The name is Hickok."

The former ranger left the table, clearly in bad cess, but without expressing it. Notwithstanding his ignorance of the other's surname, James Butler "Wild Bill" Hickok's countenance was familiar in the barracks, where a travel-worn copy of *Harper's New Monthly* had made its appearance, complete with his woodcut likeness upon its cover and accounts of his rough-and-tumble adventures on the frontier inside. In particular his prowess with knife and gun was celebrated, as in his one-man destruction of the "McCanles Gang" at the Rock Creek stage station in Nebraska Territory. Before I was very much older, I would learn that the affair was something more on the order of murder from ambush; but then this was the West, where the truth seldom impeded the progress of history in the manufacture.

In any case, skilled duelist or cunning killer, he was no man to question over his card-playing.

Now Hickok's gray eyes fixed upon me for the first time. "It seems we have a vacant chair."

I claimed it. The long months of inactivity had not been for nothing; rudimentary though my poker training was, I had a pocketful of scrip and considered it worth the price of some game-table conversation with Mr. Stanley that might lead to news from home.

"Boss Tweed is no stranger to the *Herald*," he said, when I'd managed by passive means to steer the discussion around to the man responsible for my exile. "He can be reached any afternoon for a quote at Delmonico's, where he eats a simply enormous dinner. His vest would make a suitable tent for several crippled veterans I know who sleep in doorways on the Bowery."

"Then his star has not fallen?"

"Quite the contrary. He's a director of the Erie Railroad now, thanks to some skulduggery he pulled off for Jim Fisk and Jay Gould, and he's running for state senator. The talk is he's got it. Why they're bothering to hold the election come November is anyone's guess. Form, I suppose. The old town's rotten with it. Dealer takes one."

These were unhappy tidings. I'd been feeling homesick of late, and for the first time in two years had toyed with the notion of returning home, for a brief visit at least. However, with Tweed ascendant, and more capable than ever of exacting his pound of flesh for the attack upon his man Brennan, New York was out of the question for me. If Brennan had died of the injuries I had inflicted, the complaint against me would be murder; and even if he had survived, I had only to close my eyes to feel again the heat of his crony's deep-burning gaze and know that I would never be safe inside Tweed's jurisdiction.

I lost the next two hands in silence. Then I shifted my strategy to glean what intelligence I could about my father, the judge. Claiming a slight acquaintance with the family, I asked Stanley if he knew him.

Before he could reply, Hickok uttered a filthy oath and banged his cards to the table. He had made free use of the raw whiskey sold by the sutler, and though his hand and speech remained unaffected, his wagers had grown in proportion to the amount he had imbibed. I had noticed, too, that when either Stanley or I dealt, the frontiersman lost more often than he won, while the reverse was true whenever he had charge of the deck. Since the money signified nothing, I cared not at all, but it occurred to me that the way he played poker, Hickok's skill as a pistoleer was no small asset.

Then the bugler blew Taps, and we were forced to cash in our winnings and retire to our bunks. The march was scheduled to begin at first light, and as silence was strictly enforced in the barracks after the lamps were extinguished, I did not have the opportunity that night to buttonhole Stanley upon the subject of my father; nor did I in the morning, amid the hurly-burly of "Boots and Saddles."

Torches were lit upon the parade ground. In the flickering glow assembled eleven companies of cavalry, all spit-shined leather and glittering brass aboard their curried mounts, the latter assigned by color to their various troops; seven companies of infantry in kepis with rifles upon their shoulders; a battery of artillery, squat cannon pointed rearward upon their axles; a detachment of engineers; the plumed shakos, trombones, tubas, fifes, and snare drums of the regimental band; and, bringing up the rear, the colorful disarray of civilian scouts, Delawares, special correspondents, and teamsters aboard their supply wagons, outfitted according to their own preferences from buckskins to plug hats and ladies' parasols. The air was charged, and for drama, color, and high comedy, the scene compared closely with election eve in Central Park and the Sixth Avenue St. Patrick's Day Parade.

Custer was everywhere: galloping up and down the line astride his white horse, hair and fringes flying, dove-gray campaign hat tilted rakishly, the infamous red necktie knotted to one side, pointing with his saber at this loose cinch buckle or that exposed gallus and yelping orders in his high, excited stutter. He was as nervous as any bride, and small wonder: After the orgasm of his triumphs in the late war and the letdown of his inevitable demotion and a number of petty squabbles with the Department of the Army that had delayed his reassignment to active duty, he had to be acutely aware of just how much his future depended upon the outcome of this, his first campaign against the Indians of the Plains.

I saw a touching thing. Just before he took his place at the head of the Seventh, Custer cantered up to the long porch that ran the length of the married officers' quarters and leaned down from the saddle to kiss his wife. When the kiss was completed, Elizabeth Custer—"Libby" to her husband and in the minds of hundreds of troopers who would never dare to address her so familiarly; and a better- and more noble-looking woman never set a daintier foot from civilization to join her warrior-mate since the Fall of Troy—reached behind her head, tugged loose the pink ribbon that held her hair in place, and with the dark waves cascading to her shoulders stood upon tiptoe to tie it around his right bicep. Bearing this prize as proudly as any knight-errant the scarf of his chosen lady fair, the Boy General wheeled his horse and galloped over to his place in line, the ends of the ribbon fluttering. All very picturesque and quite moving, even if the animal did choose the moment of their parting to unload a pile of apples from beneath its blond tail.

I was mounted too, aboard Dr. Reuben Samuel's reliable dun mare, but I was not going along on the expedition. My work for the army had ended when the last stubborn fife had mastered the "GarryOwen," and as Custer had made clear that he had civilians enough on his hands as it was, I was bound for places more accommodating than the prairie and the garrison, whatever those places might be. The prospect of farewell did not sadden me. The band director, a former

Prussian Army officer whose pointed beard and Heidelberg accent reminded me uncomfortably of my tyrannical childhood music tutor, was an even worse narcissist than the commander of the Seventh. He accepted my score with the exasperated air of a Fifth Avenue "swell" placing a copper in a panhandler's palm, then proceeded to trample over all its subtleties in rehearsal, hammering with drums those notes that should have been tickled with triangles and burying passages for woodwinds under tons of brass. Unfortunately, it is his version that survives. To this day whenever the march is played, usually in tribute to the martyred Custer, instead of the youthful, impudent preening of the Irish Fusiliers, I hear a blaring plagiarism of "The Campbells Are Coming."

That's what I heard that day in the spring of 1867, as the gates of Fort Riley opened to release the might of the United States Army in one direction and a lone rider, armed only with a guitar and banjo, in the other. I could hear the whirling and crashing of the cymbals for a long time after we had lost sight of each other.

TWENTY-SIX

On May 10, 1869, with two champing locomotives looking on, Leland Stanford, president of the Central Pacific Railroad, spat upon his baby-soft hands, gripped the handle of a sledgehammer, and stepped up to strike the first blow at a golden spike linking his railroad with that of the Union Pacific at a place called Promontory in the Mormon territory of Utah. A robber baron's swing being no straighter than his business practices, he missed the first time, hit the spike on his second try, and passed the hammer to his erstwhile competitor, U.P. President Thomas C. Durant. Durant pretended the spike was Stanford's head and so made his first swing count. Afterward the pair mopped their faces with white lawn handkerchiefs, clasped hands while the photographer dived beneath his black cowl and squeezed off a hod heaped with magnesium powder, and went back to their hotels as the track gang moved in to do the job right. A lot of idiots in stovepipe hats got their pictures taken standing atop the engines, and that was that.

Except now a pair of shimmering rails sutured together the recently divided North American continent from coast to coast. Supported upon oaken cross-ties laid on top of broken pieces of chat and the bones of untallied numbers of Chinese and Irish laborers lost to brawls, Indian attacks, bad whiskey, and unpredictable charges of explosives, the steel tracks cut the time required to travel from New York to California from six months to ten days. Pioneers who a scant ten years before had said good-bye forever to friends and family to farm the West could get their beans into the ground, change clothes, catch a train home, stay for a month, and be back in time to hoe the rows. Elderly Easterners could for the price of the fare visit grandchildren they had only read about in letters. Texas cattlemen weary of running the meat off their steers over the desert country that separated them from the nearest market could fatten them on grass to the railhead in Abilene, Kansas, then load them aboard cars and sell them in Chicago for ten times their investment.

For me, playing the guitar and singing with a cellist and a three-fingered fiddler in a disorderly house in Laramie, Wyoming, for bed and board and gratuities, the golden spike meant New York newspapers in my hands a week after they rolled off the press. After an absence of six years, my thumb was once again upon the pulse of my hometown and, consequently, the world (as well as the *World*).

William Marcy Tweed was a New York state senator now, without surrendering the city offices of alderman and deputy street commissioner, which he had held for years. On the first day of 1869, four Tweed men took office: Oakey Hall, mayor of New York City; Richard B. Connolly, city comptroller, with both hands in the treasury; Peter Barr Sweeny, city chamberlain, judiciary watchdog, fully in control of selecting candidates for the bench; and John T. Hoffman, governor of New York State. His influence now had spread beyond the city limits. Unchecked, he might within a few years encompass the nation. Where to hide then?

The country—no, the globe—was in flux. Ulysses S. Grant, having traded his soldier's coat for the waistcoat of a politician, was inaugurated president in March. The owner of the Cincinnati Red Stockings, an Ohio baseball team, commenced paying his players a salary, thus inventing the professional athlete. Benjamin Disraeli assumed the British prime ministry on behalf of the Tory Party, and a few months later abolished the debtors' prisons. Empress Eugénie of France, Napoleon III's beautiful and iron-willed consort, officiated at the opening of the Suez Canal, linking the continents of Africa and Asia as securely as the railroad shackled together the American East and West.

The "Smoky Hill Expedition," as General Hancock's excursion along the river connecting forts Riley, Harker, and Larned was tagged by the Eastern press, came to little, save entertainment for the plains tribes it was intended to frighten into submission and a meaningless powwow with the few braves who bothered to show up to greet Hancock and Custer outside Larned. Sometime later I heard that the commander of the Seventh managed to shoot his own horse out from under him while hunting buffalo away from the main body of troops. He did himself more credit the following year, when he swept down upon a winter encampment of the Washita River in Indian territory, killing Chief Black Kettle (who had survived the Sand Creek Massacre) and, or so the newspapers put it, "breaking the back of the mighty Cheyenne Nation."

There were laurels enough to go around. In the spring of '69, at a place called Summit Springs in Colorado Territory, General E. A. Carr and five companies of the Tenth Cavalry fell upon a party of Cheyenne dog soldiers and annihilated them at the cost of one trooper killed. A twenty-three-year-old civilian scout earned a line in print for killing the dog leader, Tall Bull. His name was William F. Cody.

I, meanwhile, was stuck in Laramie, living with a whore named Marion and taking long walks while she entertained customers in our room above the Golden Spike Saloon, rechristened from the Powder Horn after Promontory Point. Glumly, I waited out these nocturnal evictions on a bench at the station, where bad as it was the news from New York, arriving by the late train from Cheyenne, represented my lone diversion from a dissipated life.

Frequently, pulling upon the battered secondhand spirit flask that these days was my constant companion, I reflected upon my father's words to me in the only letter I had received from him since coming west: "My sole request is that you conduct yourself in a manner that will not shame you to relate to me upon our reunion." And I welcomed the excuse of a Boss Tweed to postpone that event.

To be sure, the judge would not know me at first, nor perhaps at second: Twenty-two as of the end of March, I was three inches taller than when last he'd seen me (although I was not tall as measured against the standards of a Bridger or a Hickok, who at better than six feet attracted instant notice wherever they showed themselves), had grown a beard of which I was somewhat vain, and favored the uniform of the "townie"—brushed black bowler, notched vest, striped suit, and gaiters. The last refinement had been a birthday gift from Marion, who declared that as long as I insisted upon wearing boots like some untamed mountain man I might at least cover them so people would think I had on a civilized pair of shoes. She had influenced the rest of my outfit as well. I was convinced I looked ridiculous, but then she bustled me into a photographer's studio, selected a drawing-room backdrop complete with a bust of Horace painted upon a pedestal, and made me stand in front of it while a rodent-faced gent in dirty glasses blinded me with a magnesium flash. When the picture was ready and I saw myself for the first time as others did, I was appalled. I did *not* look ridiculous, but quite natural in all the trappings of a city-bred pimp. It was after that I began to carry a flask.

Over the years I had caught myself from time to time wondering what the *real* Billy Gashade looked like—the one who had ordered his name printed upon the cards I still carried—and if by some comedy of errors he had not passed away in Bridey McMurtaugh's East River Society House, had I seen him on the street somewhere? In Denver, say, where I had entertained as vermin-infested a set of gold prospectors as ever crawled out of a hole in the ground, in a tent stinking of mildew and stale beer? Or Cheyenne, where I had turned away the amorous drunken advances of a cow moose named Martha Jane Cannary by telling her she needed a man more worthy of her, like my good friend Wild Bill Hickok, to whom I would certainly introduce her when all our paths crossed? I felt I'd have noticed Gashade in Dry Crick, a pestiferous accumulation of mud huts on the North Platte in Nebraska, where thieves ambushed me in an alley, knocked out a tooth, broke two ribs, and robbed me of my poke, forcing me to trade the dun mare to an unsympathetic stationmaster for a ticket on the Overland Stage.

However, since the incident of the photograph, I had stopped wondering. If we were to meet, and I were to see the mirror image of my stripe-suited self staring back at me, I should certainly dive back into the flask until I found oblivion.

I had confronted thoughts of this bleak nature before, in other places, and my reaction was ever the same.

Laramie was no exception. On a splintery night in December 1869, turned out from home once again with a kiss on the forehead and a tug on the scarf from Marion, I steered as always in the direction of the depot, holding down my hat against the wind razoring off the prairie. This time, however, I brought along my guitar and banjo.

TWENTY-SEVEN

Abilene!

The exclamation point this time was warranted; it had not been upon my last visit. Nothing remained of the somnolent log and-mud farming village where I had spent my first year after leaving the Missouri guerrillas. The buildings I remembered had all been torn down or burned down or rendered unrecognizable by the addition of clapboard false fronts with second-story windows through which blank sky showed from behind. The rutted streets had been graded and squared off into neat grids, hotels had been built, a depot and bank and telegraph office added, and saloons—loud, ugly, dusty, hot, smoky, tinkly, stinking, vomity, beautiful saloons —walled the vast main street on both sides. Even in winter, or so it seemed, a perpetual cloud of golden dust overhung the city, kicked up by the steady traffic of hooves and wheels and high-heeled boots and ladies' patent-leather pumps, never quite settling from the previous day before dawn brought the next day's wind from the prairie, and with it more pumps, boots, wheels, and hooves.

Especially hooves. One word summed up Abilene's change in fortunes from its Civil War languor: beef. In 1867 the Kansas Pacific Railroad had reached town, and within months appeared a sprawl of stock pens, cattle scales, barns, liveries, and offices, all still smelling of sawdust when the first bawling herd of slab-sided longhorn steers arrived from Texas, there to be counted and packed into cars bound for the slaughterhouses in Chicago, and beyond there to a postwar Eastern population starved for meat. Close behind—for animals did not drive themselves—came hotels, bathhouses, gambling hells, drinking emporia, brothels, and all the other establishments that catered to the needs and desires of men who had been deprived of civilization for weeks or months.

It was a brand-new industry, the American cattle trade, and the rules by which it was conducted, from rounding up strays to settling upon a price per head (and just what constituted a head), were still being decided upon in January 1870, when I stepped down from a day coach on the eastbound into a manure stench so fresh and warm it raised the temperature ten degrees.

I inquired of a loafer I found leaning against one of the posts that supported the roof of the depot if he knew of a place where I might find a room for the night. He was a lanky specimen in a blue flannel shirt and faded Levi's with the cuffs turned up at the insteps of his boots and a magnificent set of tobacco-stained handlebars whose curlicued tips tickled his ears.

"Wal," said he, tugging with his teeth at the drawstring of a disreputable-looking tobacco pouch, "you might could find a bunk at the Drovers' Cottage . . ."

"Drovers' Cottage." I thanked him and turned toward the platform steps.

". . . but I doubt it. She's full up."

I turned back. "What else is there?"

"Wal, there's the Gulf House, and Mrs. Childress's Boardinghouse . . ."

This time I waited while he paused to slide the tip of a gray tongue along the edge of his cigarette paper.

"They're full up too." He rolled the paper and smoothed it between his fingers.

"Is there a vacancy anywhere in town?"

He produced a lucifer from a fold of oilcloth in his breast pocket, struck it against the post upon which he was leaning, and thought while waiting for the sulfur to burn off. Then he shook his head, lighting the cigarette. "I surely doubt it. Shanghai Pierce come in last night with five hunnert head and twenty drovers. That's on top of two other outfits that was already in and a train-load of buyers from Chicaggy. Abilene's a bedbug's paradise tonight."

"I thought all the drives took place in the spring and summer."

"Them Texicans is greedy year 'round. I expect one of these years they'll be pulling 'em in on sleds."

I took my leave of him. I found in his colorful indolence a studied quality that was new to me, but then I'd noticed the fellow had a tattered copy of *Beadle's Dime Library* doubled over and thrust into his breast pocket. These slim, cheap novels printed upon rough pulp paper and bound between cardboard covers had only recently begun making their way west from presses in New York and Chicago, but were snapped up quickly from the feed stores and dry-goods counters where they were offered for sale. I suspected that my fellow pioneers were passing into a period of conscious imitation of the laconic, stalwart Western characters who appeared in them. The curtain had risen upon the second act of the drama—or was it the comedy?—that was the frontier.

As predicted, I found no billet in either the Drovers' Cottage, an impressive three-story frame structure south of the tracks, or the Gulf House, a smaller, newer hotel in town. I decided with resignation to seek a bed in one of the sprawling one-story buildings located north of the city limits where, I was told, the local harlots plied their trade. By now it may be understood that I possessed what is called "a way" with creatures of this description. Whether this was because of my music or my fast-fading lost-waif appearance scarcely mattered; with few exceptions their latent maternal instincts came to the fore whenever I appeared upon their threshold.

I was held up for several minutes by the arrival of yet another herd from the Chisholm Trail: a river of dun-colored, slat-ribbed, vapid-faced steers equipped with murderous long horns measuring at least six feet from tip to tip, bobbing its way straight down Texas Street. Here and there a rider with frost in his whiskers whistled between his teeth and quirted his reins this way and that to keep the dumb brutes from turning against the stream. A number of other would-be pedestrians were waiting patiently upon both boardwalks for the obstruction to pass, the women holding lace handkerchiefs to their noses, the men shifting their plugs from one cheek to the other and stroking the pocket watches in their palms. Less patient—and loudly vocal about it—were a number of stubble-bearded men in long buffalo coats with greasy hair to their shoulders, clustered in front of the etched plate-glass doors of the Alamo Saloon. These were buffalo hiders, and they held emphatic opinions as to who held deed to the plains, particularly when the snow was flying and the hides they sought grew shaggy, and consequently the market for them more attractive. Cattlemen in their turn resented exposing their herds and persons to Indian braves already angered by the hiders' wanton slaughter of the buffalo they depended upon to survive. Brawls between cowboys and "buffler men" were frequent diversions in saloons from Omaha to the Great Divide.

At length the way cleared and I started across the street, picking my course between disks of cow flop steaming thickly in the frigid air.

"Billy! Billy Gashade!"

I stopped and peered toward the boardwalk opposite, shielding my eyes against the sun glaring off the frosted rooftops. I saw a medium-built man in a mackinaw and fur hat of the type worn by High Plains hunters and trappers, beckoning me with sweeping motions of one arm. His dark, drooping moustaches made him appear middle-aged, but when I had mounted the boards and stood before him, I saw the clear eyes and unlined face of a contemporary. I recognized him but dimly.

"Mike Williams," he said helpfully, noting my confusion without rancor. "The Palace Saloon, Kansas City. I tended bar."

I remembered now. The Palace had been an ambitious name for that rough place, with its green-oak floorboards and Litho-printed boxers torn out of magazines and tacked to the walls for decoration. Bartender Williams's knack for enforcing order with a bung-starter and a sawed-off shotgun among the unruly clientele had quickly won him a colorful nickname.

"Iron Mike," I said, shaking his hand. "You spared me a tar-and-feathering."

"I doubt them ferry fellers would of went through with it, for all their loud talk. You couldn't know 'Dinah Won't You Blow' would set them on the prod so. I just helped them see it before they finished getting your duds off. A thing like that can get to be embarrassing, especially with ladies present."

The only "lady" I recalled had been a three-hundred-pound cigar-chewing soiled dove nicknamed Big Edna, who had cheered on the rowdies with lungs lined with leather; but I was still too grateful for his intercession to correct him. The West was not a place where men rushed routinely into situations that were not their personal concern. "If I'd known there was so much rivalry between them and the railroaders," I said, "I'd have played 'My Gal Sal.' What brings you to Abilene?"

"Money, same as you. These here cowboys don't hold on to their pay any longer'n a double handful of hot coals. I'm getting top wages at the Alamo. Where you staying?"

"I just got in. I thought I'd try my luck north of the tracks."

"The Devil's Addition? That's a far piece to walk just to get your pockets picked by as greedy a bunch in feathers as you'll find this side of a buzzards' nest."

"I'll have to take my chances. There's not a bed to be had in town."

"I can offer the other side of mine." When I hesitated, he flashed his teeth. "Don't shrink up, hoss, I ain't bent that direction. It's just till the end of the season. After the herds roll out and the drovers head for home, you can name your own rate at any hotel in town."

"Maybe just for tonight," I said. "I'm worn out from the train. Tomorrow I can start looking fresh."

He fished a watch from a vest pocket next to the handle of a large revolver and snapped it open. "My shift starts at four. Bed's all yours till two. Come on. I'll introduce you to Mrs. Childress."

"Childress's Boardinghouse?" The loafer at the station had mentioned it. Following Iron Mike down the boardwalk, I began to feel the weight of my guitar and banjo and the satchel containing all the rest of my worldly belongings. My back was sore from the hard seat—Pullman's luxurious salon car had not yet reached that stretch of the Kansas Pacific—and my head ached.

"That's the place. The lady that owns it is stiff as trade whiskey, but she's the McCoy. Just don't stare at her."

I was still pondering the meaning of this advice when we drew up before a whitewashed building, separated from its neighbor on either side by only a common wall. In appearance, however, its isolation was substantial. The windows at ground level were leaded, in contrast to the discolored panes of the saddlery on the one side and the lawyer's office on the other, and the front door painted a pleasing shade of green, with a fanlight on top and carriage lamps mounted alongside. Ornate brass numerals advertised the address from the center panel and a blue-and-white china bellpull announced visitors. Mike employed it.

Presently the door opened the width of a human face, although the face that inserted itself into the gap was scarcely human. Entirely hairless, lacking even eyebrows and lashes, it was as white as paper, with pink eyes and a cleft upper lip that completed its resemblance to a large and vaguely hostile rabbit. The creature, clad in overalls, towered over my companion full twelve inches, and Mike crowding six feet in his stockings.

"Got a boarder for Mrs. Childress," Mike informed him.

The pale giant mumbled something thoroughly unintelligible.

"It ain't for you to say whether she's taking any in," said the other. "Fetch her."

The giant remained immobile.

"It is all right, Chronus. I shall speak to them."

With the eternal slowness of a planet separating itself from its orbit around the sun, the great albino moved to one side, bringing the door with him. Mike stepped past him without another glance in his direction. I followed.

For a time I was blinded. Not so much as a lamp or a candle was burning beyond the door, and thick plush curtains covered the windows. It seemed minutes before my eyes adjusted so far as to discern the smoky outline of the woman standing near the end of the long wainscoted hallway that led from the front door to the back of the house. She was clad all in black, and to her wardrobe had been added a thick veil that covered her disfigurement; but no veil could disguise the measured Grecian tones of her speech. Recognizing me suddenly, she lifted a hand to her mouth, and I saw the familiar garnet ring upon her index finger.

Instinctively I removed my hat. "Good day, Mrs. Patakos," said I. "Or have I now the honor of addressing Drucilla Childress?"

TWENTY-EIGHT

Childress is not worth discussing," Drucilla informed me. "I married him in Ellsworth for his name and influence—he was a land speculator, and sold his property to the railroad for five times what he paid for it—and left him when he took up with a hotel cook. I understand he lost his money and went to Santa Fe to start over. I do not know what became of the cook."

I expressed surprise that she continued to bear his name.

"Patakos is too closely associated with my former profession, and my maiden name is unpronounceable to Americans. In any case, no decent unmarried woman operates a boarding house. I am the Widow Childress in Abilene. It might surprise you to learn how much better you are treated by clerks and tellers when they think your husband is dead."

Mike Williams having left us to take up his duties at the Alamo, we were alone in the dimly lit but pleasant suite of rooms Drucilla occupied at the back of the house. A spacious kitchen separated them from the dining room, where her cook served breakfast and supper to the boarders, and the parlor, where the guests relaxed and received visitors. My hostess sat in a bentwood rocker, turned from old habit to present the good side of her face to me. My seat was a horsehair sofa upholstered in faded leather, a carryover from the house in Lawrence.

"I suppose the guerrilla raid soured you on your old business," I said.

"I am certain you will not believe me when I say that I have withstood worse. In Lawrence I had an established enterprise and little competition. Out here, anyone with the price of a tent and a string of disease-ridden half-breeds can undercut you. I haven't the energy to scratch for my supper. Meanwhile, everyone needs a roof and a meal, and I no longer have to break up fights or locate a doctor who will perform operations without demanding a partnership."

"I need a roof myself. I cannot pay you until I find a job."

"Mike will find a spot for you at the Alamo. As for the roof, you are welcome to mine for nothing. But for you I would not have had one in Lawrence. The guerrillas would have torn it down brick by brick."

"Still, the result was the same. By the time I found my way back, you and Isabel and the ladies were gone. I was nearly killed by squatters."

"Dear Isabel. She died in my arms of the smallpox in Independence. We were the last to leave the house after the customers stopped coming. It was our decision, however. We made it in our own time, and not at the point of a bayonet. Thanks to you."

"Wherever did you come by Chronus?" The albino had ghosted in and out while we were talking, bringing wood for the fireplace. It was obvious by the way he behaved around his mistress that he was as devoted to her as a child.

"I bought him from a medicine drummer in Ellsworth. He kept the wretch chained to his wagon and made him dance to draw crowds. I dressed him in proper clothes and taught him to speak."

"That must have been difficult."

"Not as difficult as getting him to sleep in a bed. He was accustomed to curling up on a bit of straw in the back of the wagon. I have no idea where he came from or who his people are. The medicine drummer claimed to have bred him from a prizefighter and a she-hare. He is named for the greatest of the Titans, from the stories my father used to tell me about the old gods."

"Is he dangerous?"

"Only to those who would bring me danger. I find him better company than Panama Bob."

"It's a wonder the drummer agreed to part with him, even for a price."

"I drive a hard bargain," said she; and with those words the subject was closed forever. "You have grown, Billy. The beard becomes you. You might reconsider those tinhorn clothes before you show yourself to the cowboys at the Alamo. By the time they are ready to sit down and hear your songs, they have been skinned and skewered by slick gamblers in broadcloth and linen. A buckskin shirt and dungarees will pay for themselves in short order."

I felt myself grinning. "And will you rechristen me after one of the old gods?"

The muscles of her ruined face seemed to shift behind the veil. She might have been returning the smile.

* * *

It was a raw town, for all the brass fittings and polished mahogany in the Alamo and feathered hats and fringed white boots of the women who plied their trade along Texas Street; rougher in its way than the log village that had preceded it. Floyd, the counterman of dyspeptic memory (although mine own alone, as no one I asked had ever heard of him), would have shaken his dour head in disgust at the antics of the trail-weary cowboys, who celebrated their holiday by riding their horses into saloons, shooting the glass ornaments off the posts that flanked the entrance to the Drovers' Cottage, and scooping up wasp-waisted young women from the street at full gallop and depositing them with a tobacco-stained kiss upon the porch of some unsavory establishment.

A jail had been built, then rebuilt after rowdy cowboys tore it down. Finding the new construction formidable, with an armed guard stationed in front, the cowboys turned their attention to the mayor's office on Railroad Street, shooting out the windows on their way to the stockyards. Hardworking fellows on the ranch and along the Chisholm, they "blew off steam" in town like children set free from church and seldom damaged anything beyond property and dignity. The trail bosses, notably rough-hewn old Abel H. "Shanghai" Pierce, good-naturedly reimbursed the owners for the former, and after a night or two in jail the hungover cowboys reported with their hats in their hands to apologize to the citizens whose complacency they had ruffled.

Other infractions were less wholesome, and almost invariably committed by persons other than cowboys.

Pistol-packing professional gamblers, outlaws poured white-hot from the crucible of the Civil War, and gunmen hired by the cattle companies to guard against rustlers were a volatile enough mixture to introduce to so tiny a vessel as a frontier cow town. The addition of alcohol, women of easy virtue, and money constantly changing hands made it explo-

sive. A disagreement over cards or the affections of a female
that might in other places have ended in a torn lip or a bloody
nose commonly overflowed into the street in Abilene, where
it was settled with an exchange of bullets or, more often, by
the roar of a shotgun fired from cover. A day that began and
ended without gunfire and some miserable soul being carried
by his friends to a doctor or the undertaker was hailed as a
novelty, and celebrated in the columns of the local *Chronicle*.

A succession of town marshals—part-timers mostly, merchants and county sheriff's men seeking to make ends meet—
attempted to enforce order, only to be run off or tarred and
feathered and ridden out of town on a rail. In practice, this
last tradition was a far cry from the picture of fun drawn by
those who have never seen it. I had, in Cheyenne and again
in Abilene, and had very nearly become a victim myself in
Kansas City had not Iron Mike Williams intervened. The tar-
geted individual was dragged into the street, beaten and
stripped by a mob, immersed in scalding tar, suffocated by
goosedown feathers dumped from pillowcases, and finally
hoisted astraddle a section offence rail supported upon the
mob's shoulders, his hands tied behind him and his naked
thighs clenching the splintery wood in desperation lest he fall
and become trampled, and carried down a public street beyond the city limits, where he was dumped into a ditch or a
thorny bramble and advised not to return under threat of
death. Humanity was never so bestial as when carrying out
this barbaric and thoroughly American ritual. It is no reflection upon their courage that a number of townsmen declined the badge to avoid exposing themselves to it.

True to Drucilla's promise, Mike Williams secured for me
a position at the Alamo, playing guitar and banjo, filling in
at the piano when the regular player was off, and helping out
behind the bar when business was brisk and the staff thin.
Although I received no wages, the gratuities were generous,
especially after I followed Drucilla's advice and doffed my
"city duds" for a shirt of the softest yellow buckskin and a

broad-brimmed sombrero, which I properly "seasoned" by soaking it in alkali water and allowing it to dry in the sun. In keeping with the establishment's other appointments—triple glass doors, brass lamps with white glass shades, red felt-topped gaming tables, fat pink nudes romping about the walls, and mirrors, mirrors everywhere—I was offered the use of the stage when it was not occupied by some traveling troupe, but I turned it down in favor of a spot on the floor, where I was more approachable and my open cigar box was within reach of appreciative listeners.

Of these there were many. I played and sang the songs they crooned to the herds at night when they were skittish—"Beautiful Dreamer," "Old Dan Tucker," "The Night Guard"—and I sang songs that reminded them of the sweet-hearts they had left at home—"Cielito Lindo," "Sweet Betsy from Pike"—and I taught them the words to new songs that had swept the East while they were swallowing dust from the Panhandle to the banks of the Arkansas—"Champagne Charlie," "The Man on the Flying Trapeze," and "Little Brown Jug," whose unabashed celebration of the inebriated state never failed to raise whoops and a cry of "Do 'er agin!" On a good night the box filled quickly, and Iron Mike took it upon himself to escort me home to see that I was not way-laid and robbed.

These were my nights. My days were spent at Mrs. Childress's Boardinghouse, where I slept in a large corner room upon the second floor, comfortably furnished with a brass bed, two overstuffed chairs and a settee arranged in an intimate sitting area, a washstand, and a fine steelpoint engraving from a painting by Bierstadt of buffalo crossing a stream, framed in walnut and hung above the bed. This was the Presidential Suite, kept in reserve for surprise visitors of steep reputation, and I was pledged to vacate it the moment word arrived that Ulysses S. Grant was on his way to Abilene. I took my meals in the communal dining room, served by a garrulous Frenchwoman in her late fifties who took no heed that her prattle, delivered in her native language (for she knew no English), was understood by none of her listeners. The food was heavy, and invariably arrived swimming in wine, but the portions were generous. No one ever left the table hungry. The living arrangement was the most luxurious I had known since leaving my father's house.

The reader may be surprised, given my description of the town, that I had been in residence there for some months before I witnessed my first criminal act. The reason is I spent most of my waking hours in the Alamo, where order was strictly enforced; fights broke out from time to time, but Mike and his fellow bartenders quickly intervened, often with the aid of a bung-starter or the sawed-off double-barrel that reposed behind the bar. On occasion I had overheard gunfire from the street, indicating that the battlers had chosen a new venue and deadlier means to settle their differences, but I had enjoyed the good fortune never to be present upon the scene. I had seen enough blood shed for two lifetimes and never felt the urge to fly to a window when trouble happened.

My luck ended May 14.

It was a Saturday night. The spring cattle season was in full swing. Sixty thousand head had come through since the last snow, another twenty-five thousand were fattening on the grass outside town. Half a million were expected before winter. All the hotels were packed with drovers and buyers, with the boarders at Drucilla's sleeping two to a bed, not counting mine and Mike Williams'. (The bartender had earned special privileges when he'd evicted a drunken buffalo hider who'd insisted upon taking target practice in his room.) Players and spectators clustered like flies around the gaming tables at the Alamo and stacked up six deep at the bar, inhibiting foot traffic and causing collisions that would doubtless have led to fights had there been room to swing a fist. Tobacco smoke hung as thick as moss below the pressed tin ceiling.

I was singing and playing "Cotton-Eyed Joe" on the banjo, making little headway against the raised voices and rattling chips and clatter of the Faro wheel though my throat was raw and my fingers ached, when catastrophe occurred. It was a warm night for the season, made more so by the press of hot bodies, and the doors were propped open to let out the heat and smoke. Suddenly the room was shaken by a horrendous crash. I looked up to see one of the round felt-topped tables rolling in a semicircle on the floor like a dropped coin amid the shambles of playing cards and chips that had fallen from it. Stepping over it gingerly, like a ballerina avoiding a sand-bag dropped in the middle of her dance, was a tall, scoop-bellied horse colored that mustard shade that is called claybank, its eyes rolling white with panic, and aboard it, rak-ing its flanks with his spurs and roundly cursing its timidity in a voice thick with Missouri, a hunched rider in a linen duster with slouch hat pulled low and a blue bandanna cov-ering his face. Ducking to avoid hanging lamps, he nosed the claybank through the crowd scrambling to clear a path—hooves clomp-clomping on the hardwood floor—hauled back savagely upon the reins as he approached the bar, and, throwing aside the tail of his duster, swept a nickel-plated re-volver out of his holster and "pulled down" on Iron Mike Williams.

"Put the box on the bar!" he bellowed.

Mike hesitated only an instant. The shotgun was at the other end of the bar and the revolver was only inches from his face. With careful deliberation he hoisted the open metal strongbox containing the night's receipts from its shelf be-low the bar and placed it on top.

The man on horseback motioned him back, then reached down, fisted the paper currency, and thrust it inside his shirt. Gathering his reins, he took aim with the pistol at a lamp hanging from a chain over the bar and fired. The chain parted and the lamp plunged to the floor, shattering and spraying flaming coal oil in every direction. By the time Mike and a handful of cooperative patrons stamped out the fire, the rob-ber had turned his horse and clomp-clomped back out the way he had come in. From the street came the rattle of hoof-beats speeding away.

The county sheriff, a young man grown old in the job, assembled a posse, but there was no moon, and they lost the trail in the darkness east of town. The next day there were fresh cries for law and order, which as usual died down the moment the mayor asked who would come forward to enforce it.

I could not fault my fellow citizens. If the lawless element that claimed the streets was as bold and fierce as the man who had raided the Alamo, the job of eliminating it was far too much for any ordinary man.

For I had recognized the robber.

More specifically, I had recognized his weapon, and thus the hand that had wielded it. Seven years had passed since I had last seen it, and it had been in my possession barely a month, but I knew Corporal Templeton "Tupper" Deane's five-shot European revolver the instant it made its appearance. That, together with the rider's voice, bearing, and pale empty eyes above the bandanna, left me certain he was the man to whom I had surrendered the weapon while Lawrence burned.

Over the years I had found myself wondering upon occasion what had become of Lieutenant John Thrailkill after Anderson and Quantrill fell. I wondered no longer. And then a new question arose: If Thrailkill had come to Abilene, could Frank James and his brother Jesse be far behind?

IV

Lyric for the Lost

TWENTY-NINE

The odds being faithless, sooner or later the unluckiest of gamblers must turn up a card that favors him. Abilene's came up on June 4, 1870. On that flyblown afternoon, a square-shouldered, sunburned man of about thirty, with the regular features of an advertising graphic for gentlemen's collars and a meticulously trimmed set of moustaches, climbed the stairs to the office on Railroad Street where Ted Henry, the mayor, conducted his real estate business, and applied for the job of marshal. Henry expressed doubts about the fellow's lack of visible armament but hired him on the spot in lieu of any other applicants. Before he left, the young man handed his new employer a preprinted sign and asked him to post it where he thought best. The sign bore that day's date.

STARTING THIS DATE, CARRYING FIREARMS IS FORBIDDEN
WITHIN THE TOWN LIMITS OF ABILENE. VIOLATORS WILL BE
FINED FIFTY DOLLARS AND BE ORDERED OUT OF TOWN.
TOM SMITH, TOWN MARSHAL,
ABILENE, KANSAS

Few gave Smith much chance of remaining in residence much past midnight of that first day. The bunch that gathered in Ben Thompson and Phil Coe's Bull's Head Saloon, whose rustic appointments were more friendly to unbathed flesh and stubbled chins than the glitter at the Alamo, were said to have the tar and feathers all ready for the first time the new marshal attempted to enforce the anti-firearms ordinance.

The man was no fool. While his predecessors had patrolled

the town on foot, Smith remained on horseback during his rounds, wearing a brace of pistols concealed in shoulder holsters beneath his coat. The first time he came upon a cowboy tearing down one of his signs, however, he left the weapons where they were, leaping off his saddle and thrashing the fellow with his fists. Two or three more of these incidents, followed by a night in jail for the offender and a twenty-dollar fine for defacing city property, and the signs began to stay up. More significantly, the newly installed gun racks in the hotels and saloons filled up with checked weapons.

"They say he's from New York originally," Mike Williams informed me over tea in Drucilla's private parlor one stifling day in July. The afternoon occasions were open to her star boarders only, and although the bartender and I were indifferent to the stiff brew and soapy-tasting lemon cookies she set out, we were rarely absent. It was an hour of repose and intelligent conversation before we reported for work. "Maybe you know some of the same folks."

I was intrigued, for I had not met the marshal yet except to exchange nods when his rounds took him to the Alamo; but I said, "It's doubtful. I understand he's a career lawman. My circles and those of New York's Finest didn't intersect often."

"Well, he wasn't with the police long. I hear he shot a boy by accident and quit. That's why he's the last to pull a smoke-wagon when he's in a tight."

"His reticence will bury him."

We looked at our hostess, who seldom took part in the discussion when it turned to local figures and events; but she went on sipping her tea without elaborating. She had gathered up her veil to drink and nibble, but as always she sat in the chair farthest from the light with her left side toward us.

"It didn't bury him out in Wyoming," Mike said. "Talk is he cold-cocked this pistolero name of Montana Jones with just his fist in Bear River. Dropped him like a turd before he could go for his iron. Your pardon, Mrs. Childress." He reddened at his slip.

Drucilla was unaffected. "An admirable skill, in New York. Perhaps even in Bear River. Abilene is neither of those places. And a bullet travels much farther than a man's fist."

"Not if he makes his move before it's fired. No one ever got killed for moving too fast."

"It's enough for me that he holds Thompson and Coe in check," said I. "Whenever trouble happens it generally starts at the Bull's Head, and I never once heard of either of the proprietors raising a hand to stop it."

Mike slurped his tea. "It'd be closer to enough if Smith shut them down. Why Ted Henry ever issued them two blackhearts a license to run a saloon don't signify."

Ben Thompson and Phil Coe were poor choices to be allowed to operate a drinking establishment, at that: One was a dangerous drunk, the other a cold-blooded killer. The thick-built Thompson, an Englishman by birth with a Texas upbringing, whose speech retained a cockney edge particularly when he became agitated, had been arrested twice for shooting someone, the first time when he was thirteen years old, and had fled New Orleans before the war for killing a Frenchman in a duel. Those were the stories that circulated about him, in any case, and whether they were true or not he dressed the part of the suave duelist in a high silk hat, morning coat, and striped trousers, favoring a game leg with an ebony walking stick. Apart from keeping as much order as he bothered to maintain at the Bull's Head, his sole responsibility to the partnership seemed to be to prevent his associate from losing his temper and hurling someone through a window.

Phil Coe knew no other restraint. A shiftless fool when sober, under the sway of alcohol he flew into towering rages and had come close to killing customers on several occasions when he felt he'd been insulted. Once he was in the grip of these foaming frenzies, the only thing that would stop him was a crack on the skull with the gold head of Thompson's stick. The rest of the time the two saloonkeepers seemed to amuse themselves by feeding whiskey to sullen cowboys and turning them into a destructive mob.

"Thompson and Coe are best left where they are, and the Bull's Head kept open," put in Drucilla. "At least now the marshal knows where to look when something happens. Depriving troublemakers of a place to gather is the same as kicking apart a nest of yellow jackets."

"All the same, I'd admire to see Smith swat one or two," Mike said.

She reached for a cookie. "Bear River Tom Smith will not last six weeks."

It was an uncharitable assessment. Smith lasted six months. Early in November, while attempting to serve an arrest warrant upon a killer named Andrew McConnell in a dugout outside Abilene, the marshal was clubbed from behind by his quarry, and before he could climb to his feet the killer chopped off his handsome head with an axe.

The town seethed. A lynch gang materialized—not surprisingly, at the Bull's Head—but before it could set out after McConnell, news came from Fort Riley that the army had him in custody along with a suspected accomplice and that the pair would stand trial elsewhere to avoid hemp fever. Since their pistols were loaded anyway, the would-be stranglers proposed organizing a citizens' vigilance committee to deal with the inevitable outlaw backlash in the absence of a marshal. A town council was elected. For the first time serious consideration was given the suggestion to tell the cattle companies to bypass Abilene. Ted Henry was ousted as mayor. Replacing him was Joseph McCoy—founder of the local cattle trade, visionary, maker of fortunes, and the inspiration for the phrase "the real McCoy," which ran rampant through the regional parlance. After some deliberation, and over and above the protests of the other men on the council, McCoy selected as Smith's successor a former Indian scout, full-time professional gambler, and until recently the sheriff in Hays City, eighty miles to the west. In the spring of 1871,

Wild Bill Hickok raised his right hand and swore to uphold the law in Abilene.

In the history of the frontier, no two peace officers differed in their approach to their duties more widely than Thomas James Smith and James Butler Hickok. Smith had shot but one person in his entire career in law enforcement, and that one by accident; in Hays City alone, Hickok had shot four, killing three. How many others he had accounted for in his checkered past depended upon which tall tale you were listening to at the time. Bear River Tom had dressed and behaved quietly, melding into the background; Wild Bill was partial to low-crowned black hats with dramatic brims, Prince Albert coats, and red silk sashes tied about his waist to hold up his Navy pistols with the butts twisted forward, and conducted himself loudly and obstreperously, especially when he drank or the cards turned against him. Finally, Smith had patrolled the streets at regular intervals, but if you had business with Hickok, you either sought him out at his regular table at the Alamo or you kept it to yourself.

There he could be found day or night, seated with his back in a corner, curly hair to his shoulders, pursing his lips over the hands he was dealt and shoving his chips around with his left hand. His right was always free and rested in his lap near his pistols. Remembering the way his luck had improved whenever he had the deck in Fort Riley, I considered this a wise precaution. However, no one challenged his playing in Abilene.

For a time after he came we exchanged not a word, though night after night we were separated by only twenty feet of floor. Whenever our gazes met, no recognition flickered in his gray eyes, and I supposed he had forgotten our brief acquaintance. However, one night when I was filling in for the regular piano player, Hickok stood, scooped his winnings into his hat, slung it onto his head without spilling a chip, and came my way. He listened for a while, sipping his whiskey— the real imbibers took the stuff in slowly, letting "tenderheels" jerk it down—then placed his glass on top of the upright and asked me if I knew "The Buffalo Hunters."

"I know several songs by that title. It's a popular subject." I tried to concentrate upon my fingering. I was out of practice and his presence unsettled me.

"The one I'm thinking of has injuns in it, and something about hellfire."

"That's 'The Buffalo *Skinners*.' I know it."

He reached into a pocket, walked a silver dollar across the back of his left hand, and flipped it into the cigar box next to his whiskey. "Show me."

> *The water was salty as hellfire,*
> *the beef I could not go;*
> *And the Indians waited to pick us off*
> *while skinning the buffalo.*
> *We coaxed old Krego to pay us,*
> *but it was no go;*
> *So we left his damned old bones to bleach*
> *on the range of the buffalo.*

"It ain't that bad all the time," said he, when I'd finished. "Sometimes it's worse. The work's hard as hell. You get so you don't mind the stink, but it's no fun trying to sleep when your duds are all stiff with old guts."

"You were a hider?"

"You name it, I done it. Well, I wasn't never no streetcar conductor. Shot buff, graded track, farmed, skinned mules, fit injuns, hauled freight, tended stock, kept the peace. Spied for the Union in Missouri. I guess old Sterling Price has reason to ask the good Lord for my damnation."

"I was in Missouri during the war."

Immediately I regretted the admission. The war would never be over in the hearts and minds of many. Not a few of the young men whose fresh graves lumped the hill outside town had gone there over disagreements involving the fundamental principles of North and South, and by all accounts Hickok was not one to forget old animosities. Interested suddenly, he studied me keenly down the length of his bold beak of a nose. Then he retrieved his glass from the piano and helped himself to a long, thoughtful draught.

"Your name's Gashade, ain't it?"

I said it was. I was playing "Jack o' Diamonds"—a simple enough tune, but I gave it all the attention of a funeral mass.

"I had a hell of a time getting shut of this here lady bullwhacker when I come through Cheyenne," he said. "Name of Cannary, though she goes by Calamity Jane. She said you put her up to it."

I nearly dropped a chord. "I might have mentioned your name. She asked me if I'd introduce you. I said I would. She had me in a corner at the time. Her breath was like the alley behind a saloon."

"It is that." He emptied his glass. "Don't introduce me to no more women, hoss. I got all I can handle." He fished out another silver dollar, plunked it into my box, and strolled back to his table.

"That's the truth," said Mike Williams behind the bar, when I related the conversation to him during my break. Resplendent in green vest and sleeve garters with wax in his moustaches, he poured me a drink on the house. "He's living with a woman he knew in Springfield, and there's talk of him and that lady that come through with the circus, and I hear he's romancing that Hazell woman from the Devil's Addition that Phil Coe's sweet on. I reckon they ought to call him Three-Gun Hickok." He grinned lewdly.

I drank. "I'm certain he guessed I was not with the Union. I expected him to make an issue of it, but then he brought up that Calamity Jane business instead."

"I reckon his attitude toward the army has changed. I heard he had a run-in with some drunken troopers from Fort Hays when he was sheriffing in Hays City. Beat blue hell out of a sergeant and shot two others. Killed one. Phil Sheridan put out a warrant on him. That's why he left."

"Some men just draw trouble."

"I disagree. It's been quiet here ever since he come."

"You're just defending him because you were friendly in Kansas City."

"Friendship draws a lot of water with a man like Wild Bill. Just this week he put in a good word for me over at the Novelty Theater. They stuck me in charge of security."

"You're leaving the Alamo?"

"No, it's just part-time. I come running whenever one of them Texicans falls in love with a show girl."

I said, "It's a little more dangerous than that. The Novelty's right next to the Bull's Head."

"That's O.K." His grin was as bright as the glass he was polishing. "I like it various."

THIRTY

In the summer of '71, I was privileged to be the only reliable witness to an event that has passed into Western lore. However, my version is not the one you will find there, and few if any credit it.

Among the Texans who swarmed the boardwalks along Texas Street and the Devil's Addition that season was an underweight youth of seventeen or eighteen, with wild eyes and a sallow face broken out in suppurating pimples. His name was John Wesley Hardin, and although according to rumor he was wanted in connection with a number of shooting deaths in Texas, he was in the legitimate employ of one of the cattle companies as a "stock detective"—sanitary terminology for a killer engaged to gun down prospective rustlers. He stayed at the Drovers' Cottage and did most of his drinking and gambling at the Bull's Head. Later I heard that Ben Thompson and Phil Coe put him up to challenging Hickok, toward whom Coe held a grudge because they both shared the favors of a madam named Jessie Hazell; but it is my opinion that the incident I saw was more on the order of a chance encounter.

It was a Thursday night, and slow. The Alamo had closed early, the business being unequal to the cost of the oil burning in the lamps. The town was quiet by the time I cashed in the chips placed in my cigar box by a number of satisfied gamblers and ventured out. Mike Williams having left to attend to his duties policing the Novelty Theater, I was without an escort. I felt restless. Not ready to retire, and knowing Drucilla to be in bed and beyond reach of stimulating conversation, I paused in the shadows of the covered porch in front of the saloon to sip from my flask and contemplate the stars hanging low over the meat market across the street. The street itself was deserted but for two or three loafers like myself leaning against the porch posts and a half-inebriated cowboy making his way down the middle on foot, singing quietly to himself and walking high on his cocked heels. He had on a Sunday suit and vest, pleasantly rumpled, with no collar to his shirt and a pearl-gray Stetson pushed to the back of his head. The rest I have already described. I had no idea at the time that the fellow was Hardin. Indeed, the song he was singing was the only interest he held for me. I was straining to identify it when Wild Bill Hickok stepped out through the door of the Alamo and turned to mount the outside staircase to his room above the saloon.

He was dressed particularly fine that night, in a coat of red crushed velvet that reached nearly to his knees, encircled at the waist by a broad belt with a big square buckle like a buccaneer's. Below it a pair of checked trousers were stuffed into tall boots that gleamed with a blue flame in the light of the streetlamp. As always, the belt supported the matched Colts and his hair spilled in perfumed ringlets from under the broad brim of his flat-crowned black hat. I think that if he had outfitted himself less carefully, the meeting with Hardin would not have happened. As it was, pausing with one foot on the bottom step of the staircase to light a cheroot, he turned away from the wind to prevent a spark from the lucifer from burning a hole in his coat, and as he did so his gaze fell upon the young imbiber singing in the street.

Shaking out the match, Hickok stepped down from the boardwalk, obstructing the youth's path.

"Warm night," said the marshal by way of greeting. "I believe if there wasn't a breeze we'd all be in our shirtsleeves like a gang of shanty Irish."

"This ain't warm." It seemed to me that the other swayed a bit more than his condition warranted. "Where I come from, the water holes freeze on nights like this. The rest of the time they're pure steam."

Hickok blew on the match he was still holding, as if without attention it might rekindle. "I'm thinking your name's Hardin."

"That'd make you Hickok," said the other after a pause. "I hear how you're all the time thinking."

"Marshal Hickok."

The youth smiled slowly. I thought him young to be in possession of so many gold teeth. "How-de-do, *Marshal* Hickok. I'm *Mister* Hardin."

"Well, Mister Hardin, there's an ordinance against carrying firearms in town."

For answer, Hardin slowly curled his fingers around his lapels and spread open his coat. No pistols showed.

After a while Hickok dropped the splinter of charred wood to the ground and crushed it with the toe of his boot. It must have been the most thoroughly extinguished match in Abilene. "You gamble, Mister Hardin?"

"I have been known to wager now and again, yes, sir." He continued to hold his coat open, like a peddler showing his wares.

"Bluff much?"

"No, sir, I never do."

"Mister Hardin," Hickok said, "I'm calling the card under your left arm."

For the next twenty seconds—it seemed much longer—nothing stirred in the vicinity of the two men facing each other in the street. A block or two over, a shutter flapped in the wind. It sounded like a pistol shot, yet neither man reacted.

More gold teeth showed then. Hardin released one of his lapels and reached inside his vest with his right hand. Hickok's hand, the one not holding the cheroot, drifted down toward one of the ivory handles above his belt.

It was this hand I was watching when Hardin withdrew a pistol from the sling beneath his left arm. The fingers curled, hesitated, then relaxed. Hickok's whole body began to vibrate. In another moment I realized he was laughing.

"That's your ace in the hole?" He gasped for breath.

"Pitiful, ain't it?" Hardin actually sounded sheepish. "I bought it off a fellow in Marshall when I was in a tight. This job come up before I could find one better."

Now I looked at the pistol the young roughneck was holding by the barrel. It was an old cap-and-ball Army Colt, missing its grips and with a twist of rusted wire holding the heavy barrel to the frame. It did not look as if it could fire.

"Ever try to shoot with it?" Hickok asked.

"This greaser vaquero put a hole through my hat on the Chisholm. I kilt him fair and square, but it took two hands. There's a country block betwixt the cylinder and the firing pin."

"Lucky for you Mexicans are slow. Put it up, hoss. I don't need no more sash weights."

That was the end of the historic first meeting between Wild Bill Hickok and John Wesley Hardin, no matter what else you may have heard. The marshal told the gunman to keep his nose wiped and went up to his room. Since then I've heard many preposterous tales about the encounter, told by a couple of dozen men who claimed to have been present. The most persistent held that Hardin offered Hickok a pair of pistols, butts first, then worked the border spin, catching the lawman with his mouth open and two deadly muzzles staring at him. However, if *I* was familiar with that trick, I don't see how Hickok could not have been, given his wide experience. Legends sniff at logic.

The popular account is that the two befriended each other. Although I cannot gainsay the story, I never saw them together after that night. A few days later Hardin left Abilene by way of a window and a handy horse behind the Drovers' Cottage after shooting to death a hapless cowboy who happened to be snoring loudly in the room next to his. In Hardin's defense I must point out that a stray bullet was the cause, fired through the wall to get the wretch's attention. Instead it found his heart.

Mike Williams and I were discussing this incident over tea in Drucilla's parlor when mention of the Drovers' Cottage caused the bartender suddenly to slap his thigh.

"I forgot. Fellow come in the Alamo last night asking for you while you was out taking a leak. Beg pardon, ma'am. He's staying with a pard at the Cottage. You know 'em both, he said. I had to leave for the Novelty before you got back, so didn't get to give you the message."

I knew a chill. My first thought was that Boss Tweed's long arm had reached me at last. The news from the East had not been encouraging. Without coming out and saying it, the Eastern papers had by implication and innuendo managed to suggest that the immigrant ward heeler had every office holder in New York State strung from his watch chain, with one of his stubby fingers dipped in every public project that involved the transfer of money from one place to another. No corner of American politics was so dark it escaped the penetration of those incendiary eyes.

"What were their names?" I asked.

He tugged at his moustaches, thinking. "Bock. He said his pard's name was Howard."

The names meant nothing to me, and Iron Mike's description of the fellow who left them was so general as to encompass every third stranger whose gear found its way into the walnut wardrobes at the Drovers' Cottage. All the way over there I wondered if I shouldn't be heading instead in the direction of the depot, but as always my own curiosity was my lord and leader.

The desk clerk, a tall, balding young man named Mather, who wore his spectacles on a black ribbon clipped to his vest, was known to me. His favorite tune was "Enraptured I Gaze," and because he never failed to place a twenty-five-cent piece in my box when he came to the Alamo to listen to me during his breaks, ill though he could afford it, I felt obliged to play it whenever he was present. For this reason he allowed me to look at the register, where I learned that "J. S. Bach" and "Tom Howard" had checked into room twelve the previous day.

I was close to certain now about the identity of the man who had asked for me at the Alamo, and although I knew no one named Howard I had a fair notion whom the roommate might be. Unlikely as the situation seemed given the news reports I had read recently and the rumors I had heard, it was with the bright anticipation of happy reunion that I bounded up the thickly carpeted staircase to the second story and tapped with my knuckles upon the door marked twelve. The grim note of challenge in the voice that answered sobered me somewhat.

"Name yourself."

"I shall do better than that," said I; for I had recognized the voice. I had brought my guitar, and now I slid it around from behind my back and picked out what I hoped was a recognizable conversion of Bach's *Toccata and Fugue in D Minor*. Half a dozen bars in, the door swung open.

Frank James's appearance startled me. I knew him at once, of course, but at first glance there was nothing in him of the raw-boned Missouri plowboy I had last seen behind John Rudd's farmhouse in Carroll County. He had filled out somewhat, less lanky than slender, his hair was longer but well kept, curling at his collar, and the bristly, untrimmed chin-whiskers had given way to a full goatee of which a Southern senator would be proud. He wore a white shirt without a collar tucked into whipcord trousers reinforced with leather for riding. His braces hung and his feet were clad only in stockings, but aside from that he was prepared for visitors: His right hand held a big Smith & Wesson .44 American with the hammer rolled back. When he saw me, the broad bright grin I remembered so well broke across his long, handsome face. He pointed the revolver at the ceiling and let the hammer down carefully.

"Billy! I'll be god-damned!" Thrusting the pistol beneath his belt, he seized my hand in his knuckle-crushing grip and pulled me into the room.

It was a well-appointed chamber, as were they all in that hotel, so elegant in contrast to its tobacco-spewing, dust-slapping, four-times-yearly-bathing clientele: flock-papered and deep-carpeted, with framed lithographs leaning out from the walls and bulbous brass lamps flanking the big four-poster bed. Stretched out upon the mattress, collarless and stocking-footed like his brother, lay Jesse James—more infamous than Frank now due to the coin-flipping myth-making of the Eastern press, wanted in three states, the hero of every cheap novel that did not feature Wild Bill Hickok or Buffalo Bill Cody; the man upon whose head rested a reward (at last count) of two thousand dollars, with or without a bullet in it. That head was visibly older than I remembered it and sported a well-trimmed chestnut beard; no more need to envy my precocious whiskers, as when we were both sixteen.

He, too, held a cocked Smith & Wesson, but was slower to disarm and put it away than his brother, waiting until I was fully inside and he could see me from head to foot. Then he turned over onto his back, slid the weapon inside a fold of the Abilene *Chronicle* resting in his lap, picked up a Bible bound in worn supple leather that he had placed face down beside him on the bed, and began reading. He did not greet me, but there had been no hostility in his expression when he recognized me. We had never had much to say to each other.

Two new features I had noticed, besides the beard: The tip of the middle finger of his left hand was missing, and he had acquired the habit of blinking both eyes rapidly at regular intervals. Given his hunted state, a severed digit and a nervous tic seemed the gentlest on the long list of inconveniences.

"I heard you robbed a train outside Salt Lake City last week," said I as Frank splashed red-tinted whiskey into a hotel tumbler from a dusty quart bottle; the stuff was in such demand all over town the bartenders no longer bothered to clean the vessels before refilling them.

"We stuck up another'n in Little Rock week before that, and a bank in Michigan the same day." He handed me the glass, filled another for himself, and waved me into a tufted chair. "We're busier on vacation than when we're working, if you believe the papers."

"You're on vacation?"

Hitching up his trousers and sitting on the edge of the bed, Frank changed the subject. "When I heard you was playing at the Alamo, I just had to pay you a call. I figured you'd catch the name I left."

"Not at first. I thought it was 'bock,' like the beer. When I saw how it was spelled in the register I knew it had to be you. No one else out here knows Bach from Stephen Foster. Tom Howard?" I looked at Jesse, who turned a page and said nothing.

"That's just a handle he takes on from time to time. It don't stick in the head and that's good. You know Wild Bill?"

"Not intimately."

"They say he's dangerous." Jesse spoke without looking up.

"It's the best word you could apply to him." Alarmed

suddenly, I added, "I wouldn't test it. He's been bitten by fame and he will do anything to make it greater. He would not scruple to shoot you both in the back for the reward and the reputation it would bring."

Jesse turned back a page, paused to read something, then closed his eyes, his lips moving, as if committing a passage to memory. Then: "It's been tried. And yet here we sit."

Frank grinned. "Jess got bit too."

"It's nothing to laugh at. John Wesley Hardin got into a scrape last week right here in this hotel, and Hickok came looking for him with four deputies. He was forced to flee for his life."

"I reckon them Texicans consider four-on-one bad odds." Frank topped off his glass, offered me the bottle, and set it down on the floor when I declined. "Don't bust your blisters, Billy. We done already talked to Wild Bill."

This news staggered me. "You *talked* to him?"

"He paid us a call here this morning. I reckon our disguises ain't so good after all."

"He came alone?"

"I expect he had men posted around the hotel. He ain't *that* wild. Jess and I never let on we knowed what he was talking about, but we got the word. We stick to this end of town, he sticks to his. Oh, and don't rob the bank. He was specific about that."

"I wouldn't trust him to be as good as his word."

"Nobody's as good as his word. We're pulling out at first light tomorrow. I never did like Kansas anyway. Too many Jayhawkers."

"What brought you here to begin with? Abilene is no place to rest, even from robbing banks and trains."

For the first time a furrow appeared between Frank's brows. "We're trailing Johnny Thrailkill, Billy. He turned renegade on us."

In a flash I remembered the robbery from horseback at the Alamo. I hadn't thought about it in months.

Frank was still talking. ". . . had it out with him after Gall-
atin. It was just this little bank, figured Johnny and Jess and
me could take it quick and easy, without Cole and Jim. Johnny
went in to change a hunnert-dollar bill—get the cashier to
open the box, see. Jess was watching the door, I was on the
street. Then the shooting started. That crazy son of a bitch
Thrailkill plugged the cashier in the face and lit out with just
a fistful of cash. By this time folks was running up to the
bank and I had to open fire to back 'em off. Jesse's gray bolted
while he was trying to mount and drug him ten yards on his
face."

"Still got a pebble or two under my cheek," put in Jesse,
turning another page.

"Jess got loose finally and the gray took off. I had to ride
back through crossfire to scoop him up. We damn near kilt
that mean son of a bitch when we caught up to him. He said
the cashier reminded him of that Yankee major that bush-
whacked Bloody Bill and stuck his head on a pole. We gave
him his split and told him to pull out. Next thing we know
he's sticking up banks and saloons in all the places we go to
cool our heels. Last winter it was Mineral Springs. This year
it's the cow towns, where a man can lose hisself in the dusty
crowd if he don't stir things up. Hell, folks are saying it was
Jess bust the cap on that cashier. That crazy bastard is cost-
ing us all our friends."

"What happens when you find Thrailkill?"

Frank drained his glass. "Well, what would?"

I turned the conversation in friendlier directions. Their
mother and stepfather were in good health, Reuben Samuel
having recovered from his near-lynching at the hands of the
Federal militia. Cole and Jim Younger were resting in Texas,
but were expected to rejoin them anytime and bring their kid
brother Bob, who yearned for the bandit life. The Union's
harsh measures to "reconstruct" the South had converted
many a neutral living in the Missouri hills to the cause of
the Jameses and Youngers; let the Pinkertons scour the

countryside in vain while the gang hid out in corn ricks and laughed at them. I picked up my guitar and played some of the old tunes that had entertained us all that summer of '63 in Clay County. Jesse, perhaps remembering the one that had helped bring him out of his wound-induced coma the following year, lay aside his Bible and sat up to join us in singing "The Hunters of Kentucky." His voice remained sweet and mellow, if halting. His shyness was his central trait, despite the blood-and-thunder tales that were told about him, and could easily have been mistaken for timidity. Years later, when he was hiding out posing as a cattle speculator in St. Joseph, Missouri, I heard he was considered something of a creampuff by some of his swaggering neighbors.

He was anything but, of course; and he showed it as I was nearing the end of the song, when a rattle of gunfire drifted our way from farther up Texas Street. In the blink of a lash he was off the bed and on his feet in an animal crouch, his Smith & Wesson in hand.

Frank moved just as quickly. In an instant both lamps were blown out, and the three of us waited in darkness with the twilight describing a square patch on the floor through the window facing the street. We heard shouts coming closer, and the drumming of feet on the hard earth. Unintelligible snatches of words and names at first, and then a string of information delivered in passing from just below the window:

"Wild Bill just killed Phil Coe and Ben Thompson!"

THIRTY-ONE

As it turned out, that first report was only half right, which as rumors go was at pace with the odds.

Phil Coe was dead, or would be soon, with one of Hickok's bullets in his groin and nothing else to do but bleed to death or succumb to blood poisoning; but his partner, Ben Thompson, was recovering in Kansas City from a broken leg suffered in a buggy accident on the prairie, and had been since before the incident that took Coe's life.

It had started with an attempt by Hickok to close down the Bull's Head for violating the town's anti-obscenity ordinance with a sign displaying a bull clearly in full possession of its genitals, reached boiling point when Jessie Hazell, the marshal's female companion, moved her belongings into Phil Coe's quarters, and came to its bloody conclusion when Hickok, investigating gunfire on Texas Street, found Coe with a pistol in his hand and went for one of his own. Coe, who had taken a drunken potshot at a stray dog, fired first, knocking Hickok's hat off his head. The marshal's aim was lower and more lethal.

The second victim, originally thought to be Thompson, died instantly when he ran up with a pistol in his hand and fell with several Hickok bullets in his chest and stomach. It was Mike Williams, the bartender at the Alamo and special policeman in charge of security at the Novelty Theater, thanks to the recommendation of his friend Wild Bill Hickok.

Iron Mike's death left me empty and Abilene as shrill as it had been following the murder of Bear River Tom Smith. Friends of Coe's and Thompson's, and others who had known and liked Williams, threatened to kill Hickok on sight. The marshal took to carrying a sawed-off Stephens ten-gauge shotgun in addition to his matched Navies and the brace of derringers he was rumored to carry in his pockets. On December 12, some two months after the shootings, the town council met, and at the end of a marathon session during which tempers flared, voted above the protests of Mayor McCoy to terminate Hickok's contract. Debate commenced anew over whether to ban the cattle trade and the trouble that accompanied it from the area, and on February 8, 1872, this remarkable notice appeared in the *Chronicle*, with fifty-eight signatures attached:

> TO CATTLE DROVERS.
> We the undersigned members of the
> Farmers' Protective Association and
> Officers and Citizens of Dickinson
> County, Kansas, most respectfully request
> all who have contemplated driving
> Texas Cattle to Abilene the coming
> season to seek some other point
> for shipment, as the inhabitants of
> Dickinson will no longer submit to
> the evils of the trade.

Even a dolt could foresee that this meant the end of Abilene as a major center of commerce, and that within a year the community would have reverted to the soporific farming village it had been during the Civil War. By the time the notice had appeared in two subsequent editions, the number of signatures had grown to 366, at which point Ted Henry, McCoy's mayoral predecessor and fierce philosophical opponent, mailed copies to newspapers throughout Texas. Finally, Dickinson's representative to the 1872 state legislature persuaded his fellow public servants to tighten an 1867 law, establishing a quarantine line forty miles west of Abilene beyond which the tick-ridden Texas cattle could not be driven. After three seasons during which one and a half million long-horns had passed down Texas Street, the town's richest period came to a close.

Something in Hickok had changed as well. Even before the council stripped him of his badge, he seemed to have lost all interest in enforcing the law, and for that matter in gambling, which was his first love and sole companion (aside from his propensity to make enemies) through all his incarnations as soldier, plainsman, and peace officer. Day and night he sat glumly at his old table in the Alamo, stirring only to refill his glass and speaking only to order another bottle or hurl vile imprecations at the odd uninformed gambler who came up to challenge him at cards. His appearance suffered. Broken blood vessels turned his slate-gray eyes the color of mud, his chin stubbled over; the celebrated flowing moustaches went untrimmed; his long hair turned dull and lank and looked unclean. He wore the same yellowed shirt for days on end. His nails were bitten and dirty, and he gave off a rank odor like a lion. Of course, no one pointed out these shortcomings to him. There was that shotgun, always in plain view, and he had, accidentally or not, slain two men in as many minutes within three hundred yards of that very spot.

Apologists claimed Wild Bill was in mourning for his friend, and stricken with grief for his part in his death. My opinion was less charitable. His reputation as a great frontiersman was bound to suffer for his lack of judgment in the heat of action, and the thought that the events of a few moments could undo the cultivation of years was eating at him like an ulcer. Conscience and friendship were but abstract concepts to a man like Hickok, as remote as the Milky Way and no more real to him than the Zulu War in Africa.

As for the event itself, I cannot find it in me to blame him. Deadly gunfire had been exchanged, he was surrounded by friends of the man he had shot, and a shadowy figure came racing his way with a revolver. The reflexes and instincts of a life on the plains are not to be overcome as easily as turning out a lamp. I regretted bitterly the loss of my closest companion in Abilene, the man who had helped me find work and protected me from brigands when I carried my earnings home, but he owed his fate to his own overzealousness. "No one ever got killed for moving too fast," he had once said; whether he had had time to realize how wrong he was depended upon how much thinking he had been able to do as he fell.

* * *

"No, no sadness," said Drucilla, glancing around at the wooden crates that had taken the place of most of the furniture in her private parlor. Everything else, the items she was leaving behind to be sold or shipped later, was covered with sheets, like shrouded corpses in a mortuary. Only her rocking chair remained uncrated and uncovered, because she was sitting in it. "When you have moved as many times as I have in these past few years, every place looks the same."

She was not the last to leave Abilene, but she was far from the first. With the onset of warm weather, the residents of the Devil's Addition had led the exodus, followed closely by gamblers, barmen, storekeepers, lawyers, and blacksmiths, some of them riding in wagons with the very lumber from which their establishments had been built piled in back, to be reassembled at the end of their journey. Wild Bill Hickok had left—to join his friend Buffalo Bill's theatrical troupe back East, or so it was whispered. Most of Texas Street was boarded up, and over the entire town the dust had settled for the first time in memory, covering it as surely and finally as those sepulchral sheets.

"Where is the next place?" I asked.

"Ellsworth. That's where all the cattle are going next season. Cattlemen, cowboys, buyers, they all need a place to sleep and eat. It is the same, as I said. And where do you go, Billy? I heard the Alamo is closing."

"I haven't given it much thought. West, I suppose. I've had an offer, but I haven't decided yet whether to take it."

She nodded absently, looking away. The untouched side of her face was silhouetted against the light leaking through a space between the curtains. Suddenly she turned it full upon me. The scarred side was barely visible through her veil. "Come with me, Billy."

"What work would there be for me in a boardinghouse?"

The response was surprised out of me by the unexpected invitation.

"In my next place I intend to have an organ, or at least a piano. You can entertain the boarders."

"In Boston, perhaps. In Ellsworth they will prefer to mix their amusements."

"Then you will play and sing in a saloon, and sleep beneath my roof. I have become accustomed to your company," she added, turning her head away once again.

My chest grew tight, a sensation I had not known since my decision not to return to New York as soon as I was free of the Missouri bushwhackers. Quickly I said, "You have Chronus, who I think does not approve of me. In any case I have had my life's portion of cow towns. I never did get used to the stench of cattle."

"You will not change your mind?"

"I'm afraid I cannot."

Neither of us spoke for at least a minute. The silence outside was oppressive. Abilene did not seem Abilene without the rattle and squeak of wagons passing by, hammers clattering, saws wheezing, the lowing of steers and cowboys cursing. Then she lifted her white china cup to her lips. "What is the offer you are considering?"

"A party of buffalo hiders wants me to help with the skinning and sing to them in the evenings. I am to take a percentage of the profits in return."

She smiled then in earnest. The expression was necessarily crooked, but far from unpleasant. When she spoke, her voice was low and mellow as of old, but with a kind of playful melancholy that I had not been aware of before. "And the stench of *cattle* offends you?"

I returned the smile with a shrug. We said good-bye then. There was no place for me to sit, and so I did not have to get up to leave. I could not then guess the circumstances under which we would meet again.

THIRTY-TWO

Oh, it's now we've crossed Peace River,
and homeward we are bound;
No more in that hellfire country,
shall ever we be found.
Go home to our wives and sweethearts,
tell others not to go;
For God's forsaken the buffalo range,
and the damned old buffalo.

My sentiments, after a winter spent on the plains of Nebraska following the southward-migrating herds, were not far
different from those of the buffalo skinners of the song; substitute marrow-freezing cold for hellfire, and the least com-
panionable partners I had ever known for hostile Indians, and
the lyrics were right on the money.

None of us referred to ourselves as hunters. In truth, I never
heard the term *buffalo hunter* until the herds had thinned out
to the degree that one actually had to go looking for them. In
the early seventies, when a train passing through that Platte
River country was forced to wait six hours for a single herd
to finish crossing the tracks, the notion of ever having to
"hunt" the lumpy, woolly-headed brutes was a supreme joke.
Collectively we were "hiders." I was a "skinner," and occupied, with a bald, one-eyed fellow known only as Fetch, a
place at the bottom of a special hierarchy. Next came the
cook, a black-bearded Scot named Cockerell, with the arms
and torso of a grizzly, skinny bowed legs that until his back
straightened out late in the morning compelled him literally
to support himself upon his knuckles, and a club foot. At the
top of our society stood Van Horn, our "runner," or sharp-
shooter, upon whose keen eye and steady hand depended the
success of our venture. A lean, rifle-backed fellow of thirty

or so, born in Amsterdam but brought up on a farm in Iowa, he affected the buckskins and shoulder-length hair of the frontiersmen he read about in Beadle's, and during the twilight hours when Cockerell heated his skillet to prepare buffalo steaks seasoned with wild onions and Fetch and I scraped and salted the hides we'd spent all day stripping from the carcasses, he busied himself dismantling his prized Sharp's Big Fifty rifle and cleaning and oiling the parts, wiping them off with a square of soft sheepskin. I suspected he treated the weapon better than he had any woman, and perhaps with good reason. Smaller-bored rifles had little effect upon the thick-hided creatures, and revolvers were useless.

I had been nervous at first about the Indians. For as long as any of them could remember back beyond the time of their great-grandfathers, they had always lived upon the animals we slaughtered for the hides alone, feeding their villages, fashioning their lodges from the skins, and even grinding the bones to make their pottery. (The fact that they would often stampede a hundred buffalo off a cliff to cut out three or four for their purposes was no match for Indian logic; we were white men, we had our domestic cattle and glass plants and textile mills, and hadn't their right to waste buffalo.) I had heard of depredations in the North and South, of much larger outfits than ours shot down and scalped or captured and tortured. Against that risk, the profit we would realize when the hides were sold in Julesburg for between $1.50 and $2.50 apiece seemed tiny. When one afternoon I looked up from the bull I was preparing to skin and saw five men in feathers watching from horseback at a distance of three hundred yards—I feel no need to dissemble in this narrative—I urinated in my trousers.

"I seen 'em," said Van Horn, when I called his attention to these grim spectators. "Sioux, or I miss my guess."

He was sitting on the open tailgate of our wagon, Sharp's resting across his lap while the barrel cooled. We had come upon a small herd of forty buffalo late in the morning and he had shot almost half before the rest spooked. Fierce intelligent creatures when it came to protecting themselves from natural enemies—wolves, blizzards, and the like—they seldom reacted to gunfire, and if they did not catch the scent of blood and none of them bawled going down, had been known to stand around calmly munching grass until the last animal fell. It was the dream of every runner to experience a "stand," and this was as far as Van Horn had ever taken one. His luck had held until he rushed a shot, missing a vital organ, and the wounded cow bolted, bellowing a warning to the others. In another moment they had rumbled away over a rise to the north. Since then Fetch and I had been busy with our knives, slashing the hides of the slain buffalo at the necks and hooves; when that was done we would hitch the wagon with hooks to each and drive the mules forward, separating them from their original owners with a long steady pull. Today it was my turn to slash the more stubborn membranes as the hide came away. The work was odoriferous and filthy, and I was crawling head to foot with the ticks that infested the animals. Christmas had come and gone without notice; I hadn't bathed or slept beneath a proper roof since September. Now, having attracted the attention of the Sioux, I wondered if I ever would again.

"What do you suppose they want?" I asked.

"Meat, I reckon. It's been a hard winter for squaws and bucks."

"Do you think that's all?"

"That, or our scalps. Most like both. If we're all dead they don't have to ask."

I looked again. Sky and earth were white and dazzling. We were all burned nearly as brown as the Indians from the sun coming off the snow. The five seemed nailed to their ridge, only the feathers on their lances stirring in the wind that never stopped, never stopped blowing on the Nebraska plain. Two of them held rifles, the butts braced against their thighs with the barrels pointed straight up, and these, too, were decorated with feathers.

On the other side of the fallen herd, Fetch was at work slashing hides, but I saw him look up from time to time at the men watching from horseback. Cockerell lay snoring in the back of the wagon, wrapped in a blanket atop the stiff hides already stored there. He seemed impervious to the insects and the stench, and slept whenever he wasn't cooking or gathering chips for the fire. He'd have dozed through the Crucifixion, once the dishes from the Last Supper had been cleared away.

"Isn't there something we can do?" I asked then.

"Well, once this barrel finishes cooling I'll pick off what I can. I might get three, this being a single-shot. Wisht I'd bought that Winchester repeater I seen in Fort Kearny coming out. I didn't have the money." He spat into the snow. "I can get the two with rifles, anyways. The rest will turn tail and run."

"What if they charge us instead?"

"Wisht they would. I'd drop all three. They'll run, though. They ain't stupid just 'cause they're savages."

"What harm can three Indians do armed only with lances?"

"Plenty, when they get back to the village and tell the rest what's here. I can't shoot no hundred Sioux braves. They won't stand around waiting for it like buffler."

I watched the Indians absently, wiping the flat of my blade against my trousers, stiff as tree bark with old entrails. "Suppose we give them what they're after?"

"It's a notion," said Van Horn. "I don't think I could get along without my topknot, though. I catch cold easy."

"I don't mean our scalps. I mean the buffalo meat. All we're taking is the hides, and steaks enough for just us four. One of us could ride up there unarmed and make the offer. If they're as hungry as you say, they might let us go."

"Oh, they're hungry. Army's got 'em on the run, and they can't hunt for shit when they ain't concentrating. It is a notion," he repeated, making me think of old Jim Bridger: *Just a dumb notion, mind.* "Question is, which one of us is going to ride up there and probably be the first to give up his hair?"

"I guess I will."

The runner turned a bright eye on me, but there was no admiration there, only wary contempt. It was as if the stranger he had spent most of the night drinking with, thinking him to be of a like mind, had without warning opened his mouth and delivered a sermon against all the things Van Horn stood for. However, he said nothing. He didn't have to; the fresh spittle he shot into the snow at the foot of the wagon was eloquence enough.

I had heard somewhere, perhaps from Bridger, that it didn't do to approach an Indian empty-handed, no matter if you were offering him deed to the whole of North America. I therefore selected a buffalo robe I had pegged and cured myself—my first successful effort, which I had been intending to have made into a coat when I returned to civilization—wrapped it around a hindquarter I butchered myself, unhitched one of the mules from the wagon, and mounted it bareback, laying the bundle across my thighs. As I started toward the ridge, I was aware of Fetch watching me from across the scatter of carcasses, sitting back on his heels with a hand shielding his eyes, and of Cockerell snoring and whistling upon his green hide bed. Van Horn had alighted from the tailgate, jammed into the ground the forked stick he used for a tripod, and fished a paper cartridge out of his pocket, and as he tore the end off with his teeth to pour the powder into the firing pan of the Sharp's, said: "I was starting to get used to having music nights."

I felt neither brave nor hopeful. All I could think of was that it made no difference whether I died upon the ridge with the Indians or down among the buffalo.

The way up the grade was laborious. The snow had drifted, and the mule tried to balk, but I dug in my heels and it lunged through the chest-deep accumulation, wheezing clouds of vapor as thick as milk. The five mounted men watched without moving until I drew within ten yards of them, at which point the one in the center hoisted his rifle horizontally above his head, halting me. A moment went by, during which the icy wind skirled up under the sheepskin lining of my coat. Then they started down toward me, all at once without a signal, as if men and horses shared a single brain.

The one who had raised his rifle stopped in front of me while the others fanned out and around, enclosing me in a ragged circle. Looking into that face, round, burnished, and ageless, with hair gathered into long braids on both sides, eyes the color of smoke from which the lashes had been plucked, and a wide, well-shaped mouth drawn into a permanent scowl, I realized with a sudden dropping of the heart that we had nothing in common, neither language to communicate nor culture to understand nor experience to compare. I knew not how to begin the negotiation I had been rehearsing all the way up to the ridge. Then the leader—for I judged the rider facing me to be the man in charge—broke the silence with one earth-shattering word.

"English?"

I jumped, startling the mule into a snort. "Yes," I said. "My name is Gashade."

He did not introduce himself. I remembered Bridger's telling me that for an Indian to surrender his name was to place power in the hands of the man to whom he gave it.

"Kill buffalo?"

"I skin them."

"Eat?"

"Some." I reached for the bundle across my lap. Immediately I felt the icy touch of the muzzle of the other rifle against the bone behind my left ear. My hands froze halfway.

The smoke-colored eyes flicked to my right. The brave on that side leaned over, lifted the bundle, and unwrapped it, exposing the bloody hindquarter.

"A gift." Carefully, to avoid startling the Indian with the

rifle, I raised my right arm and gestured toward the carcasses on the flat, encompassing them with a broad sweep. "All yours. The buffalo robe too."

"Hides."

"Five hides." *Don't be too eager to give things up.* Bridger. *They'll take and take and finish by taking your scalp. It's a bad mistake to think they're not as good as us. It's a worse one to think they're better.*

"All hides."

I shook my head. "Five. We worked too hard for the rest."

I felt a tug that nearly unseated me and thought, *This is it.* However, it was just the Indian behind me, yanking at the strap that held my banjo behind my back.

"Gun?" The leader appeared to have noticed it for the first time.

Again I shook my head. "Musical instrument." Slowly I slid it off my shoulder and held it out. When he made no move to take it, I lowered it and picked out the opening bars of "Cotton-Eyed Joe," a rouser. When I finished, the brave to my right opened his mouth wide and laughed. That astonished me more than anything. Nothing I had heard or read about Indians had mentioned a capacity for mirth. I had thought them humorless and stoic. All around me there was a lifting of the atmosphere.

Now the leader put out his hands, and I placed the banjo in them. He turned it over, studying it from both sides. Stiffly he held it across his body and brushed his fingers across the strings. The strumming noise made his horse snuffle and toss its head. He patted its neck. He was grinning broadly now. I noticed he possessed few teeth, although my impression was that he was a young man.

He appeared to have a sudden inspiration, and held the banjo out to his right. The brave on that side lowered his rifle and kneed his horse forward to take the object. The leader stripped off his coat, a fine woven one with broad horizontal stripes of cream and vermilion. His naked chest was smooth and hairless, the color of an amber bottle. He folded the coat and held it before him across his forearms. Clearly, this was intended as an offering.

"Ten hides."

I regretted the loss of the banjo more than the hides we had worked so hard to acquire. Musical instruments were difficult to come by at that time on the frontier, and I did not expect ever to find a replacement. Yet I agreed to the terms without hesitation, in return for our lives. Moreover, the blanket coat was wonderfully crafted, lighter yet sturdier than the fleece-lined canvas, and stopped the wind more efficiently. We parted then.

It was the work of the rest of the afternoon to finish the skinning, and then Fetch, Cockerell, and I climbed aboard the wagon, Van Horn mounted his Appaloosa (muttering ungratefully about what a poor bargain I had made), and we left by the rusty light of the wallowing sun while the Sioux moved in behind us to harvest their bounty. One of the braves had ridden back to inform the village; women and children swarmed about the carcasses with skinning and butchering tools, chattering happily in their halting, guttural tongue.

I would not have credited it then, but the banjo would make its way back to me, much changed; by which time I would have changed quite as much. That, however, is a later verse in my ballad. There is a great deal more of it to be sung, with or without banjo accompaniment.

THIRTY-THREE

I t was an old bull, its beard worn short from years of dragging on the ground and its chest and shoulders crisscrossed with old horn scars as thick as hemp, badges of office and trophies won from many challenges to its herd leadership. Although snow was on the ground, its hide was caked with dust, matted from rolling in summer dirt mixed with its own urine, to attract cows with the pungent masculine scent. A bull's bull; Wild Bill Hickok with horns.

Remembering Van Horn's instructions, I stretched out on my chest and stomach on the ground, supporting myself upon my elbows behind his makeshift tripod, gripped the smooth walnut forepiece with my left hand, rolled back the hammer with the other, and snapped the set trigger. Little more than a breath was required now to set the mechanism in motion. I nestled my cheek against the stock, centered the grazing bull in the folding sight, drew in a breath, expelled half of it, and squeezed the rear trigger.

The heavy gun pushed against my shoulder, leaving a purple bruise, though at the time I scarcely noticed the pressure. There was a pause, then a funnel of dust leapt from the bull's coat just behind the left shoulder and it threw up its huge head and rolled over onto its side. Kicked once.

I still regret that old bull. I skinned at least two hundred buffalo that winter, but I personally shot only one, to see what it was like. It was a terrible thing to do to a brute that lived only to graze and shit and make little buffalo.

As the grim winter of 1872–73 howled to a finish, I had a great deal more to feel sorry for, beginning with my decision to come there in the first place. I hated the weather, the exposure, and the hard work. Chief of all I hated my three partners. We spent the whole of a week-long February blizzard huddled together beneath a wagon sheet, subsisting upon buffalo jerky, handfuls of snow to avoid dehydration, and bickering. We argued over everything, but kept coming back to which one of us had suggested preparing and stocking a dugout against just such an eventuality and which had vetoed the suggestion upon the evidence of a mild winter predicted in the pages of the *Farmer's Almanac*.

Van Horn, the aristocrat of our little caste, was the worst complainer. He went on bitterly about the weather, the ten hides we had lost to the Sioux, Cockerell's cooking, the slothful way in which Fetch and I went about our skinning chores, and the long litany of evil tidings that had taken him from his prosperous life in the Netherlands to this God-forsaken spot on the empty Nebraska plain. When sufficiently into the whiskey we passed around to warm the blood in our veins, he lapsed into a slurred patois of Dutch and vernacular American, from which I gleaned intermittent scraps of his life history: Shipbuilders for generations, the family's fortunes were seriously damaged when half the workforce departed for Belgium during the 1830 separatist revolution; the remains of its wealth had supported Van Horn in luxury during his childhood, then when the last of it was gone he had been forced to withdraw from school to work from daylight to dusk on a dairy farm outside Amsterdam in what amounted to indentured servitude. In 1856, at the age of fourteen, he had run away, stowed himself in the lifeboat of an American-bound clipper built by the company his father had once owned, labored in the bilge upon his discovery to pay for his passage, and panhandled on the streets of Baltimore, sleeping in doorways and living upon the scraps thrown out behind the restaurants, until he had assembled enough pennies to cover train fare as far as Iowa, on the border of the frontier and opportunity. There he found himself working on yet another farm, performing many of the same drudgeries he had had to perform back home, until he reached his full growth.

After Fort Sumter he joined the Fifteenth Iowa Infantry and fought at Shiloh, where he was invalided out with a Confederate ball in his hip that still made him miserable when it rained or snowed, as when he was telling the story. Since then he had hauled freight in Arkansas, operated a ferry in Kansas—where no doubt he remembered the much finer water craft constructed by his family in better times—and graded track for the Union Pacific in Nebraska, before deciding there was more money to be made shooting buffalo to feed the track gang. With his wages he bought a Sharp's from a runner who had made his grubstake and was going back

East to marry his sweetheart. By this time the traffic in hides was heavier and more lucrative than the one in meat, and a natural talent for marksmanship, discovered in the army, persuaded Van Horn to quit the large outfit he had hooked himself up with and organize his own. That, he now explained acidly, was before he knew how worthless a crew he had assembled. We had given up arguing with him the first day under the wagon sheet, instead possessing ourselves in patience until he passed out, knowing that when he awoke he would begin all over again.

Cockerell, the Scot, held even less regard for Van Horn than the runner held for the rest of us, and never once addressed Fetch or me directly, evidently having made up his mind sometime back that skinners were less than human and less valuable to the expedition than the mules—to whom he *did* speak, if only to damn their absence of a soul whenever they balked or (as upon one memorable occasion) one of them threw a shoe that landed square in his stewpot while he was cooking supper. I understood, mainly through a disparaging comment made by Van Horn, that he had abandoned a wife in Scotland and another in St. Louis, but could learn nothing of his past because he restricted his references to the current situation and his conviction that he would either freeze or starve to death in the worst company he had known this side of the water.

Fetch never spoke except to curse us when we disturbed his sleep or the bottle was too slow in reaching him. No one seemed to know where he had been or what he had done before he joined us, but I for one was certain that he was capable of committing any crime. There was about him an uncleanliness of a particularly vile sort that went deeper than the surface filth of the occupation he and I shared; bathe him, brush him, douse him with scent, dress him in silks and broadcloth, and within minutes his nails would be as black and he would smell as foul as if he had just returned from the killing ground. He secreted the stuff through his pores, directly from the corruption of his soul. The poisonous yellow cast of his bad eye suggested that he had once used it to look at himself in the harsh light of truth, and it had been struck blind by what it saw.

Yes, I earned the good turn Fate presented me at the end of that hellish winter. I am still uncertain as to whether it was worth the cost.

At length the blizzard stopped blowing. It was the work of most of a morning to find and uncover the wagon, after which we donned the snowshoes we'd stowed under the seat and went out in search of the mules and Van Horn's Appaloosa. When the storm had come up—suddenly, as did everything in that country—we had unhitched the team and relieved the horse of saddle and bridle, agreeing that they had a better chance of surviving the blow on the loose than tethered to the wagon. Toward dusk we located the mules, huddled together in an old wallow, emaciated and snowblind but still standing. One died during the night, another the next day. The remaining four were sound enough after three days' rest and grain feeding to return to the traces. We never found the Appaloosa and decided it had either died of exposure and been buried by the snow or stumbled into some other camp and been—well, "adopted" was a more diplomatic term than the ones Van Horn employed. We excavated and loaded the hides we'd pegged out before the blizzard and struck out for civilization, two of us taking turns walking alongside to keep from overburdening the light team.

Julesburg, when we reached it some ten days later, was a riot of activity, nearly all of it directed toward the trade in buffalo hides. There was the Buffalo Trading Post, the Buffalo Saloon—even the Buffalo Clothiers, complete with a three-piece rig and watch chain trapped out on a tailoring dummy in the display window and the name of the establishment painted upon a sign carved into a humpbacked silhouette swinging from an iron post above the door. Wagons piled high with hides jostled one another upon the street, establishments whose advertised business had nothing remotely to do with buffalo had stacks of hides enclosed in stockades built behind the stores, and nearly every pedestrian in sight, man and woman, wore a shaggy coat; at first glance they looked like small buffalo bustling along the boardwalks. The rotting stench, of course, was as much a physical feature of the town as its architecture. I guessed that in warm weather the flies would be plentiful enough to demand the vote, and get it.

My first thought was depressing. With hides in such great supply, the arrival of yet another load must be greeted with all the enthusiasm of a Pullman full of Irish politicians trundling into the New York Central station. As we drew rein before the Buffalo Great Atlantic Emporium and Western Union Office, I reduced my estimate regarding the price our cargo would bring from its early euphoric (and frankly whiskey-induced) high of $4.50 per hide by half, and prepared myself for the disappointment of an offer as low as a dollar. There was a small crowd obstructing the boardwalk in front of the store, shouting and gesticulating; I assumed this was a party of hiders calling the proprietor all kinds of a thief.

I was wrong, as I found out presently. It was not an altercation. It was an auction, and the retailers outnumbered the hiders three to one.

Changes had taken place while we were outside civilization. An Industrial Revolution was in full swing, and tough leather—acres of it, miles of it—was required to make drive belts to operate the great steam-piston machines back East. Fine buffalo robes were the fashion in Boston, New York, and Chicago, just the thing to drape across a lady's lap while riding in a carriage or skating over snow hills in the back of a sleigh: Good quality bull hides suitable for tanning brought between $100 and $175 apiece. Finally, the Department of the Army, having made up its mind to violate the Treaty of Fort Laramie and lay claim to all the Indian lands from the Black Hills to the South Platte, had decided that its best interests lay in depriving the Plains tribes of their main staple and thus shatter their fighting spirit, and in a hundred little ways encouraged the slaughter by hiders. Thousands of surplus Sharp's rifles, long the favorite of runners the frontier over, were pulled out of government warehouses where they had been gathering dust since Appomattox and dumped on the market, selling for as little as a dollar apiece. (The fact that this unfair competition employing its own product forced the manufacturer into receivership was of little interest to Washington.) Large hunting parties were offered military escort through Chief Red Cloud's Bozeman country to ensure their safety from raids by hostiles. The price of a Sharp's 420-grain cartridge, inundating the market in thousands of case lots from the same army shelves where the rifles had been kept, fell from a quarter to a dime; and to reduce even further the initial outlay by hiders planning extensive expeditions, ten cents were exchanged for each spent shell brought to post traderships at all the military forts. Never in human history had an animal been cheaper to stalk and more profitable to slay.

Between November 1872 and February 1873 we had collected four hundred hides, of which we had cured and treated twenty for robes and preserved five with the heads for mounting. The proprietor of the Buffalo Emporium, having lost out in the bidding on a big shipment of a thousand hides, intercepted us on our way into the store. Accompanying us to the wagon, he inspected five or six hides at the top of the stack, peeling them apart from the rest like sheets of tin, ran his fingers through his full white beard, and offered us six dollars for each green hide, $150 for the mountable skins with heads attached, and twenty apiece for the robes.

"I guarantee you won't get better anywhere in Julesburg," he said. "If you like, I'll give you a letter, and if anybody in town tops it and will put it in writing, I'll match his offer. I'm sick of pretenses and dickering. I can't keep a hide in stock."

"Done," said Van Horn, without bothering to consult the rest of us. I decided against objecting. The total came to

$3,400. I had ridden in to Julesburg filthy and penniless. On my way to the bathhouse I carried a poke containing $850 in paper and silver, my quarter of the winter's bounty.

That night, stretched out upon my hotel bed—my first of any kind since before Thanksgiving—smoking a twenty-five-cent cigar and digesting oyster stew and half a ham, I spread open the first of a bale of old New York newspapers I had bought for a penny from a merchant who used them to wrap purchases and read about the fall of Boss Tweed.

At the height of its power in 1870, the Tweed Ring pocketed sixty-six and two-thirds cents out of every dollar paid by the county and city to their vendors. Upon one day in April, it was estimated, between fourteen and fifteen million dollars in fraudulent bills were plundered from the city treasury, with the bulk of that amount divided among Tweed and his circle of cohorts and the rest banked by Tammany for the payment of bribes. Construction of a new county courthouse, projected to cost three million, came in at twelve; the remaining nine million was booty. During Tweed's first trial for embezzlement in 1872 (it ended in a hung jury), a bill to the City of New York for ten thousand dollars in office supplies was broken down as follows: six reams of foolscap; six reams of notepaper; three dozen boxes of rubber bands; two dozen pen holders; one dozen sponges; four bottles of India ink.

The *Times*, freed from shackles suddenly by the death of a Tweed man on its board of directors, lunged in snapping. It was fighting the Tammany machine, squads of waterfront toughs armed with revolvers and blackjacks, and Tweed's own enormous personal popularity, purchased from his illiterate constituents through years of glad-handing and charitable donation; but once it got its teeth into his fat calf—as it did with the help of a satchel full of ledgers spirited away by a disgruntled county bookkeeper named O'Rourke—it proved the most persistent of bull terriers. As the Boss's cronies fell one by one to indictment and conviction—Chamberlain Sweeney, Comptroller Connolly, Mayor Hall—the newspaper's cartoonist gleefully dipped his pen in acid and drew bloated caricatures dressed in stripes with big black iron balls chained to their ankles. In a very short time, the signature he placed upon these mean-spirited little windows into the back rooms where big-city politics were conducted would add a new adjective to our language. His name was Nast.

Tweed would stand trial again. Meanwhile the list of the incarcerated grew. It was so long, and the print so gray and smudged, that I almost missed a name at the bottom of one dense column:

Michael J. Brennan, assistant city fire commissioner; four counts, embezzlement; two counts, conspiracy to commit grand larceny; sentence, 3–5 years hard labor.

So Jehosophat had survived. I was not a killer.

My conscience was numb. Save for a sickening lapse when I awoke in the East River Society House, I had never once felt guilty for my actions on behalf of a fallen police officer and then myself. The news that I could not be arrested for murder, and that the one man who would have bothered to pursue the matter was too busy preventing him*self* from going to prison, affected me in a way far more profound. It helped me come to a decision that had begun to form the moment I learned that I was no longer a poor itinerant musician. I was going home.

THIRTY-FOUR

It was a good year to have money.

Every year is, of course—"I've been rich and I've been poor, and rich is better," Sophie Tucker once told me, then repeated it for a journalist, though she stole it from Nora Bayes—but in 1873 this was especially true, because almost no one else did.

In September, the bottom fell out of the New York Stock

Exchange. The banks in the city, fearing a "run," closed their doors. As always, the experts had reasons to offer: the sudden halt in the flow of money to, from, and through Tammany in the wake of Tweed's collapse, the shooting death by a rival the previous year of notorious stock manipulator Jim Fisk, the ouster two months later from the directorship of the Erie Railroad of Fisk's partner Jay Gould by stockholders, creating a vacuum that was filled all too quickly by chaos—any one of these incidents was sufficient to sow fear. All at once was the stuff of mass hysteria, which if you're in the habit of reading your history with a magnifying lens for the footnotes you'll see went down as the Panic of '73.

Wars, elections, and sexual indiscretions receive much more attention—squalor and despair don't offer painters much opportunity to employ cadmium red, nor writers their favorite punchy adjectives—but financial failures are far more devastating, and the ripple effect much broader. This one affected the whole of the continent, and by reflection the rest of the civilized world, for four dismal years. Independent banks collapsed. Mortgages were called in. Farms went on the block. Families separated. Heads of families committed suicide. Children were swallowed by orphanages and factories. Eggs sold for three cents the dozen.

I was aware of none of this when I took a train east from Julesburg toward New York. With money in my pocket I journeyed by Pullman salon car with arrangements for a sleeping compartment, and within a few miles determined that, fortune willing, I would henceforth travel by no other method. When it pleased me to be sociable, I joined my fellow passengers in a coach equipped with deep mohair-covered seats, room to stretch one's legs, and a footrest that swung up and out of the way when it was not desired; or I could repair to the bar or the dining car. When I wished to retire, an accommodating Negro porter would materialize outside my compartment, key at the ready to unlock and pull down a berth that was altogether more comfortable than either my lean-to at Fort Riley or the wagon sheet in Nebraska. There I lay in my nightshirt, allowing the motion of the train to rock me into a doze and wondering if that hot, dusty ride I had taken in the other direction ten years before were not just some troubling dream remembered from childhood.

New York had awaited my return for a decade. I saw no reason why it could not wait another few weeks while I took in the city of Chicago.

Upon my last trip through, I had been too young, too limited in my finances, and too distracted by my situation to appreciate any of the features the great Midwestern juggernaut had to offer. In truth, harnessed by wartime shortages and surviving almost exclusively upon its reputation as a produce-shipping center, it had borne little promise of the grand metropolis it would become following the Union victory and the ravenous craving for Western beef that swept the East in the years succeeding.

The Great Fire, two years in the past now, was a black memory to those who had lost friends, family, fortune, and that crucial intangible sense of personal security to the flames, but five million in donations from America and Europe, poured over two hundred thousand in damages, had gone a long way toward eradicating its more visible legacy. Most of the rubble had been cleared. In its place had sprung a fire-proof city of brick and steel and mortar, great spreading factories with tall chimneys in rows like rifles on parade. In the center beat its virile heart: the long barns, squat packing-houses, pens, maze of wooden chutes, and multitiered slaughtering floors of the Union Stockyards, where workers in blue overalls trotted bawling steers in one end and workers in white aprons carried sides and quarters still bleeding out the door. From there the beef was hung from hooks in freight cars packed with dry ice and sent north to Milwaukee, east to Detroit, Cleveland, New York, and Philadelphia, and south to Richmond, where carpetbaggers sold it for pirate prices to gentry in frayed cuffs sipping green whiskey in the empty rooms of plantation houses in need of shingles and paint. A black pall of coal smoke, locomotive exhaust, and coke residue, thick and gritty, overhung the vast gray sprawl on Lake Michigan like God's brow over Sodom.

Paradise, for a healthy twenty-six-year-old male with jingling pockets, no attachments, and a winter of hardship behind him.

I checked into the Palmer House—plush floral carpets, brass bedsteads, a separate bath on every floor—reported to Marshall Field's to be measured for a new wardrobe, made an appointment at a photography studio to have my picture taken when the clothes were ready, and bought a ticket for that evening's performance of the first play I had seen since coming west, a thing called *Scouts of the Prairie*, featuring none other than William F. "Buffalo Bill" Cody, Hickok's friend and the celebrated slayer of Tall Bull, the Cheyenne chief, whose infamy seemed to have increased since his death at Summit Springs. After a dinner in the gaslit hotel dining room of roast duck and red wine, topped off with a delight called Iced Cream, I hailed a two-wheeler and alighted at Nixon's Amphitheater just in time for the overture.

I daresay that proscenium, hung with olive curtains and broken out in gilded cherubs, death's-heads, angels with trumpets, and the obligatory masks of Comedy and Tragedy, never saw anything to compare with *Scouts of the Prairie* since the fire. Penned, the rumor went, in an alcoholic three hours by a scoundrel operating under the alias Ned Buntline, the play consisted mostly of windy campfire monologues by its star player Cody, another lanky authentic frontiersman named Texas Jack Omohundro, and its paunchy author, decked out in buckskins and a preposterous wig. These were punctuated by the odd Indian attack and romantic interludes between Texas Jack and a "Cheyenne princess" identified in the program as "Mlle. Morlacchi." Of course it was all claptrap, and its hero a humbug, but the snapping and blue flame of the blank pistols shook the audience out of the torpor created by the overheated poetastry of the dialogue, and when the savages seized, bound, and stood Buntline over a genuine smoldering fire, the delirium was electric. A New York house, I thought, would have applauded good-naturedly, laughing behind its programs. At the Novelty Theater in Abilene the liquored-up cowpokes would have whooped and fired their pistols into the ceiling, provided they could be restrained from taking potshots at the actors. In Chicago, the crowd of Friday-nighters stamped, whistled, pounded their hands, and demanded curtain call after curtain call until the proprietor came out to announce that an additional performance had been appended to the Saturday schedule. More cheers greeted this announcement, and then the chattering, rib-nudging exodus was under way.

As it turned out, I was wrong about the New York audiences. When the show toured there, the Broadway columnists were disdainful, but the theater was sold out for its entire run. It seemed the farther one traveled from the actual arena, the higher grew the level of interest in the doings out West. Cody himself, pale-faced with stage fright while taking his bows but looking very much at home in his exaggerated fringes and ten-gallon hat, appeared overwhelmed, although that far into the production he might have been expected to have grown accustomed to it. Recalling that impressive figure in his long chestnut locks and the reaction to his ridiculous little melodrama, I was not greatly surprised a dozen or so years later when his Wild West extravaganza swept across Europe like Napoleon's Grand Army.

Outside, it was a pleasant autumn evening, with the gas lamps aglow and a smell of burning leaves in the stiff breeze coming off the lake. I ignored the horse cabs drawn up before the theater and began walking toward the hotel. I wore my striped suit from Laramie, somewhat the worse for wear but freshly brushed and pressed, and I was approached three times by panhandlers within five blocks. One I assumed was a veteran, displaying the iron hook he wore in place of his right hand, but the others appeared whole and healthy despite their dirty faces and shabby dress; one was younger than I. I gave each a coin, for I had known their misery once. Farther on I saw shapeless figures heaped in doorways, and when I passed a small fenced-in park I noticed that every bench was occupied by a supine form. These were sobering indications of the grim economic period through which we were passing. I wondered, with so many so close to desperation, if it had been a wise choice to walk, and began looking for a cab.

No sooner had I developed this course of action than someone came up quickly from behind and slid an arm inside one of mine. In self-defense I turned—and found myself looking into an enormous pair of blue eyes ringed in artificial shadow and overhung by a charming hat, slanted steeply to one side and trimmed with ostrich plumes and lace. The dress the creature wore was just as becoming, snug at the waist, open to the collarbone, and decorated down the front with velvet frogs in imitation of military fashion; not that any gouty old general ever cut a figure as fetching as the tiny specimen of femininity clutching my arm. She was five feet and ninety pounds, not an inch nor a grain more, under thirty, with golden tendrils framing her face, and it occurred to me that if she were not careful with the white lace parasol that rested upon her shoulder, the wind would pick her up and carry her all the way to Des Moines.

Which, I decided, would be tragedy for me.

Naturally, she was a harlot. There was, however, a world of difference between the women who quartered the streets of that city and those who hiked their skirts for every hider and saloon swamp in the territories. Out there, where men outnumbered women twelve to one, being female was the only criterion (and I had been to places where even that was waived under certain circumstances); bad teeth, prominent moustaches, and surplus flesh lay outside the notice of a man who had spent the last six weeks in the company of unshaven drovers and ticky cattle, or one who had just stumbled blinking into the sunshine from an underground shaft with only a whiskey glass full of gold dust to compensate him for ten months of heartbreak. Chicago, for all its cattle stunners, boat-pullers, barrow-bellied police officers, and robber barons, was a woman's town, with ten gorgeous, buxom, salon-coiffed, Paris-gowned females hanging upon the arms of every monopolist. The plush parlors in the Loop daily turned away women who could set all of Denver scrambling to carry their hatboxes, had they but known it. The fishing in public waters was not as costly as in the private ponds, but the catch was not much less impressive.

Thus I spent my first night in the Windy City.

There is a trunk in storage in San Francisco, if it has not been sold to pay for the rent I owe upon it. Buried inside, beneath a moth-eaten striped suit, stacks of yellowed song sheets, and a woven coat of Indian manufacture wrapped carefully in blue tissue and sprinkled with camphor, is a photograph still in its cardboard studio frame. The model is a wicked-looking young blade in full evening dress complete with tails, posed incongruously before a sylvan backdrop with an empty two-seater glider hanging from an apple tree branch. A silk hat is cradled in the crook of one arm, while his other hand clutches a pair of gray kid gloves upon the silver crook of a brand-new cane. His hair is longish, although not so long as an Indian scout's or a Wild West show entrepreneur's, his beard is trimmed into a neat Vandyke, and there is a youthful arrogance about the way he stares fixedly at the camera, as if to say that he has money or that he has recently slept in the arms of a desirable, naked woman.

Both statements are true. Yet there is something else about that young fellow that disturbs me greatly in my old age, and that is that I don't know him, not from Adam, and although

I can guess what thoughts are passing through that slick head, I cannot fathom why he harbors them, or what makes him reckon them worth holding on to. At the time the picture was developed I remember being quite pleased with it—certainly more so than I was with the one I'd had taken in Wyoming— but I'd choose the other over it now, if only because what it showed about me had had the power to upset me. That's why the Chicago photo is in storage, and if it's gone at auction, whoever bid upon it is welcome to do his own guessing.

I had intended to stay three weeks, then press on east. I stayed six months. Had my money held out, I might have stayed even longer, for I had discovered an indolent streak, and was curious—that old bugbear—to see where it would lead.

My guitar gathered dust upon the top shelf of the wardrobe in my room at the Palmer House; I had not sat down at a piano since Abilene. Others could entertain me. I attended Wagner's *Tristan und Isolde* at the Opera House, in which Christine Nilsson sang the female lead, heard Sarasate play with the Symphony, returned to *Scouts of the Prairie* and saw an entirely different play with the same performers portraying the same roles, and became something of a connoisseur of the better brothels along Fifth Avenue, which in 1870 had been rechristened from Wells Street to spare the memory of Captain Billy Wells, an early local martyr to the Indians who had originally settled the lake basin; the women at the Metropole were better-looking, but the ones at Madame Fleauville's were more well mannered, and the cigar-chewing Negro who played the piano at the Dearborn House was the most accomplished musician I had ever seen, performing exercises upon the keyboard that my old dragon of a tutor had insisted were "impossible, *jung Meister;* concentrate upon the things of this world, and leave the fantastic to *Herr* Robert-Houdin." The man's mastery, beside which I was a backward student, made me sick at heart, all the more because it came to him naturally; he admitted to me that he had never learned to write his own name, let alone read music.

In this manner, along with meals, my hotel accommodations, cigars, and whiskey, my funds drained away at a rate that fascinated me. Although I supplemented them from time to time with winning wagers at the racetracks outside town and a plethora of gambling halls—banned, by order of the city fathers, but easy to find, and still easier to get into, provided one had cash to show—I celebrated my twenty-seventh birthday in the bar of the Palmer House with a glass of whiskey I bought out of the last of the original $850 I had carried away from Julesburg and studied the train ticket that would take me back West in the morning. I had pawned my new clothes and some odds and ends of jewelry I had acquired—ruby stickpin, platinum watch and chain, gold ring—and pocketed enough to set myself up for a few weeks in whatever town was printed upon the ticket. The whiskey had not been my first of the evening, and reading was something on the order of a chore.

Needless to say, I felt low. Money stuck to me no better than it did to those poor wretches who begged coins from me whenever I went out in my city finery, and I hadn't a crippling injury or a nationwide depression to hold responsible. Indeed, if I clung to any sort of pride, it was my refusal to blame my financial condition for denying me a reunion that season with my father and mother in New York. If I had a thousand dollars, if I had ten thousand, I should have spent it on anything but a ticket home. The manner in which I had conducted myself during my brief prosperity had demonstrated that I was not the kind of man with whom my father would choose to associate, much less have for a son. I had stared into this abyss before, of course, but then I'd had my music for compensation. Now, having seen and heard what a genuine artist could accomplish, which practice as I might I could never hope to approach, I doubted that I would ever again find the courage to take up a musical instrument. I would tend bar for my living, or hand out towels in a bordello. It was high time I took up a profession in keeping with my low character.

"Mr. Gashade?"

I looked up from the bottom of my glass—swam up would be a more appropriate description—into a round, hairless face beneath a soft hat, with an egg-shaped pair of spectacles straddling its nose and a Pickwick collar tickling the largest and fleshiest ear-lobes I had ever encountered. Their owner stood at my elbow, both hands clutching a dilapidated leather portfolio in front of him like a bird balancing itself upon a telegraph wire.

"I have that honor," said I. "May I stand you to a libation? Today is the anniversary of the day of my birth."

"Indeed, sir? Many happy returns. Unfortunately, I must decline your generous hospitality. I am a man of temperance." He cleared his throat, a demure ripple. "The desk clerk told me I might find you here. I left my card upon two previous visits, with a note asking you to pay me a call. My name is Whitstead. I am the bookkeeper at the Cook County Fairgrounds."

I remembered the name. I had supposed he was a creditor. "You have an excellent racetrack. I have made down payments upon a number of horses there."

"That brings me to the reason I am here. There is a matter involving a wager you placed last fall."

I reached the end of my tether. Placing my back against the bar, I snatched my old cowhide poke from my pocket and spread it open under his nose. "Take it all, Mr. Whitehead; the poke too. It is not enough that I have squandered a small fortune at your facility. Since you must hound me at my place of residence for more, you may as well own that you are a thief and pick my pocket." There was no cash in the pouch. I did not feel the need to mention the grubstake I had in the hotel safe.

To my astonishment, the bookkeeper thrust his portfolio under one arm and took the poke. "Whitstead is my name, sir. This is what I need to see, if you have not—Ah!" He separated a cardboard stub from the jumble between the folds. "Here it is, October twenty-fifth, sixth race, horse number nine: Buffalo Skinner. It paid twenty to one." Keeping the stub, he returned the pouch. "Normally, we at the fairgrounds consider an unclaimed ticket to be the bettor's responsibility. However, because there is a substantial sum involved, unlikely to be overlooked indefinitely by the winning party, and because it is essential that our books balance at the end of the fiscal year—"

"How did you find me?"

He had untied his portfolio and was rummaging inside. "Your calling card stuck to the banknote with which you placed the wager. Because of the amount, I inquired at all the best hotels." He withdrew a check and placed it on the bar. It was made out to me in the amount of four hundred dollars.

"'Entertainments,'" he mused, while I studied it. "Are you in the show business, Mr. Gashade?"

"No. It was a bad joke."

Wishing me a pleasant birthday, he left. I felt nothing. What value hard work and probity in a world that rewarded indolence?

". . . help overhearing your glad tidings. May I interest you in a proposition?"

I looked into the pleasant, ruddy face of the stranger who had inserted himself into the space next to me. He had black side-whiskers under a bowler hat and prominent front teeth that clamped his lower lip like a hasp.

"I'm not interested in purchasing any gold bricks today." I folded the check into my poke.

His chortle, like his accent, was distinctively British. "I am not a confidence man, but a purveyor, and at the moment I am without a partner. If you will allow me to serve you from the bottle at my table, I shall explain myself."

"What happened to your partner?" I was mildly amused. He reminded me of a caricature of a Limey in a variety house in Brooklyn.

"He was arrested." The hand he offered was freckled and soft, with pink skin showing beneath the nails; there was none cleaner west of Albany. "Delmar St. George Dibble. All my partners call me Del. I should be honored, Mr. Gashade, if you would follow their example."

THIRTY-FIVE

Del Dibble claimed to be sixty, but I didn't credit it any more than his insistence that he'd served under Lord Cardigan in the Crimea—as quartermaster, of course. Although he might have dyed his hair and muttonchops, the rest of him would have had to have been preserved in the same vinegar that pickled his heart. More times than I can count I saw him spring aboard a wagonload of contraband to test a knot or adjust the sheet, all in one motion from ground to tailgate, while I at twenty-seven made use of the sideboards to pull myself up.

On the other hand, threescore years seems scarcely enough for anyone to have grown so wicked.

Forty or sixty, he's dead by now—hanged, shot, or (as seems most likely) gone in his sleep with that same contented half smile he shone upon me that day in Chicago, while measuring me for a square yard of stone floor in Isaac Parker's dungeon in Fort Smith. In that hole I cursed him by the day, yet from this distance I bear him no grudge. If he was the instrument of my fall, no one put my thumbs in a screw to persuade me to take him up. Shark that he was, he cruised the waters of the bars, brothels, and elevated railway of the city, moving in swiftly the moment he smelled blood.

"The procedure is simple, and you won't even need a map

to get where you are going," said he, over a bottle of aged and mellow whiskey at his corner table; perhaps the best that can be said of him is that his taste in the finer comforts was irreproachable, and that he was not stingy in sharing them. "I have an arrangement with the proprietor of the House of Lords Saloon in Fort Smith. He needs only to see my face to turn over his inventory—that, and a hundred fifty dollars American."

"Arkansas?"

"That's just the jumping-off point. After we say good-bye you will drive the wagon along the South Bank of the Arkansas River into the Indian Nations, then follow the Canadian when it forks to the south. Three days after that you will be in Indianola, where Ed White Turkey will give you three hundred in gold for the cargo. I shall be waiting when you return to Fort Smith with the empty wagon. The profits will be divided down the middle."

"What's the penalty for transporting liquor in the Indian territory?"

"My friend, there is none. The federal court in Arkansas is a political boondoggle, as crooked as any man in Grant's cabinet. Most of the marshals traffic in liquor on the side. If you are stopped, the chances are they will confiscate the shipment and turn you loose."

"And if they don't?"

"Even better. Judge Story peddles dismissals at a fixed rate. For a little more he may even return the liquor."

"Still, the risk seems steep for seventy-five dollars."

"It's one hundred percent profit. Those Creeks and Cherokees are starving for whiskey; Ed White Turkey will take as much as we can supply. You can make six trips in a season. That's four hundred fifty dollars, and you won't have to peel hides or worry about your scalp. The Five Civilized Tribes have worn trousers and spoken English for forty years."

"If it's so simple, why don't you drive the wagon?"

"I am too old. I can barely handle a one-horse buggy. You

took your turn with a six-hitch team in Nebraska. In any case our little enterprise requires someone with an established reputation to show himself in all the respectable places in Fort Smith. How would it look if Cornelius Vanderbilt were seen mounting to the cab of Old Number Nine, wearing a cap made of ticking with a red bandanna dangling from his hip pocket?"

I don't know now if Del Dibble actually saw himself as a robber baron on the grand scale of a Vanderbilt. It's not impossible. The most successful confidence men begin by selling themselves their own bill of goods.

It doesn't signify, as they used to say in Missouri; I became his creature. To give him his due, I must point out that throughout the first summer and autumn of our association, nothing transpired to dispute what he had told me of Fort Smith and the Indian Nations.

I have not visited there since long before it became the State of Oklahoma, but from stories I hear, admission to the Union has not changed the place demonstrably. In my time it was the home of domesticated Indians, outlaws on the run, and human predators not far removed from our animal ancestors. Only last year, federal agents cornered bank bandit Charles Arthur "Pretty Boy" Floyd, an Oklahoma native, in a farmer's field in Ohio and shot him to pieces, exactly as U.S. marshals hunted down and destroyed Ned Christie in the northeastern section of the Nations a generation earlier. Both were accused of the ambush murders of federal men. The territory was set aside by Andrew Jackson for members of the Cherokee, Chickasaw, Choctaw, Creek, Quapaw, and Seminole Nations—the so-called Five Civilized Tribes (plus one)—who were torn from their homes and prodded over the Trail of Tears, conveniently out of sight of white society. Governed by the federal court in Fort Smith, Arkansas, its seventy-four thousand square miles were patrolled by a handful of native peace officers and an even smaller number of deputy United States marshals, making its rocky hills and tangled forests a haven for every blackguard and brigand with a price on his head and a rough idea of its boundaries. No one will ever know the full extent of the crimes and depravities that took place there. Most of the ones we know about were too despicable even for the dime novels. The motion picture industry will not touch them.

The musical profession is different. I heard three separate ballads about Ned Christie's vendetta the first year following his demise; and I understand my old friend Woody Guthrie is composing one about Pretty Boy Floyd.

Music was beyond my ken in the Year of Our Lord 1874. I had pawned my guitar in Chicago along with my jewelry and wardrobe—not for the two additional dollars it brought, but with the air of a man ridding himself at last of a pious and quarrelsome companion—and for the first time in ten years I decamped for the sparsely populated regions without so much as a harmonica for my personal amusement. I hoisted my single portmanteau into the brass rack above my Pullman seat, swung down the footrest, and stretched out, waiting for the regret. I waited all the way through Illinois's furrowed fields and while changing trains in St. Louis; gave up waiting somewhere among the steep green hills of the Ozarks, and by the time the car in which I was riding swept through a ravine and the whistle blew for the Fort Smith station, I had forgotten I ever knew F major from a sixbrace.

I made eight trips between Fort Smith and Indianola throughout June and November. My traveling companion was a half-Creek, half-Negro murderer (I was convinced) named Charlie Stone Bucket, flat-faced and dusky-skinned, with dead black hair worn long and chopped off square at the corners of his jaw and across his forehead, like an Aztec warrior in an old woodcut. He wore smoked glasses to protect his weak eyes and rode next to me with a ten-gauge shotgun across his knees for close work and a big Remington rolling-block rifle behind the seat for use at a distance. Del Dibble said Charlie was there to secure the shipment from highwaymen, but I suspected he was guarding it from me as well, lest I decide to set myself up in competition with my partner.

The half-breed was poor company. Journey after journey he wore the same calico shirt, corduroy trousers, broken-down Wellingtons, and stained Yankee kepi, and the continuing decrepitude of trousers and shirt suggested he had not had them off between trips. He emitted an eye-watering odor of stagnant sweat and rancid bear-grease—the latter to ward off mosquitoes, or so he claimed. Certainly it repelled almost everyone with whom he came into contact, although I myself was immune thanks to my recent occupation in Nebraska. His sole topic of conversation was the legions of women he had known, with and without their consent. I loathed him, and he in turn distrusted me. Camping along the Canadian, whenever I returned from relieving myself in the woods I found him sitting up in his bedroll with his shotgun in both hands, eyes glittering in the moonlight.

Three times we were waylaid.

The first was by a party of deputy U.S. marshals escorting a wagon containing a half-dozen men with their ankles bound and their hands tied behind their backs. It was my impression that federal law enforcement appointees had to be in top physical condition, but the spokesman was morbidly fat, sunken in rings of suet like a raccoon aboard his big shaggy chestnut, with a filthy bowler jammed down to his ears and a stout cigar screwed into a corner of his mouth. His badge, a small silver star in a circle, sagged from one pocket of his flannel shirt with a thick fold of arrest warrants thrust inside. It was clear from the way his muck-colored gaze kept sliding toward our cargo of barrels that he coveted it; but when Charlie Stone Bucket, fingering the ten-gauge in his lap, informed him that we were about Del Dibble's business, he nodded, puffed at his cigar, and snarled to us to stand aside for officers of the court and their prisoners. Obviously, Dibble had made prior arrangements.

Another time, while we were picking our way down a rocky grade, three horsemen burst from behind a nearby stand of sycamore, plainly bent upon stampeding our team and upsetting the wagon. However, when a blast from Charlie Stone Bucket's shotgun carried away the lead rider's left sleeve and most of his ear, he and his companions fell into confusion. I unfurled my bullwhip over the heads of our horses and we rattled down the rest of the grade and away, losing two barrels off the back. I kept up the pace for two miles, but we were not pursued.

We were not so lucky the third time. Admittedly, upon this occasion our vigilance slipped. We had left the Arkansas River ferry only that morning and were not four hours into the Nations; consequently we considered ourselves relatively safe when I drew rein to give the road to a group of drovers evidently bound for the saloons and brothels of Fort Smith. My companion, who dismissed all "cow-scratchers" as beneath contempt, pulled out the tail of his disreputable shirt to wipe his glasses as they passed. Suddenly there was a rattle of forestocks and a crunch of hammers, and we looked around to find ourselves inside a semicircle of revolvers and rifles, all pointed at us.

"What's in the wagon?" one of them demanded, in a tone that told me he knew the answer.

"Flour," I replied. Indeed, that was what was stenciled upon the lids of the barrels.

One of the riders near the back of the wagon leaned out of his saddle and gave one of the barrels a shake, sloshing the contents around inside. "I got sad news for you, peddler," said this one. "Your flour done got wet."

Another rider thought this was the funniest thing he had ever heard. His laugh was a high hard bray.

I don't know if Charlie Stone Bucket tried to make a fight. I was busy looking at the man who was doing most of the talking when one of the others swept his rifle stock across the half-breed's face, shattering his nose and his glasses. He clutched the seat to keep from falling while the man who had assaulted him grasped the shotgun by its barrels and slid it off his lap. Charlie Stone Bucket kept still after that, covering the lower half of his face with both hands to control his nosebleed.

"You want the same or worse, peddler," said the one with the words, "you go right on staring."

I lowered my eyes. I *had* been staring at him. He'd filled out some, grown a sparse beard and his fair hair to his shoulders, but it would take more than that, or the broad brim of the black hat he wore with an eagle feather in the band, to prevent me from recognizing John Thrailkill. Even had I failed to note the deadness of his eyes—blank buttons, doll's eyes—I could have picked out the shiny, slim-handled revolver he held from a pile of similar weapons. He had used it in Abilene when he stuck up Mike Williams at the Alamo Saloon, and had carried it all through the war after taking it away from me in Lawrence.

Now he reached over, grasped my chin with his free hand, and turned up my face. Looking into the empty holes through which he saw, I tried to keep my mind empty, lest it communicate anything about our past association. I saw puzzlement cross his features, an attempt to remember. Finally he let go and leaned back.

"All you whiskey peddlers look alike," he said, but he sounded unconvinced. "I got good news. You boys are walking back to Fort Smith."

"Aw, shit." This from the man who had struck Charlie Stone Bucket. His face was narrow and rodentlike, with a predatory nose and boils in his beard. "Cain't we at least take target practice on the breed?"

"We can't risk the shots this close to town. Them marshals'd shoot us all trying to escape for a load half this size."

We alighted from the wagon, my companion glaring murder over his hand with blood welling between the fingers.

Looking down at me from horseback, Thrailkill said, "Was you in the war, peddler?"

"No, I was too young."

He stared at me hard for another moment, then shook his head. "Get to walking. First one of you turns his head carries it back."

I have never taken a longer walk in my life than the one that carried me around the bend and out of John Thrailkill's sight behind a stand of hardwoods. At any moment I expected him to remember the youth who had humiliated him before his fellow Missouri raiders with the border spin, and put a slug between my shoulder blades.

Fort Smith was a quiet place to spend the winter. The cattle drives were over, the steamboats put in less often, and all thirty saloons hunkered in for the long dead spell before spring. The Fort Smith *Herald* occupied itself with reports of suicide on First Street—locally referred to as "The Row"— where the harlots found time at last to take stock of their lives and decide whether they were worth the trouble of continuing, and the periodic arrival of a wagonload of prisoners from the Nations bound for the courthouse attracted curious crowds, but for these diversions the place might have been Abilene before and after the boom. I took a room in a boardinghouse—clean, with a hearty breakfast and dinner provided, but the proprietress, a hefty Scotswoman whose skinny, put-upon husband chopped firewood out back and carried it to the rooms, was no Drucilla; her conversation was even more limited than Charlie Stone Bucket's, and scarcely as entertaining. Charlie himself wintered somewhere in the Nations and Del Dibble returned to Chicago.

Accomplished liar that he was, he had told the truth about the law in Fort Smith. John Sarber, the United States marshal appointed by President Grant to enforce the law in the Indian territory, was a sloth and probably corrupt, taking no official interest in the larceny that ran rampant through his deputies. District Attorney Newton J. Temple, it was rumored, had been subpoenaed to testify in Washington about irregularities in the system by which certificates of payment were issued to jurors (and not paid), and while the reports were probably untrue that Judge Story kept a list of bribery amounts for certain offenses posted in his chambers like a restaurant bill of fare, it was widely accepted that dismissal of charges for any crime including murder was merely a matter of negotiation in the Fort Smith court. He, too, was under investigation; but the local wisdom was that things had always been this way and were not likely to change, regardless of who wore the robes.

I whiled away the cold months along the Row and in the saloons, where I ignored the piano players and guitar pickers, drinking alone and catching up on the news of the world as it was reported off the wires in the columns of the *Herald*.

Boss Tweed had exchanged his table at Delmonico's Restaurant for a cell in the New York County Penitentiary on Blackwell's Island. Although he had originally been sentenced to serve twelve years, the Court of Appeals had ruled that although the defendant had been convicted on 204 counts of criminal fraud, no punishment in excess of that prescribed for one offense could be inflicted. However, the State of New York had announced its intention to bring suit to recover six million dollars of the plunder that had been traced to Tweed, and when he was released in January 1875, he was rearrested and confined in the Ludlow Street Jail in lieu of three million dollars' bond. Manipulate how he might the system that had made him rich beyond all pretense of decency, Tweed's reign was clearly over.

That same month, acting upon information that Frank and Jesse were inside, Pinkerton agents surrounded the Clay County, Missouri, home of Dr. Reuben and Mrs. Zerelda Samuel. When their demands for surrender went unanswered, a detective lobbed a cast-iron device, shaped vaguely like the base of a lantern, through a window. Moments later a tremendous explosion blew out all the panes, carrying away Mrs. Samuel's left arm below the elbow and the life of Archie, her nine-year-old son by the doctor.

Pressed by reporters, a Pinkerton spokesman identified the device as a smoke bomb intended to drive the occupants outside; it had evidently exploded when someone swept it into a fireplace, igniting the kerosene. The spokesman's name was Captain John Terrence Fabian, my old acquaintance from Abilene and before that the train station in Indianapolis.

Frank and Jesse had been nowhere near their mother's house at the time of the raid. The Pinkertons had hoped to take the James boys away in chains and thus bring them down to human size for those who would erect statues of them. Instead they managed to strengthen even further the Jameses' support among the Yankee-hating hill people of Missouri.

I thought of that remarkable woman, correcting her grown sons' English and calmly describing her husband's lynching by the federal militia. I doubted the mere loss of an arm would quench that fiery spirit.

Change was abroad in Fort Smith as well. Under threat of impeachment, Judge Story resigned, and for his replacement the president turned to a thirty-six-year-old former United States congressman from Missouri. Although Isaac Charles Parker had a reputation as a teetotaler and an ardent supporter of Indian rights, the general opinion around town was that he would prove to be as corrupt as his predecessors, or at best ineffectual. The federal bench in the Western District of Arkansas, with jurisdiction over the Indian territory, had a reputation for grinding a man's resolve down to pebbles.

This was the atmosphere in which I set out, in May of 1875, to deliver the first load of whiskey of the season to Ed White Turkey in Indianola. With me, nose decidedly askew but brand-new shotgun in place and a host of new female conquests to share, was Charlie Stone Bucket.

I found him easier company, for all that. I was both rested and restless after the long hiatus. The sycamore were heavy with leaves, the birds and frogs were in full voice, and a warm breeze was puffing up from Texas, combing my beard and bringing with it the scent of blue lupine and morning glories. I had the strongest possible dose of spring fever.

In my euphoria, I felt no great alarm, shortly after crossing the tracks of the Missouri, Kansas, & Texas Railroad—affectionately known in those parts as the Katy Flyer—when two riders came into view a hundred yards down the road and, spotting us, drew rein. They wore the tall-crowned hats of drovers, but neither had been among John Thrailkill's band the previous autumn, and in any case the scattered buildings of Indianola were visible behind them. Civilization was too close for an ambush.

It was a great surprise, then, when lifting his shotgun into a wary position, Charlie Stone Bucket was thrown over the back of the seat by a blast from the rifle of the man mounted to the right, and quick as thought his partner bounded ahead of him and leveled the barrel of an enormous Colt at me across his forearm. "Stand still for arrest!" he bellowed through his handlebars. I raised my hands. "I work with Del Dibble." The handlebars formed a grim line. "Well, fancy that, *I* work with Judge Parker, and you'll meet him in Fort Smith. That is, if you don't jerk a piece like your friend and save me the freight."

THIRTY-SIX

The federal courthouse was a two-story brick building set at an eccentric angle to the Arkansas River and partitioned into a courtroom, jury rooms, and offices for attorneys, clerks, and U.S. Marshal James F. Fagan, who had succeeded the indolent John Sarber during the housecleaning that took place in the wake of Judge Story's resignation. It was an official-enough-looking building, wainscoted in golden oak and lit by lamps in bowls suspended from the ceilings, with only the bars on the windows in all rooms and corridors accessible to prisoners to remind the visitor that it was a place of justice in a land that regarded the law as something to be ignored or eradicated.

Below ground level, the genteel trappings vanished altogether.

The basement was eight feet deep, stone-paved, and separated by a solid stone wall into two compartments, each twenty-nine by fifty-five feet. Chains were stapled to the walls at ten-foot intervals, a kerosene barrel cut into two halves served as bathtubs, and buckets stood in the bases of the old chimneys for purposes of sanitation. This was the federal jail, where some prisoners were interred awaiting trial, others awaiting execution. It was my home for five months.

I was not chained, but assigned to a filthy straw pallet teeming with vermin. At first I avoided it, but the stone floor was clammy and hard, and after two nights I no longer paid attention to the bites and itching, although they troubled me fresh after my monthly bath. By then I had grown accustomed to the hideous stench of the place, an evil mix of offal, urine, perspiration, mildew, and despair. Each day I asked the guard who brought food and water (about which the less said the better), a heavy-shouldered brute armed with a short truncheon, when I could expect my case to come to trial. His reply was ever the same: "You got about six dozen rapists and murderers ahead of you. Wait your turn." After a month I stopped asking.

I wasn't lonely. At any given time I had eight to ten inmates with whom to converse upon my side of the partition, some of them quite personable, including two or three who were considered enough of a risk to chain to the wall. They came and went, however: acquitted, remanded to a court in a different jurisdiction, convicted and sent north to the Federal House of Corrections in Detroit; or, as in the case of six men at once on September 3, declared guilty and suspended by their necks from the infamous Fort Smith gallows.

Although there was a room upstairs where prisoners could confer with their lawyers, I never saw it. I had no attorney, and Del Dibble never offered to provide me with one, and for that matter never visited me. Incensed at first, I eventually came to realize that nothing had been said about what might happen in the event of my arrest, and that no promises had been made. He had probably left for Chicago within a day of my incarceration, and was even now haunting the city's drinking establishments in search of a new associate. Had my predecessor been rotting away in this same dungeon as we were sealing our partnership? It seemed likely. If I had not asked the questions I should have when it counted, it wasn't because they hadn't occurred to me. I simply had not wanted to hear the answers.

In August, I think it was—I reckoned the passage of time by information carried by fresh inmates—a fanfare of blows and curses announced the arrival of additional company. A new prisoner had tried to push his escort off the top of the stairs and been soundly trounced by two guards with their fists and truncheons. By the time they dragged him into my half of the basement and fixed the shackles to his wrists and ankles, he was unconscious, his face a mass of bruises, and his long fair hair streaked with blood. I knew him instantly, however. The Great West was vast, but it seemed it was not so large I could wander in it for long without encountering John Thrailkill.

Several yards separated us, and at high noon the dugout windows near the ceiling allowed only gray twilight into our world, and so I was not greatly concerned that he would recognize me, having failed to do so in broad daylight on the other side of the Arkansas River. As the days passed and he recovered from his injuries in so far as to engage some of the other prisoners in conversation, I learned that he was under a charge of murder and rape. The murder victim, a white farmer living in the Cherokee Nation with his Indian wife, had shot and killed one of Thrailkill's companions during an attempted robbery along the Canadian River. Thrailkill boasted that he had tracked the man to his cabin, lured him outside by gobbling like a wild turkey, and shot him from ambush. Then he had gone into the cabin, pistol-whipped and raped the widow, and left with eighty-six dollars he found stashed in a tobacco tin behind the cookstove. "Parker's marshals," as the deputies working under Marshal Fagan were coming to be known, caught up with him on the road and surrounded him.

He stood trial shortly thereafter—I envied those arrested for capital crimes only because justice came to them more quickly than to a lowly rumrunner—and was sentenced to hang. As the last of the first half dozen condemned by juries since Parker's appointment, he was scheduled to join the other five in a swift gesture of official retribution.

Such a burden would have been impossible for any ordinary gallows to accommodate. For Fort Smith, this was operating at only half capacity. The scaffold was eighteen feet long, with a single trap running its entire length, and had been designed to suspend twelve men at a time. It was the talk of the West; some said it had been inspired by the efficiency with which the packinghouses in Chicago dispatched, quartered, and packaged cattle even before the life heat had passed from the carcasses. Until now it had been little more than a curiosity, receiving infrequent use, and then only to hang one man at a time.

That was about to change. No more momentous marriage was ever engineered than the one that united Isaac Parker and the Fort Smith gallows.

Thrailkill seemed unaffected by his sentence. If anything he became more loquacious, striking up spirited conversations with some of those scheduled to join him upon the scaffold, notably Daniel Evans, who had shot a nineteen-year-old boy through the head for his horse and saddle, then had the temerity to wear the boy's fancy high-heeled boots throughout his trial, and James Moore, a horse thief who had killed eight men in the course of his career, the last a deputy marshal. They seemed to consider themselves charter members of an exclusive club.

Which, in a way, they were; for from the moment they dropped through the trap, Congressman Parker of Missouri would cease to exist and the legend of the Hanging Judge would be born.

I did not, of course, seek Thrailkill's attention. Neither did I avoid it, knowing furtive action to be the surest way to shine a beacon upon oneself. He did look my way upon occasion; however, having learned by way of the grapevine the nature of all the infractions that had brought our little community together, he made no attempt to draw me into conversation, doubtless considering a mere whiskey runner to be no fit company for a murderer. Once or twice, stirring from a doze, I opened my eyes to find him gazing my way pensively through the gloom, yet I had no way of knowing if he was sorting through his memory for my features or simply brooding upon his fate, and staring at me in lieu of the wall opposite. I had the misfortune during one of these episodes to be asked by a wife-beater with whom I had become conversant, Alvin Sixkiller by name, if from my vantage point I could see where the sun was in the sky, and to be addressed as "Billy" within Thrailkill's hearing; but as he showed no reaction I assumed his reverie was impenetrable.

Two nights later I awoke strangling, with a chain around my neck and John Thrailkill's voice whistling in my ear. "What good's your border spin now, you Yankee pissant?"

Sliding my way across the floor, he must have found just enough slack in the chain that married him to the wall to sling it over my head. I clawed at it with both hands, but the iron links were biting into the skin. I couldn't get my fingers underneath.

"Guard! Gua—" The chain tightened, sealing off my croak.

"Go ahead and holler," said he, but he made no attempt to loosen the bond. "Time it takes to bash in my brainpan with their damn clubs, you'll be done for, and I'm dead either way."

I felt my face swelling with blood. Black checks obscured my vision.

"I knowed it was something about you when I put the bulge on you across the river. You growed up some. I should of tied you up and cut off your business and fed it to the magpies."

His words thrashed inside my head, tangled with the blood surging in the arteries at my temples. I heard shouting, blows struck, but it was all very far off. They might have been remembered sounds, flying away from my memory as it tore loose and spun through my skull. New York, fire bells and chopping axes; Lawrence, cries and shooting; Pilot Knob, pounding hooves and sabers clashing; Cheyenne, Laramie, Abilene, the buffalo range, Julesburg, Chicago, the Nations. Fort Smith . . .

"—choke you all over again in hell, you Jayhawking son of a—"

I fell in darkness.

"**H**ow does the defendant plead?"

I stood before the high oaken bench, hands folded in front of me as if for protection. I had on a cheap new flannel shirt, scratchy but clean, and an old pair of patched overalls donated by the Fort Smith Ladies' League, of which Mrs. Parker was a prominent member if not its president. My worn old boots were the only items on my person that belonged to me.

The room was done all in oak, from the picture rail near the ceiling to the railings that enclosed the jury box and separated the court from the spectators' gallery, and the pew-like benches beyond, where some of the curious had gathered to see what Parker was about this day. The effect, enhanced by the strong tobacco odor that permeated the place, was of standing inside a gigantic cigar box.

"Guilty, Your Honor," I said.

It was October. John Thrailkill was as dead as Bloody Bill, as dead as Quantrill and the Southern Confederacy; as dead as his heart, which had been buried with the woman he had intended to marry before hell came to Missouri. On the third of September, 1875, he had joined the five other men whose hearts had been interred long since, dropping through the twelve-foot slit behind the courthouse into eternity. There had been talk of a postponement after a gang of guards had seized his limbs and swung a truncheon square across his face to separate us before I finished strangling; but as announcements had already gone out and Parker's views were clear upon the "cruelty" of false stays, he had appeared before his Maker upon the appointed day with his nose broken and swollen and a black eye upon either side.

Later, when jail trusties came with lanterns and a mop to tidy the area he had occupied, they found a mural meticulously rendered with a stub of gray chalk upon the stone wall that supported his shackles. The former artist had sketched in silence while the rest of us slept, unaware of the work of art taking shape within arm's length. Summoned down to take a look, Parker had ordered it to be scrubbed off immediately. The glimpse the picture offered inside the mind of its creator, of scaly, half-human demons feeding upon (and copulating with) decaying corpses in a craterous battlefield, was disturbing by any standards, particularly those of the judge's stern Methodism; yet I believe I was the only one who noted the resemblance between the features of both the ghoulish victimizers and their hollow-eyed victims and those of the artist himself. A short drop at the end of a stout rope, a few swipes with a wet mop, and a lifetime of self-violation disappeared as if it had never been.

As for me, two days' rest in the Fort Smith infirmary and I was declared recovered sufficiently to resume my incarceration. However—in deference, perhaps, to my ordeal, or simply because it served to remind someone of my existence—a date for my arraignment was fixed shortly thereafter. Even so, I am told that five months awaiting disposition of my case was far from the record for that overworked court.

A tall man, Judge Parker looked taller still behind his elevated bench, broad across the chest in his pleated black robes, with his chestnut hair brushed to a sheen and threads of wiry gray in his chin-whiskers and moustache, although he was just in his middle thirties. He had strong bones and chilly blue eyes, like silver coins in the bed of a clear mountain stream. His lids were heavy, his voice low but not unpleasant; it was said he could be heard clearly above the dozens of worshipers who sang "Praise God from Whom All Blessings Flow" every Sunday.

"Have you anything to say in your defense before I consider your sentence?" he asked.

"No, Your Honor."

"Have you a permanent address in or near Fort Smith, Mr. Gashade?"

"No, Your Honor."

"Honest employment?"

"No, Your Honor."

He fingered his whiskers. "You place me in a difficult position. After nearly half a year in confinement, you oblige me to return you to jail until sentencing. An unemployed transient is scarcely a fit candidate to be released upon his own recognizance. My views upon the certainty of punishment are well known."

"I am sorry, Your Honor."

"You are convinced there is no one to claim responsibility for your conduct pending a date for sentencing?"

"I have no friends in Fort Smith." *Or anywhere else*, I added silently.

"Very well." He raised his gavel. "This court orders the defendant to be returned—"

"I'll look to him," someone spoke up from the back of the gallery. It was a strong female voice.

THIRTY-SEVEN

Her name was Alma Barnstable.

She was small and slight, but wiry strong within the limits of her unpredictable fits of energy; I saw her go as long as fifty hours without a break, and flag soon after rising from a full night's sleep. She was extremely fair—her skin was almost blue, with the shadowy veins visible beneath, like one's own fingers behind a fine china plate—with pale green eyes, a long, straight nose as delicate as stem crystal, and blond hair cut boyishly short and worn in bangs across her high forehead. She was twenty-two when we met. She looked younger and seemed much older. I never saw her wear anything but the same ivory-and-black high-topped shoes, worn at the heels but always freshly polished, an unadorned white dress that hung from her collarbone to her toe-caps with only a hint of waist, and a lace-trimmed bonnet to prevent sunburn, of which she was in great danger after only a few minutes' exposure; not that it prevented her from venturing out often for many hours at a stretch as she pursued her special calling. The bonnet didn't go with the dress, nor the dress with the shoes. I'm convinced that had she been informed of this, she would have changed nothing. She cared less about what people thought of her than most women I've known, and any man.

She was the daughter of Christian missionaries sent by their church in Maryland in 1860 to minister to the faith of the Five Civilized Tribes. Her father, a practical man, as adept with a hammer and plane as he was with a hymnal, and her mother, a trained nurse who set the arms of Choctaw and Cherokee women broken by their drunken husbands and stitched and bandaged their sons' knife wounds suffered in brawls outside the establishments where liquor was sold, had operated a combination meetinghouse and infirmary on the other side of the Arkansas for four years, then died of the cholera within ten days of each other. Orphaned at eleven, Alma was taken in by a Seminole woman who operated a laundry in Fort Smith. From her, the young girl learned the ancient Creation beliefs that still wound their way among the Christianized standards of the peoples whom her parents had regarded chiefly as converts and patients; discovered the healing properties of yarrow, snakeroot, and elderberry bark; and, helping the old woman peg shirts and suits of underwear to the clothesline behind her ramshackle house, listened to stories of brutality and depravity from white and Indian households upon both sides of the great river that would have drained the blood from the face of a longshoreman in Baltimore. By age nineteen, at which time the old woman died after a lengthy decline, Alma retained few illusions about the enlightened nature of the human spirit.

Why she chose to accept custody of a confessed rumrunner had, I suppose, something to do with this altered awareness. In any case, the decision was in keeping with the methods by which she had conducted her life in the three years that she had been on her own. That those methods had established a reputation in the community was evident by the deference with which Judge Parker addressed her in his court that day.

"Miss Barnstable?" It seemed the jurist raised himself slightly from his seat behind that high bench to locate the sparrowlike creature who had spoken from the last row of the gallery.

"Yes, Judge."

"Miss Barnstable, everyone in Fort Smith is aware of your altruism. However, the defendant is not an underage orphan in need of nurturing and moral guidance. He is an adult, and by his own admission he is a criminal. To offer to take him in as if he were some stray—"

"Judge, who is in need of moral guidance if not a criminal? Anyway, you asked for someone to claim responsibility. I am claiming it."

Stern lines fissured his face. "It is not seemly for an unmarried woman to share quarters with an adult male. Furthermore, it is not legal."

"If that is the case, Judge, I know of eight citizens of this community who should be in jail."

In all his twenty years on the Fort Smith bench, I doubt that anyone else—lawyer, supplicant, or witness in the dock—got away with addressing Parker by any other title but "Your Honor." It was not that Alma didn't respect him; it was merely her way to confront everyone, panhandler and prince, eye to eye. As for her declaration, the ripple of gasps and titters that swept through the gallery indicated that many of those present were aware of the identities of the eight citizens to whom she had alluded.

Parker gaveled for silence, then delivered a brief lecture upon the subject of immorality versus the appearance of same, but the argument was clearly over. He set a long date for sentencing, waggled a finger at me to remind me that abuse of my freedom would be a far more serious crime than the one to which I had confessed, and remanded me into "the good, but, this court is convinced, misdirected custody of Miss Alma Barnstable, of this city," snapped his gavel again, and called for the next case.

"Miss Barnstable," said I, when the two of us were alone in the corridor outside the courtroom, "I don't—"

"My name is Alma. And you will be Billy. Do you know how to chop wood?"

"Chop wood? Yes."

"I don't require anyone for that. Elmer is good at it, and one or two of the others are of age. I only asked because a man who knows how to chop wood is usually good for most of the chores that need doing. I intend to put you to work, Billy. If that doesn't suit you, the jail will continue to accommodate you. I'm not operating a hotel for loiterers."

"What *are you* operating?"

"Behind schedule," said she, consulting a tiny brass watch

pinned to her bosom; she wore no other jewelry. "Come with me." She struck out for the stairs at a masculine pace, obliging me to trot to catch up.

"I have possessions," I protested.

"I'll send Elmer back for them. It's time for Coral's lesson."

Grateful as I was to be free of that dungeon, I felt that I had been manipulated into indenturing myself as some kind of unpaid servant, and wondered if my diminutive keeper made a habit of recruiting her household staff from the arrest rolls. Her brusque manner was not far removed from that of the guards, and as she paused outside to retrieve a lace-trimmed handkerchief from the tiny reticule she carried on a loop around her wrist, I was somewhat surprised not to see at least a small pistol inside.

The house to which I accompanied her, half a mile or so from the courthouse, was large by local standards, with a long porch in front furnished with rocking chairs, and smelled of pine sawdust and fresh whitewash. A pair of girls, aged about ten and fourteen, were sweeping the porch and front steps with homemade brooms; at Alma's approach they stopped and curtsied, pulling out the hems of their dresses as decorously as if they were at dancing school.

"Come inside, girls," said Alma. "I'm calling a meeting."

Inside was a parlor, airy and comfortable-looking, although shabbily appointed: The rug was threadbare, the upholstery patched, and the curtains were made inexpertly from flour sacks. Sewing baskets littered the room and an Autoharp, the one visible nod away from the raw basics, leaned in the corner by the fireplace. There a boy around sixteen clad in overalls was sweeping the hearth. I felt a pang of lost youth. He was the age I had been when I came west.

"Elmer, where are James and Otis?"

The boy grazed me with a look that fixed me somewhere below the level of the ashes in his dustpan, then slanted his head toward the back door. "Jimmy's out mending fence like you said. I don't know where the hell Otis is."

"Say that again, please."

Her tone was deadly calm. To my astonishment, this young hulk, who was nearly twice the woman's size, ducked his head as if he'd been struck. "Sorry, ma'am. I don't rightly know where Otis is. I think he's upstairs loafing."

"Find him, will you, please? And please call James and tell him I wish to see him. I want to talk to all of you."

He stood his broom and pan against the mantel and went out through the back.

"Elmer's father was hanged last year," Alma said. "Teaching manners to an angry boy is difficult."

I said I didn't mind.

"I wasn't apologizing. I was explaining."

Presently we were in the company of five youngsters. Aside from Elmer and Otis, a younger, less fully developed boy who shared the other's thick brown hair and hooded eyes, I could tell at a glance that none of them was related to the others. Coral, the youngest, was thin, black-haired, and chewed her nails all the time she was in the room. The other girl, Augusta, was hefty, with red in her hair and that troublesome look of a child who is close to becoming a woman and growing impatient with the wait. James, twelve or thirteen and towheaded, with the remains of a recent sunburn flaking away from his cheeks and the bridge of his nose, was a big-knuckled, scrawny outdoors type who would probably have climbed a tree as readily as any of the rest of us would walk through a doorway.

Alma's speech was brief. "I want you all to meet Billy. He'll be with us for a while, so you're not to go treating him as a guest."

Coral took her fingers from her mouth long enough to ask where I would sleep. Alma said there was a mattress in the attic and no one would have to give up his or her room.

Elmer evaluated me once again, coming up with the same low figure. "I look after the young ones," he announced.

"That's our agreement, whenever I'm out," Alma assured him. "This won't change that."

Otis said, "He's old."

James peeled a large patch of dead skin from below his left eye. "Was your daddy a law or a jailbird?"

"You shut up!" snarled Elmer.

Grinning, James closed his hands around his neck, crossed his eyes, and stuck out his tongue as if he were choking. Elmer lunged toward him. Alma stepped between them with the reflexes of a trained referee.

"James, finish fixing that fence. Elmer, go out on the porch and move the rockers so Augusta can finish sweeping."

Augusta said, "What about Coral?"

"It's time for her lesson."

"I ain't through cleaning the fireplace," Elmer protested.

"It will still be dirty when you get back."

The two would-be combatants went their separate ways.

"Otis, your brother said you were upstairs resting. Are you ill?"

"No'm." The boy stared down at the scuffed toes of his shoes. They appeared to be two sizes too large.

"I'm glad to hear that, because the cistern needs filling."

He shuffled out. Watching his back, Alma shook her head slightly.

"James's father was a deputy marshal," she said. "A squatter shot him as he was entering a cabin to get in out of the last big snow up in the Winding Stair Mountains. He thought the shack was abandoned. James suspects everyone who ever spent time in the Fort Smith jail. He will come around to you in his season."

"I think I can defend myself from a boy."

"Don't be too sure. I've been missing a butcher knife for a month." Her eyes were cool. "It isn't you I'm concerned about, although I may be when I know you better. James's father would not want him to walk off Parker's scaffold."

The subject needed changing. I asked her if the house was an orphanage.

"It is a place of reclamation."

Before I could inquire into that, she said that I must be hungry and that I would find a loaf of fresh bread in the pantry and a pot of beans warming upon the stove in the kitchen. Then she told Coral to find her slate.

The girl's lesson, overheard from the kitchen, was arithmetic; but there was no mention of apples or of trains approaching each other from distant stations. Alma was teaching Coral how to make change. During later lessons, the girl would learn how to calculate percentages by figuring out the shipping fees in a harness manufacturer's catalogue.

"This will all go to waste if Coral marries an Astor," said Alma when I inquired about her methods. "In case she does not, she will be able to support herself as a clerk. If Greek and Latin had a practical application in today's world, I would teach her those as well."

The house was indeed a place of reclamation. I never knew whether Alma during the many months she spent nursing the dying Seminole woman had thought consciously of how she would spend her life; but immediately after the old woman was buried, the room in which she had expired was occupied by the six-year-old daughter of a man who had been sent to the Detroit House of Corrections to serve twenty years for attempting to rob the Fort Smith post office. After eight weeks the girl's aunt and uncle arrived from Ohio to claim her, but by then two more children were living in the house. One, the fourteen-year-old son of a horse thief hiding out somewhere in the Nations and his Indian mistress who had died of consumption, ran away. The other was Augusta, whose father had slashed her mother's throat with a bowie knife before plunging it into his own breast in a tiny cabin on the Canadian.

Little Coral was the only resident whose parents were both still living, or believed to be. While traveling by train from

North Carolina to California, the couple had quarreled bitterly over who was responsible for the child's bed-wetting, and achieved peace by leaving the sleeping girl on a bench in the Fort Smith station when they moved on.

"She's forgotten them now," Alma said; "and she hasn't wet the bed since her first week in this house."

The house was not the one where the Seminole woman had died. A year later Alma had pestered and shamed the community into pooling its resources to build a more spacious and comfortable place in which to shelter the disenfranchised. Now she supported herself and the children through donations, gifts of food and clothing, and odd jobs taken on by the boys, who pocketed a percentage of their earnings and turned the rest over to the household account. "I've tried to teach the girls sewing for the same reason, but I never acquired the knack for it myself. My parents were too busy converting the pagan. The old woman mended some of the shirts she washed, but I suspect she never taught me because she was afraid I'd set myself up in competition."

"I have to ask why you choose to sacrifice yourself for the children of strangers," said I. "Most people would not, particularly for the offspring of criminals."

She was silent long enough to convince me she had never before taken time to contemplate her motives. Finally she said, "The law is an imposing machine, especially with men like Judge Parker at the controls. The gears are too big. Things—people fall between the sprockets. Who will reclaim them if I do not?"

I slept in the attic, dined in the kitchen upon meals prepared by the girls (which were barely adequate, cooking being another skill that Alma lacked the ability to pass on), and did whatever work required a man's strength: rehung doors, unstuck windows, dug the well deeper when it went dry, moved furniture so the girls could sweep under it. Someone was always sweeping somewhere. When the cistern was full, the grass trimmed, and the window-panes sparkled, there was always something to be swept. During the hours of daylight, no one sat in the house except to eat or take lessons.

I worked as hard as the lot of them and was never commended until the day Alma rose from the gallery in Judge Parker's courtroom and told him how valuable I had become to her household. Parker listened, his face as unreadable as a cedar Indian's. Then he read out my fate.

"For the crime of transporting and selling liquor in the Indian territory, this court sentences the defendant to serve twelve months at hard labor." He lifted his gavel. "Paroled in recognition of time served." Bang.

As relief flooded into my extremities, he waggled a finger at me. "You, Mr. Gashade, will remain in Miss Barnstable's charge for the seven months remaining in your sentence. If during that time you violate any law, or leave this jurisdiction without the permission of this court, your parole will be revoked and you will serve the full twelve months in Detroit."

In Alma's company I walked out into the blustery air of December a free man by most standards. I did not consider myself such. After two months beneath the same roof, I was in love with my warden.

THIRTY-EIGHT

1876.

The year cries out to be pounded through the skulls of imbecilic schoolchildren as relentlessly as 1066 and 1492; perhaps more so, for those dates introduced but a single Norman invasion and the mere discovery of a New World, while the Year of the American Centennial bulged to bursting with momentous events that have been reenacted, argued over, wagered upon, and fought for the honor of across poker tables and over fences throughout our continent every day for nearly sixty years—and will be, I suspect, for sixty more.

Who but a tenured professor can tell you the age of William the Conqueror when first he set booted foot upon English soil, or Christopher Columbus' response when the cry "Land ho" boomed out above the mutinous mutterings of his verminous crew? Conversely, who does *not* know the significance of Northfield, the reason for Jack McCall's infamy, or the images connected with the oxymoronic name Little Big Horn? None of these appellations was familiar to the public at large in 1875; by 1877 they had become fixtures in the historical mosaic.

Each of them touched me personally, and perhaps uniquely, for I really believe that I alone could claim close acquaintance with the principals involved in all three events. However, 1876 affected me upon a level entirely more visceral. I began it as a criminal, under threat of the pentitentiary, and ended it as the man I am now, older and less certain that there is order to the universe, sadder but at peace.

When I fell in love with Alma is a question of no consequence, even were I able to provide an answer. Irritated at first by her cool manner, representing as it did the assumption that I would carry out all the menial tasks with which she greeted me each morning, I came grudgingly to admire her for her very self-assurance, to marvel at her single-minded determination to bring her charges through one more day, and yet the next when that day was done, and finally to appreciate the beauty of her person, within and without. When, as happened infrequently, she was late rising, or excused herself to her room when dusk was barely upon us, I found myself strangely bereft, precisely as if a heavy curtain had been drawn between myself and the sunlight. Gradually, I began to notice her lithe silhouette beneath the white dress when she passed before a bright window; the delicate line of her throat when she raised her head to see why one of the girls was taking so long beating the dust out of the rugs in the backyard; the way the lamplight wrapped itself around the bones of her face when she turned up the wick in the evening. She was by every standard a handsome woman, and though she scarcely required adornment, would draw every male eye and no small amount of female envy in a Chicago restaurant the moment she crossed the threshold in silks and feathers and with a light application of paint.

At these times I looked at her with the wonder of discovery, pride in our acquaintance, a measure of masculine lust, and, particularly when my bones were weary from a day of exertion and I felt the weight of my twenty-nine years, curiosity over what our children would look like. The first time this occurred to me I realized what I suppose I had known for some weeks without bringing it out for study, that I was in love for the first time in my life, and probably the last.

It was on a dismal day in late January that I told Alma how I felt. Late in the morning one of those freak blizzards that catch Arkansas by surprise once every two or three years had passed through like an enormous flour sifter, flattening fences, heaping roofs ill-prepared to support the weight of a heavy snow, and sweeping eight-foot drifts against the walls of barns and houses and arbitrarily along ridges so slight one scarcely noticed them when stepping over them in mild weather. Night had fallen, the doors and shutters were barred against the gales that came in hinge-rattling gusts first from this direction, then that; the children were asleep beneath heavy counterpanes sewn by the Fort Smith Ladies' League; and the pair of us were sharing a pot of tea at the scarred and much-repaired table in the kitchen before retiring. The tiny flame in the lamp upon the table flared and dimmed with the passage of the razorlike drafts that found their way through flaws in the siding, painting crawling shadows upon Alma's unlined face. She was looking away when I spoke.

"That pane needs putty," she said when I finished. "One good blow from the northeast and it will pop out."

"Alma—"

She stood. "The snow will stop soon. You'll want to rise early to shovel."

"Alma, did you hear what I said?"

"I have no such feelings for you." She gave me the coolness of her gaze for a beat, then turned and left the room.

I did not speak of the matter again that winter.

The snow did not stop soon, but continued to fall for two days, by which time Fort Smith was paralyzed. For the first time since his appointment, Parker suspended testimony in a trial while waiting for witnesses bogged down in their journey from the Nations. Upon the afternoon of the second day, unable to venture outdoors and having exhausted all inside chores for the time being, I picked up the Autoharp out of boredom and laid it across my knees. Rusty as I was and unfamiliar with the idiosyncracies of the instrument, it took me some time to master the scale. By accident I found the opening bar of "Bringing in the Sheaves," and so I continued it, employing the triangular gutta-percha pick that rested atop the mantel. When I looked up, Alma was standing in the kitchen doorway watching me.

"It belonged to my mother," she said. "No one's played it since she died."

"I'm sorry." I got up to return it to its corner.

"I didn't mean that. I tried to sell it, but Fort Smith is a poor market for unnecessary merchandise. It's been the only item in this house that served no purpose. Until now."

Thus another duty was added to my roster. As the snow receded and the first green shoots appeared among the tangles of brown grass, I entertained the household in the evenings. It seemed everyone had a request except Elmer, who sat glum and unresponsive through the recitals until one night I asked him if there wasn't something he wanted to hear that he hadn't heard in a long time.

"No." He stared at his hands folded in his lap.

"I know one!" James's face lighted with evil glee. "'Hing, hang, hung!'"

"You shut up!" Elmer leapt to his feet.

"'Hing, hang, hung,'" James sang, "'see what the hangman done.'"

Elmer lunged. I slung out one arm, grasped him from behind by his overalls, and told him to sit down.

"'Hung, hang, hing, see the bad man swing.'"

I let go. Elmer closed the distance in a stride, fell upon James where he sat on the patched settee, and the two of them tumbled to the floor grappling.

"Otis! Girls! Stop them!" Alma was glaring at me.

Otis grabbed his brother by the shoulders and Augusta and Coral got hold of James and separated them. One of Elmer's shoulder straps was broken. James had a bloody nose.

"Why did you let them fight?" Alma demanded.

I started another tune. "The only way to stop a fight is to let it be fought. This one has been building up too long. If you don't let them use their fists, someday it will be done with guns."

"This evening is over. I want everyone in bed in five minutes."

For the rest of the week Alma did not speak to me except to tell me what work she wanted done. As time went by, however, and there were no more incidents between James the lawman's boy and Elmer the son of a condemned criminal, I sensed a softening in her silence more eloquent than anything she might have found to say. Not that the taunting stopped; but a lighter note of good-natured teasing had appeared in James's offhand comments, and Elmer was learning to banter back. It was armistice of a kind, as much of one as boys—or even most men—were likely to acknowledge.

One evening, quite by accident, I discovered the piece Elmer wanted to hear, a sprightly reel from the Scots Highlands that his late father had been wont to hum when occupied with some labor in the days before life went sour. The boy confessed this to me in private after he had left the room blinking hard the first time I played it. After that I made it a fixture. It never again made him cry. Sometimes he smiled, and I knew he was remembering something specific.

"I didn't know you were a musician," said Alma one night, when the children had been shooed off to bed and I was putting away the instrument.

"I am not, although I thought I was for most of my life." I told her about the colored piano player in Chicago, omitting the nature of the establishment in which he played.

She was not taken in by the subterfuge. "You're probably the only patron who appreciated him. Meanwhile, you have brought a measure of happiness to a boy who has known nothing but misery for two years. Who is the greater musician?"

"Elmer is not a typical audience."

"In every audience there is at least one Elmer. You have a God-given gift. It's a sin to conceal it."

"If it is a sin, it's one of my lesser ones."

"Don't be bitter, Billy. You haven't the right."

"You don't know that. You know nothing about me."

"I love you."

She said it on her way to her room. Her back was turned, and I spent the rest of that night arguing with myself over whether I had heard her correctly. In the morning, she was as she had been every day since we'd met, and there was no asking her about what she had said. I decided to wait until the moment returned.

And if it did not—what?

The columns of the Fort Smith *Herald* fed me news from both coasts and the great space between. In December 1875, Boss Tweed, who had enjoyed the privilege of a daily supervised visit to his Manhattan mansion to soften the rigors of life in the Ludlow Street Jail, had disappeared. Broadsides were issued throughout the United States and Canada offering a reward of ten thousand dollars for his delivery to the authorities. That night I had a nightmare: Tweed—noose-shaped beard, burning eyes, diamond stickpin, and all—appeared upon Alma Barnstable's doorstep, his heavy stick raised to thrash the assailant of Jehosophat Brennan. With dawn the apparition vanished, and I knew him to be cowering in some secluded room eight hundred miles away, awaiting clandestine passage to some latitude from where he could not be extradited. However, the fact that I had been troubled by him at all demonstrated clearly that all my old ghosts were with me yet.

Six months later, nearing what appeared to be a moderate-size village of renegade Indians among the swells of the Little Big Horn Valley in Montana Territory, Lieutenant Colonel George Armstrong Custer divided his Seventh Cavalry into three units to surround the lodges. Charging what he believed to be the end of the camp, he found instead that he was attacking the center of a community of some fifteen thousand Sioux, Cheyenne, and Arapaho, which bent in the middle to encompass his two hundred cavalrymen and swept them from the face of the earth. As details attending the death of one of America's anointed heroes filtered eastward, I learned that upon this occasion the Boy General had left the regimental band behind at Fort Abraham Lincoln; still, as from beyond a distant hill, I heard the whirl and crash of the "Garry-Owen," and saw the flicker of interest in the gray-blue eyes of the young commander the first time he heard it, surrounded by his soporific greyhounds at Fort Riley.

Had his hemorrhoids troubled him to the end?

In August, while James Butler Hickok was playing poker in a saloon in Deadwood, Dakota Territory, a cross-eyed saloon swamp named Jack McCall crept up behind him and punched a pistol ball through that head of splendid curls. According to later accounts, the hand held by Wild Bill contained a pair of aces and a pair of eights. I wondered if at the moment of death he had been cheating.

Then came September, and Northfield, Minnesota.

Frank and Jesse James, accompanied by the three Younger brothers and sometime companions Bill Chadwell, Clell Miller, and Charlie Pitts, raided a bank in that prosperous farming center and stirred up a hornets' nest. When the shooting was over, Miller and Chadwell were dead and the wounded Youngers were in jail. The Jameses alone managed to slip through the various posses who winnowed the countryside and were believed to be in hiding somewhere in Missouri, or Texas, or California. A rumor circulated, gaining momentum as time passed and no further robberies occurred bearing the distinctive James stamp, that Jesse was dead.

I doubted the rumor. He had been wounded several times in the war, twice badly enough to be despaired of by his doctors, and he had survived a dozen years of national notoriety without spending so much as a day behind bars. It was not in Jesse's cards to pass out of existence quietly. As for Frank, it was the central truth of his nature that no one with whom he traveled would come to harm so long as he was able to place himself between it and his companion. Separate from him, one's chances were no more than equal; with him, they automatically improved fifty percent. If Jesse was dead, so was Frank, and Frank James dead was a situation ludicrous to contemplate. It would take more than the Pinkertons and the authorities of four states to extinguish that broad guerrilla grin.

I devoured each fresh journalistic speculation in the only waking hour I had to myself, by the lamp in the kitchen after the rest of the household had retired. One night toward the end of my court-enforced stay, I was climbing the stairs to my attic cell, my head filling with the latest report that Jesse was in Colorado posing as a mining engineer, when I heard the unmistakable sounds of sobbing. The house was full of children who had lost their parents, and it was nothing unusual in that hour when one is most alone to overhear an expression of grief. This was no child crying, however. The sounds were coming from Alma's room.

THIRTY-NINE

Her bedroom, I was surprised to note when she opened the door at my knock, was the largest in the house, although scarcely better furnished than any of the others. There was a fine old four-poster bed with a feather mattress, but the washstand needed a new finish and age cracks checked the basin. Framed miniature portraits of a woman in a high-necked blouse and a man with a full beard encircling his jaw—her parents, I assumed—hung upon the wall opposite the bed, and a lamp and Bible and the schoolbooks Alma used to educate the children stood upon an unremarkable chest of drawers. There was no other furniture, not even a chair. The message conveyed was that the room served no other purpose than a place to sleep.

One look at Alma confirmed that she had not been sleeping. Dark thumbprints showed beneath her eyes and she appeared gaunt, almost transparent, with the lamplight seeming to shine through her from behind. She had thrown on a white cotton dressing gown over her muslin nightdress and thrust her tiny feet into a pair of satin slippers that were anything but new, and probably acquired secondhand. Her eyes and nose were red.

"I wondered if you were all right," I said.

"I need to sleep. So do you." She started to close the door.

"Are you ill?"

The door stopped eight inches from the jamb. Her eyes were luminous in the gap. "Yes."

I knew then: her periods of exhaustion, her sometimes erratic hours. A faint medicinal odor reached my nostrils from the depths of her bedroom. "Should I get a doctor?"

"No. I have seen enough of doctors to last me"—she laughed shortly—"the rest of my life."

The floor seemed to open beneath my feet. I pushed at the

door. She let go, and as if she had lost her balance she fell against me. My arms closed around her. A great shudder racked her body. When at length she pulled away, her features were composed. Her will was iron from first to last.

"I have a disease of the blood." Her tone was the one she used to explain a new chore to one of the children. "None of the doctors I've seen know much about it. They agree on one thing."

"It's that bad?"

"Yes."

"There are specialists in Chicago—" I began.

"Not in this."

A moth flung itself against the window. "How long?"

"That's one of the things they didn't agree on. According to the least hopeful, I am already in the churchyard." She placed a hand upon my arm for support. "I need to lie down."

I closed the door behind me and helped her to the bed. She lay on her back beneath the covers, staring up at the canopy. "I sent away for medical journals. Half the articles claim it's caused by a poisonous miasma. The other half say it grows from inside, like a carbuncle. They will have to come to some sort of conclusion before they can begin to treat it. Someone who isn't born yet may benefit."

Suddenly I was filled with rage. "You're twenty-two years old!"

"I turned twenty-three last month. What is that? My mother and father were thirty and thirty-five."

"People live to be eighty. Useless people. Wicked people."

"Good people too. It's not a question of arithmetic."

"It's not fair!" Her calm acceptance drove me to fury.

"I said the same thing when they told me. It is fairer than you think. I might have been run over by a wagon, and then where would the children be? This way I have had time to make the necessary arrangements. Mrs. Parker and the Fort Smith Ladies' League will take over the operation of this house when I am gone."

"Do the children know?"

"Yes."

That surprised me. "Even Coral?"

"I think you'll agree they all have a closer acquaintance with death than most children their age."

"When were you planning to tell me?"

"I wasn't."

I let my next question pass unspoken.

"You're leaving at the end of this month. Judge Parker himself has said you will be free to go then. You are not a child in need of care and guidance. What would have been the point?"

"Love. We love each other."

"I don't love you."

"You said you did. Did you think I didn't hear?"

"Go away, Billy. Leave this house tonight. Go away from Fort Smith. Judge Parker won't send anyone after you for the sake of a few days. Not to bring back a simple rumrunner."

"Who will take care of you if I go?"

"The same person who has taken care of me since the old woman got sick. Her disease required a good deal more attention than mine. Augusta is the same age I was then. She will see to my needs when I can no longer leave this bed."

"You're a fool."

She smiled up at the canopy. She did not smile often. When she did she lit the corners of the room untouched by the lamp.

"Every beast recognizes its own kind," she said. "What were you planning to do when peddling whiskey lost its romance? Would you hold up banks and trains like your heroes Frank and Jesse?"

I was caught off-guard. "What do you know about Frank and Jesse?"

"I am not blind. I've seen how you sit up straight whenever you come upon a reference to them in the newspaper. Leave it there, Billy. Life on the scout is not for you."

I was standing over her. She was as pale as the pillow upon

which her head rested. "You don't know as much about people as you think you do, Alma Barnstable. I have been on the scout since I was Elmer's age."

I told her my story then, all of it. She was silent for a time after I finished.

"We're both fools. You are the greater one. Go home, Billy. Talk to your father."

"What shall I say? 'Good day, Judge. I have whored and drunk whiskey and run with bad men and broken the law of the land. Is my old room ready?' "

She looked away. "I'm sorry."

"Please don't be."

"I'm not sorry for you." She looked back at me. "I'm sorry for your father. He can't be much of a judge. Even Parker, who hangs men five and six at a time, does not expect perfection. To lack compassion is a serious failure in a jurist."

"My father is a great man."

"Great men are not always good men."

"He is the best man I've ever known. If I were as good I'd never have left New York. If I were half as good I would not hesitate to return."

"I need to sleep now." She closed her eyes. In a moment the even rise and fall of the counterpane told me the conversation was indeed ended.

The next day she was up before me, and the routine was as always. It was as if the subject of our discussion had never arisen. The children sensed a difference, however. Not so much as a word was spoken of the matter, but whenever Elmer's gaze met mine I felt an arc of understanding, and when I asked Augusta to fetch water from the well so I could wash the window in Alma's room, her reply that she would do it right away carried a tone I had not heard before. I had never before sensed such a matter-of-factness concerning death in the company of people so young, and hope never to sense it again. They were incredibly old, these children, most of whom had not been born when first I laid eyes upon a poor corpse dangling by its neck from a rope above a street in Manhattan; in their eyes and upon their faces could be read the tragic wisdom of centuries.

Alma began to fail at the same time as the leaves upon the trees that grew along the Arkansas. The mornings when she was unable to descend the stairs grew together. The time between these late descents and her early retirements narrowed, then disappeared entirely. Two days, three days, a full week she spent in her room, where Augusta brought her meals and carried out her chamber pot. A week became two. The doctor, a tall, stoop-shouldered fifty-year-old who had signed many a certificate of death so that Judge Parker's condemned could be cut down and carted away, came and went. No one else saw her but the daughter of parricide and suicide, who merely shook her head when I asked if I could visit. Yet the routine of the household went on. Augusta never came downstairs without bearing instructions for each member. Alma seemed determined to remain in charge, if in fact it was not just habit. Either way it was unnecessary. Her influence was so much a part of the residents' lives, and every task had been carried out so many times before, that the work would have proceeded on schedule if she never said a word.

Then came the day when each of the children was summoned, one by one, to climb the stairs. Each visit consumed no more than five minutes, and then a congested and contorted face would reappear upon the ground floor and another name would be called.

Coral was the last child to emerge from her room. The muscles of her face were working, but she did not cry, nor did she speak. Her eyes sought mine. I nodded and ascended the stairs.

"Please open the curtains."

The room was indeed dark, and reminded me of Drucilla Patakos and her eternal twilight. When I spread the curtains, coppery autumn light spilled in.

"That's much better. The doctor closed them, I can't think why. I will have my fill of darkness soon enough."

I was surprised to see that she was sitting up slightly, a pillow wedged behind her back for support. She wore the white cotton dressing gown. Her pallor now was marblelike. The dark smudges were gone from beneath her eyes, which had acquired a wonderful luminescence. She was beautiful, achingly so. My throat closed. I could not have spoken even if I could think of something to say.

"Your sentence was over last month," she said. "Did you forget?"

I shook my head.

She looked beyond me, toward the window. "Winter will be here soon. I hope it's milder than the last one."

"I'll help the children through it," I managed to say.

"That's exactly what I don't want. It's why I asked you up here."

She was looking at me now. I waited.

"The Ladies' League will find it difficult enough teaching the children to recognize their authority without another adult around to confuse them. Every time the children are told to do something they'll look at you for confirmation."

"You're asking me to leave."

"It's only a matter of time before Mrs. Parker or someone else tells you to leave. My way is more polite, but my reasons are the same. You will be doing the children a favor. Their loyalties have been jostled around enough." She closed her eyes. The counterpane rose and fell. Plainly the effort of speaking was claiming all her strength. "Promise me you'll go."

"I promise." I waited again, but she did not speak. "Is that all you wanted to see me about?"

"Of course not." Her eyes opened. "I need you to promise something else. I think you know what it is."

"My father."

"No, that's something you must decide to do for yourself. If I force you, you'll resent it, and that will poison the reunion."

"My music."

She smiled faintly. This time she failed to light the room's corners. "How possessive you are. Music belongs to everyone. I'm referring to your gift. I want you to use it. The Autoharp is yours."

I hesitated.

"Don't thank me," she said. "You know how I feel about having unnecessary things around. Once you're gone it will collect nothing but dust."

"It's a difficult instrument to travel with."

"You won't have to carry it far. Mr. Cooper at the general merchandise thinks he has a customer for it. He has a guitar someone gave him to settle a credit bill. I spoke with him last month. He will accept the Autoharp in trade for the guitar."

After a moment I smiled. "It seems I have no choice."

"The last choice you made did not serve you well." She glanced away then; her eyes had started to fill. "I'm so frightened, Billy."

I sank down on my knees beside the bed, embracing her for the second and last time.

V

Rebel's Requiem

FORTY

I played the Autoharp once more only, leading the mourners at Alma Barnstable's graveside in the Fort Smith Cemetery in "Bringing in the Sheaves." The turnout was large, including the mayor, who had celebrated the life of the deceased in full, rounded phrases at the funeral in the Methodist church; the redoubtable members of the Ladies' League, black-cloaked and -hatted against the first icy breath of winter; and Isaac Parker, who stood a little apart from his wife wearing a caped overcoat and holding his soft hat before him in both hands. I could not help thinking that a donation of a dollar from each of those present would have elevated the standard of living of all the members of Alma's household; but respect costs nothing in dollars and is always in ample supply for the dead.

The children wept quietly and undemonstrably, in contrast to a number of women in the group whom I had never seen within five hundred yards of Alma's house. Upon her death it had suddenly become the fashion to claim intimacy with her. A column in that day's *Herald* had celebrated "the good Christianity of Fort Smith's late lamented citizen." There was talk of erecting a statue before the courthouse, dedicated to her memory and bearing the legend "The Angel of Fort Smith" chiseled into the base. I never found out if anything came of it.

Eustace Cooper, behind the counter at the general merchandise, was an honest man. For the Autoharp he traded a guitar that had seen better days and made up the difference in cash, with which I purchased a ticket on the next train west. I told the children good-bye and rolled out at nightfall.

My heart was a stone, its weight pulling me farther into the interior of the continent, whose great spaces separated the fleeing from the sadnesses and mistakes of the past. I seldom spent more than a week in one place. Often I was gone the next morning without having unpacked my threadbare valise. I played in saloons whose names I never bothered to learn. I was as a man on the run.

Weeks, months, seasons tumbled into the gap between my heels and the last town: winter in Fort Worth, where the gaunt, whiskey-flushed faces of cowboys beseeched me silently for a tune that would play in their heads when the blizzards found them riding the fenceline; spring in Dodge City, where I saw a buffalo hider disembowel a cowboy in the Lone Star Dance Hall during a dispute involving their respective occupations. The proprietor, a self-styled dandy in a figured vest with tobacco spittle glittering on one lapel, continued dealing faro without making a move toward the shotgun leaning in the corner at his elbow. After thrashing around for a while in bloody sawdust, the injured cowboy was removed by his friends to a doctor's care, whereupon the fellow at the faro table directed his bartender to mop up the mess. (The proprietor's name was Masterson. I understood he was a sometime peace officer, celebrated for the wisdom of his reticence.) Summer in Denver, and a short stint at the piano on the ground floor of the Rocky Mountain Hospitality House, operated by a cheroot-chewing harridan who called herself Colorado Jo, but owned by the county sheriff, three hundred pounds of tax-supported corruption with a bad case of gout and a habit of laying harlots open to the bone with a horsewhip when he suspected them of pocketing the house receipts. A brick supported one corner of the piano where the leg had been shot from under it by a drunken miner.

A great gift, music. It was forever placing me in high company.

October found me in Nebraska. There I stopped at Fort

Robinson after revisiting a portion of my history on the plains. Those long silken grasses grew now through the bleached rib cages and empty eye sockets of a million buffalo, scattered across the prairie like pieces of broken crockery. The great herds were thinning out at a rate that seemed marvelous; already the concept of a train being forced to wait a day for a slow-moving river of humps and horns to cross the tracks recounted like a tall tale told by toothless old men.

The post trader, a sallow-faced cadaver whose tuft of gray chin fuzz reminded me of cheese mold, demanded twenty-five percent of my gratuities in return for his consent to let me occupy a stool in the corner of his establishment. I agreed with a sigh. The congressional decision to replace the old sutler's system with post traderships overseen by the local fort commanders had ushered in a new era of greed. "Liquor's extra," he added, almost as an afterthought.

"I don't drink." It was not a falsehood. I had not tasted liquor since my arrest in the Indian Nations.

He spat, though he wasn't chewing. "Penny a cup for coffee."

Raising my eyes in exasperation, I noticed a familiar-looking object lying atop a high shelf behind the counter. "Is that banjo for sale?"

He turned to look up at it, as if surprised that such an object could be in his possession. He turned back with an expression of disgust.

"That was in some truck General Crook brung in with a Sioux buck last month. Buck got hisself bayoneted trying to escape. The army took his guns."

I felt a tingle. "May I see it?"

"It's all junked up."

"I'd like to look at it anyway."

He scratched his head, delaying. His natural instinct to make money was at odds with his unwillingness to climb the ladder that leaned against the shelves. Finally he expelled a great lungful of stagnant air and dragged it over.

When he alighted, I resisted the urge to snatch the instrument from his hands. It was painted all over with spiritual symbols in primary colors, the catgut strings had been replaced with sinew, and the parchment had been torn and then patched with a square of animal membrane and some kind of native glue. However, the changes could not disguise an object I had carried for years. Instantly I was transported to a ridge three days' ride east of Julesburg, where the gift of a banjo had made the difference between safe passage for myself and my partners and our scalps hanging from a pole in a Sioux lodge. I saw again the interest in a pair of smoke-colored native eyes when callused fingers brushed its strings.

"Five dollars gold," said the trader.

"All I have is silver."

This put him out as much as the notion of having to scale the ladder. "I should of stood in Cincinnati," he whined. "I can't get ahead out here. This here's genuine injun workmanship."

"A moment ago you said it was all junked up."

"You want it or not?"

I gave him five silver dollars. In Chicago, banjos were selling fresh from the factory for two apiece, but I'd have paid fifty for that one and considered it a bargain. I strummed it once. Although it needed tuning, I was surprised by the mellow tone the crude strings offered. I thought of a question.

"What was the Indian's name?"

"Crazy Horse."

I didn't hang around Fort Robinson long. The Department of the Army was engaged in a full-scale campaign to round up the Plains Indians. There would be no more nonsense about sovereign nations or noble savages or ignorant children in need of spiritual guidance from the Great Father in Washington; it was hem them in, shoot their horses, burn their lodges, imprison or hang those who could definitely be iden-

tified as participants in the Custer massacre, and pen the rest
up on government reservations. The spectacle of those arrogant bands reduced by starvation and bombardment to crawl
to the fort under military escort, weaponless, dragging all
their earthly possessions behind them upon travois, was too
painful for one who had seen them in their full-blown pride.
I thought of that long-ago party of horsemen, balancing a
worn old banjo and a small stack of hides upon the one hand
and the lives of a handful of interlopers upon the other, and
deciding for whatever reason to let them go on living. It wasn't
because of the offer I had made; they could have slain us and
taken everything, including our horses and weapons. Their
kind had done as much or worse upon other occasions, as had
ours. I liked to think there was a spark of humanity in their
leader that made him say that for this day at least, the killing
would stop. Whether he was indeed Crazy Horse, the great
Sioux general who had sent Custer to his grave while Sitting
Bull claimed the credit, or (as seemed more likely) he was
just some anonymous minor chieftain whose musical prize
had made its way from one red hand to another until it wound
up in the leader's possession, was immaterial. A spirit that
was capable of mercy in a savage season was too great to see
laid low by a column of illiterate troopers.

In truth, the man who gave him that instrument would not
have felt this way. Still congratulating himself upon his savvy
horse trading ("Think of it; three thousand in hides for a
broken-down banjo. Stupid heathens!"), he would have stayed
to see the show. I was not that man, merely a distant relation.
He had never lain in the dank of Judge Parker's dungeon, listening to the *squee-thump* of the gallows trap dumping open
under the feet of six of his fellow transgressors, nor held the
head of a nearly grown boy to his chest in the night when the
boy awoke from a frightening dream, calling for his executed
father. He had not known himself for a coward, afraid to present his own father with the image of the man he had allowed
himself to become. Certainly he had never loved, nor been

forced to stand by watching while the woman he loved faded from this life. I was a more solemn man, but an improved one. Like my banjo I wore indelibly the markings of my passage; the music I made was more mellow.

The next year I was in New Mexico Territory, playing and singing in a general store in Lincoln owned by a lawyer named McSween. The lawyer's partner, an expatriate British rancher by the name of Tunstall, had been slain in a dispute with his rural neighbors. Tension was thick in the store whenever employees of rival cattle companies were present. Upon these occasions I selected music of a neutral nature, evoking pastoral memories of times a century removed from the current troubles, of countries a hemisphere away. They had their effect upon my listeners, or seemed to. No incidents took place upon the premises when I was there to witness them.

Once indeed, John Chisum, an oak-hewn old rancher, erect as a fence rail tamped squarely into the center of the affray, snapped a nod of approval in my direction when he paused at the counter to order nails by the keg and ammunition by the crate. He had with him a willowy youth scarcely over five feet tall, buck-toothed and talkative, attired in a plug hat creased upon one side of the crown and a heavy ribbed sweater tugged down over his waist in an unsuccessful attempt to conceal the pistol he carried upon his right hip.

This fellow took a liking to my music and came around often after that, sometimes upon a ranch errand, but usually just to pull up a stool and listen. His name was William— Billy to his friends, who, in order to avoid having both of us turn our heads when only one of us was hailed, took to calling him the Kid. I was fond of the young man, despite his larcenous streak; more than once I saw him slip some unimportant item from the counter where it was displayed into his sweater pocket when he imagined no one was looking. It seemed a minor failing on the part of one so good-humored and charming. I confess I doubted the speaker when the story reached me, a month after I made his acquaintance, that the

Kid and his cronies had just gunned down the county sheriff and one of his deputies in the street.

I left soon after. The Lincoln County War was then in full cry, I had seen and heard enough of battle to last me all my days, and the gratuities were not likely to continue flowing as long as customers were afraid of being chopped to pieces by bullets the moment they showed themselves out-of-doors. I heard later McSween was killed in a siege upon his home from which the Kid shot his way out. This was the beginning of his notoriety, which even so would not spread much beyond New Mexico for another dozen years, long after he was in the ground.

In the fall of 1879 I took my first vacation ever, hiring a horse and trap in Socorro and heading south into old Mexico, where I spent two weeks drinking lemonade in the shade of an adobe cantina in a place called Casa Negrita and reading month-old newspapers from the States. Jesse James was not dead, it appeared; he and Frank had been positively identified among the men who held up a train in Glendale, Missouri, in October, pistol-whipped a guard, and vanished into the hills with six thousand in cash and securities. Pinkerton Captain Jack Fabian discounted earlier inflated estimates of the amount and reported that the reward for information leading to the capture of Frank and Jesse had gone up to five thousand dollars apiece, with a matching sum offered for the conviction of each.

I worked my way north to Tucson the next year, then followed the circuit down to Tombstone. Playing guitar there in the orchestra pit of the Birdcage Theater, I learned Billy the Kid had been killed by a man named Garrett, but by then I was packing once again, and too preoccupied with where I should go, to give him anything more than a passing reflection. So many had died since making my acquaintance that if I dwelt upon the subject I might have condemned myself for a Jonah: Jim Bridger, infirmity and old age; Wild Bill Hickok, an assassin's bullet; Quantrill and Bloody Bill Anderson, fire from ambush; John Thrailkill, a long drop at the end of a short rope; and now Billy, the youngest of all. Boss Tweed, the ogre of my exile, was gone, dead of his own enormous appetites in a guarded bed following his recapture in Spain. The news left me feeling strangely detached, as if my old music tutor, bane of my childhood, had succumbed, far too late to bring me any joy.

Tombstone, rich in silver as it was, had become too various for me. One of my strings had broken at a crucial point, causing Eddy Foy to miss a step while dancing onstage, which prompted a sardonic comment from a drunken cowboy in the audience. A sometime dentist and full-time gambler named Holliday, also drunk and watching from a box, told him in a loud voice to shut up. One of the cowboy's friends produced a pistol and fired it toward the box. The dentist drew his own weapon, but before he could return fire another man in the box grasped his arm and escorted him out. I believe the man was one of four brothers, gamblers who sometimes kept the peace, but whether it was James or Virgil or Wyatt or Morgan I cannot now say; all those Earps looked alike.

I rode the next day's stage back to Tucson, and there caught the first train heading east. It happened to be bound for Missouri.

FORTY-ONE

St. Joseph was as prosperous a city as existed in the beleaguered State of Missouri. Built of brick and frame upon orderly streets facing the great river, surrounded upon three sides by a green-and-yellow checkerboard of dairy fodder and wheat, it sheltered some forty thousand souls, who visited its shops and gathered at the quay in neckties and bright bonnets to see what and whom the great stacked steamboats brought down from Omaha and up from Joplin. Its room rates were too steep for a poor itinerant musician, and so I commuted by means of an aging mare I had bought in Platte City between the public house where I performed and my room upon the second floor of a farmhouse in what was called the Crackerneck section of Clay County, less than an hour's ride from the James-Samuel farm of misty memory.

Passing the cutoff that led past the farm, I thought invariably of that strong woman, rearing her sons and caring for a husband broken by his brush with death, steeped in her hatred of the Union but maintaining her good humor throughout. She would be elderly now, doing her chores one-handed, embittered further by the loss of an arm and her youngest son to a Pinkerton bomb. I knew not if she would welcome me now, with my Northern origins still so plain upon my countenance and in my manner; but it was more than this uncertainty that prevented me from taking that side of the fork. Going back was not in my nature.

The public house—or so I continue to call it, for its quiet, shaded atmosphere of male companionship put me more in mind of what I had read about the taverns of London than the smoky, noisy saloons of my past experience—was a place of hanging oil lamps and framed steelpoint engravings upon the walls of prizefighters in tights, of captain's chairs around dark oak tables with initials carved into their tops, and billiards in the back room. It was cool and pleasant, smelling of spilled beer and cigars and the gamey musk of the mounted elk's head moldering above the stone fireplace. There were times when even the gentlest of music was an intrusion. At these times I filled my coffee cup from the pot simmering on the heating stove behind the bar and took it to a corner table to sip and reflect. I think it was the very Englishness of the place that drew a large young man into it in the damp spring of 1882, wearing a flamboyant coat trimmed in purple velvet and his hair to his shoulders. Inside the door he struck a pose with one hand upon his ample hip, making eye contact with each patron who raised his head to stare at the newcomer. Spying me sitting with my coffee, he strode over, swinging his stick with the confidence of a man approaching the very fellow he had come there to see.

"I beg your pardon, old sport, but would you mind terribly if I joined you?"

"There are empty tables," said I, for I had been thinking of Alma and did not much care for company. His Irish accent scarcely endeared him to me. It reminded me of Jehosophat Brennan.

"Empty heads as well, I fear. I find both depressing. You hold it in your power, sir, to spare me a fate worse than indifferent tailoring. Yours is the only cultivated face upon the premises. If I hear the words 'Howdy, stranger, take a load off and hunker down hyar' one more time, I shall scream."

I sat back, mildly interested. His face was heavy and his lips were thick, but he seemed to consider himself uncommonly handsome, a difficult combination that required years of effort. He might be diverting, at that. I inclined my head toward the chair opposite. He scraped it out and threw himself into it as if he had been on foot for a week. "I am in your debt, sir. May I buy you a whiskey?"

"Coffee's my drink."

"My compliments upon your abstemiousness. As for me, I can resist everything except temptation. Innkeeper!" He thumped his stick. "A fresh pot for my friend, and a bottle of bourbon for myself."

The bartender, a horse-faced crank named Cy who suffered from shingles, thumped down a bottle and a glass and topped off my cup from the evil-looking pot. The Irishman paid him and he hobbled away upon spraddled legs.

My benefactor lifted his glass. "To your president, whoever he may be at present."

"To your queen." I drank from my cup.

He emptied the glass in a long draught, then refilled it. "Ah, yes, the queen. Had she given me the chance, I'd have voted for her." His lively eyes alighted upon my guitar and banjo leaning in the corner. "Are you a musician?"

"For want of a more precise title."

"A difficult art. If one plays good music, people don't listen, and if one plays bad music, people don't talk." He held out a large and meaty hand, beautifully manicured. "My name is Oscar Wilde."

"I know." I shook it. "Billy Gashade."

"Am I so famous, then?" He appeared delighted.

"I read in a broadside that you were lecturing in Leavenworth. The moment you walked in I said to myself, 'This must be Wilde.' No other man in this part of the country would have the nerve to wear that coat in public."

His laugh was loud and booming, a surprise in view of his reputation. I'd expected a titter. Abruptly he stopped, studying me over his drink. "I sense you also are not from this part of the country."

"I was born and raised in New York."

"New York, yes. I approve of the place. The hotels are above reproach and the morals are beneath contempt. Also my lecture there was a sellout."

"If I thought I would be received as warmly, I would return," said I.

"How long have you been away?"

"Nineteen years."

"All the more reason to go back. All your enemies are likely dead. I have always said that a man cannot be too careful in the choice of his enemies."

"It is not my enemies I fear."

"Your friends, then. That I cannot help you with, having none myself."

"I am speaking of my parents."

"I regret that I can offer you no sympathy. To lose one parent may be regarded as a misfortune. To lose both seems like carelessness." He drained his glass again. Again he refilled it. "Forgive me. I am not a facetious man by nature, merely by experience. I would hear your story."

It was my turn to study him. He had a guileless look, for all his pretension. I suspected the show of arrogance concealed a fragile spirit.

"Have I your word you will not use it in your fiction?"

"Certainly not! What earthly good is a conversation off the record when material is so hard to come by?"

We shared our secrets then, Oscar Fingal O'Flahertie Wills Wilde and I; or as many as anyone does with a stranger, which amounts to more than he will confide to a companion of longstanding. Nothing important, of course—our respective darkest demons remained securely locked in their cages—but enough that we came away with a better understanding of each other than I warrant we had of ourselves. Years later, in his time of trouble, when his very name was spoken in vile whispers like that of some loathsome disease, I thought of that conversation, and hoped he remembered it and found in it some measure of the solace I felt at the time. It is the supreme tragedy of the human condition that we are so quick to crush the beauty from the butterflies in our midst.

While we were talking, the room had begun to fill. Dusk was upon us. Cy, waddling beneath the burden of his painful affliction, lit more lamps and served the newcomers from a tray bristling with glasses and bottles. Beyond Wilde's shoulder I observed a pair of men in business suits and bowlers enter and sit down at a table in the opposite corner. The older of the two wore a chestnut-colored beard neatly trimmed after the fashion of physicians, and when he removed his hat and placed it on the table I saw that his hair was receding at the temples. He blinked rapidly while giving his order to the bartender, as if to accustom his eyes to the artificial light.

I drank the last of the coffee. Wilde was speaking; I waited for him to pause. "Would you excuse me for a moment? Someone just came in whom I haven't seen in years."

"Go to him, by all means. The only way to get rid of a temptation is to yield to it."

As I approached, the bearded man saw me and leaned back in his chair. His right hand rested upon a folded copy of the *St. Joseph Gazette*, or rather inside it. The click of the hammer was smothered by the din of voices that filled the room. Alerted, his companion twisted to face me, groping inside the side pocket of his coat. He was a pale young man, dark-haired, with shifting eyes and the kind of schoolboyish good looks that certain women find difficult to resist, even as their purses are being rifled.

I stopped, holding my hands out from my sides. "This is no way for old friends to greet each other." I forced a smile.

The bearded man blinked. "Billy?"

"Have I changed so much?"

"Is this a wrong fellow?" The younger man possessed one of the less fortunate regional accents, thin and twangy. His eyes remained upon me.

"Have a seat, Billy. I hardly ever see any of the old outfit these days."

I borrowed a vacant chair from a nearby table and sat. The strangeness of the situation was like a fourth member of the party. Here he was, the most wanted man in America, sought by the authorities from Boston to the Barbary Coast, calmly conversing in a place of public commerce less than a day's ride from the farm where he was born. The years of gun battles and midnight rides, of suspicion and months spent in hiding, showed in the lines of his face and the threads of silver at his pink temples; at thirty-five we were the same age, but he could have been mistaken for a man in his forties. For all that he looked to be in good condition, flat-bellied and sinuous in his movements.

"Is it still Tom Howard?" I asked Jesse.

"It is. The name has brought me luck and I see no reason to change."

"How is Frank?"

"I don't see much of Buck these days. He is playing farmer and reading Shakespeare."

"You left Abilene in such a hurry we never got to say good-bye."

"The place was becoming various. We were supposed to be on vacation." He leaned forward then, removing his hand from the newspaper. "Billy, this here is Bob. Bob Ford, Billy Gashade."

To my surprise, a broad grin lit the young man's face and he offered me a slender hand. "Did you and Jesse ride together in the war?"

"We rode in the same direction at the same time," I said. "However, I was no guerrilla."

"Those must've been some times. I wish I was old enough to run with Bloody Bill."

Cy appeared then, with beers for Jesse and Ford, and we stopped talking. Jesse raised his eyebrows in my direction, but I shook my head. He paid for the beers. When we were alone: "You're working in Saint Joe?"

"Now and again. I take it you live here."

"I got me a little place on Woodland. You ought to stop by. Zee gets restless with just me and the children to talk to. Zee, that's my wife. I'm a family man these days."

I congratulated him. I felt uneasy. Here was an affable Jesse I had never seen. Except for brief moments when I was playing one of the tunes he remembered from his mother's song sheets, I had never known him to lay down his guard so completely. It occurred to me that he was growing weary. A hand can bear the weight of a cocked pistol only so long before it begins to weaken.

"You know Buck's married too," he said. "Nice girl."

"I hear that's the best kind."

Now his forehead wrinkled. "I reckon you're still un-hitched or you wouldn't still be on the move. You ought to find someone."

"I did."

"Well, hooray!"

"Then I lost her."

"I'm sorry. Truly I am. There are other women."

I shook my head, smiling. "I never thought I'd live to see the day I'd be getting advice to settle down from Jesse James."

Bob Ford shushed me, but no one could overhear us in that buzzing room.

Jesse scowled down at the newspaper in his lap. "I've been at this twenty years almost. I can't hardly remember why I started, except every time I go to visit Ma she reminds me. I think if I was to retire she'd take my place. She always did have more rebel in her than Buck and I put together." He sipped his beer. "You get tired. You get the awfullest kind of tired."

He was staring at the opposite wall, or rather through it. I thought I knew at what. "I read about that business in North-field," I said.

"That was Cole's idea from the start. 'Them scandihoov-ian farmers got more money than they can carry in two buck-ets,' he said. 'We ought to ride on up there and give 'em a hand.' Every gun in that town was on us when we come out of the bank. They chopped Chadwell and Clell Miller clean to pieces. The Youngers too, only they survived. Not that they'd want to, rotting in a Minnesota pen for life." He moved his shoulders. "Never stick up a place you don't know. You can tell 'em Jesse said so."

"They'll never get you, Jesse." Bob Ford was beaming.

"They wouldn't have much if they did. Not no ten-foot-tall desperado with Colts growing out of both fists like they expect."

The company was depressing me: an aging bandit afraid of his shadow, and his callow companion, fairly slobbering for a pat on the head from his god. I pushed back my chair.

"Good luck to you, Mr. Howard. Give my regards to your brother."

"I don't see much of Buck these days. You know he's mar-ried now."

I looked at him closely, suspecting some of that Missouri humor that so often escaped a listener from the East. There was no light in his eyes. In that moment he reminded me of no one so much as his stepfather, defeated so many years before by forces he didn't understand. I wanted to warn him, *Go to Frank; there is safety.* Instead I said nothing.

Oscar Wilde had made serious inroads upon the bourbon in his bottle when I rejoined him. However, his eyes were clear and his voice steady.

"Doubtless an old friend. They insist upon coming back despite our best efforts, like the detachable collar."

"Just someone I'd heard was dead," I said.

And I had heard right.

Our conversation wandered. After ten or fifteen minutes, Jesse James and Bob Ford got up from their table and left. As they passed a man seated near the door, Ford glanced his way. Immediately the man shifted positions and spread his copy of the *Kansas City Times* in front of his face.

That face troubled me. If it was him, he had put on considerable weight, becoming absolutely stout, and grown a crepey beard. However, Jesse James and Captain Jack Fabian in the same room at the same time was too great a coincidence to accept.

The next day I was playing "Londonderry Air" for an Irish laborer when someone burst through the door with news. Jesse James dead . . . right here in St. Joe . . . his own parlor . . . back of the head . . . Bob Ford.

I had never composed a song. That night, lying against the pillows in my Clay County bed with my guitar across my lap, I began picking out the bars of a standard ballad, the words dropping into place as I sang them, as if from a great height:

> *Jesse James was a lad*
> *who killed many a man.*
> *He robbed the Glendale train . . .*

FORTY-TWO

New York had changed, perhaps as much as I.

I was prepared for physical growth. The seven-story city I remembered had stretched upward and northward, bumping the sky with great Gothic spires and creeping up past the forties and fifties, encompassing the wilderness that had become Central Park, with no sign that it would quit before the tip of the island forced it to do so. All this I had heard about or suspected, but nothing I had read or imagined could embrace the *noise* of the place as it charged into the last two decades of the nineteenth century. The rustling of the crowds upon the sidewalks, the jangling trolleys, the brisk trotting of horses pulling hansoms and four-wheelers, the braying whistle of the elevated train as it roared overhead, releasing a gusher of sparks and cinders to the pavement— the very earth vibrated beneath the din. My head was splitting long before I alighted in front of the familiar old brownstone on Fifth Avenue and paid the driver his exorbitant ransom.

The building appeared unchanged, although it seemed to have grown smaller after all those blocks of skyscrapers, and oddly provincial, having been the center of my world for so long. I climbed the front steps, took a deep breath—and turned and nearly left, seized suddenly with a panic I had not known since that interminable trek from the buffalo camp to the ridge where a band of Sioux sat considering the fate of the trespassers. I turned back and tugged at the bell before I could change my mind again. The door was opened after a moment by a man in overalls whose gray, drawn face I had never before seen.

"Nobody by that name living here," he said when I inquired for my father. "They cut this place up into apartments five years ago. I don't know who owned it before that, nor where they went."

I tried two other doors in that block. The liveried maid who answered the next was ignorant as well. When no one answered the fourth time I rang the neighboring bell, I started to leave. I came back when I heard the door open.

Instantly I recognized the old woman who asked me what I wanted. She was whiter-haired, perhaps, and more shriveled than I remembered, but she had been ancient for as long as I had been aware of her. The lace at her throat was costly and the diamond upon the wedding finger of her left hand was the size of a thirty-two-caliber bullet, the band sunk deep into the old flesh. She was hard of hearing and almost blind, but nothing was wrong with her memory.

"Your father lost everything in the Panic," said she, once I'd succeeded in convincing her of my identity. "He sold the building to pay his debts. Had to resign from the bench then, because he didn't have a residence in the city. I heard he and your mother moved in with his brother on Long Island."

I winced at the bitterness of the situation. At the time I'd left home, my father and my uncle had not spoken to each other for years. They had broken over the latter's unethical business practices.

I took the train to Long Island. I had not been there since I was a child, but I remembered the big house and fourteen-acre estate at Southampton. The footman, whose powdered wig and silk stockings told me his employer had surrendered none of his conceits, took me to my uncle, a short, bald man with massive side-whiskers, who looked me up and down suspiciously, fired off a series of questions designed to trip me up over vagaries in the family history, harrumphed over the correctness of my answers, rang for the butler, and instructed him to take me to my father.

"What about my mother?" I asked.

"Dead these three years. I told him he'd never amount to anything, married to a sickly woman."

I bridled, stung by grief and his callous attitude. "A district judge doesn't amount to anything?"

"Pah! A public servant is still just a servant. He isn't even that any more, just a burden on the brother he was too good for when he was riding high."

Fearing that I would be ejected without being allowed to see my father, I held my tongue and accompanied the butler to a hall bedroom, where a nurse with a wart on her chin informed me that the judge had suffered a stroke some months before and was unable to speak, although she believed he understood things that were said to him.

I scarcely recognized him. He looked as small as Alma in a wheeled bath chair with a rug drawn across his knees; withered, white-haired, and vacant-eyed. The right side of his face was slack. I told him who I was. He showed no reaction. I told him again, this time grasping the pale, spotted hand that rested atop the rug. It seemed I felt a faint pressure. When I identified myself a third time, his eyes rolled my way and appeared to fix themselves. I recognized then the directness of the old jurist. He opened his mouth and tried to speak. Plainly the effort excited him, for he was trembling. The nurse took his pulse and asked me to come back later.

My uncle, it developed, had been divorced from his first wife for many years. The woman to whom he was now married was half his age, a pleasant solidly built woman with black hair and great sympathetic brown eyes, who told me her husband was not as bad a fellow as he seemed to want people to think him. I was still upset and replied that he must want people to think him very bad indeed. At this point she excused herself, and I thought I had offended her. Presently, however, she returned to the spacious living room, whose windows looked out upon the Atlantic, and handed me a bundle of papers five inches thick, bound with faded blue ribbon.

"They are letters from your father. He kept on writing, even though he didn't know where to send them when they started coming back."

The one on top bore an 1863 date. My throat closed. "He might not want me to read them. I'm not the same person he addressed them to."

"Read them. I've had the north room aired out and the bed made. Of course you're staying."

I stayed, and I read the letters. When I had finished, I returned to my father's room. The nurse, who was capable of greater human feeling than her appearance indicated, left us alone, and there in the gray silence I told my father everything that I had done and seen since the day I left. I do not know how much he heard or understood. He lay in bed, his eyes open. When the nurse came back, I rose and touched his hand again. Again I felt a faint squeeze.

He died the second week in December, in his sleep, without having said a word to me in nearly twenty years. I felt, however, after reading his letters and presenting my life to him with all its many shortfalls, that we stood upon the same level.

I declined my uncle's halfhearted offer to bear the cost of his burial. Instead I used the last of the money I had saved to purchase a walnut casket with a gray silk lining and arrange for a modest service at the Marble Collegiate Church at Fifth Avenue and Twenty-ninth Street, just down the street from our old home. It was attended by a number of Father's legal associates and fellow club members, a small group of less than two dozen. He was interred in the churchyard beside my mother, beneath a granite headstone I had ordered bearing his name and the dates of his birth and death, together with this inscription:

"For this my son was dead, and is alive again; he was lost, and is found."

—LUKE 15:24

My song is almost ended. Yet there are a few more verses to be sung.

The era of the New York music hall was then just beginning. On the basis of the popularity of "Jesse James"—crude ballad that it was, it swept through the Midwest from saloon to saloon like a brand of cheap potent whiskey, and had been heard in San Francisco—I obtained a position as house lyricist with the Mellow Memories Song Sheet Company, three flights up from Forty-fourth Street at the corner of Broadway. Very soon I learned I could supplement my income by selling work on commission to my employers' competitors. My career as a full-time freelance composer began when Mellow Memories discovered my duplicity and fired me. When the royalties began coming in I moved out of my uncle's house into an apartment on Forty-second. There, the cacophony of a hundred pianos clattering out a hundred parlor tunes day and night prompted deafened local journalists to dub the neighborhood Tin Pan Alley.

I was working steadily and making more money than I ever had in my life, but something was missing. I found it when I walked into a dank, brick-walled drinking establishment in Greenwich Village one Saturday night and talked the proprietor into allowing me to play and sing a few of my songs in the corner by the stove, where patrons never sat because the heat was oppressive. The audience response, modest though it was, fed an appetite I hadn't realized I'd acquired all those years I sang for my supper in every watering hole between St. Louis and Cripple Creek. I came back the following Monday and every night after that. When new people began coming in because they'd heard there was music, the proprietor put me on salary, on top of which I was free to claim all gratuities.

Since Jesse's legendary death, the James brothers were front-page news even in New York. Frank surrendered himself to Governor Crittenden of Missouri six months after St. Joseph. Tried three times for robbery and murder and acquitted, he walked out of an Otterville, Missouri, courtroom a free man in February 1885. He was never again to my knowledge associated with any criminal activity, and died a respectable farmer in 1915, leaving behind a tidy nest egg contributed to by his personally guided tours of the James farm at fifty cents a head. Bob Ford and his brother Charlie, who had conspired with the Pinkertons to kill Jesse, were convicted of his murder and sentenced to hang, only to be pardoned immediately by Governor Crittenden and set free with five hundred dollars of the promised reward of five thousand in their pockets. Four years later, Charlie committed suicide. In 1892, after being hounded through the West, it was said, by the line in my song, "that dirty little coward, that shot Mr. Howard," Bob Ford was cornered in his own saloon in Creede, Colorado, by a James admirer named Ed Kelley, who blew his head off with a shotgun.

About this time I was moved to visit the site of the East River Society House, where nearly thirty years before I had recovered from injuries sustained in the draft riots while Boss Tweed's men were scouring the city for Jehosophat Brennan's assailant. The building was gone, the lot where it had stood surrounded by a ten-foot board fence behind which a construction crew was laying the foundation for yet another skyscraper. A policeman I spoke to on the corner informed me that the old building had been demolished after the roof collapsed during the great blizzard of '88. He had been on the beat only three years and had never heard of either Bridey McMurtaugh or Templeton "Tupper" Deane of the Invalid Corps.

Relaxing at home on a Sunday, I read in the *World* that a company formed by Thomas A. Edison was at work in the New Jersey countryside, photographing models in action for the new motion-picture process invented by the company's founder. These "photoplays" had started to pull in nickels from candy stores where they were projected upon bedsheet screens and from hand-cranked viewing machines installed inside smoke shops and soda fountains, and public demand for complete and coherent stories had prompted Edison to re-create daring exploits from the West for the camera. My old curiosity intact, I journeyed out there the next weekend, only to be told by a harried employee in riding breeches carrying a megaphone that motion-picture-making being a silent process, the company had no need for a musician.

I discovered, however, that a rival company was shooting in the area. The man I spoke to there was intrigued with the concept of providing music on the set to establish the proper mood for the models, whom he referred to as actors, and put me to work on the spot. His employers were so pleased with the results that within a month I found myself the director of a quartet including a violin, a bass fiddle, and a spinet piano.

One morning I reported to the barn outside Union City where the equipment was stored and copies of the day's shooting schedule were given out, only to find the door padlocked and a notice tacked up explaining that the building and its contents had been confiscated by the county sheriff. The Edison Company, which claimed exclusive patent to the motion-picture process, had filed infringement charges against all its competitors; any further violation would result in arrest for each member of the offending company and destruction of its equipment.

At the end of that week, a meeting was convened in the downtown office of the company's owner, who announced that the operation was moving to California, outside the reach of Edison's long arm. The sleepy residential community of Hollywood, located just outside Los Angeles, had been selected, and any member of the company who cared to relocate was invited to come along. That weekend I closed out my apartment and gave notice at the saloon in the Village. I had been in one place far too long as it was for a man who had spent most of his life wandering.

The train ride through the country of my awakening was uneventful. Electric fans cooled the cars, train changes were efficient and infrequent, the sleeping berths were a good deal more comfortable than many I had been forced to put up with for months at a time. I was growing into a time of life that celebrated the convenience, but I was still close enough to my youth to decry the loss of a sense of adventure. If the mechanics of travel continued to improve, I postulated, one would soon cross the continent as easily as he crossed the street, without reflection upon the men and women who broke their hearts and lost their lives during the same journey.

Hollywood, a sun-washed section of reclaimed desert made up of small stucco-and-tile houses on streets lined with palms and orange trees, had begun to bustle: Other outlaw production companies had preceded us, and dusty cowpokes from all over the West had set up camp outside town as casting calls went out for extras, wranglers, and stunt riders to enliven the backgrounds of westerns being shot. As the great ranches broke up and cow work became scarce, the news of opportunities for employment had made of this unlikely place a boomtown every bit as raw and wild as Abilene in its heyday. A few weeks after I had settled in, I stepped outside my rented bungalow in time to see a foreman employed by William Ince shoot down a stand-in with the Griffith company in the middle of La Cienaga Avenue. During the inquest that followed, testimony revealed that bad blood had existed between the pair ever since they had fought over a lower bunk at the King Ranch in Texas.

That aside, I was working hard and enjoying myself, but I craved recreation. An Essanay extra with whom I'd been friendly in Fort Worth when he'd worked for Shanghai Pierce told me of an establishment in the San Fernando Valley that specialized in female escorts who bore a close resemblance to well-known motion-picture queens. "You could have you a fine time, if the old lady that runs the place don't put you off your feed."

The house, a cool, sprawling mansion of timber-reinforced adobe with a red tile roof, occupied twelve acres of an old Spanish land grant dating back to King Philip. Mary Pickford, attired only in a big hair bow and a diaphanous peignoir, was entertaining a pair of moguls-in-the-making on the sofa in the front parlor, and Mabel Normand and the Gish sisters cruised the halls and staircases in brassieres, panties, and garter belts studded with rhinestones. They were close matches to the originals, provided one didn't stare too hard through the careful makeup.

I became bored with the conceit quickly and sat down at the piano in the parlor to play some tunes I was in danger of forgetting. I had been at this for some time when a huge Negress in the black dress and white lacy apron and cap of a housemaid tapped me on the shoulder.

"Beg pardon, mister, but the lady of the house say she'd admire to speak with you upstairs."

She escorted me up the sweeping carpeted steps to the second floor and rapped lightly upon a door at the end of the hall.

An instant before a voice answered from inside, I had a premonition. "The lady of the house" was known to me.

The dimensions of the room were difficult to determine in the gloom created by the thick curtains that covered the windows. The voice that greeted me from somewhere near the back, however, was as clear as if the speaker were standing at my side.

"Well, Billy, you are getting quite gray."

"I wish I could claim it's premature," said I.

A small electric lamp came on with a snap upon a plain writing table ten feet away. She, too, had aged. Her hair was entirely white, and a mass of wrinkles marred the hand that wore the garnet; but the undamaged side of her face, turned toward me, was largely unchanged. An extra line here and there could not affect the handsome bone structure I remembered so well.

I said, "I see you've given up the boardinghouse business and returned to the basics."

"The rents here are too cheap. I cannot compete. You might be surprised to learn how many famous and desired people make use of my services, when it seems they could have anyone they wanted without paying a fee."

"Perhaps they prefer your Theda Bara to the real article."

"I have a Ramon Novarro as well, and a Francis X. Bushman. My clientele is nothing if not diverse. Are you revolted?"

"A frontier town is a frontier town. None of the old rules apply when the money's standing around in bushels and the Mexican border is so close."

"You are growing tolerant in your old age, Billy."

"I've lived some since Abilene."

"Any regrets?"

"Almost nothing but."

She nodded slightly. "This is good. I do not trust the man who says he would live his life the same way if he had the chance to repeat it. And there is hope in the 'almost.' As for me, I would change everything."

I shook my head. "If you did that, I would not have the 'almost.' "

"Perhaps there is hope for me also," she said after a moment.

"There's always hope." I spread my arms, smiling. "Isn't that what this is all about?"

The shadow of the ghost of a smile touched the one visible corner of her lips. "Good-bye, Billy. Enjoy the hospitality of my house tonight. I should be very disappointed in you if you choose to come back."

"Not even to visit you?"

"Especially not that. I am your past. You cannot visit the past, only live there. To live there is to die. Remember that as the last counsel I will give you."

She snapped off the lamp.

T he motion-picture industry has changed nearly as much as the American West, and I was there to see it happening. Talkies came in, and after a period of jabbery "message" pictures and tinny musicals, the camera learned to move again and westerns came back, with the bonus of loud gunfire, hammering hooves, and singing cowboys. The money's not so good now: A Depression is on, and as I approach my ninth decade I have to submit my work through younger songwriters of indiscernible talent, whose names appear in the credits identifying them as the authors. Arthritis in my hands keeps me from playing my own compositions. Myra, the landlady's daughter, finds the chords I want on her mother's piano and writes them down for me—when she isn't out with some producer who will never give her a speaking role, not even if she performs an unnatural act upon him during the lunch rush at the Brown Derby.

I pawned the guitar last year, but I've made arrangements to leave the banjo to Myra, along with a letter authenticating it as one of the items found in Crazy Horse's possession when he was killed. A wealthy collector of western memorabilia may pay her enough for it to finance her own studio.

I've changed my thinking since my final meeting with Drucilla Patakos. I don't regret much. I've known some of the best and worst men of my time, survived events that sent better men than I to their graves more than half a century ago, and, as I was told by one of the strong, intelligent women who have charted the course of my life, I have my gift. Unlike its composer, the song I wrote fifty-three years ago grows stronger each year. A month hardly passes that I don't hear it on the radio or in a supper place with a live performer, usually at the request of one of the patrons, even if whoever sings it usually leaves out the last verse:

This song was made by Billy Gashade
Just as soon as the news did arrive.
He said there was no man with the law in his hand
That could take Jesse James when alive.

Not a bad epitaph for either of us, if I do say so myself.

B.G., Hollywood, California,
April 3, 1935